S. L. FARRELL

A Magic of Dawn

A Novel in *The Nessantico Cycle*

DAW BOOKS, INC.
DONALD A. WOLLHEIM, FOUNDER
375 Hudson Street, New York, NY 10014

ELIZABETH R. WOLLHEIM
SHEILA E. GILBERT
PUBLISHERS
www.dawbooks.com

First Paperback Printing, April 2011
1 2 3 4 5 6 7 8 9 10

DAW TRADEMARK REGISTERED
U.S. PAT. AND TM. OFF. AND FOREIGN COUNTRIES
—MARCA REGISTRADA
HECHO EN U.S.A.

PRINTED IN THE U.S.A.

Acknowledgments

I've read several books for inspiration and reference in writing this series. The books I read prior to starting the Nessantico Cycle as well as those read during the writing of *A Magic Of Twilight* and *A Magic Of Nightfall* are listed in those books; obviously, they too have also influenced this one. I've continued to read historical and other nonfiction texts for inspiration and research—it's something I enjoy, in any case. Here are the books read during the writing of this book, all of which to some degree influenced this story.

- *The Lucifer Effect* by Philip Zimbardo. Random House, 2008
- *Paris In The Middle Ages* by Simone Roux, University of Pennsylvania Press, 2009

A trip to France in 2005 also served as inspiration for much of the Nessantico Cycle. In particular, the Loire Valley region, with its chateaux and lovely countryside, sparked several ideas, as did our days in Paris. I would like to recommend that anyone going to France see the Loire Valley and spend time exploring not only the chateaux, but the small villages in the surrounding countryside such as Azay le Rideau or Villaines les-Rochers. Nessantico is not specifically France, but many details are drawn from our experiences there. Hopefully they have enriched the book.

*   *   *

It may sound strange to acknowledge a piece of software, but I will. Early in writing *A Magic Of Nightfall*, I stumbled across the most useful novel-writing software to have ever graced my computer: Scrivener. For those of you on the Macintosh platform, I can't recommend it highly enough. Scrivener thinks the way I think, and allowed me to manage the monumental task of writing an epic fantasy far, far better than any word processor ever could. Thanks, Keith Blount, for creating this program! This book, in all its drafts and revisions, was written using Scrivener. For the curious, Scrivener can be found at http://www.literatureandlatte.com/

My gratitude to my first readers, Denise Parsley Leigh, Bruce Schneier, Justin Scott, and Don Wenzel, who labored through the draft (Denise, through *all* of them!)—thanks for your input, folks. It was much appreciated!

Many thanks, as always, to my agent Merrilee Heifetz of Writers House, who has been my partner-in-writing for many years now—without her, none of this would have been possible.

And lastly (but certainly not last in importance) I'd like to express my gratitude to Sheila Gilbert, a most excellent editor and someone I also consider a friend. We've now worked together on several books, and her input and criticism has made each a richer book than it would have been otherwise. Thank you, Sheila!

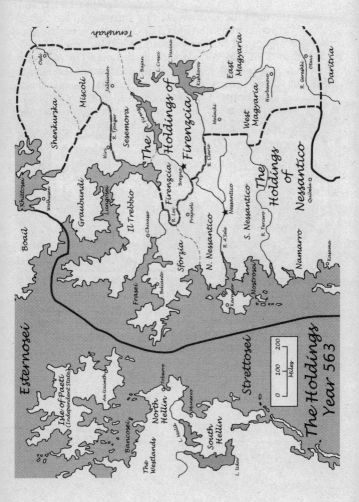

The Holdings
Year 563

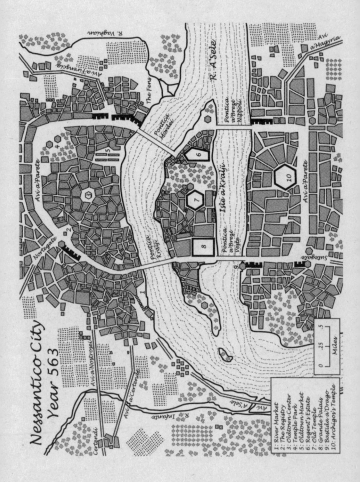

Nessantico City
Year 563

1: River Market
2: The Registry
3: Oldtown Center
4: Temple Park
5: Oldtown Market
6: Regent's Estate
7: Old Temple
8: Grande Palais
9: Basilica a'Drego
10: Archigos' Temple

0   .25   .5
Miles

Table of Contents

Prelude: Nessantico

IF A CITY CAN HAVE a gender, Nessantico was female . . .

She had experienced the flowering of all her promise and her beauty during the long reign of Kraljica Marguerite. In that magnificent half century, Nessantico's long childhood and even longer adolescence culminated in mingled elegance and power, unmatched anywhere in the known world. For fifty years, she brooked no peer. For fifty years, she believed that this glorious present would be eternal, that her ascent would—no, *must*—continue.

Her superiority was ordained. It was destined. It would last forever.

It would not.

Kraljica Marguerite, like all those who ruled within Nessantico's confines, was human and mortal; Marguerite's son Justi and then Justi's son Audric, both of whom inherited the Sun Throne, didn't possess Marguerite's gifts. Without Marguerite's strong guidance, without her guile and her wisdom, Nessantico's flowering was sadly short-lived. The blossom of Marguerite's promise withered and died in far less time than it had taken it to bloom.

Worse, rivals rose to challenge Nessantico. Firenzcia betrayed her: Firenzcia, the brother city who had always envied her; Firenzcia, who had always been her companion, her strength, her shield, and her sword. Firenzcia left her to form its own empire.

And from the unknown west strode a new, harsher challenge: an alien, unguessed empire as strong as Nessantico herself. Stronger, perhaps; for the Tehuantin—as they were called—not only ripped away Nessantico's hold on their shores, but sent an army over the sea to plunder and rape and destroy the cities of the Holdings and to shatter the walls of Nessantico herself.

The assault left Nessantico shaken and afraid. She was stained by the soot of magical fire and twice trampled by the boots of foreign soldiers: first the Tehuantin, then the Firenzcians. The architectural beauty of her buildings morphed into toppled columns, broken domes, and roofless husks. The A'Sele was clogged with bodies and refuse.

Nessantico . . . she was a woman exhausted by her struggles, worn by her cares, and clothed in the shredded tatters of her old supremacy. Her sense of security and inevitability was lost, perhaps—she feared—forever. The smell still lingered in her streets: a malodorous stench of rotting flesh, blood, and ash.

A lesser entity would have collapsed. A lesser entity might have looked at her sad reflection in the fouled waters of the River A'Sele and seen a skeletal death mask staring back. A lesser entity would have given up and ceded her supremacy to Firenzcia or to the unglimpsed cities of the Tehuantin.

Not her.

Not Nessantico.

She gathered the tatters around herself. She drew herself up and cleansed herself as best she could. She cloaked herself in pride and memories and belief, and vowed that one day, one day, the rest of the world would again bow to her.

One day . . .

But not yet today.

LAMENTATIONS

Allesandra ca'Vörl
Varina ca'Pallo
Sergei ca'Rudka
Allesandra ca'Vörl
Nico Morel
Brie ca'Ostheim
Allesandra ca'Vörl
Rochelle Botelli
Sergei ca'Rudka
Jan ca'Ostheim
Varina ca'Pallo
Niente

Allesandra ca'Vörl

GSCHNAS—THE FALSE WORLD BALL—swirled below Allesandra in the Grand Hall of the Kraljica's Palais. The hall was still partially under construction, but that only lent depth to the ambience.

After all, the False World Ball was where reality was turned on its head. Costumes—the stranger and more creative, the better—were required of all attendees. The cracks in the walls had been filled with sculptures of demons or miniature pastoral landscapes, as if the foundations of reality itself had broken, the cracks providing glimpses of entire new worlds set at odd angles to their own. A flock of flightless birds had been brought in from Far Namarro: as tall as a man, with tufts of grandly colored plumage rising from their rumps. They wandered among the revelers. Several téni from the A'Téni's Temple had been set to keeping a river of crystalline water flowing in a sweeping curve above the dancers' heads, with large goldfish swimming placidly in the magic-driven currents. The musicians sat on chairs perched within a huge gilded frame hung on the wall at one end of the room, their backdrop a beautifully-painted landscape, so it appeared that a painting of musicians had magically sprung to life.

Gschnas: a fantasy created for the entertainment of the ca'-and-cu'—the wealthy and important people of the city and of the greater Holdings. They had come bearing the Kraljica's gilded invitations: they packed the floor below Allesandra bedecked in their glittering costumes: A'Téni ca'Paim, the highest ranking téni of the city; Comman-

dant Telo cu'Ingres of the Garde Kralji; Commandant
Eleric ca'Talin of the Garde Civile; Sergei ca'Rudka,
once Regent and now Ambassador to Firenzcia; all of
the members of the Council of Ca' except the Numetodo
Varina ca'Pallo, who was home with her desperately ill
husband . . .

"Kraljica, you look stunning." Talbot ci'Noel, her aide,
came up alongside her as she peered over the balcony at
the gathering. He was dressed as a monkey, an ironic costume for a man who was always exceedingly proper and
elegant, and who ruled the palais staff with a fist of iron
and a voice of fire. Behind the furred snout of the mask,
his lips smiled. "Are you ready for your entrance?" Already, the dozen or so téni had begun their chanting. Talbot
tested—for what seemed the hundredth time—the ropes
attached to the harness concealed in Allesandra's gown: a
flowing, billowing fantasy of chiffon and lace ribbons, so
that when she moved, trails of shimmering color rippled in
vain pursuit.

"I'm ready," she told Talbot. Two servants came forward, each with a glass ball enchanted with Numetodo
spells—Talbot was a Numetodo himself, and Varina, the
A'Morce of the Numetodo, had herself placed the spells
in the glass balls. Allesandra took one in each hand. Talbot gestured to another of the servants on the floor below,
who in turn signaled the musicians. The gavotte they had
been playing abruptly ended, followed by an ominous, low
roll of the drums like thunder. The chanting of the téni
increased, and the ceiling of the palais was suddenly obscured by dark, roiling clouds from which lightning hissed
and arced. Allesandra spoke the spell-word Varina had
given her, and the globes in Allesandra's hands blossomed
with pure, white light—so bright that Allesandra, wearing
glasses with smoked lenses as protection, could barely see
for the coruscating brilliance. Anyone looking up at these
sudden twin suns was momentarily blinded. Allesandra
felt the ropes pull and lift her: she was gliding up and over
the balcony rail, then descending slowly toward the floor.
The glass globes were cold in her hand with the Numetodo
magic, and the globes now flared brilliant trails of sparks,
as if two slow meteors were descending from the heavens
to earth, a human figure trapped in their intense radiance.

Allesandra heard the applause and cheers welling up to greet her. Her feet touched the marble floor (she was certain she could almost hear Talbot's sigh of relief), and the light within the globes blossomed—an iridescent and almost painful blue, followed by pure, aching gold: the colors of the Holdings. At the same time, servants hurried from the sides of the hall to remove the ropes from the harness catches and take her glasses. The ropes were hastily pulled up as the globes maintained their brilliance, then finally went dark.

And there, as eyesight slowly returned to the onlookers, was the Kraljica, her crown on her head. The ovation was pleasingly deafening. "Thank you all," she said as they bowed and cheered. "Thank you. Now, please—enjoy the ball!" She gestured, and the music began once more, and the couples on the dance floor bowed to each other and resumed the dance. The ca'-and-cu' pressed around her in their costumes, bowing and murmuring their appreciation, and she smiled to them as she passed among them.

She saw Sergei and gestured for him to join her. He bowed—awkwardly, his arthritic body no longer as supple and flexible as it had been when she'd first known him—and he came over to her, leaning heavily on his cane. He smiled at her, the reflective silver paint on his face cracking slightly as he did so. Sergei's silver nose—the false one he always wore to replace the one of flesh he'd lost in his youth—seemed almost to be part of him tonight. A patchwork of small mirrors covered the bashta he wore. Crazed, broken reflections of herself and the dancers and crowd behind her moved madly around him. The lights of the hall flared and shimmered in the tiny mirrors, dancing from the nearest walls.

"That was quite an entrance," Sergei said. Allesandra slowed her pace to his as they moved through the crowds.

"Thank you for suggesting the method, though you had poor Talbot terrified that something would go wrong. I must say, however, that I'll need to retire for a bit soon to have my attendants get rid of the harness; it's rubbing my poor skin raw."

He smiled. "The Kraljiki's entrance should always be dramatic," he said, smiling. "A little discomfort is fair payment for a stunning appearance. You should know that."

"That's easy for you to say, Sergei, when you don't have to endure it."

"I've always loved the Gschnas," Sergei told her. "I'm glad you've brought back the tradition, Kraljica. Nessantico *needs* her traditions, especially after the last few years."

Especially after the last few years. The comment tightened her lips and narrowed her eyes. "You needn't bring *that* up now, Ambassador," she told him. The history was never far from anyone's mind in Nessantico: the horrible cost of recovery after the Westlanders nearly destroyed the city, the continued separation of the Holdings and the Coalition nations, and most recently, the political and military disaster in West Magyaria.

"Then I won't," he answered. "Though I do need to talk with you about the Firenzcian spy that Talbot believes he's discovered . . ." As Sergei talked, she looked away from the images of herself on his clothing to the crowd that pressed in around them. She saw a man staring at her. He was handsome, his skin somewhat darker than most of those in the hall, his head entirely shaved, though his beard was full and midnight-black. His clothing was loose and wildly-colored, and feathers sprouted from the shoulders as if he were some exotic bird. His eyes—behind a beaked demi-mask—were strangely blue and light, his gaze piercing and keen. He saw her attention and he nodded slightly toward her.

Sergei was still talking. ". . . already has the traitorous servant in the Bastida, so he'll be no more trouble. But there are still the Morellis—" He stopped as she raised her hand.

"Who is that man?" she whispered to Sergei, glancing again at him. "He looks Magyarian."

Sergei followed her gaze. "Indeed, Kraljica. That is Erik ca'Vikej. He's just come to Nessantico yesterday. There's undoubtedly a note on your desk from him requesting an audience. I haven't had the chance to speak to him myself yet."

"Stor ca'Vikej's son?" The man had truly wonderful eyes. He continued to regard her, though he made no move to approach.

"The same."

"I will see him," she told Sergei. "In the south alcove, a mark of the glass from now. Tell him."

Sergei might have frowned, but he bowed his head. "As you wish, Kraljica," he said. His cane tapped on the marble floor as he left her side, his costume sending motes of light fluttering. Allesandra turned away, nodding and conversing with others as she moved slowly around the hall. Talbot came to her side, having paid and dismissed the téni who had helped with her descent, and she told him to clear the south alcove. She continued on her procession around the room. A'Téni ca'Paim, the head of the Faith in Nessantico, dressed tonight as one of the Red Moitidi, was approaching. "Ah, A'Téni ca'Paim, so good of you to attend, and your téni have done a wonderful job this evening . . ."

A mark of the glass later, Allesandra had made a circuit of the hall and moved past the line of servants Talbot had set around the alcove to keep away the crowd. She took a seat there, listening to the music. A few moments later, Sergei approached, with ca'Vikej just behind him. "Kraljica, may I present Erik ca'Vikej . . ."

The man stepped forward and performed a deep, elaborate bow. She remembered that bow: a Magyarian form of courtesy. The ca'-and-cu' of West Magyaria had bowed the same way for her late husband Pauli, who had become Gyula of West Magyaria after their rancorous separation, only to be assassinated by his own people eight years later. Two years ago, Eric's vatarh, Stor, had tried to step into the vacuum left by Pauli's death.

Allesandra had made the decision to back him. That choice had turned out to be a poor one, the full extent of which was still be determined. She'd made the choice to send only a small part of the Holdings army to support Stor ca'Vijek's own troops. That had doomed them, and the effort had ended in a military defeat for the Holdings at the hands of Allesandra's son, Hïrzg Jan.

"Especially after the last few years . . ." Sergei's comment still rankled.

"Kraljica Allesandra, it is my pleasure to meet you at last." The man's voice was as stunning as his eyes: low and mellifluous, yet he didn't seem to notice its power. He kept his head down. "I wanted to thank you for your support of my vatarh. He was always grateful to you for your championing of our cause, and he always spoke well of you."

Allesandra searched his voice for a hint of sarcasm or

irony; there was none. He seemed entirely sincere. Sergei was looking carefully to one side, hiding whatever he was thinking. Close, she could see the gray flecks in ca'Vikej's beard and the lines around his eyes and mouth: he was not much younger than she was herself—not surprisingly, since Stor ca'Vikej had been elderly when he'd tried to take the Gyula's throne. "I wish events had gone differently," she told him. "But it wasn't Cénzi's Will."

The man made the sign of Cénzi at that statement—he was of the Faith, then. "Perhaps less Cénzi than circumstances, Kraljica," he answered. "My vatarh was . . . impatient. I'd counseled him to wait for a time when the Kraljica and the Holdings could have supported us more openly. I told him then that the two battalions you sent were the most he could expect unless he waited, but . . ." He shrugged; the motion was as graceful as his manner. "I warned him that Hïrzg Jan would come down with the full fury of the Firenzcian army."

Yes, and Sergei told me the same thing, and I didn't believe him. She nodded, but she didn't say that. Handsome, modest, polite, but there was ambition in Erik ca'Vikej as well. Allesandra could see it. And there was anger toward the Coalition for his vatarh's death. "You are more patient than your vatarh, perhaps, Vajiki ca'Vikej, but yet you want the same thing. And you're going to tell me that there are still many Magyarians who support you in this."

He smiled at that: graceful, yes. "Evidently my head is entirely transparent to the Kraljica." He swept a hand over his bald skull. He managed to look almost comically bemused. "Next time, I should perhaps wear a hat."

She laughed softly at that; she saw Sergei glance at her oddly. "Supporting your vatarh as much as I did nearly brought me to war with my own son," she told him.

"Family relationships too often resemble those between countries," he answered, still smiling. "There are some borders that must not be crossed." He cocked his head slightly as the musicians started a new song out in the hall. He held his hand out toward Allesandra. "Would the Kraljica be willing to dance with me—for the sake of what she meant to my vatarh?"

Allesandra could see the slight shake of Sergei's head. She knew what he was thinking as well: *You don't want reports*

*to get back to Brezno that you are entertaining Stor ca'Vikej's
son . . .* But there was something about him, something that
drew her. "I thought you were a patient man."

"My vatarh also taught me that an opportunity missed is
one forever lost." His eyes laughed, held in fine, dark lines.

Allesandra rose from her chair. She took his hand.

"Then, for the sake of your vatarh, we should dance,"
she said, and led him from the alcove.

~

Varina ca'Pallo

IT WAS DIFFICULT TO BE STOIC, even though she
knew that was what Karl would have wanted of her.

Karl had been failing for the last month. Looking at him
now, Varina sometimes found it hard to find in the drawn,
haggard face the lines of the man she had loved, to whom
she'd been married for nearly fourteen years now, who had
taken her name and her heart.

Because he was so much older than her, she had feared
that their time together must end this way, with him dying
before her.

It seemed that would be the case.

"Are you in pain, love?" she asked, stroking his balding
head, a few strands of gray-white hair clinging stubbornly
to the crown. He shook his head without speaking—talking
seemed to exhaust him. His breath was too fast and too
shallow, almost a panting, as if clinging to life required all
the effort he could muster. "No? That's good. I have the
healer's brew right here if that changes. She said that a few
sips would take away any pain and let you sleep. Just let me
know if you need it—and don't you dare try to be brave
and ignore it."

Varina smiled at him, stroking his sunken, stubbled
cheek. She turned away because the tears threatened her
again. She sniffed, taking in a long breath that shuddered
with the ghost of the sobs that racked her when she was
away from him, when she allowed the grief and emotions

to take her. She brushed at her eyes with the sleeve of her tashta and turned back to him, the smile fixed again on her face. "The Kraljica sent over a letter, saying how much she missed us at the Gschnas last night. She said that her entrance went better than she could have wished, and that the globes I enchanted for her worked perfectly. And, oh, I forgot to tell you—a letter also came today from your son Colin. He says that your great-daughter Katerina is getting married next month, and that he wishes ... he wishes you ..." She stopped. Karl would not be going to the wedding. "Anyway, I've written back to him, and told him that you're not ... you're not well enough to travel to Paeti right now."

Karl stared at her. That was all he could do now. Stare. His skin was stretched tautly over the skull of his face, the eyes sunken into deep, black hollows; Varina wondered if he even saw her, if he noticed how old she'd become as well, how her studies of the Tehuantin magic had taken a terrible physical toll on her. Karl ate almost nothing—it was all she could do to get warm broth down his throat. He had difficulty swallowing even that. The healer only shook her head on her daily visits. "I'm sorry, Councillor ca'Pallo," she said to Varina. "But the Ambassador is beyond any skill I have. He's lived a good life, he has, and it's been longer than most. You have to be ready to let him go."

But she wasn't ready. She wasn't certain she would ever be, *could* ever be. After all the years she'd wanted to be with him, after all those years when his love for Ana ca'Seranta had blinded him to her, she was to be with him only for so short a time? Less than two decades? When he was gone, there'd be nothing left of him. Karl and Varina had no children of their own; despite being twelve years younger than Karl, she'd been unable to conceive with him. There'd been a miscarriage in their first year, then nothing, and her own monthly bleeding had ended five years ago now. There were times, in the last several weeks, when she'd envied those who could pray to Cénzi for a boon, a gift, a miracle. As a Numetodo, as a nonbeliever, she had no such solace herself; her world was bereft of gods who could grant favors. She could only hold Karl's hand and gaze at him and hope.

You have to be ready to let him go ...

She took his hand, pressed it in her fingers. It was like holding a skeleton's hand; there was no returning pressure, his flesh was cold, and his skin felt as dry as brown parchment. "I love you," she told him. "I always loved you; I will always love you."

He didn't answer, though she thought she saw his dry, cracked lips open slightly and then close again. Perhaps he thought he was responding. She reached for the cloth in the basin alongside his bed, dipped it in the water, and dabbed at his lips.

"I've been working with a device to use the black sand again. Look—" She showed him a long cut along her left arm, still scabbed with dried blood. "I wasn't as careful as I should have been. But I think I may have really stumbled upon something this time. I've made changes to the design and I'm having Pierre make the modifications for me from my drawings . . ."

She could imagine how he might answer. *"There's a price to pay for knowledge,"* he'd told her, often enough. *"But you can't stop knowledge: it wants to be born, and it will force its way into the world no matter what you do. You can't hold back knowledge, no matter what those of the Faith might say . . ."*

Downstairs, she could hear the kitchen staff beginning to prepare dinner: a laugh, a clattering of pans, the faint chatter of conversation, but here in the sickroom the air was hot and still. She talked to Karl mostly because the quiet seemed so depressing. She talked mostly because she was afraid of silence.

"I spoke to Sergei this morning, too. He said that he'll stop by tomorrow night, before he goes off to Brezno," she said in a falsely cheery voice. "He insists that if you won't join him at the table for dinner, he's going to come up here and bring you down himself. 'What good is Numetodo magic if you can't get rid of a little minor illness?' he said. He also suggested that the sea air in Karnmor might do you some good. I might see if we could take a villa there next month. He said that the Gschnas was ever so nice, though he mentioned that Stor ca'Vikej's son has come to the city, and he didn't like the way that Kraljica Allesandra paid attention to him . . ."

She realized that the room was *too* still, that she hadn't

heard Karl take a breath for some time. He was still staring at her, but his gaze had gone empty and dull. She felt her stomach muscles clench. She took in a breath that was half-sob. "Karl . . . ?" She watched his chest, willing it to move, listening for the sound of air moving through his nostrils. Was his hand colder? She felt for his pulse, searching for the fluttering underneath her fingertips and imagining she felt it.

"Karl . . . ?"

The room was silent except for the distant clamor of the servants and the chirping of birds in the trees outside and the faint sounds of the city beyond the walls of their villa. She felt pressure rising in her chest, a wave that broke free from her and turned into a wail that sounded as if it were ripped from someone else's throat.

She heard the servants running up the stairs, heard them stop at the door. The sound of her grief echoed in her ears. She was still holding Karl's hand. Now she let it drop lifeless back to the sheet. She reached out and brushed his eyelids closed, her fingertips trembling.

"He's gone," she said: to the servants, to the world, to herself.

The words seemed impossible. Unbelievable. She wanted to take them back and smash them so they could never be spoken again.

But she had said them, and they could not be revoked.

~

Sergei ca'Rudka

THE BASTIDA A'DRAGO STANK of ancient molds and mildew, of piss and black fecal matter, of fear and pain and terror. Sergei loved that scent. The odors soothed him, caressed him, and he inhaled deeply through the nostrils of his cold, silver nose.

"Good morning, Ambassador ca'Rudka." Ari ce'Denis, Capitaine of the Bastida, greeted Sergei from the open doorway of his office as Sergei shuffled through the gates.

He moved slowly, as he always did now, his knees aching with every step, wishing he hadn't decided to leave his cane in the carriage. Sergei held up a piece of paper in his right hand toward ce'Denis. Under his left arm was tucked a long roll of leather.

"Good?" Sergei asked. "Not so much, I'm afraid." He could hear his age in his voice, also: that unstoppable tremor and quaver.

"Ah, yes," the Capitaine said. "Ambassador ca'Pallo's death. I'm sorry; I know he was a good friend of yours."

Sergei grimaced. His head ached with the worries that assailed him: the deteriorating relationship between the Holdings and the Firenzcian Coalition over the last few years; the Kraljica's cold reception to his suggestion to repair that rift finally and completely; the rising presence of Nico Morel and his followers in the city; even the way that Erik ca'Vikej had dominated the Kraljica's attention during the Gschnas . . .

Poor Karl's death had merely been a final blow. That had been a reminder of his own mortality, that soon enough Sergei would have to face the soul-weighers and see what his own life had come to. He was afraid of that day. He was afraid he knew how heavy his soul would be with his sins.

"It's Ambassador ca'Pallo's death, yes," Sergei answered, holding up the paper again as he approached the Capitaine. "Certainly. But it's also this. Have you seen it?"

Ce'Denis peered myopically at the paper. "I noticed some of these posted around the Avi on my way in this morning, yes. But I'm afraid I'm a plain man of battle, Ambassador. I don't have the skills of letters, as you undoubtedly remember."

"Ah." Sergei scowled. He *had* forgotten—ce'Denis' illiteracy had been one of the reasons that he was only the Capitaine of the Bastida and not an a'offizier in the Garde Kralji or Garde Civile; it was also the reason he wasn't a chevaritt and why his rank was only ce'. Sergei's hand fisted around the parchment, crumpling it with a sound like brief fire, and tossing it on the ground. Deliberately, he stepped on it. "It's a repulsive piece of trash, Capitaine. Vile. A proclamation from that damned Nico Morel, railing against the Numetodo and insulting the memory of Ambassador ca'Pallo. Gloating at my good friend's death . . ."

Sergei grimaced. Memories of Nico Morel came back unbidden even as he railed. The boy he'd known a decade and a half ago during the great battle for Nessantico had little resemblance to the charismatic, raving firebrand who had surfaced recently. Still, those had been awful times, and Nico had been lost during them—who knew what the boy had experienced? Who knew how life might have twisted him?

Life twisted you, didn't it? Sergei's headache pounded at his temples. "Nico Morel believes he's the incarnation of Cénzi himself," he said, rubbing his brow with one hand. "I swear, Capitaine, I will have Morel here in the Bastida one day, and I will take great delight in his interrogation."

Ce'Denis pressed his thin lips together. He looked up at the skull of the dragon, mounted on the wall and glaring down at the courtyard in which they stood. "I'm sure you will, Ambassador ca'Rudka."

Sergei glanced at the man sharply. He wasn't sure he liked ce'Denis' tone. "I want you to take any of your gardai not on duty and send them out along the Avi," he told the Capitaine. He nudged the paper on the ground with his foot. "Have them tear down any of these proclamations that they find. That will be the request of Commandant cu'Ingres when I return to the palais, but if you could start before the order comes, I would appreciate it. The fewer people who see this filth, the better."

"Certainly, Ambassador," ce'Denis said, saluting. "Will you be with us long this morning?" He glanced at what Sergei carried under his left arm.

"Not long," Sergei answered. "My day is busy, I'm afraid. And ci'Bella?"

"He is two levels down of the tower, Ambassador, as you requested." Ce'Denis inclined his head to Sergei and went back into his office, calling for his aide. Sergei shuffled toward the main tower of the Bastida, saluting the gardai who opened the barred door for him. He moved slowly down the stairs that spiraled into the lower chambers, bracing himself with a hand on the stone walls and groaning at the strain on his knees, wishing again that he'd brought his cane. At the landing, he reached into the pocket of his overcloak to pull out a small ring of keys; they jingled dully in his hand.

Two levels down he stopped, allowing the pain in his head and his knees to subside. When it had, he thrust the key into a lock—there were flakes of rust around the keyhole; he made a mental note to mention that to Capitaine ce'Denis when he left—there was no excuse for that type of sloppiness here. As he turned the key in the lock, he heard chains rustling and scraping the floor inside. He could see the image in his head: the prisoner cowering away from the door, pressing his spine to the old, damp stone walls as if they might somehow magically open and swallow him.

Suffocation in the embrace of stone might have been a more pleasant fate than the one that awaited the man, he had to admit.

Sergei glanced around before he opened the cell door. A garda was approaching from the lower levels. He nodded to Sergei without saying anything. The capitaine and the gardai of the Bastida knew that Sergei usually required an "assistant" when he visited the prison; those who had the same predilections as Sergei often helped. They understood, and so they said nothing and pretended to see nothing, simply doing whatever Sergei asked of them.

He pushed open the cell door.

"Good morning, Vajiki ci'Bella," he said pleasantly to the man as the garda slid into the cell behind him. The prisoner stared at the two of them: Aaros ci'Bella, one of the many minor aides in the Kraljica's Palais. The man still wore the uniform of the palais, now soiled and torn. Sergei set the ring of keys on the hook just inside the cell door, leaving it open. Ci'Bella stood against the rear wall, the chains that bound his hands and feet loose—the chains, looped through thick staples on the back wall, had just enough slack to allow him to come within a single stride of the door but no more. If the man charged at Sergei, all Sergei had to do was step back and he could not be reached— though the garda would undoubtedly stop the man if he dared make such a foolish move. The prisoner who would do that was rare. "Old Silvernose," as Sergei was known derogatorily, had his reputation among the enemies of Nessantico and those in the lowest strata of Holdings society. He could already sniff the apprehension rising in the man. "May I call you Aaros?"

The man didn't even nod. His gaze traveled from Ser-

gei's nose to the thick roll of black leather under his arm to
the silent garda. Sergei set the roll down near the cell door,
untied the loop holding it closed, and laid it out flat it with
a flick of his hand, grunting with the motion. Inside, snared
in loops, were instruments of steel and wood, their satin
patina showing much use.

Looking at the display, ci'Bella moaned. Sergei saw a
wetness darken the front of his pants and spread down his
leg, followed by the astringent scent of urine. Sergei shook
his head, *tsking* softly. The garda chuckled. "Ambassador,"
ci'Bella wailed. "Please. I have a family. A wife and three
children. I've done nothing to you. Nothing."

"No?" Sergei cocked his head. He removed the overcloak from his shoulders, brushed at the soft fabric, and
placed it carefully on the peg with the keys. He grimaced
again as he knelt down, his knees cracking audibly and his
leg muscles protesting. *Once, this would have taken no effort at all . . .* His fingers—knobbed and bent with age, the
skin loose and wrinkled over the bones and ligaments—
stroked the displayed instruments. He could feel the silken
coolness of the metal through his fingertips, and it caused
him to inhale deeply, sensually. "Tell me, Aaros. What would
you do if a man harmed your wife, if he raped her or disfigured her? Wouldn't you want to hurt that man in return?
Wouldn't you feel justified in taking revenge on that man?"

Ci'Bella seemed confused. "Ambassador, you're not
married, and I did nothing to your wife or to anyone's . . ."

Sergei raised a white, heavy eyebrow. "No?" he said
again. He allowed himself a gap-toothed smile. "But you
see, I *am* married, Aaros. I'm married to Nessantico. *She* is
my wife, my mistress, my very reason for living. And you,
Aaros, you have assaulted and betrayed her. Talbot told
me what he'd discovered. You spoke to an agent of the Firenzcian Coalition. Certainly you remember him? Garos
ci'Merin? I had the . . . pleasure of talking to him yesterday,
here in the Bastida." Sergei smiled at ci'Bella; the garda
snorted with amusement. "He told me how *kind* you were
to him. How helpful."

"But I didn't know the man was a Firenzcian, Ambassador," ci'Bella protested. "I swear it by Cénzi. He seemed
lost, and I only escorted him through the palais . . ."

"You showed him through the corridors for the palais

staff, the corridors that only authorized staff are permitted to access."

"It was the quickest way . . ."

"And it was also a way that someone wishing to harm the Kraljica or to prowl about the palais would desire to know and use."

"But I didn't *know* . . ."

Sergei smiled. He rubbed at the carved nostrils of his false nose, where the glue holding it to his face itched. "I believe you, Aaros," he said gently, smiling. "But I don't *know* if that's the truth. Perhaps you're a skilled liar. Perhaps you've helped other people find their way through the palais corridors. Perhaps you're an agent of Firenzcia yourself. I don't *know*." He plucked a set of clawed pincers from their loop and stood with an effort, his knees cracking once more. The garda pushed himself off the wall, moving forward to Aaros.

"But I *will* know," Sergei told the man. "Very soon . . ."

~

Allesandra ca'Vörl

ALLESANDRA KNEW THAT there would be a backlash to her decision to hold a state funeral for Ambassador Karl ca'Pallo. She just hadn't expected it to be quite so vitriolic nor so rapid.

Her aide Talbot entered her chamber with a quick warning knock. "I apologize for interrupting your breakfast, Kraljica," he said with an elegant half-bow as her *domestiques de chambre* diplomatically left the room. "A'Téni ca'Paim is here to see you. She insists it is 'vital' that she see you immediately." Talbot frowned. "I swear, the woman doesn't know how to speak in anything but hyperbole. If her breakfast is late, it's a crisis."

Allesandra sighed and set down her fork. "It's about our request to use the Old Temple for Karl's funeral?"

"I sent your request over to A'Téni ca'Paim's office less than a turn of the glass ago. So, yes, I suspect that's why she's come. A'Téni ca'Paim seems . . . well, rather nervous and upset." Talbot's pale eyes glittered with a hint of amusement, a corner of his thin mouth lifting. But then, Talbot was a Numetodo, which meant that he might believe in other gods than Cénzi or no god at all. Being a Numetodo rather than a follower of Cénzi had become nearly fashionable in Nessantico in recent years—the fact that ca'Paim was the leader of the Faith in Nessantico mattered not at all to him.

Allesandra pushed the silver tray away from her. Cutlery rattled, tea shivered in the cup. "Since the a'téni herself has come rather than sending one of the lesser téni over, I assume she feels this can't wait?"

"A'Téni ca'Paim said that she was—and I quote the woman—prepared to stay here until the Kraljica can find time to see me.' Though if the Kraljica wishes to make her wait until this evening or even tomorrow, I'd be pleased to give A'Téni ca'Paim that message."

"No doubt you would," Allesandra said; Talbot flashed another grin. "And to bring her blankets and a pillow, too. But I suppose I might as well get this over with. Wait half a turn so I can finish my breakfast, then bring her up. Ply her with those candies from Il Trebbio, Talbot; perhaps that will sweeten her mood."

Talbot bowed and left the room. Allesandra glanced up at the painting of Kraljica Marguerite, a masterpiece by the painter ci'Recroix. The painting, like most of the city of Nessantico, had undergone extensive restoration from the damages it had sustained a decade and a half ago, when the Tehuantin had sacked Nessantico. Rips in the canvas had been meticulously glued together, the smoke stains carefully cleaned and the burned sections repainted, though the restoration work was visible if one looked closely at the canvas: even the best painters still could not match ci'Recroix's subtlety (or literal magic, if one believed the tales) with the brush. Archigos Ana, Allesandra knew, had insisted that the painting had been ensorcelled and was responsible for Kraljica Marguerite's sudden death. Certainly Kraljiki Audric had displayed an unhealthy relationship with the painting of his great-matarh, treating it as if the portrait were the Kraljica herself. Allesandra occasionally found herself glancing uncomfortably at the painting, installed over the mantel in the reception room of her apartments in the rebuilt palais. Marguerite always seemed to be gazing back at Allesandra, the painted highlights glistening in her eyes and an inscrutable expression of half-disgust touching her lips, as if the sight of a ca'Vörl bearing the crown and ring of the Kralji pained her.

Perhaps it did, in whatever afterlife the woman inhabited. No matter what the truth of the painting's history might be, Allesandra found that the piece served as a reminder of what Nessantico had been under her rule, and what perhaps it might become again.

"Does it bother you, Marguerite?" she asked the painting.

There was no answer.

She finished her meal and called the *domestiques de chambre* to take the tray, telling them to bring a new tray with tea and scones for the a'téni. Talbot knocked again on the outer door just as the servants brought in the tea. "Enter," Allesandra said, and Talbot stepped into view.

"A'Téni ca'Paim," he said, bowing more formally this time. He started to step aside to allow ca'Paim to enter the room, but she pushed past him. Only Allesandra saw the roll of Talbot's eyes

Soleil ca'Paim was a portly woman in her mid-forties, with dyed dark hair showing white at the roots and a complexion that the emerald green of her robe rendered pasty. She had the harried look of a matron with too many children—and indeed she had birthed ten children in her time—but Allesandra knew it would be a mistake to think of her as soft, ineffectual, or unintelligent; a mistake many had made during her career. Soleil had risen quickly within the ranks of the téni from her beginnings as a lowly e'téni in Brezno, to her current position as the representative of the Faith for Nessantico. There was talk that, should Archigos Karrol's ill health take him, the Concordance of A'Téni might elect her as Archigos. Certainly Archigos Karrol had shown her favor in giving her charge of Nessantico.

"Kraljica," ca'Paim said, inclining her head. The woman was breathing a bit heavily, and Allesandra waved to the chair set across from her.

"A'Téni, it's so good to see you. Would you like tea? These scones are still warm from the oven and our new

pastry chef, I have to say, is excellent . . ." Allesandra waved
to the servants, standing against the wall, and they scurried forward to serve the tea and hand the a'téni a plate
adorned with several scones, drizzled with honey. A' Téni
ca'Paim was not one to turn down food: she ate a scone,
then another, while the two of them talked pleasantries, circling around the subject they both knew must be broached.

Finally, ca'Paim set down the plate, dusted with sticky
crumbs. "I received your request this morning, Kraljica,"
ca'Paim stated in her flat, somewhat nasal voice. "While we
of the Faith readily acknowledge Ambassador ca'Pallo's
long service to Nessantico and the Holdings, that doesn't
alter the fact that neither the Ambassador nor any of the
Numetodo believe in Cénzi as we do, and the usage of Concénzia Faith's facilities would amount to a *de facto* acceptance of their heretical beliefs."

Allesandra set her own plate down. She put a hand on
either side of it. "I must remind you, A'Téni, that the Old
Temple was rebuilt at least partially with funds given to the
Faith by the Holdings."

Ca'Paim acknowledged that with an inclination of her
head. "And for that the Faith is extremely grateful, Kraljica.
We have tried to give back to the Holdings what we can.
I'd remind the Kraljica that our light-téni donated their
services to the Holdings for five years in thanks. Archigos
Karrol, in particular, has been most generous with his attentions to the Holdings, making certain that the Faith is as
well-served here as it is in the Coalition. But *this* . . ." Her
lips pressed together, and Allesandra could see that the
woman was concealing a genuine indignation, not something feigned because it was forced upon her. "This is a
matter of *faith,* Kraljica, as you must see. Surely the Grand
Hall here in the palais could accommodate the crowds that
might wish to pay their respects to the Ambassador."

Allesandra ignored the comment. "A'Téni, the
Ambassador—and the Numetodo—have also given to the
Faith. Your war-téni now use techniques developed by the
Numetodo, in particular those created by the Ambassador
and Councillor ca'Pallo both. Archigos Ana certainly saw
the value of their work."

Ca'Paim's lips pressed together even tighter at the mention of Ana's name, then she smiled, though with some ef-

fort. "One might think you're deliberately trying to goad me, Kraljica."

"One would be correct," Allesandra said. "You have to admit it worked, Soleil. It always does."

"And you always push the knife in as deeply as you can, Allesandra," the woman answered, and the two of them laughed. Allesandra saw the woman visibly relax, sitting back against the cushions of her chair and taking another scone. "These are quite good," she said to Allesandra. "Tell your pastry chef that he must send the recipe to my baker." She took a bite. Swallowed. "Archigos Karrol would tell you the same as I've told you."

"No doubt. But I haven't asked *him*, have I?—not that there would be time to do so, in any event. I'm asking you."

"I truly don't like this, Allesandra, for several reasons. I wish you wouldn't force the issue. It puts both me and the Faith in an awkward position."

It's your reputation you're worried about. Not the Faith. Allesandra smiled again at the older woman. "The Old Temple is better suited for the crowds than the Grand Hall here in the palais. You have to admit that; you saw the hall at the Gschnas."

"Yes, but the Old Temple is dedicated to Cénzi's worship, and as a Numetodo, the Ambassador was outspoken in his disbelief in our tenets. He believed there were no gods at all."

"Yet—again—he *has* helped your Faith, and he was also Archigos Ana's great friend. Whatever you might think of Ana, you can't say that she wasn't bound to the Faith's beliefs. I'm not asking you to give Karl the funeral rites of the Faith—and Varina would rightly howl in protest if I did. I'm asking to use the best venue in the city for the occasion. That's all. Cover the murals if you wish. Take all the trappings of the Faith out from beneath the Great Dome. The Grand Hall here is large enough, yes, but it's still under construction—that was fine for the Gschnas, but not for the dignity demanded by this funeral. The funds we could spare went first to the reconstruction of the Old Temple and Cu'Brunelli's Dome, not to the Kraljica's Palais."

A grimace. "I can't offer you my staff's help. Not openly."

Allesandra knew then that she had won. She wondered if ca'Paim could hear the satisfaction in her voice. "Talbot can reach out to your aide for procedural details and to decide how many of my own staff we need to assign to ensure everything goes smoothly. We'll use palais staff and the Garde Kralji for crowd control. And you can tell Archigos Karrol that I bullied you into accepting this by threatening to withhold the final payment on the building funds."

"Would you do that?"

Allesandra brought one shoulder toward her cheek. "Is it necessary?"

One of ca'Paim's fingers stroked the golden summit of another scone. The woman sighed. "No. I suppose not, though I still don't like it."

"Good," Allesandra said. "And you'll be there, Soleil? Seated next to me?"

Another sigh. "You've become shameless as you've aged, Allesandra. Absolutely shameless. I will attend since you insist, but I won't speak. I cannot."

"That's understood." Allesandra leaned forward and patted the woman's hand. "Thank you, Soleil. I'll tell Varina what you've done; she'll appreciate the gesture."

"What about Nico Morel's followers?" ca'Paim asked. "He's the one you should be worrying about. You know how deeply that man hates the Numetodo. They are sure to protest, and demonstrations by the Morellis have turned violent before. Have you read the proclamation he and his people posted all over the city yesterday about the Ambassador's death? They'll be railing against any display of support for the Ambassador, and there might well be worse trouble with them."

This time it was Allesandra who frowned. "Ambassador ca'Rudka showed me the proclamation, and it was vile and disgusting. You're probably right. Perhaps Commandant cu'Ingres might give Vajiki Morel and his local troublemakers free lodging in the Bastida for a few days, assuming we can find them before the ceremony. In any case, I'll make certain the Commandant's posted sufficient gardai in case there is an issue. And if you would have your téni tailor their Admonitions today and tomorrow against the Morellis . . ."

"Fine," ca'Paim told her. "That much I'm happy to do. But I have to tell you, Kraljica . . ." ca'Paim frowned sternly. "There are téni here, especially the younger ones but even those high in the Faith, who have an unhealthy amount of sympathy for Nico Morel and his philosophy. Far too many of them than I like."

"I know," Allesandra told her. "That infection is among the populace as well, I'm afraid. The man's influence is is becoming increasingly dangerous. Soleil, I appreciate your cooperation in this. I know it's not what you want, and I know that it will cause you grief with Brezno, and for that I'm genuinely sorry."

Ca'Paim nodded to that and plucked another scone from the plate. "Archigos Karrol and Brezno I can deal with," she said. "I only hope this turns out to be what *you* want, Allesandra."

~

Nico Morel

NICO STARED AT THE YOUNG MAN who had brought the news. "You're certain of this?" he asked. "Certain?"

The man—an e'téni of the Concénzia Faith, still wearing his green robes—bowed. "Yes, Absolute Nico. A'Téni ca'Paim announced it to the staff this afternoon." His gaze kept skittering away, as if he were afraid that Nico's temper might erupt and leave him a charred husk. Nico took a long breath—the news *did* burn in his gut, furious and hot. It was an outrage, an insult to Cénzi to have Ambassador ca'Pallo's funeral at the Old Temple. A Numetodo, resting in that sacred place, being praised there ... But he managed a grim smile for the e'téni. "Thank you for coming to tell us," he said. "And may Cénzi's Blessing come to you for your efforts." He gave the man the sign of Cénzi.

The e'téni smiled quickly at that and bowed his way from the room, closing the crooked wooden door behind him. Nico turned to the window: between the gaps of the warped shutter, he looked down on an Oldtown alley, the central gutter clogged with waste and trash. The house they were using was on a street with two neighboring butcher shops, and the offal and stench from the carcasses was sometimes overpowering.

It was nearly dusk; the light-téni would soon be setting alight the famous lamps of the Avi A'Parete, the wide boulevard that ringed the old confines of Nessantico. He saw the flash of green as the e-téni emerged from the house and scurried back to his duties at the Old Temple, dashing between two whores walking toward the taverns on the next street. Nico could smell the piss and shit on the streets below: the scent of corruption.

That odor defined Nessantico to him.

Strangely, these weren't the smells he remembered from his time in Nessantico before the Tehuantin. In those childhood memories, Oldtown was warm and comfortable, tasting of spices and the perfume of his matarh and the sweet odor of her sweat when he hugged her on hot summer days. It was the scent of the herbs his Westlander vatarh had used in the brass bowl he'd always carried. *That* Nessantico was bright and colorful, alive with hope and promise.

That Nessantico was utterly gone. That Nessantico had died when he'd been snatched away from his matarh.

"Absolute?" The call came from Ancel ce'Breton, one of the few Morellis he trusted implicitly, and one of the two people in the room with Nico. Ancel was gaunt, with a hollow-looking face patchworked with a scraggled dark beard, his long fingers scratching at his cheap linen bashta with cracked, dark fingernails—even more than Nico, he had the appearance of an ascetic. "What are your thoughts?"

"I think, Ancel, that this is a slap to Cénzi's face," he said without turning from the window. "I think that A'Téni ca'Paim's soul will be torn and weighed by the soul-shredders and found wanting when she dies—and I hope that day comes soon. I think that once again the Concénzia Faith has shown its weakness and its degeneracy."

He felt a gentle hand brush his shoulder: Liana. She pressed against him from behind and he felt the swell of her belly against his spine. "What do you want us to do?" she asked him. "Will you preach against this? Will we act?"

"I don't know yet," he told them. "I have to think, and I have to pray." He turned away from the window. The anger was still there in the pit of his stomach, like banked coals that would never go out, but he smiled to Ancel and reached out to brush the hair from Liana's wonderful face. "I will spend the night in meditation, and hopefully Cénzi will come to me with His answer by tomorrow."

Ancel nodded. "I'll let the others know, especially the téni who are with us. They'll be ready to do whatever you ask of them, Absolute."

"Thank you, Ancel. Without you, I don't know what I'd do." Nico saw the compliment lend momentary color to the man's pale face. His eyes widened slightly as he bowed his head and gave Nico the sign of Cénzi.

"I am your servant as you are Cénzi's," Ancel said. "I'll send in one of the others in a turn of the glass with your suppers."

Nico inclined his head as the man closed the door behind him. He heard Ancel call out: "Erin, bring the Absolute and Liana their meals, please . . ." Now that they were alone, Liana rubbed her rounded stomach and finally came closer, pressing her body against his; he wrapped his arms around her body and kissed the top of her head and the glossy, dark-brown curly strands there. *Not as dark as Rochelle's hair, which was as black as midnight, but the same tight curls . . .*

He shook away the memory. It was no good thinking of his sister Rochelle. She was lost, along with the rest of his past. Nico tightened his embrace on Liana, and could feel the nagging pull of healing ribs from where the Garde Kralji had kicked him two days ago: he'd been preaching to a crowd near Temple Square. They'd shoved him down on the soiled flags and circled around him, their booted feet lashing out as he covered his head and his followers screamed invectives and tried to pull the gardai away from him. "No!" he'd shouted to them. "Don't worry! Cénzi will protect me!"

He'd wanted to use the Ilmodo then. He'd wanted to call down a storm of lightning on them, or set them afire, or sweep them away with a howling wind. He could have done any of those, easily. But he dared not—not in public, not with the téni watching. If they saw Nico use the Ilmodo, the magic of the téni, they would have invoked the laws of the Divolonté, the code by which the Concénzia Faith lived. By that code, as a defrocked téni, Nico was subject to the harshest penalties if he used Cénzi's Gift again: he would have his hands cut off, his tongue ripped from his mouth so that he would never again use the Ilmodo. Only the téni were permitted to call upon the magic of the Second World.

And because Nico truly believed in the Divolonté, because he *was* a faithful téni, he obeyed. He had not used the Ilmodo for three years now, though he had been the best of them: the most talented, the strongest with the power. Even Archigos Karrol would have admitted that. Yet Nico took no pride in his prowess: it was Cénzi who had made him that way, Cénzi who had made him the Absolute. Not Nico himself.

The Faith had cast him out unfairly. They cast him out because they were jealous of him. They cast him out because they were afraid. They cast him out because he spoke the true, pure words of Cénzi and they felt it even as they denied it. They cast him out because they heard the power in his voice, and they saw how easily he gathered followers to him.

All the a'téni, even Archigos Karrol in Brezno, now allowed the Numetodo to spew their poison. They were not like Archigos Semini, who had set the bodies of Numetodo heretics swinging in their gibbets in Brezno Square. No, the current Archigos and his a'téni might complain about the godlessness and false beliefs of the Numetodo, but they permitted them to mock Cénzi with their own magics. The téni adulterated the Faith's own magic by using Numetodo techniques themselves. They tolerated members of the Numetodo serving on the Council of Ca' and whispering into the Kraljica's ears. They listened to the nonsense the Numetodo spat out, about how all things in the world could be explained without resorting to Vucta or Cénzi or even the Moitidi. The Numetodo claimed that logic always trumped faith, and ...

The
Faith
Said
Nothing.

The Numetodo infuriated Nico. Neither they nor the people of Nessantico herself saw how the sack of Nessantico by the Tehuantin—themselves heathens and heretics who worshiped false gods—had been Cénzi's great punishment, a dire warning to them of what must happen when people turned their backs to Him.

Nico would show them. He would lead them along the correct path. They would hear his voice and heed him.

That was what Cénzi demanded of him. That was what he would do.

"Nico, where are you?" Liana was looking up at him with eyes the color of well-steeped tea—that was not like Rochelle either, who had pupils of the palest blue. Nico started, torn from his reverie. "Is He speaking to you?"

He shook his head down at her. "Not yet," he told her. "But I know He's close. I can feel His strength." He hugged her and leaned down to kiss her mouth, which yielded softly under his pressure. He felt the flicker of her tongue against his and a tightness under his bashta.

"Then let me comfort you for now," Liana whispered to him as they broke the embrace. "For a turn of the glass only . . ."

He touched her belly. "Should we . . . ?"

She laughed up at him. "I'm pregnant, my love, not made of glass. I won't break." She took his hand, and Nico allowed her to lead him over to the bed.

There, for a time, he lost himself in earthly passion and heat.

~

Brie ca'Ostheim

BRIE RAISED HER EYEBROW toward Rance ci'Lawli, her husband's aide and thus the person responsible for the smooth running of Brezno Palais. "She's the one, then?" she asked, pointing with her chin to the other room—a drawing rooms in the lower, public levels of Brezno Palais. Several of the court ladies were there, but one was seated on the floor with Elissa, Brie's oldest child, the two of them working on an embroidery piece.

Rance nodded. He towered over Brie as he towered over most people: Rance was long and thin, as if Cénzi had taken a normal person and stretched him out. He was also extraordinarily ugly, with pocked skin, sunken eyes, and the pallor of boiled rags. His teeth seemed too big for his mouth. Yet he possessed a keen mind, seemed to remember everything and everybody, and Brie would have trusted him with her life as she trusted him now. "That's Mavel cu'Kella," he whispered. It sounded like the grumbling of a distant storm.

"I suspected as much; I noticed Jan paying a lot of attention to her at the ball last month. And you're certain of her . . . condition?"

A nod. "Yes, Hïrzgin. I have my sources, and I trust them. There's already some whispers among the staff, and when she starts obviously showing . . . Well, we can't have that."

"Does Jan know?"

Rance shook his elongated head. "No, Hïrzgin. I came to you first. After all . . ."

"Yes," Brie sighed. "It's not the first time." She stared at Mavel through the sheer fabric of the curtain between the rooms. The woman was younger than Brie by a good ten years, dark-haired as most of Jan's mistresses tended to be, and Brie envied the trim shape of her, though she imagined that she could see the slight swell of her belly under the sash of her tashta. After four children, Brie struggled to keep her own figure. Her breasts sagged from years of feeding hungry infants, her hips were wide and her stomach was crisscrossed with stretch marks. She was still holding much of the weight she'd gained with Eria, her youngest from almost three years ago. Mavel had the litheness that Brie had once possessed herself.

She wouldn't keep that long. Not now.

"The cu'Kella family has some land holdings in Miscoli. She could stay with her relatives there during her confinement," Rance said. "I've had dealings with her vatarh; he was supposed to be on the list to be named chevaritt, but now . . ." He shook his head. "That will have to wait. We'll see if one of the minor Miscoli families might have a younger son they need to marry off, who would be willing to call the child his own. I'll make the usual offer for the girl's silence, and draw up the contracts for her vatarh to sign."

Brie nodded. "Thank you, Rance. As always."

He gave her an awkward half-bow. "It's my pleasure to serve you, Hïrzgin. Send Vajica cu'Kella to my office, and I'll talk with her. She'll be gone by this evening. I'll give the staff some convenient reason for her absence to counter the gossip." He bowed again and left her. Brie took a breath before the curtain then entered the drawing room. The women there rose as one, curtsying to her as she approached, while Elissa grinned widely and ran to her. Mavel rose slowly, and Brie thought she saw a hesitation in her curtsy, and a cautious jealousy in her eyes. The young woman's hand stayed on her stomach.

Brie crouched down to hug Elissa and gather her up in her arms, kissing her. "Are you enjoying yourself, my darling?" she asked Elissa, brushing back the stray strands of gold-brown hair that had escaped her braids.

"Oh, yes, Matarh," Ellisa said. "Mavel and I have been embroidering a scene from Stag Fall. Would you like to see?"

"Certainly." Brie kissed Elissa's forehead and put her down on the floor. She glanced at Mavel, who dropped her gaze to the rug, with its black-and-silver patterns. "But I was just talking to Rance, and he has asked that Vajica cu'Kella come to his office. Some family news." That brought the girl's head up again, and now her eyes were large and apprehensive. "I'm sure you'll excuse her," Brie said to Elissa.

There was a moment of silence. Brie could see the other ladies of the court glancing at each other. Then Mavel curtsied again, hurriedly. "Thank you, Hïrzgin," she said. "I'll go immediately." She gathered up her sewing, and left the room, brushing past Brie with the scent of almonds and flowers.

"Well, then," Brie said to Elissa. "Let's see that embroidery . . ." She smiled as she let Elissa take her hand, and the other women of the court smiled in return. Brie wondered, behind the smiles and idle talk, what they were really thinking.

But that, of course, she would never know.

~

Allesandra ca'Vörl

ALLESANDRA ATTENDED THE THIRD CALL service at the Old Temple, as was her usual pattern while in the city. The Admonition, delivered by A'Téni ca'Paim herself, was pleasingly stern, though Allesandra noticed that several of the téni attendants seemed to frown at her rhetoric against "those who would follow the teachings not of the Archigos of the Faith, but of self-styled disciples of Cénzi," an obvious reference to Nico Morel and his followers.

She also found herself pleased to see Erik ca'Vikej at the service, seated several rows behind the royal pew reserved for the Kralji. Despite knowing that Sergei would be upset, and that A'Téni ca'Paim would undoubtedly include the incident in her weekly report to Archigos Karrol in Brezno, she had one of her attendants go back and invite ca'Vikej forward to sit in the pew with her. He bowed to her as he took his seat near her. His smile dazzled, his eyes sparkled. Allesandra felt again the pull of the man—the people she'd set to checking his background had already told her that he was one of those individuals that people would easily follow—a natural leader.

They had also told her that he was a widower, whose wife had died birthing the last of his three children, who were currently living with relatives in exile in Namarro.

He would be a fine Gyula, should the Moitidi who governed fate ordain that for him. And if that happened . . . well, Allesandra, like Marguerite before her, believed that marriage was a fine weapon to wield. And if one's spouse was at least pleasant to be with, that was a bonus.

After the service, she allowed ca'Vikej to take her arm as they proceeded first from the temple, Allesandra nodding to those she knew as she passed them. "A stern warning from the A'Téni," he commented. His voice was warm and low, his breath smelled pleasantly of some eastern spice. "Thank you, Kraljica, for allowing me the privilege of sitting with you."

"I was surprised to see you there, Vajiki," she said.

"I once thought of becoming a téni myself," he told her. "My vatarh talked me out of it, but ever since . . ." She felt him shrug. "I still find great comfort in the Faith. And besides, I knew there was a good chance you would be attending."

"Ah? And why would that be important, Vajiki?" she asked.

He laughed at that, deep and throaty and genuine. She liked that laugh, liked the way it deepened the lines around the man's eyes. "I never had the chance to properly thank you for the dance at the Gschnas, Kraljica."

"That's all? Are all Magyarians so aggressively courteous, Vajiki?"

Again, the laugh. They were approaching the doors, and the téni there opened them wide. The western sky above the buildings that fringed the plaza was touched with red and orange, as if the clouds were afire. They entered out into a cool evening. A crowd of citizens had gathered—some who had come out of the side doors of the temple to see the Kraljica, as well as the usual curious tourists. Allesandra's carriage was waiting several steps away, the driver already holding open the door for her. They cheered as she emerged from the temple, and Allesandra lifted her hand to them. "No, I'm afraid not," ca'Vikej answered as the crowd roared. "But they don't have the incentive of your beauty. As you can see, even your subjects are overcome."

Now it was Allesandra who laughed, stopping momentarily. "You've inherited your vatarh's golden tongue, I see, but I don't flatter that easily, Vajiki. Forgive me if I say that I suspect your motives are more *political* than personal."

"In that, you'd be—" he began to reply. But a shout from the front of the crowd interrupted him.

"Don't be a traitor to your own faith, Kraljica!" a male voice shouted. His voice was strangely loud, as if enhanced by the Ilmodo, and all heads turned toward it. The gardai holding back the crowd were suddenly shoved aside as if some invisible, gigantic hand had pushed them sprawling to the flags of the pavement, and a green-clad téni, the slash of his rank on the robes telling Allesandra that he was an o'téni, stepped through the gap. She recognized him, though she didn't know his name; his was a face she'd glimpsed among A'Téni ca'Paim's staff. "You defile Cénzi if you bring the body of a Numetodo heretic into this sacred place. Cénzi will not allow it!" The o'téni stalked closer. Allesandra felt ca'Vikej's arm leave hers. "Those who are truly faithful will stop this travesty if we must!" The man's face was twisted as he shouted, and now he began to chant, his hands moving in the pattern of a spell. But Allesandra heard the whisper of steel being drawn from a scabbard, and ca'Vikej had rushed from her side. One muscular arm was around the téni's head and a dagger in his hand was pressed against the man's throat.

"Another word," she heard him say in the téni's ear, "and you'll have no throat with which to talk."

The téni's hands dropped and he stopped his chant. The gardai, regaining their feet, were now around him as well, several of them stepping between Allesandra and the téni. She heard shouts and cries. Hands hurried her to her carriage. Past uniformed shoulders, she saw the téni being dragged away, still screaming. "*. . . betraying the Faith . . . no better than a Numetodo herself . . .*"

She stepped up onto the carriage, and saw ca'Vikej, the dagger taken from him, also being hurried away. "No!" she shouted. "Bring Vajiki ca'Vikej here."

They brought him to her, a garda holding each arm. "You may release him," she told them; they reluctantly let go of ca'Vikej. "Give me his dagger," she said, and one of them handed it to her. "Vajiki, in my carriage, please."

As the door of the carriage closed and the driver urged the horses forward, Allesandra glanced at ca'Vikej. He was disheveled, his clothing torn, and there was a long scratch on his shaved head with beads of darkening blood along it. She lifted his dagger from her lap—a long, curved weapon, crafted from dark, satiny Firenzcian steel with a carved ivory handle. She turned it in her hand, admiring it. "Very few people are permitted to bear a weapon in the presence of the Kraljica," she said to him, keeping her face stern and unsmiling. "Especially one made in the Coalition."

He inclined his head to her. "Then I beg your forgiveness, Kraljica. I will remember that. Please, keep it as my gift to you; the blade was forged by my great-vatarh—my vatarh Stor gave it to me before . . ." She saw a brief flash of teeth in the dimness of the carriage. The springs of the seats groaned once as they jounced over the curb of the temple plaza onto the street.

She allowed herself to smile, then. "I thank you for your gift," she said. "But in this case, I think it's better to return it. Let that be my gift to you." She handed the dagger to him.

He hefted it in his hand, touched the hilt to his lips. "Thank you, Kraljica," he said. "The blade is now more valuable to me than ever." She watched him sheathe it again in the well-worn leather hidden under the blouse of his bashta.

"Are you hungry, Vajiki?" she asked him. "We could take supper at the palais, and then . . ." She smiled again. "We could talk, you and I."

He inclined his head in the deep Magyarian fashion. "I would like that very much," he said. His voice was like the purr of a great kitten, and Allesandra found herself stirring at the sound of it.

"Excellent," she said.

~

Rochelle Botelli

SHE HADN'T EXPECTED TO FIND HERSELF IN Brezno. Her matarh had told her to avoid that city. "Your vatarh is there," she'd said. "But he won't know you, he won't acknowledge you, and he has other children now from another woman. No, be quiet, I tell you! She doesn't need to know that." Those last two sentences hadn't been directed to Rochelle but to the voices who plagued her matarh, the voices that would eventually send her screaming and mad to her death. She'd flailed at the air in front of her as if the voices were a cloud of threatening wasps, her eyes—as strangely light as Rochelle's own—wide and angry.

"I won't, Matarh," Rochelle had told her. She'd learned early on that it was always best to tell Matarh whatever it was she wanted to hear, even if Rochelle never intended to obey. She'd learned that from Nico, her half brother who was eleven years older than her. He'd been touched with Cénzi's Gift and Matarh had arranged for him to be educated in the Faith. Rochelle was never certain how Matarh had managed that, since rarely did the téni take in someone who was not ca'-and-cu' to be an acolyte, and then only if many gold solas were involved. But she had, and when Rochelle was five, Nico had left the household forever, had left her alone with a woman who was growing increasingly more unstable, and who would school her daughter in the one best skill she had.

How to kill.

Rochelle had been ten when Matarh placed a long, sharp knife in her hand. "I'm going to show you how to use this," she'd said. And it had begun. At twelve, she'd put the skills to their intended use for the first time—a man in the neighborhood who had bothered some of the young girls. The matarh of one of his victims hired the famous assassin White Stone to kill him for what he'd done to her daughter.

"Cover his eyes with the stones," Matarh had whispered alongside Rochelle after she'd stabbed the man, after she'd driven the dagger's point through his ribs and into his heart. The voices never bothered Matarh when she was doing her job; she sounded sane and rational and focused. It was only afterward . . . "That will absorb the image of you that is captured in his pupils, so no one else can look into his dead eyes and see who killed him. Good. Now, take the one from his right eye and keep it—that one you should use every time you kill, to hold the souls you've taken and their sight of you killing them. The one on his left eye, the one the client gave us, you leave that one so everyone will know that the White Stone has fulfilled her contract . . ."

Now, in Brezno where she had promised never to go, Rochelle slipped a hand into the pocket of her out-of-fashion tashta. There were two small flat stones there, each the size of a silver siqil. One of them was the same stone she'd used back then, her matarh's stone, the stone she had used several times since. The other . . . It would be the sign that she'd completed the contract. It had been given to her by Henri ce'Mott, a disgruntled customer of Sinclair ci'Braun, a *goltschlager*—a maker of gold leaf. "The man sent me de-fective material," ce'Mott had declared, whispering harshly into the darkness that hid her from him. "His foil tore and shredded when I tried to use it. The bastard used impure gold to make the sheets, and the thickness was uneven. It took twice as many sheets as it should have and even then the gilding was visibly flawed. I was gilding a frame for the chief decorator for Brezno Palais, for a portrait of the young A'Hïrzg. I'd been told that I might receive a contract for *all* the palais gilding, and then this happened . . . Ci'Braun cost me a contract with the Hïrzg himself. Even more insulting, the man had the gall to refuse to reimburse me for what I'd paid him, claiming that it was *my* fault, not his. Now he's telling everyone that I'm a poor gilder who doesn't know what he's doing, and many of my customers have gone elsewhere . . ."

Rochelle had listened to the long diatribe without emotion. She didn't care who was right or who was wrong in this. If anything, she suspected that the *goltschlager* was probably right; ce'Mott certainly didn't impress her. All that mattered to her was who paid. Frankly, she suspected that ce'Mott was so obviously and publicly an enemy of ci'Braun that the Garde Hïrzg would end up arresting him after she killed the man. In the Brezno Bastida, he'd undoubtedly confess to having hired the White Stone.

That didn't matter either. Ce'Mott had never seen her, never glimpsed either her face or her form, and she had disguised her voice. He could tell them nothing. Nothing.

She'd been watching ci'Braun for the last three days, searching—as her matarh had taught her—for patterns that she could use, for vulnerabilities she could exploit. The vulnerabilities were plentiful: he often sent his apprentices home and worked alone in his shop in the evening with the shutters closed. The back door to his shop opened onto an often-deserted alleyway, and the lock was ancient and easily picked. She waited. She watched, following him through his day. She ate supper at a tavern where she could watch the door of his shop. When he closed the shutters and locked the door, when the sun had vanished behind the houses and the light-téni were beginning to stroll the main avenues lighting the lamps of the city, she paid her bill and slipped into the alleyway. She made certain that there was no one within sight, no one watching from the windows of

the buildings looming over her. She picked the lock in a
few breaths, opened the door, and slid inside, locking the
door again behind her.

She found herself in a storeroom with thin ingots of
gold—"zains," she had learned they were called—in small
boxes ready to be pressed into gold foil, which could then be
beaten into sheets so thin that light could shine through—
glittering, precious metal foil that gilders like ce'Mott used
to coat objects. In the main room of the shop, Rochelle
saw the glow of candles and heard a rhythmic, dull pounding. She followed the sound and the light, halting behind
a massive roller press. A long strip of gold foil protruded
from between the rollers. Ci'Braun—a man perhaps in
his late fifties, with a paunch and leathered, wrinkled skin,
was hunched over a heavy wooden table, a bronze hammer in each of his hands, pounding on packets of vellum
with squares of gold foil on them, the packets covered with
a strip of leather. He was sweating, and she could see the
muscles in his arms bulging as he hammered at the vellum.
He paused for a moment, breathing heavily, and she moved
in the shadows, deliberately.

"Who's there?" he called out in alarm, and she slid into
the candlelight, giving him a small, shy smile. Rochelle
knew what the man was seeing: a lithe young girl on the
cusp of womanhood, perhaps fifteen years old, with her
black hair bound back in a long braid down the back of her
tashta. She held a roll of fabric under one arm, as if she'd
purchased a new tashta in one of the many shops along the
street. There was nothing even vaguely threatening about
her. "Oh," the man said. He set down his hammers. "What
can I do for you, young Vajica? How did you get in?"

She gestured back toward the storeroom, placing the
other tashta on the roller press. "Your rear door was ajar,
Vajiki. I noticed it as I was passing along the alley. I thought
you'd want to know."

The man's eyes widened. "I certainly would," he said.
He started toward the rear of the shop. "If one of those no-
good apprentices of mine left the door open . . ."

He was within an arm's length of her now. She stood
aside as if to let him pass, slipping the blade from the sash
of her tashta. The knife would be best with him: he was too
burly and strong for the garrote, and poison was not a tactic

that she could easily use with him. She slid around the man as he passed her, almost a dancer's move, the knife sliding easily across the throat, cutting deep into his windpipe and at the side where the blood pumped strongest. Ci'Braun gurgled in surprise, his hands going to the new mouth she had carved for him, blood pouring between his fingers. His eyes were wide and panicked. She stepped back from him—the front of her tashta a furious red mess—and he tried to pursue her, one bloody hand grasping. He managed a surprising two steps as she retreated before he collapsed.

"Impressive," she said to him. "Most men would have died where they stood." Crouching down alongside him, she turned him onto his back, grunting. She took the two light-colored, flat stones from the pocket of her ruined tashta, placing a stone over each eye. She waited a few breaths, then reached down and plucked the stone from his right eye, leaving the other in place. She bounced the stone once in her palm and placed it on the roller press next to the fresh tashta.

Deliberately, she stripped away the bloody tashta and chemise, standing naked in the room except for her boots. She cleaned her knife carefully on the soiled tashta. There was a small hearth on one wall; she blew on the coals banked there until they glowed, then placed the gory clothes atop them. As they burned, she washed her hands, face, and arms in a basin of water she found under the worktable. Afterward, she dressed in the new chemise and tashta she'd brought. The stone—the one from the right eye of all her contracts and all her matarh's—she placed back in the small leather pouch whose long strings went around her neck.

There were no voices for her in the stone, as there had been for her matarh. Her victims didn't trouble her at all. At least not at the moment.

She glanced again at the body, one eye staring glazed and cloudy at the ceiling, the other covered by a pale stone—the sign of the White Stone.

Then she walked quietly back to the storeroom. She glanced at the golden zains there. She could have taken them, easily. They would have been worth far, far more than what ce'Mott had paid her. But that was another thing her matarh had taught her: the White Stone did not steal

from the dead. The White Stone had honor. The White
Stone had integrity.

She unlocked the door. Opening it a crack, she looked
outside, listening carefully also for the sound of footsteps
on the alley's flags. There was no one about—the narrow
lane was as deserted as ever. She slid out from the door
and shut it again. Moving slowly and easily, she walked
away toward the more crowded streets of Brezno, smiling
to herself.

~

Sergei ca'Rudka

"HAVE YOU HAD A CHANCE to speak with Varina yet? The poor woman—she's taking her loss
so hard."

Sergei nodded to Allesandra. "I took supper with her
yesterday, Kraljica. She's not sleeping well at all, judging
from the circles under her eyes. I sent my healer over to
her with a potion."

"You're such a kind man, Sergei."

She was facing away from him, and her comment was
carefully modulated. He couldn't tell if her words had been
laced with irony or not. He suspected that they were. "I pray
that when Cénzi's attendants weigh my soul—soon enough
now—that it will float in His arms, however slightly, Kraljica.
But I'm afraid it will be a rather delicate balancing act."

They were sitting on the balcony of Allesandra's outer
apartments in the Grande Palais, overlooking the gardens.
The wind-horns had sounded First Call a turn and a half
ago. Below them, the grounds staff prowled in the morning
sun, watering plants and pulling the weeds that dared to
raise their green heads in the manicured beds. To their left,
workers swarmed the scaffolding where the facade of the
north wing was still under construction. The uneven per-
cussion of hammers and chisels kept the birds from roost-
ing easily in the trees.

Allesandra lifted her cup of tea and sipped. She appeared to be watching the workers shaping the granite blocks. Sergei drank his own tea. He had little doubt that Allesandra knew his vices; as he'd aged they'd become, if anything, stronger and more compulsive. When he was in Nessantico, he visited the Bastida a'Drago nearly every day—many of the offiziers within the the the Bastida staff were men who had come up through the ranks while he had been Commandant of the Garde Kralji and then the Garde Civile; Capitaine ce'Denise was a recruit he had hired nearly forty years ago. They allowed him to prowl the lower levels, to "visit" the occasional prisoner there, and if they heard the howls of pain, they ignored them (or, often enough, were there with him). In Brezno, in his capacity as Special Ambassador to the Hïrzg, there were certain grandes horizontales Sergei would hire who could serve his particular needs in consideration of the considerably higher fees he paid for their pain and their silence.

Sergei prayed to Cénzi frequently to take these impulses away from him, but He had never answered. He had tried to stop, a thousand times, and each time had lost that battle.

He could command an army to victory but it appeared that he could not command himself.

To the public, "Old Silvernose" was generous. He was kindly in person, he was known for his charitable contributions, and praised for his long service and dedication to the Holdings. To his friends, he was loyal and he would give of himself all that he could. That part of him, too, he had strived to enhance over the years, as a balance to the other.

He wondered which side of him would be remembered, once he was gone. He wondered which side Cénzi would weigh the most. He would find out, soon enough, he suspected. There wasn't a joint in his body that didn't have issues of one sort or another. He shuffled rather than walked. It took him several breaths to rise from a chair, and his back sometimes refused to straighten. The prosthetic metal nose glued to his face stood out more than ever in the wrinkled bag of flesh in which it sat. Sergei had outlived nearly all his contemporaries. He existed in a world where everyone seemed to be younger than him. For them, the events he had witnessed and participated in were history rather than memory.

"I understand you've convinced A'Téni ca'Paim to

allow the Old Temple to be used for the funeral, despite the confrontation yesterday."

Allesandra nodded. She set down her cup and turned to him. "I did—in fact, the confrontation may have helped; she felt guilty that one of her téni was involved in such an assault. Still, I'm glad that Vajiki ca'Vikej was there."

Sergei sniffed at that. He knew that ca'Vikej had stayed for several turns of the glass at the palais, and he hoped that wasn't for the reason he suspected—but that was a question he couldn't ask. "I interviewed the téni along with A'Téni ca'Paim. He's a follower of Nico Morel, but claims he was acting on his own. I believe him."

"I'm sure you coaxed the truth from the man," she said with a strange inflection in her voice, but she hurried past the comment before Sergei could remark on it. "A'Téni ca'Paim seems to think Archigos Karrol will still be suitably outraged at the use of the temple to honor a Numetodo."

Sergei lifted an aching shoulder. "Oh, he'll pretend to be so. He has to. But he also realizes that without Karl and Varina's help, the Tehuantin might still be feasting in the ruins of Nessantico or conceivably walking the streets of Brezno. Karrol doesn't like the Numetodo beliefs—I don't either—but he understands that they've made themselves useful occasionally."

"Hmm." Allesandra put her hand atop his. Once, years ago, Sergei had thought that Allesandra might have even been attracted to him despite the differences in their age. That would have been a horrible and awkward situation, and he'd been pleased that she had never moved to take their relationship beyond friendship. Now he wondered whether she'd found another infatuation with ca'Vikej. "I do worry about the Morellis, Sergei," Allesandra said. "We're taking precautions, but . . . All the reports indicate that Nico Morel is somewhere here in the city, and his attitude toward the Numetodo is quite clear."

"Clear and entirely unreasonable," Sergei spat. "Karl and Varina were nothing except kind to him as a boy, and now he's turned on them because what they believe isn't what he believes. I assume you've alerted Commandant cu'Ingres."

"I have, and I've suggested to the Commandant that

he should step up the attempts to find Morel and hold the young man in the Bastida until after the funeral."

The Bastida. That brought images of dark stone and . . . other things. Sergei stirred uneasily in his seat. "That's sensible. We don't want a repeat of what happened last Day of Atonement. Allesandra, despite Varina's objections, I think you're going to need to move against our self-proclaimed prophet and his Morellis soon. Varina may feel that he's redeemable, but Nico Morel is too charismatic and dangerous, and too many people are beginning to listen to him. The problem is that Archigos Karrol is half in sympathy with the boy—the Faith won't do more than slap him on the wrist. If Archigos Karrol or Hïrzg Jan can see a way to use the Morellis against you, they will. At best, he's an unnecessary distraction at the moment; you don't want him to become more."

Allesandra nodded but said nothing. Her hand had gone back to her own lap. "Ambassador ca'Schisler of Brezno will attend the funeral," Sergei said. "I spoke with him before I came here. I was a little worried that the Coalition wouldn't be represented, and that would have been a terrible insult to Karl's memory."

Another nod. She was staring out toward the garden again.

"What are you thinking, Kraljica?" he asked. "Your mind is a thousand miles away."

That garnered him the hint of a smile. "We've done awful things in our time, Sergei—things that at the time we felt we had to do, but awful. I once even . . ." She stopped. A muscle twitched along her jawline as she closed her mouth. The years were beginning to take their toll on Allesandra as well, Sergei thought, especially in the last few years. There were deep wrinkles there, and around her eyes, and her hair was liberally salted with gray. "I suppose we can hardly blame others for being willing to commit violence for their own cause."

"Blame them, no," Sergei answered. "But stop them if they threaten Nessantico? Imprison them or execute them if necessary to deal with them? Yes. And without any regrets."

"You say that so easily."

"I believe it."

"I envy you your convictions, then." She seemed to shiver in the morning chill, pulling the thin cloak she wore over her tashta tighter around her shoulders. "I wanted this so much, Sergei. I wanted to be Kraljica. I imagined myself as the new Marguerite, and the Sun Throne ablaze with its former glory and more."

Sergei stirred—for the last few years, since the debacle with Stor ca'Vikej and West Magyaria, he had been pushing Allesandra to reconcile with her son. She had always pushed such hints aside angrily. But now . . . "You still have three decades and more to match her," Sergei said. "Ask the historians how troubled her first several years were if you don't already know. You can still *be* her, if that's what you want. There's plenty of time."

"I appreciate the sentiment."

"And you don't believe me."

"I know what you're going to say next, Sergei. You needn't bother. We shouldn't try to delude ourselves at this stage, not about anything." She patted his hand again. "What's my legacy to be? I'm Kraljica Allesandra, who betrayed her own child to take the Sun Throne—isn't that what they'll say of me? Kraljica Allesandra, who—if I were to make the Holdings whole again—would have to destroy her own offspring to do it. Kraljica Allesandra, who made a mistake backing Stor ca'Vikej and nearly plunged us into full war with the Coalition."

"Make sure that you don't make another mistake with Stor's son." He went too far with that; the glance she shot him was as keen as the knife on his belt. He hurried to speak again. "It's too early in the morning to be this maudlin, and neither one of us is drunk enough."

He was relieved to hear her laugh once through her nose, her mouth closed. "Karl's dead. I don't know what it is about his death that's hit me more than all the others, but it has. I'm feeling suddenly mortal. Sergei, I haven't seen my own son in five years; he only talks to me through you, my friend. He sits on an opposing throne. He calls me his enemy. Meanwhile, I've done little with the Sun Throne except to try to repair the damage the Westlanders caused."

"Maudlin," Sergei repeated. "Let's have the servants bring us some wine, so at least we have an excuse."

"It's not a joke."

"Oh, but it is, Allesandra. It's just not funny to us. But Cénzi no doubt finds it tremendously amusing. As for mortality—look at me." He spread his hands wide. "I've been feeling it for a long time. In fact, it's a wonder that I'm still moving at all. Compared to me, you've no room for complaint. You still have all your teeth. And your nose." He tapped his own false nose with a fingernail so that it rang metallically. He saw her fighting a smile, which made him grin himself. "As for your son," he continued, "I'll talk to him when I'm next in Brezno. I've suggested this before, as you know: maybe it's time the two of you sat down together, to see if you can come to an understanding. He does love and respect you, Allesandra, even if he won't say it."

"He has a strange way of demonstrating it. How many border skirmishes have there been, and more numerous now than ever since the debacle in West Magyaria? He thought that he'd give me the Sun Throne and watch the Holdings continue to fall apart. That's what he wanted."

"And instead you've kept the Holdings together," Sergei answered, "which is what I've been trying to point out to you. The Holdings have survived, despite the fact that without your guiding presence the various countries would have broken away or let the Coalition absorb them. You very nearly brought West Magyaria back to the Holdings."

"And that angers my son."

"Perhaps," Sergei admitted. "But it also makes Jan respect you, however grudgingly."

"You think so?"

"I know so," he told her. It was a lie, but he was used to lying and he did it convincingly.

He could use this. He could twist it to his advantage.

Later. For now, he patted Allesandra's hand, and he smiled again at her. "Let me talk with Jan," he repeated. "And we'll see."

Jan ca'Ostheim

JAN WASN'T CERTAIN that he could believe the story. "She's here in Brezno again? Are you *certain*?"

Commandant Eris cu'Bloch of the Garde Brezno nodded, stroking one end of his long, elaborate mustache. "It certainly appears so, my Hïrzg. Or someone is trying to create that impression. The goltschlager ci'Braun was found with a light-colored stone over his left eye, just as with your onczio, and none of the gold had been disturbed—all of the ingots were found still there. A common murderer or thief would have taken the gold. I'm afraid all signs indicate that this was indeed a contract murder by the White Stone."

Archigos Karrol, who had been at the palais when the news came, sniffed loudly. "There have been no White Stone murders in a decade and more. I think this is a fraud. The real White Stone is dead or retired."

Commandant cu'Bloch turned his bland gaze to the Archigos. The Archigos, approaching his sixtieth birthday, had once been the A'Téni Karrol ca'Asano of Malacki, until Jan had discovered that then-Archigos Semini ca'Cellibrecca had betrayed Firenzcia. Archigos Karrol had been a burly man whose presence and booming voice dominated a room, though most of his earlier brawn had evaporated over the years except for the paunch he retained in front. His hair had thinned and receded to leave his skull bare; his long beard was an unrelenting white, his skin was spotted with brown age marks, and his spine curved so much that, when walking, the Archigos seemed to be eternally staring at the floor and the cane he required to support himself. Currently, he sat perched on a chair, frowning.

"That's certainly possible, Archigos," the Commandant answered. "But, regardless, in the last year or two I have been given three or four reports from inside the Coalition that match this one. Perhaps the White Stone tired of her retirement, or perhaps she has trained a replacement."

"Or someone wants to profit from her reputation and is pretending to be her," Karrol retorted.

Cu'Bloch shrugged. "That's also possible, yes, but does it matter, either way?"

Jan lifted a hand and both men turned to him. "It's not as if the White Stone is too old. She was only a few years older than me when she killed Hïrzg Fynn," Jan commented. He couldn't keep the hopefulness from his voice; he saw Karrol glance at him strangely. "She'd be in her late thirties now; no more than forty at the most. This still may be the original White Stone."

Cu'Bloch bowed to Jan. "I have already given my offiziers a description of the way she looked at that time, my Hïrzg, though fifteen years changes a person, especially if that person wishes to change. She may look quite different now."

Jan remembered very well how she had looked then: "Elissa ca'Karina," she'd called herself at the time, and he had been deeply in love with her. He'd thought that it had been the same for her—he'd believed in their mutual affection so strongly that he'd asked his matarh Allesandra to open marriage negotiations with the ca'Karina family. Before the ca'Karina family had responded with the news that their daughter Elissa had died as an infant, the White Stone had killed his matarh's brother Fynn, then newly crowned as the Hïrzg, and fled the city. He'd glimpsed her one more time: in Nessantico during the war with the Tehuantin.

There, she had saved his life, and he could never forget the last glance they had shared. He was certain he had seen his love for her reflected in her eyes.

Even though he had married since, even though he felt a deep and abiding affection for his wife and for their children, when he thought of Elissa, something still stirred within him. He still looked for her, in the mistresses he took.

Why would she come back here? Why would she return to Brezno?

He found himself torn by conflicting feelings—as he had when he'd thought of her in that first year or two after he'd taken the crown of the Hïrzg. He was repelled by what she'd done to Fynn, whom he'd loved as he might have an older brother, yet he was drawn to her by the memory of her laugh, her lips, her lovemaking, by the pure joy of being with her. He had tried to reconcile the conflicting images in his head countless times.

He had always failed.

Jan had sent agents searching for her in the years afterward. He wasn't certain why, wasn't certain what he would do with her if she were captured. All he knew was that he *wanted* her, wanted to sit down with her and discover the truth. Of everything. He wanted to know if she had loved him as he had her, wanted to know if she had only used him to get close to Fynn, wanted to know why she'd saved him in Nessantico.

Sergei ca'Rudka had suggested that Elissa—whatever her real name might be—might have been responsible for abducting the young Nico Morel from his matarh during the Sack of Nessantico. But when Jan had interviewed the young téni Morel who had at the time been assigned to the Archigos' Temple in Brezno, Morel claimed to have no idea whether the woman—whom he called Elle Botelli—had ever been the White Stone, or where she might be now. "We always moved around," Morel had told Archigos Semini, when asked. "She never stayed longer than half a year in any one place, and usually less than that. The woman was touched; I can tell you that—the Moitidi inflicted her with voices. That was Cénzi's punishment for her sins."

Morel—he was an enigma himself, no less than the White Stone: an incredibly charming and talented acolyte and téni who had been marked from the beginning for rapid advancement. But he'd become an eloquent and stubborn troublemaker who ended up cast out from the ranks of téni when he claimed that Archigos Karrol and the Faith were no longer supporting the tenets of Cénzi. Archigos Karrol, the upstart had insisted, must either acknowledge his errors or be forcibly removed from the throne. The young man had come closer to succeeding than either Jan or Karrol had expected. There were still téni within the Concénzia Faith who would follow the charismatic Nico if he called on them.

Jan shook away his thoughts. "Find this assassin—whomever she is," Jan told the Commandant. "I don't care what resources it takes. The White Stone or someone pre-

tending to be her was in this city no more than a day ago.
She may still be here. Find her."

The Commandant bowed, smoothed his mustache once
more, and left them.

"It can't be her," Karrol persisted. "It must be an impostor. It might not even be a woman."

"Why? Why can't it be *her*?"

Karrol sputtered momentarily. He wiped at his mouth
with a large hand. "This just doesn't *feel* right," he grumbled.

Jan scowled. It shouldn't matter, one way or the other.
He was long married now, and if the affection he had for
Brie ca'Ostheim didn't burn as hot and bright as his love
for Elissa had, he did respect her and enjoy her company.
Her family had excellent political connections; she understood the duties, obligations, and societal niceties of being
the Hïrzgin. She had produced four fine children for him.
She seemed to genuinely love him. There was a friendship
between them, and she knew to look the other way with the
occasional lovers he took. He should be content.

But Elissa . . . There had been more there. He still felt
the passion occasionally, like the pulling of an old scar long
thought to be healed. Now, that ancient scar felt entirely
ripped open. *The White Stone has returned . . .*

There was nothing more he could do about it. Cu'Bloch
would find her, or not. Jan took a long breath, let it out
again. "Enough of this," he said. "Archigos, what is it you
wanted to talk to me about before the Commandant distracted us?"

Karrol lifted his head. The movement seemed painful;
his knuckles tightened around his staff. "Ambassador Karl
ca'Pallo of Paeti, the Numetodo A'Morce, has died."

"I know that," Jan said impatiently. "I saw the news in
Ambassador ca'Rudka's last dispatch. What of it?"

"I know you were reluctant to have the Faith move
against the Numetodo considering the aid that ca'Pallo
gave to both you and your matarh in the past. But . . . I
wonder if now . . ."

"If now *what*?" Jan interrupted. It was the old, old
conflict—one that Karrol's predecessor Semini had believed in, that Semini's marriage-vatarh Orlandi had
fought as well: the Numetodo were a threat to all of those
within the Faith—with their usage of forbidden magic,

with their lack of belief in any of the gods, with their reliance on logic and science to explain the world. It was the battle that Nico Morel championed too, more voraciously and harshly than even the Archigos. Jan was far less convinced. For him, belief in the Faith was a necessity of his title and little else—it was like a political marriage. "You want to be become a Morelli now, Archigos, and begin persecuting the Numetodo again? I find that a bit ironic, myself, since it's one of the things Morel wanted the Faith to do all along."

"Morel was stripped of his title as o'téni because he would not accept the guidance of his superiors," Karrol answered. "He was insubordinate and impatient and believed himself better than any a'téni or even myself. He claims to speak directly with Cénzi. He's a madman. But even the mad occasionally say things that make sense."

"You know my feelings on this."

"I do. And I know your allegiance to the Faith is strong, my Hïrzg." Jan chuckled inwardly at that; Jan was no longer sure what he believed, though he made the required motions. "But—if I may be permitted a bit of blunt honesty, my Hïrzg—you listen too much to Ambassador ca'Rudka. The Silvernose believes in nothing that doesn't advance his own interests."

"And you would have me listen more to you, is that it, Archigos?"

"I flatter myself that I know you better than the Silvernose, my Hïrzg." Jan sniffed at that. Flattering himself was one thing the Archigos did very well indeed. "Your matarh attaches herself to the Numetodo," Karrol continued. "The reports I get from A'Téni ca'Paim—"

"I see those same reports," Jan interrupted. "And I know my matarh. Better than you."

"No doubt," Karrol answered. "You undoubtedly know that Stor ca'Vikej's son Erik is in Nessantico, also—no doubt he is looking for her help to gain the throne his vatarh couldn't take. Each day Allesandra remains on the Sun Throne, she becomes stronger, my Hïrzg."

Jan scowled. He tended to agree with Karrol on that, even if he'd never admit it. He had given her the title she'd coveted for so long when Nessantico was broken and shattered. It had seemed an appropriate punishment at the time, an irony he couldn't pass by. But she had managed somehow to turn that irony on its head. He had expected her to wither and fail, to realize her errors and beg his forgiveness and help; she'd done none of those things. She'd rebuilt the city and she'd managed to hold together the fragile connections between the various rulers of the countries that made up the Holdings. With Stor ca'Vikej, she'd nearly wrenched West Magyaria back to the Holdings—she *might* have succeeded, had she actually sent the full Nessantican army in support of the man's ragtag army of loyalists. As it was, he'd had to put all of Firenzcian's military might to bear in order to put down the rebellion.

The Firenzcian Coalition had been unable to profit from Nessantico's misfortune. Il Trebbio had briefly joined the Coalition in the wake of the Tehuantin invasion, then a few months later had returned to the Holdings when Allesandra had offered them a better treaty and married one of the ca'Ludovici daughters to the current Ta'Mila of Il Trebbio. Nammaro had entered into negotiations with Brezno, then pulled away from them also.

No, his matarh had shown herself to be all too well-skilled politically, and Jan should have known. He should have seized the Sun Throne himself, should have brought the Holdings forcibly into the Coalition with his army still in the city. He could have done all that. But he'd been young and inexperienced and blinded by the chance to humble his matarh.

It wasn't an opportunity he would pass up again. And if Silvernose ca'Rudka was right, he might have that opportunity. Soon.

There was a discreet, soft knock on the door—that would be Rance ci'Lawli, his chief secretary and aide, letting him know that the Council of Ca' was in their chamber waiting for him. And there was a question he wanted to ask Rance, in any case: he had not seen Mavel cu'Kella for two days now . . .

Jan smiled, grimly, at Karrol. "Leave my matarh to me," he told the Archigos, "and concern yourself with the work of Cénzi, Archigos. Now, I have other duties . . ."

Karrol, with little good grace, rose from his chair. Bent

over, he gave Jan the sign of Cénzi. "The works of Cénzi
extend even to matters of state, my Hïrzg," he said.

"So you always tell me, Archigos," Jan retorted. "Inter-
minably."

~

Varina ca'Pallo

THE DAY OF THE FUNERAL was appropriately
gloomy. Heavy, slumbering clouds sagged low in a
leaden sky, flailing at Nessantico with occasional spatters
of chilling rain. The ceremony in the Old Temple had been
interminable, with various dignitaries spouting eulogies
praising Karl. Even the Kraljica had stood up and delivered a speech. Varina had heard little of it, honestly. All
their lovely, ornate phrases had run together into meaningless noise.

She sat in the first pew with Sergei and the Kraljica surrounding her, and she stared at the bier on which Karl's
body lay. She felt dead herself, inside. All the oiled and
polished words of admiration might as well have been
spoken in some foreign language. They did not touch
her. She stared at Karl's body. He looked *wrong,* as if the
corpse was some poor waxen sculpture laying there. Perhaps Karl was standing elsewhere in the temple, laughing
at what was being said about him. Sergei leaned over toward her at one point and whispered something into her
ear. She didn't hear him; she just nodded and he eventually leaned away again.

There was a mourning mask on her lap: a white, expres-
sionless face of thin porcelain, the closed lips too red, the
open eyeholes shimmed with wisps of black fabric, a black
lace veil glued to the top and draped over the front. The
mask was mounted on a long stick so she could fold her
hands on her lap and still have the mask cover her face if
she felt the need to be private. The mask seemed too much
effort to lift, and it seemed wholly inadequate to cover her
grief.

The murals of the newly-rebuilt Great Dome of cu'Brunelli had been draped with silken curtains: all the images of Cénzi and the Moitidi hidden because a Numetodo—a heretic, a horrible unbeliever—lay beneath them. She realized that without really seeing it. The sacred vessels and embroidered cloths had been removed from the altar on the quire, even the bas-reliefs carved on the thick buttresses had been veiled.

She should have been amused, noting that. Karl would have been, certainly. She *was* amused, somewhere distantly. She felt as if "Varina" were somewhere outside, observing this dull, wooden simulacrum of herself.

Varina realized that the people were standing around her, that several of the Numetodo had moved to their positions alongside the bier. The plan was for the bier to move in procession through the streets around the Old Temple to the outer courtyard of the Kraljica's Palais, where the pyre awaited the body. It was a relatively short distance of about two and a half blocks in the Isle a'Kralji—far, far shorter than the grand processions for Kraljica Marguerite or Kraljiki Justi, which had followed nearly the entire circle of Avi a'Parete around the city.

Nessantico was still careful about celebrating the Numetodo too much.

She would watch his body be consumed by the flames, and afterward . . .

Varina didn't want to think about that. She didn't want to contemplate the rest of the day, returning to the Ambassador's residence on the South Bank where Karl's ghost would haunt every corner and every memory, where she would constantly be reminded of the loss she had suffered.

She would never sleep next to him again. She would never hold him again. Never talk to him. She felt emptied of everything important, felt dead herself. Someone could cut off her hands or drive a knife into her heart and she would feel nothing.

Nothing.

She was standing with the others. She realized that belatedly, wondering whether she had risen herself or whether someone had helped her up. She didn't remember. She blinked, heavily. The bier with Karl's body, resting with hands folded atop his fine white bashta and the green sash

of Paeti, was passing her; she shuffled out directly behind it
with the others following. Sergei remained at her side, his
silver-tipped cane tapping on the flags, his silver-tipped face
gazing sternly forward; Kraljica Allesandra and A'Téni
ca'Paim were directly behind them, then the various ca'-
and-'cu' of the city, the diplomatic representatives living in
Nessantico, and finally those of the Numetodo.

The doors of the Old Temple were pushed open. Even
under the dreary sky, the light made Varina narrow her
eyes. She could taste rain in the air, and the flags of the
plaza were damp. The curious had come out as well: they
crowded behind the ranks of Garde Kralji and utilino who
were keeping a wide corridor open for the invited mourners to pass through. Varina could feel their stares on her,
and she lifted the mourning mask to her face, closing out
the world.

The carriages were there, waiting, along with the flat-
bedded funeral wagon drawn by three white horses in a
four-horse harness, the left front space glaringly vacant.
Behind the funeral wagon were two of the Kraljiki's carriages drawn by black horses, one carriage for Varina and
Sergei, who would ride with her; the other for the Kraljica
Allesandra. A'Téni ca'Paim's carriage was next, without
horses, only a driver-téni in white mourning robes sitting
on the seat, ready to turn the wheels with the power of
the Ilmodo. The remainder of the mourners would walk
behind—those who wished to follow the procession to the
pyre. Many would not, Varina knew—they had already
been seen, which was primarily why they were here: so
the Kraljica and A'Téni ca'Paim noticed their faces and
knew they had performed their social duty and paid their
respects.

A servant opened the gilded door of the carriage for her
and proffered a hand to help her up. She felt the suspen-
sion dip under her weight, then dip again as she settled into
the plush leather seat and Sergei put his weight on the step
and ducked to enter. She let the mourning mask fall back
into her lap. He smiled gently at her as he settled into the
seat with a groan while the attendant closed and latched
the door.

"How are you doing, my dear?" he asked. He groaned

again as he shifted position on the seat. She heard his knee
crack as he flexed it.

For a moment, she heard nothing but nonsense syllables.
It took her a breath to process the question and have it
make sense. "I don't know," she admitted. "But I'm glad
you're here with me. Karl . . . Karl would have appreciated
it."

He leaned forward and touched her knee with a thin
hand momentarily—the gesture of a confidant. Shadows
slid over his silver nose, around the much-wrinkled face.
"He was a good friend to me, Varina. Both of you have
been. The two of you literally saved my life, and I will never
forget that. Never."

She nodded. "That debt, one way or another, was paid
and repaid between you and Karl. You needn't worry."

"Oh, I don't," Sergei answered, and she pondered that
remark before letting it waft away like the rest. Unim-
portant. The carriage lurched, one of the horses snorting,
and they began to move. She could hear the steel-rimmed
wheels clattering on the uneven paving stones of Old Temple Court. She sat silently, neither looking at Sergei nor at
the view outside, but inside her own head, where Karl's
face still lived. She wondered if she would begin to forget
the familiar lines, the crinkled smile, and his eyes. She wondered if he would fade, and one day when she tried to con-
jure up his face she'd be unable to do so.

She heard voices outside the carriage, but she paid them
no attention. Sergei, however, had straightened in his seat
across from her and moved the curtains aside with a hand,
his silver nose pressed against the wavy glass there. Past
him, she could see the lines of onlookers beyond the gardai,
and beyond them . . .

A huge person had appeared: a giant dressed in green,
his head larger than the carriage in which they rode and his
shoulders as wide as three men abreast, clad in an imitation
of téni-robes and his eyes glowing with a red fire that sent
shadows racing out toward the carriage from the people
between them. The chanting voices seemed to come from
that direction, and she realized that it wasn't a person but
some sort of gigantic puppet, manipulated from below by
poles. It bobbed and weaved over the heads of the onlook-

ers, who were turning now toward it rather than the funeral procession.

She realized who it must represent in that moment: Cénzi. She had seen images of the god done that way, with his eyes glowing as he cast fire at the Moitidi who opposed him. The puppet-god wasn't staring at Varina, however, but at the space before her carriage—the space where Karl's bier moved.

"Sergei?"

Sergei had opened the carriage window and called to one of the gardai on the line, who ran over to him. "Who is doing this?" he asked.

"The Morellis," the garda answered. "They assembled behind the crowd, and when the bier approached, all of a sudden that *thing* went up."

"Well, get it down before—" That was as far as Sergei got.

The puppet-god roared.

The sound and heat of its call washed over her. It lifted the carriage—she heard horses and people alike screaming even as she felt herself rising—and sent Sergei tumbling backward into her. He struck her hard, and then the carriage, lifted in the wind of the puppet-god's scream, fell back to earth hard.

There must have been more screams and more sound, but she could hear nothing. She was screaming herself; she knew it, felt it in the rawness of her throat, but she heard no sound at all. She could taste blood in her mouth and Sergei was thrashing his limbs as he tried to untangle himself from her, and he was shouting, too. She could see his lips mouthing her name—"Varina!"—but all she heard was the remnant of the puppet-god's roar, echoing and echoing.

Then she remembered. "Karl!" she shouted silently, pushing at Sergei and trying to rise from the wreckage of the carriage. She could see the street and horses on their sides, still in their harnesses and thrashing wildly at the ground, and bodies of people here and there.

Especially around the bier.

Which burned and fumed and smoked in the middle of the courtyard.

~

Niente

THE ISLAND CITY TLAXCALA gleamed like white bone on the saphire waters of Lake Ixtapatl, but Niente didn't see it. All his attention was on the bronze bowl before him and the water shimmering there.

The scrying bowl. The bowl that held all the possible futures. They swam before his eyes, blotting out reality. He saw war and death. He saw a smoking mountain exploding. He saw a queen on a glowing throne, and a man on another throne. He saw armies crawling over the land, one with banners of blue and gold and the other of black and silver. He saw an army of warriors and nahualli coming against them. Yet beyond that war, down a long, long path, there was hope. There was peace. There was reconciliation. *Go to war, and you will find peace.* That was what the god Axat seemed to be saying to him. The images surrounded him, warm and gentle, and he basked in their heat ...

"Taat Niente?" *Father Niente.*

The query was accompanied by a touch on his shoulder that broke his concentration, and Niente grudgingly lifted his head from the futures swimming in the bowl's waters. The emerald light illuminating his face faded with the spell's passing, and his soul returned to the city with a shudder. He was standing atop the Teocalli Axat, the high, stepped pyramid that was the temple of the moon-god Axat. The Teocalli Axat wasn't the highest structure in the city—that honor belonged to the Calli Tecuhtli, the House of the King, though the Teocalli Sakal, the sun-god's temple, was only a few spans lower. Still, from the summit on which Niente stood, all of Tlaxcala was laid out before him: the canals that served as streets glistening straight as spears and crowded with *acal,* the small, paddled watercraft used for transportation within the island city; the huge plazas bustling with people on their unguessed er-

rands; the market with its thousands of stalls. Beyond the
market rose the Calli Tecuhtli, its facade decorated with
the bleached skulls of vanquished warriors. Out beyond
the city and the lake in which it sat, the great valley was
ringed by snow-capped peaks, with a trail of fuming ash
wind-smeared across the summit of the volcano Poctlitepetl and its neighboring mountains. The sun had already
slid behind the slopes though the western sky was still
ablaze, the flanks of the lower clouds touched with the colors of burning while the east was a deep purple in which
the first stars glimmered.

The magnificent view from the summit of Teocalli Axat
never failed to stir Niente, never failed to make his heart
beat harder in his chest. He loved this land. His land. And
he was grateful to Axat for giving him hope that it could
become the seat of a greater empire yet.

"Taat?" *Father.*

He turned finally to the young man, panting from his
long climb up the steps of the temple, his arms crossed over
his chest—Niente's son. "I hear you, Atl," he said. "It's later
than I thought. I'm sorry. Did Xaria send you?"

Atl grinned at him. "Na' Xaria says if you don't get
home soon, she'll throw your supper to the dogs and you
can fight them for it. She also said that you'd be sleeping
with the dogs as well."

Niente smiled in return. The expression pulled at the
scars of his face. He knew what that face looked like, knew
what his decades of casting Axat's spells and peering into
the scrying bowl had cost him, as it had cost every nahualli
who utilized Her power so deeply. His left eye was a white,
blind horror, his mouth sagged on that side also, as if his
flesh had melted there. Ridged, hard scars furrowed his
face and body; his muscles wobbled in sacks of skin as if
they had shriveled inside him. He appeared at least two
hands of years older than he was.

But none of the other nahualli would dare to challenge
him and try to wrest the title of Nahual from him. No. He
was the famous Nahual Niente, whose spells had driven
the army of the Easterners from their cousins' land along
the coast, who had accompanied Tecuhtli Zolin across the
Great Sea to the Easterners' land, the empire of the Hold-

ings, who had burned their great capital city, and who had warned Tecuhtli Zolin of the consequences of his pride even when the Tecuhtli had refused to listen to him. He was Nahual Niente, who with Tecuhtli Citlali had razed the last Easterners' fortress in the Hellins—the city of Tobarro—to the ground and ended the Holdings' occupation of the Hellins forever.

He was Nahual Niente whose fame approached and even exceeded that of the great Mahri.

No, the nahualli were content to let Axat take Niente when She would. They were content to watch his body burn slowly away at her bidding, a little bit each day. The nahualli who might want his title were content to be patient, to wait.

Even his own son, who was also one of the nahualli.

Niente rubbed the golden bracelet around his right forearm: the sigil of the Nahual. Atop the teocalli, the youngest nahualli were lighting the oil cauldrons which would burn all night. They inclined their heads to Niente—"Good evening to you, Nahual Niente!" they cried, and he could almost believe the sincerity in their voices. The cauldrons were already lit on the other teocaltin of the city and atop the Calli Tecuhtli. All over the city, lanterns clawed at the night. Tlaxcala glowed yellow in the darkness of the valley, a city that never slept.

Niente slapped Atl on the shoulder. At two hands of age, his son had an athlete's body, and though he was trained as a nahualli, he could as easily have entered the warrior caste. "Let's get home," Niente said to him. "I'm hungry enough to eat those dogs if they get in the way."

He threw the water from the bowl onto the stones and wiped the brass with the hem of his robe. He slipped the bowl into its leather pouch and slung it around his neck. The two started down the long, steep staircase, Niente moving carefully and noting that Atl stayed close to his elbow. Had Atl been any other of the nahualli, he might have been insulted, but he was glad for Atl's attentiveness.

As they descended, Niente saw a young man in the blue garb of the Tecuhtli's staff hurrying up the stairs toward them—one of the Tecuhtli's pages. Niente paused, letting the boy approach. The page bowed, prostrate on the nar-

row stone steps, at Niente's feet. "Up," Niente told him.
"What's your message?"

"The Tecuhtli requests your presence, Nahual."

Niente laughed aloud at that, which startled the boy.
"I guess the dogs will be well fed tonight," he said to
Atl. "Tell your Na' Xaria that it's the Tecuhtli's fault, not
mine."

The Calli Tecuhtli was in the next *calpulli,* the neighbor-
hoods into which the city was subdivided by the canals
and large boulevards. Niente followed the page along
the terra cotta flank of one of the aqueducts that provided fresh water to the city—the waters of Lake Ixtapatl
being rather brackish—and over one of the many arching bridges of the island city to the plaza before Calli
Tecuhtli. Ahead of him, the pyramid of the Calli rose like
Poctlitepetl itself, its summit also smoking, not with ash
and lava but with the fires of oil cauldrons. The plaza was
bustling with people: visitors from the other cities come
to see the glory of the capital Tlaxcala; citizens petitioning one or another of the innumerable bureaucrats who
actually ran the city; scarred and tattooed High Warriors
who served the Tecuhtli. All of them stepped aside before
Niente with inclined heads and muttered greetings as he
followed the page up the steps. At the third level of the
pyramid, the page stopped, leading Niente to a curtained
alcove a little way down. He tapped on the call drum outside and lifted the thick, woven tapestry, gesturing to Niente to enter.

The room—the outermost room of the Tecuhtli's
apartments—was lavish. The walls were brightly painted
with figures of birds of prey and solemn warriors. Warm
woven rugs covered the floor. Citlali sat in a carved wooden
chair cushioned with many pillows, a table with several
dishes steaming in front of him. "Ah, Nahual Niente. Sit.
Eat with me; no doubt poor Xaria has already given up on
you for supper."

The red-dyed tattoo of an eagle, the insignia of the
Tecuhtli, seemed to wriggle on Citlali's wide, shaved head
as he spoke. He gestured to a chair set on the other side of
the table. "Thank you, Tecuhtli," Niente told him, sinking

into the chair with a sigh. "I'm afraid I forget the time too easily."

"You look more tired than usual."

"I am," Niente admitted. "Axat is a hard taskmaster, and She doesn't care what happens to Her servant."

"And what did you see in the scrying bowl today?"

Niente leaned forward and lifted a cover from one of the dishes. He took a flat corn cake and slathered meat on it, folding it over. He gnawed at it hungrily. *The battle raging in the waters of the scrying bowl . . . The strange architecture of the buildings . . . The enemy in their steel and shields . . . The blood, the fire, the death . . . And the long path of peace . . .* And the cost of that Long Path; he knew that also. "I saw enough," he said as he swallowed, "to guess why you've asked me here, Tecuhtli." He sighed. "I don't look forward to crossing the Lesser Sea again."

Citlali laughed, clapping his hands together once. "You guess well," he said. "I thought it would be enough for me to send the Easterners running back home like a pack of frightened dogs. I thought when I stood on the burning embers of their last fortress here on our cousins' lands of the Hellins that I'd be satisfied. But I find I'm not. I keep dreaming of their cities and the loss we suffered there. I keep thinking that we haven't yet paid for the souls of those great warriors and nahualli who died there."

"More warriors and nahualli will die if you do this, Tecuhtli. Many more." Even though he had seen the Long Path, no future was certain. He had also seen that there would be peace—for a time—if Citlali stayed here. But not forever. The Holdings would be back, and this time they would bring an army that would be terrifying.

"I know. Yet isn't that what the true warrior desires?"

"There are still wars to fight here. Not all of our cousins beyond the White-Peak Wall pay tribute to Tlaxcala—you can add their skulls to the rack."

Citlali nodded as Niente spoke, but his gesture was tempered with a shrug. Niente could see the vision of the scrying bowl in the Tecuhtli's eyes, glimmering there in his pupils. He could almost hear Axat's laughter. *This is what She wants of you. You want to deny it, but you know it.*

"I hear Tecuhtli Zolin in my dream," Citlali said. "His

spirit calls to me from the land of the dead to finish what he started."

"Zolin is too proud even in death, then," Niente said, and Citlali barked laughter at that.

"Zolin refused to listen to you, Niente. I'll listen. If you tell me that Axat says I shouldn't go, I won't."

Niente sat, silently. *Do you throw this to me as a test, Axat?* he asked, and thought for a moment that he heard the response of Her sinister laughter. "I can't tell you that, Tecuhtli," he said.

Citlali laughed again, this time with satisfaction. He clapped his hands together loudly enough in his pleasure that the page outside lifted the flap of the tapestry and peered in momentarily. "I was certain you'd argue against this, Niente," he roared. "I thought you would warn me of what you saw in the scrying bowl as you did Zolin, and tell me that I was being foolish. I thought you would say that I tempt the gods, and they would strike me down for my arrogance and pride, as they did Zolin."

Niente smiled, taking another bite of meat as Citlali spoke. No, he would not tell Citlali what he'd seen in the bowl, because Axat had made it clear to him that he must not, not if he wanted the vision of the Long Path to come to fruition. He only bowed his head to the warrior. "I will be at your side, Tecuhtli Citlali, as I was at Zolin's. I will be your Nahual, and I will look again on the Easterners' land."

Citlali rose from his seat—his body was still that of a muscular warrior, but there was the beginning of a paunch around his waist. That explained much of his eagerness to Niente: unlike the Nahual of the nahualli, the Tecuhtli—the highest of the High Warriors—rarely reached old age before a rival arose to challenge and kill him. If Citlali wanted his name to be remembered long after his time, he needed to make his mark on the world.

Ambition: it had killed many of the Tehuantin over the centuries.

"Page!" Citlali called, and the boy slid into the room from outside. "Call the High Warriors—tell them to come here tonight. The Tecuhtli and the Nahual wish to meet with them." The boy made an obeisance and hurried away. Citlali turned back to Niente, and Niente saw him draw in his stomach self-consciously. "This will be a time of greatness for the Tehuantin," he said. "Is that what you saw in the bowl, Nahual?"

To that, Niente could nod. "Indeed," he said. "That is what I saw. Greatness."

INCARNATIONS

Nico Morel
Varina ca'Pallo
Allesandra ca'Vörl
Niente
Sergei ca'Rudka
Brie ca'Ostheim
Varina ca'Pallo
Jan ca'Ostheim
Rochelle Botelli
Varina ca'Pallo

Nico Morel

THE BLAST FROM THE BLACK SAND was more powerful and stunning than Nico expected.

The concussion hit his chest like the fist of Cénzi. It fluttered the drapes of the puppet, pummeling the papier-mâché head so strongly that none of them could hold it upright. The puppet toppled as people screamed and pieces of the Ambassador's funeral bier began to rain down around them.

"Away!" Nico called to his followers. "Scatter! Quickly!"

The crowd was already fleeing; the gardai were confused and stunned. The Morellis evaporated into the crowd, lost in a few moments. Nico waited a few breaths, staring at the destruction. There were several people down, mostly the Numetodo who had been around the bier—he had no sympathy for death or injuries to them at all. Still, there were onlookers who had been hurt by flying debris. "I'm sorry," Nico whispered to one of them, a woman bleeding profusely from a cut to the temple. "No one intended for you to be hurt. Cénzi will bless you for the blood you've spilled here today, and for your pain."

He felt Liana tugging at his sleeve. "We have to go," she said urgently. Nico glanced up. Ambassador ca'Rudka was rising clumsily from the twisted frame of the carriage following the bier; ca'Pallo's heretic wife Varina was already out, staring in horror at the destruction of the bier. The horses pulling the Kraljica's carriage had bolted and the driver was trying to bring them to a stop farther down the court, with gardai chasing after them. The blast had knocked the a'téni's driver from his seat and ended his chant; her carriage had halted untouched well back from the rest.

Nico smiled at that—he hadn't wished A'Téni ca'Paim any harm.

Where Karl's body had lain, there was a black hole torn in the stone flags, with debris sprayed for a dozen strides all around. "Thank you, Cénzi," he prayed, making the sign quickly. "Thank you for permitting me to do Your bidding." He wondered if Varina would understand the irony of using black sand—the invention of Westlander heretics and recreated by Karl and Varina—against them.

He nodded as Liana tugged at his sleeve again. She was holding the swell of her stomach. "You're all right?" he asked her, suddenly concerned that she'd been injured.

"I'm fine," she told him, "but you need to go. Now!"

He shook his head at her. "Go on," he said to her: calmly, quietly. "I'll meet you at the house." She hesitated, and he waved his hand toward her. "Go!" he said again, and this time she obeyed, hurrying away with the waddle of the heavily pregnant.

Nico turned back to the chaos. He watched the gardai from behind a screen of those who had also stayed behind, snared by the sight of all the destruction. He listened to Old Silvernose's shouting as he tried to organize the rescue. He couldn't entirely hold back the exultation he felt, though he tried since that was only his own foolish pride tugging at the corners of his mouth. Finally, he walked away slowly, calmly, at peace—as if out for a simple morning stroll.

They could catch him only if Cénzi willed it to be so, and if Cénzi willed such, then Nico would be comfortable with His decision. He was beyond the Kraljica's or the Archigos' authority. They could do nothing to him on their own.

So he walked away leisurely, his face solemn. Cénzi held him in His protective hands.

When he reached the safehouse the Morellis had established in Oldtown, a turn of the glass or more later, he entered into an ongoing celebration. Ancel slapped his shoulders; Liana hugged him desperately as the others gathered in the room shouted and grinned.

"A full hand of them dead, that's what the word on the street is," Ancel said. "And that bastard ca'Pallo's body is strewn in bits over the Temple Court for the téni to clean up—that'll teach the A'Téni to cozy up with the heretics. Too bad thc blast spared ca'Pallo's wife and Old Silvernose."

Strangely, the glee in Ancel's face soured Nico's good mood. He looked at them, at their pleasure, and Cénzi moved in him. He frowned, his face darkening. "Why are you laughing? Why do you grin?" he asked them, and the scorn in his voice wiped the celebration from their mouths. The room went rapidly quiet. Liana released him; Ancel took a step back, his face suddenly crestfallen.

"I'm sorry, Absolute," Ancel said, spreading his hands in apology. "Didn't we do as Cénzi asked us to do?"

"We did," Nico answered him. "And we succeeded only because we have His hands over us. Should we celebrate that? Yes, we've sent several of the heretics to Him for His judgment, but we've taken away childrens' vatarhs and matarhs, we've shattered their families. We've brought hardship on those close to them, and many of them are *not* our enemy. Many of them are believers. Should we be *pleased* that we've hurt them, that we've caused them pain?"

"I didn't think—" Ancel began, and Nico cut him off with a wave of his hand.

"No, you didn't. None of you did. Not even me." He took a breath, and he felt Cénzi's words filling his mind. "These are *lives* we're talking about. These are people who are little different from us. Yes, they're heretics. Yes, they poison the Holdings and the Faith with their very presence. Yes, they're our enemies. But they are *people* nonetheless, and when we cause them pain, we bring pain upon ourselves at the same time."

He could feel hot tears welling in his eyes, and he didn't care that they spilled over and ran down his cheeks as his disciples watched. "I don't mourn a broken cup. I don't grieve if the strap on my sandal breaks. But I *do* cry for the Numetodo. I cry because they failed to see the truth. I cry because I could not convince them to follow the truth. I cry because it was given to me to be their executioner. I cry because it pains me to see the waste of their great potential."

Then he felt Cénzi lift him, and he dragged his sleeve over his eyes as the anger left him. "Ancel," he said. "I'm

sorry. I'm not angry with you. I'm not. You are my right
hand, and you've done well today. All of you have, and
we should be pleased that we were able to demonstrate
Cénzi's power to those who control the Holdings and the
Faith. We have been good servants today. But it's our task
to *always* be good servants, to be ready to run when the
Master calls us and to do His bidding no matter what he
asks of us."

Nico opened his arms, taking a step toward Ancel and
enfolding him in his arms. He kissed the man's cheek. "You
know this. I know you do, and it wasn't my place to scold
you. Do you forgive me, my friend?"

Ancel grimaced, then let out a breath through his nose.
He nodded, and Nico grabbed his head and kissed the
crown of it. He clapped the man on the back. He smiled at
them all. Liana embraced him again, pressing her stomach
and their child to his.

"We've *all* done well today," he said to them, his gaze
sweeping over the people gathered in the room. "You are
all blessed."

~

Varina ca'Pallo

HER EARS WERE RINGING and she could barely
hear the voices talking to her through the din. That
was an improvement, at least: immediately after the blast
she'd found herself entirely deafened. She'd been carried
to the nearest building—one of the Holdings' bureaucratic offices that dominated the Isle A'Kralji. Healers
had been sent for; gardai had flitted in and out asking
questions of her and Sergei. Even Commandant cu'Ingres
had seen her, and the news he had brought her was grim.
Kraljica Allesandra and A'Téni ca'Paim were both shaken
but unharmed, but of the dozen Numetodo who had been
accompanying Karl's bier—all of them friends, most of
them longtime members of the group—five were dead,
and three more were seriously injured. Even if they lived,

they would suffer from the effects of this day for the rest of their lives.

Varina cried for them more than she cried for Karl, who was beyond suffering.

Talbot had been among those escorting the bier; luckily, his injuries had been minor.

Varina frowned in concentration toward Sergei, who was leaning over her solicitously. She could see her warped reflection in his silver nose; her face was scratched, a long line of dried blood slicing across her forehead, and her right cheek was dark with a rising bruise. "The deafness should be temporary, the healers tells me," he was saying. She had to concentrate on his lips to understand him. "That's good news for both of us—my hearing has suffered enough in the last few years. They also tell me that none of your injuries are likely to be serious, though you're going to be stiff and sore for several days. You don't appear to have broken bones, though you should let them know if you feel sharp pain inside, or if your cuts start to grow red or foul."

"It was Nico who did this?" she asked.

Sergei scowled. "Yes," he said. "He and the Morellis. One of the gardai swears that he saw Nico in the group below the puppet."

"Why would he do this? Karl and I never . . . never . . ." She bit at her lower lip, the tears threatening again at mention of his name.

"Hopefully you'll get to ask the man yourself, when we find him," Sergei told her. "And they *will* find him. I've already told Commandant cu'Ingres that I will personally oversee the search for Morel if he's not already been captured by the time I return from Brezno."

"You're still going? You're all right?"

"I'm old and tough—it will take more than a bit of black sand to stop me. I've already started an investigation into how they acquired the black sand; I suspect that someone within the Armory is a Morelli sympathizer. But with the recent border incursions, I have to go . . ." The smile collapsed as if under its own weight, and he placed his hand on Varina's shoulder. "I'm so very sorry, Varina. This should never have happened. Karl deserved far better than this."

The weeping overtook her then, and she could not speak. Sergei patted her shoulder, but his gaze was elsewhere. "Karl's . . . body?" she managed to say, finally.

"Karl's body," he said, and she could see by the tightening of his lips that he wasn't telling her everything, "has been recovered and is already on the pyre at the Kraljica's Palais. The Garde Kralji have been stationed around it, and there are several Numetodo there as well, who say they won't leave until the pyre's been lit."

"I need to go there, then." Varina started up. She could feel her muscles protesting the movement, but she managed to sit. The room lurched around her, then settled.

"Varina, Kraljica Allesandra said she would light the pyre herself. The healers have said you should stay—"

"I need to go there," she said, more firmly, and Sergei sighed. He nodded.

"I told the Kraljica that would be your answer. I'll accompany you there . . ."

"Varina . . ." Kraljica Allesandra enveloped her as she stepped from the carriage after Sergei. "I am so sorry. I must take the blame for this atrocity. We obviously didn't take all the precautions we should have, and that's my responsibility."

Varina shook her head. "It wasn't your fault," she said simply. Behind the courtiers and chevarittai who flanked Allesandra, she saw Mason ce'Fieur, a Numetodo and friend, and one of her students within the group. He nodded to her grimly. "Excuse me, Kraljica," she said to Allesandra, and went to Mason. They embraced.

"A'Morce Numetodo," he said, and the use of the title startled her. Karl had been the nominal head of the group for as long as she had been with them. She'd never considered that with his passing, the title might pass to her, but it seemed it had. "We've been waiting, all of us."

She glanced toward the pyre. There were the ca'-and-cu' in their finery—the palais sycophants who wanted the Kraljica to see them—but there were also the Numetodo of the city, most of them ce' or less: two hundred or more of them, faces she recognized, people she had worked with and taught. They stood there now, silent and patient.

The pyre was three people high, and the smell of oil was

strong in the courtyard between the scaffold-latticed wings
of the palais. At the top of the pyramidal stack of timbers,
a closed wooden coffin had been set—no longer the body
draped in the flag of Paeti. Varina's lips tightened at the
sight and her stomach overturned, sending acid burning in
the back of her throat. She swallowed hard, once. "Let's do
this," she said. "We'll have more pyres to light for the rest
of our fallen soon enough."

With Sergei on her left, the Kraljica on her right, and
the Numetodo closing ranks behind her, she advanced to
the base of the pyre. She looked up at the coffin and for a
moment had to pause, overwhelmed by memories of Karl.
Her stomach churned anew, and she closed her eyes briefly.

She opened them again, finding in her mind the spell
she'd prepared last night. It sat in her head like an egg on
the edge of bursting, and she caressed it with her thoughts.
This was the way of the Numetodo: like the téni, they used
a pattern of words and hand movements to shape the
spell—a formula that must be followed. Like the téni, the
effort of spell-casting cost them in exhaustion and weakness. Unlike the téni, they did not call on Cénzi or attribute
the power to any deity at all; unlike the téni, they did not
have to cast their spell immediately upon finishing the in-
cantation. The Numetodo knew how to hold the spell in
their minds, to be released with a word and a single gesture
much later. The Numetodo could thus "pay in advance" the
weakness that came with spell-casting and not be affected
later. They could cast a prepared spell in the moment it
took to speak and gesture.

She did that now. Standing before the pyre, she opened
the spell. *"Tine,"* she said in the language of Paeti, Karl's
homeland. *Fire.* She made a motion as if casting a stone at
the base of the pyre. A sun erupted within the center of the
pyramid, yellow-white and so hot that the wavering shim-
mer of it struck the onlookers like a hurricane wind. The
oiled timbers caught with an audible *k-WHOOMP,* and
flames leaped toward the sky, twirling tornadoes of sparks
ahead of them. A fume of smoke followed, drifting toward
the distant rooftops of the palais where a wind tore at the
column and smeared it westward toward the Old Temple
and the River A'Sele.

Already, the furious blaze was licking at the coffin that

held Karl's remains. As Varina watched, the flames slid upward along the sides until the wooden box was obscured by flame and veiled in smoke. "Good-bye, my love," Varina whispered. "I will always miss you."

The tears were streaming unashamedly down her face, the fierce heat of the pyre drying them quickly. Someone was hugging her, and she didn't know if it was Sergei or the Kraljica or Mason.

It didn't matter. She watched Karl's remains spiraling upward into eternity.

She stood there until the pyre collapsed, several minutes later, into a heap of ash and coal as dead and as charred as her own self.

~

Allesandra ca'Vörl

ALLESANDRA WATCHED SERGEI PACE in front of the portrait of Kraljica Marguerite. The portrait's stern eyes seemed, to Allesandra, to track the Ambassador's limping progress from side to side. Commandant cu'Ingres didn't watch at all; his gaze was fixed determinedly on the small fire in the hearth, intended to take the evening chill from the room. A'Téni ca'Paim sat near the table of pastries, with a full plate on her ample lap.

Allesandra had no appetite herself. The carnage she'd seen during the funerary parade had stolen that. Her hands still trembled, remembering. *So cowardly, the use of the black sand. Such an awful death . . .* There was still a faint ringing in her ears from the blast.

"We can't permit another incident like this, Kraljica," Sergei declared as he passed beneath the portrait yet again. "The message this sends to the populace; the message this sends to the Faithful . . . We can't allow it."

"There was no téni-magic involved in this," A'Téni ca'Paim declared sternly. "Morel understands the consequences if he would use the Ilmodo. That's why he used

black sand—though one of his followers probably set off
the black sand with a spell as the bier passed over it."

"That's exactly the point," Sergei answered. "He was
able to disrupt a solemn ritual of the Holdings *without* the
Ilmodo. Without magic. The use of black sand was a message: that the Faith is useless and weak, that the Holdings
can be held hostage by anyone who can create black sand,
that the Numetodo are more dangerous than any téni.
That's worse than if he *had* used the Ilmodo."

Ca'Paim's face wrinkled in a moue of disgust. "The Faith
is *not* weak," she responded primly. "The Faith is stronger
than it has been in decades. Archigos Karrol has seen to
that."

Allesandra noticed that ca'Paim pretended not to hear
Sergei's audible sniff of disdain at that statement. "You
think that Morel isn't intelligent enough to understand
the symbolism of his actions?" Allesandra asked her. "It
seemed clear enough to me. That blasphemous puppet of
Cénzi was staring directly at the bier when the black sand
exploded. I think Morel *would* have used the Ilmodo to the
same effect—except that he was obeying the laws of Faith.
Apologies to you, A'Téni ca'Paim, but the man believes he
follows the tenets of the Toustour and the Divolonté far
more closely than any of us a'téni and Archigos Karrol."

"His message may be read differently by different people, Kraljica," Sergei persisted, "and that's even more of an
issue. Yes, to the Faith he is saying 'Look, I obeyed your
rules even though I find them supremely foolish.' To the
Numetodo, he says 'I find your beliefs vile and heretical.'
But I think the general populace—who is neither téni nor
Numetodo—takes away an entirely different statement. I
think some of them might look at what happened and think
'I can do that. Why, *anyone* could do that.' *That's* dangerous. That's not what we want the people to believe, especially those who might have reason to oppose us."

Ca'Paim bit savagely into a pastry, chewing furiously.
Cu'Ingres watched the dance of the flames. "So what would
you have me do, Sergei?" Allesandra asked.

"We must find Morel. We must execute him savagely
and publicly," Sergei answered. "Then your answer to his
message is: 'If you try this, you die.'"

"Is that what Varina would tell me to do?" Allesandra asked.

"No," Sergei admitted. "It's not. But I'm your adviser, not the A'Morce Numetodo. My loyalty is to you, Kraljica: to Nessantico, and to the Holdings—as it always has been. I tell you what will best serve those loyalties. We need to deal harshly with Nico Morel and his followers."

"I agree with the Ambassdor entirely," ca'Paim said. She rose, still holding the plate of pastries. "My people will aid you in that in any way we can. I can begin by questioning those suspected of having Morelli sympathies . . ." She gave the sign of Cénzi, one-handed, to Allesandra and the others. "Do you think Talbot could have someone wrap these up for me, Kraljica?" she asked, holding up the plate. "I hate to see them go to waste . . ."

A'Téni ca'Paim made her exit with a parcel of sweets, and Commandant cu'Ingres accompanied her from the room. Talbot—who had insisted on returning to work despite the cuts and scratches he'd sustained—sent in a trio of servants to clear the tables and take the trays back to the kitchens.

Sergei had made no motion to leave. Allesandra watched him, his attention seemingly on the servants as they went about their tasks, one hand behind his back, the other leaning on a silver-knobbed cane that nearly matched his nose. A stripe of the candle later, the last servant bowed and left the room, closing the door behind her. "What, Sergei?" Allesandra asked then. "I have Erik ca'Vikej arriving for lunch in a half-turn. He wants to discuss how the exiled West Magyarian government might respond to the Morelli issue."

Sergei turned to her. She saw his eyes close briefly and his lips press together, as if the movement pained him—or as if the mention of ca'Vikej bothered him. "You're toying with black sand and fire there, Kraljica," he said. "As Ambassador to the Coalition, I have to caution you against appearing to openly support the man."

He seemed to swallow something else that he might have said, and she wondered if he realized the other feelings she had for Erik. "As Ambassador to the Coalition, I expect you to support me, however I tell you to do so," she answered sharply, and he inclined his head; mostly, she suspected, so she could not see his eyes.

"Forgive me, Kraljica—that is, of course, my duty. I will be seeing your son in a few days. But I would like to offer him an olive branch rather than a naked sword."

Allesandra was already shaking her head before he finished. "You're becoming predictable, Sergei," she told him. "And you're getting soft in your dotage."

"Then you've decided against my proposal to reconcile with him?"

"I appreciate the thought that went into it, Sergei. And your intent."

"But?"

"I don't intend to capitulate so my son can take the Sun Throne."

Tap, tap . . . Sergei took a few shuffling steps toward her. His quilted face was earnest, and she could see the reflection of the hearth's fire flickering in his polished nose. "You wouldn't be capitulating, Kraljica, only naming your son as your heir upon your death."

The laugh she gave was more of a cough. "I fail to see the difference, Sergei. If I name Jan as heir, I lose my power as Kraljica. Everyone will start to look east to Brezno and the Hïrzg with any proclamation I might make, to see if he agrees. The Council of Ca' here will be more concerned with how their rulings are perceived by Jan than by me. I intend to live a long life yet, Sergei. What did you tell me the other day—that I have decades yet to match Kraljica Marguerite?" She rose from her seat—*let him see that our conversation is done.* She spoke now distantly and sternly, as if giving an order to Talbot. "Well, I intend to do exactly that. You will support me, or someone else will be my Ambassador."

She watched his face, though Sergei's expression rarely betrayed his private thoughts. It did not do so now. He bowed a bit awkwardly and stiffly, but his face was bland and his eyes seemed to hold nothing but respect for her. "I will always serve Nessantico and whomever sits on the Sun Throne," he said. "Always."

She nearly laughed again—*so carefully said.* "Then tell my son that he toys with black sand and fire, as you said, with his recent border excursions, and that my patience is ebbing. Tell him that I expect them to stop immediately, or that I'll be forced to respond in kind. Remind him that West Magyaria is his only because I failed to send the full Garde Civile to support Stor ca'Vikej—that's a mistake I won't repeat."

His face showed nothing as Sergei bowed. "As the Kraljica wishes," he answered.

"Good," she told him. "I'll have Talbot draw up a list of demands for your meeting, and my responses to the questions that you're likely to receive from the Hïrzg."

The Hïrzg. Not "my son." Allesandra had a sudden memory of Jan: holding him as an infant, watching him suckle at her breast and the close, intense pleasure of feeling her milk come; his first words; his first staggering steps; the times he'd come to her crying because of some injury or perceived slight and she'd held and comforted him. *Where did that change? Why did I let that happen?* She sucked in her breath. Sergei was watching her, his rheum-touched eyes on her face. "We're done," she told him. "I'll send Talbot with my instructions."

"Yes, Kraljica," he said, and she hated the sympathy he allowed to pass over his face, hated that he had noticed the emptiness inside her, that made her cry sometimes alone at night, that troubled her dreams. He bowed his way out, but she was no longer paying any attention to him. It was Jan she saw, as he was when she had last seen him. She wondered what he was like now, what her great-children might be like, whom she had never hugged or kissed or dandled on her knees. *So much you've missed. So much you've lost.* Her vision wavered, the tapestry-lined walls going briefly liquid, and she wondered whether Sergei might be right. Perhaps it *was* time.

There was a soft knock on the door, and she blinked, wiping at her eyes quickly with her sleeve. "Come," she said, and Talbot stuck his head in the doorway.

"The Ambassador said you would want me, Kraljica."

She sniffed. "Yes," she told him. "Come in, but first have one of the servants bring parchment and ink. And if Vajiki ca'Vikej has arrived, tell him that I will be with him shortly."

"I was terrified when I heard, worried that you might have been injured . . ."

Erik was pacing back and forth in front of the windows of the apartment. Their lunch steamed on the table untouched. Allesandra watched him from her chair at the table, staring at him: at the worry in his face, at the way the muscles lurched on his bald skull.

It's real, the concern he has for you. It's not faked, it's not based on his own agenda: it's genuine. She hoped she was right in that. She also realized that she'd made a decision, all unbidden and unasked for. It was wrapped in her own loneliness, in her estrangement from Jan, in the mistake she'd made with Erik's vatarh, in the intense grief she felt when she was with Varina, in her anger with the Morellis. She hoped her decision was the right one.

"I'm fine, Erik," she told him. "I was shaken but not injured. The attack wasn't directed at me."

He nodded fiercely. "Had you been hurt, I would have gone out myself and found this Nico Morel, and . . ." He stopped, turning away from the windows to look at her. His face and his voice softened. "My apologies, Kraljica. It's just that I was so worried . . ."

"I'm fine," she repeated. "And here, while we're alone, I would prefer you call me Allesandra."

"Allesandra," he said, as if tasting the name. He smiled. "Thank you. But don't underestimate these Morellis. They're a danger to you, whether you believe it or not. They're fanatics, and they threaten anyone who doesn't believe as they believe."

"Are *you* a fanatic, Erik?" she asked him gently. She gestured to the chair next to her right.

He sat before he answered. "About West Magyaria, you mean?" His hand cupped his wineglass, shivering the ruby liquid in it. "No, not about that. In politics, I'm more of a pragmatist than my vatarh. I believe that West Magyaria would be better off as part of the Holdings. I believe that I would be a good Gyula, if Cénzi desires that to happen. I'm willing to work as hard as I need to make that happen, but I also know that sometimes sacrifices and compromises must be made to accomplish things, and that sometimes the best result isn't the one you would like to see. So, no, I'm not a fanatic but a realist." He lifted the glass and set it down again. "That's not to say that there aren't things that I care deeply about or that I'm not a passionate man, Kralji—"

A breath. "Allesandra. When I come to love something, or someone . . ."

His hand left the glass and lay on the linen tablecloth. She reached out her own hand and put it on top of his. She heard him draw in his breath. His lovely pale eyes held her own gaze, unblinking, almost as if in challenge. His fingers opened, then laced with hers.

"I *am* passionate," she told him softly. "Nessantico and the Holdings are my passion. And I am also dangerous because of that. So this . . ." She pressed his fingers lightly. ". . . would not be a decision to make lightly. Or, if you prefer, we can eat the dinner that's set here for us."

He nodded. He lifted his hand, still holding hers, to his mouth, and kissed the back of her hand. His breath was warm on her skin, the touch of his lips soft and exciting. "Are you hungry, Allesandra?" he asked.

This is what you want . . . This is why you asked him here today . . . "I am," she answered. She rose from her chair, still holding his hand.

She led him away.

~

Niente

THE WATERS OF MUNEREO BAY swarmed with ships anchored together so densely that it seemed a person might walk entirely across the great bay without getting wet. Their sails were furled and lashed on their masts, and they huddled together under a low sky with the clouds racing west. Fleeting shafts of dusty sunlight pierced the clouds and slid over the bay, sparkling on the distant waves and the bound white cloth on their masts.

Niente had never in his life seen so many ships gathered in one place, had only once before seen so many warriors of the Tehuantin gathered together.

He heard a gasp from his side as his son Atl came along-side him. "By Axat's left tit," he breathed, the profanity loud in the chill morning air, "that is something new in the world."

"It certainly is," Niente told the young man. He blinked, trying unsuccessfully to clear his blurred vision—even his remaining eye's sight was beginning to fail. They were standing on a hill outside the city walls, not far from the main road down to the harbor. The road was thick with soldiers, marching down to the boats. The few hundred nahualli, the spellcasters that would be accompanying the invasion force, were gathered in their own group a little farther down the hill, just off the road. They would be among the last to board the ships, just before Tecuhtli Citlali and his High Warriors.

Behind Niente and Atl, the thick walls of Munereo were still pockmarked and stained by the vestiges of the battle that had raged here a decade and a half ago, when the Holdings forces had been defeated by the army of Tecuhtli Zolin, Citlali's predecessor. Niente had been here for that battle, had seen the black sand roar and the stones fly, had helped to sacrifice the defeated Easterner leaders to Axat. And he had sailed with Tecuhtli Zolin from this very harbor across the sea to the Holdings itself.

So long ago. It felt like another lifetime to Niente.

A lifetime he was now forced to revisit if he wanted to achieve the vision he'd glimpsed in the scrying bowl. *How many of these warriors will die for this? How many souls will be sent to the underworld because of what I'm doing? Axat, please tell me that I can do this, that it will be worth the guilt my own soul will have to bear. Help me.*

"Taat?"

Niente shook himself from reverie. "What?"

"I thought you said something."

"No," he answered. *At least I hope not. No one could know this vision. Not yet.* "I was clearing my throat; the air this morning is hard on my lungs." He gestured out toward the ships and the bay. "Tomorrow, we'll be sailing toward the sun when it rises."

"And there will be good winds," Atl said, and the confidence in his voice made Niente turn to his son, his eyes narrowing.

"You *know* this?" he asked.

Atl smiled briefly, like the touch of sun through the clouds on the ships below. "Yes," he answered.

"Atl—" Niente began, and his son lifted a hand.

"Stop, Taat. Here, I'll finish it for you. 'Look at me. Look at how Axat has scarred me. Leave the scrying to some other nahualli. Axat is hardest on those to whom She gives Sight.' I've heard it all. Many times."

"You *should* look at me," Niente persisted. He touched his blind, white eye, stroked the sagging muscles of the left side of his face, the ridges of scarred, dead skin: a mask of horror. "Is this what you want to look like?"

Atl's gaze swept over Niente's face and departed once more. "That took many years, Taat," he said. "And the oath of the nahualli binds us to do what Axat asks of us. And your scrying got you that also." He pointed to the golden band around Niente's right arm.

"You musn't do this," Niente persisted. "Atl, I mean it. When I'm gone, do as you wish, but while I live, while I'm your Taat and the Nahual . . ." He put his hand on Atl's shoulder. The contrast of their skin startled him: his own was loose, painfully dry, and plowed with uncountable tiny furrows; Atl's was smooth and bronzed. "Don't call on Her," he finished. "That's *my* task. *My* burden."

"It doesn't have to be yours alone."

"Yes, it does," Niente said, and the words came out more sharply than he'd intended, snapping Atl's head back as if he'd been slapped. The young man's eyes were slitted, and he shot a glance of raw fury at Niente for a moment before turning his head slightly to stare deliberately out toward the bay. *"Take care of him,"* Xaria had told him before they left. *"He loves you, he respects you, and he admires you. He wants so much to make you proud of him—and I worry that he'll do something foolish in the effort . . ."*

Xaria didn't understand. Neither did Atl, and he could tell neither of them. He couldn't allow Atl to use the scrying spells, not because of the cost of them—though that was signficant—but because he knew that Atl had the Gift as he did, and he could not let Atl see what he saw in the bowl. He could not. If Atl saw what he saw, Niente could lose the Long Path. Axat's glimpses of the future were fickle, and easily changed. "I'm sorry," he said to Atl. "But it's important."

"I'm certain it is," Atl said, "because the Nahual is always right, isn't he?" With that, Atl gave a mocking obeisance to Niente and stalked away toward the other nahualli even as Niente stretched out his arm toward him. Niente blinked; through his remaining eye, he saw Atl stride into the group.

He could feel them all, staring back up the hill toward him and wondering: wondering if Atl would soon challenge his Taat as Nahual, wondering if perhaps they should do it first.

Their gazes were appraising and challenging and without any mercy or sympathy at all.

~

Sergei ca'Rudka

FROM THE STREET, SERGEI WATCHED Commandant cu'Ingres' squad crowd around the door of the shabby, rundown building in Oldtown in the gray dawn. The stench of the butcheries up the street filled their nostrils. There were four men at the front, another three around the rear door, and two each in the space between the house and its neighbors. There was also a quartet of war-téni lent to them by A'Téni ca'Paim—they huddled around the front door, already beginning chants of warding.

The morning was chilly, and Sergei wrapped his cloak tighter around his shoulders. The street was empty—there was an utilino stationed at the nearest crossroads to stop people from entering, and crowds had gathered behind them to watch. Those neighbors who had noticed the Garde Kralji moving in stayed judiciously in their houses. Sergei could see the occasional flicker of a face at the curtains, though there'd been no movement at the house they were about to enter.

That twisted his lips into a frown. The tip had come from a good informant, and had been "verified" by the interrogation of two suspected Morelli sympathizers in the Bastida. Sergei was hopeful that this sweep would catch Nico Morel. Yet . . .

"Now!" cu'Ingres shouted, waving his hand. One of the war-teni gestured, and the door of the house exploded into slivers of wood, accompanied by a loud boom and dark smoke. The Garde Kralji rushed inside, brandishing swords and shouting for anyone inside to surrender.

Sergei heard their calls go unanswered. He scowled and started across the street, his cane tapping on the cobblestones—Commandant cu'Ingres following at Sergei's measured, careful pace—even as the o'offizier in charge of the squad came to the door, shaking his head. "I'm sorry, Ambassador, Commandant," he said, standing aside as Sergei entered the house, his knees cracking as he stepped up onto the raised threshold. He could hear gardai searching the rooms upstairs, their boots loud on the floorboards above. "There doesn't appear to be anyone here."

"No. They knew we were coming," Sergei said. The room in which he stood was sparsely furnished: a table whose scarred surface a square of stained linen did little to conceal; a few rickety chairs with wicker seats in need of recaning. It seemed that if the Morellis had lived here, they hardly lived in luxury. He went to the hearth in the outer room and crouched down, groaning as his legs protested. He held his hand out over the ash: he could feel heat still radiating up from the coals underneath. He stood again. "They were here only last night. Someone warned them."

He scratched at the skin near his false right nostril. On the mantel above the hearth, there was only a neatly-folded piece of parchment; lettering looped over the front and Sergei leaned in closer to read it: his own name, written in an elegant, careful script. He snorted laughter through his metal nose.

"Ambassador?" Cu'Ingres was peering over Sergei's shoulder. "Ah," he said. "Then our informant was right."

"Right about the location. Wrong with the timing," Sergei said. He plucked the paper from the mantel and opened the stiff parchment.

Sergei—I'm sorry to have missed you. Cénzi tells me that someday you and I must talk. But not today. Not until I've accomplished the tasks He has given to me. I would like to think that perhaps now you'll see that I am only doing His work, but I suspect your eyes, like those of the Kraljica and the A'Téni, are blinded. I'm sorry for that, and I will pray for Cénzi to give you sight. It was signed simply "Nico."

"We won't find anything here," Sergei told cu'Ingres. "Have your men search the place thoroughly in case they've missed something important, but they won't have. The Morellis have an informant of their own, either in the Garde Kralji or—more likely—within the Faith. We've missed them."

He poked at the ash in the fireplace with the tip of his cane until he saw glowing red. He let the note drift from his hand onto the coals. The edges of the paper darkened, lines of red crawling over it before it burst into flame. "I won't let this happen a second time," he said: to cu'Ingres, to the paper, to the ghost of Nico.

The paper went to dry ash, fragments of it lifting and rising up the flue. Sergei shrugged his cloak around his shoulders. He slammed his cane hard once on the floor of the house, and left.

"We'll be successful next time," Sergei said. "I promise you that."

He watched Varina shrug in the light streaming in between the lace curtains of the window. The patterns of the lace speckled her face and shoulders with dappled light and put her eyes in deep shadow. "I know this isn't what you want to hear," she said, "but part of me is glad Nico escaped you, Sergei. I think Karl would have felt the same."

The teapot on the table between them clattered as Sergei adjusted himself in the chair. "Your compassion is admirable, and is what makes everyone—including Karl—love you."

"But?" Varina put down her teacup. Lace-shadow crawled across the back of her hands.

Now it was Sergei who lifted his shoulders. "Compassion isn't always good for the State."

"Would you have said that back when the Numetodo were called heretics and condemned to death?" Varina retorted softly. She looked out to the curtained window and back again. "Would you have said that when Kraljiki Audric and the Council of Ca' named *you* a traitor?"

Sergei put his hands up in front of him as if to stop an

onslaught. He remembered the time he'd spent in the Bastida after Audric's condemnation of him all too well: how frightened he'd been that what he'd done to many others would now be done to him, and how it had been Karl and Varina who had saved him from that fate, at the risk of their own lives and freedom. "I yield," he said. "The lady has taken the field."

Varina almost smiled at that. The expression was momentary, but Sergei grinned in response—it was the first time he'd seen her show a trace of amusement since Karl's final illness. He reached out and patted her hand; the skin sagging around his bones made her hands look youthful by comparison. "The boy's had a hard life," she said. "Snatched away from his poor matarh by that horrid madwoman, the White Stone. What kind of life could the boy have had? We have no idea what horrors he might have experienced with her."

"I agree, we can't know that. However, he's no longer a boy but a man who must be responsible for his actions," Sergei said, then lifted his hands again as he saw Varina start to answer. "I know, I know. 'The child shapes the man.' I know the saying, and yes, there's truth to it, but still . . ." He shook his head. "Nico Morel isn't the boy we knew, Varina, no matter how much you'd like that to be true. His last action killed five of your friends and injured many others."

"I know," she answered sadly. "And I'm not saying he should have no punishment for that. Nor do I think him the monster you'd make him out to be, even after what he's said, even after what he did to—" She stopped there. He heard the catch in her voice and saw the moisture gather in her eyes, and he knew what she wouldn't say. Varina sniffed and gathered herself. "But *compassion* . . . You're wrong about that, Sergei. You're wrong about what I'm feeling. A dog gone mad can't be blamed for its madness, but it still must be dealt with for the good of all. I understand that, Sergei. But if the dog is *mine*, then it's my duty to deal with him. Mine."

Her voice was fervent, and Sergei wondered at the urgency he heard there.

"Just promise me that if you hear from Nico, for any reason, that you'll tell Commandant cu'Ingres immediately," he said. "He's promised to watch over you while I'm in Brezno, but I worry about the Morellis, especially after Karl's funeral. Cénzi knows what they're capable of doing. Dealing with him yourself would be risky. From what Archigos ca'Paim has told me, his skills with the Ilmodo are positively frightening, if he would choose to use them. Promise me you'll be cautious. Promise me that you won't make any effort to contact him. This particular mad dog threatens everyone in the city; let the city deal with him."

Another smile, this one far fainter than the last. "You sound like Karl now. I've always believed that caution was overrated," she said, and the smile broadened suddenly. "And you, Sergei—you'll be careful yourself?"

"Hïrzg Jan, though it probably shows his lack of judgment, seems to like me despite the frigid relationship between him and his matarh," Sergei told her. "And in any case, I'm only the messenger for Kraljica Allesandra." *And sometimes the messenger is blamed when the message isn't the one they want to hear* ... Sergei smiled even as the doubt crept into his mind. Jan wouldn't like Allesandra's message, that was certain. He suspected that Allesandra was going to dislike Jan's reply just as much.

You're getting too old for this ... That thought kept rising to the surface, more and more. He *was* tired, and the thought of several days in a carriage on the road and the pounding his body would take from that, and the discomfort of the inns and strange beds along the way ...

Too old ...

"Take care of yourself, Varina," he said. "Be careful, and please remember what I said about Nico." Grimacing, Sergei pushed his chair back and rose. He took up his cane, leaning against the table. Varina rose with him, going to him and hugging him. One-handed, he returned the gesture.

"And you take care of yourself," she told him. "And watch yourself with the court ladies, Ambassador. I hear that in Brezno, they aren't as ... discreet as we are here."

It won't be ladies of the court with whom I consort ... "I'm afraid that when they look on me, the court ladies wish to do nothing more than flee the room," he told her, touching his nose. He pressed her tightly once more, then released her. "I'll call on you again as soon as I return. I promise."

~

Brie ca'Ostheim

KRIEGE SHOULDN'T HAVE BEEN in their dressing room at all, but he had a habit of slipping away
from the nursemaids who watched him. Brie would have to
talk to them later.

Brie was awakened when she heard the servants' door
to the dressing room creak open. She heard Kriege's feet
padding over the carpet. She slid from her bed and into the
dressing room both she and Jan shared. Kriege was standing in front of Jan's dresser, his hands busy with something
that his body masked. Brie smiled indulgently, rubbing
the sleep from her eyes. "Kriege," she said, "what are you
doing?"

Krige spun around, startled, and she saw the dagger in
his hand, the blade out of the scabbard, the edges of the
dark Firenzcian steel glinting. His mouth opened in an "O"
of surprise, and his face colored as he realized that he was
still holding the weapon.

"Kriege," she said. "Put that down. Carefully now. Your
vatarh would be terribly angry if he saw you with that."

The nine year old's eyes widened. She saw his lower lip
start to tremble. "I'm not angry with you, Kriege. Just put
it down."

He did so, a little too hastily, so that the blade clattered
against the wood and rattled the boxes there. She slid forward quickly and grabbed the dagger, sliding it back into
its well-used scabbard. Kriege watched her movements: he
watched everything that had to do with things martial—in
that, he was unlike his vatarh and more like her own vatarh,
who had an obsession for edged weapons and possessed a
collection of swords and knives that was the envy of even
the museums. Kriege's true name was Jan—for his vatarh
as well as his great-great-vatarh; he'd quickly acquired the
nickname "Kriege"—warrior—for his stubborn and col-
icky personality as an infant. The name had stuck; he was

"Kriege" to everyone in the palais. Now it seemed he might be intending to live up to the nickname.

Brie herself had inherited her vatarh's fascination for weaponry; in fact, she'd first come to her husband's attention when she'd demonstrated her skill with swordsmanship at a palais affair she'd attended with her vatarh, dueling and defeating a chevaritt who had made a disparaging remark when she'd commented on his weapon. She generally carried a knife somewhere on her person, still.

But this wasn't her weapon; it was Jan's. She put the dagger back in the rosewood box where Jan kept it when it wasn't on his belt, then crouched down in front of Kriege. The boy's brown, curly locks tumbled over his forehead as he lowered his head, and she lifted his chin with a hand, smiling at him. "You know you aren't supposed to be in here, don't you?"

He nodded, once, silently. "And you know you shouldn't be going through your vatarh's things, don't you?"

Another nod. "I'm sorry," he said.

"What are you sorry for?" The voice came from behind them; Brie looked over her shoulder to see Jan standing in the door of his own bedroom, still in his nightshirt, his hair bed-tousled. He yawned sleepily, rubbing his bearded face.

Brie hesitated, but Kriege was already slipping past her, grabbing his vatarh's legs. "Vatarh, it was your dagger. I wanted to see it . . ."

Jan glanced at Brie, still crouching in front of the dresser. She shrugged at him, shaking her head. "My dagger, eh? Well, come here . . ." He took Kriege by the hand and walked to the dresser. He opened the rosewood box and took out the weapon and its soiled, stained sheath. The pommel end of the hilt was decorated with semiprecious stones—Brie suspected that was what had attracted Kriege in the first place—the hilt itself carved from hard blackwood. The blade was double-edged, tapering to a precise and deadly point. An exquisite weapon. With an exquisite history.

Jan held the knife, sheathed, in his hand. "This is what you were after?"

Kriege nodded his head energetically.

"What do you know about this knife?"

"I know you always wear it, Vatarh. I see it on your belt nearly every day. And I know it's old."

Jan smiled at Brie over Kriege's head. "It's *very* old," Brie told him. "It was made for your great-great-great-vatarh Karin when he became Hïrzg, almost seventy years ago, and he gave it to your great-great-vatarh Jan when he was young man, and Jan gave it to . . ." She stopped, glancing at Jan, who shrugged. ". . . your great-matarh Allesandra." She didn't mention that Allesandra had used the dagger to kill the Westlander magician Mahri. Reputedly, both Karin and the first Jan had also killed someone with the same dagger. Her Jan, too, had found a reason to feed the steel with an enemy's blood—when his sword had broken in the midst of a battle against the army of Tennshah. "And Allesandra gave it to your vatarh."

Kreige's eyes had gone wider and wider as Brie had given the history of the weapon. "Will you give it to me one day, Vatarh?" he asked Jan, and then his face clouded and he scowled. "Or will stupid Elissa get it 'cause she's the oldest?"

Brie stifled a laugh as Jan opened his mouth, then clamped it shut again. "No one is going to get it until they're much older," he said finally. "It's not a toy or a plaything."

"I want a knife of my own," Kriege persisted. "I'm old enough. I won't cut myself. I'd be very careful."

"I'm sure you would," Jan told him. He took a breath, glancing again at Brie, who shook her head slightly. *No,* she mouthed.

"I'll tell you what," Jan said to Kriege. "I'll tell Rance to have a talk with the weapons master for the Garde, and see if he can give you lessons on the proper handling of a knife. If he tells me you understand and have learned all of his lessons, then perhaps for your next birthday we might talk about something you could wear on state occasions."

"Oh, thank you, Vatarh!' Kirege burst out, hugging Jan again. He broke away, then. "I'm going to go tell Elissa and Caelor. They're going to be so jealous!" He ran from the room, calling for his siblings.

"Don't," Jan said, raising a hand as Brie started to speak. "I know what you're going to say. I know. Elissa will be in here in a few minutes, demanding to know why she can't have a knife, too, and Caelor will be right after her."

"And what are you going to tell them?"

"That Caelor needs to wait until he's as old as Kriege."

"And Elissa?"

"I think lessons in handling a weapon would be good for her. It's a skill she may need one day." He put the knife back in its box, closing the lid. "You don't agree?"

It's one of many skills she'll need, she might have retorted, remembering Mavel cu'Kella, who was by now on her way to relatives in Miscoli. Brie was certain that Jan knew what had happened, and who had sent her away, though neither of them had spoken about it. Jan had come to her room last night, which told her that no one had shared his bed last night. "Sometimes," she said to him, "you can't have everything you want. Even the Hïrzg." His gaze rested on her more sharply with that, and she added: "Or Hïrzgin. If that should be her fate."

"Indeed," he said. "Still, I think it might be good for her—and for her to take those lessons with Kreige. They might start getting along better."

He lifted his head. They both heard the pounding of feet in the hall, the nursemaid calling sleepily and futilely after them (yes, she would need to speak to the woman, and perhaps replace her), and Elissa's voice: "Vatarh! Where are you, Vatarh?"

Jan sighed, and Brie put her hand on his. "She's your daughter," she said. "Like you, when she wants something, she finds a way to get it. You can't blame her for that."

He might have answered, but Elissa came bursting into the room through the servants' door in the next breath, with her younger brother Caelor trailing behind. "Vatarh, it's not *fair!*" she exclaimed, stamping a foot.

"I'll leave you to answer that one," Brie told Jan, chuckling. "I'm going to call the domestiques de chambre to help me dress. I need to have a chat with the nursemaid . . ."

~

Varina ca'Pallo

"HERE IT IS," PIERRE GABRELLI SAID handing the device to Varina. "I hope this works for you," he added with a wry grin.

She took the device in her hands, marveling. "Pierre, this is *gorgeous* . . ." His grin widened.

She'd put together most of the experimental versions of the piece herself, scrounging bits and pieces from here and there in the city and cobbling them together. Her own devices had been functional but ugly and clumsy in the hand. Pierre was a metalworker and artisan as well as a Numetodo. What he had given her wasn't a crude facsimile of the idea in her head, but a piece of artwork.

She turned the "sparkwheel," as she'd decided to call it, in her hands to examine it from all sides, marveling. The device was deliciously heavy and solid, yet well balanced enough for her to wield in one hand. A straight, octagonal metal tube—thicker this time than the last—extended a hand's length out from a curved wooden handle. Varina's barrels had been plain and unadorned; this one was incised with curling lines of vines and leaves, the metal burnished while the lines were stained a satin black. Where the barrel met the wood, the leaves flared out, fitting neatly into niches in the wood carved to receive the leaf pattern. And the wood: Pierre had taken several different woods, laminating them together, the varied grains creating a lovely, warm pattern under hard, gleaming varnish. The pan that held the powder was no longer a crude device screwed lopsidedly onto the top: here it nestled into its own niche in the handle, and Pierre had added a metal door to keep out the weather and enclose the pan. The finely-ridged steel wheel protruding slightly into the pan was chromed and polished; the small clamp above the pan reflected the leaf-and-vine pattern on the barrel, with a fine piece of iron pyrite grasped in its jaws. A trigger guard—also in the shape of a leaf and chromed—enclosed the firing mechanism.

Staring at the piece, she for a moment forgot the grief that had lain over her like a dark shadow for days. For a moment, there was light in her world.

"I'm afraid to try this," she told Pierre. "I'd hate to ruin it."

"It's all to your specifications, which were, I must say, ingenious; I just added decoration to make it look pretty. Go on—pull the clamp back. Put your thumb on that leaf and press it back ..."

Varina did: she heard mechanisms click smoothly as the pyrite lifted away from the pan, heard the spring attached to the wheel purr as it was extended, felt the trigger slide forward and lock. She curled her finger around the trigger and pressed it: the trigger *snicked* back cleanly; the wheel spun madly; the pyrite clamp slammed down against the rim of the wheel, and she saw sparks fly into the pan.

She could imagine the rest: the sparks setting off the black sand in the pan; the explosion propelling a lead ball from the round hole bored into the barrel ...

At least, that was the theory. Her last, far cruder, version had nearly worked, as she'd told Karl. Nearly—she still bore the scars from that experiment. The barrel of the device had been too thin or the metal flawed or her hole bored at a slight angle. The explosion of the black sand had caused the barrel to rupture, spraying the room with metal fragments, one of which had cut a deep gash in Varina's arm—two hands higher and it would have hit her face, a hand to the side and it might have penetrated her chest. She could've been blinded or killed—that's what she *hadn't* told Karl.

With the thought of his name, the pall threatened to return, and she forced herself to smile at Pierre and pretend. "Pierre, I should have had you craft this long ago. This is far more elegant than the contraptions I was making myself. All this lovely work. It's just ... What if it breaks like the last one?"

"Then you can tell me what I need to do to make the next one work better, eh?" He grinned again. "Go on. Try it. I'm dying to see." His eyes widened suddenly as he realized what he'd said. "A'Morce, I ..."

Varina smiled at him, touching his hand. She shook her head. "I don't know," she told him. Until now, she'd conducted all her experiments alone. The other Numetodo knew that she was experimenting with some kind of device to deliver black sand, but no one—not even Karl—had known the specifics. "Pierre . . . it's dangerous. If . . ." Excuses. That's all they were. She didn't *want* him to be there; she could see from the way the lines of his face fell that he understood that.

He frowned. Shrugged. "Whatever you wish, A'Morce," he said. He moved to the door of the room; almost, almost she called out to him, feeling guilty, but the lethargy that had wrapped her for the last several days made her sluggish and slow, and she did not.

The door closed behind him.

She was in a basement room of the Numetodo House on the South Bank, one of the several laboratories there. *Her* laboratory. It was here that Varina, years ago, had ferreted out the formula for making the Tehuantin black sand. It was here that she had worked on developing the Westlander magic as well: the physically-demanding ability to enchant an object to hold a spell. She had spent many long hours here. Too many, she thought sometimes. It sometimes seemed that her entire life had been spent here. Alone, most of that time. Every mark, every scratch on the furniture, every stroke of paint on the walls reminded her of the past.

Varina had set the room carefully: at the longest end stood a fabric-filled dummy, wearing a set of old, battered plate mail Commandant cu'Ingres had given her. At the other end, she'd placed a table with a heavy wooden vise. One of the things she'd learned in the course of this experiment was that the device would recoil when the powder was set alight. During one of the experiments, she'd injured her wrist when a version of the sparkwheel had slammed hard against her hand when fired. Since then, she'd used the vise to hold the various incarnations of sparkwheels, using a string tied around the trigger mechanism to set them off—it was that arrangement that had probably saved her from further injury when the barrel had shattered on the last one.

She took Pierre's sparkwheel over to the table. Gently,

carefully, she filled the pan with black sand. She'd prepared paper "cartridges" with more black sand and a lead ball; she tamped that into the barrel. She folded a cloth around the barrel—"It's so beautiful I don't want to scratch it in the vise," she would have told Pierre, had he been there— and clamped it down, making certain it was aimed directly at the dummy's chest. She cocked back the pyrite clamp and tied a string to the trigger. She moved behind the table, holding the string.

The barrel of the sparkwheel pointed ominously at the mail-clad dummy. She tugged the string.

The wheel spun, sparks flew. There was a loud *bang* and white smoke poured from the end of the barrel and the pan. From the other end of the room, she heard a distinct, metallic *ping*.

Varina waved at the acrid smoke. She peered at the dummy: in the middle of the chest plate, a dark hole had appeared. Varina shuffled over to it as quickly as she could, leaning over to examine it. There was a hole as thick around as her index finger, the edges torn and pressed inward. She put her finger into the hole—she could not feel the bottom of it, and the hole expanded as it burrowed into the dummy's stuffing. Somewhere deep in there, pieces of the lead ball were buried. Varina realized that she was holding her breath.

A sword cut would have been turned by this armor. An arrow from a bow would have rebounded. A bolt from a crossbow might have penetrated it, but not so deeply.

It worked. Had that been a garda standing there, he would be on the ground, bleeding terribly and perhaps dead . . .

She could imagine it, and it wasn't a pleasant vision; she'd seen too many people die in battle. She straightened. She went back to the table, looking closely at the spark-wheel in its vise. It appeared whole and unaffected, the barrel still straight and untouched except for a smear of black soot around the end. There were soot marks around the pan as well, but otherwise the weapon appeared to be intact. Varina unclamped the vise, picking up the device again. She held it out at arm's length, sighting down the barrel at the dummy.

Well, old woman, there's the obvious next step, if you want to take it . . . It sounded like Karl's voice, chuckling as

he admonished her. The rememberance brought tears to
her eyes, and she had to stop for a moment and fight back
the grief. She laid the sparkwheel on the table, and after
a few moments, began to refill the pan with more black
sand and tamp another paper cartridge into the barrel.
She picked up the weapon, pulling back the pyrite clamp
to cock it. Her hands were trembling slightly as she aimed
the weapon. She brought her other hand up to steady it as
she sighted down the barrel. She wondered, for a breath, if
she was being reckless and foolhardy, if she should wait and
repeat the experiment as before, but even as the thought
came to her, she pulled the trigger, closing both eyes as she
did so.

The report of the sparkwheel was terrible, and the
weapon bucked in her hand, though not so terribly as she
remembered. She lowered the weapon, peering at the
dummy. Yes, there was a second hole in the armor, this one
on the other side of the chest plate and higher.

Someone knocked on the door of the laboratory.
"A'Morce, are you all right?" a voice called faintly.

"Yes," she said. "I'm fine. Everything's fine."

She sat in the single chair in the room, cradling the sparkwheel in her lap. It was warm, and a thin trail of smoke still
wafted from the barrel. She stared at it: her creation.

*Anyone could wield this. It takes little skill and a few mo-
ments to learn. With this, anyone could kill another person
from a distance, even a garda in armor.* She had always been
able to imagine possibilities; Karl had always said that was
what had made her a good researcher for the Numetodo.
"You have imagination," he'd told her. *"You can see possibilities where no one else does. That's the best magic of all
to have."*

The line of research that had produced the sparkwheel
had been due to that kind of serendipity—she'd been experimenting with a new mixture of black sand, a few years
ago. She placed a small amount of the black sand in the
bottom of a narrow metal container; she'd tamped it down
with a stone pestle; she hadn't noticed that the pestle was
cracked, and that she'd left behind a chunk of the pestle
in the container. She used a fire spell to set off the black
sand . . . and the fragment of pestle had been propelled
out of the end of the container to slam against the ceil-

ing of the laboratory. The gouge in the wooden beam was still there, above the table. She'd realized then that might be another use for the black sand than simple unfocused destruction.

An army of soldiers with sparkwheels . . . She could imagine that, and the vision made her hands tremble.

That could change warfare. That *would* change warfare. Completely. As the black sand itself was beginning to render the use of war-téni far less important, so skill with a heavy blade would no longer matter, not when all one needed was the strength to pull a trigger and eyes to sight down a barrel.

Anyone could be a warrior. Anyone could dispense justice.

Anyone could exact revenge. Or slay a mad dog.

Anyone could murder needlessly. For the worst or most trivial of reasons.

Anyone. Even herself.

What have I done this time, Karl?

She blinked. Her hand stroked the silken varnish of the handle. An irony, that: a beautifully-crafted instrument dedicated entirely to destruction.

She rose from the chair finally and went to the table. She stoppered the vial of black sand, gathered up the paper cartridges she'd prepared. She placed the vial, the cartridges, and the sparkwheel in a leather pouch and slung it over her shoulder. She blew out the lanterns that illuminated the room, opened the door, and locked it again behind her.

The pouch heavy around her shoulder, her hands still remembering the feel of the sparkwheel as it had fired, she ascended the stairs.

~

Jan ca'Ostheim

" . . . OUR TROOPS WERE EASILY a day's
march past Il Trebbio's borders before we
had any sign that we'd been noticed. We did have a small
skirmish with a company of Holdings chevarittai. Two of
them were killed by our war-téni, and they turned and fled
after that; none of our own people were seriously harmed.
Given our last discussions, after a day there I brought the
battalion back over the border. From everything we've
learned in the last several months, Hïrzg Jan, it would
appear that the Holdings borders are rather porous, and
Il Trebbio is certainly one of the weaker points. Kraljica
Allesandra doesn't have enough—"

Armen ca'Damont, Starkkapitän of the Firenzcian
Garde Civile, halted his report to Jan as the door to the
room burst open, the doors slamming hard against their
stops. A trio of children entered in the wake of the distur-
bance, trailed distantly by one of the staff servants with
another, smaller, child in her arms. "Vatarh!" Kriege, Jan's
eldest son, was the first into the room. He stamped his foot,
glaring back at his older sister. Caelor, a year younger than
Kriege, stood beside his brother, nodding vigorously and
echoing the glare. "We were playing Chevarittai, and Elissa
cheated! It's not fair!"

The nursemaid rushed in, looking harried, and bowed
awkwardly to Jan and ca'Damont with Eria, Jan's youngest,
now in her arms. "I'm so sorry, Hïrzg," she said, not looking
up. "The children were playing fine and I was dressing little
Eria, and there was an argument and they were running to
find you . . ."

"It's fine," Jan said, grinning at ca'Damont. "Don't worry
yourself. Now then, Kriege, what's all this about cheating?"

"Elissa *cheated*," Kriege repeated, scowling so fiercely
that it was nearly comical. "She did."

"Elissa?" Jan said sternly, his gaze moving to his daughter.

Another child might have looked at the floor. Jan knew that Caelor would have, with even the hint of a rebuke, and even Kriege looked away now. But Elissa gazed placidly back, glancing once at ca'Damont's thin face marred and disfigured with the ridged memories of old battles, then fixing on Jan. She brushed back brown-gold strands of hair that had escaped her braids to flutter around her eyes. "I didn't cheat, Vatarh," she said. "Not really."

"Yes she *did,*" Kriege interrupted, stamping his foot again. "She *lied.*"

Elissa didn't bother to look at Kriege. Her regard stayed with Jan. "I did lie, Vatarh," she admitted. "I told Kriege that I'd help him if he attacked Caelor's keep with his soldiers."

"She said she'd use her war-téni on her next turn and help me," Kriege interrupted again. "And she didn't. When it was her turn, she attacked *me* instead and I lost all my keeps and most of my chevarittai. She cheated."

Jan glanced again at ca'Damont, who was stifling his own grin. "Is that true, Elissa?"

She nodded. "It is," she said gravely. "You see, Caelor had the most keeps and soldiers left on the board, and Kriege and I had about the same. I knew I couldn't beat Caelor by myself, so I told Kriege that I'd help him because I knew Caelor would take lots of his soldiers and Caelor would lose enough of his so that he couldn't attack me, and then, when it was my turn, I could take most of Kriege's keeps and capture enough soldiers that I'd probably win the game." She glanced at her brothers. "And I would have, too, if Kriege hadn't gotten mad and knocked the pieces all over the floor."

Ca'Damont's snicker was audible, and he turned his blade-scarred face away for a moment. Jan had to fight to hold back his own amusement, though it was tempered by just how much Elissa was like her great-matarh Allesandra. Jan could well imagine her doing the same as a child; it was what he'd watched her do as an adult.

"So . . ." Jan said to her, "you offered your brother an alliance that you didn't intend to keep so you could win? Is that right?"

A nod. Jan looked at the two boys. "I think your sister has just taught you an excellent lesson," he told them. "In war, sometimes a person's word isn't enough. Sometimes your enemy will lie to you in order to gain an advantage. And there's more to war than simply moving your soldiers about. You should remember this. Both of you."

"But she *cheated!*" Kriege insisted, stamping his foot again.

Jan stroked his beard, trying not to laugh. "What do you think, Starkkapitän?" Jan asked ca'Damont. "Should I punish Elissa for her cheating?"

"No, my Hïrzg," ca'Damont answered, and Jan saw Elissa's face relax slightly—so she *had* been worried about what he might do. "But I would say that there also is a lesson for her from this—that when one gives her word, others will be upset if that word's not kept, and sometimes their reaction may prevent one from gaining the advantage they'd hoped to gain. Now no one will ever know which one of you might have won the game."

Jan clapped ca'Damont on the shoulder. "There, you see," he told the children. "You have it from the Starkkapitän himself. He knows war better than any of us. I hope you've learned well, so when one of you is Hïrzg . . ."

"Let's pray to Cénzi that isn't for many decades yet, my husband." The voice lifted up Jan's head, and he saw Brie standing in the doorway and smiling in at the scene. He went to her, kissing her and embracing her briefly. She smelled of jasmine and sweetwater, and her hair—once the same color as Elissa's, but darkening now—was soft even in the tight Tennshah braids that were currently so popular. If her figure had become heavier after bearing their children, well, that was like the scars on ca'Damont's face: a sign of the sacrifices she had made.

Rance had told him that it was Brie who had sent away Mavel cu'Kella, and why. After his initial irritation, he was pleased: it saved him the trouble of doing the same.·

"What's going on here?" Brie asked. She looked at the children, at the servant holding Eria, at the nursemaid. "Rance told me you were still in conference, and we're to be at the temple for the Day of Return blessing in a turn of the glass." She shook her head, though the expression on her face was indulgent and serene. "And none of our children are dressed yet."

"I'm sorry, Hïrzgin," the nursemaid said, curtsying. "It's my fault. I'll get them ready. Elissa, Kriege, Caelor—come with me now. Quickly . . ."

Brie hugged each of them as they passed (Kriege still frowning and flushed with anger, Elissa with a tight-lipped smile of triumph, Caelor as always dour and pensive). "I should take my leave also," ca'Damont said, bowing to Brie and Jan. "I'll have my scribe write up the full report for you this afternoon," he said to Jan. "And we'll see what Ambassador ca'Rudka has to say when he arrives. I'm sure word will have come to him on his way here. Hïrzg, Hïrzgin . . ."

He bowed again and left them. As the doors to the chamber clicked shut, Brie went to Jan and hugged him again, tilting her face up for his kiss. She leaned back slightly in his arms, plucking at the collar of his shirt. "You're wearing *this* to the ceremony?"

"I was considering it, yes. It's comfortable."

"You look so handsome in that new red one, though."

He smiled at her. "Then I suppose I'll have to change to the red, just to please you."

She kissed him again. "Armen had no trouble in Il Trebbio?"

"Less than I expected, actually."

She nodded, her head against his shoulder. "The children have never seen their great-matarh, Jan. They only think of her as that awful woman in Nessantico who sometimes sends presents. I think you should consider what Sergei wants to offer her."

"*She's* the one responsible for the estrangement," Jan said. "And Rance agrees with me that there should be no treaty with the Holdings. If she wanted peace, she shouldn't have supported Stor ca'Vikej in West Magyaria, and she shouldn't be letting his son hang around the court of the Holdings. She stuffed the mattress on which she lies; if she finds it uncomfortable, well, she's the one responsible."

"I know," Brie whispered. "I know. But I still wish . . . Children should know their relatives, and not as enemies."

"Then let her give up the Sun Throne entirely, rather

than letting Sergei propose this nonsense of naming me as A'Kralj."

"*You* put her on the throne, my love." The rebuke wasn't as harsh as it could have been, and she softened it by touching her hand gently to his cheek. "I know. You did what you thought was right at the time."

"I was young and foolish," Jan said. He opened his arms, releasing her. "And I don't want to talk about this. Not now." He grasped her hand and kissed it. "Let me have my *domestiques de chambre* find this red shirt you like so much, and we'll go to the temple to make our appearance . . ."

He heard the sigh she stifled, but she smiled up at him and stroked her hand down his chest, stopping just at his belt. "Don't call them just yet," she said. She raised up on her toes to kiss him again as her hand remained where it was. "There's still time, isn't there, my love?" she asked.

He laughed. "As much as we like. They can't start without us, can they?"

He kissed her again, more urgently. He felt her body yield to his, and that drove away any other thoughts for a time.

~

Rochelle Botelli

THE CEREMONY STARTED LATE, since the royal party was tardy arriving at the temple. Rochelle, in the press of the common, unranked folk at the rear of the temple, had found respite in the lee of one of the interior half-columns on the back wall, leaning there with her eyes half-closed, her nostrils flaring at the stink of incense and her ears full of the prayer chants and the choir's singing. She heard the seated ca'-and-cu' rising from their seats as the wind-horns sounded their mournful call from the temple dome and the great front doors of the temple opened to admit the Hïrzg and his family. Bright sunlight streamed into the half-gloom of the temple. Rochelle opened her eyes fully; she stepped up onto the base of the half-column, allowing her to see over the heads of the congregation.

The procession was headed by Archigos Karrol and several o'téni, wrapped in a fog of aromatic smoke from the censers, with four chanting light-téni bearing lanterns that burned with yellow flames brighter yet than the sun. The Archigos walked slowly, an o'téni on either side in case he stumbled—Karrol was seven decades and more of age, and though he was still as sharp-witted as ever, in the last few years his physical health had begun to decline and his attendants were always vigilant with him around steps and stairs, or when—as today—ritual demanded that he walk for a significant distance, though he was supported by the Archigos' staff he clutched in his right hand, the bejeweled cracked globe of Cénzi at its summit. He wore green robes trimmed with golden thread, the patterns glistening in the brilliance in which he was bathed, his long white hair seeming to glow under the mitered crown. He lifted his free hand in greeting to the crowd, his mouth curving into a smile under his beard.

Starkkapitän Armen ca'Damont and his family followed next, then the members of the Council of Ca' with their spouses and families. Rochelle rose on her toes to see better as Jan entered. Rochelle remembered her matarh—in the fewer and fewer lucid moments before the voices in her head overwhelmed her completely—talking about Jan, how handsome he had been, how he had held her, how he promised her that he would always love her.

How Jan had been her vatarh.

Rochelle's matarh had loved Jan until her death, as she had also hated Kraljica Allesandra for having torn them apart.

Rochelle had seen paintings of him, and she had stared at the image, trying to see in it some hint of the features she glimpsed when she looked into a polished plate or still water. Perhaps that long, sharp nose? Or those high cheekbones? Her skin, duskier and more deeply and easily bronzed in the sun; did it speak of the Magyarias and the south where the Hïrzg had been born? Did those features come from her vatarh, and from her great-vatarh?

She had never seen him this closely in person—less than

a stone's throw away as he entered the temple. She peered anxiously in his direction.

He *was* handsome: a thin, dark beard along a firm jawline, a sharp, narrow nose (yes, much like her own), skin darker enough that it stood out among the Firenzcians in the temple; dark and intense eyes; hair curled and so dark as to be nearly black, though the sun sparked bronze-and-red highlights from it.

Like her own hair. Like the face she sometimes glimpsed looking back at her.

Yes, he could truly be her vatarh. The tales that her matarh had told could be true. She felt her breath catch in her throat as he glanced around, as his gaze swept momentarily over hers. She raised her hand; he seemed to nod toward her, ever so slightly.

Next to him was the Hïrzgin Brie, and Rochelle saw Jan's hand cup her waist as he leaned toward her and whispered something. She laughed, and Rochelle saw the affection in the woman's eyes as she glanced at her husband. At Rochelle's vatarh. And behind . . .

Behind were the children. Rochelle knew their names; everyone in Firenzcia knew them. She stared at them, her half sisters and -brothers. She yearned to call out to them. *"It should have been me with him,"* her matarh had said, *"with you as the eldest, the one he would dote on, the one who would always bring that smile to his face. He had such a wonderful smile . . ."*

Rochelle smiled at Jan but he was no longer looking in her direction and now he was past her, striding down the main aisle of the temple toward the quire where Archigos Karrol was already waiting. He was bowing to the ca'-and-cu' in the pews toward the front.

Rochelle imagined herself walking with him. Imagined the applause breaking over her. Imagined that Jan was tousling her hair rather than that of Elissa.

"That was my name: when I knew him, when we were lovers. That's the name I'd taken at the time—Elissa. He named his firstborn after me. He did . . ."

The family—the family that might have been, *should* have been hers—was distant now, sliding into the empty seats before the High Lectern at the front of the temple, under the dome and the painted figures gazing down on the assembly from their frescoes. The e-téni at the rear of the temple were chanting, the energy of the Ilmodo closing the massive bronze doors, and Rochelle let herself drop from her perch to the floor. Moving lithely and quietly, she slipped outside before the doors closed.

She hurried into the older and poorer sections of the city where she lived. That was another piece of advice from her matarh: *"Living among the rich makes you too visible. That was the mistake I made with your vatarh ..."* She heard the temple wind-horns sounding Second Call and the end of the Day of Return blessing as she moved deeper into the narrow and twisted lanes that curled around the hills of Brezno, hurrying because she was late to an appointment.

Someone wanted to hire the White Stone: Josef cu'Kella, who belonged to a rising family that seemed to have its hands in several businesses within the city. She wondered what excuse the man had used to avoid being at the temple this morning.

He should be waiting already outside the Blue Wisp, a tavern on Straight Lane—aptly named, for it arrowed up the steep slope of Hïrzgai Hill, on which sat the ruins of the first palais, burned and abandoned three centuries ago. The Blue Wisp was located halfway up the hill; she'd chosen it because she could approach it from either the top or bottom of the lane, giving her a good line of sight to determine if it were safe to approach or whether she should walk on past; in the last week since she'd completed the contract for the *goltschlager* ci'Braun, the utilinos and the Garde Brezno had been asking questions, carrying out strange raids, and taking certain women into custody throughout the city: women who nearly always were the age her matarh would have been if she were still alive, women who had the same general build and complexion as her matarh. It was obvious to Rochelle that they were hunting the White Stone. It was possible that cu'Kella was the bait in a trap meant to capture her.

She wondered, again, if she should be meeting the man at all, even if he was no more than a potential client. He was cu', which meant that she could charge him handsomely for her services, but matarh had long ago warned her that the White Stone could perform two or, at the most, three contracts in a city before she would have to move on. She wanted to stay in Brezno, now that she'd seen Jan. She wanted to know more about him, wanted to know him better. Wanted to meet him. It would be best if she let the White Stone stay idle; she had coins enough in her purse.

But the truth was that she didn't *want* to stay idle. There was an excitement to being the White Stone, to the hunt and the eventual kill.

One more contract. That would be all.

She could see cu'Kella already, wearing—as he'd been told—a red bashta and a hat with a blue feather in it. He looked uncomfortable, scanning everyone who passed as he stood shuffling outside the tavern's door. Rochelle glanced to either side of the street; no utilino, no gardai of the Garde Brezno; no one standing close by pretending to be doing something else where they could easily watch the man. That didn't mean there weren't gardai hiding in the nearby buildings and watching, but so far everything seemed safe and normal. Rochelle continued to walk toward the man, deliberately not looking at him as she approached, pretending to be interested in the wares in the shop windows. In her peripheral vision, she saw him glance at her appraisingly, then look away again. She passed behind him, putting her hand on the hilt of the knife under her cloak. "Walk with me, Vajiki cu'Kella," she whispered as she passed. She continued to walk on up the lane, slowly.

The man started visibly. Then he stirred, turning to walk alongside her. "Are you . . . ?"

"I'm the one you're waiting for," she told him. She glanced behind: no one emerged from any of the buildings around them; no utilino whistled alarm, no squad of Garde Brezno appeared. Rochelle relaxed slightly, though she continued to watch to see if they were followed—the side streets off Straight Lane were tangled and many, and she felt she could lose pursuers there easily at need. She kept the hand on her knife hilt, in case cu'Kella himself tried to attack her, but his hands were visible and he didn't appear to have a sword.

"What is your name?" the man asked her.

She laughed at that. "You don't need my name, Vajiki. We're not conducting business, and even if we were, it's

of the type where names aren't needed. It's enough that I
know yours, and it's not me, after all, you want to talk to."

"So you're not . . . Of course not, you're so young . . ."

"No, I'm not the one you'd like to hire," she said firmly.
"I know how to contact her, if that's what you want. That's
all. But even I don't know what she looks like, or who she
might be." He stopped, and she glanced over her shoulder
at him. "Keep walking, Vajiki, unless you've changed your
mind."

He seemed to shiver, then took a step to fall in alongside
her again. "Good," Rochelle said. "So tell me, who is it?"

"Who is it?" cu'Kella asked dully, then shook himself
again. "Oh, that. I'd rather not say. Only to . . . the person
you're contacting for me."

They were at one of the cross streets, and Rochelle
paused. "Then we're done," Rochelle told him. "Good day,
Vajiki." She started to turn left, away from the lane.

"No, wait!" he called after her, and she paused, allowing herself a small smile. *So typical.* She started walking up
Straight Lane again, saying nothing, and cu'Kella hurried
after her, close to her elbow. "I . . . I'll tell you. It's Rance
ci'Lawli."

She could not entirely keep the surprise from her voice.
"Ci'Lawli? The Hïrzg's chief aide?"

A nod. "The same."

*You shouldn't do this. To kill someone so close to the
Hïrzg.* Yet . . . It would necessitate her being near or in the
palais, where she would have to be in proximity to her vatarh and his family . . . Something pulled at her inside, made
her burn with a yearning she couldn't quite define. "Why
ci'Lawli?"

A sniff. "As you said, Vajica, there's no need for names
here, nor for tales. I'll tell the Whi—" He stopped. "The
person you know. If she cares."

Rochelle shrugged. "As you wish." She took cu'Kella's
arm, as if they were lovers strolling the lane, pulling him
close to her. She whispered into his ear: a location, a day,
and an amount of money in gold solas.

He pulled away from her. "So much?" he said.

"So much," she answered. "Be there with the solas if
you're interested, Vajiki," she told him, "and you'll meet
her."

Varina ca'Pallo

SHE KNEW SHE SHOULDN'T HAVE DONE THIS, knew that Sergei would be irritated when he found out—and she knew he would find out. She just hoped it would be afterward, when it was too late.

One of the gardai assigned to watch her at Sergei's request had let slip the address of the house in the Oldtown district raided by the Garde Kralji. She made certain that her errands the next day took her past that house, and she called out to the carriage driver to halt. The garda (who was not the one who had given her the address) looked concerned when she opened the carriage door and descended. "Vajica ca'Pallo, I don't advise . . ."

"Then don't," she told him, interrupting him. The raising of his eyebrows at the rebuke might have pleased someone else; it only made Varina feel guilty, but she continued, trying to soften her tone. "I only want to see this place where the Morellis lived. Just a glimpse; you can come with me if you must."

"The Commandant will have my neck for this."

"I'll tell the Commandant I gave you no choice."

The garda looked unconvinced, but he preceded Varina to the door of the house. She allowed him to enter first. She thought she could feel eyes watching them, staring at her from somewhere. Without trying to hide the motion, she took a small box from under her cloak: finely-crafted, carved from oak, and varnished to perfection, a master's work. She placed the box on the sill of the window nearest the door, feeling the cold chill of the Scáth Cumhacht clinging to the wood. Then, quickly, she followed the garda into the house.

She spent little time there, since she'd already done what she'd come to do. Still, she tried to imagine Nico here, tried to imagine his voice and his presence in the rooms, or sleeping in one of the beds. There were religious icons of the Faith everywhere in the house, and someone with a fair artistic hand had painted the cracked globe of Cénzi on the side wall of one of the bedrooms, while from the opposite wall leered the demonic forms of the demigod Moitidi, misshapen and twisted parodies of humanity. Varina shivered, looked at them, wondering how someone could stand to sleep here, with their leering, grinning expressions and clawed hands. Even the garda shook his head, looking at them. "They have a strange view of the Faith, these Morellis," he said. His fingers were curled around the pommel of his sword, as if he was afraid that one of the painted figures might leap out at him. "They say that Archigos Karrol has some sympathy for them, though I swear I don't understand it."

"I don't either," Varina told him. "I can't imagine the Nico I knew . . ." She stopped. "I'm ready to go," she told him.

"Good," the garda answered, too quickly. "That painting makes the hairs stand on the back of my neck. It's an ugly thing."

They left quickly, the garda closing the door behind them. Varina kept herself carefully between the man and the windowsill where the box sat, making sure that he wouldn't see it. The carriage's driver was on her staff; he would say nothing.

The garda opened the carriage door for her; she stepped in as the garda closed the door behind her and pulled himself up to sit next to the driver. The small hatch above her head lifted and she saw the driver's face looking down at her. "To the house," she told him; he nodded and let the hatch close again. The carriage lurched into motion.

Varina looked out as they drove off. She could see the box on the windowsill, the varnish on the golden wood gleaming in the afternoon sun.

"The Kraljica and Ambassador ca'Rudka would be terrifically disappointed in you." They were the first words he said to her, smiling as he spoke.

In her mind, Nico had to some extent remained the child she'd known. Yes, she knew the boy had grown into manhood in the intervening fifteen years. She'd followed his career when he'd suddenly reemerged so unexpectedly as a rising téni in the Archigos' Temple in Brezno, an acolyte whose skills with the Ilmodo, whose charisma and power of personality impressed all who met him. She—as well as Karl—had tried to reach out to him then: through letters, and when those went unanswered, through Sergei via his frequent travels to Brezno. Sergei had managed to talk to him there, but Nico had made it obvious that he had no interest in contacting either Karl or Varina. "He said this," Sergei told them on his return. "'Tell the two heretics that they are anathema to me. They mock Cénzi, and therefore they mock me. Tell them that when they see the errors of their beliefs, then perhaps we might have something to say to each other. Until then, they are dead to me, as dead as if they were already in their graves with their souls writhing with the torment of the soul shredders.' And he laughed then," Sergei continued. "As if he found the thought amusing."

Despite the disappointment, Varina had continued to follow his career. She had been worried when he and his followers had directly challenged the authority of the Archigos and Nico had been defrocked as a téni and forbidden to use the Ilmodo ever again on pain of the loss of his hands and tongue.

Then Nico had left Brezno, wandering for a time and continuing to preach his harsh interpretation of the Toustour and the Divolonté—the sacred texts of the Concénzia Faith—until he had finally come to Nessantico. Now he stood in front of her, and she could still see the boy's round face that she remembered in the thin, ascetic, and bearded visage in front of her, with his smoldering, burning gaze.

"The Kraljica and Ambassador ca'Rudka would be terrifically disappointed in you." All those years, all that time, and this was how he began. She could feel the heavy weight of the sparkwheel in the pouch on her belt.

"Why would they be disappointed?" she asked. She gestured around at the Oldtown tavern in which they were sitting. Around them, the patrons were talking among themselves and drinking. A group of musicians were tuning their instruments in a corner. The noise lent them privacy in their booth. Nico sat across from her, his hands folded together on the scratched and rough wooden surface of the table between them, almost as if he were praying. He wore black, making his pale face seem almost spectral in comparison, even with the dim lighting of the tavern and the single candle on the table. "Because there aren't any gardai here to try to trap you?" she said to him. "Do you think I hate you that much, Nico? I don't. I don't hate you at all. Neither did Karl."

"Then why the elaborate setup?" he asked. "Leaving an enchanted box . . . I have to admit that was clever and certainly got my attention, though my friend Ancel didn't heed the warning not to open it. He told me that he thought his hands were going to blister, the wood became so hot." Nico shook his head, *tsking* as if scolding a child. "You really should be more careful with the gift Cénzi has given you, Varina."

She took a long breath. "You *killed* people, Nico. My friends and my peers. Karl was already dead; you couldn't hurt him anymore. But the others—they were *people,* with husbands and wives and children. And you took their lives."

"Ah. That." He frowned momentarily. "It says in the Toustour that '. . . if they fight you, then slay them; such is the reward of the unbelievers. Fight with them until there is no persecution, and the only religion is that of Cénzi.' I'm sorry for the pain I've caused the families of those who died. I truly am, and I've prayed to Cénzi for them." He sounded genuinely apologetic, and nascent tears shimmered at the bottom of his eyes. He closed his eyes then, his head tilting upward as if he were listening to an unseen voice from above. Then his chin came down again, and when his eyes opened, they were dust-dry. "But am I sorry that a few Numetodo have gone on to be judged by Cénzi for their heresy? No, I'm not."

"The Toustour also says '. . .O humankind! We created you and made you into nations and tribes that you may know each other, not that ye may despise each other.' "

Nico's mouth twisted in a vestige of a smile. "I wouldn't expect a Numetodo to quote from a text in which she doesn't believe."

"I believe—like any Numetodo—that knowledge is what will ultimately lead to understanding. That includes knowing those who consider you to be an enemy, and knowing what they believe and why they believe it. I've read the Toustour, all of it, and the Divolonté as well, and I've had long and interesting talks with Archigos Ana, Archigos Kenne, and A'Téni ca'Paim."

"You've read the Toustour, but you've evidently failed to see the truth in it."

"Anyone can write a book. I'm a Numetodo. I need evidence. I need incontrovertible proof. I need to see hypotheses tested and the results reproduced. Then I can allow myself to believe." Varina sighed. "But neither one of us is going to convince the other, are we?"

"No." He spread his hands, palm up, on the table. "Though I must admit that you Numetodo can occasionally be useful: the Tehuantin black sand, for instance. It's rather ironic, if you reflect on it: had I and my people been permitted to use the Ilmodo, then I wouldn't have needed to use black sand and your friends would likely still be alive. The Ilmodo, at least, can be a precise weapon."

Varina flushed at that, and her hand caressed the stock of the cocked and loaded sparkwheel in her belt-pouch.

"So why am I here, Varina," he continued, "if you're not planning to hand me over to the Garde Kralji and have me thrown into the Bastida?"

"I wanted to see you again, Nico," she told him. Her finger curled around the metal guard of the trigger. "I wanted to hear you." The cold metal tongue on her finger warmed quickly at her touch. "Because I needed to know . . ." *Just a tightening of a muscle. That's all it would take.*

". . . if I'm the monster that the Faith makes me out to be?" he finished for her. *It would be so easy:* under the table, slip the sparkwheel out and point the open metal tube toward Nico; pull the trigger mechanism to spin the wheel and set the sparks aflame to touch the black sand in the enclosed pan. A single breath later, and . . . *The holes in the armor; what would this do to an unprotected body?* "No one thinks of himself as a monster," Nico was saying. "Other people may deem what a person does as evil, but *they* think that they are doing what they must do to correct the wrongs they perceive. I'm no different. No, I'm not a monster." He gave her a smile, and his face and eyes lit up in a way that reminded her of the old Nico, the child. "Neither are you, Varina. No matter what you might be thinking of doing to me."

Her finger uncurled. She brought her hand out from the pouch. "Nico . . ."

"Varina," he said before she could gather her chaotic

thoughts, "you tried to do what you thought best for me during the Sack of Nessantico. I appreciate that, and I will be forever grateful to you for your efforts, even if you don't realize that you were following the will of Cénzi. When I pray to Cénzi, I ask Him for forgiveness for both you and Karl. I pray that He will lift the blindness from your eyes so that you may see His glory and come to Him. But . . ." He slid from the booth and stood alongside her. His hand touched her shoulder once and slid away. His eyes were full of a quiet sadness. "We are on opposite sides in this. I wish it weren't so, but it is. There can be no reconciliation for us, I'm afraid. For what you did, I will always love you. Because you, too, are Cénzi's creation, I will always love you. And because of the path you've chosen, I must always be your enemy." His sadness on his face deepened. "And it's far easier to hate an enemy you don't know than the one you do. So good-bye, Varina."

He gave her, without any apparent irony, the sign of Cénzi and turned his back to her. *The mad dog . . . You could take care of it now.* She clenched her right hand into a fist; she tried to hear Karl's voice, but there was nothing. Nico began to walk away slowly.

Now, or it will be too late . . .

Varina sat unmoving in her seat, staring at the black cloth of his back as he made his way through the tavern patrons to the door.

Nico opened the door and left. From somewhere in the street, she heard the barking of a dog. It seemed to mock her.

PROGRESSIONS

Niente
Sergei ca'Rudka
Nico Morel
Varina ca'Pallo
Allesandra ca'Vörl
Rochelle Botelli
Varina ca'Pallo
Jan ca'Ostheim
Brie ca'Ostheim
Niente

Niente

THE SEA WAS CALM, and the nahualli that Niente had set to bring the winds were working their spell-staffs hard, the prows of the ships carving long trails of white water. Niente gazed out from the aftcastle of the *Yaoyotl,* which had begun life as a Holdings warship before its capture fifteen years ago. The *Yaoyotl* had made this crossing once before, when Tecuhtli Zolin had made his foolish and fatal invasion of the Holdings. Now, it was cruising eastward once again, this time accompanied by over three hundred ships of the Tehuantin navy, three times the number Zolin had used, with an army aboard the size of that which had crushed the Holdings forces in Munereo and the other cities of their cousins' land on the shore of the Eastern Sea. Niente could look out over the rails of the *Yaoyotl* and see the sails, like a flock of great white sea birds covering the ocean.

The sight was formidable. When the Easterners saw it approaching, they would tremble and quake. Niente knew this to be the truth; he had seen it in Axat's visions in his scrying bowl. He saw it again now, as he brought his gaze down to the brass bowl in front of him. He had dusted it with the magical powder, and he had used the power of the X'in Ka to open the path-sight. Now, he peered into the green-lit mists, with his son at his side and his attendant nahualli watching him carefully. In the mists, scenes flitted by him: he saw the great island of Karnmor sending a great fume of smoke and ash into the sky as the ground trembled and the sea itself writhed in torment. He saw the great Te-

huantin fleet ascending the mouth of the River A'Sele, saw
their armies crawling the shore, saw the walls of Nessantico
and its army arrayed there.

But he frowned slightly as he stared; before, the scenes
had the hard-edged clarity of reality. Now, they were
smudged and slightly indistinct, as if he were seeing them
more with his own eyes than with Axat's help. It troubled
him.

*Where is the Long Path? Why do You hide it from me,
Axat?*

No, there it was . . . Once again, he saw the dead Tecuhtli
and the dead Nahual, and beyond them, the Long Path.
But it, too, was no longer as clear as it had been. Interfer-
ing visions slid past between him and the path, as if Axat
were saying that movements were afoot that had twisted
and snarled the threads of the future. Niente peered more
closely, trying to see if he could still find the way to the
Long Path. He moved backward in time, saw the myriad
possibilities unfolding . . .

He could feel his son Atl close to his shoulder, staring
into the scrying bowl and holding his breath as if afraid
that it would pierce the mists and destroy the vision. Niente knew what came next; he also knew that he could
not let Atl see it. Niente exhaled sharply, the green mist
swaying, and grasped the bowl. With an abrupt motion
he sent the water cascading over the rail and into the
sea, hissing coldly. At the same time, Niente felt the weariness of the spell strike him, causing him to stagger as
he stood there. Atl's arm went around his waist, holding
him up.

He took a long breath, setting the scrying bowl back on
the table. He straightened, and Atl's hand dropped away
from him. "Clean this," he said to the closest of his attendants; the man scurried forward and took the brass bowl,
bowing his head to Niente and hurrying off. "I will rest
now," he told the others, "and talk to Tecuhtli Citlali afterward. There was nothing new in the vision."

They bowed. He could sense them watching him: *was he
weaker than he had been? Were the lines carved deeper in
his face, were his features more twisted and deformed than
before, his eyes more whitened with cataracts? Was this the*

time to challenge him, to become Nahual myself? That's what they were thinking, all of them.

Perhaps his son no less than any of the others.

He could not let that happen. Not yet. Not until he had fulfilled the vision he'd glimpsed in the bowl. He forced himself to stand as upright as his curved spine allowed, to smile his twisted smile, and to pretend that his body hurt no more than was usual for a man his age.

The nahualli, with polite protestations, began to drift away to their other tasks.

"You stopped the vision before it was finished," Atl said quietly.

"There was nothing more to see."

"How do you know that, Taat? Haven't you told me that Axat sometimes changes the vision, that the actions of those in the vision can alter the futures, that you must always watch for changes so as to keep to the best path?"

"There was nothing more," Niente said again. He could see the skepticism in his son's face, and the suspicion as well. He forced anger into his voice, as if it were twenty years ago and Atl had broken a bowl in the house. "Or are you ready to challenge me as Nahual yourself? If you are, then ready your spell-staff." Niente grasped for his own, leaning against the table on the aftcastle, the knobbed end polished with decades of use, the carved figures dancing underneath his fingers. He leaned on the spell-staff as if it were a cane, letting it support his weight.

Atl shook his head, obviously not willing to let go of the argument. "Taat, I have the gift of far-sight also. You know that. You can fool most of the other nahualli, but not me. You've seen something that you don't want me to see. What is it? Do you see your death, the way you did that of Techutli Zolin and Talis? Is that what it is?"

Niente wondered whether that was fear or anticipation he heard in Atl's voice. "No," Niente told him, hoping the young man couldn't hear the lie. "You're mistaken, Atl. You haven't learned the far-sight yet enough to know."

"Because you won't let me. 'Look at me,' you always say. 'The cost is too high.' Well, Taat, Axat has given me the gift, and it would be an insult to Her not to use it. Or are you afraid that I *will* want to be Nahual in your place?"

The salt wind ruffled Atl's long, dark hair; the canvas above them boomed and snapped. The captain of the *Yaoy-otl* called out orders and sailors hurried to their tasks. "You *will* be Nahual," he told Atl. "One day. I'm certain of that." *I've seen that* . . . He thought the words but would not say them for fear that saying them would change the future. "Axat has gifted you, yes. And I've . . . I've been a poor taat and a poor Nahual for not teaching you all I know. Maybe, maybe I've been a bit jealous of your gift." He saw Atl's face soften at that: another lie, for there was no jealousy within him, only a slow dread, but he knew the words would convince Atl. "I would like to start to make up for that, Atl. Now: this evening after I've talked to Tecuhtli Citlali. Come to my cabin when they bring me my supper, and I will begin to show you. Will that do?"

In answer, Atl hugged Niente fiercely. Niente felt him kiss the top of his bald head. He released him just as suddenly, and Niente saw him smiling. "I will be there," Atl said. He started to turn, then stopped. He glanced back over his shoulder. "Thank you."

Niente nodded, and gave his own lopsided smile in return, but there was no passion in it, no joy.

He wondered how long he could keep Axat's vision secret. He wondered—if Atl came to realize what that vision meant—if he would be able to achieve that vision at all.

~

Sergei ca'Rudka

THE FIELDS ALONG THE AVI A'FIRENZCIA were bright with the tents of the Coalition army. "On maneuvers," the aide from the Brezno Palais staff who escorted Sergei from the border to Brezno told him, but both of them knew what it really was: a mustering and a direct threat. A communiqué had come to Sergei from Il Trebbio before he'd crossed the border, informing him of the incursion of a battalion under control of Starkkapitän ca'Damont into Il Trebbio territory. The battalion had withdrawn, but it had obviously been probing to see what response it might provoke.

And now this massing of troops near the border of Nessantico . . .

Jan, what are you up to? Do you really want to poke at the Holdings with this stick?

Sergei knew already, as his cane tapped along the marbled flags of Brezno Palais on his way into his meeting with Hïrzg Jan, how it would end. The strap of a small diplomatic pouch was looped over his shoulder, and he had gained enough skill over the years to have opened the sealed letter inside and read what Allesandra had written there. The Hïrzg's aide Rance ci'Lawli bowed as Sergei approached the outer reception room of the Hïrzg's apartments. His face was pleasant, but underneath, there was a disdain: Sergei knew that Rance was one of those advising the Hïrzg to keep the Coalition intact and to refuse any compromise with the Holdings. "The Hïrzg is just inside," Rance said, "but he begs the Ambassador's indulgence, as he's with the Hïrzgin and his children. A mark of the glass . . ."

"I would love to see them myself," Sergei told Rance, "so I could bring a report to their great-matarh on their appearance."

Rance shrugged and favored him with an insincere smile. "A moment, then, and I'll inform the Hïrzg," he said. He turned to one of the hall servants. "If you would escort the Ambassador into the outer room and fetch some refreshments for him." Rance bowed again and vanished down the hall. Sergei followed the servant into one of the waiting rooms, accepting a glass of wine and a plate of sweet cheese rétes. Not long after, Rance returned and escorted him down a short hall to another door. On the other side, Sergei could hear several voices and the laughter of children. Rance knocked twice firmly, and then opened the door.

The two oldest children, Elissa and Kriege, were playing at a chevaritt board set on the table, with the Hïrzg looking on; the younger son, Caelor was watching from behind his brother's shoulder. The youngest, Eria, was sitting on

her matarh's lap near the window, toying with the knitting
piled there, while a nursemaid folded diapers and clothes
on a bench near one of the doors leading out of the room.
"The Ambassador ca'Rudka," Rance announced as Sergei
stepped into the room, the sound of the cane muffled by
the thick rug there.

Elissa turned to look. "Vatarh, it's Old Silvernose!"

"Elissa!" Jan shot Sergei a look of apology. "That's terribly rude."

"Well, that's what Starkkapitän ca'Damont calls him,"
she answered, her face twisted into a scowl, her arms
crossed over her chest. One of the game pieces, a war-téni,
was still clutched in her hand.

"You still need to apologize to the Ambassador," Jan
told her, but Sergei coughed gently, interrupting him.

"That's not necessary, Hïrzg. I've been called far worse,
and at least both parts of that nickname are true. By the
way, there are presents for the children from their great-
matarh in my rooms at the embassy; I'll have them sent
over this afternoon."

"Presents!" The shout came from all three of the oldest
children at once, and even Eria glanced up from her efforts
to tangle Hïrzgin Brie's knitting.

Sergei laughed—in truth, Jan and Brie's children did
amuse him. They were bright, engaging, and healthy. It was
a shame that Allesandra didn't know them as well as he
did. "If you go tell Rance, I'd wager he'd send a messenger
over to fetch them for you now—if that's all right with your
parents."

"Vatarh? Matarh?" Elissa immediately shouted. "May
we?"

Brie smiled indulgently, glancing at Jan. "Go on," she
told them, giving Eria to the nursemaid. "And wait for them
in the playroom, please. Don't keep pestering Rance."

The children went out with their nursemaid, calling for
Rance. "They're lovely children," Sergei said as they left.
"The two of you have been very lucky."

"That's what people say who aren't parents themselves,"
Brie told him, smiling.

"I'm certain that all of your children are perfectly be-
haved all of the time."

Both Jan and Brie laughed at that. "We'll lend them to

you while you're here, Sergei," Jan said. "That will change your mind." Then the smile collapsed, and he waved Sergei to one of the chairs at the table. Sergei saw his eyes glance down toward the diplomatic pouch at Sergei's hip. "But I'm certain you didn't come here to compliment us or to deliver presents. What has my matarh to say? The last time you were here you said that you hoped to broker a compromise and have her name me as A'Kralj. Has she agreed to that?"

Sergei glanced at the chevaritt game in progress before him before answering. They were playing two-sided, and the number of pieces still on the board were about equal. Yet Sergei saw a flaw in the way Kriege's pieces were set: if Elissa moved her vanguard three spaces, she could be behind Kriege's lines. He would have to bring three of his chevarittai over to protect himself—and that would leave two of his keeps open to siege from the other flank.

He wondered whether Elissa had seen that, also. From the positions of the pieces, he suspected she had.

"Elissa always wins," Jan said, evidently noticing Sergei's attention to the board. "I like to think that, in the game at least, she is demonstrating her heritage." His fingers spread, Jan moved the pieces of her vanguard: three spaces forward. Sergei looked up, stroking the side of his nose.

"Ah, then you see it also."

Jan smiled. "In the same way that the fact that you haven't answered the question I asked you also tells me how the Kraljica has responded."

Sergei reached into his diplomatic pouch, removing the resealed letter. He placed it on the table, his forefinger tapping the thick paper near the red wax seal. "The Kraljica has tendered a . . . counteroffer."

Jan glanced at the letter without reaching for it. "Then let's hear it. I assume you've read it already, even though the seal is still intact."

"That would be improper of me, Hïrzg," Sergei said. He heard Brie clear her throat. He glanced at her; her regard was on her knitting. She seemed to feel the pressure of his gaze and spoke without looking up from her needles.

"Allesandra says that if we continue to threaten her borders, she will take action," Brie said. "She sees the offer

Jan has made as a 'capitulation,' not a compromise. She suggests instead that the Hïrzg should dissolve his foolish Coalition and again become the 'strong right arm' of the Holdings."

Sergei nearly laughed. "Do you have an ear in the Palais, Hïrzgin? 'Capitulation' is exactly the word the Kraljica used."

Brie set down the knitting in her lap, looking up. "I know how she thinks," she answered. Amusement lurked in the corners of her mouth. "It's the same way my husband thinks."

"Brie—" Jan began to protest, and her gentle laugh silenced him.

"That's not a criticism, my love," she said. "I admire you; I always have. But you *are* your matarh's son." She returned to the knitting, the needles making a sound like distant swords clashing. "And that's the problem—if one or the other of you were a poorer leader, then there would not be a Holdings or a Coalition, but only one empire."

"That was my mistake," Jan said. "I could have achieved that fifteen years ago. I could have taken the Sun Throne myself." He glanced at Sergei, who had arranged his face in careful neutrality: no nod, no expression of agreement or disagreement. "But I was young and I wanted to teach my matarh a lesson. Instead, I have found myself the student."

Again, that faint amusement slid over Brie's mouth. "You both want the same thing—you always have. Unfortunately, you also both feel your vision of the world is the correct one." She set the knitting down on the bench alongside her and rose, going to Jan. She took his arm, leaning into him and kissing his cheek. "I love you, my dear, and I share your vision. But I also understand how your matarh might see things."

Jan's arm went around her, pulling her tightly to him. Sergei rose from his chair, his knees cracking like dry twigs underfoot. He leaned on his cane and tugged his overcloak around himself. "I'll leave the two of you to read the Kraljica's reply and compose an answer for me, though I can guess what it might be. If you'd like, we could discuss the letter and what possibilities there might be for coming to

some more equitable terms—would the two of you be willing to take supper in the embassy tonight? I'm told we have
a new chef who specializes in delicacies from Navarro . . ."

"We'd be delighted," Brie answered, and Jan nodded a
moment later.

"Then I will see you tonight—a turn of the glass after
Third Call? Good . . ."

He bowed to the couple, and went to the door, knocking
against it with his cane. One of the hall servants opened the
door for him. He wondered, as he walked down the hall to
the gate where his carriage waited, how long it would be
before son and matarh were again at war.

~

Nico Morel

THEY'D HASTILY ERECTED THE PODIUM in
Temple Park, not far from the ancient temple there—
the oldest (and smallest) of the temples of the Faith in Nessantico. Originally, they'd agreed that Ancel would be the
speaker and that they would remain there no more than
a mark of the glass—not enough time, hopefully, for the
utilino nor the Garde Kralji to respond, though Nico had
arrangements for distractions should they arrive. Nico
himself would not speak; he would watch from behind
the podium with Liana and the rest of the inner circle of
the Morellis, ready to flee and vanish into the warrens of
Oldtown if there was an assault by the authorities on their
gathering.

But the crowd was larger than anticipated. News of the
gathering had spread through word of mouth, through
cryptic postings on the walls of Nessantico that only their
followers would understand, but the response was greater
than any of them had expected. Nico was certain that, yes,
some word of the gathering would have leaked out to
the Commandant's people, but they'd watched carefully
for any signs that they would be prevented from speak-

ing. Nico was not surprised to see none: Cénzi Himself protected Nico, who was his Absolute Tongue. After his meeting with Varina, he'd gone home with his head aching and his feelings confused. He'd spent the rest of the day praying, and that night, in his dreams, Cénzi had spoken to him: clearly and without mistake. He had told Nico what must be said.

Cénzi would speak through Nico today. And Nico would obey, as any servant must. He'd written the words that Ancel would speak; Liana had already placed the scroll on the podium. What amazed Nico was that even as his followers had begun assembling the small platform, the crowd had begun to gather. The first to arrive were the Morellis of the city, those who were already believers. But the crowd continued to swell, well beyond the numbers of those who had already openly given their allegiance to him. Dotted throughout the crowd were green robes: the téni of the city, most of them of e' status—the new téni, those who may have heard of him since he'd come to Nessantico but hadn't yet heard him speak. Now, as the wind-horns of the temple sounded the Second Call, when many in the crowd might be attending services, they were instead here. Three hundred at least, and perhaps more.

Here. To listen to Cénzi's word.

You must speak. They have come to hear you, to hear My words through the gift of your voice.

The realization came to him hard, like a blow to his temple. He nearly reeled from the impact of it. Liana clutched at his arm, feeling his reaction. "Nico . . . ?"

"I'm fine," he told her. "Cénzi has just spoken to me."

He heard her intake of breath. "Is there danger?"

"No," he said, almost laughing. "Quite the opposite. He wants me to speak."

"You can't," Liana protested. "Everyone has said it's too dangerous."

"There's no danger to me; not while I have Cénzi's protection." He patted her hand, then the slope of her belly. He felt the child stir underneath his hand, and he grinned. "I'll be fine. Please, don't worry." She frowned, but her hand left his arm. He smiled at her and kissed her cheek, then quickly ascended the two steps to the small stage where Ancel was already unrolling the scroll. A roar from the crowd greeted him; Ancel looked up from the scroll at the sound and stared at the sea of pointing hands, turning his head abruptly.

His voice could barely be heard above the crowd's roar. "Absolute? I thought . . ."

Nico gave him the sign of Cénzi. "It'll be fine, Ancel. But I'd appreciate if you stay here with me and watch for the gardai. Cénzi . . . Cénzi wishes me to give our people His message in my own voice."

Ancel's eyes widened and he bowed low to Nico with the sign. "The scroll . . . Here it is." He held out the paper to Nico, but Nico smiled at his friend and shook his head.

"I won't need it. Cénzi will give me words."

Another bow. Nico went to the podium as the crowd redoubled their noise. He lifted his hands, his eyes closed as he looked to the sky. He could feel the sun on his face, could feel the crowd's adulation strike him like a physical blow. "For you, Cénzi," he whispered. "For you."

He opened his eyes, and gestured to them to be quiet. Slowly, they obeyed. "Cénzi blesses you all today," he said, and he heard Cénzi enter his voice, heard it sound loud and booming over the park like an a'téni using the Ilmodo to amplify his Admonition, yet Nico had created no such spell. No, this was Cénzi's presence, warping the Second World around his words so that everyone could hear him.

"I have prayed, my people," he said, "and I have listened, and I have heard Cénzi's Voice." His last phrase was a roar that lashed the audience and seemed to sway the very trees of the park, and the people roared back at him wordlessly. "The time is coming, He has told me, when we must make a choice, when we must decide if we follow His path or that of weak humans. The time is coming—and it is coming soon, my friends, very soon—when we must show Him that we have heard His words and that we will obey them. The words are there for us. We hear them in the Toustour and the Divolonté. We have heard them read in the Admonitions in the temples. We have heard them in prophets and through the téni, but . . ." He paused momentarily, closing his eyes and lifting his face again. "The end times approach us. They come slowly, unstoppable. The téni of the Faith no longer hear Cénzi's words. Oh, they say them, but they don't *hear* them, they don't *feel* them. The words of the Toustour and the Divolonté should strike you like the very fist of Cénzi. They tear at your soul and rebuild it anew, if you let them. I tell you: this is what we need now. We need to open ourselves to Cénzi and let Him make us into his spear!"

The words were fire in his mouth. The heat of them blasted the people before him, and they again shouted their affirmation. "Tell us, Absolute One!" someone shouted, and they all took up the chant. "Tell us! Tell us!"

Nico listened to them for several breaths, his chest heaving from the effort of speaking. He lifted his hands finally and they went silent again. In the hush, in the quiet, he began to speak, and though his voice was but a whisper, they could all hear him. He could hear his voice rebounding from the temple walls on the far side of the park.

"Cénzi has told me that we can no longer tolerate the heretics among us. We can no longer even tolerate those who wear the green robes but who fail to hear Him when He speaks. The Archigos and his a'téni speak with false tongues. We can no longer tolerate those whom this world has blessed with power and money but who do not see that those blessings derive from Cénzi, not themselves. He has told me this: He will give us a sign. He will bring fire and destruction. He will bring death and darkness. He will demonstrate to us our folly so that we may all see it, and when He does . . ."

Another pause. He enunciated each of the next words clearly. Slowly. Each in its own breath. "We. Must. Respond."

They shouted, they applauded, they raised their hands. But Nico, looking over them, could see at the rear of the crowd Garde Kralji in their uniforms, squadrons of them pouring into Temple Park. "The sign is coming!" he shouted. "We will know it soon! I promise you this because He has promised it to me. But, look—" he pointed then to the Garde Kralji, "—there are those who want to prevent you from hearing my words. They would stop me from speaking Truth, because Truth is their enemy. Look!"

The crowd turned. They saw the Garde Kralji and they shouted. As the gardai pressed forward, trying to reach the stage, the crowd pushed back. The gardai, armed with batons, responded. Some of the crowd went down under the assault. One of the e'téni in the crowd unleashed a spell: a blast of fire that went howling into the ranks of the gardai.

Suddenly, it was chaos—many in the crowd pushing through the new gap in the gardai's ranks. Batons rose and fell, and there was now open fighting in the park. Utilino whistles shrilled, and the Ilmodo was now being wielded against the crowd. A controlled blast of wind hit near the front of the stage, sending the closest onlookers sprawling onto the dirt and grass of the park, as well as blowing Nico backward into Ancel. "Absolute!" Ancel shouted above the din of the fray. "We must leave! Now!"

Nico stared outward. There was nothing he could do here, and Cénzi was silent in his head. "They don't listen to me," he said. "This is unnecessary. The Faithful should not be fighting each other."

More gardai were coming into the park, some of these in the uniform of the Garde Civile, and armed with swords and spears rather than batons. He saw bloodied heads. Nico started toward the front of the stage, but Ancel took his arm. Liana had clambered on stage now, along with several others of his inner circle, and they were all around him. "You will see!" Nico shouted toward the crowd, but his voice was only his voice now, and if they heard, they paid him little attention. He was exhausted, as tired as if he'd been using the Ilmodo. He sagged in the hands of his people and they hurried him to the rear of the stage and down the steps. "We're done here," Ancel told them. "Now we must protect the Absolute One and get him away. Quickly."

Nico took Liana's hand as his followers closed ranks around him, and they fled into the depths of Temple Park toward the maze of the Oldtown streets.

~

Varina ca'Pallo

PIERRE'S WORKSHOP WAS IN THE REAR GARden of the Numetodo House grounds on South Bank. It stank of iron, oil, wood, and varnish, as well as Pierre's unfinished sausage, which sat half-eaten on a side table in the cluttered room. Every work surface was filled; no wood showed on any of the tabletops. Instruments and strange devices sat around in various stages of assembly. Varina could only guess at what half of them might be. The room was lit by sun streaming in from several ivy-fringed skylights; the sheets of light illuminated air that was full of wood dust: Pierre was sanding a board set in a vise on one of the tables.

"A'Morce," he said, suddenly noticing her standing at the door. He dropped the sanding block in a flurry of bright motes. "I wasn't expecting you."

As she entered, Pierre plucked up a half-dozen wood chisels from the seat of a chair, and shooed away the cat that had been curled in their midst. He gestured for Varina to sit, as the cat hissed in irritation and went under the nearest table to lick her paws and sulk.

"I understand the Morellis caused a full-scale riot in Temple Park yesterday," Pierre said. "At least a dozen dead, from what I heard, but that bastard Morel escaped."

Varina nodded silently. The complex guilt gnawed at her her again: for having let Nico live when she could have killed him; for allowing herself to think she could be his judge and executioner; for having failed Karl; for still having maternal feelings for Nico after all these years; for thinking that there was something about the young man that was redeemable; for the strange sympathy she found she had for him.

For what she was about to do now.

Karl, is this what I should do? Is this what you'd have done as A'Morce? The grief washed over her again at the thoughts and she had to turn away from Pierre for a moment. Everyone had warned her it would be this way: that the mourning would ebb away only slowly, that for a long time she'd suddenly remember Karl and the sorrow would take her again.

Pierre must have thought she'd caught a speck of dust in her eye. "Morel said there'd be a sign from Cénzi." he continued. "Something about fire and destruction and death, from what I hear." He sniffed. "If that's all prophecy is, well, then any of us could make a living as a prophet. There's enough fire and death and destruction in any given year for a double handful of vague prophecies like that. You'd think that if Cénzi were really as powerful as Morel seems to think, then he'd make such signs unmistakable and his prophecies more specific—why, if he told me the sun would rise in the west tomorrow and it did, *that* might just convince me to turn to the Faith." He grinned at his own joke.

Varina smiled politely. She wiped at her eyes quickly.

Pierre seemed to take the smile as encouragement. "What bothers me," he said, "is that there were evidently quite a lot of people listening to them, and some of them were téni, too, if you can believe it. I tell you, the troubles for the Numetodo may be ready to start again."

"Nico can be quite charming and convincing," Varina said. "He has quite a presence." *And if I'd had any doubt of those reports, then meeting him again confirmed them.*

Pierre shrugged. "From what I heard, the crowd actually resisted the Garde Kralji when they showed up and allowed the *bastardo* to escape. There's going to be blood between the Morellis and us Numetodos, A'Morce. Mark my words on that—and call me a prophet, too." He grinned again, then shrugged. "But forgive me, A'Morce, for rattling on. I take it you had a chance to try the device I made for you. Did it work? Did it survive the experiment?"

"It did," she told him; he nodded, and she saw a fierce satisfaction slip over his face. "I was very pleased with it," she continued. "That's why I'm here. I want more of them. Several hands of them, in fact."

Now his eyebrows climbed his thin face. He absently brushed sawdust from the front of his bashta. His gaze skittered about the workroom. "Several hands of them," he muttered, almost inaudibly. "A'Morce, all the work I have here to do . . . The requests from the other Numetodo for instruments and devices for their studies . . . I don't know how I could possibly . . ." He lifted his hands; she could see the scars and calluses on them.

"Hire yourself some competent apprentices," she told him. "I will pay their wages myself, whatever you feel is fair. Buy the material you need and bill it to me. The devices needn't be as . . ." She stopped and smiled at him. ". . .beautifully crafted as the one you made for me. Good solid workmanship would suffice. Have them work under your supervision; you can even have them help you with your other work at need. I don't care. But I want the devices soon—within a month, and as many as you can make." She took a breath that shuddered. "Pierre, this is necessary for the protection of all Numetodo."

"A'Morce, I haven't heard—"

"That's because I've said nothing to anyone else. And you shouldn't either. I can count on your discretion, I trust?"

The eyebrows climbed higher. "Of course, A'Morce. Of course. Only . . ."

"Yes?"

Pierre shook his head. "Nothing, A'Morce." He brushed at his thighs, raising a cloud of dust that billowed into the nearest light shaft. "I will do as you ask, and I hope you'll be pleased with the results."

"Good," she said. "Thank you, Pierre. I'll stop by next Draiordi and see what progress you've made." She rose from her seat, shrugging her overcloak over her tashta. "I hope that I'm wrong and that none of this is necessary," she told him. "That's actually what would please me the most. But I doubt that I will have that pleasure."

Allesandra ca'Vörl

COMMANDANT TELO CU'INGRES of the Garde Kralji and Commandant Eleric ca'Talin of the Garde Civile both stood at uneasy attention before the Sun Throne. The courtiers and the public had been sent from the room, and the usual monthly Council meeting had been cut short. The Council of Ca' sat to the throne's right, but other than the servants against the walls waiting to jump to any request, there was no one else there to witness Allesandra's displeasure at their reports.

No one aside from Erik ca'Vikej, who was seated behind the Council. Allesandra saw them struggling to ignore the man's presence; their discomfiture was almost pleasant. Of the councillors, only Varina seemed to take little notice of him. Varina seemed to Allesandra to be lost in her own thoughts; she'd said nothing at all during the meeting.

"Nico Morel is able to make a public speech—one that attacked both the Faith and the Sun Throne—and yet we were unable to capture him." Allesandra sniffed. The bright yellow glow of the Sun Throne enveloped her; she could see it radiating around her fingers as she clenched the crystalline arms of the throne. She could see the cracks in the carved, translucent stone where the throne, damaged in the assassination of Kraljiki Audric, fifteen years ago, had been repaired. The cracks did not glow but remained stubbornly opaque despite the best efforts of the light-téni. "This is not what I wished to hear." She heard Erik snort in cold amusement at her remark.

"Nor is it what we wished to report, Kraljica," Commandant cu'Ingres said. "I was in charge of the operation, not Commandant ca'Talin, who had agreed to support the Garde Kralji, and thus he should be blameless in this. I have no adequate excuse, and will make none."

"Then it's good that I had other reports from the scene, Commandant," Allesandra told him. "I know that your gardai were attacked by the crowd, and that they used admirable restraint in not responding in kind against citizens of the Holdings." Cu'Ingres inclined his head toward her in acknowledgment. "But I think that the time for restraint against the Morellis may have passed," she continued. "In the future, both of you have my permission to use whatever force you feel is necessary." Allesandra looked at Varina with that statement. She made no sign, staring at the hands folded in her lap. Allesandra wondered if she'd even heard what had been said.

"Nico Morel is to be found and brought to justice for the murder of citizens of Nessantico, and for the damage he has done here," she said to the Commandants, to the councillors. The Commandants bowed their heads, receiving their orders as any good soldier should, but the five members of the Council of Ca' were less in agreement. Varina was lost in her own thoughts. Allesandra's cousin Henri ca'Sibelli was nodding, the wattles of his neck swaying with the motion. But the other three . . . Simon ca'Dakwi's hand prowled his white beard, his mouth twisted as if he'd tasted something sour; Anaïs ca'Gerodi leaned over to Edouard ca'Matin and whispered something in his hair-tufted ear, to which the man scowled vigorously, his head shaking with the palsy that afflicted him.

Have I misjudged Nico Morel's support here? Allesandra found herself wishing that Sergei were still in the city; she needed his unvarnished honesty. But she looked instead to Erik.

He was scowling as well, but his irritation was directed at the Council: she saw that he'd noticed their reaction. "Are we in agreement?" she asked the councillors.

"We are, Kraljica," ca'Sibelli answered, but his was the only voice. The others said nothing; if they felt otherwise, they weren't going to say it here, then, in front of her.

"Good," Allesandra snapped—if they were too unsure to voice their discontent, then let them be discontented. She rose from the Sun Throne, and the glow from within the crystal died. The room seemed suddenly dim. "We're done here. Commandants, Councillors, thank you for your time." The Commandants bowed themselves quickly out, their boot heels clacking loudly on the tiles of the Sun Throne's hall; the councillors glanced at each other, uncertain, then finally rose from their chairs with various groans and mutterings. They bowed to Allesandra, then—hesitating—bowed also to Erik before, more slowly than the two soldiers, beginning to make their way from the room. "Varina," Allesandra called out, "a moment, if you would . . ."

When the last of the councillors had made their way from the hall and the hall servants had closed the doors behind them, Allesandra went to Varina. She took the woman's hands. "How are you?" she asked. "I worry about you. You said nothing today at all."

"I'm sorry, Kraljica."

"You're recovered from your injuries?"

"My injuries?" she asked, as if uncertain what Allesandra meant. Then: "Oh, my injuries. Yes, entirely. Thank you for your concern."

Her voice was dull, and she appeared more tired and worn even than usual. The left side of her face seemed to sag slightly, and the eye on that side was clouded. Allesandra was reminded of other longtime couples she'd known, and how after one spouse died, the other often followed into Cénzi's arms soon after. She wondered if that would be the case here. "I'm going to send my healer over to you this evening," she said to Varina, and waved off the beginning of the woman's protest. "No, I won't hear any excuses from you, my dear. I insist. I know you have the Numetodo to look after you, but Talbot tells me that you're burying yourself in work, keeping yourself locked up in your laboratory. That's not healthy, Varina. You should be out in the air, enjoying yourself and your friends."

"I'm afraid that I'm feeling my mortality, Kraljica. I don't have much time left, and there's so much to do, so much to understand."

"You will be here for years and decades yet," Allesandra told the woman. It was a polite lie, and they both knew it. "You missed the Gschnas tending to poor Karl, and that's a shame. I will have another party soon; you'll be invited, and I will insist you come. I won't hear of any excuse."

"The Kraljica is too kind," Allesandra said. "Of course I'll come. But I do need to return to the Numetodo House. An experiment I'm conducting . . ." She gave Allesandra the ghost of a curtsy and began to turn, then stopped. "Kraljica?"

"Yes?"

"I always told Karl that Nico could be reclaimed, that if we only had the chance to talk to him . . ." She licked dry, cracked lips webbed with wrinkles. "I was wrong."

"You've actually spoken to him?" Allesandra asked.

Varina nodded. "Nico is convinced that he is right and the rest of us are wrong. And he's more dangerous than any of us thought."

With that, she gave her abbreviated curtsy again and shuffled away toward the doors, moving like a woman two decades older than she was.

"She's right, you know."

The voice startled her; she'd forgotten that Erik was still there with her. She felt his hand on her shoulder and she trapped it with her cheek.

"I know," she told him. "And that frightens me."

~

Rochelle Botelli

"THAT *BASTARDO* CI'LAWLI took me off the list for chevaritt," cu'Kella said, swearing under his breath. As Rochelle had instructed the man, he didn't turn around to look into the shadows where she stood. "He sent my daughter away, who was carrying the Hïrzg's child, and they're offering me almost nothing, *nothing,* in return. Why, I'd have been ca'Kella when the Hïrzg made the announcement if it hadn't been for ci'Lawli's interference. I may even have become a councillor in time. Now ci'Lawli has to pay—for me, for my daughter, for my family's fortune."

It was an old tale, a variation on one she'd already heard a hand of times in her short career as the White Stone, one that her matarh had no doubt listened to innumerable times. "If that's what you wish, Vajiki," Rochelle said to the man, casting her voice in a low and ominous tone, "then leave the solas and the stone I told you to bring as a sign, and go home. Within the month, the man will be dead. I promise you that."

He'd left the bag of gold coins and the pale, flat stone. Rochelle had taken it.

Rance ca'Lawli. Killing him would mean being close to her vatarh. She could feel the thrill inside her at the thought.

She manufactured an identity for herself. Matarh had shown her how the White Stone did that. She already had four or five false identities ready for use, a few she'd used in the past: girls who had been born within a few years of herself, but who had died in infancy. They were everything from common, unranked people to those of ca' status. For the latter, she knew their genealogy, knew their parents, their towns and their titles, and who they knew. Matarh had warned her how careful one had to be with false identities, especially as one climbed the social scale to the ca'-and-cu'. She'd given Rochelle the cautionary tale of how she'd nearly been exposed, here in Brezno, when Matarh had called herself Elissa ca'Karina, when "Elissa" and the A'Hïrzg Jan had been lovers.

When Rochelle herself had been conceived.

"The elite know each other," Matarh had said to Rochelle, after Rochelle's second or third kill as the White Stone, not long before Matarh died. "Oh, shut up—you don't know what you're talking about." That last had been an aside to one of the voices in her matarh's head; Rochelle had learned to filter out such comments. "They're a closed group, many of them related to one another, and family relationships are important to them—and because of that, they know them. You must be careful what you say, because the slightest misstatement can reveal you. Yes, I know that, you idiot. Why do you keep tormenting me this way? Shut up! Just shut up!" She clasped her hands to her ears as if she could stop the interior dialogue, rocking back and forth in her chair as if in pain.

Two days later, Matarh was dead. Killed by her own hand.

Rochelle didn't need that caution here. She presented herself to Rance ci'Lawli as Rhianna Berkell, an unranked young woman of Sesemora who had come to Brezno seeking her fortune, and who looked to make her start on the palais staff. She had in hand recommendations on the stationery of three chevarittai of Sesemora, with whom she'd supposedly worked. The stationery and the names on them were genuine, the paper stolen when she'd been in Sesemora with her matarh years ago; the recommendations were, of course, entirely false. But Rochelle was an accomplished actress: she knew what to say, how to present herself, and what skills would put her in the best situation on the palais staff. She also knew how to flirt without being obvious, and ci'Lawli was susceptible to the attentions of a young, handsome woman. Three days later, the summons came to the inn where she was staying: she was to be hired. Aide ci'Lawli placed her on the royal staff, who cared for the Hïrzg's wing of the palais and who worked directly with ci'Lawli. Over the next several days, she made certain that her work was superior, and she watched. She watched ci'Lawli so that she could learn his habits and routines.

She also found herself occasionally in the same room as her vatarh. Once or twice, she thought she noticed him looking at her strangely, and she wondered if he felt the same pull she felt. But most of the time, especially if his wife or children were in the room, he paid no more attention to her than to the paintings on the walls; she was—like the rest of the staff—simply part of the furniture of the palais.

Today, she'd been sent to clear the reception room outside the main rooms of the Hïrzg's apartments. The children were elsewhere, but Jan and the Hïrzgin had taken breakfast with Ambassador ca'Rudka of the Holdings, who was leaving Brezno today.

As she entered from the servant's door with a tray to clear the table, ca'Rudka—whose face made her shudder, with that horrible silver nose glued to his wrinkled skin—was bowing to both Jan and Brie. ". . . will convey to the Kraljica your letter as soon as I return."

"By which time, you'll have no doubt read it yourself, just to make sure it matches what I've told you," Jan said. He chuckled. Rochelle loved the sound of his laughter: full of rich, unalloyed warmth. She liked the sound of his voice as well. She wished she had known it in her childhood, had heard him whispering to her at night as he wished her good night, or as he cradled her in his arms in front of a fire, telling her stories of his own youth, or perhaps the tales of the long history of Firenzcia and their ancestors.

"Now, Jan, don't go giving the Ambassador ideas," the Hïrzgin interjected. Rochelle wasn't sure how she felt about the matarh of her half-siblings. Hïrzgin Brie seemed to genuinely care for Jan, but Rochelle had already heard comments and seen glances that made her wonder how well-reciprocated that affection might be. There was the palais gossip also, but Rochelle wasn't yet privy to the details of the carefully whispered suspicions.

"Don't worry," Sergei said to the two of them. "The Hïrzg has already told me exactly how he feels, but I trust he's couched it more *diplomatically* in the letter to the Kraljica. At least I hope so." The three of them chuckled again, but the amusement was short this time, and tinged with something else that Rochelle couldn't quite decipher. Sergei's voice was suddenly serious and muted. "I truly hope that we can find some way through this without resorting to violence. A new war would not be good for either the Holdings or the Coalition."

"That depends entirely on my matarh," Jan answered.

"And it depends on the Coalition not provoking her in the meantime," Sergei responded. He nodded, and bowed to the two of them. "I'm away, then. I'll send a response by fast-courier as soon as I've spoken with Kraljica Allesandra. Give my love to the children, and may Cénzi bless both of you."

He bowed again and left the room as Rochelle continued to pile dirty dishes on the tray. "I'll go see to the children," Brie said to Jan. "Are you coming, my dear?"

"In a few moments," he told her.

"Oh." The strange, dead inflection of the single word made Rochelle glance up from her work, but Brie was already walking toward the entrance to the inner chambers, her back to Rochelle. She bent down to her work again, the dishes clattering softly as she stacked them.

"You're new on the staff."

It took a moment for Rochelle to realize that Jan had addressed her. She saw him gazing at her from the other side of the table. She curtsied quickly, her head down, as she'd seen the other servants do in his presence. "Yes, my Hïrzg," she answered, not looking up at him. "I was hired only a week ago."

"Then you've obviously impressed Rance, if he's put you on palais staff. What's your name?"

"Rhianna Berkell."

"Rhianna Berkell," he repeated, as if tasting the name. "That has a pretty sound. Well, Rhianna, if you do well here, you might find yourself one day with a ce' before your name. Rance himself was ce'Lawli only two years ago, and now he's ci'Lawli. He'll almost certainly be cu'Lawli one day. We reward those who serve us well."

"Thank you, sir." She curtsied again. "I should get these back to the kitchen . . ."

"Look at me," he said—he said it gently, softly, and she lifted up her face. Their eyes met, and his gaze remained on her face. "You remind me of . . ." He stopped. His regard seemed to drift away for a moment, as if he were lost in memory. ". . . someone I knew."

He reached out, the fingertips of his right hand stroking her cheek—the touch, she thought, of a vatarh. She dropped her gaze quickly, but she could still feel the touch of his fingertips on her skin for long breaths afterward. "The tray, my Hïrzg," she said.

"Ah, yes. That. Certainly. Thank you, Rhianna. I appreciate it."

She lifted the tray and stepped toward the servants' door. She could feel his gaze on her back as she pushed the door open with her hip. She didn't dare look back, afraid that if she did, she would blurt out the secret, that she would call him by the name she longed to use.

Vatarh . . .

She could not do that. Not now.

Not yet.

~

Varina ca'Pallo

SHE'D SET UP THE DEMONSTRATION in the main hall of the Numetodo House. There were two hands of the long-standing Numetodo there with her: among them Pierre Gabrelli, who was grinning, already knowing what Varina intended to show; the Kraljica's chief aide Talbot ci'Noel; Johannes ce'Agrippa, perhaps the most skilled of the Numetodo's magicians, whose study of magical forms pushed the boundaries of Karl and Varina's own discoveries; Niels ce'Sedgwick, whose interest was not in any magic at all, but in the rocks of the earth and what they spoke of the history of the land; Leovic ce'Darci, whose graceful drawings of buildings and engineering marvels were not only a delight, but were beginning to change Nessantico's skyline; Nicolau Petros, who studied the stars and their movements with a device based on the one Karl had seen the Tehuantin spy Mahri use; Albertus Paracel, the scribe and librarian who was creating an already-monumental compilation of all knowledge gained from Numetodo research and experimentation. All of them were essential to the primary task of the Numetodo—to understand how the world worked without the veil of superstition and religion, to use reason and logic to fathom the mysteries that surrounded them.

They were those Nico Morel and his ilk found so terribly threatening.

There were a few who were missing, though—those that Nico had already killed, those who had actually been closest to Karl and her. She could do nothing for them except mourn their and Karl's aching absence.

Varina had continued her own experiments with the sparkwheel. She'd refined the mixture of black sand and the shape and composition of the lead bullet the device delivered; she had Pierre create a few new experimental pieces as well. Each day, she saw the frightening potential of the sparkwheel more clearly. Each day, she was more convinced that this device could change the very sinews and fiber of the society in which they lived.

She wondered, sometimes, if this was really something she wanted to unleash.

"You can't hide knowledge." That was what Karl had said, many times over the decades. *"Knowledge refuses to be hidden. If you try to bury it, it will only find a way to reveal itself to others."*

Fine. Then she wouldn't hide it.

"Thank you for coming," Varina said to the assembly. "You're all familiar with black sand. You all know the terrible destruction it can cause when ignited in large amounts.

My experiments recently have been with far smaller amounts than those used in war, and with no use of magic to set it off at all. And ..." She stopped, stepping to the table she'd set up, covered in a black cloth. Several strides away, a ripe sweetfruit had been set up on a stand in front of an upended oaken table serving as a backstop: a fruit the size of a man's head, enclosed in its marbled, yellow-and-green tough rind. *A head as hard as a sweetfruit*—it was an old saying in the Holdings. She could see everyone looking at the setup curiously. "Well, it's easier to simply demonstrate," she said to them.

She nodded to Pierre, who flicked the cover from the table. Pierre's original sparkwheel sat there, gleaming and beautiful, already primed and ready. Varina plucked it up without a word, cocked it, and aimed at the sweetfruit.

She pulled the trigger.

The sparkwheel clicked. The black sand in the pan flashed and flared; the sparkwheel bucked in her hand with a loud report. At the end of the room, the sweetfruit seemed to explode, spattered chunks falling to the floor as the broken remnant jumped in its stand. In the silence that followed, they could hear the bright red juice of the shattered sweetfruit dripping to the floor.

The symbolism, as Varina had expected, was lost on none of them.

"No magic?" Talbot muttered. "None?"

Varina shook her head. The report of the sparkwheel still rang in her ears; a thin line of white smoke curled from the muzzle. "No magic," she said. "A few pinches of black sand, a lead pellet, and Pierre's craftsmanship. And it's repeatable. Back away ..." She called out to the others, some of whom had gone to examine the broken sweet-fruit or the oaken planks behind it, where the pellet was embedded. She reloaded—the work of a few breaths— cocked the sparkwheel and fired it again. This time the rest of the sweetfruit collapsed entirely and the stand fell backward. Varina put the sparkwheel back on the table.

"Pierre has made a sparkwheel for each of you here," she said, "and I will teach you how to use it."

"A'Morce, this . . ." Talbot said. He was looking at the ruined sweetfruit on the floor. "Why?"

"I'm afraid that the Numetodo are about to be under

attack again," Varina said. "With these, you don't need skill with a blade, physical strength, or magic to defend yourself. All you need do is aim the device and pull the trigger. I'm afraid we will need all the protection we can arrange."

Leovic had gone to the table. He was turning the spark-wheel in his hands, examining the mechanism. Varina could already see his mind at work. He glanced at her. "It's warm," he commented. "What if that were a garda in armor?"

"He would fare little better than the sweetfruit," she told him. "I can show you, if you'd like."

Muscles bunched in Leovic's jaw, as if he were holding back the reply he wanted to make. "Any competent crafts-man could make something like this," he said finally. "If not as ornate as Pierre's creation. And learning to use it?"

"I can show all of you in a few marks of the glass," Varina answered.

"You can give us all the potential to kill someone from strides away, even if they were in armor?" That was Johannes, his voice hushed and almost reverential.

"Yes," she answered.

"You truly want to release this power?"

"It's already been released," she answered. "That power was loosed when the Tehuantin created the black sand. If we destroyed the sparkwheels right now and never said anything about them again, someone else would come to the same realization I did and make them again. You all know Karl's . . ." At the mention of his name, her voice choked and broke. She swallowed hard, apologetically. Talbot nodded to her in sympathy. ". . . Karl's saying that knowledge can't be hidden. Even those of the Faith have a saying for it: *'Once the Moitidi has been created, there can be no Unmaking.'* This is no different."

"Still, A'Morce . . ." That was Niels, shaking his gray, long locks. "The possibilities . . ."

"I can imagine them as well as any of you here," Varina answered. "Believe me, they've haunted my dreams since Karl's funeral and the Morellis' murder of our people. But I can also imagine what might happen if we *don't* have all the resources available to protect ourselves. And that scares me more."

She nodded to Pierre, who brought out a long box from the side of the hall. He set it down by the table and opened it. Inside, steel and wood gleamed. "There's a sparkwheel there for each of you," Varina said. "Take one, and a vial of the black sand, and a packet of the paper cartridges, and I will show you how to use them . . ."

~

Jan ca'Ostheim

"THE YOUNG WOMAN on our personal staff named Rhianna," Jan said to Rance. "What do we know about her?"

The aide raised a single eyebrow. He had just brought in Jan's daily calendar of meetings, going over the plans for the day—it was, as always of late, too crowded and full. It was one of those days when Jan felt the weight of his responsibilities; it was one of those days that he felt old before his time; it was one of the days when he felt restless and trapped.

But the young woman . . . He had thought of her more than once since their encounter, and he found himself looking for her when he entered a room. There was often a faint smile on her face whenever she saw him, though she never broke propriety, never tried to approach him or talk to him, but concentrated on her work and left when it was finished.

He liked that. She knew her place. It boded well.

"She's from Sesemora," Rance told him, "though she has very little of the awful accent, thankfully. She had excellent references from the ca'Ceila and ca'Nemora families. She takes direction well and works hard. I could use a dozen more servants who perform as well as she does. And," he added, "she's not difficult to look at, as I'm sure the Hïrzg has noticed."

"I had, in fact," Jan said. This was a dance that he and Rance had performed more than once over the years, and they both knew the steps.

"Would the Hïrzg prefer that I assign her to your personal quarters?"

"That might be good. She seems an excellent fit."

"Then I'll do that," Rance said. "I've heard whispers that the Hïrzgin thought Felicia was rather short with her last week; Rhianna might make a good replacement. I'll have the change made today."

Jan shrugged. "Whatever you think best, Rance. It's your staff to run. I'll leave it to you. Now, is there something we can do about the audience with the A'Gyula? Perhaps the Hïrzgin could see him. He's such a tedious boor . . ."

"Good night, children . . ." Jan kissed each of them in turn: Elissa, Kriege, Caelor, and little Eria. He nodded to the nursemaid, and she began to shepherd the children out of the room. Elissa hung behind stubbornly, a fierce scowl on her face. "I should be allowed to be at the ball tonight," she said. "I'm not even the least bit sleepy, Vatarh."

"Next year," he told her.

"Next year isn't until *forever*," she answered, with an emphatic stamp of her foot.

Jan heard Brie snicker. He was sitting in the chair at Brie's bedroom desk. She stood behind him, her hand on his shoulder. She wore only her shift, her hair unpinned and her jewelry on the dressing table. Jan could smell the perfume she'd just applied as she leaned down close to his ear. "She's *your* daughter," Brie whispered. "I hear you in her voice."

Jan smiled. He gestured to Elissa to come to him. She did so, with a dramatic pout on her face. "If I say that you can attend the ball, then I'm going to have Kriege saying he should be allowed to be there, too."

"Kriege's only nine," Elissa answered. "He's practically a baby. I'm eleven. Nearly twelve."

Jan felt Brie's fingers tighten on his shoulder. He grinned. "I know," he told her. "I'll tell you what. If you go with the others now, I'll have the nursemaid get you up and dressed in a turn of the glass, and you can come down to the ball for a bit. But you mustn't let your brothers know."

Elissa beamed and clapped her hands once together, then dropped them to her sides, putting a comically solemn look on her face. "Yes, Vatarh," she said loudly, for the benefit of her brothers, still in the doorway with the maid. "I'll just go on to bed, then." Impulsively, she stood on her tip-toes and kissed his cheek, then her matarh's. "Goodnight, Vatarh, Matarh."

She pattered off with her siblings. Jan watched them leave, a helpless smile on his face. "If we were artists, we could not have created anything more beautiful than our children," Brie said.

"I would agree," Jan said. He turned in the chair to face her, his hands going to her hips—he could see the years and the costs of bearing the children in her body: she was no longer the slim, smooth beauty he'd married. Her body had widened and thickened over the years, lines had invaded her face, and the skin under her chin sagged. Her stomach was paunched, her breasts larger and heavier.

He had changed as well, he knew, but change was eas-ier to see in others. He stroked the well-rounded flanks of her body, and she smiled down at him, pressing closer to him. "There's still time," she said. "I could have that new girl—what's her name? Rhianna?—help me dress quickly. If you'd like . . ."

She leaned down. Her lips were still soft, still yielding, and after a moment he lost himself in the kiss. Her hands cupped his head, brought him up standing without break-ing the embrace, then hugged him fiercely. As one, as if in a slow, passionate dance, they moved to the bed. Brie fell onto its cool softness and he allowed her to pull him down on top of her. He kissed her this time, a kiss that was harder and more insistent, and her hands moved lower on his body as he lifted the hem of her shift.

Afterward, they lay together in the tangled sheets. She smiled at Jan, her hand caressing his cheeks and brushing the hair back from his face, and he traced the line of her breasts, circling the aureoles with a forefinger and watching the sensitive skin respond. "That was nice," he said to her.

"Yes." She kissed him again—only a brush of lips this time. "Perhaps we'll have created something new again."

"Perhaps," he told her, and he smiled though in truth he felt nothing at the thought. Children he had—those he could acknowledge and those he didn't know at all, fathered on the occasional paramour who had to be sent away with a pouch of gold solas as a memory. Like Mavel cu'Kella.

"Sergei should be back in Nessantico today or tomorrow," she said.

He laughed. "Where did *that* come from?"

"I don't know. I was just thinking. The children . . . It might be nice if they knew their great-matarh. Really knew her."

Jan grunted wordlessly. His hand stopped moving, resting on her abdomen.

"Do you think she'll agree to what you asked? Do you think Sergei can convince her to name you A'Kralj?"

"I don't know," he answered. "Besides, Rance would tell me that's what I want anyway, that it's not good for Brezno." That was no more than the truth. He didn't know. Part of him agreed with Rance and wanted her to refuse, so that he would have an excuse to move against her. And part of him . . . Yes, part of him hoped she would agree, hoped that they might reconcile.

He just wasn't sure which part was the stronger.

"The choice is Matarh's," he said. "It's out of my hands now. I've made the offer; she can take it or not."

"I hope she does," Brie said. "It's time. A family should not be so estranged." She kissed him again, and rolled away from him. She glanced at the large sand-clock on the desk. "You should go back to your own room and get dressed," she said. "We don't have much time. I'll call the hall attendant to fetch Rhianna and send someone to help you . . ."

She slid her shift and robe over her body and padded toward the hall door. Jan watched her, then pulled on his own clothes as she opened the door and called out softly to the hall servant there. Jan stood; Brie came back and hugged him.

There was a soft knock on the door. "Go on," Brie told him. He went to the rear door that led to his own bedroom but stood there with his hand on the knob. Rhianna opened the door and slipped into the room. She curtsied to Brie.

"You wish help dressing, Hïrzgin?" she said. She noticed Jan at his door; he thought she smiled faintly then in his direction, but she returned her attention quickly to Brie and didn't look toward him again. "Here, let me get these under-lacings for you . . ."

He opened the door and left the bedroom. He smiled, though he wasn't certain why.

~

Brie ca'Ostheim

"YOU WISH HELP DRESSING, Hïrzgin?" Rhianna said. Brie saw Rhianna's gaze slide quickly to Jan, then just as rapidly return. She didn't look at Jan again, though Brie felt Jan hanging in the room behind her. "Here, let me get these under-lacings for you . . ."

Brie turned, allowing Rhianna to reach the laces of the back-closed corset. Jan's attention was somewhere over Brie's shoulder, but he seemed to shake himself to find Brie's eyes. He smiled at her, a bit guiltily, Brie thought, then opened the door of the dressing room. He nodded to Brie as Rhianna tugged on the lacings and closed the door behind him. Brie glanced at the mirror on her dresser, watching Rhianna through the silvered surface. She hadn't looked up to watch Jan leave; that pleased Brie. *Maybe I'm wrong* . . . The girl—no, the young woman—was handsome enough, with strangely muscular arms. Her hair was raven-black and the eyes were such a strange light blue against the hair and olive-complexioned face . . .

Nearly all of Jan's affairs had been with dark-haired women, Brie realized. She wondered what he was trying to find in them.

Rhianna was perhaps five or six years older than Elissa. No more.

"There," Rhianna said behind her. Her voice held the slightest of accents, one Brie couldn't quite place. "Does that feel comfortable, Hïrzgin? I could loosen them a little if they're too constricting . . ."

"It's fine," Brie told her. "Bring me my tashta—there, the one on the bed . . ." She watched Rhianna pick up the tashta, carefully rolling up the hem in her hands. "So Rance has assigned you to our personal staff?"

"Yes, Hïrzgin. I have to admit that I was surprised by that, so soon after being hired, but he said I'd done well in my other duties and there was an unexpected opening."

"Yes, trust Rance to be ever-vigilant for openings that will benefit the Hïrzg," she said. "It's one of his better qualities, I'm sure."

Rhianna looked puzzled, as if she sensed the subtext but didn't quite know how to respond to it. She brought the tashta to Brie and placed it over her head as Brie lifted her arms. "Here, let me find the sleeves for you, Hïrzgin. I'll be careful of your hair . . ." She slid the tashta slowly down, and Brie stood to allow the folds to fall over the rest of her body, Rhianna went to her knees to tie the sash at Brie's waist. "This is lovely cloth, Hïrzgin. Such a beautiful pattern and color, and it goes so well with your coloring . . ."

"Rhianna," Brie said, "you don't need to flatter me."

Rhianna's face reddened. Brie saw no guile at all in her, only a genuine embarrassment. 'Hïrzgin, I didn't mean . . . I was only saying what I was thinking . . . I'm sorry . . ."

Brie brought a finger to her own lips, smiling gently. "Shh. You needn't apologize, dear. I would hope . . . Well, I would hope that if we're to be together often, that we could come to trust each other."

If anything, Rhianna's blush deepened at that. She hesitated, seeming to search for a response. "Oh, you *can* trust me, Hïrzgin," she said.

"Then," Brie said, still smiling, "if, say, the Hïrzg were to say something to you that I should know about as his wife, you'd tell me, wouldn't you?"

The blush darkened even further, which told Brie all she wanted to know. *He's already approached her* . . . "Why, yes, Hïrzgin," Rhianna stammered. "I would. Of course."

"Good," Brie told her. She touched the young woman's cheek. *So smooth, so untouched* . . . but then her fingers found a rippled scar along Rhianna's jawline. *A knife stroke?* She wondered at that, but she lifted the servant up with her hand. She sat again on the chair before her mirror and opened a jewelry box, lifting out a necklace. "Here," she said, handing it to Rhianna. "I think this will go well with the tashta. Put it on for me, please . . ."

As the servant put the necklace around her throat and set the clasp, Brie watched her face, and she wondered.

~

Niente

THE FIRST TIME THE TEHUANTIN had taken Karnor, the main city of the island Karnmor, they had entered the harbor with their ships hidden in a magical fog. This time there were far more ships in their fleet, and Niente had the nahualli call up a spell-storm as soon as they glimpsed the volcanic cone of the island rising on the horizon. The storm drove just ahead of their vanguard of warships, a blackness of pelting rain and violent lightning that shielded them from being sighted too quickly by the Holdings navy, a storm intended to entice the enemy into anchoring their vessels in the safety of the harbor.

Which, when the nahualli dispelled the storm, would suddenly no longer be so safe, for a trio of the largest of the Tehuantin warships lurked at the harbor mouth, preventing any of the Holdings ships from escaping to warn the mainland. At the same time, the majority of the fleet broke away and sailed north, then east around the curve of the island, all but one of the ships—the *Yaoyotl* on which Niente and Tecuhtli Citlali sailed—staying well away from the shore.

The *Yaoyotl* anchored just offshore on the north side of the island at dusk, several miles from Karnor, while the rest of the fleet sailed on. Niente, with Atl and several more of the nahualli, as well as a large contingent of warriors, disembarked from their ship in rowboats laden with leather packs. They climbed the flanks of Mt. Karnmor, the volcano on whose slopes the city was built.

Niente had spent days peering into the scrying bowl. He had seen this scene several times, and it felt strange to actually live it now. As they ascended in the early night, from the far side of the mountain they could see flashes of light: the nahualli aboard the ships guarding Karnor Harbor were lobbing black sand fireballs toward the enemy fleet, as if preparing for a frontal assault on the city. All of that was a feint and a diversion—to keep the Easterners' attention on the harbor and not the mountain behind their city. If what the scrying bowl had told Niente was at all correct, the city would be destroyed, but there would be no assault on it.

The land itself would destroy the city.

Niente comforted himself with the thought that the descent would be far easier than the climb. He was exhausted quickly during the ascent, even though he himself carried nothing but his spell-staff, while the others bore the leather packs. His legs and his hips ached, and his sandals were torn and frayed. The rocks left long scratches on his legs and arms from his occasional missteps, the blood now scabbed and dark. It was an effort simply to put one foot in front of the other, and he was wishing that Axat had never shown him this path. His son stayed close to him, helping him occasionally, but he tried not to rely on Atl—it was not good for the Nahual to show weakness. If the other nahualli sensed that he was vulnerable, one of them might challenge him for the title, and he could not risk that now or everything he had gambled would be lost.

He forced himself to keep moving, to stifle the groans that threatened to escape his lips.

"We're almost there," Niente said to Atl finally, exertion breaking the words into separate breaths. "Just there, around the shoulder of the mountain." Where Niente pointed, a plume of smoke marred the moonlit sky. He knew what he would see there, when they rounded the ridge to the southern side of the mountain: a steaming, hissing fumarole belching its sulfuric, yellow breath from the earth. There were several such vents in this area, well above and directly overlooking the city—and that was their destination.

"Good." Even Atl seemed out of breath. He looked back down the slope, at the line of nahualli and tattooed warriors following them. In the far distance, glimmering in the moon-shimmered water, the *Yaoyotl* awaited their return, sails for the moment furled. "The Tecuhtli didn't seem entirely happy with you," Atl commented.

"Tecuhtli Citlali would rather we assaulted the city," Niente answered. "Like all warriors, he prefers the clash of steel, the smell of blood, and the cries of those who fall before him. What we're doing seems unfair to him." Niente paused, resting a moment and allowing himself to lean against Atl. "I promised him that Axat has shown me that there will be ample opportunity to display his skills as warrior."

They could not only see the flashes of light from the black sand bombardment of the Holdings ships; they could hear, strangely disconnected and belated, the thunder of their explosions. Niente climbed around and over a rock shelf, and he could see the lights of Karnor well below them, spreading along several shelves from the lower slopes to the water.

There were no Holdings troops here guarding the city, as Axat had promised in Her visions. In the distance, the shimmering waters of the harbor were lit by the fires of burning ships. As Niente watched, another fireball arced from the harbor's mouth toward the cluster of Holdings warships there, and exploded in their midst. The sound came to them a full two breaths later, a low rumble that he could almost feel in his chest.

"Hurry!" he told the others, who were coming around the ledge. They stood on a slight incline where Mt. Karnmor seemed to swell outward, a landscape dominated by steam-holes that hissed and burbled. Niente, with Atl's help, directed the nahualli to place spell-staffs, that had been made just for this purpose and prepared with potent earth-shaping spells, in a large circle around the area of the vents. The packs filled with black sand, carried by the warriors, were set in a single large pile: a man high and two men across. Atl, alongside him, shook his head. "So much black sand," he said. "We could bring down the Teocalli Axat with that."

"With this," Niente said, "we will bring down their entire city."

"I hope you're right, Taat. If this fails . . ."

"It won't fail. Axat has promised it. I saw it."

"I know. But I've been looking in the water, as you've shown me, and I saw nothing of this."

Niente clapped his son on the shoulders. "Axat's visions come slowly and in Her own time," he told the young man. "Be patient. She'll speak to you soon enough. You'll know it when it happens; Her voice is harsh and painful to hear." *And I pray to Her that when the time comes, you won't see what I've seen. You won't see what I'm doing.* That, he did not say.

Atl nodded. Niente, grunting with the effort, wedged the spell-staff he'd carried in the wall of black sand, the knob carefully facing the east. Niente looked over the landscape. He nodded—yes, this was what he had seen.

"We're done here," he called out to Atl and the others. His voice shook with weariness. "It's time to return to the ships."

Tecuhtli Citlali shook his bald head, the red-and-black tattoo of a fierce eagle clawing at his skull and over his face. His eyes were snared in the bird's talons, and they glared at Niente. "Nothing has happened," he spat. "We could have taken the city by now with our ships and warriors. We could be holding the entire island. If you have wasted the black sand . . ."

"Be patient, Tecuhtli," Niente told him. "It's not yet dawn. And what will happen will terrify the Easterners more than any assault."

The *Yaoyotl* and the entire fleet, under Citlali's reluctant direction, had sailed away from Karnmor during the night. The island was an empty blackness against the lingering stars over the lightening western horizon as the Tehuantin fleet—with steady easterly breezes—sailed north into the Strettosei, as Niente had requested, as far away from the island as they could reach. The vision in the scrying bowl had been clear, the possibility for this future nearing certainty as long as Niente followed the path Axat had shown him. The High Warriors gathered around Tecuhtli Citlali, grumbling and scowling. The highest-ranked nahualli, with Atl among them, were also watching, and their gazes were far more appraising, searching as always for any sign of fatal weakness in their Nahual.

He'd give them no such sign; Axat would not allow it. Axat had shown him the weakness of the mountain. She had whispered to him that the mountain was nearly ready to stir to terrible life again on its own, much like the smoking mountains of their own land. With Her help, he could hasten its awakening. Niente looked to the east, where golden bands in the sky heralded the sun's imminent arrival over the blue-hazed hills of the mainland. The eastern sky was glowing now. Niente shaded his eyes as the rim of the sun hauled itself over the horizon. Golden beams arrowed through the gaps in the clouds, spearing toward Karnmor and the west.

Niente turned to the island. He waited. *Axat, don't abandon me . . .*

The tip of Mt. Karnmor was touched with sunlight now, the sunlight sliding downward toward the scarves of white steam cloaking it. Niente could imagine the light touching the knobs of the spell-staffs set there, even though that side of the volcano was now hidden from them. The spell-staffs had been enchanted. so that when the sunlight touched them, they would release the spells inside. The bulging earth there would open, a new crater appearing, and the black sand would cascade downward into it, the powdery contents spilling from the pack even as the spell-staff Niente had planted saw the light and spat fire . . .

The steam-scarves about Mt. Karnmor were ripped asunder, replaced by a gout of darker smoke. There was no sound, not for several long breaths, not even as the black smoke itself was consumed by a far greater explosion of red, orange, and yellow that shot from the side of the mountain. A monstrous fountain of gray smoke began to climb toward the sky, the eastern breezes tearing at its edges even as it lifted.

They heard the sound then: the sharp report of the black sand, and then the godlike wail of the mountain itself in torment. The sound battered them like a fist: as Tecuhtli Citlali joined it in a roar of his own, as the warriors and nahualli cheered, as their cheers were echoed by those in the other ships. Niente could see thick fire sliding down Mt. Karnmor toward where the hidden city lay, and he imagined the lava pouring down on the terrified inhabitants, setting fire to everything in its path. The city would be caught in panic, and after the fire, there would come the thick ashfall . . .

The ship shuddered as if the sea itself had lifted them up and dropped them again. White-capped waves surged northward. The fleet bobbed in the long waves, their masts dipping and swaying. The great cloud lifted ever higher so that their heads had to crane far back to watch it, blocking out the brightening morning sky and stretching dark, boiling arms toward the east.

This would be a dark day, and hot ash would fall from

the sky rather than rain, but they were away from the worst of it.

"Nahual," Citlali shouted against the continuing roar of the volcano's eruption. "I shouldn't have doubted you." His mouth was open in a wide grin. "You are indeed the greatest of the Nahual, and with you, there can be no doubt of our victory." The warriors and the nahualli all shouted their agreement, cheering. His son's face was proud.

He should have felt exultation. Instead, he had to struggle to smile in return.

ERUPTIONS

Sergei ca'Rudka
Nico Morel
Sergei ca'Rudka
Allesandra ca'Vörl
Varina ca'Pallo
Niente
Rochelle Botelli
Varina ca'Pallo
Brie ca'Ostheim
Jan ca'Ostheim
Rochelle Botelli

Sergei ca'Rudka

SERGEI TURNED OVER THE arguments in his mind as he rode in his carriage toward the Kraljica's Palais. The luncheon meeting, he suspected, would not go well. Allesandra did not seem inclined to accept her son's proffered olive branch if it included naming him as her heir. Having Erik ca'Vikej as her confidant and (Sergei feared) her lover certainly wouldn't help. Nor did Jan, in his turn, seem inclined to listen to Brie's more moderate view and cease prowling the borders with the Firenzcian army.

There would be war if Sergei could not broker an agreement between matarh and son, and war would be disastrous for Nessantico. He feared he did not have much time or energy left for the effort. He felt old. He felt tired. He felt empty. As the carriage jounced along the cobbles of the Avi a'Parete, he sensed every movement as if it were a blow to his ancient body.

He slid his fingers under the flap of the diplomatic pouch on the seat next to him to touch again the sealed letter there. How could he best frame Jan's intemperate words? How should he respond to Allesandra's expected anger on reading them? Again, he played over the expected conversation in his head, closing his eyes and leaning his head back against the cushioned seat.

He realized suddenly that the carriage had stopped. He opened his eyes, lifted his head. "Are we at the palais already?" Sergei called out to the driver, surprised. Had he fallen asleep? Was he that exhausted?

"No, Ambassador," the man said. "I think . . . I think you should see this."

Sergei lifted the flap over the carriage window and stuck his head out, peering around. They were still on the Avi, just approaching the southern end of the Pontica a'Brezi Veste. A few other carriages had stopped as well, and many within the crowd were gaping westward. On his seat above Sergei, the driver pointed in the same direction.

Over the roofs of Nessantico, a blackness had risen from the west. It was already beginning to blot out the sun: like a wedge of strange, coiling, and rolling storm clouds without lightning and thunder, and moving so rapidly that they seemed to outrace the wind. Already the edge of it was directly above Sergei, masking the sun. A false dusk came, and the air under the storm was strangely warm. Something was falling, as well, but it was not rain: gray flecks that almost looked like impossible snow. Sergei caught a few flakes in his palm, touching them with his fingertips: they smeared on his skin like ash, dry. "Driver! Move on," he called. "Hurry, man!"

The driver nodded and flicked the end of his whip over the back of the horse. "Hey-ah!" he called to the beast, and the carriage began to move again, lurching wildly. Sergei let the flap fall back over the window.

He hoped he was wrong in his surmise.

At the palais, he disembarked into what seemed an early night. The ash was falling more heavily now, and the clouds covered the sky entirely. Servants were running about, lighting lanterns, and Talbot rushed from the palais entrance to Sergei's carriage. "This way, Ambassador," he said. "The Kraljica is waiting." Sergei grabbed the diplomatic pouch and, hurrying as fast as he could with his cane, shuffled along after Talbot, who escorted him through the private corridors and up a flight of stairs to a chamber on the western side of the palais. There, Allesandra was standing near the open balcony of the chamber. Erik ca'Vikej was with her. Sergei bowed to both of them as Talbot announced him and closed the chamber doors, and he went to where Allesandra stood. She was gazing out over the grounds of the palais, which were already dusted as if by a gray snowfall.

"Mt. Karnmor," Allesandra said as he came up to her.

Her voice was muffled by the lace handkerchief she held over her nose and mouth. "That's what this must be. Talbot says that the records talk about how in Kraljiki Geofrai's time, the north face of the mountain exploded and fell down. They claim that the ash fell as far away as Brezno."

"And Karnor?" Sergei asked.

She shook her head. "We haven't had word yet from them. That may not come for days." He heard her breathe; he could taste the ash in the air. "If at all." She turned from the balcony; Erik closed the curtained balcony doors. That did little to change the illumination in the room, lit only by candles and a téni-lamp on the mantel. "This is a horrible omen. We should pray for those in Karnor and all the cities of the island. For that matter, if what Talbot suspects is true, then things may even go badly for those as far away as Fossano." Sergei saw ca'Vikej stroke Allesandra's arm furtively, on the side away from Sergei. *Yes, they're now lovers* . . . Allesandra seemed worried and tired. She took another long breath, tucking the handkerchief into the sleeve of her tashta. "You have something for me?" she asked.

Sergei handed her the pouch. She took the letter from it and examined the seal, then broke the wax away from the paper and opened the envelope. She read the document slowly. Ca'Vikej read over her shoulder; she didn't seem to care or notice. Sergei could see the tiny muscles of her jawline clenching as she read.

"You know what this says?" she asked finally. She refolded the parchment, put it back into the envelope.

Sergei looked deliberately at ca'Vikej without answering. Allesandra waved the envelope. "You can speak," she said. "After all, as a claimant to the throne of West Magyaria, Erik has a vested interest in the answer."

"Erik . . ." She calls him by his familiar name. "Then yes, Kraljica, the Hïrzg told me what he intended to say to you."

"So nothing has changed."

Sergei shrugged. He stroked a finger along the edge of his false nose. "The Hïrzg holds to his original offer—name him as your heir, and upon your death the Holdings will automatically become one with the Coalition again. I told him that was unacceptable, but . . ." Another shrug. "I was unable to convince him of the wisdom of your alternative offer."

"Unable to convince him," she repeated, her lips pursed.

"No doubt you gave it an impressive effort." She made no attempt to hide the mockery in her voice.

"Kraljica, I've made no attempt to hide my preferences in this. I think that naming the Hïrzg as your heir would be best for the Holdings. But, as Ambassador, my feelings are of no concern. I represented you and the Holdings to the best of my poor abilities." He spread his hands. "If you feel someone else could fare better, then you may have my resignation this afternoon."

Ca'Vikej turned away quickly, going over to the balcony door and holding the curtain aside to gaze out at the falling ash. Allesandra stared at Sergei. Then her head shook almost imperceptibly. "That won't be necessary," she said. "I believe you, Sergei." She glanced over to the balcony, where ca'Vikej was still looking out. "It's this horrible day. It has me on edge. A few of the servants were saying that very early this morning, they heard a series of low rumbles in the west, and then this . . ."

He inclined his head to her. "Thank you, Kraljica. I'd hate to think that you believe I've misrepresented you or the Holdings." He paused. She had crumpled the letter in her hand. "Perhaps," he suggested softly, "we might tentatively agree to the Hïrzg's offer to negotiate in person at Ville Colhem? If he believes that we are moving toward some kind of reconciliation, the Hïrzg might become less aggressive with his excursions over the Holdings' borders."

She sniffed. She waved her hand. Ca'Vikej had returned to stand near her. Sergei saw her lean slightly toward him. "Perhaps," she said. "I will have to think on this and consult with the Council."

And with ca'Vikej, Sergei thought. He smiled to her and bowed again. "Then I'll leave you to your consultations, with your permission. Kraljica, Vajiki." He nodded to them and shuffled his way to the door. He tapped on it with the knob of his cane and the hall attendant opened it. He gave them a final bow and left the chamber. Not long after, he was outside in the false night, where the gray ash drifted down from a gray sky over gray buildings.

His carriage clattered up to the entrance of the palais. The driver held the door for him. He would go to the Bastida. That would suit his mood.

It was a day for pain. A day for loss.

~

Nico Morel

THE FALSE NIGHT LINGERED into afternoon, and merged with its true cousin.

The citizens of Nessantico tied cloths around their noses and mouths to keep out the ash, coughing in the fetid air. Some of those, the ones who were already having difficulty breathing, labored more than the healthy or even succumbed. A'Téni ca'Paim sent out the light-téni to light the lamps of the Avi a'Parete not long after Second Call, and had to send them out again to renew their glow after Third Call. The denizens of Oldtown slogged through ash almost as deep as the first joint of Nico's forefinger.

And Nico prayed. He gave thanks to Cénzi for sending this sign, this incontrovertible signal that He was angry at the Faith for their failure to follow the Divolonté and the Toustour, for their tolerance of those who denied Him. They would remember Nico's words—those who had heard him speak in the park, and those who had been told his prophecy at secondhand—and they would realize the truth that he had spoken.

Cénzi's truth. The eternal truth.

Death and darkness. Cénzi had wrapped them in both.

"Nico?" He felt Liana come up behind him as he knelt before the altar in his room, felt her hand gently touch his shoulder. He shivered, his open eyes coming back to focus on the room. He coughed, the grit tickling his throat. He had no idea how long he'd been kneeling there—he'd heard the wind-horns sound Third Call, but that could have been turns ago. There seemed to be no time at all in this gloom. "The ash has stopped falling," she told him. The mask she'd been wearing was looped around her neck. "There are people in the street outside. Lots of them. Ancel said I should come and get you."

He tried to rise to his feet and found he could not; his legs wouldn't cooperate. Liana put her hands under his armpits and help him to stagger to the bed, where she rubbed life back into his legs. "You haven't eaten anything for two hands of turns," she told him. "I've brought some bread, cheese, and wine. Eat a bit first . . ."

He did as she suggested, the first bite telling him how drawn his stomach was. He cut slices of cheese from the pale yellow block and tore at the loaf. The wine soothed the grittiness in his throat. "Thank you," he told Liana, "I'm better now. How have you been with all this?" He lifted her from where she knelt in front of him.

She gasped as he did so. "The baby just kicked," she said. "Here, feel . . ." She put his hand on the slope of her stomach, and Nico felt the push of hand or foot against his fingers. He was certain that if he'd looked at her stomach, he might have seen the outline of that limb on her own stretched skin. "It won't be long now, little one," Liana crooned to the child. "You'll be coming out to see your va-tarh and matarh."

Nico leaned over to kiss Liana, and she smiled up at him. "You said Ancel . . ."

She sighed and took his hand. He stood, his legs still tingling from his long sojourn at prayer, and followed her from the room.

Ancel was waiting for them on the stoop of the house they'd taken in the depths of Oldtown. Above, the stars and moon were still masked in cloud and ash, but the ashfall, as Liana had said, had stopped. Still, the railings of the stoop were coated with it, and their feet raised cloudlets as they walked.

And on the street . . .

There were at least a hundred people there, perhaps more—it was difficult to tell in the darkness, but they filled the narrow street and spread out between the houses on either side. Mixed in among them, Nico saw several green robes, their color muted by darkness and smears of ash. They were of all ages, both men and women. They gazed at the house, silent, but he stayed to the shadows of the stoop as he looked out at them.

"How did they find us?" he asked Ancel, who only shook his head.

"I don't know, Absolute. They started gathering around Third Call. I watched, afraid that the Garde Kralji would come, but so far . . ." He shrugged, and ash slid from the folds of his cloak. "I've asked them to leave, told them that they're putting us in danger, but they won't go. They say they're waiting to hear from you."

Nico nodded. "Then let me talk to them," he said. He stepped to the edge of the stoop, Liana and Ancel just behind him, several other Morellis emerging from the house to stand with them. The crowd called out, seeing him in the glow of the lamps on the supports of the porch. He heard his name shouted, and Cénzi's, but he raised his hands and the crowd quieted again.

He looked out on the landscape, dark and ominous, interrupted only by the pools of light cast by those carrying lanterns, as if the stars had abandoned the sky for the ground. "If you believe that I am pleased by what has happened, you would be mistaken," he said—slowly and softly, so that they leaned forward to hear his words. He cleared his throat, coughing once, and felt Cénzi touch his voice, so that it strengthened and swelled. "Yes, I said Cénzi would give a sign to us, and He has done so. He has given us an unmistakable and grim sign. The end times are coming, if the Faithful will not listen! What you see around you is the death of thousands, all of them martyrs so that we of the Faith might see the error of our current path, so we might see what awaits the world if we fail to heed Cénzi. I weep for each of those who have died. I weep because it had to come to this. I weep because you would not listen. I weep because you could not follow Cénzi's words without His needing to give us this terrible punishment. I weep that we still have so much of His work to do. I weep that even as the ash coats Nessantico, those who rule her *still* do not see the truth of what we say."

He paused. In the audience, he could hear them coughing. "I know why you have come here," he said. "But I tell you that you already know what you must do. It's here in your hearts." He touched his own chest, the words a fire in his throat burning away the taste of ash. "It's in your souls, that Cénzi already holds. All you need to do is listen, and feel, and be open to Him. As Cénzi has been fierce in His sign, so we must be fierce in our response."

He paused, and his next words shredded the air like black claws. "It is time!" he roared to them. "That is what

I have to tell you. It is *our* time. Now! It will be *His* time,
or He will bring death down upon all of us! Now—go and
show them!"

He pointed southward, toward the Isle a'Kralj, toward
the Old Temple, toward the Kraljica's Palais, toward the
South Bank with the houses of the ca'-and-cu'. They roared
with him. He could feel Cénzi's touch depart, leaving him
weary and his legs again weak. But the clouds parted momentarily, releasing a shaft of blue moonlight that painted
the crowd and illuminated their faces. "It's another sign!"
someone cried within the crowd, and they all began shouting. The crowd surged away from the house and away.

Nico leaned against one of the supports of the porch,
not caring that the ash stained his face, as he watched them
move away. "Should we go with them, Absolute?" Ancel
asked. "If that is what Cénzi wants of us . . ."

"No," he told them. "We must stay hidden a while yet—
but soon. Soon." He looked up; the clouds had closed once
again over the moon and the street seemed darker than
before, the shouting of the crowd fading in the distance.

"Tonight, there's something else we must do."

~

Sergei ca'Rudka

COMMANDANT TALOS CU'INGRES GESTURED
harshly at his offiziers. "You, take your squad to the
River Market; I need you and you to use your men to control the Avi so that the fire-téni can get in and do their
work. The rest of you, get your people to push the mob
back up the Avi away from the Pontica—join up with the
gardai coming in from the north if you can. Once we push
them away from the Avi, they'll break up in the smaller
streets where we can control them. Use whatever force is
necessary. Now, go! Go!"

The offiziers bowed and hurried away from the Garde
Kralji command center hastily set up on the North Bank at
the Pontica Kralji. It was a few turns before dawn, though

time was nearly impossible to gauge in this gloom. Sergei—listening from inside his carriage, opened the door and went over to where cu'Ingres stood, leaning over a table with a map of the city spread out on it, his staff placing markers as messengers hurried in with the latest reports. Beyond, well up the Avi, Sergei could see fires sending black smoke coiling up to join the gray ash clouds. Everyone, cu'Ingres included, looked as if they'd been rolling in a fireplace.

"I heard about the mob," Sergei said. "I thought I'd see if I could be of assistance."

"Ambassador," cu'Ingres said wearily. "I appreciate the offer, and I'm sure I can benefit from your experience. However, I think we finally have the fires and the mob under control. There's no longer any danger to the Isle or the South Bank." He nodded to the glow of the conflagrations. "The fire-téni from the Old Temple are making some progress with that, though sometimes I think it would serve them right if they ended up burning Oldtown to the ground."

"The Morellis?"

Cu'Ingres nodded. "I had a report of a crowd gathering at a house, supposedly where Nico Morel was hiding. I had one of my a'offiziers and his people heading to the area to investigate, but then they were set upon by a mob that was moving toward the Avi and the Isle. They were setting fires and looting as they went—shouting about signs and the end of days and the usual Morelli garbage. Morel had worked them up into a frenzy about all this, though Morel himself and the people close to him weren't with them." He kicked at the drifts of ash on the street. "It's been a shit of a day, if you don't mind my saying so. First all the problems with the ash, then this."

Sergei clapped the man on the back. "You've done well, Talos, and I'll let the Kraljica know that. Casualties?"

"Nothing serious, thank Cénzi. A few injuries from thrown rocks and the skirmishes with the mob: bloodied heads and broken bones, the usual. A few of the fire-téni have been overcome with smoke and exhaustion; that's only going to get worse until these fires are under control, but A'Téni ca'Paim is sending more téni to help. There were a few of the Morellis killed in the skirmish and several injured. We have several hands of prisoners."

"Prisoners. Ah." Sergei found himself stirring with the familiar old passion at that. "Where are they?"

He thought that cu'Ingres hesitated a breath too long before replying. Then he inclined his head toward the northern end of the bridge. "Over there. I was going to have them transported to the Bastida as soon as I had enough gardai to spare."

"They should be able to tell us where Morel is now," Sergei said.

"I'm sure they can," cu'Ingres answered blandly. "I'm sure they will."

"Carry on, Talos," Sergei told him, "but have a full squad of gardai ready to leave within a mark."

A salute. "As you wish, Ambassador."

Sergei saluted the man and moved painfully toward the bridge. He found the prisoners easily, seated on the ash-smeared cobbles near the bridge and ringed by sullen gardai. The o'offizier in charge saluted as Sergei approached, stepping aside so that Sergei could look at the captured rioters. Some of them glared back at him, others simply stared with heads down at the pavement. "I need to know where Nico Morel is," he told them. "I know at least some of you know. I need one of you to tell me."

There was no answer. The closest of them to him—an e'téni, his green robes of office torn and stained with ash and soot, blood smeared across his face—scowled and spat in Sergei's direction. The man's hands were bound—so he could not use a spell to escape or attack the gardai. "We won't tell you, Silvernose," he said. "None of us will. We won't betray him."

Sergei smiled gently toward the man. "Oh, one of you will. Willingly. And you're going to help me. Take him," he said to the e'offizier. "Bring him over here."

Sergei stepped back, waving his cane to the driver of his carriage, who slapped the reins on the horse and came clattering over to where Sergei stood. "I need rope," Sergei said, and one of the gardai ran to fetch a length. "Tie his feet also," he said, pointing to the téni and knowing that all the prisoners were watching. When the gardai had finished binding the feet as they had his hands, Sergei had them lash a short length of rope from the man's hands to the back of the carriage. The e'téni watched, his eyes widening.

Sergei tapped the cobbles of the Avi at his feet with the brass ferrule of his cane, and the téni glanced down. "These stones . . . These are the very soul of Nessantico. The Avi wraps the city in its embrace—and as you know as a téni, defines the city with its lamps. The people who made the Avi did so with care and with a love for their work. Look at these cobbles; they were carved from the granite of hills south of here and brought to the city by the wagonload, and placed carefully. It took sweat and labor and care, but they did it. They did it not only because they were paid, but because they love this city." The téni was staring at him; both prisoners and gardai were listening to him. "But . . . These stones, ancient as they are, remain rough and hard. Eternal—like this city and the Holdings, I like to think. Why, these stones are so stern and unforgiving that I must have a wheelwright replace the rims of my carriage's wheels twice a year, and they're made of steel. Can you imagine what these stones would do to mere flesh if, let us say, someone were dragged over them like the wheels of this fine carriage? Why, it would tear and rip and flay the skin from that person, break his bones, and pull him apart, piece by piece. That would be an unpleasant and horrible death. Don't you agree, e'téni?"

The man's mouth had opened as he realized what Sergei was saying. Sergei could feel the man's fear; he could *taste* it, and he savored the sweet spice of it. "Ambassador," the man stuttered. He held out his bound hands in supplication. "You wouldn't do this."

Sergei laughed; a few of the gardai chuckled as well. "I would do whatever I need to do to serve the Holdings and Nessantico," he told the man. "Right now, to serve her, I require Nico Morel's location from you. So . . . Will you tell me?"

The man licked his lips again. "Ambassador . . ."

Sergei lifted his cane. The driver shifted in his seat, and the téni lifted his bound hands again in supplication. "No!" he nearly shouted. "Please! The Absolute . . . He . . . He is in a house on Lamb Street, on the south side two down from where Herringbone crosses. I . . . I swear it. Please, Ambassador . . ."

"You see," Sergei told the téni. "I knew you would tell me."

He gestured again with his cane, hard this time, and the driver slapped his reins at the horse. "Hey, up!" the driver called, and the téni shouted as the rope suddenly tightened and the carriage lurched away, gaining speed. The man screamed as he was pulled from his feet, as his body bounced along behind the carriage and the stones began to tear at him. Even in the darkness, they could all see the dark, wet trail that his body left on the cobbles. The téni's voice was a long, wordless wail as the carriage made the turn and headed across the bridge: shrill and terrified, then eerily and horribly silent. The carriage continued on its way across the A'Sele.

"My driver will return shortly," Sergei told the other prisoners, his voice calm and almost gentle. "Now, it's possible that our e'téni was lying about the location. I'm certain that—to avoid his fate—you all will tell me whether that's the case or not, won't you?"

He smiled as they shouted affirmation back to him, their voices a loud, terrified jumble.

Faintly, the wind-horns of the temples were sounding First Call, though there was little sign of the sun in the eternal ash-dusk.

Sergei knew before they ever entered the house that he was too late. Again.

"I'm not going in," he told cu'Ingres. "They've already left."

The Commandant gave Sergei a long stare. "You killed a man for this. A téni."

"I did," Sergei told the man easily. "And I would do it again, without a regret. And I chose the téni deliberately, for the effect it would have on the others—if I would kill a téni, I would kill them just as easily." He shrugged and tapped his cane on the street as the gardai, moving swiftly, encircled the house. Yes, this was the correct address: he could see the new footprints in the ash; the mob had gathered here, first. "They *were* here, but they're not here now, Talos. I'm sure someone is watching to bring a report to Nico. I can feel it. But . . . Go on. Do what we must."

Cu'Ingres sniffed. Almost angrily, he tore his gaze away from Sergei and gestured harshly toward his offiziers, who gave quick orders. Several gardai rushed the front door of the house and broke it down. Swords drawn, they entered.

A few minutes later, one of them emerged again; he shook his head.

Sergei drew a long breath that tasted of the dead ash in the streets. "Tell Nico Morel that I *will* find him," he said loudly, turning as he did so to face the other dwellings along the street. "I *will* find him," he repeated, "and he will face justice for what he's done. Tell him."

There was no answer to his call. Sergei turned back to cu'Ingres. "Have your people tear the house apart. They may have left something behind that will tell us where they've gone. Have a report on both my desk and the Kraljica's by Second Call," he said. The Commandant saluted without a word, though his eyes were still full of quiet accusation.

Sergei started toward his waiting carriage.

They would find nothing in the house that Nico didn't want them to find. He was certain that Nico was too careful for that. But he would keep his promise to the young man. He vowed that much.

~

Allesandra ca'Vörl

ALLESANDRA STOOD ON THE BALCONY of her rooms and stared out over the grounds. The ashfall had stopped two nights before, and the sunset tonight was stunning. Yellow-and-white clouds billowed near the horizon: wind-streaked, brushed in scarlet and orange-gold, and caught in a deep azure sky while the sun threw shafts of brilliant golden light through the gaps between them. The land underneath was caught in gold-green light and purple shadow. Fragments of saturated color seemed to lurk wherever she looked, as if a divine painter had smeared his palette across the sky.

Below her, workers were still sweeping the walkways of the stubborn gray and brushing the clinging ash from the bushes and plants of the formal garden her apartments overlooked. It had mercifully rained earlier in the day—

already, the palais grounds were beginning to look as they once had, but Allesandra could smell the ash: astringent and irritating in her nostrils. The entire city, the entire land stank of it.

The ash, the Morelli insurrection two nights ago, Jan's curt insistence that he be named her heir: it all weighed on her despite the beauty of the sunset.

"A'Téni ca'Paim wants you thrown into the Bastida," Allesandra said.

Sergei, who was ignoring the sunset and staring instead at the painting of Kraljica Marguerite on the wall, snorted audibly through his metal nose. "No doubt she does. What did you tell her?"

"I told her that the téni you killed had been a Morelli, had broken the laws of the Holdings, and was deliberately withholding information from you. I said that there wasn't time to consult her; you took the action you felt was necessary to try to capture Morel."

Sergei seemed to bow more to Marguerite than to Allesandra. "Thank you, Kraljica."

"I also read Commandant cu'Ingres' report. He doesn't seem to feel that killing the téni was required."

Sergei shrugged at that. "Two offiziers don't always agree on tactics. Had Talos done as I did a turn or two earlier, we might actually have caught Morel. Did he mention that in his report?"

"I know you, Sergei. You didn't kill the man as a tactic. You did it for the pleasure it gave you."

"We all have our faults, Kraljica," he answered. "But I *did* do it to capture Morel. At least partially."

"Gyula ca'Vikej doesn't feel you can be trusted anymore. He thinks your predilections and your ambitions have put you in opposition to me."

If Sergei was worried by that, he didn't show it. "You know my weaknesses, and I freely admit them to you, Kraljica. All of us have them, and yes, sometimes they can interfere with our best judgment for what is right for the Holdings. And as Ambassador to Brezno and the Coalition, I would prefer that no one else hears the Kraljica refer to ca'Vikej as Gyula. But then *I* haven't taken the Gyula-in-exile of an enemy state into my bed."

The surge of anger through her was hot and as bright

as lightning. She scowled, her fists tightening so that her fingernails carved crescent moons into her palm. "You *dare* . . ." she began, but Sergei put his hands out in supplication before she could say more.

"I'm simply pointing out—clumsily, I admit—that the choices we make aren't going to be universally beloved; that we make them for reasons that make sense to us but not necessarily to everyone. Forgive me, Kraljica. We have a long history together, but I shouldn't presume upon it. You know that my loyalty is to the Holdings and to her ruler. Always and forever."

I know that your loyalty is to the Holdings. But as to the other . . . Allesandra bit her lip, thinking the words but not saying them. She owed Sergei: she knew it; she knew he knew it. He'd saved her life and that of her son. The sting of his remark still cut at her, but the anger was cooling. She still needed Sergei. She still valued his advice.

But when the time came, she would not hesitate to throw him into the Bastida that he loved too much.

"I would be careful what you say and who you say it to," she told him, "if you want to escape the fate you'd give to others. You're lucky that—"

There was a discreet knock on the door of the chamber; a breath later, the door opened and the side of Talbot's head appeared, carefully not looking in their direction. "Kraljica," he said. "A messenger has come. I think you should hear what he has to say."

"What message?" Allesandra asked, the irritation still warm in her voice. "Tell me."

"I really feel you should hear it from him, Kraljica," Talbot said.

Allesandra scowled. "Fine. Send him in to us."

The door closed and reopened a moment later. Talbot ushered in a bedraggled man, his clothing stained with mud and ash, his face streaked, his eyes sunken in the midst of dark pouches. His hair was white, his hands curled in with huge, knotted knuckles. She guessed him to be five decades old or more, someone who had seen too much work in his time. "Please, sit," Allesandra told the man immediately, and he sank gratefully into the nearest chair after a sketch of a bow. "Sergei, pour some wine for this poor man. Talbot, see if the cook still has some of the stew from dinner . . ."

Talbot bowed and left the room. Allesandra stood in front of the man; she heard wine gurgling into a cup, then Sergei's cane on the floor as he handed the man a goblet. He drank thirstily. "What's your name," Allesandra asked the man.

"Martin ce'Mollis, Kraljica."

"Martin." Allesandra smiled toward him. "Talbot said you had news."

The man nodded and swallowed. "I've been riding for the last few days after sailing my boat from Karnmor."

"Karnmor." She glanced at Sergei. "Then you saw . . ."

He nodded, then shook his head. "I saw . . . Kraljica, I live on the northern arm of Karnmor Bay, well out from Karnor. I saw the ships coming in one afternoon—first a storm like nothing I'd seen before, then suddenly they were just *there*, painted ships attacking our navy in the bay—Westlander ships. I saw them tossing fireballs into the city and our ships there as the sun began to set. I knew some-one had to come, had to tell you what was happening. I'm just a fisherman now, but I served in the Garde Civile in my time, so I went to my boat and kept close to the shore and sailed around the northern end of the island in order to make for the mainland. I saw another Westlander warship anchored just off the shore, and a line of lights descending Mt. Karnmor as if people were there and moving down. I anchored where I was sheltered and watched, and the lights came down to the shore, and a small boat came out to the Westlander warship. After that, the warship pulled its anchor and left—I saw out on the horizon there were more ships waiting, Kraljica, more than I could count, and all of them sailed away from Karnmor as if Cénzi were chasing them, as if they knew . . ."

Martin licked his lips and drank again. "Thank Cénzi that they didn't pay any attention to me, didn't see me. I sailed on all night, staying close to shore and finally crossed the channel and landed on the mainland before dawn. There's a small garrison there, and I was telling the duty offizier what I'd seen just as the sun was rising. Then . . ."

He stopped. He gulped at the wine again. "Then Mt. Karnmor woke. I watched that awful cloud rising high in the air, felt the thunder hit us like a wall of hard air, and then the ash, so hot it burned the skin where it touched . . ." He shivered, and Allesandra noticed the reddened and blistered skin of his arms. "They gave me a horse, told me to ride here as fast as I could. Don't stop, the offizier told me. I didn't, either, except to steal another horse when the one I was riding died under me. I came here as fast as I could, Kraljica. You had to know, had to know . . ."

He took another sip; Sergei, wordlessly, refilled his glass. "*They* did it," he said finally. "The Westlanders. They brought their ships there, and their magic made the mountain explode. They *knew*. They *knew* it was going to happen—that's why they went north with their fleet that night. They knew what was going to happen, and—"

Talbot entered with a tray; the man stopped. "Talbot," Allesandra told him, "take our good friend Martin with you. Feed him, let him bathe, and put him in one of the guest rooms. Send for my healer to make certain he receives any treatment he might need. Martin, you've done a great service for the Holdings, and you'll be rewarded for it. I promise you that." She smiled again to him, and the man rose from his chair and bowed unsteadily. He let Talbot lead him away.

"The Tehuantin are back . . ." Sergei breathed the words as the door closed behind them. "This changes everything. Everything."

Allesandra said nothing. She went back to the window. The sun bathed the horizon in rose and gold.

"There will be panic in the streets as soon as this gets out. And if he's right, if Mt. Karnmor's eruption wasn't simply a coincidence . . ."

The sun spread a column of orange high into the haze as the searing yellow disk slipped behind the buildings of the city. The gilded dome of the Old Temple was silhouetted against the fiery colors. Third Call was sounding from the wind-horns; in a mark of the glass, the light-téni would be walking the city, illuminating the lamps of the Avi a'Parete so that the city was snared in a necklace of light. "*I will give it to you,*" her vatarh had told her once, referring to Nessantico and those lights. He had failed in that, but she had taken the city and the Holdings for herself. She had the city, had the pearl of lights as her own, had been washed in the light of the Sun Throne.

It was hers, and she had to do what she must to keep it.

"You'll be going back to Brezno," she said to Sergei. "There's a message you need to deliver to my son."

~

Varina ca'Pallo

"**. . .A**ND IF WHAT HE'S SAYING IS TRUE, then I worry about the Holdings in general." Talbot shook his head as he, the mage Johannes, and Varina walked along the Avi a'Parete. They were walking from the Numetodo House on the South Bank—near what was still called the Archigos' Temple, even though no Archigos had resided there since the unfortunate Kennis—toward one of the fashionable restaurants near the Pontica a'Brezi Veste. The street had been cleaned vigorously, but Varina could still see ash drifts along the gutters, and the cobblestones had a vaguely gray appearance.

Johannes was shaking his head. "I don't know of any magic that could cause a volcano to spontaneously erupt, and if they can do *that,* then . . ." He seemed to shudder. He pulled his cloak tighter around him. He glanced at Varina, bushy white eyebrows like thunderheads over his dark, hidden eyes. "You know the Tehuantin capabilities better than any of us," he said. "You're being awfully quiet, A'Morce, and that's making me uneasy."

Varina favored him with a wan smile. "I don't have better information than either of you," she said. "Maybe it was simply coincidence, or maybe the man's mistaken about what he saw."

Talbot shook his head. "Not all of it. We've had other fast-riders coming in who have also seen the Tehuantin fleet. They're definitely out there and heading toward the A'Sele by all indications. I thought I should tell you, A'Morce, since anything that happens could end up affecting the Numetodo also. The general populace will know in a day or two—this can't be kept silent . . ."

His voice trailed off. Varina, who had been walking with

her head down—as she nearly always did now, since her balance was sometimes as unstable as someone two decades older—glanced up. They had passed the long northward turn of the Avi, passing a short segment of the original city wall of Nessantico as they approached the Bastida. To their left, several small streets led off to the poorer area of South Bank. A knot of several young men had come out from one of the lanes onto the Avi, directly in front of them. They spread out in a ragged line, blocking their path even though there was more than ample room in the Avi.

"Move aside," Talbot said to the nearest of them. "Unless you want more trouble than you can handle. You don't know who you're accosting."

"Oh?" the man replied. "It's nearly Third Call, Vajiki. Shouldn't you be on your way to Temple? But no, I would have remembered seeing the Kraljica's aide at Temple, or the dead Ambassador's wife, or this owl-faced trained monkey you have with you." He laughed at that, the others joining in. Varina felt her stomach muscles contract at the sound: this was deliberate. They knew who they were confronting.

"Don't make a mistake here," Varina said to them, looking from one to another, trying to see in any of their faces reluctance or fear. She saw neither. She glanced around for an utilino, for a garda, for anyone who might help, but the eyes of the other people strolling the Avi seemed to be elsewhere. If anyone noticed the confrontation, they ignored it. She had to wonder if that, too, was deliberate.

"Mistake?" the same young man said. He had pox scars mottling his cheeks, and he was missing one of his front teeth. "There's no mistake. Nico Morel said there would be a sign—and the sign came, as he said it would. But you don't believe in Cénzi and His signs, do you? You don't believe that Cénzi speaks through the Absolute One."

"This isn't a discussion to have here, Vajiki," Varina told him. "I would love to discuss it with Nico in person. Tell him that. Tell him that I will meet with him whenever and wherever he wants. But for now—let us pass."

The pox-cratered man chuckled, the sound echoed by his companions. "I don't think so," he said. "I think it's time that the Numetodo were given a lesson."

As the Morelli spoke, Varina saw his companions sliding

around to surround them. "Don't do this," Varina said. "We don't want to hurt anyone."

In answer, the pock-faced man brought a cudgel from under his cloak. Raising his hand, he struck at Varina. The stick caught her on the side of the head, knocking her to the pavement before she could even bring her hands up to protect herself. She managed to get her hands up before she hit the cobblestones; the stones scraped and bloodied her palms, but still the impact knocked the breath from her. She felt something (a foot?) strike her side, and she felt more than saw the flash of a spell as Johannes shouted a release word. Talbot was casting a spell also, and so were others. She could taste the ash that her fall had kicked up. Blood was running into Varina's eyes (had she cut her forehead also, or had the cudgel done that?) She tried to push herself up. Everything was confused, and her head was pounding so hard she could barely remember the release words for the spells that she—like most Numetodo—had prepared for defense. Something had dug hard into her side when she'd gone down: the sparkwheel she carried under her cloak. Blinking away the blood, caught in the tumult of the scuffle, she grabbed for it.

Another spell flashed and Varina smelled the ozone of the discharge as someone—one of the Morellis?— screamed in response. There were more spells going off; at least one of the Morellis must have been téni-trained, she realized. Somewhere distantly, someone was shouting and she heard the shrill of an utilino's whistle.

Her own breath was the loudest thing in the world.

She had the sparkwheel out now. She cocked the hammer and rubbed at her eyes with her free hand. She saw the pocked-cheek man to her left, his cudgel up and about to come down on Johannes.

"No!" she shouted, and at the same time, her finger convulsed on the trigger.

The report was shrill, the sound echoing from the remnants of the city wall and rebounding, fainter, from the buildings up the Avi; the sparkwheel's recoil tore her hand up and back, and at the same time, the pocked-face man grunted and fell, the cudgel flying from his hand as an invisible spear seemed to rip flesh, bone, and blood from his face. "Back away!" Varina shouted from her knees to those closest to her. Blinking, she brandished the now-useless sparkwheel, which was trailing smoke and the strange, astringent odor of black sand.

The command was unnecessary. With the weapon's firing and the sudden, violent death of their leader, the others dropped their weapons and fled. Varina felt Talbot's arms under her, lifting her up. There were people coming toward them, among them an utilino. "Can you stand, A'Morce? Johannes, she's been hurt . . ."

"I'm fine," she told them. She wiped at the blood again. There were three people laying on the Avi. One of them was groaning and struggling; the other two were eerily still. There was no doubt as to the fate of the pock-cheeked man. Varina turned her gaze quickly away from him. She was still holding the sparkwheel. Talbot noticed it; standing close to her so that the utilino and the others coming toward them could not see, he put it back under her cloak. "Better not to let anyone know," he whispered. "Let them think we used magic."

She was too confused, too hurt to argue. Her head was throbbing, and she kept wanting to look at the mangled face of the man she'd killed. "Talbot . . ." she said, but the world was lurching around her, and she could not stand.

That was the last she remembered for a time.

~

Niente

IT'S AS IF THE ASH HAS MUDDIED everything, Taat," Atl said. "I haven't been able to see well since." Atl's voice was weary, his face was drawn, and he sagged in the chair in Niente's little room on the *Yaoyotl* as if he'd run all the way across the great island of Tlaxcala.

Niente grunted. The ashfall had been so dense it seemed that the fleet moved through a solid fog. The sky had first turned a strange, sickening yellow before the ash had become so thick that it had turned day to night. Lightning and thunder furiously wrapped the expanding cloud, and the

warm ash smelled of burning sulfur. The stuff was so fine
and powdery that it had insinuated itself everywhere. Their
clothing was full of it; it was in the food stores; it lingered in
every pore of the wood despite the efforts of the sailors to
clean it away. The sulfurous smell lingered as well, though
by now they were all accustomed to it. The ash was also
abrasive—one of the Tehuantin craftsmen had collected
several pouches of the ash, saying that he could use it as a
polishing agent.

And yes, the ash had tainted the purity of the water and
the herbs that Niente used for the scrying bowl. Since the
ashfall, Niente's own attempts to glimpse the future had
been nearly as clouded and useless as Atl's.

He hoped they were still on the same path, the same
route through the possibilities of the future that could lead
to the Long Path he'd glimpsed. The Tehuantin fleet had
entered the mouth of the A'Sele without any resistance
from the Holdings navy, though he was certain that by now
word must have come to Nessantico of what had happened
and of the appearance of the Tehuantin ships. If Axat's vision still held, then they would have linked the eruption of
Mt. Karnmor with their arrival.

For now, the wind that touched his nearly bald skull and
his ravaged face was cool and smelled of sweet, fresh water
rather than salt. They moved through a jarringly mono-
chrome landscape, the distant hills on either side gray when
he knew they should have been green and lush. Streams of
the finest ash floated by in the currents, heading out to sea
and back toward its source. They moved through a landscape touched by death: Niente saw the carcasses floating
past: birds, waterfowl, the occasional sheep or cow or dog,
even—once or twice—a human body. This close to Karnmor, the devastation had been terrible. There were only a
few gulls winging hopefully alongside them, far fewer than
Niente remembered from his last visit here.

Atl tossed the water from the scrying bowl over the side
of the *Yaoyotl*. That brought Niente back from reverie.
"What did you see?" he asked his son. "Tell me."

"The images came so fast and they were so dim . . ."
Atl sighed. "I could hardly make them out. But—once I
thought I saw you, Taat. You, and a throne that gleamed
like sunlight."

Niente felt himself shiver at that, as if the wind had sud-
denly turned as cold as the snowy summits of the Knife
Edge Mountains. He had seen that moment also, and more.
"You saw me?"

"Yes, but only for a breath, then it was gone again." Atl's
eyebrows rose. "Is this what you've seen also, Taat?"

*He stood in the hall, surrounded on all sides by the dead
of the Tehuantin and the dead of the Easterners. The place
stank of death and blood. He saw the Shadowed One—
the one who ruled here—but the throne glowed so brightly
that he couldn't see the face of the person who sat on the
throne, didn't even know if it was a man or a woman. Niente had his spell-staff in his hand, and it burned with the
power of the X'in Ka, so vital that he knew he could have
blasted the Shadowed One, could have broken the glowing throne. Yet he held back and didn't speak the words
though he could hear the Tecuhtli screaming at him to do
so, to end this.*

*Behind the Shadowed One an even greater presence rose,
one whose powers were so fierce that Niente could feel them
pulling at him: the Sun Presence. That being held a great
sword, and raised it as Niente waited. But the sword did not
come down. Instead, the Sun Presence touched the sword
and broke it in half as if it were no stronger than a slice of
dry bread, giving one part to Niente and keeping the other.*

*Niente walked away from the throne, the Tecuhtli and the
warriors screaming curses at him, calling him a traitor to his
own people . . .*

"No," Niente told Atl. "I've not seen that. I think your
vision was confused and wrong. It was only the ash speaking, not Axat."

Atl looked disappointed. "Give me the bowl," Niente
told him, holding out his hand. Atl handed it to him, the
brass heavy. "I'll clean it and purify it myself. We'll try
again, perhaps in a few days. You should rest."

"Rest?" Atl scoffed. "A few days?" He waved at the fleet
around them, at the gray land. "We need Axat's vision now
more than ever, Taat. Tecuhtli Citlali asks you constantly if
you've seen anything—"

"The ash obscures our vision," Niente said harshly, cutting him off. "Even for me, but especially for you, who are
still learning how to read the bowl. I tell you that we must

wait a few days, Atl. If you can't learn patience, you'll never learn to read the bowl."

Atl glared at Niente. "Is this more of your 'look at me, don't do what I did' lecture, Taat? If so, I've heard it too many times already."

"I told you I would teach you to use the bowl, and I will," Niente answered, but he cradled the bowl possessively to his belly. "You must show me that you're ready to accept the lessons."

"There are other nahualli who can teach me."

"And none of them are Nahual," Niente answered, more sharply. "None of them have my gift. None of them can show you as well as I can." Then, afraid of the expression on Atl's face, as if his son's face had been carved of stone, he softened his voice. "You will be Nahual one day, Atl. I know this. I've *seen* this. But for that to be, you must listen to me, and obey—not because you're my son, but because there are still more things you must learn." He pressed the bowl to him with one hand and reached out toward Atl with the other. "Please," he said. "I want you to know everything I know and more. But you must trust me."

There was a hesitation that tore at Niente's heart. Atl's mouth was twisted, and even through the boy's weariness, Niente could see his desire to use the bowl again.

He remembered that desire—he'd had it himself once, when he was his son's age, when he'd realized that Axat had touched and marked him, when he'd realized that he might be a successor to Mahri, that he might even rise to Nahual.

He knew what Atl was feeling, and that frightened him more than anything else.

But Atl finally shrugged as Niente continued to hold the bowl, and took Niente's hand, pressing his fingers once in Niente's palm. "I'll do as you ask," he said. "But, Taat, I won't wait forever. If I need to, I'll find another way."

He released Niente's hand. He stalked away, and Niente could see him forcing his body not to show the exhaustion he must be feeling.

It was what Niente himself would have done, in his place.

~

Rochelle Botelli

T HE DAYS WERE SPENT CLEANING, because the
    ash that caused such beautiful sunsets also dusted ev-
erything in Brezno Palais. Rance ci'Lawli drove his staff
relentlessly to keep surfaces clean. From rumors that Rochelle heard, Brezno's experience was insignificant. Here,
the ashfall was a fine coating like a week's worth of dust on
the furniture. But she heard whispers that people coming
from the west talked of drifts as thick as a winter's snowfall,
so heavy that roofs collapsed and animals choked to death.
She didn't know how many of the rumors were simply ex-
aggerated tales meant to entertain and how much truth
they contained, but it was apparent that something cata-
strophic had happened in the far west of the Holdings. "Mt.
Karnmor has awakened again after centuries of sleep," was
the most persistent rumor. "Thousands have died there."
Here, the person speaking would most often shake his
head. "They should have known better than to build the
city on the slopes of a volcano. It was a disaster waiting to
happen . . ."
    So she cleaned, and she made certain that the drapes
remained closed over the windows when they were open.
And she waited. She waited because the ashfall disrupted
the routines of the palais; they disturbed the patterns that
ci'Lawli made through his day and until they settled again,
she could not safely kill the man and fulfill her contract. She
found she didn't care; she toyed, in fact, with the thought
of handing Josef cu'Kella's money back to him—the solas
were hidden in her tiny sleeping room here.
    *"The White Stone can't fail a contract, and can't refuse
a contract,"* her matarh had said, in one of her lucid moments when the voices didn't torment her. *"If the people
feel the White Stone works for one cause or another, then the
Stone isn't a ghost to be feared, but just another garda in the
uniform of the rulers. The people love and fear the Stone be-*

cause she strikes anywhere, anytime. We are Death, coming for someone without remorse and without thought."

"Why doesn't Matarh like you?"

Rochelle was cleaning Elissa's bedroom, wiping down the girl's furniture with a damp cloth. She stopped, straightening and glancing at the child, who was sitting on her bed playing with a doll. Rochelle had noticed that the girl was snared in that awkward space between childhood and adolescence, when she was as likely to want to do "adult" things as to play with the toys that had once fascinated. The doll—which showed by the wear on its cloth arms and legs and porcelain face that it had long been a favorite—was now mostly abandoned except in moments like this.

"What do you mean, Vajica?" Rochelle asked Elissa, genuinely puzzled. Hïrzgin Brie had never seemed to show any dislike for Rochelle—in fact, after their talk the other day, she had even begun to think that the Hïrzgin might like her more than she did many of the dozens of servants who were in her presence each day. "She doesn't think I do my work well?"

Elissa shook her head vigorously, the doll's limb swaying with the effort. "It's not that," she answered. "I heard her tell Vatarh that she didn't like the way he acted around you. He said he didn't know what she was talking about. 'You know what happened before,' is all Matarh told him, and Vatarh just grunted. He told Matarh that she worries too much, and walked away, but Matarh still had on her mad face, like she did with Maria and Greta. Are you going away like them?"

"Maria and Greta?"

A nod, as energetic as the head shake. "They were servants that Rance hired, like you. Greta was here when I was nine and Maria last year. They were nice, and Vatarh liked them but Matarh didn't."

Rochelle found her hands trembling suddenly. She remembered the conversation with her vatarh the other day, the way he'd touched her face, the words he'd said, the interest he'd taken in her. *You fool* . . . It might have been her matarh's voice whispering in her head. *You stupid girl* . . . "Oh," she said, the exclamation flat and dead. It seemed to lay on the carpet between them, like a bird with its neck broken.

She'd been with men before. She'd been in love, been in lust, had twice now felt a man's weight on and inside her. She'd heard the glittering, bejeweled lies that they would say to convince her to share her bed, and had experienced the emptiness afterward when she realized how vacant and false those words had been. She had learned to hear the lies and to ignore them, and how to turn them aside so that they seemed a harmless flirtation—unless she wanted more.

She'd learned to expect the emptiness that followed the temporary moments of closeness and passion, and to accept it.

You fool . . . She should have realized . . . She'd heard the words Jan had spoken, but she hadn't thought of him that way, hadn't seen him as one of *them,* the ones who wanted the warm, hidden treasures under her tashta. She knew now why it had been so easy for Rance to place her on the private family staff. She recalled the Hïrzgin's conversation, and she understood.

She also heard Jan's words again in her memory, and they were changed and altered. Those words were gilded lead. They were empty boxes. They were blank parchment.

He was no better than some man looking for a night's anonymous companionship in a tavern.

Fool . . . No wonder the Hïrzgin had warned her.

"I should have been Hïrzgin," her matarh had raged when Jan had married Brie. Rochelle had been younger than Elissa then, but she still remembered the rage and madness that consumed Matarh at the news. *"He loved me, not her! She's just some piece of ca'-and-cu' trash, another title to add to his list. He loved me . . ."*

Rochelle wondered how much longer she could even stay here. "I'm not Maria or Greta," she told Elissa. *"Elissa. That was my name, the name he knew me by. He named his daughter for me . . ."* "I would never do anything to hurt your matarh. I hope she knows that."

"I'll tell Matarh," Elissa said, hugging the doll. She seemed to realize what she was doing and released the doll, letting it fall carelessly onto her lap.

"Tell her what?" Another voice interrupted them, the sound startling Rochelle. She hadn't heard Jan enter the room. That was troubling all on its own; how many times had her matarh cautioned her that the White Stone must always be alert, no matter what the situation. Yet Rochelle had been so lost in her own thoughts that she hadn't heard Jan enter, though now she recalled having heard the shuffle of his footsteps on the carpeting.

"That she should keep Rhianna," Elissa said. "I like her."

"I do, too," Jan said. His gaze was on her, and Rochelle forced herself to smile, as he undoubtedly expected. "Elissa, I think your matarh wanted to see you." He kissed the top of her head, but his gaze was still fixed on Rochelle. "But I'll tell you what, darling, let's not say anything about Rhianna to her just yet. Go on, now." He tousled Elissa's hair, and she jumped down from the bed, the doll falling to the floor. Elissa left it there. She padded away without a word.

Rochelle put the cloth into the bucket. She wiped her hands on the apron of her servant's uniform and picked up the bucket. "You're leaving, too?" Jan said.

She curtsied, keeping her gaze on the floor. "I'm finished here, Hïrzg," she said, "and I have other rooms that need attention."

"Ah." He paused and she waited, thinking he was going to say more. He stood there and she could feel him staring at her. She started to move toward the servants' door and the rear stairs. "You really do remind me of, well, someone I knew once. Someone who meant a great deal to me. It's very strange."

That stopped her, despite her trepidation. *"It should have been me . . ."* "May I ask who she was, Hïrzg?" Rochelle found herself saying, despite herself. She glanced at him once, saw his eyes, and dropped her gaze slightly.

He gave a one-shouldered, casual shrug. "I'm not really certain who she was, honestly. At best, she was a beautiful pretender who loved me, but became caught in the web of her lies; at worst . . ." He stopped again, giving the shrug once more. "At worst, she was an assassin."

By Cénzi, he knows! The thought yanked her head up to him once more, her eyes wide. He seemed to mistake her response for fear. He smiled as if in apology. "If she *was* that," he said, "then I became Hïrzg because of her. Maybe that's what she intended all along."

Rochelle nodded. Jan took a step in her direction and she retreated the same distance. He stopped. "You remind me so much of her, even the way you move. Maybe I should be afraid of you—are you an assassin, Rhianna?" He chuckled at his own jest. "Rhianna, you shouldn't be afraid of me. I think we—"

"Jan?" They both heard the call from the adjoining room—Brie's voice. The door to Elissa's bedroom started to open. "A fast-rider has come from Nessantico with some urgent news . . ."

Jan's head had turned at the sound of his name, and Rochelle took the moment. She grabbed the bucket and fled for the servants' door. She closed the door, cutting off Brie's voice.

She was trembling as she hurried down the stairs.

~

Varina ca'Pallo

"THIS WON'T HAPPEN AGAIN," Allesandra said, her voice full of concern and anger. She patted Varina's hand. "I promise you." Varina saw the woman glance at her bandaged head, and Varina reflexively lifted a hand to touch the bandage. The loose sleeve of her tashta slipped down her arm, revealing the brown-scabbed scrapes there. The bruises on her face, which she'd seen this morning while taking her bath, had turned purple and tan.

"Thank you, Kraljica," Varina told her. "I appreciate your concern, and thank you for sending over your personal healer—her potion eased the headache quite well."

Allesandra waved a hand in dismissal. The two women were seated in the sunroom of Varina's house, alone except for the two attendants who had accompanied the Kraljica, standing silently by the door. This room had been Karl's favorite in their house; he would often sit here, looking over old scrolls or writing down some of his own observations at the little table facing the small garden outside. His cane still leaned against the desk he'd used; Varina had left it there—seeing the familiar items made her feel as if he might walk into the room.

"Ah, there's my cane," he would say. *"I was wondering where I left that . . ."*

But she wouldn't ever hear that voice again. The thought brought tears shimmering in her eyes, though they didn't fall. Through their wavering veil, Varina saw Allesandra lean forward. "You're still in pain?"

"No." Varina wiped at her eyes. "It's . . . nothing. The sun in my eyes—though I suppose I shouldn't complain. It's good to finally see the sun again."

"The thugs who attacked you have been executed."

Varina nodded; it was not what she'd wanted—Karl had always said, and she believed herself—that harsh retribution only fed the anger in their enemies. But the news didn't surprise her, and she found that she could summon little sympathy for them.

Sympathy? What sympathy did you have when you shot your attacker? That image remained with her still. She didn't think she would ever forget it. Yet . . . She would do it again, if she had to, and the next time the act would be easier. She would protect herself if she must, and she would do that in whatever way she could—through magic or through technology. To her, they were no different: both were products of logic and thought and experimentation.

Magic and technology were the same, at the core.

The sparkwheel was in the drawer of Karl's desk now, reloaded. She could almost feel its presence, could imagine the smell of the black sand.

Allesandra evidently attributed her silence to acquiescence. She nodded as if Varina had said something. "I spoke to A'Téni ca'Paim and told her how serious I consider this incident to be. I warned her that she must deal harshly with the Morellis in the ranks of her téni, and that I expected the Faith to continue to support the rights of the Numetodo, and not to return to preaching oppression and persecution."

"With all due respect, Kraljica, that command needs to come from Archigos Karrol, not you or even A'Téni ca'Paim. I'm afraid the Archigos doesn't share your enthusiasm for the Numetodo, and his distaste for the Morellis stems mostly from his fear that Nico Morel might actually have enough power take his place, not from any particular disagreement with their philosophy. In that, they seem rather aligned."

A small moue of irritation flickered across Allesandra's lips, but was quickly masked by a smile. "You're right, of course, Varina. As usual. But it's what I could do, and hopefully A'Téni ca'Paim agrees with me. So perhaps we can do some good." She reached over to pat Varina's hand again. "I should leave you to your recovery," she said. "If you need anything, please let me know. We—the Holdings—will need the Numetodo, I'm afraid."

"The Tehuantin?" Varina asked. "It's true, then, the rumors—the Westlanders have returned?"

The single nod was all the answer Allesandra gave. It was enough. "I should go," the Kraljica said, rising from her chair. "No, don't get up. I can see myself out. Don't forget—tell me if you need anything. The Holdings is in your debt for your service, and for Karl's." The attendants stirred, opening the door to the sunroom as Allesandra pressed a hand to Varina's shoulder in passing and left. Varina heard her own servants bustling as the Kraljica moved down the hall toward the main door and her carriage. She heard the doors open, and the clattering of the horses' hooves and steel-rimmed wheels on the drive's cobbles.

She didn't move. She stared at the windows and the garden, at the desk with Karl's cane, at the ornate pull of the drawer where the sparkwheel was nestled.

The front door shut again. Her downstairs maid knocked softly on the door. "Do you need anything, A'Morce?"

"No, thank you, Sula," Varina told her without looking at her. She heard the sunroom door close softly again. She felt the breeze of it, like a caress on her cheek.

"I miss you, Karl," she said to the air. "I miss talking to you. I wonder what you would tell me to do now. I wish I could hear you."

But there was no answer to that. There never would be.

~

Brie ca'Ostheim

*J*AN WAS KISSING SOMEONE, *and Brie felt an immense tug of jealousy and irritation because he hadn't
even bothered to hide it. He was in the audience chamber
of the palais, and everyone was watching Jan embrace his
lover: Rance, Starkkapitän ca'Damont, Archigos Karrol,
the children, all the courtiers and ca'-and-cu'. She couldn't see
the woman's face, but the hair was long and black, and the
sound of their passion was loud enough that Brie could hear
a beating like that of a heart . . .*

The quiet but insistent knock came from the servants'
door, and it shattered the dream. "Enter," Brie said sleepily. She rubbed at her eyes, squinting toward the balcony,
where the thin drapes swayed with only false dawn's light
behind them. Brie yawned as the door eased open and Rhianna stuck her head in. "Hïrzgin, Rance sent me up. The
Ambassador ca'Rudka has returned to Brezno."

"Sergei?" Brie gestured to the young woman to come
into the bedroom, sitting up in the bed. She did so almost
shyly, standing with her head down at the foot of the bed.
"He's back so quickly?"

Rhianna nodded. "Yes. Aide ci'Lawli said that the runner from the Holdings embassy said that the Ambassador would be arriving at the palace as soon as he bathed
and dressed. He has an urgent message from Kraljica
Allesandra."

Rhianna's face seemed to twist as she said the last, as if
the name tasted sour in her mouth. "I take it you don't care
for the Kraljica, Rhianna?"

Rhianna shrugged. "I'm sorry, Hïrzgin. It's not me. It's
my matarh. She . . . Well, she had dealings with the Kraljica.
Before I was born. Exactly what her issues were I don't
know, but Matarh never spoke the Kraljica's name without a curse following it. I'm afraid her attitude has affected
mine."

Brie laughed at that. "Well, a child should listen to her matarh, and your matarh's attitude wouldn't be all that unusual in this household, I'm afraid. Is your matarh still living?"

Rhianna shook her head. "No, Hïrzgin. She passed to the Second World three years ago now."

"Ah, I'm sorry to hear that. It must have been hard for you." Brie pushed the covers down; the sky was beginning to lighten beyond the drapes. "Did Rance tell you what the Ambassador was in such a hurry about?" Brie was certain she already knew the tidings that had brought Sergei hurrying back to Brezno—a fast-rider from their own Ambassador ca'Schisler had come to Brezno from Nessantico not long after the ashfall, but Rance and Jan had scoffed at the rumors that ca'Schisler had given them.

They were about to be confirmed. Brie was certain of it.

Rhianna gave another shake of her head. "Aide ci'Lawli said only that the Ambassor claimed the message was urgent, and he asks you to come to the lower reception room as soon as you're able. Aide ci'Lawli is having breakfast sent there; I'm told the Hïrzg is already present and the Starkkapitän and the Archigos have been sent for as well."

"Hmm ..." Brie sighed and tossed the covers back completely. *If this is true, if the Westlanders are coming again ...* "You'll help me dress, then, Rhianna. In the closet in the dressing room, I'd like the blue tashta with the black lace trim. Go get it; I'll be there in a few moments."

Rhianna curtsied and left the room for the adjacent dressing room. Brie sighed as she swung her legs over the side of the bed.

The morning air was chilly on her bare feet, and through the drapes she could see clouds that promised rain.

Jan ca'Ostheim

"**Y**OU'RE CERTAIN OF THIS? Absolutely *certain?*"
Jan stared at Sergi ca'Rudka as he asked the
question, watching the man's face and trying to ignore
the distraction of the silver nose. Not that one could ever
see a lie in the Ambassador's ancient, lined, and practiced
face, but he still watched. Sergei only nodded, slowly and
carefully.

Jan heard the massed sigh from the others around
the conference table: Archigos Karrol, Starkkapitän
ca'Damont, Brie, his aide Rance.

"Oh, it's certain," Sergei answered. His voice sounded
tired, and his travel cloak was still stained gray with the
ash kicked up in his travel from the Holdings capital. He
reached into the leather pouch that sat on the table before
him and placed a stack of bound papers on the polished
oak. "I have the transcripts here with me of the several
fast-riders who came to Nessantico immediately after the
ashfall—many of them are firsthand reports of having seen
the Tehuantin fleet. The Kraljica has sent riders heading
west to verify the sighting, but we're certain what we'll find.
I came as fast as I could, but by now . . ." Sergei shrugged.
"The Westlanders may have already landed their army.
We've lost Karnmor to them; Fossano could already be
under attack, or they could be heading past that city upriver toward Villembouchure."

Jan found himself still wanting to deny the news. How
was it possible that Westlander magic could have brought
Mt. Karnmor to life? How could they have destroyed the
Holdings fleet and the city of Karnor, how could they have
caused thousands of deaths and this horrifying ashfall?

"Could the eruption of Mt. Karnmor have been a fortunate coincidence for the Westlanders?" Jan asked. "They
didn't necessarily *cause* that to happen."

Sergei sniffed. "They didn't land their army on the island. They took their fleet well north of Karnmor when it would have made more sense for them to move directly toward the mouth of the A'Sele. One of our eyewitnesses saw a Tehuantin ship at anchor at the flank of Mt. Karnmor the night before the mountain exploded, and lights on the slopes going to and from the ship. That doesn't sound like a coincidence to me, Hïrzg."

And if they could do that, what else could they do? That's what they were thinking, all of them in the room. "When the fast-rider came from Nessantico, I didn't want to believe this," Jan told him. "I thought perhaps—"

"I told you that your matarh wouldn't dare use such an outrageous lie," Brie interrupted.

"Yes, you did," Jan answered, though he didn't bother to hide the irritation in his voice. "Though I'm certain that the fact that it's true won't stop her from trying to take whatever advantage she can from the situation. So what is it that my matarh wants, Ambassador, that she'd send you so quickly back to Brezno?"

"She asks for the help of Firenzcia and the Coalition," Sergei said simply.

"Asks for or demands?" Jan interrupted. Sergei spread his shriveled, delicate hands wide.

"Does it matter, Hïrzg Jan? The Garde Civile of the Holdings couldn't stand alone against the Tehuantin fifteen years ago and defeat them. They still cannot."

From the edge of his vision, Jan saw Starkkapitän ca'Damont allow himself a momentary smile at that. "So now she *wants* our army to enter Holdings territory. How terribly amusing and ironic."

"We have no obligation to help them," Archigos Karrol said. The elderly man's voice quavered, and he cleared his throat noisily afterward, phlegm rattling in his lungs. "The Tehuantin wish to attack the Holdings? Well, let them. They won't come here, or if they do, we'll deal with them at that time, when their supply lines have stretched too far and their forces are weak."

"No obligation to help?" Sergei responded. "Only the obligation that Cénzi gives us in the Toustour, and also by the rules of the Divolonté. 'It is the duty of the Faithful to help those of the Faith who are in desperate need.' I believe that's an accurate quote—or has the Archigos decided to abandon those of the Faith who happen to live in the Holdings?"

"If your Kraljica hadn't decided to interfere in issues of faith and coddle and legitimize the Numetodo, then perhaps Cénzi wouldn't have sent this trial to her."

"Now you sound like Nico Morel, Archigos. I must say I find *that*—to use the words of your good Starkkapitän—terribly amusing and ironic."

Jan slapped his hands on the table. "Ambassador, Archigos, enough!" His hands tingled with the force of the impact. Archigos Karrol's mouth slammed shut with an audible grating of teeth; Sergei simply leaned back in his chair, his hand wrapped around the knob of his cane. "What does my matarh offer, Ambassador? Because she must be offering something in return."

The man's nervous ticks were at least predictable—he rubbed at the side of his metal nose as if it itched. "She is willing to give you what you've asked for," Sergei said, and Jan felt a sudden pressure in his chest. "She will name you A'Kralj," Sergei finished.

Jan felt Brie's hand on his arm. "Where is the knife blade hidden under those silken words?" she asked Sergei.

The Ambassador did smile at that, briefly. Then he leaned forward in his chair. "In return for the title, the Kraljica requests that Firenzcia dissolve the Coalition and immediately return to the Holdings. The other Coalition countries would be invited to rejoin the Holdings. If they refuse . . ." Sergei leaned back again. "Then the Kraljica, after this crisis is over, might be inclined to have them returned forcibly, with the aid of Firenzcia and the A'Kralj's—and Hïrzg's—army."

The pressure in his chest released once more, and Jan felt himself laugh, a sound that was almost a cough. Archigos Karrol chuckled broadly. Both Rance and Starkkapitän ca'Damont shook their heads. Brie's hand left his arm, leaving behind a chill. "So the old bitch still gets what she wants," Jan said.

"It *is* a compromise," Sergei responded. "You both get a portion of what you wanted. And you, Hïrzg Jan, get the final prize: you'll eventually be Kraljiki of a united Holdings."

"While she gets to play Kraljica for the rest of her

life." He scoffed again. "And if she lives for decades yet, I get to play Justi to her Marguerite, waiting patiently for her to die so I can receive my inheritance."

Sergei's mouth twitched; Jan couldn't decide if it was amusement or if he simply expected that objection. "I believe that I can persuade her to put a time limit on her reign, Hïrzg. After all, Allesandra will be sixty in 570; she might be persuaded to resign her title in favor of the A'Kralj at that point—which is only seven years from now."

"Which would be adequate time for, ahh, some unfortunate accident to befall our Hïrzg," Rance broke in. His smile showed no teeth, his lips pressed together as he inclined his head toward Sergei. "Such things seem to have a habit of occurring to those involved with the Kraljica, after all," he added.

"Yet somehow I've managed to live," Sergei answered, spreading his hands wide. "Kraljica Allesandra has her faults, I'll admit, but let's not fall prey to conspiracy rumors and attribute every misfortune to her influence. With the Archigos' forgiveness, she's hardly the Moitidi that some would make her out to be."

Jan had only half-listened to the exchange. "Is she still bedding the pretender Erik ca'Vikej?"

Sergei sighed. "Yes," he answered simply.

"I suppose she wants him on the throne of West Magyaria, and perhaps even married to her. Another ally to keep her on the throne."

Sergei said nothing. Finally, Jan sighed. *It's this or war. It's this or allowing the Westlanders to ravage the Holdings once again—and make it worthless to you.* He glanced at Brie; she nodded to him. "She would do what you said?" Jan asked Sergei. "She would abdicate the Sun Throne on her sixtieth birthday?"

"That isn't the offer she made, but I believe I can convince her of the wisdom of that choice," Sergei answered. "Whatever you might think of your matarh, Hïrzg, or her choices in lovers, she truly does want what is best for the Holdings. She knows that means the Holdings needs to be one again."

"Hïrzg," Rance interrupted, "forgive me, but I still don't like this. There is no reason that Firenzcia needs to bow to Nessantico. If anything, it should be the other way around,

with you dictating the terms . . ." Rance stopped as they
heard a knock on the servants' door to the chamber. "Ah,
that will be the additional refreshments. A moment . . ."

Rance rose from his chair, bowed to Jan, and went to the
door. Rhianna was among the servants who entered, Jan
noticed immediately, with a cart laden with glasses, a tray
of pastries, and bottles of wine. She seemed to notice Jan
at the same time, dropping her gaze as she pushed the cart
toward the end of the table.

Brie noticed her as well. Jan felt Brie watching him as
he regarded Rhianna, and heard the quick intake of breath
through her nose. The conversation around the table turned
to the ashfall, to Sergei's journey here—safe subjects—as
the servants placed the glasses and dishes in front of each
of them, opened the bottles and poured, and put the pastries within easy reach. Jan pretended to listen and take
part in the talk, glancing deliberately and often at Brie as
he did so, turning carefully away from Rhianna when she
came quietly to his side to place his glass and then hurry
away. He saw Brie glance at the girl, saw the narrowing of
her eyes and the flare of her nostrils as she watched Rhianna even while she smiled at Jan. He forced himself not
to look away even though he wanted that. There was something about the girl that made him want to talk to her, to
listen to her voice and stare into her face, and, hopefully, to
know her much better . . .

But if he wanted that, he had to be patient. He had to
be careful.

Patience.

He laughed, suddenly, startling Brie and the others. Brie
touched her face quizzically, as if wondering whether the
kohl around her eyes had decided to smear. "Is something
wrong, my love?"

"No, no," he said. Rhianna, with the other servants,
were already exiting the room, ushered out by Rance,
who closed the door after them and returned to the table.
"Starkkapitän, I want you to muster three divisions of the
army—one at the Loi-Clario Pass, and two near Ville Colhelm; Archigos, you will coordinate with the Starkkapitän
to make certain that he has sufficient war-téni for full-scale
operations. Rance, we will be leaving Brezno for Stag Fall
in two days, and we will wait there for further news."

"Then you are accepting the Kraljica's offer?" Sergei said, and Jan shook his head.

"No," he told the man. "I am preparing my country for possible war against the Westlanders—because what you have told me of Karnmor is terrifying. Perhaps that war will be brought to us . . ." He waited, picked up the goblet that Rhianna had put at his side and took a sip of the wine. It was tart and dry, and as red as blood. "Sergei, if you can convince Matarh that she would be more comfortable if she stepped away from the Sun Throne on her sixtieth birthday—and if she would declare such publicly and in writing to both me and the Council of Ca' for both Nessantico and Brezno—then perhaps Firenzcia might find the war wherever it is at that point. I can be that patient, I suppose."

Sergei nodded. He lifted his cane and slammed it hard against the floor. "Then, Hïrzg, I will take enough time to eat and get the rest of this damned ash from my clothes and body, and I will immediately be returning to Nessantico."

~

Rochelle Botelli

IF SHE WAS TO BE THE WHITE STONE, if she was to be what her matarh had taught her to be, then she could not wait much longer. The Hïrzg and Hïrzgin, their family—along with Rance ci'Lawli and the personal staff— would be leaving in two days, and that would ruin all the planning she'd done.

She'd been slow because she wanted to be here, wanted to know her vatarh better. But she had to act now, if she were going to act.

If she fulfilled the contract and killed Rance ci'Lawli as she had killed the others, then she might also have to leave the palais just as swiftly, and in leaving the palais, leave behind forever her vatarh.

Rochelle knew some of the same emotional conflict must have torn at her matarh in her day: pregnant with

Jan's son, in love with him, yet forced to flee—because if he knew who she was, that knowledge would also destroy the love and any chance she had. Rochelle fingered the stone that hung in a leather pouch around her neck, the white pebble that Matarh believed held the very souls of those she had killed. *I understand, Matarh,* she thought. *How hard that must have been for you . . .*

But she was not her matarh. She wasn't tormented by voices. She had only begun to be the White Stone. And her matarh had been too enamored of the knife and of watching her victims die.

There were other ways to kill someone, and if she did it right . . . Well, she might fulfill the contract and not need to flee the scene. All she needed was a sufficient proof of her innocence.

To that end, she had seduced Emerin ce'Stego, one of the trusted palais gardai. In the past week, she had spent as many nights as she could with him in her small bedchamber in the lower levels of the servants' wing, as both of them were generally on day duty and the palais gardai were permitted to occasionally spend nights away from the barracks. Emerin was pleasant enough, and gentle enough, and not much older than Rochelle herself. He also had wonderful green eyes; she enjoyed watching him as they made love, seeing the surprise in his face as he found his release. The first few nights, she made certain to get up in the middle of the night, jostling their bed and making enough noise that he would wake sleepily and talk to her. "You sleep so lightly, love," she told him. "It must be your training."

He'd smiled at that, almost proudly. "A garda needs to be alert, even when he's sleeping," he told her. "You never know when you might be called, or when something might happen."

"Well, I'd never be able to sneak away from you at night. Why, I was trying so hard not to disturb you at all . . ."

Matarh had known knives and other edged weapons, but she had also known the rest of the assassin's repertoire, and Rochelle had paid close attention to that portion of her education. It was easy enough, the night that the Ambassador of the Holdings left, to slip a potion into Emerin's wine goblet—a slow-acting sleeping draught. They made love, and he had drifted off to sleep. Rochelle slipped from the bed and dressed, taking with her the blade Matarh had given her, her favorite dagger, its edges blackened with a tar she was careful not to touch herself.

Rochelle had acquainted herself with the patterns of the palais and the servants' wing. The night staff would be at work; the day staff sleeping. Rarely would anyone be moving in the corridors. She was able to quickly slip to the single outside door, then sidle along the wall in the moonless, cloudy night to the window of Rance's bedroom. She could see the campfire of the gardai near the gate, and the forms of the men there—staring outward, not back toward the palais, and their night vision ruined in any case by the flames.

The staff rotated the duty of cleaning Rance's rooms; it had been Rochelle's turn three days ago, and she had taken the time to replace the metal lock of Rance's casement with one she'd fashioned from painted, dried clay. It was the work of a moment to push hard against the window. The clay cracked and crumbled easily; the two windows swung open. She could hear Rance snoring inside—Rance's snore was nearly legendary among the servants. She hoisted herself up and slipped inside, dropping almost silently to the floor. She pushed the windows shut again.

She needed no light; she'd familiarized herself with the room. Rance invariably slept alone. "*No one could actually* sleep *with that racket in the same bed*" was the usual laughing response from the staff if anyone speculated on the aide's love life. She heard more ominous gossip—that Rance had been injured in an accident as a young man and no longer possessed the requisite equipment for such activities.

Whatever the reason, Rance always slept alone. Rochelle's eyes had already adjusted to the gloom; she could see the hump of his body under the covers—not that anyone needed more than ears to locate him. She padded over to the bed. He had tossed one of the pillows on the floor; Rochelle picked it up. She slid the dagger from its sheath. Then, in one motion, she plunged the pillow over Rance's face and slid the the dagger along his side, the cut shallow but long—the depth of the stroke didn't matter, only that the black poison on the blade entered his body.

Rance immediately jerked awake, his hands scrabbling

blindly, but Rochelle pressed all her weight down on him. The poison on the blade was already doing its deadly work; she could hear the choking rattle in his muddled cries and the flailing hands began to jerk spasmodically. A breath later, and they had dropped back to the bed. Carefully, Rochelle lifted the pillow from Rance's head. In the dimness, she could see his mouth open, the tongue black and thick and protruding from his mouth, vomit smeared along his chin. His eyes were wide, and she quickly removed the two pebbles from the pouch laced around her neck: the White Stone's pebble, and the one that Josef cu'Kella had given her. Her matarh's stone she placed on the man's right eye, cu'Kella's on the left. After a moment, she plucked the one from his right eye and placed it back in the pouch. She cleaned the dagger on the bedding before sheathing it again.

Moving to the window, she quickly replaced the metal latch and tied a string around it. She climbed back outside, then pulled the twin windows shut; pulling the string, she brought the metal latch over to snug itself in the opposite latch, and a tug on the string pulled it through the crack between the two segments of the window.

A few minutes later, and she was back in her bed next to Emerin.

It was not until dawn that a scream awakened them both.

REALIZATIONS

Niente
Jan ca'Ostheim
Brie ca'Ostheim
Allesandra ca'Vörl
Varina ca'Pallo
Nico Morel
Rochelle Botelli
Niente
Sergei ca'Rudka

Niente

ATL HAD COME TO HIM THE NIGHT BEFORE.
"I saw the battle, Taat," he said. His voice was solemn,
his face serious. He sounded on the verge of exhaustion;
the skin under his eyes was puffy and dark. "In the scrying
bowl, I saw it."

They were standing on the rear quarterdeck of the *Yaoyotl*.
The sun had set with another spectacular blaze, as if sinking into
a burning city just over the horizon. The fleet was anchored,
nearly filling the A'Sele from bank to bank and blockading the
harbor of the city Fossano. Niente had consulted with Tecuhtli
Citlali, had told him what he'd seen in the scrying bowl, then
Niente called together the chief nahualli of each of the ships
to give his instructions for tomorrow. They had left less than a
stripe of the candle before, and he still sat here, the crew studi-
ously avoiding him as he stared out toward the distant lights of
the city. He rubbed at the gold bracelet of the Nahual around
his right forearm; it seemed to chafe his skin.

Now Atl's words chilled Niente though the night air
was warm enough. He felt as if snow blanketed his spine.
If Axat had granted the boy far-vision, of what lay well
ahead of them—it all could still unravel, the entire Long
Path, like a poorly-tied weaving. "What battle?" he asked.
"In Nessantico?"

Atl shook his head. "No, not the great city." He pointed
over the water to the light. "This one. Fossano." With that
admission, the coldness and unease began to recede and
Niente found himself relaxing hands that had curled defen-
sively into fists. "Tell me," he said to Atl, more calmly now.

"Have you seen it also, Taat?" Atl asked, and Niente
nodded to him.

"Yes. Axat has granted me that sight. Tell me what you
saw, so I know whether you saw true."

"I saw the ships anchored here close to the shore, and
the warriors spilling out onto the land like furious black
ants. I saw Holdings ships at our rear, and fire arcing from
our boats to theirs and setting them afire. There were two
battles, really—one here on the water and another on the
land. Mostly I saw the one on the land. I was there, and you,
Taat, and Tecuhtli Citlali. The city walls were tall and thick,
but the black sand tore into them and knocked them down.
I saw their war-téni sending fire back toward us, and the nahualli's spell-staffs responding. But their war-téni wearied
eventually, and they couldn't stop the catapults that threw
black sand at the walls. The great stones tumbled down
and their portcullis was shattered. Tecuhtli Citlali sent up a
great cry, and our warriors rushed into the city."

Niente saw Atl's throat move as he swallowed then.
"The vision began to shift then, and Axat only gave me
quick, fleeting sights. All of it was short and bloody. We
took their city, we slew the Eastlander warriors until their
courage broke and they fled in whatever direction they
could. We took the spoils from their houses." He flushed. "I
saw their women raped and their young men killed if they
dared to protest, though the High Warriors stopped that
where they could. I saw their children wailing and crying. I
saw their city in flames. And I saw *you*, Taat, and Tecuhtli
Citlali—I saw you sacrifice the tecuhtli of their city to Axat
and Sakal in gratitude."

"And then . . ." Niente prompted him, but Atl shook his
head.

"There was no more, Taat. Only a glimpse of warriors
coming back to the ships. That was all that Axat granted
me." He shook his head. "Was Her vision true, Taat? Is this
what you saw also?"

That was all . . . Niente sighed in relief, though Atl's expression fell, as if he thought that Niente were disappointed
in him. Niente forced a smile; it ached in the muscles of his
face. "I saw the same," he told his son, and Atl beamed.
"Axat also granted me to see the water battle, and we sent
a dozen of the Easterner ships to the bottom of the harbor;

the rest were damaged and retreated to the west down the A'Sele. This will be a great victory for Tecuhtli Citlali. Axat has ordained it." He stopped, and this time the smile was genuine. "I saw you also, Atl. I saw you leading the nahualli with your spell-staff; I saw you still strong when other nahualli were weak, and I saw you leading the warriors into the city. I saw Tecuhtli Citlali's pride in you afterward."

He could see Atl struggling not to grin, to remain stoic and serious. He would not tell Atl of the fate he'd seen for him later. Instead, he clapped his son on the back, then clasped him to him, kissing him on the cheek. "I love you, my son," he whispered into the young man's ear. "You should know that I'm proud of the person you've become."

The night air was cool around them. There were stars struggling to be seen through the persistent high clouds, and a moon that cloaked itself in a luminous mist. There were the yellow lights of the city glistening in the blackness of the land. Waves slapped the hull of the *Yaoyotl* like erratic hands on a drum, and Niente could smell the sweet oil on Atl's skin and the heavier musk of the river. He felt like a child holding an adult. He felt shriveled and frail and tiny against his son's muscular body.

"Go, and fill your spell-staff," he told Atl. "Then rest as best you can. Tomorrow—tomorrow we will go and fulfill Axat's vision." He kissed Atl again, then pushed him away. "Go," he said. Atl clasped Niente once more, kissed him as Niente had him, then gave him the moon-sign of Axat.

"Tomorrow," he said to Niente, and left.

Niente watched him go. "Tomorrow," he whispered after him. "There's at least that."

~

Jan ca'Ostheim

"THE PEBBLE ON THE LEFT EYE—that's the signature of the White Stone. How she entered Rance's apartments, we don't know. The door was locked when Paulus arrived; the windows are all latched from the inside." Eris Cu'Bloch, Commandant of the Garde Brezno, shook his head. "I'm sorry, Hïrzg. He was long dead when they found him. There was nothing to be done."

A raw, sickening fury enveloped Jan. He stared at Rance's body on the bed, the pebble still over his left eye, his right clouded and open. Paulus ci'Simone, one of Rance's trusted assistants, sat with his head bowed and hands clasped between his knees in a chair. In the outer room, the door to Rance's apartment hung askew on its hinges from where it had been broken in by the palais staff, and occasionally one of the staff would walk past hurriedly, face averted.

"There's blood, but not enough," Jan commented.

"No," cu'Bloch agreed. "Nor does it look like he struggled much with his attacker." He lifted Rance's bloodied nightgown: it had been sliced open along the side by a sharp knife, and Jan could see the long cut on the man's side, but the cut was not so deep as to have been fatal. "If you look closely, you can see a dark, oily substance in the cut. If you touch it, it burns. I think the blade that did this was poisoned, though with what . . ." Cu'Bloch shrugged. "I don't know of a poison that works quickly and effectively enough that Rance wouldn't have had time to defend himself, but perhaps the White Stone does."

Jan pressed his lips together. "Cover him," he said to cu'Bloch. "Paulus, he was this way when you found him?"

Paulus lifted his head and nodded mournfully. "Yes, my Hïrzg. Rance was supposed to go over the day's kitchen menu with me at First Call, and when he didn't arrive, I knocked on his door and found it locked. He didn't answer our calls, so I found two of the staff gardai and we broke in. I saw him in his bed, just like that, his skin cold . . ." Paulus stopped. His eyes glistened suddenly and a tear tracked down his face. "We called for the Commandant and you."

"You don't know how the White Stone might have gained entry?" Commandant cu'Bloch asked. Paulus shook his head.

"It doesn't matter," Jan said. "This was the White Stone. She's here." He scowled.

She's here. As she'd been here when Hïrzg Fynn had been assassinated. He felt as if his hands had suddenly gone cold: that death had been his matarh's doing. It had been

Allesandra who'd hired the White Stone; he'd learned that to his disgust, and that had been one of the reasons he'd abandoned her and the Holdings when the moment had been there to reunify the empire.

And there had been the even more terrible realization that Elissa—who had vanished the same terrible evening that Fynn had died—had been the White Stone. He had wanted to deny that; he'd wanted to tear that knowledge from his head and remember only the Elissa he'd loved.

He glanced again at the body on the bed, the bloodied sheet covering Rance. "Where's Rhianna?" he asked suddenly. "Has anyone seen the girl? Bring her here. Now." Cu'Bloch gestured, and one of the garda in the room rushed back out. Jan heard Rhianna's name being called in the corridor.

In truth, he expected the answer to come that she could not be found, that she had vanished from the palais. That would explain everything. And the assassination . . . Could it have been Allesandra who had again hired the assassin? Rance had always advised flatly against any reconciliation with Nessantico; Sergei would certainly have mentioned that to Allesandra. Could Allesandra have wanted Rance dead as a result? Or could the White Stone's client have been Sergei himself, ridding himself of an obstacle? Rhianna had been there when Sergei had met with them; she could have overheard, or perhaps Sergei could have given her some signal that told her to murder Rance . . .

The possibilities spun in his head like kitten-tangled yarn, the threads of his thoughts so interwoven that he couldn't find the ends of them. Cu'Bloch was talking to Paulus, but Jan heard nothing of it. When he heard footsteps in the outer room, he turned. The garda had returned, with Rhianna and another garda, a face Jan vaguely recognized—was he named Enid? Emero? Emerin? Rhianna was gazing around her as if confused, glancing back at the broken door, then seeing Jan, the Commandant, and Paulus.

"My Hïrzg," Rhianna said, curtsying deeply to him. "I was told . . . You wanted . . ." She was looking past him now, to the bed and its covered form. Her hand went to her mouth as her eyes grew wide and frightened, and the garda with her put his arm protectively around her. The gesture made Jan scowl. *She has a lover here, then?* "Oh, no! By Cénzi, is that . . . ?"

"Yes," Jan told her. "Rance has been killed. The murderer would have us think that the White Stone did it."

Rhianna seemed to stagger, her legs unsteady, and the garda held her more tightly. "The White Stone . . ." Jan watched her; her stunned reaction seemed genuine. He saw her lower lip trembling as if she were about to cry. Then she seemed to shake herself, and her gaze went quizzical. "Why does the Hïrzg wish to talk to *me*?" she asked.

"Where were you last night?" Jan asked her.

"Why, I was with Emerin," she said. A flush crept up her neck from under the collar of her robe. "He and I . . ." She stopped. "My Hïrzg, you can't possibly think . . . I was with Emerin all night, and Vajiki ci'Lawli and I were on excellent terms."

"Hïrzg, may I speak?" Emerin asked. He had straightened, tugging at his nightclothes as if it were his uniform. Jan glared at him. He nodded. "It's true she was with me," he said hurriedly.

"You never slept, then?" Jan asked. "You watched her all night?"

Emerin's blush matched Rhianna's. "Yes, I slept, my Hïrzg. But I sleep very lightly. Everyone knows that—ask Rhianna. Or better, ask my fellow gardai at the barracks. The slightest noise wakes me, and I never woke last night. Rhianna went to sleep before I did, and she was still asleep this morning when you summoned us here."

"Indeed," Jan said. "Then neither of you know anything of this?"

They both shook their heads simultaneously.

"You don't know anyone who would have wanted Rance dead?"

Again, he received the same response. Jan pursed his lips, staring at Rhianna. *So like her* . . . She would not look at him; she kept her face down, gazing at the floor. Her hands were coupled together as if she were praying, and Emerin's arm never left her shoulder. "All right, then," he said. "We will be questioning all the palais staff. Someone must know something. If anything occurs to either of you, no matter how minor, you will immediately tell Commandant cu'Bloch. Is that understood? Paulus, you also."

Rhianna curtsied again; Emerin gave a salute; Paulus rose slowly from his chair. "You may all go," he told them. Rhianna and Emerin hurried away; Paulus followed more slowly. Jan glanced back at cu'Bloch.

"Do you know something I don't, my Hïrzg?" the Commandant asked.

"No," Jan answered. "It's just that Rhianna ... She's new to the staff, and frankly, Brie doesn't like her for some reason." He saw cu'Bloch's chin lift slightly at that, and his eyes seemed to nearly smile. Jan ignored that. "You know this garda she's involved with?" Jan asked the man.

"Emerin? Yes. He's someone I've been watching for promotion—a good young man who seems trustworthy. And he's right, my Hïrzg; he has a reputation as an extremely light sleeper. I believe him. Besides, if the girl was somehow the assassin—and she seems rather young to have that kind of skill—I doubt she would have stayed."

Elissa didn't stay. She fled . . . Jan grunted assent. He looked again at poor Rance's covered body. "I leave this to you then, Commandant. Interrogate the staff; see if anyone has seen or heard anything that could lead us to the White Stone or the person who hired her—and if that path seems to lead back to Nessantico, tell me immediately. No one here in the palais can rest easily now. We will proceed with our plans to leave for Stag Fall tomorrow; I'll have Paulus take over Rance's position for the time being."

The Commandant saluted as Jan left the bedchamber with a last glance at the bloodstained bed. Maybe he was wrong. Maybe Rhianna's uncanny resemblance to Elissa was more in his head than reality; after all, it had been a decade and a half since he'd last seen Elissa. Would he even recognize her if her saw her now? Did he truly remember what she'd looked like or was he romanticizing the memory he had of her? Perhaps he was only seeing what he wished to see.

Down the corridor, Emerin was talking to Rhianna. She glanced at Jan as he exited Rance's chambers, looking quickly away when she noticed his attention. It was difficult to tell in the dimness of the servants' corridor, but the look on her face as she turned ... it wasn't the fearful respect he usually saw in his staff's faces; it was something else, some-

thing more wistful and possessive, and he wondered at that
as he made his way back to his own apartments, trying to
decide how he was going to tell Brie and the children what
had happened.

~

Brie ca'Ostheim

SHE FOUND RANCE'S MURDER difficult to process, and even more terrifying when she considered
the import: an assassin loose in the palais, a skilled and
relentless killer able to find her way into a closed and
locked room and kill Jan's trusted aide and councillor in
his sleep.

If the White Stone could do that, then none of them
were truly safe. After Jan had told her, Brie had gone immediately to the playroom to make certain the children
were unharmed. They'd seen the concern on her face, the
tears in her eyes, and she'd explained to them that Rance
was dead and that they'd be leaving the palais tomorrow
for Stag Fall. She wasn't certain they really understood.

She hugged Elissa, Kriege, and Caelor fiercely, then gestured to the wet nurse to bring Eria to her. "Matarh, it's
all right," Kriege told her. "I'll protect you. Why, if I had
Vatarh's dagger . . . I've learned so much already from the
arms captain. More than Elissa."

"Have not," Elissa retorted. "Why, I know ever so
much more, Matarh. The captain says I'm a natural, and
he doesn't say that to Kriege." She stuck her tongue out in
Kriege's direction.

Brie knew then that they really didn't understand, that
they wouldn't until Rance's absence became apparent to
them. Brie smiled wanly at them, feeling the dried tears
pull at the skin of her face. "Commandant cu'Bloch has
put his gardai all around the palais," she told him. "I think
we're safe enough for now."

She wasn't certain she believed that. She knew she
would be less certain tonight: in the darkness. She didn't

want to sleep alone. Not tonight. She would ask Jan if he would spend the night with her, and the children also ...

"Matarh, what's wrong?" Eria tugged at her tashta, and Brie crouched down next to her, cradling her in her arms, smiling into her inquisitive face.

"You'll be safe, little one," she crooned. "I promise."

There was a knock on the servants' door and Brie stood up, sucking in her breath. She nodded to the nursemaid, setting Eria down on the floor and reaching under the sash of her tashta for the knife she had there, curling her fingers around the hilt. The nursemaid opened the door; Rhianna entered, carrying a tray. The garda in the corridor outside glanced in, then closed the door again.

"Rhianna," she said. "It must have been terrible, this morning."

Rhianna nodded before she answered, almost furtively. "It was, Hïrzgin," the young woman answered. There were dark circles under her eyes, as if she hadn't slept well, and her manner was distracted and nervous. She placed the tray on the table near Brie's chair. She wiped her hands on the apron over her plain tashta. "It just doesn't seem possible. Aide ci'Lawli gave me my chance here and I worked with him so closely, even though I didn't know him for as long as other people on the staff. I'm shocked and I still expect to hear him calling for me ..." She took in a long, slow breath. "The Hïrzg said to send wine up for you, and some fruit for the children ..."

"The Hïrzg?" A quick flash of jealousy surged through Brie, burning for a moment through the grief. Rhianna seemed to sense it. She took a step back and lowered her head, and that made Brie wonder even more.

"Yes, Hïrzgin," the girl was saying. "I mean, the Hïrzg told Paulus, and Paulus told me ..."

"Ah." Brie sniffed. "I see." The jealousy subsided, allowing the sadness and fear to return with a shiver. "The White Stone ... Here, in this palais. I simply can't believe it. The last time ..."

She stopped. The last time, the White Stone had killed the Hïrzg. She couldn't say that, afraid that saying it might cause history to repeat itself.

"Please don't worry, Hïrzgin," Rhianna said. "You've nothing to fear."

Brie looked at the young woman. The words had
sounded so firm, so certain, her face lifting, though now she
flushed again, lowering her gaze once more. "I mean," she
continued, "that with all the gardai on alert . . . The White
Stone is surely gone by now . . . Paulus thinks she was most
likely hired by somebody with a personal grudge . . . The
White Stone wouldn't . . . wouldn't . . ."

Brie continued to stare at her as Rhianna's voice faded
and went silent. "You should leave the staff gossip and
speculations at the door, Rhianna," she said to her. "It's
been a stressful day, but that doesn't excuse spreading
rumors."

Rhianna flushed furiously, curtsying at the rebuke. "I
apologize, Hïrzgin. I'm sorry."

Brie waved her silent. "Don't let it happen again," she
said.

"I won't, Hïrzgin. Ma'am, Paulus also told me to have
your domestiques de chambre and those of the Hïrzg
start packing for Stag Fall. With your leave, Hïrzgin, I
should go find them and tell them."

"Yes, certainly," Brie said. "Go on with you, then."

Rhianna curtsied again. She turned and hurried away.
Brie stared at the door for several breaths after it closed
behind her. Then she sighed. "Come, children. Your vatarh
has sent up some fruit. Let's eat, and then perhaps we can
have a game of chevaritt . . ."

~

Allesandra ca'Vörl

ERIK ROLLED AWAY FROM HER, leaving her
body momentarily chilled. Allesandra reached down
and pulled the blanket up over herself. She glanced over at
Erik, panting next to her. "Satisfied?" she asked. His body,
in the candlelight, was heavy and dark, the light glimmering
from the polished flesh of his skull and glinting from the
white hairs snagged in his midnight beard.

From above the fireplace at the foot of the bed, Kraljica

Marguerite stared down at the lovers from her painting, her expression severe.

Erik groaned and nodded. "By Cénzi, woman, you're a tigress. A danger to all men. You've destroyed me entirely." His voice was a purr, a low growl, and his eyes regarded her possessively.

She smiled at that. But he didn't ask her the same question she'd asked him; he never did. She wondered if that would begin to do more than annoy her one day. She wondered if he looked at her, saw her age and the way her breasts sagged and her stomach rounded, and whether he wished he were with someone younger, someone who could give him children. She would never give him that, even if she wanted it; her monthly flow had ended a few years ago. The seed that filled her belly now could do nothing.

But she could offer him things that no younger woman could, that no other woman in the world could. She wondered again if she would make that offer to him.

"Perhaps."

"Hmm?"

Allesandra laughed, not realizing she'd said the word aloud. "Perhaps you would like some refreshment, my love? I could ring for the servants . . ."

"No, not unless you want something for yourself." There was silence for a moment; she wondered whether he was falling asleep. "Allesandra?"

"Yes, love?"

"This offer to the Hïrzg. If he accepts it. What then happens with me?"

He was staring at her; she could feel his gaze. She held it in the darkness. "I've already told you that when the Holdings are one again, I will make certain that a true Gyula sits on West Magyaria's throne. You shouldn't worry yourself."

"Yet I do. When the Holdings are one again, the Kraljica might not want to cause yet more dissent."

"You talk of this Kraljica as if she were some other woman."

His hand stroked her side. "My family has been involved in the politics of the Holdings all my life, by necessity. Forgive me for saying this, but one thing my vatarh always told me was that the promise of a Kralji could not buy a beer in the tavern: even a barkeep knows that the Kralji might

decide that the folia is better spent somewhere else, and
leave you with the tab."

"You believe I'm that cold?" she asked, and she knew he
could hear the warning in her voice. "You think you mean
that little to me?" His hand stroked her arm and found her
hand, but she didn't return the pressure of his fingers. He
hurried to answer.

"No, of course not." A breath. A sigh. "I would be lost
without you. Truly. Being with you, well, I've never felt this
way with anyone, not even the matarh of my children. I just
hate to think . . ."

"Then *don't* think," she told him. Her voice snapped
more sharply than she intended, and she softened her tone.
"Just feel what I tell you, and accept it."

He laughed then, and his hands roamed the slope of her
side, falling into the hollow of her hips. His hands tightened
there, and he pulled her toward him. His mouth sought
hers, his beard brushing her skin. His hands cupped her as
he brought her on top of him. She looked down at him, and
he seemed vulnerable and almost boyish.

She smiled at that thought. She brought her head down
and kissed him deeply, her mouth opening, her hands on
either side of his face. When she finally pulled away, gasping, she leaned on her elbows, a cloud hovering above his
landscape. Firelight rippled across his face and she saw the
eager expression there. "No more thinking, and no more
worrying," she told him. "At least not for a bit . . ."

Sergei sat in his chair like a wizened toad, one hand clutching the end of his staff, his silver nose reflecting the morning light from the window overlooking the palais gardens.
Erik was seated near him, and his face was dark and red
with a flush. Allesandra had left her own chair behind her
desk, pacing near the balcony entrance.

"I wonder, sometimes, if you aren't conspiring with my
son, Ambassador," she said. "I thought that you believed
you could convince him to accept the offer we tendered."

"I told you, Kraljica, that I thought he would listen to it
sympathetically. And he did exactly that."

"Yet he requires that I abdicate the throne in seven
years in favor of him."

Sergei gave a nod that sent motes of light scattering along

the wall like bright cockroaches. "Yes," he answered simply. "If you agree to that and state so publicly, the Hïrzg will dissolve the Coalition, freeing the member countries to make whatever choice they wish: to rejoin the Holdings or remain independent." Sergei smiled slightly. "Like you, Kraljica, he doesn't expect any of them to choose the latter course. And he will bring the army of Firenzcia here to help defend Nessantico against the Tehuantin."

"What of West Magyaria and the false Gyula he set on its throne?" Erik interjected before Allesandra could respond. "What does the Hïrzg say of that?"

Sergei glanced over at Erik. He seemed to look the man up and down with a smirk of disdain. "Of that he said nothing at all," he said. "He didn't seem to consider the throne of the Gyula important enough for comment or negotiation."

"Then he's a fool," Erik spat. "With West Magyaria at the Kraljica's side, the Holdings wouldn't need Firenzcia at all."

"The Hïrzg, I believe, would disagree with you, Vajiki ca'Vikej. For that matter, so would I. And I note that the Kraljica didn't send an Ambassador to West Magyaria asking for their help."

Erik sucked in a breath through clenched teeth, and Allesandra whirled to face them. "Be quiet, both of you," she snapped. "Your bickering makes my head ache so that I can't think." She kneaded her forehead with a hand. She felt confined, trapped, as if the palais walls were constricting around her. *You have no choice in this.* The thought hammered at her skull in time with her pulse. *You really have no choice. The Holdings can't stand alone against the Westlanders, and the Holdings can't survive another long recovery.*

She stared out the window, to the walls where she could still see the marks of the repairs that had been done after the Tehuantin bombardment. She remembered how the city had looked in the days and weeks and months after the Firenzcian army had finally smashed the Westlander forces and sent them reeling back across the Strettosei. She remembered the misery and the pain of those times. She remembered how desolate she had been herself then, abandoned by her own son.

"We're stronger now," she said to both of them. "We no

longer have half of our army fighting a war across the sea."
She tried to say it with confidence, but even she could hear
the uncertain quaver in her voice.

"And the Tehuantin, from all reports, are also stronger—
they've brought easily three times the ships they had before," Sergei answered. "Between Karnmor and Fossano,
they've already destroyed most of our navy. Kraljica, if I
thought that Commandant ca'Talin could defeat the Tehuantin alone, I would counsel you to ignore the Hïrzg's
counteroffer. But I can't do that, not in good conscience.
Not as a loyal subject of the Sun Throne, who wishes nothing more than the Holdings' success. I wish I were wrong in
this, but I fear that I'm not." She wasn't looking at him. She
didn't wish to see his face. "And I think that you know it as
well," he finished.

She continued to stare out at the palais grounds. She
could feel her fists clenched at her waist, as if she'd eaten
bad shellfish and was trying to quell a rebellious stomach.
The damnable man was right; the Garde Civile would fight
courageously and well, but in the end, they would fall. And
Jan, as he had before, was in position to sweep in and clean
up the mess. If he wanted the Sun Throne, he could have
it in mere months; all he need do was wait and do nothing
until Nessantico was taken and Allesandra herself dead or
fled.

"Don't listen to him," Erik was saying. "You should be
Kraljica for the rest of your life. This offer; it is an insult."

"Insult or not," she told the air, "I have no choice." She
turned to the two men. "Sergei, you will have Talbot draft
the agreement; I will sign it this afternoon. A'Téni ca'Paim
will read the proclamation at service tomorrow. We'll also
send it by fast-rider to Brezno; you will follow as soon as
you can, and you will remain with the Hïrzg as my representative until he arrives here in Nessantico with his army."

She watched Erik's face as she spoke. She saw the anger
he tried to hide. She suspected it was not rage at the decision, but a fear that he might not have what he wanted.
Which one of us is using the other? She told herself that she
had no answer to that question, but a voice deeper inside
laughed at that evasion. *You don't just want to admit the
truth . . .*

"Why are you both still sitting there?" she barked at the two men. "We're done here."

With that, she waved her hand and turned back to the landscape outside once again. She listened as they bowed and hurried away, Sergei's cane tapping at the marble flags. She stared at the isle and at the buildings of Nessantico, and they no longer seemed hers alone.

~

Varina ca'Pallo

"**HOW HAVE YOU BEEN RECOVERING?**" Sergei asked her. "You certainly look well, like you're a decade younger than you are."

Sergei had come to the Numetodo House, and Johannes had escorted him down to Varina's workroom. Varina saw him eyeing the sparkwheel prototype she had set in a vise, pointing at the straw dummy at the far end of the room. This version of the sparkwheel had a significantly longer barrel; she had wondered whether that might improve the accuracy of the shot. Varina flipped a sheet over the apparatus as she laughed at the blatant compliment. "I have to believe that your eyes are failing in your old age then, Sergei. But thank you for the lie."

"Karl saw your beauty, as I do—though it took him longer than it should have."

She managed to smile at that, remembering. *In the midst of the war, in the midst of death and terror, there had been Karl, and that had made it all bearable.* Yet now it seemed those times were to return, and Karl was gone. She didn't know how she was going to live through another war and more battles.

She wasn't certain she wanted to.

"The Morellis are becoming more than a simple nuisance, I'm afraid," Sergei was saying. "Unfortunately, I need to leave the city again, so I can't join the hunt for Morel himself. However, I'll make certain that Commandant

cu'Ingres understands the importance both the Kraljica
and I place on tracking down the man. You were lucky that
you were with your people. I understand it was your magic
that killed one of them—I hope that you're not too upset
by that. You truly had no choice." She thought that his gaze
was strangely intense on her as he said the last, as if he were
watching her for a reaction. She wondered what he'd heard,
what he suspected. She forced herself not to look at the
covered sparkwheel.

Not magic. Something more dangerous.

"I regret that it came to that," she told him, truthfully.
"If I could have avoided it, I would have. But . . ." She
lifted a shoulder. Over her warped reflection in his nose,
Sergei's gaze flicked to the sheet on the table and back
again. He leaned heavily on his cane, his back bowed.

"You wouldn't be who you are if you didn't feel that
way," Sergei said, "but I assure you that no one blames you
in the slightest. The man brought his death upon himself.
He has no one to blame but himself and his actions, and—
you'll pardon my saying this here—Cénzi will give him the
eternal punishment he deserves."

"Mentioning Cénzi in the Numetodo House seems almost sacrilegious."

"It does, doesn't it?" he answered, chuckling. "I'll admit
I was surprised to find you here. I called at your house, and
your house servant said that you'd been working here for
the last several days and often staying overnight. I worry
about you, Varina, especially after what you've been
through."

"A few aches and pains is all," she told him, "and I had
those in plenty before the attack. It comes with age, you
know."

"As we *both* know." His gaze went back to the covered
apparatus again. "Varina, I think you should leave Nessantico. Go north, perhaps. Maybe go to Il Trebbio. Or even go
visit Karl's homeland. I hear the Isle of Paeti is gorgeous."

"You think it's going to be that bad, Sergei?"

His fingers tightened around the knob of his cane. His
tongue licked his upper lip. "Yes," he said. "And no. When
Jan brings the Firenzcian army, we should prevail, but that
still won't be without loss and it won't be without hardship, and it may be that the battle will take place *here* again,

in Nessantico. I hope not, but if the Tehuantin ships move quickly . . ." He nodded, as if he were agreeing with a new thought he'd had. "I think it would be best if you were gone from here."

"If the battle does come here, then here is where I'm needed."

He glanced at the sheet again with that. "Talbot could be A'Morce Numetodo for the time being. He can lead and direct them. Unless . . . Unless there is something that only you can do."

"You're not very subtle, Sergei."

"And you're not very good at keeping secrets, Varina."

She stared at him blandly. "The Numetodo don't keep secrets. We want knowledge to flourish. I gave the formula for black sand to you and the Kraljica, if you remember. Freely."

"Yes, you did. And Nico Morel stole some and used it against you."

Varina flushed at the memory. "It's ignorance and secrecy that causes problems with the world," she said. "Not knowledge."

"What causes problems is what people do with the knowledge."

"Strange how often it's the ca'-and-cu' who always say that. It's underneath half the platitudes I hear from the rich: they feel that the lower ranks should be kept uneducated and ignorant."

Sergei's eyebrows rose at that. "What strange philosophies have you been listening to, Varina? Next I know, you'll be claiming that the peasants should enjoy everything that the ca'-and-cu' have."

"I grew up in a ce' family," she answered. "I know what it's like to be on the bottom of society."

"And now you're ca', and you also know that it's possible to be rewarded for your hard work and your intelligence. You're an example of what every unranked and ce' person can aspire to accomplish."

"Possible, perhaps," she said, "but I would argue that I am the exception rather than the rule, and that there are many unranked and ce' who deserve better, and ca'-and-cu' who deserve less."

Sergei lifted a hand. "No doubt. But who is to determine

which? We have to leave that to Cénzi—ah, sorry. There I go again—or, as I suppose you would say, to an accident of fate." He chuckled again. "And this is an argument neither of us will win, and I've no desire to leave you in a poorer mood than I found you. Varina, promise me that you'll consider leaving the city."

"I will consider it," she told him. She didn't tell him that she had already considered it and made up her mind. Instead, she smiled and put her own hands atop his. Her hands were like his: knobby and wrinkled, the flesh loose on the bones; the hands of an ancient. "Come," she told him. "Let's go upstairs where it's more comfortable, and we can continue our talk over tea and scones."

Gently, she ushered him from the workroom, locking the door behind them.

~

Nico Morel

THEY SNUGGLED TOGETHER IN THE BED, and Nico kissed the slope of Liana's shoulder, tasting the salt of her sweat. Her arms and her legs clutched him tightly, as if she wanted to hold him there forever, though he was held back by the surprising mound of her stomach. He laughed, stroking her hair and staring into her eyes. They were the color of rich earth after a rain, and he could see his own thin, bearded face reflected in them.

For a moment, his vision blurred and darkened, and it was as though there were a third person in the room with them: small and frail, a heart that could be heard above the pounding of his heart and Liana's, and he thought he saw a form drifting away from them, leaving the room: a child's form. A girl. He could feel the cold heat that he associated with Cénzi at the same moment. He closed his eyes, opened them again.

"Nico?" Liana asked him. She sounded worried. "You were so far away . . ."

Her arms had loosened around him. He tried to smile at her. "I'm sorry. It's just . . ."

"What did you see?"

He shook his head. "Nothing. Or rather, I don't know." He stroked Liana's abdomen. "I thought I saw . . . *her.*"

"Her?"

Nico gave a small nod. "Her." He tried to smile, but found it difficult. Something about the brief vision bothered him. Why was the child leaving? Why did she vanish? Why did he not see either himself or Liana in the vision? "A girl."

Liana was suddenly weeping, but it was a cry of joy. She flung herself at him, her arms going around his neck as she kissed him. "A girl. Are you happy?" she asked. "Is that what you wanted?"

"No," he said, then laughed at the face she made. "I mean, it doesn't matter at all to me. Son or a daughter. All that matters is that the child is ours." He gestured at the shabby room around them, another in the sequence of houses they'd fled to in Oldtown. "I have so little to offer you," he said, and now it was Liana who laughed.

"Do you think that's of any consequence to me?" she told him. "If you do, then Cénzi didn't tell you everything." Her arms gathered him to her again. "You offer me all that I want. I want you to be happy. I want us to be happy," she whispered into his ear. "That's all."

"And I am," he told her. "Liana, we should marry. I will ask Ancel—"

She surprised him then. "No," she told him, shaking her head. Her hair drifted around her shoulders with the motion. "We should not."

"Liana?"

She leaned back slightly, still holding him. Her gaze was serious and unblinking. "I know you love me, Nico. I know because you would never lie—not to me, not to anyone. You've no guile in you at all. I'm content with your love. And it may be that the Absolute—especially if he becomes what I believe Cénzi intends him to become—may need to marry someone for reasons other than love. He may have to do as the Archigi have done before, and marry to keep the Faith safe."

He was shaking his head, but he could hear Cénzi inside his head: a deep, low approval, and he knew that she
was right. Marriage could wait; it made no difference to his
commitment to Liana or their child.

"I don't deserve you," he said to her, and she laughed.

"Perhaps not, but you have me, Nico, and I don't intend to let you go."

There were a half dozen of the war-téni of Nessantico gathered in the room, as well as a double-handful of the other
téni from the city's three temples. Most of them were young,
most of them were e'téni, though a few, especially among
the war-téni, had the rank of o'téni. Nico surveyed their
faces as he entered the room behind Ancel and Liana. His
arm was around Liana's waist protectively; he saw some of
them notice that and smile, as if they were pleased to see
that the Absolute of the Morellis, Cénzi's Voice, the Sword
of the Divolonté, was as human as them, that he could love
someone and produce an heir.

Nico kissed Liana's cheek and smiled at her as she and
Ancel moved to the side of the crowded room—the largest
of three small rooms in their current refuge in Oldtown.
The place stank of mold and rat feces, and the boards
creaked and groaned under their weight, but Cénzi had
told him that none of the Garde Kralji would find them
here for now, so it must do. Nico gave them all the sign of
Cénzi, which they returned.

They bowed their heads to him as well, every one. Nico
nodded at that. He could feel Cénzi's presence: a heat in
the core of his body and a fire in his voice.

"Cénzi has told me that I can trust you," he said without preamble. "He has shown me the heart of each one of
you, and I know you. You have taken a great risk tonight
to be here, and He knows this and blesses each of you for
your devotion, and I appreciate it as well. I know that you
hold the Toustour and the Divolonté to be the true Word of
Cénzi. I know that you feel, as I do, that leaders of the Faith
have lost their way. Archigos Karrol, A'Téni ca'Paim: they
have abandoned Cénzi for the secular world, listening too
much to Kraljica Allesandra and Hïrzg Jan and too little to
the Great Voice. I tell you . . ."

Nico paused, looking at each of them in turn, holding

their gazes. He could sense Cénzi's power building inside him. He let it do so, let the energy sear the words he would say. They emerged from his mouth as if he were spitting red coals and fire. The words raged in the tiny, dingy room; it wreathed them with Cénzi's anger. "Cénzi said He would give us a sign, and He has sent us an unmistakable one. He has shown us in fire, in ash, and in blood how angry He is with the Faith. It was not enough that the Faith has coddled the unbelievers, the Numetodo, who deny Him entirely. No. Now He has sent the Tehuantin, heathens who worship a false god, to punish us for having fallen away from Him. There is but one way to save us. To cool Cénzi's displeasure and to end His punishment, we must take our Faith back. We must take back the Faith for Cénzi, and for the people who truly believe. We must take it back *now*!"

Nico paused, gathering the energy once again. They were listening to him, rapt in the power of Cénzi's words. Nico drew himself up, He raised his hands and his face to the bowed ceiling. He let Cénzi take his voice fully. "It is time," he roared. "It is time to rise up and throw off the Archigos and a'téni who refuse to follow Cénzi's path."

The command snapped their heads up, pulled them from their seats. For a moment, it was chaos in the room, with dozens of voices contending as Liana and Ancel tried to calm them. It was only when Nico raised his hands that quiet returned. Nico pointed to one of the war-téni, the slashes of an o'téni on his green robes. "You," he said. "Tell me why your face is so full of fear."

The war-téni rubbed a hand through short, dark hair. He glanced around at the others before answering. "Absolute," the man answered. "You ask us to go against the oaths we have all taken as téni—the oaths that we made to Cénzi."

"I know that oath. I have taken it myself," Nico answered. "I pledged to obey the Archigos and to follow the Toustour and Divolonté, as did you. That is why I no longer use the Ilmodo even though Cénzi's Gift burns within me. But listen to me now: it is the *Archigos* and the a'téni who listen to him who have broken their oaths, for they make it impossible for us to both obey them and obey the Toustour and Divolonté. If the Archigos, with his orders, demands that we break with the Toustour and Divolonté, which come to us through Cénzi, then it is *our duty*—as téni and by the oath we've all taken—to refuse to obey them."

The o'téni was nodding before Nico finished speaking, and he turned to the others. "Do any of you have more objections? Come, let us hear them."

One of the e'téni lifted a tentative hand, and Nico gestured to him. "Absolute, there are those who say that you only wish to be Archigos yourself."

Nico smiled at that, clapping his hands together. "I wish to serve the Faith however Cénzi demands that I serve it. If Cénzi would one day bring me to the Archigos' throne, then I would be a poor servant if I refused Him. But I'd also be a poor servant if I let pride and desire govern my actions." He pointed to the téni, then let his finger sweep over all of them. "I would tell you, all of you, that you should watch me as I watch the Archigos, and if you see me ever, *ever* acting in my own interests rather than those of the Faith, then you should raise your voices against me. Do you wish to do that now? Do you?"

They were silent. Nico let the quiet reign, listening to the sounds of their breaths, the noise their feet made on the rough boards under their feet. Finally, he gave them the sign of Cénzi again. "I thank you," he said. "And Cénzi thanks you. Now—listen to me. Here is what we must do . . ."

~

Rochelle Botelli

STAG FALL WAS MORE BEAUTIFUL than any description she'd had of it.

The palais sat in the center of hundreds of acres of mountainous forest, clinging to the side of one of the tallest slopes like a limpet, with arms of thick-hewn timbers that supported its many balconies and wings. The approach to the villa was long and arduous, the road winding back and forth across the face of the heavily-wooded and ancient mountains of the range. The switchbacks would have drawn any enemy laying siege to Stag Fall into long, vulnerable lines, and there were cliffs above many of the sections where defenders could easily send boulders, arrows, and spells down upon hapless attackers. Morning and night, thick, white mists rose from the valleys, so dense that they muffled all sound and confused any sense of direction.

The palais itself was built from rich oak and adorned with other precious hardwoods. It was polished and gleaming, its dark-paneled rooms large with huge inviting hearths that were used year-round; even in summer when Brezno would be sweltering, the nights here still held a chill. Rochelle had thought Brezno Palais foreboding: a fortress of cold stone. Stag Fall was a glimpse into another world, a forest world. Stag Fall was softer and more inviting than Brezno Palais, but it was no less formidable and no less a fortress.

A caretaker staff remained permanently at Stag Fall to care for the villa when the Hïrzg or other notables were not there, but with the Hïrzg and his family arriving, the permanent staff was placed under the control of the Hïrzg's personal staff. Paulus ci'Simone was no Rance ci'Lawli, and it showed in his rough and almost territorial interaction with the two staffs. Rochelle had seen Rance's ability to smooth ruffled feathers between staffs; Pauli was far less polished, and tended to bark orders rather than listen to explanations. Rochelle witnessed it daily.

"Damn it, woman, the Hïrzgin won't eat the venison cooked that lightly. Do you know absolutely nothing about how your mistress prefers her meat? Another half-mark of the glass on the fire, at least! There should be no red left in it."

Paulus glared at the cook, who slapped the cut of meat back onto a spit and thrust it over the open fire again. Paulus made a sound of disgust. "Rhianna!" he barked. "As soon as this incompetent has the meat acceptably cooked, make certain the meal gets up to the Hïrzgin's room while it's still hot. She's been waiting too long already. I can't waste my time here any longer—I have to see to the Hïrzg's attendants now; they seem to have misplaced his riding leathers."

Rochelle curtsied, and Paulus stalked away from the kitchen. "Bastardo!" she heard the cook mutter as soon as he was safely out of earshot. She was a stout woman of middle years, the skin hanging under her arms wobbling as she moved. "He thinks he's already ca'-and-cu'. I'll spit in his food tonight—see how he likes that." The rest of the kitchen staff chuckled.

"He's just scared," Rochelle told her. "He knows he's swimming out of his depth."

"Well, he's no Rance ci'Lawli, that's certain, may Cénzi rest his soul," the cook responded. She shook her head and turned the spit. Grease hissed and crackled as it dripped into the cook fire. "That was a terrible thing, his murder. The White Stone, they say. Wouldn't surprise me if that worm Paulus was the one who hired her, just to take old Rance's position." Her voice dropped to a conspiratorial husk. "They say Rance was laid open from throat to cock like a filleted fish, and every wall of his bedroom was covered in his blood." The skin under the cook's chin was as loose as that under her arms; it swayed as she glanced back at Rochelle. She pushed back the red turban wrapped around her head to absorb the sweat from the kitchen fires. "Did you see any of that, girl?"

The image of Rance open-eyed in death came back to Rochelle, and she shivered. She touched the pebble in its pouch under her tashta. *At least I don't hear his voice . . .*

"No," she said, then shook her head. "I mean, I saw the body, and it was nothing like that. There was very little blood. I was told that he was killed by a poisoned blade."

Eyebrows clambered toward red cloth. "You saw his body? Truly? Well, I suppose you would know then." The way she said it, Rochelle was fairly certain that no one in the kitchen staff preferred the image of Rance's actual death to the cook's more gory and visceral one. She suspected that the blood-bathed version was the one that would prevail in staff gossip. "Well, this meat should be done enough for the delicate tongue of the Hïrzgin, eh?" The cook lifted the skewer from over the fire, the thick sleeve of her soiled tashta around the iron bar, and slid the meat onto a plate with a large fork. "There you go, girl. You'd better hurry. You've a bit of a climb to the Hïrzgin's quarters . . ."

Rochelle nodded and placed the plate on the tray with the rest of the Hïrzgin's meal, covered it, and left the close heat of the kitchen. The servants' corridors of Stag Fall were narrower than those in the Brezno Palais, and cold after the kitchen. She moved quickly up several flights of stairs, occasionally passing another of the staff with a nod or a quick greeting, until she reached the royal family's level. There were a pair of gardai there, of the Brezno Garde Hïrzg, and one of them examined her tray while the other watched with a hand on the pommel of his sword. Finally, the garda nodded toward the door and, with a clatter of plates, Rochelle moved on.

She wasn't happy that Paulus had assigned her to the Hïrzgin. She still wasn't certain whether the Hïrzgin entirely trusted her. It was almost as if she knew the connection between Rochelle and her husband. And the Hïrzg—for all the interest he'd shown in her at first, now he acted cold and distant toward her. He ignored her if she were in the same room with him, and a few times she'd caught him staring at her with an appraising look on his face.

He knows who you are. He knows, and the knowledge terrifies him. The thought seemed to come to her wrapped in the voice of her matarh.

She knocked on the door to the Hïrzgin's chambers. The door opened a moment later, and Rochelle was looking down at Elissa. "Hello, Rhianna," the girl said. "Matarh has gone to see Vatarh. She said for you to put the dinner on the table in the outer room and leave it."

Rochelle felt muscles relax in her back and abdomen, and she realized that she'd tensed without realizing it. She smiled at Elissa. "Then that's what I'll do," she said. Elissa opened the door wider, and Rochelle entered, moving through the bedroom and into the outer reception chamber. She placed the tray on the table there and arranged the cloth over it to keep it warm and any ambitious flies away. She started back toward the servants' door.

"Matarh is going with Vatarh to see the troops, then come back here later to be with us," Elissa said. "I heard Vatarh tell Paulus that he wanted you to be on the staff that goes with them."

"Ah . . ." Rochelle smiled at Elissa, though she wasn't certain how she felt about the news. "And what did your matarh say to that?"

"She wasn't there," Elissa answered.

Rochelle nodded. *He wants me to go with him.*

"I'll miss you, Rhianna," Elissa said. "So will Kriege and

Caelor, even if they wouldn't say so. Eria won't, though."
Elissa's face twisted into a frown. "She's too little and
stupid."

Rochelle laughed. "Don't say that about your sister,"
she said gently. "She's still learning, that's all. You should
teach her—she looks up to you."

"I'd rather have a sister like you," Elissa said.

Rochelle caught her breath. In that moment, she could
have blurted it all out. The words burned in her throat. *I* am
your sister, Elissa . . . But instead, she nodded. "Thank you,
dear one," she said instead. "That would be wonderful if it
could be that way, and I'd be the best big sister you could
have. But Eria is growing up—and walking and talking and
getting into things—and you'll need to be the big sister for
her. You'll need to show her everything, and help her so
that she learns what she needs to learn. She'll be watching
you, and wanting to do what you do, just as you do it."

"Did you have a big sister?" Elissa asked her.

"No. I had a big brother, though he was much older than
me, and he left before I was very old. And I didn't have a
little sister—or brother."

"You would be a good big sister, Rhianna. You would
teach her everything you know."

Rochelle touched the stones under her tashta. "No," she
said. "I don't think I could." She curtsied to the girl then,
hurrying to finish before the girl asked any more questions. "I have to go now, Elissa, or Paulus will be wondering
where I am. Is your matarh coming right back, or should I
send one of the other maids up to be with you?"

"She'll be right back," Elissa said, and they both heard
the outer door begin to open in the same moment. "Oh,
there she is now," the girl said, running to the door. "Matarh,
Rhianna has brought your supper . . ."

But that was all Rochelle heard. She hurried to the servants' door, closing it quickly behind her before Brie could
see her or call out after her. In the dimness of the corridor beyond, she leaned against the door, and her fingers
caressed the stone in its pouch.

Niente

*T*HE PATH HAD BEEN SO CLEAR *back in Tlaxcala.*
Every step had been laid out, and now it's all confused
and diffuse. The Sun Presence dominates everything, hiding
the Long Path from me . . .

Niente bowed his head over the scrying bowl, immersing himself in the green mist that boiled up from the water, praying to Axat fervently, begging Her to give him clear sight, to show that the Long Path had not already been destroyed by the actions of those in the present. That was the danger: the future was malleable and changeable, and a single act by someone might alter everything.

There . . . That was Villembouchure, the city they had taken once before, and Niente saw the possibilities of battle there. He stirred the water with a hand, dissolving the image and pushing his mind further into the mists of the future. He didn't want to see Villembouchure; he knew what should happen there—the path was wide and difficult to turn away. He wanted to see again the great city: Nessantico.

He wanted to see again the fate that awaited him there, the fate that would affect both Tehuantin and Easterner, that might shape the world with his own mold.

There . . . There was the great city, its strange, majestic
buildings rebuilt, so unlike the stepped pyramids of Tlax-
cala. But the mists around this future were heavier than they
had ever been before, and the visions came too fast, too fleet-
ing. There was his son's face, and he was shouting at Niente,
his face full of anger and fury. There was the glowing throne
of the great city, but the shape sitting on it was uncertain: one
moment it was a woman, then a man, then another, and there
was a young man standing alongside it, wearing green robes,
and from his hands boiled more mist that obscured Niente's
sight. For a moment Niente felt a stirring in the mists: was
this a glimpse of the Sun Presence?

Where was the Long Path? Had it vanished? No, there it was again, but now faint, so faint, and overlaid with a dozen other possible futures when before it had been clear and certain. There was Atl again, and he walked yet another future. There was a paper, with strange writing on it, and the scroll was in flames, the words going to gray ash. There was a young woman with a pale-colored stone in one hand and a dagger in the other, and she governed yet another path. Faces wafted up toward him from the mist and vanished again: a man of middle years with a crown on his head, an old man with a metal nose, an old woman from whose hands sparks flew like a fire-rock striking metal, and again the young, green-robed man from whose mouth fire emerged, as if he were a dragon.

Niente had never seen these figures before—or at least not so clearly—but now they rose up in opposition to him, confusing Axat's sight and seeming to bar him from the path he'd chosen. He sought to find it again, staring into the mists of the bowl and searching for a way past these specters. *There . . .* He saw it again, at last, but this time he also saw Atl laying still on the ground before the path, his head bloodied, and he recoiled in fear. *No, Axat!* he prayed. *You can't demand that of me . . .* But the vision remained, and it was only beyond Atl's corpse that the future he'd wanted lay . . .

The Long Path.

It still led to his own death as well, but he welcomed that. It would be a release from eternal pain. He welcomed the thought of falling into Axat's embrace at last, of leaving behind the shriveled, tormented, and pained shell of his physical body. That would be no great sacrifice. He'd lived long decades, and he had been Axat's devoted servant, and he had been both rewarded and punished for that. No, to find his own death would be sweet and he could embrace the Great Winged Serpent without fear, if beyond his death there was still the vision She had granted him. If his death sealed the Long Path.

In his visions atop the Teocalli Axat, Niente had glimpsed a world at peace for a time, a world where East and West respected their individual boundaries, where trade between them was open and free, where the best of both cultures merged into a new whole, where even the worlds of the gods seemed to come together. Yes, there were still battles and strife in this world, but the conflicts were smaller and more easily resolved. People being what they were, it wasn't possible to find a path where there wasn't bloodshed and conflict. But down that Long Path, the world as a whole was more benign, more accepting.

Now, Niente looked for that future. It was still there, but the vision was murky and disordered, and he was no longer certain he could find the way to it in reality.

"Taat?"

He heard Atl's voice, and with the interruption, the green mist dissolved and he was merely staring at his own ugly, shimmering reflection in the water of the bowl. A droplet—like rain—hit the surface of the bowl, rings radiating out from it, touching the edges and rebounding in complex patterns, and Niente realized that he was weeping. He brushed at his eyes with his gnarled, clawed hands. "What?" he asked, blinking and raising his head. The back of his neck was stiff; how long had he been gazing into the bowl?

Atl was staring at him, and Niente wondered how long his son had been there. Perhaps he'd been muttering to the visions in the scrying bowl, as he sometimes did—what might Atl have heard? "What, my son?" Niente asked again, trying to soften his voice.

"The fleet is approaching the next large city, and Tecuhtli Citlali would like to speak to you regarding the vision you have had for this battle."

"Yes, I'm sure he would," Niente said. He sighed. Groaning with the effort of moving, hating how his back was bowed and how he shuffled like an old man, he lifted the scrying bowl and took it to the small window of the tiny room. He opened the shutter that kept out the spray and wind, and tossed the water out into the A'Sele. He wiped the bowl with the hem of his robe and handed it to Atl. "Take the bowl and purify it," he said to his son as if he were an apprentice. "Tell Tecuhtli Citlali that I've just asked Axat to grant me Her visions, and that I'll come to him as soon as I've rested for a stripe of the candle."

"He won't like that."

"Indeed he won't. And that's part of why I do it." Niente attempted a smile; he wondered if it showed on his face at all. "One thing the Nahual must teach the Tecuhtli is that we are equals, despite what the Tecuhtli likes to believe. We won't reach Villembouchure for another day and more. There's nothing he can do right now to seal our victory. Therefore, he can wait long enough for me to recover my strength."

Atl grinned at that. He clutched the bowl to his chest. Niente saw Atl's fingers close around it, almost possessively, stroking the incised figures of animals around the rim with familiarity. *He is going to look into the bowl again, too.* The realization came to him as a certainty. "I'll do as you say, Taat," Atl said. "I'll give Tecuhtli Citlali your message."

Niente nodded. Almost, he started to caution Atl not to use the bowl again so quickly, but he did not. *You can't stop him, any more than you could have stopped yourself. Say it, and you only guarantee that he will use it more.*

So he said nothing. The vision of Atl laying dead overlaid his true vision. It was as if a corpse walked from the room, and he found himself weeping again and cursing the gift that Axat had given him.

He could not let his son die. That was not something a Taat who loved his son could do, no matter what the consequences. It didn't matter if saving Atl destroyed the Long Path.

Please don't set that before me, he prayed to Axat. *Please don't force me to make that choice.*

He thought that he heard a distant chuckle in his head as he prayed.

∼

Sergei ca'Rudka

THERE WAS A SMELL TO THE LOWER LEVELS of the Bastida: the stink of human desperation, the stench of pain. The very stones were saturated with the odor. Sergei thought that if the Bastida were torn down, a century later the ruins would still exude that foul reek.

It was a smell that he'd loved, in a strange way, for it was a smell that he'd had no small part in creating over the decades. It had been his hand—many times, *too* many times—that had sent terrified shrieks echoing here, that had caused men and women to lose control of their bladders and bowels, that had spilled blood upon the flags.

His own spirit, he thought, must smell the same. When the soul shredders finally took him, would they recoil from the odor as their claws ripped his immortality from his flesh? Would their nostrils dilate at the sewage he contained?

He wondered about that more and more. But there was nothing he could do to change it. The sickness was as much a part of him as it was a part of these stones, of the Bastida itself.

His body was a Bastida also, a tower that imprisoned his own soul, shrieking unheard in terror in his depths.

His cane made a persistent, steady beat on the stone stairs as he descended. His hips ached, his back pained him with every step until he reached the level footing of the lowest floor of the tower. The air here was dank and cold. It didn't matter whether it was summer or winter above; what lurked here was an eternal, dead autumn. The only light was that of two torches guttering in iron rings on a wall. The two gardai on duty saluted him, but Sergei also saw the knowing glance they gave to the roll of old, soiled leather under Sergei's arm, and the smirk the two exchanged with each other. "Good evening, Ambassador," one of them said. "A pleasure to see you, as always. I thought the Kraljica had sent you back to Brezno."

"I leave tomorrow," he said. "The Morelli?"

"There." The other gardai pointed to the nearest cell. "Should I open the door, Ambassador?"

Sergei nodded again, and the garda took a thick steel circle adorned with keys from his belt, and thrust one of them into the lock. It turned with a metallic protest. The hinges made a similar complaint as he pulled the cell door open.

"Do you need one of us to stay, Ambassador?" the garda asked. "I can stay if you like."

The man's face showed nothing, but Sergei knew what he was thinking. He nodded as the garda placed the keys back on his belt. "Your friend may take his lunch, then,"

he said. The two gardai exchanged glances again before
the other saluted and left them. Sergei stepped over the
threshold of the cell onto a floor strewn with dirty and
soiled straw. A man was huddled in chains at the rear of
the cell: hands bound tightly together, and a silencer af-
fixed around his head so that he couldn't speak—a cage
of metal helmeting his head, with a cloth-wrapped piece
protruding into the man's mouth so that the tongue was
covered and held. Flickering shadows from the torches in
the hall outside clawed at the darkness of the cell. The
man's eyes, dark in the hollows of his face, stared at Sergei with desperate hope, which dimmed as the man saw
the leather roll. He moaned around the metal piece holding his tongue down. Saliva glistened on the black metal
framework.

The stench in the room grew.

"You're a war-téni?" Sergei asked. He laid the roll, still
tied together, at his feet, groaning with the effort of bending over that far—the roll dropped the last few fingers to
the straw, and a muffled clink of metal came from it. "A
war-téni?" Sergei repeated as the man's eyes widened. The
garda chuckled behind Sergei.

The prisoner nodded.

"Ah," Sergei replied. He leaned on his cane, peering at
the man. "And a Morelli sympathizer, also?"

A hesitation. Then another, smaller, nod.

"You are O'Téni Timos ci'Stani?"

A final nod.

"Good," Sergei told him. "We should have no lies between us, Timos. May I use your familiar name? You can
think of me as Sergei, if you like. You see, Timos, lies always
cause pain. Even out there in the world, a lie is eventually a
poison that causes violence. But lies are especially volatile
here in the Bastida. Here in the donjon, there must only be
truth. Do you understand me?"

This time there was only a stare, but Sergei continued.
"Good. Now, I would be willing to remove the tongue gag
from you if you swear to Cénzi that you will not use the
Ilmodo. Do you swear?"

A nod, more desperate this time, accompanied by a
strangled, muted "'ethh" from his mouth.

"Fine. I'll accept that oath, though for safety we'll keep

your hands manacled. Here, let me unlock th
from around your head ..."

As a war-téni, ci'Stani had power that could leave
a blistered, charred husk. Unless the man had learned to
use Numetodo magic, which required only a single word
and a limited gesture to cast, there was no real danger in
removing the silencer. Téni magic took time, and the few
links of chain between the man's manacles would prevent
him from making the necessary gestures to create magic.
Carefully, even gently, Sergei removed the device from the
prisoner, ci'Stani gagging once as the prong holding his
tongue was removed. Sergei felt a thrill pass through his
body as he did so. Perhaps the man had learned enough of
the Numetodo methods to cast a spell ...

The danger was part of the excitement. Part of the thrill.

The man spat dryly, taking in great gulps of the fetid air
and working his jaw. "Thank you, Ambassador ca'Rudka,"
the man said, giving him the sign of Cénzi awkwardly, the
chains holding his hands rattling. "May Cénzi bless you."

"Let us pray that's so, Timos," Sergei answered fervently.
"Commandant cu'Ingres tells me that you were captured
in Oldtown two nights ago, that there were, strangely, many
téni with Morelli sympathies missing from the temples that
night. And, strangely, when Commandant ca'Talin left to
confront the Tehuantin at Villembouchure the morning
after your capture, most of those same war-téni failed to
appear, despite A'Téni ca'Paim's orders."

"I don't know about that, Ambassador," the man told
him.

"Then speak for yourself, Timos," Sergei said. "Why
were you in Oldtown? Would you have been one of those
missing war-téni, Timos, had we not—" He glanced at the
man's chains. "—otherwise detained you?"

"I ..." The man stopped, licked at cracked lips. There
were bruises on his face, Sergei noted, and a white-stumped
gap in his front teeth from a broken tooth. "I was in Oldtown because I have a lover there. I was returning to the
temple after visiting her."

"You weren't at a meeting of the Morellis, then? You
weren't with Nico Morel?"

Ci'Stani shook his head vigorously. "No, Ambassador. I
was not."

Sergei nodded. "I want to believe you, Timos," he said. "I truly do. But you see, my friend, the Commandant captured more than one téni in Oldtown that night, and they have told already him that there was a meeting with Nico Morel that night, and confessed that you were among those in attendance."

That was a lie—there was no other captive. An utilino on patrol had found O'Téni ci'Stani in Oldtown and knew the war-téni should have been asleep in the temple. Ci'Stani had fled when the utilino had tried to detain him, and the utilino had used a spell to subdue him. Ci'Stani had given the utilino the same tale he'd given to Sergei about a lover in Oldtown, but the utilino had been suspicious and summoned the Garde Kralji rather than the temple staff.

Following Sergei's orders, the Garde Kralji hadn't yet notified A'Téni ca'Paim that they'd captured one of her missing war-téni. That could come later, when Sergei knew what the man knew.

Sergei watched the téni closely. Despite the chill, beads of sweat had formed along ci'Stani's hairline. Grimacing at the pain in his knees, Sergei crouched down by the leather roll. He started to untie the strings holding it. "You see my quandary, I'm sure," he told the téni. "Someone is lying. And as I said earlier—lies create pain."

With that, he flicked open the roll of leather, displaying the well-used instruments there in their loops: the pincers, the drills, the tongs, the punches, the keen-edged knives. The téni stared at them. He heard the garda let out a breath. Sergei opened a pocket in the roll, bringing out a thick brass bar with a hole drilled in the middle of it. The end of the bar was slightly flattened and scratched, as if it had seen significant use. He plucked a length of tapered wood from the same pocket, thrusting it into the hole in the middle of bar and tamping it down. He held up the crude hammer, turning it in the dim light coming through the cell doorway.

He told himself that he did it only to frighten the man, and he knew it for the lie it was.

Lies always cause pain.

Ci'Stani stared at the brass hammer. "Please, Ambassador . . . Yes, yes I was with Nico Morel. I confess it freely. I was with him in Oldtown. I could tell you where, but he won't be there now—the Absolute moves constantly, and none of us know where he is now." Ci'Stani licked his lips again, the words tumbling out almost too fast for him to keep up with them. "I would take you to him if I could, but I can't, Ambassador, and that's Cénzi's truth. I swear it. He spends a night here, a night there. One never knows. There will be a notice of where to meet, but he gives us only a bare few turns of the glass notice . . ."

Sergei hefted the bar, then slammed the end of the brass onto the floor. The impact jolted his muscles through to the shoulder, but he showed nothing of that to ci'Stani. Even through the muffling straw, the sound was terrible. "Oh, please, Ambassador. I've told you the truth," ci'Stani said, his voice breaking with a sob.

Sergei nodded. "I'm certain you have, Timos," he said softly, almost as if he were crooning to a lover. "Though you haven't said *why* Nico Morel wanted you there, or what he said to you."

The man visibly blanched, the color leeching from his skin. "Please, Ambassador. I swore an oath to Cénzi that I wouldn't reveal that, that I wouldn't betray the Absolute or the Morellis . . ."

"You swore also that you would obey the Archigos and a'téni, and you've already—by your own admission—violated that oath. I have A'Téni ca'Paim's permission to do whatever I find necessary to gain the truth from you." That was also a lie. The man would be returned to ca'Paim after his interrogation was complete. Sergei was certain that ca'Paim would not be pleased with his condition, nor with what he had to say. "So—which of your oaths do you wish to keep, Timos? Choose carefully."

The man's head dropped down, as if he been struck. His eyes were closed, his mouth moving. Sergei thought he might be praying.

"Tell me, Timos," Sergei said. Softly. Almost a whisper. A plea. "Tell me."

The head came up. Ci'Stani's eyes were wet and de-feated. "All right," he said. He began to speak then, and what he said startled Sergei so much that he did nothing but listen. When the man had finished, Sergei could only shake his head in mingled anger and sorrow. He would need to speak to the Kraljica again, and to A'Teni ca'Paim as well. Very soon.

But now now. He could feel the old urge taking him again, his breath coming faster as he thought of it, as he tried to fight it. *Now. You have everything you need. You know he's told you the truth. So let this be the time that you turn and leave. This is the moment you can change.*

But he could not. His legs trembled as he remained crouched in the straw before ci'Stani, but they would not move. They forced him to remain there.

"Tell me, Timos," he said to the man. "You have the skill of letters?"

Ci'Stani looked at him, confused. "Ambassador?"

"You can write? You would sign a confession if I gave it to you?"

A slow nod.

"Good. And with which hand do you write?"

"Why, the right . . ." ci'Stani began, then stopped. He glanced again at the hammer in Sergei's hand. "Ambassador, I told you what you wished to know. I told you everything. Everything. I swear it."

"I know you did, and for Nessantico's sake, I thank you." He lifted the hammer. "I require your left hand, Timos. I'm sorry. I truly am." Sergei wondered if ci'Stani could hear the sincerity in his voice, or if he believed it. He nodded to the garda, who stepped forward and grasped ci'Stani's left wrist, placing the hand flat against the stone floor. Ci'Stani struggled, his right hand rattling as he tried to pull away. The garda put his knee on the man's right arm.

"Ambassador. You can't do this. No!"

"I can't?" Sergei asked. His voice became more stern, more eager—and the eagerness disgusted him. *You can stop this,* a still part of him declared. *You already have what you need. Stop now, as you say you want to. As you should.* But desire shouted louder.

"Oh, I *can*," he told Timos. "I assure you of that. I also assure you that you'll regret your lack of cooperation, and you will like even less the parts of you I choose to torment if you don't. Now—Timos, is there anything else you need to tell me?"

Ci'Stani stared, straw bunching around his hand as he tried again to pull it away from the garda, the chains that held his hands together clinking against stone like dull, mournful bells. The garda struck him in the face with an

elbow; Sergei heard the nose break and saw blood spray.
"You heard the Ambassador," the garda said. "Keep still,
or this will go worse for you."

The prisoner moaned. His left hand flattened against the
stones. Sergei found the screams that followed delightful,
and he hated the delight he felt.

MANEUVERS

Niente
Sergei ca'Rudka
Nico Morel
Brie ca'Ostheim
Allesandra ca'Vörl
Rochelle Botelli
Niente
Sergei ca'Rudka
Varina ca'Pallo
Jan ca'Ostheim

Niente

*T*HERE WERE SNARES IN THE WATER, *cables with steel claws that tore at the wooden hulls of the ships, sending cold river water into the holds. The lead ships of the fleet canted over, unbalanced, their masts dipping toward the A'Sele's surface and sending men screaming into the water . . .*

"I have seen certain victory, Tecuhtli," Niente told Citlali. The Highest Warrior reclined in a nest of cushions in his cabin. The red eagle of the Tecuhtli on his bald skull seemed to flex its wings as he reached for a goblet of the strong beer on the table before him. His chest was uncovered, and Niente could see that Citlali's body showed his age: the chest sagging like a woman's breasts; the muscles of his arm still thick but not as sharply defined as those of other warriors; his belly rounding into a comfortable paunch. The High Warrior Tototl, Citlali's second-in-command, sat to Citlali's right, his face impassive.

Tototl's body was hard and lean. Niente thought that if Tototl challenged Citlali for the title of Tecuhtli, his wager would not be for Citlali, despite the man's long years of experience. The decline of age struck the warrior caste far harder than it did the nahualli. For the nahualli, experience and age was more often an indication of power and skill.

Niente sat on his own cushions across the low table from Tecuhtli Citlali, his own drink untouched before him. Atl stood behind him, as silent as High Warrior Tototl.

"Certain victory," Citlali echoed, as if tasting the words. Niente nodded. "I saw our banner flowing over the city.

I saw their defenders fleeing in droves into the land beyond the city walls. I saw the bodies of the defenders on the broken walls. But . . ." Niente paused. He leaned forward on the table, hoping it would ease the pain of his bowed back and painful joints. "This victory won't be like Karnmor or Fossano, Tecuhtli, where we overwhelmed them with numbers and surprise. This victory doesn't come without cost. The Easterners know that we're here, and the Kraljica has sent troops here to bolster the garrison of the city. I have seen that they have learned the secret of black sand as well, which our spies have also told us. They will use black sand against us. I see victory, yes, but this one will not be an easy one."

Niente heard Atl stir restlessly behind him. He didn't dare look back, and he prayed that the boy would remember his place and stay silent. Tecuhtli Citlali frowned slightly at Niente's admonition. "Were there other paths in your vision, Nahual Niente?" Citlali asked. "A better way for us than this one? Some of the warriors are grumbling that it's time we leave the ships to the sailors and take to the land, where we can forage for fresh food and meet these Easterners sword to sword, if they dare."

Niente heard Atl's intake of breath even as he shook his head. "There were other paths, yes," he told the Tecuhtli. "But I tell you that they all led to worse outcomes than this. In one, our ships were scattered and destroyed entirely and we couldn't return home. I saw the path where the warriors took too early to the land, and it was not good—the army of the Easterners awaited us there, and though there was victory for us, it was so costly in the end that it might as well have been defeat."

Atl's breath exhaled loudly behind Niente, as if he were about to speak, and Citlali's gaze drifted up to Niente's son briefly, as did that of Tototl. But Atl remained silent. Niente hurried to continue.

"Keep to the strategy we have discussed, Tecuhtli, and I promise you the best result. And now," he said, getting to his feet with difficulty, noting that Atl did not offer to help him, "I should see that the nahualli are all prepared and that the black sand is mixed as it should be, so that we're ready tomorrow when we reach Villembouchure. We have taken the city once before, under Tecuhtli Zolin. It will be ours again, I promise you. From there, yes, the warriors can remain on land and march on to Nessantico and the prize you seek."

Citlali beamed. He drank the rest of his beer and slammed the goblet down on the table. "Excellent!" he shouted drunkenly. "Go, then, and do as you need, and I will tell the warriors that we will leave the ships tomorrow."

They will be doing exactly that. They will have no choice.

Niente bowed his way out of the cabin. He didn't look at Atl as he moved down the short corridor and up the stairs to the ship's deck. He blinked in the sunlight, taking in great draughts of the cool, sweet air which no longer tasted or smelled of the ash or of sea salt, only of the land and the river. On either side of them, the land of the Holdings spread out, blurred in his poor, crippled vision—green, lush hills (though still largely grayed with ash); the occasional small villages, most of them abandoned with the news of the oncoming invaders; the sparkling mouths of smaller streams and rivers spilling water into the great river. This was a beautiful land, nearly as beautiful as his own.

The ships of the fleet filled the A'Sele, a long line three or four ships wide that vanished around the sweeping curves of the river. The wind was in their favor, blowing strongly eastward, and the sails billowed and snapped above them, the sailors adjusting the lines as the deck officers called out orders. Under their prows, white water curled and spread out. The *Yaoyotl* was near the front of the fleet, though there were ships out ahead of her. Niente looked at the high aftdecks and imagined them as he'd seen them in the vision.

"Taat!" Niente felt his son's hand on his shoulder. He turned, knowing what he had to say and hating it. "Why did you tell the Tecuhtli not to land the troops now? I saw that path in the scrying bowl. You must have seen it, too. That was the best choice of all. I saw an easy victory afterward."

Niente forced himself to look into his son's eyes. "Then you misread the vision," he said, but Atl was already shaking his head in denial.

"No, Taat, it was very clear to me. There was no army waiting for us along the road, as you told Tecuhtli. They expect us to attack from the river, and that's where they've put their strength. I saw them surprised and in disarray. I saw another quick victory for us. I saw us moving toward their great city with all our strength intact."

"You saw incorrectly," Niente persisted, "or you misunderstood what it was you saw."

Atl was shaking his head. "It was *clear,* Taat. The mists cleared and I *saw* the path, as if I were there. Perhaps . . ." He bit his lower lip quickly, though Niente knew what he wanted to say. *Perhaps* you *were the one who was mistaken.*

Niente knew that Atl had seen correctly. Niente's own vision had the same clarity as Atl's, and had been no different. But he could not admit that now. For the Long Path to be gained, the Tehuantin forces had to be pared down here or they would overwhelm both Nessantico and the Long Path—if it still existed. *Axat, please show me that I'm not wrong in this. Let me see it again, as clearly as I once did. And please, show me that Atl can be spared, as he once was . . .* Niente would still seek to follow the Long Path, but he wasn't sure if he could sacrifice his son for it. If Axat required that . . .

"Perhaps?" Niente repeated, making the word a mocking retort. "Do you wish to accuse the Nahual of being unable to read Axat's visions? Do you believe that you can see what I cannot? Is that what you're saying, Atl? Do you want to go back to Tecuhtli Citlali and tell him that you, after a bare few days learning the scrying skill, are now my superior, that the decades I have spent poring over the waters are nothing compared to the great power of Atl? Do you wish to tell him to abandon my counsel and take yours? Are you so proud and arrogant?" The words lashed the young man like the snap of a whip. Atl's eyes narrowed, his lips pressed together in a tight line.

"No," Atl said at last, though the word was grudging, a mere grunt. "But you should look into the bowl again, Taat. Tonight, before we reach this city."

"Why?" Niente snapped. "Do you think I'll see *your* vision and not my own?"

A shrug.

"I will look," Niente told him, "but I know what I will see. I've already been shown. Go—fetch me the bowl and the powder. I will do this now."

Atl nodded and hurried off. *I know what I will see.* He would see what Atl had seen, and he would lie again.

Sergei ca'Rudka

A GRAY MOOD HAD CLOAKED SERGEI at the Bastida, as he rolled up his leather packet of torture devices and left behind the bleeding, moaning wreck of the war-téni ci'Stani. It had wrapped around him tighter that evening, as he prepared for his departure to Brezno. It had pressed down upon him as he'd slept, and his night had been filled with nightmares and horrific visions. In the red visions, it had been his body laying chained in the Bastida, and the cell door had opened, and it was himself who stood before him, who knelt there and crooned a false sympathy and who advanced on him with the instruments of pain. He had screamed himself awake three times, his bedclothes drenched with sweat and wound tightly around him, his heart slamming against the cage of his chest and his lungs heaving. During the last dream, his thrashing had torn the nose from his face; he'd found it lying in the bedding, gleaming in the dim grayness of false dawn.

He'd not been able to go back to sleep. The mood, the sense of despair, had stayed with him. He wasn't even certain why he went to see Varina again, this time at her house. There was no reason to do so; he'd said what he'd needed to say to her already. But he found that he could not walk into the temple and pray to Cénzi; that somehow seemed wrong. And he had no desire to confess to any of the téni what he had done: the day before, or for years and years now.

It was enough that he knew. It was enough that others suspected.

The mood darkened. It surrounded him. He imagined as he walked that he was pooled in an eternal night, even as the sun glared down on him.

"I talked to Talbot," Sergei told Varina, pretending nonchalance as he sat in the chair across from her in the sunroom of her house. "He told me that you've refused to leave the city, despite his agreeing with my advice." He *tsked* as he gazed at Varina, shaking his head. "A'Morce, I am disappointed in you."

She laughed. "Don't you go lying to me, Sergei. I've known you for far too long now. You never expected me to leave; you just wanted it off your conscience that you'd given me fair warning so you could say 'I told her so.' Well, you've done that. Your conscience can rest easily."

His conscience . . . The words speared him, as if a knife twisted in his gut.

But he ignored the burning. Sergei spread his hands as if he'd been caught stealing a roll from the kitchen. "Obviously, I am entirely transparent to you, Varina. But that doesn't mean my advice wasn't sound. And it's not too late. I'm leaving in just a few turns of the glass myself, and we expect that the Tehuantin may attack Villembouchure at any moment. If Commandant ca'Talin can't stop their advance there—and I don't believe that he has the troops or the support to do so, especially since A'Téni ca'Paim had difficulty finding war-téni willing to join him—then the Westlanders will be advancing on Nessantico within the week."

Varina sighed at that. "I know. I've already given my house staff leave and told them to make arrangements to stay with friends or family far to the north or south." She gestured at the table in front of them on which a pot of tea steeped, surrounded by a small pile of stale cookies. "That's why my hospitality is so poor, I'm afraid. I scrounged what I could from the kitchen. I'm moving into the Numetodo House for the duration this evening."

Sergei's head shook again. He rubbed at his nose, making certain that the glue he'd applied this morning was still holding the metal form tightly to his face. "We're old, Varina, and we've gone through enough trials in our lives. This shouldn't be our battle any longer."

"Says the man leaving for Brezno in a few turns."

The darkness deepened around him. He could not laugh. "I'm required to go—it's my duty to the Kraljica," he said. "You don't *have* to stay."

Varina leaned forward, pouring herself more tea. She blew over the hot liquid, her lips pursed so that all the fine lines of her face gathered there. *Old* . . . "There's something else troubling you, Sergei," she said, sitting back in her chair again and taking a sip. "We've already discussed my leaving and we both know the answer. So what is it you really want to say?"

He wondered if he'd been hoping she would notice, that she would ask. And he wondered if he dared answer. "All right. I have a question for you: I want to know what you hold onto. If you don't believe in Cénzi or any other god, if you don't believe there's some higher purpose to things, what *do* you look to for solace and guidance?"

"That's a conversation that would take far longer than a few turns of the glass, Sergei," she answered. "And it's a strange question for you to ask—or is it that you're doubting your own faith?"

"I don't know," he told her honestly. "I'm . . . I'm not what the Faith would call a good man, Varina. I have done things . . ."

She shook her head and set down her cup. Leaning forward, her hand grazed his and fell away again. "Sergei, none of us are perfect. None. We've all done things of which we're ashamed. I have seen you do things that are heroic and brave, also. That should offset a few character flaws."

He laughed, bitter and dark. "You don't know," he told her. "You don't know what I—" He stopped, taking a deep breath. "I'm sorry," he said finally. "I should be going . . ."

"Sergei," Varina said, and he halted in the midst of reaching for the cane leaning against his chair. "The Numetodo don't have a single creed or set of beliefs. There are some of us who still believe in gods—even Cénzi, if not the Cénzi of the Faith, but a more absent and uncaring deity. There are others who think there may be some 'guidance' to this world, some intelligence that is part of the Second World itself, which gives power to the Ilmodo or Scáth Cumhacht or whatever you want to call that energy. But . . . both Karl and I believed that there were other, and better, explanations for why things are as they are—a truth that the Faith couldn't offer. Both of us believed that death is final, that there was nothing beyond that—I've never seen any compelling proof for me to think otherwise, even when—since Karl died—I might have reason to hope for that. I believe in no gods, no afterlife. But . . . I understand the solace that someone can find in believing there *is* something greater

than us, something that tries to direct us. My parents believed; I was brought up to believe."

"What changed that for you?"

Varina shrugged. "None of the mythology made sense to
me—or, rather, I kept stumbling over the contradictions in
the texts. But I continued going to temple for years, more
from habit than anything else. Then I heard Karl speak,
and I started talking to Mika ci'Gillan, who was A'Morce
Numetodo here at that point, and what they were saying
fit together for me. It made sense. All those tales from the
Toustour were just attempts to explain the way the world
was, but here were people saying 'No, there's another explanation that doesn't require divine intervention, only
nature itself, and that somehow felt *right* to me. I found
they were right about the Ilmodo, for instance: The Faith
insisted that it was only through Cénzi that one could perform magic, yet I could do that—me, who had no training at
all from the téni and who no longer believed in Cénzi . . ."

She paused, and he sat there. He'd heard her words, he
could even recall them if he tried, but they didn't penetrate.
They rolled from his body like water. "Sergei," she continued after a moment, "how can I help you, my friend?"

"You can't," he told her. "It's something only I can do
for myself."

"I don't believe that."

He smiled toward her and lifted himself from the chair,
pushing hard on the cane's head. "I glad you don't. It's
good to know that someone cares."

"You were always a great friend to both Karl and me,
Sergei. That's something I will never forget. I will always be
there if you need me."

It was difficult to maintain the smile, knowing that had
he ever needed to betray her or Karl's friendship to save
himself, he would have done so without hesitation. But he
managed it. "I will never forget either," he told her. "And I
will come to you first, if I need help."

"Good," she said, rising with him. She embraced him,
and he closed his eyes, trying to feel her affection and her
trust. But there was nothing. Everything was empty and
cold. There was no heat, even in the glare of the sun. "Stay
safe," she told him. "You are one of the few true friends I

have left. I can't afford to lose you. I'll worry about you the entire time you're gone."

"And I will worry for you," he told her, "because you're here."

Bowing his head to her, he shuffled from the sunroom.

He wanted her to call after him: to stop him from leaving, to force him to confess it all, to spill out the poison inside him so that perhaps, having to confront it, he could come to understand it.

But she did not.

Nico Morel

THE CROWD BEGAN TO GATHER well before First Call, as if the day were one of the High Days where attendance at temple was required of all the Faithful. In the cold hours before dawn, they came to the plaza outside the Old Temple on the Isle a'Kralji: a few hands of people at first, milling near the temple entrance, then small groups of others. They were young and old, many of them—from the tattered and worn appearance of their dress and the state of their hair and teeth—the ce'-and-ci' or even the unranked dregs of Oldtown, though there were a few better-dressed folk scattered among them, and the occasional green flash of téni-robes.

They gathered as the eastern sky began to turn pale mist-gray and then a tentative orange. By the time the sky beyond the black silhouette of cu'Brunelli's famous dome had gone to golden hues and the téni responsible for sounding the wind-horns had clambered up the long stairs to their station, gaping in surprise at the crowded, shadowed plaza far below, the crowd had grown to a few hundred.

That was when Nico arrived, huddled in the midst of his close Morelli companions. Liana held to him as if she were afraid she might lose him in the crush, her arm around his waist—she had insisted on coming, even though Nico had urged her to remain behind. He knew that by now someone must have alerted A'Téni ca'Paim about the odd gathering outside the temple, but none of the higher téni appeared to be watching from the doors or windows of the Old Temple. In fact, except for the gathering of the Morellis and their sympathizers, everything seemed strangely, almost eerily quiet. Those of the Faith who were coming into the plaza for the regular First Call service stopped, puzzled at the gathering and uncertain whether they should continue forward or not.

Nico grinned. Cénzi had told him it would be like this. He had prayed; he had spent turn after turn of the glass on his knees asking for insight before he had met with those of the Faith who believed in him, and finally the vision had come: Cénzi had told Nico that they would be betrayed, that a confession would be wrung from one of them too weak to resist, that the Garde Kralji and A'Téni ca'Paim would know what had been planned.

And that knowledge was enough. It was enough.

Liana pressed close to Nico, and now Ancel also approached him. "We're ready?" Nico asked, and Ancel nodded, tight-lipped. He could feel their trepidation as they walked out into the square: twenty or so of his disciples—those closest to Nico, those who had been with him since the early days in Brezno when the Faith had first embraced, then rejected him. Around them, a buzz of excitement was growing as people recognized him. Nico could hear the whispers: "Look, it's the Absolute . . . It's him . . ." Then the chant began to rise: *"Nico! Nico! Nico!"* It was a pulse, a beat, a rhythm. Even the wind-horns, beginning their mournful announcement of First Call could not drown out that call. *"Nico! Nico! Nico!"* It pounded against the walls of the Old Temple and rebounded from the gilded dome, spearing into the dawn sky.

As if summoned by the call, the Garde Kralji appeared, emerging from the temple and from the buildings attached to it, squads appearing at the street entrances, surrounding the crowds: the gardai in their uniforms, their pikes ready; the utilino, with their cudgels and—undoubtedly—spells prepared to control the crowd. Those of the Faithful who had come for the service realized that something violent was about to happen—most of them scrambled through the lines of the gardai and away. Commandant cu'Ingres and A'Téni ca'Paim appeared at the balcony above the main doors of the temple: at cu'Ingres' gesture, an aide sounded a trumpet, shrill and high above the continuing drone of the wind-horns, while two gardai on the balcony waved signal flags.

The Garde Kralji began to advance, closing the circle around the Morellis. Nico nodded to one of the téni with them: the woman gestured and chanted, and light burst high over the plaza, sending long shadows scurrying over the stone flags and over the people there. The gardai and utilino paused. Even the wind-horns' moaning sagged and failed.

From around the plaza, outside the ring of the Garde Kralji, several people now emerged from the street entrances or the buildings, most of them green-robed: téni of the Faith, yes, but téni who knew Nico for what he was: Cénzi's prophet, Cénzi's Absolute. Many of them were war-téni, the war-téni who had vanished at the time of A'Teni ca'Paim's call to join Commandant ca'Talin and the Garde Civile to defend Villembouchure. Nico could see—above the columned entrance to the temple—A'Téni ca'Paim pointing and gesturing to Commandant cu'Ingres as she realized what was happening. Cu'Ingres turned desperately to his aides, and the trumpet sounded a new, frenzied call as the signal flags waved frantically.

They were too late. The war-téni of the Morellis had already begun their chants, and now they gestured. Fire and smoke bloomed in the dawn light, arcing up and then falling into the ranks of the gardai, exploding as if the wrath of Cénzi Himself was falling on the wretched Moitidi who had disobeyed Him. There were screams and shouts from everywhere around the plaza as gelatinous flame fell among the gardai, clinging to their clothes and skin as it burned: téni-fire of the worst kind. The Garde Kralji normally dealt with crowd control and small groups; unlike the Garde Civile, they were unused to large-scale organized battles, and now their ranks fell apart entirely as they scrambled for safety away from the flames. "Now!" Nico shouted, and again the téni sent a spear of white light to explode above the plaza. "To the temple!" Nico shouted, and his voice was louder than the screams, louder than the trumpet, louder than than the wind-horns. His voice echoed like booming thunder from the buildings around the plaza. "We will take back what belongs to the true Faithful!"

His disciples surged forward toward the main gates, and the others who had come at his summons moved with them. The gardai at the temple entrance lowered their pikes, but the attackers were too many: the crowd slipped past them or struck down their weapons. The gates were wrenched open with a metallic shriek. Inside, Nico could glimpse the gilded-and-frescoed walls; the ornately-carved columns bearing the immense weight of the arched, distant roof; the rows and rows of burnished pews; the brazier burning with the scent of strong incense; the massive, impossible dome, painted with the images of Cénzi struggling with the Moitidi, the quire and High Lectern far underneath, seemingly tiny against the massive space. Nico breathed it in—this holy space, this reverent palais built to honor Cénzi which not even the heathen fire of the Westlanders could entirely destroy.

This place was sacred. This place was history incarnate, and here he would begin to make his own history.

His disciples had moved aside, none of them entering yet. The crowd stood at his back. Out in the plaza, the soldiers writhed in pain or lay dead or had fled.

Nico took a step. Another. He crossed the threshold of the place he had been forbidden to enter again as téni, and as he did so, he let his cloak slide from his shoulders to the ground, revealing the green robes of a téni underneath.

He would take back his title and his rights. He would be téni again, as Cénzi had told him to be.

The interior of the temple seemed brighter than the dawn outside, the flames of the braziers around the sides of the space sending heat and light shimmering up the fluted walls and gleaming in the polished marble of the floor. He stood ensconced in gold and warm browns, breathing an air spiced and fragrant and achingly familiar. He lifted his head looking up to the dome far above at the end of the long aisle.

There were people moving there, scurrying under the beauty of the fresco like mice: a group of téni, with the green-trimmed golden robes of A'Téni ca'Paim just behind them, Commandant cu'Ingres at her side and gardai spreading out along the walls to either side. Nico could hear someone behind him—Liana, he thought—beginning a chant, and he held up a hand.

"Hold!" he said. "There is no danger here for the Faithful. There's no danger here for me." With the temple's fine, legendary acoustics, he could hear his words whispering to the farthest corners.

"How *dare* you!" The words sliced harsh and bitter through the temple. A'Téni ca'Paim stepped forward on the raised steps of the quire, standing next to the prow of the High Lectern as if she were about to ascend and give a stern Admonition to the assembled Morellis. "How dare you step into the temple wearing the robes that were taken from you by the Archigos himself? How dare you come into this holy place after you've just murdered dozens outside? You are *damned* in the sight of Cénzi, Nico Morel, and I will have your tongue and your hands for this outrage!"

"My tongue and hands?" Nico responded. His voice sounded deep and rich after the shrill, breathless outcry of the older woman. "My tongue speaks the words of Cénzi Himself, A'Téni, and my hands hold His affection. They are not yours to have. They will never be yours." He advanced down the aisle toward her, still talking. He could see the gardai along the walls, armed with bows, and he saw them fit arrows to their strings. He smiled. "I have listened to Him," Nico said, "and He has told me that the time has come for me to reclaim my place, and that if you, A'Téni, or Archigos Karrol himself, will not see the truth of what I say, then He will cause you to curse your blindness and wail as the soul shredders tear your imperfect souls from your bodies."

"You *threaten* me?" ca'Paim sputtered. "Here in my own temple, in front of Commandant cu'Ingres and my staff? You're a fool as well as a heretic."

"I don't threaten," Nico told her, still walking forward. He could hear the creaking of leather bowstrings under tension. His voice was calm. His voice was kind. His voice held a full measure of sympathy and understanding. "I give you a last chance, A'Téni, a chance to see the error of your thinking, to go to your knees and give the sign of Cénzi and ask Him for forgiveness."

Nico thought for a moment that she had heard Cénzi in his voice, that she—finally, belatedly—understood. A'Téni ca'Paim said nothing. She stood there, her mouth open, and Nico saw her body trembling as if she were possessed of a fever. Her face lifted for a moment to cu'Brunelli's dome above her, to the images painted there. Under the heavy, gold-threaded robes, her legs seemed to give way, to bend, and Nico thought that she *would* go to her knees there.

But the trembling ceased, and she stood straight again. "No," she said aloud. "I will not."

Nico sighed sadly. "I'm genuinely sorry for that," he said. He lifted his hands. He began to chant.

"No!" ca'Paim, and this time it was a shout. "You are *forbidden* to use the Ilmodo. Stop him!" she said to cu'Ingres, and the Commandant gestured. Bowstrings sang their deathsong, and Nico heard Liana cry out in fear.

But it was already too late. Nico gestured, full of Cénzi's power, and the arrows went to fire and ash before they could touch him. A wave—visible in the air—rippled outward from him in a great arc to the front and sides, and what it touched, it destroyed. Pews lifted and were hurled as if by a hurricane wind, slamming against walls and gardai alike. The plaster on the walls cracked, the fire in the braziers guttered and nearly failed.

And on the quire, the téni attendants, A'Téni ca'Paim, and Commandant cu'Ingres were also tossed and thrown. Nico saw ca'Paim's body hit first the railing at the back of the quire, breaking it into splinters, then a sickening, dull *clunk* as her head collided with one of the columns. Her body slumped to the floor; blood smeared all the way down the column.

The spell passed, vanishing as if it had never been there, and Nico shivered for a moment in the cold and normal exhaustion of spell-casting. The interior of the temple was silent except for the moaning of injured gardai and téni. Cu'Ingres was trying to regain his feet, though from the way he cradled his left arm, it must have been broken. Ca'Paim did not move at all, and Nico knew then that she never would, nor would several of the gardai and téni. His eyesight wavered with tears: such a tragic, but necessary, waste . . . "May the soul shredders be kind to you,"

he whispered toward ca'Paim's body. "I forgive you your
blindness."

Liana came up to stand alongside him, her arms supporting him as the weariness of using the Ilmodo this strongly
trembled his legs, and he could hear the others entering as
well. Nico looked at Ancel and pointed to the Commandant. "Take him," he said, "and bind his wounds. Have the
healers among us look at him and the others." He spat directions to the others. "Liana, make certain that the main
doors are barricaded and barred. Tell our people to use
whatever they can. You, and you—clear the plaza of our
Faithful and get the the war-téni inside. You three—secure
the rest of the doors into the temple once everyone's inside.
Everyone else, let's clean up this place and make it a fit
House for Cénzi again . . ."

He watched as his followers began to move. Then Nico
sank to his knees and clasped his hands to his forehead in
the sign of Cénzi, and he prayed.

The first step back had been taken. Now would come the
rest of the journey.

~

Brie ca'Ostheim

"RHIANNA, I WANTED TO TALK WITH YOU . . ."
Rhianna put the quartet of tashtas she was carrying on the bed, smoothing the fabric of wrinkles—she and
the domestiques de chambre had been tasked by Paulus
with packing Brie's clothing and essentials for the trip to
the army's encampment, and several trunks were scattered
about the room, half-filled. The two other servants—older
women who kept the Hïrzgin's bedchamber and attended
to her needs there—continued to work after curtsying once
to Brie. They pretended to ignore her presence with the
long practice of servants at being invisible when required.

"What did you want, Hïrzgin?" the young woman asked,
brushing her hands on her apron and tucking a strand of
her black hair behind an ear. She *seemed* guileless enough,

but Brie had been watching Jan and Rhianna whenever
the two were in the same room with her, and there was
no doubt in her mind that Rhianna was certainly someone
that her husband would bed if the opportunity presented
itself. But she was relatively convinced it hadn't happened
yet. There was a skittishness to Rhianna whenever Jan was
around, and she always kept herself a careful arm's length
from him. She didn't act like someone who was already on
intimate terms with him. Still, it was familiar, this dance;
Brie had seen it too many times before: sometimes with
servants, sometimes with one of the court ladies. Yet this
time it was different, too. Rhianna didn't seem as eager as
the others to be caught, and that both pleased and worried Brie. She wondered what it was that Rhianna would
want from Jan in return for the pleasures of her body, if she
prized the gift so highly.

"I've been considering whether I should have you remain with the children here at Stag Fall," Brie told her. She
watched Rhianna's face carefully. Yes, there was the hint of
a frown, even though she tried to disguise it by wiping her
brow with a sleeve.

"Paulus said that I would be going with the staff to the
encampment," she answered, and Brie smiled at her.

"Yes," she said. "I know. But you're so good with the
children, Rhianna. Elissa especially likes you, and the
nursemaids will have their hands full."

Rhianna's face was impassive. Carved from stone. The
domestiques de chambre kept their heads down, intent on
their own tasks: invisible. Brie knew that they had heard
this conversation played out in one form or another before
as well. "Whatever the Hïrzgin wishes, of course," Rhianna
said, but the response was slow in coming and toneless.

"Unless, of course," Brie continued, "the Hïrzg would
rather you were with us."

Rhianna's head came up, her eyes widened, and Brie felt
the sickness tighten in her stomach. *Such a strange look:
fear and anticipation all at once, as if she doesn't know what
she wants* . . . Brie kept the well-practiced smile on her face.

With Mavel cu'Kella, with the servants Maria and
Greta, with the other women she'd known about, the decision would have been easy. Had Rhianna been like one
of them, Brie would have her remain here, then dismiss

her on her return. When lovers became too close to Jan, too bound up with him, they became a danger to Brie as well. With Rhianna, it wasn't clear yet what was going to happen. *Perhaps that's better. If I sent her away, then Jan would just find someone else: someone I might not know about for too long. At least with Rhianna, I know who to watch, and I can always end it. She's just one of the unranked, after all . . .*

Brie nodded, as if to herself. "I'll talk with the Hïrzg," she told Rhianna. "I'll ask him what he thinks."

The girl nodded. "I'll . . ." She cut off whatever it was she might have said. "I should finish the packing in the meantime," she said.

"Yes," Brie told her. "I'll leave you to that."

She wouldn't talk to Jan. She would allow the girl to come along as Paulus had wished. And she would watch.

She would watch very carefully.

~

Allesandra ca'Vörl

A'OFFIZIER PIERRE CI'SANTIAGO was obviously uncomfortable with the news he brought to Allesandra. Under curls of raven-black hair matted and unruly from the pressure of his uniform cap, now twisting in his hands, ci'Santiago's gaze kept sliding away from Allesandra's face like feet on slick ice. A glance toward the windows, then off to the painting of Kraljica Marguerite in its place over the mantel. Ci'Santiago seemed to shudder momentarily at the sight of Marguerite, perhaps remembering the madness of Kraljiki Audric years ago. "The Commandant has been captured by the Morellis." Back to her, his eyes widening, then away again. "We're not certain of his condition, but the body of A'Téni ca'Paim as well as those of several other téni and gardai were delivered to us." Back, and this time moving down to his own feet. "The war-téni who had failed to ride with the Garde Civile force you sent to Villembouchure were there. All of them, when it was thought that they had fled the city rather than serve. Neither Commandant cu'Ingres nor A'Téni ca'Paim could have foreseen that."

"No? Is that what you think, A'Offizier?" Allesandra asked. Her stomach burned as if she had swallowed a hot coal. "Isn't anticipating the movements of the enemies of the state the Commandant's job? Isn't anticipating the movements of the enemies of the Faith the task of A'Téni ca'Paim?"

Ci'Santiago swallowed hard. "Well, yes, I suppose it is, my Kraljica, but . . ."

He stopped, as if uncertain what to say next, and she waved aside whatever objection he was concocting. She wished that Sergei were here—the man might be twisted and dangerous, but there wasn't a better tactician in either of the Gardes. And if not Sergei, then Commandant ca'Talin, who was directing the action at Villembouchure. The attack on the Old Temple begged for leadership of the Garde Civile, leadership she suspected she wasn't going to see from ci'Santiago.

"So A'Téni ca'Paim, my good friend and the leader of the Faith here, is dead," she said before ci'Santiago could comment again. "And Nico Morel and his riffraff hold the Old Temple. What do you intend to do about that, A'Offizier, now that it would seem that you are in charge of the Garde Kralji?"

Ci'Santiago shook his head. "Kraljica, retaking the Old Temple would be costly in lives and perhaps in damage to the structure itself. With the war-téni and other téni Nico Morel has at his disposal, a frontal attack is nearly impossible. I have people contacting the architect cu'Brunelli for his architectural drawings of the temple, so that we can perhaps plan an attack from an unexpected quarter, but it may well be that the téni Morel has with him know the hidden ways of the Old Temple—especially the ancient sections of it—as well or better than cu'Brunelli, who after all was concerned mostly with the dome and the main temple area. We're also looking for old maps or texts in the Grande Libreria as well. I've surrounded the Old Temple and the attached complex with my people. The Morellis have trapped themselves. They can't escape and we will also keep out his people and food supplies, though the kitchens of the Old Temple complex were undoubtedly full."

"So you're telling me that he's won, that the best we can do is lay siege to the Old Temple and hope to starve out the Morellis. One day maybe months from now. You're telling me that, a quarter turn's walk from the palais, we no longer control one of the most important buildings in the city?"

Ci'Santiago heard the heavy sarcasm in her voice. His gaze flittered away again. "To some degree, that's an accurate assessment, Kraljica," he said. "Unless you can commit some of the chevarittai and the Garde Civile to this, the Garde Kralji doesn't have the resources to deal with this large and this powerful an insurrection." He finally looked at her face again, and this time his gaze was hard and unblinking. "I'm simply being honest, Kraljica. I wish it were otherwise."

She sighed. "I know. What does Morel want? Have we received demands from him yet?"

"His demands were pinned to A'Téni ca'Paim's robes," he answered, almost apologetically. He reached into a side pocket of his uniform jacket and handed a folded piece of parchment to Allesandra. She unfolded the stiff paper; the writing there was clear and bold, in a fine, small hand.

To Archigos Karrol, Kraljica Allesandra, and Hïrzg Jan— Cénzi will wait no longer for the Faith to come to its senses and return to His teachings. He has demanded that I be His Voice and His Hand, and I am but His humble and obedient servant. Up until this moment, I had obeyed the unfair and misguided restrictions that the Archigos and the Faith placed upon me. I had not used the Ilmodo, I had not worn the robes I had earned, I had not represented myself as a téni or even as a member of the Concénzia Faith. But Cénzi has ordered me to throw off the chains you would place around me and serve Him as He wishes.

I have obeyed.

Know that A'Téni ca'Paim's death was her own fault for having attempted to defy Cénzi's will; neither I nor any of my people intended her death. It was Cénzi who called her back to His arms. Commandant cu'Ingres has been injured, but my people are caring for him and we will do no further harm to him, nor to any of the other prisoners in our charge. If some of these captives die of the injuries they've already sustained, we will return the bodies so that their families can grieve and bury them; those who are healthy and those we are still caring for will, unfortunately, need to remain here for the time being, as I'm sure you can understand.

All of you must be curious as to what I hope to gain by this. I personally hope to gain nothing; I leave it to Cénzi to tell me what He wants of me. What He has said is this:

1) Those who have participated in today's acts will not be prosecuted or punished for their actions, which were necessary because the Faith turned blind eyes and deaf ears to the pleas of those who saw the Faith falling away from the true teachings of the Toustour and the Divolonté. We weep for the death and injury that has been caused, and we wish it did not have to be so. But when those in authority no longer obey the tenets they have pledged to uphold, they must be cast down. If that requires violence, then Cénzi will bless those who do His bidding.

2) The seat of the Faith must return to Nessantico where it properly belongs.

3) Archigos Karrol must step down; a Concord A'Téni will convene immediately to elect a new Archigos for the Faith.

4) No heretical views will be tolerated within the Holdings nor the Coalition. Those preaching such views will meet the justice of the Faith. All secular cooperation with groups such as the Numetodo will immediately cease. Those heretics who recant their ways and accept Cénzi will be forgiven; those who do not will quickly meet Him.

5) The Concénzia Faith does not concern itself with secular affairs except where such conflict with the tenets of the Faith. Thus, the Faith does not care that Kraljica Allesandra remains on the Sun Throne or that Hïrzg Jan bears the crown of Firenzcia. However, both Kraljica Allesandra and Hïrzg Jan must acknowledge the supremacy of the Faith in all matters that impinge on the Toustour and the Divolonté, or the Faith will cease to cooperate with them. No téni will be allowed to assist them in any way: the war-téni will not fight with their armies; the light-téni will not illuminate their streets; the utilino will not patrol with the Garde Kralji nor the Garde Brezno; the lower téni will not toil in the industries of the state.

These five demands are not open to negotiation. They reflect Cénzi's Divine Will and will not—can not—be abro-

gated. *If any of these demands are not met, then the wrath of Cénzi will fall upon you as it has A'Téni ca'Paim.*

We await your replies.

The document was signed with a bold flourish: Nico Morel.

Allesandra folded the paper again, staring at it in her hand, resisting the temptation to crumple the document and toss it into the fire in the hearth. "Well, the young man is certainly arrogant enough," she commented. Ci'Santiago said nothing. "I'll have Talbot make a copy of this for Hïrzg Jan and Archigos Karrol and send it by fast-rider to them. They might be amused. They'll undoubtedly be terrifically entertained by the fact that Morel could take over the Old Temple and we seem to be unable to root him out."

"I'm sorry, Kraljica," ci'Santiago said. "I'll consult with the other offiziers and perhaps some plan can be devised . . ."

She waved him silent.

"No. Let Morel have the Old Temple. All I ask is that you keep him there. Right now, there are more important matters: let's see what happens with Commandant ca'Talin at Villembouchure. When we know how he's fared, we can decide what must be done with Morel. Just keep him there, snared in a hole of his own making. Can you do that much, A'Offizier?"

Ci'Santiago flushed and nodded quickly. "Is there an answer I should send to Morel?" he asked.

"I think that the lack of an answer will be all the answer he needs," she said. "That is all I require of you for the moment, A'Offizier. Please send in Talbot on your way out . . ."

Ci'Santiago saluted her and spun on the balls of his feet. She watched him leave, glancing at the portrait of Marguerite as he closed the door. "I'm sorry," she told the stern face in the painting. "I'm sorry I ever thought it would be easy to be on the Sun Throne. Every day, I appreciate what you accomplished all the more."

Kraljiki Audric might have thought that the painting of his great-matarh could speak and respond, but it did nothing for Allesandra. Kraljica Marguerite only stared at her, frowning and eternally stern.

"If you don't act, the people will start to think you

weak." The voice came from the direction of her bedroom.
The door had opened and she saw Erik there, dressed in
one of the robes she'd had Talbot bring up for him.

"I know," she told him. She tried to keep the sudden an-
noyance she felt out of her voice: at the tone of his voice,
at the nonchalant and confident way he leaned against the
doorway. Something about his demeanor gigged her; she
told herself that it was because of the news, because of
ci'Santiago's uselessness and cu'Ingres' incompetence and
ca'Paim's death. "And I *will* act," she finished.

"Let me talk to this ci'Santiago," Erik continued. He
pushed off from the wall, coming toward her with his arms
opened. She allowed his embrace but did not return it. His
voice was a low growl in her ear, his Magyarian accent
more pronounced than usual. "Or give me command of the
Garde Kralji in his place. I have experience commanding
an army, my love. I can tell them how to take down this
Morel. Let me help you, Allesandra, as you have helped
me."

*I have seen your vatarh command his army, and I have
watched him go down to defeat . . .* She did not say that. Instead, she allowed herself to relax in his arms. "Talk to him
if you'd like," she told him. "Tell him that I've asked you
to consult for me. But do nothing without telling me first."

He kissed the top of her head. "I will do that. Immediately." He kissed her again and released her, striding
quickly toward the bedroom. He paused there a moment,
looking back at her. "We make good allies, you and I," he
said. "Perhaps even of the more permanent variety, eh? We
don't *need* the damned Firenzcians."

It did not seem to occur to him that she herself was Firenzcian. He left the room. She could hear him dressing,
humming some Magyarian folk tune.

He was right, she knew. She had to act, and forcefully.
But the prospect did not please her.

Nor, at the moment, she was afraid, did Erik.

Rochelle Botelli

THE ENCAMPMENT WAS LOUD, dirty, and malodorous. It stank of horses, mud, men, and fires; it
boomed with orders, curses, laughter, and a seemingly
eternal hammering of smithies. The tents of the Firenzcian
army covered a rolling field not far from the Nessantican
border town of Ville Colhelm. The field might once have
been lush and beautiful, dappled with grass and wildflow-
ers. Now it was a muddy, torn mess rutted with makeshift
lanes between the canvas ramparts of a portable city. It was
impossible to stay clean here. Just walking to the kitchen
tents caked Rochelle's legs halfway to the knee. A midden
had been set up downwind of the encampment, but on still
days, one could catch the odor of rot and filth.

The soldiers themselves grumbled about the inaction,
fretting over their wait while the offiziers endeavored to
keep them busy with maneuvers, with drills and meetings,
and with keeping their equipment in order.

But there was tension in the air. They knew that they
might be going to war at any moment, and that made everyone here nervous and short-tempered. There was no escaping the foul mood of the soldiers, the chevarittai, or the
royal family.

The Hïrzg and Hïrzgin's quarters were commodious and
luxurious, comparatively. There, the muddy ground was
covered by rugs, the furniture had been carted from Stag
Fall, and paintings were hung on the walls of the several
tents which, together, made a traveling "palais" for them.
There was a pretense that the royal couple were simply at
yet another of their estates—at least for the moment—and
the usual routine should be followed despite the circumstances. The small personal staff, under Paulus' relentless
and tedious direction, brought in meals and refreshments,
made certain that the tables and chairs were stable despite

the rather uneven ground underneath, and that the worst of the mess stayed outside the tents.

The staff was nearly as unhappy as the soldiers. Keeping up the pretense was far harder work than actually being at the palais.

Rochelle grumbled with the rest of them because she knew it was expected, but her efforts were half-hearted. True, she could not avoid Hïrzgin Brie and her suspicious glances, but here the Hïrzgin could hardly fault Rochelle for being around Jan. Her vatarh, for his part, seemed to take a renewed interest in her. He would nod to her if she passed him among the tents, and she often caught him glancing her way as she served the two and their guests—usually Starkkapitän ca'Damont and others of the high-ranking of-fiziers, as well as the occasional adviser from Brezno.

She hated that. She hated that Hïrzgin Brie invariably noticed, and that it obviously bothered her.

As within the palais, though, she tried to avoid being alone with him. Part of that was the memory of what had happened at Brezno Palais, part of that was to avoid Brie hearing of it and sending Rochelle away. The conflict tore at her. Rochelle wanted to be with Jan, wanted contact with the man who had given her life, yet she was certain that if he knew the truth, if somehow she blurted it out to him, he would deny it. He would be angry. He would want nothing to do with her.

She knew that her matarh's advice had been right, that she should never have sought him out, yet, knowing that she should leave, she still stayed.

They had been there nearly four days already when Paulus handed Rochelle a sealed letter that had just ar-rived by fast-rider. "Take this to the Hïrzg," he told her. "I have to deal with a crisis in the kitchens."

"But you're the chief aide. Aide ci'Lawli would have taken it himself . . ." Rochelle started to protest. But Paulus cut her off.

"I don't care what you think, girl," he snapped. "Just do it."

Rochelle bowed as required, and hurried to the Hïrzg's tents.

The servant stationed at the door to the series of royal tents, set somewhat apart from the others, told her that

Hïrzg Jan was in his "private office," a tent set in the middle of the complex. "And the Hïrzgin?" Rochelle asked.

The man shrugged. "Starkkapitän ca'Damnot invited her to oversee today's maneuvers down near the river. Said that the men would perform better if they knew she was watching."

Rochelle nodded and hurried past him. The hubbub of the rest of the encampment was muffled and distant-sounding here. She moved through the "rooms" of the palais, seeing no one else about. Rochelle tapped at the board hung by the flap, then went in at Jan's muttered "Enter."

He was alone. She noted that immediately. The "office" tent was small, with room for only two or three people. He was seated behind a traveling desk that took up much of the available space, the front painted with ornate battle scenes. Papers and maps were scattered over it, and Jan was poring over them with one hand cupping his forehead. Rochelle thought that he looked worried. "A message from a fast-rider, my Hïrzg," she said, curtsying and handing him the sealed parchment as he stood up. Jan glanced at it. He gave her a smile.

"Kraljica Allesandra's seal," he said. "Wonder what she has to say, eh?" He let the missive fall to the desk as he came around the side. "The rider gave this to you rather than Paulus?"

Rochelle shook her head. He was an arm's length from her. She could smell the cologne Paulus had put on Jan's bashta this morning. She lowered her eyes, staring at the tapestry that covered the grass. There were mud tracks from Jan's boots, smearing across a mountain meadow in which a unicorn pranced—a rug she might well have to clean this evening. The beast's crown seemed to spear a clump of the mud. Rochelle found herself wondering—strangely—if the mud would come out of the tapestry or if the fibers were to be eternally stained. "Paulus gave the message to me to deliver. He said there was a problem in the kitchens that demanded his attention."

She could hear the frown in Jan's voice, though she didn't look up. "The kitchens are more important than a communication from the Ambassador?" She heard his sigh. "Paulus is no Rance, I'm afraid. I need someone more competent to be my aide. Could that be you, Rhianna?"

Unexpectedly, Rochelle felt his right hand touch her arm, and she gasped, her head coming up. His fingers were gentle around her, but they also did not release her as she started. "So muscular," Jan said, as if that were what he expected. "Somehow I'm not surprised by that, Rhianna."

She could feel herself tensing. He was so very close, his face bending above hers, but he didn't pull her arm away. "I don't know what you mean, my Hïrzg."

His hand moved, sliding up her arm past the elbow. His fingers grazed the outside of her breast. "You remind me so much of her," he said. His hand was at her shoulder now. Then, before she could respond: "I know that the Hïrzgin treats you suspiciously, and I'm sorry for that. But I can handle Brie, if it comes to that. She knows when to ..." He smiled down at her; his eyes were those of a hawk. "... look the other way if she must."

"My Hïrzg," she breathed. "I love Emerin ..."

"Ah, him." Another smile. "I can guarantee his advancement in the Garde. Maybe even set him on the path to be a chevaritt. He would like that, wouldn't he?"

She knew then that he would accept no answer but yes, and she could not. *"I'm your daughter,"* she wanted to scream at him, but he would ignore that as well, thinking she was saying it only to stop him. There was an eagerness in his face that she had seen before in men, and it was not a pleasant sight. She tried to pull away from him; his fingers tightened around her arm and started to pull her toward him.

She had no choice. No choice.

She surprised him by letting herself fall into his pull. He laughed, thinking that she was submitting, but her hands had gone to the scabbard at his waist and the ancient leather scabbard there, holding the dagger with the bejeweled pommel. She slipped the weapon from its sheath and brought it up quickly, pressing the double-edged blade against the side of his neck hard enough that he could feel it, that a thin line of blood trickled down from under the dark Firenzcian steel. "Back away," she told him. "Back away, or I'll kill you here and now."

She wondered whether that was at all true, if she would have the resolve to follow through on her threat. It was not what she wanted. She felt tears starting in her eyes, and she blinked hard to clear them, sniffing.

His hands loosened around her. Holding his hands up as if in surrender, he took a step back, but his eyes were laughing and there was a smirk on his lips. She moved with him, keeping the dagger near his throat. "Not a sound either," she told him. "If you shout or call out, I swear you'll have a second mouth a moment later."

"Rhianna . . ." He said her false name quietly. She was neither Rhianna nor Rochelle now; she was the White Stone. The tears had dried up, and her hand was steady on the knife's hilt. It felt good in her hand, solid and well-balanced, a piece as deadly as it was beautiful, the ebony handle ancient and much-handled. She glared at him as he stared at her, his hands still up in mocking surrender. She could see him considering whether to snatch at her knife hand; she wondered if he dared that—he was a soldier as well as the Hïrzg, and he had fought many times. Her matarh had told her how brave he was in battle, how good with weapons, how skilled.

If he tried to prove his bravery now, could she kill him? She had attacked the Hïrzg; Rochelle knew neither of them could ignore that, going forward. Her decision had changed everything, irrevocably. She wasn't certain just how, yet.

"I only want to leave," she told him, hoping that might make him reconsider his options. "I don't intend to hurt you."

He nodded, very slowly. The line of blood touched the collar of his bashta, the fabric blooming red. "Rhianna, I didn't mean . . ."

"It's too late now," she told him. "It's your fault. You've made everything impossible." Suddenly, she lifted the knife from his neck. "I'm your daughter," she told him. The words rushed out, and she could not stop them. "I'm Elissa's daughter. The White Stone's daughter."

She knew the words would stun him, that it would take him a few breaths to process what she'd told him. She ran, still clutching the dagger. "Wait!" she heard him call after her, but she didn't wait. She ran through the palais tents that she knew well, knew far better than Jan himself. She slipped into the space between two of the tents, a well-masked passage she'd found a few days before. She heard Jan call after her—"Rhianna!"—and his footsteps pursuing her, but she was already gone, already slipping out at the rear of the encampment near the line of trees, already slipping into the cover of the trees with his dagger, Jan's dagger, in the belt of her tashta.

She was the White Stone, and the White Stone knew better than any how to hide, how to escape pursuit, how to change appearance and name at need, how to blend in.

They would not find her. Not if she wished to remain hidden.

~

Niente

THE DESOLATION WAS NEARLY MORE than Niente could bear. The glare of his son sliced him open to his very bones.

He stood in the central square of Villembouchure, where he had stood once before in victory. The city walls were a tumbled ruin near the water, as were many of the buildings. On the hills outside those walls, the army of the Holdings was in retreat, though the farsighted among the Tehuantin claimed they could see lines of the Easterner warriors on the ridges overlooking the city. They might have retreated, but that retreat had been orderly and measured and they had not gone far.

If this was victory, it was a cold and bitter feast. That was what the Long Path demanded, but it didn't make it any easier for Niente to stomach.

The Tehuantin warriors, their faces painted with the dark lines of battle and their bodies spattered with the blood of the Easterner defenders, trudged wearily through a gray landscape punctuated with fires and smoke. The city was theirs but it had cost them greatly; it had begun even as they approached. Nearby, Tecuhtli Citlali was huddled with the Tototl and the other High Warriors, his face grim and the glances he cast Niente were venomous.

There were too many bodies on the ground, and too many of them were Tehuantin. Their dead, gaping faces all seemed to accuse Niente. He remembered . . .

*   *   *

They could see the Easterners on either side of the A'Sele as they approached, just as the walls of Villembouchure tantalizingly appeared beyond the river's bend. No one but Niente and perhaps Atl realized what the Easterners intended, nor the import of two crude stone buildings that had been erected on either side of the A'Sele.

Niente knew, and he braced himself. As the lead ships came abreast of the buildings, winches whined inside the structures and steel cables lifted menacingly from the brown waters of the river. The cables snagged the hulls of the lead ships. Great snarled hooks on the cable scraped and screeched, tearing gouges into their wooden hulls as the warriors and sailors shouted alarm, ripping planks and seams open so that the cold water rushed in. More cables lifted behind them, clawing at the ships behind.

Niente saw the first ships lift and cant over, stopped and snared to block the river. They took on water rapidly, the mast spars touching the water as men—warriors and sailors—spilled into the river, the lines and sails snarling and tangling in the mast of the nearest ship and bringing them down. The captains of the ships behind, tried to turn, tried to drops sails, tried to avoid colliding with the ships ahead of them in their way, but several could not—including the *Yaoyotl,* which crashed into the ship ahead of it, masts and spars snagging and breaking. Niente felt the impact, which knocked him from his feet despite his bracing. Through the screams and frantic shouting, through the smoke of fires started as lamps and cook fires were disturbed, he could see the A'Sele clogged with wreckage and disabled ships.

He could also hear the cheers of the Easterners on the shore . . .

"Taat!" Atl's call brought him back to the present. His son's tone was accusatory. He stirred, leaning heavily on his spell-staff, still warm from use. He felt older than the hills around them, older than the channel the river had carved in the land, as tired and ancient as the stones which were the bones of the place.

"Atl," he answered. "Here I am."

His son also showed the weariness of the battle, his face

drawn and pale, smeared with soot. Atl thrust the end of
his spell-staff hard into the ground before Niente. His glare
was hard and accusing. "It did not have to be this way," he
said.

"We have won a victory, as I promised Tecuhtli Citlali,"
Niente told him. "The path I was shown was true."

"There was another path," Atl insisted. "I saw our ships
caught. Why didn't you see that? I saw their troops waiting
for us at the shore. Why didn't you see that also, Taat? Why
did you tell me that I'd seen wrong, and why did I believe
you?"

"Why didn't you see that?" Memory assaulted him again.

They lost too many warriors to the river, as the warriors
were already dressed in their armor for the coming assault.
The weight dragged down those who fell into the water
even if they could swim. The ships that managed to drop
sail and anchor in time sent out their small boats to rescue
those they could. Everyone could see the Easterner warriors on the walls of the city, so tantalizingly close, and even
Niente shuddered, waiting for the fire of their war-téni to
come shrieking down on the disabled ships and the helpless
warriors and sailors. They were a dead, unmoving target,
and the téni-fire would be devastating. The river would become a conflagration, a death trap.

That was what Niente himself would have done, in their
place: he would have rained death on the helpless enemy,
ripe for the plucking. Impossibly—as Axat had shown him
in the bowl's water—only a very few spells were actually
cast, and the nahualli easily turned them.

The ships at the end of the fleet's long line turned away
from the wreckage, sliding toward the shore well below Villembouchure's walls, and the small boats poured out from
the rest of the fleet, the warriors shrieking and pounding
their shields as they landed, a furious Tecuhtli Citlali leading the charge. Niente was with him, as was his place, and
his spell-staff cast fire toward the walls that shattered them
and sent men screaming to their death. The catapults from
the closest stable ships tossed their black sand, though
much of it fell short.

The gates of the city opened, and the army of the Easterners poured out, then Niente's world was enmeshed in the chaos of battle, all the plans the Tecuhtli and the High Warriors had devised gone to ash. The fight was brutal and bloody, but they had the advantage of numbers, of magic, and of the black sand.

In the end, they prevailed at great cost, as Niente had known they would.

"Axat showed me that if we had landed the fleet a day's march from Villembouchure, we could have marched in on them intact—without having our fleet fouled and blocking the A'Sele, without the great losses we sustained there and in the initial attack," Atl insisted. "Why didn't you see that in the scrying bowl, Taat?"

"I'm sorry, but you saw wrongly, Atl," Niente insisted again, hating the lie. But he had no other choice.

Atl was already shaking his head, glancing over toward Tecuhtli Citlali, who was staring in their direction. Atl's voice was raised and heated, and his gestures were as sharp as a dagger's edge. "I had one of the metalsmiths make me my own bowl, Taat, since you're so reluctant to let me borrow yours. In that bowl and in yours also, I saw the same events, and they were *clear*. Had we landed the fleet earlier, this would have been a far easier victory, and the A'Sele would still be open to us. Your path was the wrong one, and it cost the lives of too many good warriors and sailors and has taken away our water path to the great city. Taat, I'm concerned. I look at you and I see how Axat has crippled your body; I see how weak you've become. I wonder . . ." He gave a *huff* of exasperation, or perhaps it was only concern. "I wonder if your far-sight has become as poor as your true sight."

No, Niente wanted to tell him. *My future sight has become sharper than ever before, and I can see further down the possibilities that Axat reveals than you can. And that is the problem . . .* But he could say nothing of that to Atl. He wouldn't understand and he wouldn't believe. Niente wasn't entirely certain that he understood it himself.

"What is this?" a gruff voice interrupted: Tecuhtli Citlali. He had come over to them; behind him, Tototl and two others of the High Warriors stared at Niente and Atl impassively. Citlali's broad head, the red eagle bright against his flesh, turned from one of them to the other. The bamboo ridges of his armor were scratched and scarred from the battle, many of the steel rings set in it missing. "What are you saying to the Nahual, Atl?"

"I was asking Taat if perhaps there hadn't been a better path for us to take, Tecuhtli," Atl answered.

"He promised us victory," Citlali said. "We have that." He glanced around, his nose wrinkling at the odor of death and smoke. "Though not a pleasant one."

"Yes, we do," Atl answered. "But sometimes there is more than one road that can be traveled to the same place, and one might be easier than the other."

The Tecuhtli's regard turned back to Niente. "Nahual? What is the young man saying?"

Niente looked more at Atl than at Citlali. "I gave the Tecuhtli advice that led to our victory. If he wishes to follow another path next time, that is his choice. I am the Nahual, and I speak with Axat's voice, as I always have. I *know* that Axat has given me true far-sight. I have proved that too many times already, at great cost to myself." His voice was quavering at the end: an old man's tired voice. His emptied spell-staff trembled in his hand. Niente stared at his son, and finally the young man's gaze lowered.

"The Nahual found victory for us," Atl said. "What else can be said?"

Citlali stared, but Atl kept his own gaze to the ground. Finally, the Tecuhtli coughed up phlegm, spitting on the ground and using his booted heel to grind it in. "Good," he said. "Then there is no more discussion." He gestured with his head to the High Warriors and they moved off. Tototl stared for a moment longer, then moved away to join Citlali. Atl lifted his head again, but there was no remorse and no apology in his eyes.

"I hope your victory pleased you, Taat," he said. The words were thick with sarcasm, and they clung to him as if Atl had spat upon him. He turned and left, stalking away through the blue-gray smoke and the stones and bricks strewn over the square.

Niente sat on the ground, abruptly. The exhaustion rolled over him and he felt as if he couldn't breathe. He huddled with his spell-staff clutched in his hands, and when one of the nahualli came to see if he could help, he simply grunted and sent the man away.

He stared at his wrinkled, ancient hands, and he tried to think of nothing at all.

～

Sergei ca'Rudka

HE FOUND THE CAMP IN AN UPROAR. The Hïrzg's new aide, Paulus, gave him the news in a rush. "The White Stone murdered Rance, my predecessor, back at Brezno Palais. We moved to Stag Fall, then out here into this forsaken emptiness, and now Rhianna, who was one of the most trusted servants we had, has stolen a dagger that dates all the way back to Hïrzg Karin, taken it from the Hïrzg and threatened him with it, and now she's gone. I'm terribly understaffed as it is, and out here where there's just *nothing,* and the Hïrzg and Hïrzgin are in a terrible upset, and it's just an *impossible* situation . . ."

Sergei soothed the whining man as much as he could—thinking that Paulus wouldn't last another turn of the glass as aide if it were up to Sergei—and asked that word be sent to the Hïrzg that he had arrived.

The journey from Nessantico had been long, made even more tedious by finding that the Hïrzg had abandoned Brenzno first for Stag Fall and then the southern border with the army. He'd followed that trail, escorted by a few dozen chevarittai from the north of Firenzcia who were be-latedly joining the army.

He'd expected that Jan and Brie would be delighted by the agreement he carried in his diplomatic pouch. Now, he was not quite so certain. Jan, behind his field desk, had a dour look as Sergei entered. Despite that, Sergei caned his way into the tented room and set the pouch on the desk. He opened the lock—noticing how old his hands looked, holding the key—and slid out the rolled parchment inside. "Your treaty, Hïrzg Jan," he said. "Signed by the Kraljica. She has agreed to all the major points and had it read publicly in the temples of Nessantico. All it needs is your signature and the Holdings and the Coalition will be one again."

Jan stared at it. His finger stroked the seal that held it closed. "Tell me, Sergei," he said. "Do you think that the past must always haunt the future? Do you think we can ever escape what we did before?"

Sergei frowned. "I'm not certain what the Hïrzg is asking, I'm afraid. If you're referring to your relationship with your matarh ..."

"We tell ourselves that we'll make our own history, that we can completely change things. But all we do is continue to weave from the same threads we've been using all along."

Sergei waited, silent. Jan took a long breath, seeming to stare through Sergei. "The White Stone killed Rance."

"I heard that from Paulus."

"You wouldn't know who hired her, would you, Sergei?"

The accusation buried there was obvious—and startling. Sergei straightened himself as well as he could, pushing against the knob of his cane. In truth, he had complained to Allesandra about Rance's stubbornness, and had laughingly suggested that if the man slipped down the palais stairs and died, he wouldn't mourn. He wondered, for a moment, if perhaps Allesandra *had* hired the White Stone. But he allowed none of that suspicion to show on his face. "Hïrzg Jan, I assure you that I had nothing to do with Rance's death."

"Rance advised me against this treaty and against any reconciliation with the Holdings," Jan interrupted, tapping the scroll. His eyes smoldered with a dark fire. "You knew that, and you knew the high regard I had for Rance's opinion. Perhaps it wasn't you who hired the Stone, but surely you told Matarh about Rance's stance. Perhaps *she* decided to silence the man? Perhaps she would decide to silence me as well, once this treaty is signed—that would relieve her of any obligation to abdicate the throne, wouldn't it? Did you happen to mention *that* to her, Sergei?"

Sergei was already shaking his head. "Hïrzg, who has been whispering this poison to you? Is it Paulus? Frankly, I don't think the man's competent to judge whether his eggs are sufficiently cooked ..."

Jan stopped Sergei with a sharp slice of his hand, half-rising from his seat. The field desk shivered with the motion, the scroll rolling across the polished surface. "Not Paulus," he said. "The man's a dullard; I know it. I'll replace him as soon as I can. But I have my reasons for this suspicion, I assure you."

"Then tell me what they are, so I can refute them. Hïrzg Jan, I had *nothing* to do with Rance's death. I swear it before Cénzi."

"And my matarh? You can swear for her also?"

Sergei lifted a hand from the cane, let it drop again. "No, but I believe that if Kraljica Allesandra were responsible, she would have told me her plans, and she has said nothing." That, at least, was the truth. He was fairly certain that Allesandra would have told him. At least, he hoped so.

Jan sniffed derisively, as if he'd read Sergei's mind. "Oh, believe me, Matarh is quite skilled at keeping her intrigues to herself. I know *that* one from my own history. I know it very well." He tapped the treaty again. "I don't know that I'll be signing this, Sergei. I might be signing my own death notice."

"Hïrzg, I assure you—"

Jan scowled and stiffened in his chair. "With all due respect, Ambassador, your assurances mean very little at the moment. I will look at the document with the Hïrzgin, and we will talk."

Sergei nodded. "Then I will meet with you tomorrow, Hïrzg. It's been a long ride here . . ."

But Jan was shaking his head. "Not tomorrow. I'll give you my answer in my own time, when I've had a chance to investigate other matters, or when . . ." He stopped. Frowned. "You may return to Stag Fall or Brezno if you wish, Ambassador, or wait here. I don't care which. I can have Paulus give you field accommodations, if you feel you can trust him that far."

Stag Fall would be far more comfortable, and Brezno would be more pleasing in other ways, but Sergei shook his head. He had no choice here; over the decades, Sergei had become well-versed in the reading of faces and the lies and half-truths concealed in words. There was something Jan wasn't telling him, something else that was driving his conviction that Allesandra had hired the White Stone. Sergei couldn't entirely deny the possibility, but found it unlikely.

He'd never mentioned Rance in such ominous terms that
Allesandra would have felt compelled to take action. No, if
the murder *had* been the White Stone's work and not that
of some impostor, then there was another explanation.

And if there was something else driving Jan's anger and
irritation. Sergei couldn't uncover that in Brezno or Stag
Fall. "I'll remain, Hïrzg," he said. "I would like to talk with
you further on this—the choice we make here is crucial for
both the Holdings and the Coalition, and is time critical.
The Tehuantin attack is an issue that can't wait."

"That's an issue critical for the Holdings, yes," Jan
agreed. He tapped the scroll again, staring at it as a miner
might inspect a chuck of rock for the presence of gold. "But
for the Coalition?" He shrugged. "I assure you, Ambassador, the Coalition will survive that problem, whether the
Holdings does or not. Good day, Sergei," he said, and point-
edly began to examine a map laid out on his desk.

Sergei watched him for a breath, then bowed to him. His
cane pressed deeply into the carpet-hidden grass as he left.

~

Varina ca'Pallo

"**I** NEED YOUR HELP, VARINA."

It was not a statement that a person expected
to hear from the Kraljica. In the years that Varina had
known Allesandra, she'd come to consider the woman
a friend, yet there was always a necessary distance and
deference to that friendship due to her title. Allesandra
wasn't someone who asked for help; rather, she generally
expected help to be offered without the necessity of a request, or she would instead issue an order for the aid. Yet
here was Allesandra, sitting in Varina's sunroom as if on a
social visit, and asking.

The room was warm with the sunlight pouring through
the glass, and full of the scent of blooming flowers. Varina
had watered them little since sending the servants away,
and the stress and neglect seemed ironically to have star-

tled them into bloom. She had never seen the room so vibrant and alive.

It was almost a mockery. The plants flaunted their color and brilliance against the gray, wrinkled bag of her own flesh and against the gray plain of her continuing grief.

"*I need your help.*" Varina was afraid that she knew exactly what Allesandra wanted, and she wasn't certain it was something she could do. "If this has to do with Nico and the attack on the Old Temple . . ."

"It does," Allesandra replied flatly. She stroked the yellow petals of a sunrise flower on a stand alongside her chair. "Very pretty," she said. "The ones in the palais garden are just beginning to bud." She laid her hand back in her lap, her gaze on Varina again. Varina could see the steel of the ca'Ludovici line in her face: the sharp nose, the jutting chin. "Nico Morel doesn't only threaten the Faith and me," Allesandra said. "He also threatens you and the Numetodo, and he does so directly. If he has his way, the persecution of the Numetodo by the Faith would begin once again. He wants to see your tortured bodies hanging in cages from the Ponticas, as they did when Orlandi held the Archigos' throne."

"You wouldn't allow that, Kraljica," Varina answered. "I know you that well."

Allesandra gave an audible sniff, as if searching for the perfume of the flowers in the room. "I wouldn't, no. But if Morel has his way, then my refusal would be mean that there would be someone else on the Sun Throne, a lackey who would bow first to the Archigos' throne rather than to the people of the Holdings, who would place religious issues before political ones. If that happens . . ."

"How can it?" Varina said. "Nico can be charming and persuasive; I know that well. But this tiny group of followers taking over the Faith?" She shook her head. "Surely that's not a serious threat."

"You underestimate both Nico, and the Morelli influence among the téni and the populace. They aren't a 'tiny group,' Varina. When A'Téni ca'Paim called for the war-téni of the Holdings to join the Garde Civile to defend Villembouchure, few of them answered. Most of those who ignored her are now in the Old Temple with the Morellis. My people are telling me that the Garde Kralji doesn't have the capacity to deal with the raw power Morel has gathered there. I suspect they also don't have the *will* to do so—I know that some of the offiziers within the Garde are actually sympathetic to the Morellis and their stance."

The bright colors of the sunroom plants filled the air behind Allesandra, discordant. Varina's hand had gone to her throat. She felt a sour burning there, deep inside: a remembered fear that she'd thought long extinguished and forgotten. She remembered Sergei's advice to her; she wondered whether she should have listened, if once again he'd been right when everyone else had been wrong. "It's that serious? How did we miss this?"

"When things don't go well, people look for scapegoats to blame. They never blame themselves, they never blame Cénzi, they never blame circumstance, they never blame chance. They blame others."

"And the Numetodo have always been convenient scapegoats. Is that what you're saying?"

A nod. "The way to ensure that the Numetodo survive is to make certain that the Nico Morel and his people receive the justice they deserve. Strength is the other quality that people respect. If you show that the Numetodo are stronger than the Morellis, then you'll see the blame shifting the other way; all the talk will be about how it's the Morellis who have caused the problems and who are endangering the Holdings. Not you. Not the Numetodo. The affection of the people is fickle. We can change it."

"You've become a skeptic, Kraljica. Or a pragmatist."

She shook her head. "I haven't changed at all. In this, I've always been a realist. And I'm right. That's why you need to help me."

"How?"

She turned slightly and stroked the soft petals of the sunrise flower once again. Varina watched the bloom bend and spring up again under the Kraljica's hand. "It's simple enough. I can't fight war-téni without magic of my own; you're the A'Morce Numetodo. If I no longer have the Faith as my ally, if I can't trust the téni there, then my only hope is to turn to the only rival to them—the Numetodo: your magic, your knowledge, your black sand. And whatever else you have that would change the equation."

Varina glanced at her desk, on which a weeping violet

drooped small, purple flowers like bloody tears. Below the plant, in the drawer of the desk, was her sparkwheel. "Kraljica, we've been friends for a long time now ..."

"We have," Allesandra answered. "Which is the other reason I've come to you. I ask for friendship's sake, too. You know what Morel asks—no, *demands*—of us?"

Varina shook his head. Allesandra took a scroll from her pocket, and what she read to Varina stunned her to the core. Her hand trembled at her throat and she wished, at least momentarily, that the shock would sweep over her and take her, that she could join Karl in the sweet oblivion of death. She glanced again at the desk, at the weeping violet and the drawer. It seemed that she could smell the weapon there, the scent of burnt black sand.

The odor of violence and death.

"He can't be serious," she said. "He can't really expect you to accept those terms. That's madness."

"Nico Morel *is* mad," Allesandra answered. "And he believes that Cénzi will make this happen." She rose from her seat, and she moved into the sunlight streaming through the window, Varina could see the age in her face: the wrinkles, the sagging of her chin, the gray that was beginning to show in the hair. For a moment, Varina saw Allesandra as she might look in another decade. Then the sun slid over her face and left her in shadow again, and the moment was gone. Varina started to rise with her, but Allesandra waved to her to keep her seat.

"No, don't get up. Varina, I can't wait, as some in the Garde Civile have advised me. I have to take care of this quickly, because I fear that Commandant ca'Talin won't be able to hold back the Tehuantin, and I can't have this distraction while trying to fight a greater enemy. I tell you again—I need your help. Nessantico needs our help. I need the Numetodo, and I promise you that if you give me the aid I ask for, then the Numetodo will never have to fear persecution within the Holdings ever again. Will you help?"

She knew how Karl would have answered. She could almost hear his voice. *I know you love Nico, but he's not the child that we knew. He's changed, and he's been terribly damaged, and he's dangerous. He's brought this upon himself.* "Yes," she told Allesandra. "I'll have to talk to the others, but I'm certain they'll agree. I'll arrange with Talbot to coordinate things."

Allesandra nodded. Her face seemed to relax. "Thank you," she said. "You won't regret this, Varina. I promise."

Varina pushed herself up from her seat, and Allesandra embraced her gently. "Thank you," she heard the Kraljica whisper again. Allesandra's lips brushed Varina's cheeks momentarily, and the Kraljica turned to leave.

The wake of her passage smelled of flowers and damp earth.

~

Jan ca'Ostheim

WHEN JAN READ SERGEI THE CONTENTS of the missive from his matarh, the Silvernose didn't seem startled at all, which told Jan that Sergei already suspected what it said.

"Morel thinks that he has divine guidance," Sergei said, rubbing—as he too often did—at the metallic nose glued to his ravaged, wrinkled face. "When one truly believes that Cénzi has set you on a course, you have no limitations. It's a lesson many of the Kralji have had to learn. Now it's Allesandra's turn."

They were gathered at the table in the dining "room" of the palais tents. Hïrzgin Brie was there, as was Starkkapitän ca'Damont and Archigos Karrol, who had come down from Brezno. Jan had invited Ambassador ca'Rudka to join them, not only because of the communique from Nessantico, but also because he enjoyed watching Sergei annoy both the starkkapitän and the Archigos.

"You speak like a Numetodo," Archigos Karrol said to the man, but Sergei shook his head slowly, his jowls wobbling with the motion.

"I believe in Cénzi, Archigos, as firmly as do you," the Ambassador said, and Jan thought he heard a strange sadness in the man's voice, almost a regret. "I know that I will go to Him when I die, and the soul shredders will weigh me before Him. I believe." Then he seemed to shiver, and his gaze wandered away from the Archigos and found Jan's. "It's not *faith* that's the problem, Hïrzg Jan, only blind fanaticism. Morel insists that there is only one true path, and that's *his*. Therefore, all the rest of us are wrong. The greater problem is that you have too many téni within the Faith who agree with Morel rather than you."

Archigos Karrol spluttered at that. He lifted his bent head against the resistance of his curved spine. His long, white beard waggled; his brown-spotted fist banged at the table, rattling crockery. "*I* am the authority within the Faith, not this damned Morel. He's already doomed himself by using the Ilmodo against my direct orders. His hands and tongue are forfeit for that, and his life is mine for the death of poor A'Téni ca'Paim."

Jan heard Sergei sniff, saw his eyes, now enveloped in tired folds of skin, widen slightly. "Yes, we in Nessantico saw how well the war-téni obeyed A'Téni ca'Paim, whose authority derives from yours, Archigos. I wonder, if you order the war-téni of Firenczia to move against Morel, will you get the same obedience?"

The Archigos' bald skull was pale against the angry flush of his face. He scowled, turning his head sidewise to glare at Sergei. "My war-téni will do as I tell them to do," he said. Spittle flew with the comment; he didn't seem to notice. He looked over to Jan. "Hïrzg, Hïrzgin, I find that my appetite has left me, and I need to speak with the téni here to give them the news about A'Téni ca'Paim and arrange for services in her memory. If you'll forgive me . . ."

Without waiting for an answer, he gave the sign of Cénzi and pushed away from the table. Two o'téni in attendance rushed to help him. They handed him his staff and he shuffled away, his head facing the carpeted ground as he padded from the tent.

"I apologize, Hïrzg, Hïrzgin," Sergei said after the servant had closed the tent flaps—painted in trompe-l'oeil fashion as a massive, carved wooden double set of doors— behind the Archigos. "I only told him the truth."

"The truth is often unappetizing," Brie answered. She glanced at Jan with that, a quick, sharp look. "I'm surprised any of us can eat at the moment." Jan set down the knife he was using to cut the slice of roast on his plate. Brie smiled at him blandly. "I'd have the servants take that away," she said, "but there are so few of our private staff left here. I wonder what keeps driving them away?"

Jan returned the same meaningless smile to his wife.

Sergei didn't seem to have noticed the exchange. He stirred in his seat. "Archigos Karrol is deceiving himself if he doesn't think that there are téni who are sympathetic to the Morellis—especially among the war-téni."

"Our war-téni are *here*," Starkkapitän ca'Damont interjected. "They're actively working with me."

"They're here *now*," Sergei answered. "But will they be tomorrow, or the day after? The news from Nessantico is just now arriving, and if it *was* Morel who asked the war-téni to stand down, as he claims, then perhaps that request is only just reaching them."

"Sometimes, Ambassador," ca'Damont retorted, "I believe you're like an old black crow, with nothing but bad news and gloom to relate. You stink of the prisons you like so much."

Jan looked over sharply at ca'Damont with the crude remark, but Sergei lifted a hand, shaking his gray head slightly. "You'll be happy to know, Starkkapitän, that you're hardly alone in that opinion," Sergei told him. "But then, I'm a crow who over the years has dined on the remains of many victims who failed to listen to me or who said I was mistaken. I never take much satisfaction in that sort of meal, but it's one I suspect I'll continue to enjoy. Perhaps soon."

The man's fork scraped along his plate. Brie snickered nasally. Jan hurried into the conversational gap. "Villembouchure has already fallen, Ambassador. Nessantico will fall, too—again—if Firenzcia doesn't come to her aid. Do you agree with that?"

Sergei nodded. "I do. Emphatically. Commandant ca'Talin is an excellent leader and I have nothing but respect for his martial skills, but he doesn't have the resources he needs."

"Why should I provide them?" Jan asked. "Why shouldn't I let the Tehuantin flail against Matarh's Garde Civile? Even if they *do* take the city, they'll be so wounded in the process that I could take them with half the army I have here, and take the Sun Throne for myself—without waiting, without this treaty she's sent. The Tehuantin will likely even take care of the Morelli problem. That's what

Starkkapitän ca'Damont and Archigos Karrol are advising me to do." From down the table, ca'Damont grunted assent. "Why shouldn't I follow their advice, Ambassador?"

Sergei sat silent for a moment. Then he leaned back in his chair. He rubbed his nose. "Because you're a better man than I am, Hïrzg," he said. "If it were Brezno facing invasion, and Kraljica Allesandra were considering whether to come to your aid, I might give her the same advice the Starkkapitän and Archigos are giving you now. Remain aloof; let the invaders wear themselves out first, then go in and take everything for yourself afterward. But I know her as well as I know you. She wouldn't take that advice from me, any more than you will. She would come to your aid, if circumstances were that dire."

"You're awfully confident in your assessment."

"I'm the Crow. I'm Old Silvernose," Sergei answered with a wry, gap-toothed smile. "And I know that you, Hïrzg, even if you *were* willing to abandon your matarh entirely, you don't care to inherit a broken empire and a broken city, so ruined that repairing it will make Firenzcia herself a pauper nation. Nessantico holds your heritage, as it does the heritage of everyone in the Holdings *or* in the Coalition. It is too precious a jewel to simply cast away."

The man was warped and twisted. His predilections were odious. But Jan knew of no one alive who knew the intrigues of the nations so well—and the man had once saved his life, as well as his matarh's. And, in this, he was right.

Jan nodded. With Sergei's words, the decision had come to him, falling into place and erasing all the doubts. "That is why I will sign the treaty," he told them. "I will take Matarh's offer, and we will ride to Nessantico—if only to preserve the empire that will one day be mine."

ILLUMINATIONS

Niente
Rochelle Botelli
Varina ca'Pallo
Jan ca'Ostheim
Allesandra ca'Vörl
Sergei ca'Rudka
Nico Morel
Brie ca'Ostheim
Varina ca'Pallo
Niente

Niente

CITLALI WAS NOT ONE TO HIDE HIS ANGER
and displeasure. Niente suspected that was true of all
Tecuhtli—when everyone is below you in stature, there's
no need to conceal your feelings.

Citlali's face was nearly as ruddy as the eagle tattooed
on his bald skull. Even the black, geometric lines of the
warrior across his body were dimmed. Behind him, the
well-muscled form of the High Warrior Tototl loomed. Citlali pointed at Niente as he entered the tent. "You've lied
to me," he said without preamble.

Niente grasped his spell-staff tightly, feeling the power of
X'in Ka trapped within it, and wondering if he would need
to use that today. He forced his bowed back to straighten as
best he could. He ignored the screaming of his muscles and
the urge to sit down. He lifted his face to Citlali and Tototl,
let them see the scarred and withered horror that his use
of the scrying bowl and the deep enchantments made in
the name of the Tecuhtli over the years had made of him,
how he aged far more than his years in the service of the
Tehuantin. His blind and white left eye stared at Citlali.
"Tecuhtli, I have never—"

"Your own son tells me this," Citlali interrupted. That,
Niente realized, explained why Atl had avoided him this
morning, remaining far down the army's column from the
Tecuhtli and Nahual's escorts. "He says that he also has the
gift of Axat's far-sight," Citlali continued, "and he insists
that your path at Villembouchure nearly led us to disaster.
No, be silent!" he roared as Niente started to protest. "Atl

said that had we followed the path that Axat showed him, we would not have needed to leave our fleet blocked and tangled in the A'Sele, that we wouldn't have had the losses we had in the river or at Villembouchure. He says we could have gained an easy victory there, and have sailed with the fleet on up the A'Sele to Nessantico."

"And after that?" Niente asked, almost afraid to voice the question. "What did he see past that point?" If Atl could glimpse the twisting paths of the future that far ahead, there was nothing he could do. He would fail in his task, now, and the future he'd seen would slip away entirely.

Tototl's face was impassive, but Citlali shrugged. "Atl said that Axat granted him no glimpse of the future past that point. Still, an easy victory at Villembouchure, not having to abandon the river for the road . . ."

The army of the Tehuantin had taken all they could from the ships, the deep channel they needed hopelessly blocked by the wreckage of the lead vessels of the fleet, the A'Sele effectively barricaded by their own wrecked, half-sunken ships. Now it was the army who carried everything on their backs, or on groaning, scavenged carts pulled by stolen horses and donkeys. Where the wind could have carried them on the backs of the ships without effort, now they were obliged to walk the long miles to Nessantico, to arrive later, to endure the constant attacks of the defenders who would sneak toward their lines, shower them with arrows or attack them with black sand and vanish again.

Niente understood Citlali's foul temper.

"If Atl could see nothing beyond Villembouchure, that is the issue," he told Citlali and Tototl, and that statement deepened the scowl on the Tecuhtli's face. "Atl does have Axat's gift. And I forgive him for coming to you—it was his duty to tell you what he's seen, Tecuhtli, and I'm pleased that he understands his responsibility. But his far-sight isn't as deep as mine, and that's where he's mistaken. As he admits, he doesn't see far into the mist. Yes, there was another path that would lead to victory, one that seemed easier and better. But had I advised you to follow it and had you taken that advice, it would have led to our destruction later. We would never have taken Nessantico."

Citlali narrowed his eyes, the wings of the eagle moving in concert, and Niente hurried to continue his explanation—to give Citlali the lie he'd prepared against this. His voice was quavering; that only seemed to lend verisimilitude to the tale: the worried Taat explaining the mistakes of the inexperienced son. "In a few days, the remnants of the Easterners' own fleet would have caught us—from both behind and forward. We would have been snared in their trap, and our army would have drowned in the A'Sele without being able to fight. *That* was the fate that awaited us, Tecuhtli Citlali. Now . . ." Niente lifted his hands. "Now our ships hamper those coming up the A'Sele in pursuit and the rest of the fleet can turn to handle them; with our army on the road, the rest of their ships can do nothing to us. This *is* the way of victory, Tecuhtli, as I told you. I never promised that it would be an easy path, or is it that the High Warriors are now afraid of the Easterners?"

The last was a calculated risk—the Nahual *should* be outraged that his skill was being questioned. There *should* be anger in response to anger, and if he could blind Citlali by the accusation, then perhaps the lie might be accepted easily.

"Afraid?" The roar was the response Niente had expected; the flush deepened on Citlali's face, as well as on the face of Tototl. Tototl's hand was on the hilt of his sword, ready to hew Niente's head from his shoulders should the Tecuhtli order his death. Niente grasped his spell-staff tighter.

This was one of the futures he'd glimpsed, and in it, his life was exceedingly short from this point . . .

But Citlali laughed, suddenly and abruptly, and Tototl's fingers loosened on his sword hilt. "Afraid?" Citlali roared again, but this time there was no fury in his words, only a deep amusement. "After the dead Easterners I've already left behind me?" He laughed again, and Tototl laughed with him, though Niente saw him gauging Citlali closely— Tototl would undoubtedly be the next Tecuhtli, if they all lived long enough. "You promise me that you see me in their great city, Nahual Niente?" he asked. "You promise me that you see our banner flying over their gates?"

"I promise you that, Tecuhtli Citlali," Niente told him. His hand had loosened from his staff, and he let his head droop and his spine sag.

"You need to speak with your son, Nahual," Citlali said.

"A son should believe his Taat, and a nahualli should believe his Nahual."

"I will do that, Tecuhtli." *I will, because this was far too
dangerous a moment* . . . Niente bowed to the Tecuhtli and
the High Warriors. "I will indeed."

When he returned to his own tent, Niente pulled the scrying bowl from his pack. He filled it with fresh water, took
the scrying powders from the pouch at his belt and sprin-
kled them over the surface once it had stilled. He chanted
over the bowl, the ancient words of the X'in Ka coming
unbidden as he called upon Axat, praying to Her to show
him again the paths that might be. The water hissed, and
the emerald light burst from somewhere in the depths, the
mist rising above the water. He leaned over the bowl, opening his eyes . . .

*There was the great city, with its odd spires and domes,
and there was the fire of spells and black sand trailing smoke
in a grim sky. He was outside the walls with the rest of the
nahualli, and like the rest of them, he was exhausted. They
couldn't hold back the assault. A fireball screamed down
from above them, and though Niente raised his spell-staff
to block it, there was nothing there. The fire descended like
a shrieking carrion bird, and it slammed into him, and in
that future, even with the Tehuantin razing Nessantico to
the ground, in the mists beyond that time he also saw the
pyramids of Tlaxcala tumbled in smoke and ruin and the
eagle banners cast down, with Easterners walking amidst the
rubble . . .*

*. . . In the mists, he sought the path that he'd seen be-
fore, but the landscape had changed and the futures were all
tangled and snarled, the mists rising high in all but that first,
terrible vision. He could still see it, vaguely: the two armies
clashing in fire and blood, the battle turning suddenly and
unexpectedly as Niente—was it him? The mist made it difficult to see—raised his spell-staff a last time . . . And beyond,
in the the future of that path, a city rising higher than before in the east, and the pyramids of Tlaxi strong against the
backdrop of the smoking mountain . . .*

*. . . but there was a figure standing before that path, bar-
ring it, and Niente tried to pierce the mist around the man. It
was his own face gazing back at him . . . No, it was a younger*

version of himself, the features shifting . . . Atl! It was Atl, his
spell-staff raised in defiance, and lightnings crackled around
him, licking hot and fierce toward Niente . . .

Niente lifted his head from the bowl with a gasp. The green mist was swept away, vanishing in the sun and leaving Niente staggering in the midst of a reality that seemed thin and unreal. He shook his head to clear it, allowing himself to come back from the vision. His legs threatened to stop supporting him, and he sank onto the ground, the rickety table that held the scrying bowl falling over. The water spilled from the bowl, the brass bowl rang as it hit the stony ground, and one of the nahualli stuck his head through the tent flaps. "Nahual?"

Niente waved him away. "I'm fine," he said. "Go away." The nahualli stared for a moment, then withdrew.

Niente sat there, hugging his knees to himself. *Atl . . .* It was Atl who now made the path he'd glimpsed difficult to find. It was Atl who blocked the way.

Atl. "You can't give me this burden," he said. He was weeping—from the exhaustion, from the fear, from his love for his son. "You can't expect me to pay this price."

Axat, if She listened, remained silent. Niente stared at the bowl, upturned in the grass, and he shuddered.

~

Rochelle Botelli

BEFORE SHE'D LEFT THE ENCAMPMENT, she'd gone back to her own tent, taking the coins she'd hidden there—the money she'd received for killing Rance and the others she'd slain in her short career. She'd bound the coins under her clothing so that they made no noise; Jan's dagger was sheathed just above her boots under her tashta.

She watched the encampment for a few days from a clump of trees near the royal tents, twice having to evade searchers beating the brush for her. She saw Hïrzgin Brie, saw that fool Paulus, saw the Starkkapitän. She saw the Archigos and Sergei arrive. And finally, she saw her vatarh.

She stared at him until his figure wavered in the tears forming in her eyes.

Then, finally, she slipped away.

It had been easy enough to evade the patrols looking for her—they were noisy and large, giving her ample time to conceal herself. She was good at that, at blending in. She found a bitter-eye tree and stripped long peels of the bark from it, boiling them in a small pot she stole from a farmhouse she passed, and washing her hair with the pale, caustic extract until her black hair became a paler nut-brown. The bitter-eye extract made her hair brittle, coarse, and untamable, her natural curls gone, but that only enhanced the effect. She looked like some ragged, unranked young woman, a farmer's daughter. She took on the accent of the region; she stole a chicken and basket from another farm, and walked the road with that as if she were on her way home or to a market. Once, as a test, she even stayed on the road when a quartet of chevarittai in Firenzcian livery came by on their warhorses, greeting them as if she had no idea they were searching for her. They looked at her, talked among themselves for a moment, then asked her if she'd seen a dark-haired woman about the same age. Rochelle shook her properly-downcast head shyly, and after a moment, they cantered on.

She held back the angry laugh until they'd gone.

She moved south and west, crossing the border into Nessantico at Ville Colhelm. There she took a room at one of the inns, calling herself "Remy." She remained there, restless but not yet certain what she must do.

The nights were the worst. She could hear the revelry in the tavern downstairs, and yet it repulsed her. People should not be happy here, not when her own mind was in such turmoil. Her dreams were haunted by memories of that final confrontation with her vatarh. Sometimes Matarh was there with her. "I told you," she said, her face touched with sadness as she looked from Jan to Rochelle. "I told you not to go there . . ."

"But he's my vatarh, and I knew you loved him," she answered, and they were no longer in the tent-palais, but in the home she remembered best, the cottage in the uplands sheep country of Il Trebbio. "You should have known that I'd be drawn to him."

"I know, and *they* know," she answered. She touched the stone she kept around her neck, the pale stone that held all the voices that haunted her, that drove her mad, and Rochelle pressed a hand to her own neck to where the same stone hung, its presence reassuring. "They told me that you would be the one to finally pay for my sins, and I'm sorry, I'm so sorry for that." She was sobbing, and her tears dissolved the daub-and-wattle side of the cottage. The smell of burning peat was heavy in her nostrils, but the scene had shifted again, and she and her matarh were standing in a meadow under a starlit, moonless sky, with silvered clouds hurrying along the horizon as lightning licked at the distant hills with white snake tongues. Thunder growled imprecations and curses around them.

"But you've not done what I've asked," Matarh said, and she was no longer weeping. The fury of madness was on her face now, and her fingers gripped hard at Rochelle's shoulders. She was thirteen again, still a few fingers shorter than her matarh but more muscular, her first few kills already behind her. Her matarh lay back on the bed, and they were no longer on the hilltop but in that last home they shared, in Jablunkov, Sesemora. The painted, great oaken timbers loomed over them. Matarh was gasping for air, on her deathbed. She'd picked up the red lung disease and begun coughing up blood a week before. The healers had all shaken their collective heads at the symptoms and told Rochelle to prepare for the worst. "Listen to me now," her matarh said, still grasping Rochelle's shoulders as she leaned over the soiled rag she'd held over her mouth and nose.

"Listen to me, Rochelle. There is one responsibility that I place on you, something that—no, just shut up! You can't stop me from telling her . . ." That last was to the voices in her head. Matarh shook her head as if trying to dislodge a persistent fly. She turned her head to cough, loosing a spray of red flecks that coated the pillow. ". . . something I intended to do myself, but now . . . No, I will *not* be with you, you bastards. I killed you all, and I'm going to where your voices will be silent forever. Do you hear me?"

Then Matarh's eyes cleared again and her fingers tightened on the cloth at Rochelle's shoulders. "I wanted to kill *her* for what she did to me," she husked. "If it weren't for *her,* I could have been happy, could have stayed with your vatarh. I wanted to hear her scream in torment in my head as she realized what I'd done—not because someone paid me to do it, no, but because I *wanted* it. I could have been happy with him, Rochelle. Your vatarh . . . The voices were gone when I was with him, but *she* . . . She ruined it all, for me, for Jan, for you too, Rochelle. She ruined it . . ."

Her hands loosened, and she fell back on the bed. For a moment, Rochelle thought that Matarh was dead, but her breath shuddered in again and her eyes focused. Her hand, trembling, lifted to touch Rochelle's cheek. "Promise me," she said. "Promise me you will do what I couldn't do. Promise me. You will kill her, and as she dies, you will tell her why, so she goes to Cénzi knowing . . ."

"I promise, Matarh," Rochelle husked, crying.

The smell of peat overcame the odor of sickness. Rochelle sat up, startled, in her bed in the inn. She could hear the wind blowing outside as a storm came through, the chimney to the hearth in her room losing its draw and the smoke from the peat chunks glowing there wafting back into the room. Then the wind changed and the smoke was sucked upward again. The wind screamed, and Rochelle thought she heard a fading whisper in it. *"Promise me . . ."*

She'd not yet kept that promise. She'd told herself that she would, that one day she'd go to Nessantico as the White Stone, and there she would find the woman who had ended Matarh's affair with her vatarh.

Allesandra. The Kraljica.

Why not now? Jan would be going there, also, she was certain. That was what all the offiziers and gardai were saying. He would be taking the army to Nessantico.

She could be there first. She could keep the promise to Matarh, and Jan would know who had done it, and he would understand why.

Rain spattered against the shutters of the room. Thunder boomed once. Rochelle brought the covers around her, suddenly awake.

"I will go to Nessantico, Matarh," she whispered. "I promise." The peat hissed in response.

~

Varina ca'Pallo

THE SPARKWHEEL WAS HEAVY ON THE BELT under her cloak, a constant reminder, and her mind burned with the spells she'd cast the day before, holding them for this afternoon. On the far side of the plaza, looking ominously abandoned and empty, the Old Temple's golden dome gleamed even in the rainfall, as water spilled from the copper gutters into the mouth of gargoyle rainspouts, which disgorged white, loud streams into the plaza far below.

There were lights in the Old Temple and the attached buildings: the light of normal fires and téni-light both. They had all seen faces staring outward; those eyes could not have missed the massing of the Garde Kralji around the plaza and the arrival of the Numetodo. There could be no surprise here. This would be a frontal assault into the face of a well-prepared enemy.

Talbot, Johannes, Leovic, Mason, Niels, and others of the Numetodo were gathered near her, all of them grim-faced. A'Offizier ci'Santiago of the Garde Kralji approached them as they waited. "My gardai and utilinos are all in position," he told them. "The Kraljica is also here to observe." He pointed to a window above them, one of the government buildings that bordered the plaza. "You're certain that you want to try speaking to Morel first, A'Morce?"

"I have to," Varina answered.

Talbot shook his head. "No, you don't, A'Morce. We could send in someone else with the message. I would go myself, willingly . . ."

Varina smiled at Talbot. "No," she told him, told all of them. "I know Nico. He'll recognize me, and he'll talk to me. I'll be safe. He's the head of his group as I'm the head of mine. He'll see us as peers. This is the way it needs to be."

"And if you're wrong?" Ci'Santiago asked.

"I'm not," she told him firmly, though she wondered

herself about that possibility. "Wait here. All of you. If this goes well, we can end this siege without bloodshed."

She could see the disbelief on all of their faces. None of them shared her optimism. In truth, she had little hope herself.

She nodded her head to them, then started across the plaza. As she walked, her footsteps splashing through puddles, she spoke a release word. Light bloomed above her head, illuminating her as she made her way across the dark, wet flagstones in the false night of the storm. Despite the rain, she kept down the hood of her cloak so that her white hair shone in the light and her face could be recognized. She looked back once, when she was halfway across the open area: her friends appeared to be little more than specks in the darkness. All around the plaza, she could see torches alight: the waiting gardai. She turned back, walking slowly toward the Old Temple's main doors. "I am Varina ca'Pallo, A'Morce of the Numetodo," she shouted out loudly as she came near. "I need to speak to Nico Morel."

In the storm-gloom, her voice echoed from the buildings around the plaza, sounding weak and lonely and thin. A head peered down at her from a window high in the temple and vanished again. She could almost feel arrows pointed toward her or spells being chanted. She felt old, frail. *This was a mistake . . .*

But she heard a small door open to the side of the main doors, one without light behind it, and a figure stood there: a shadow in deeper twilight. "Varina," a familiar, gentle voice said. "I'm here. The question is, why are you?"

"I need to talk to you, Nico."

She thought she saw the flash of teeth in the darkness. The shadow moved slightly, and a hand waved. "Then come inside, out of the rain."

With a final glance backward, she moved past him into incense-perfumed dimness. She was in one of the side chapels off the main nave of the temple. Down a wide corridor, she could glimpse the torchlight vista of the main chapel underneath the great dome. There were people there, many in téni-robes, some of them staring in her direction. She could see the main doors of the temple, barricaded and barred.

She heard Nico close and lock the door again, sliding a

heavy wooden beam across it. Another person was there with him: a young woman with a heavily pregnant curve to her stomach: very noticeable as her téni-robes pressed against her as she stood next to Nico. He must have noticed Varina's attention on the woman; he smiled again. "Varina, this is Liana. She and I . . ." He smiled. "We are married, even though Liana insists that I should remain free of the actual rite."

"Liana," Varina said. Varina wondered if she had ever looked that young and that obviously in love. Varina touched her own belly: *if I'd known Karl back when I was young enough* . . . "That's a lovely name." Then she looked back to Nico, whose arm had gone around Liana. "Nico, you can't win here. Kraljica Allesandra has made the decision that the Old Temple must be retaken. She doesn't care about the cost—in terms of lives or in damage. She's massed the Garde Kralji and those chevarittai who are still in the city, and they are ready to attack."

"And the Numetodo?" Nico asked. "Are they out there, too?"

Varina nodded. "We are. You can't stand against us, Nico. Not even with the war-téni you have here. We have our own magic, and we have black sand in quantity. This will be a massacre, Nico. I don't want that. At the very least, I would ask you to release Commandant cu'Ingres as a sign that you're willing to negotiate an end to this. Let's talk. Let's see if we can come to some sort of agreement."

"You want me to release cu'Ingres so that the Garde Civile might have some competent leadership." He smiled at her, his arm tightening around Liana. "You forget that I have Cénzi on my side. I know you don't believe, Varina, but you have no idea what you *really* face here. He has told me that He will send down fire from the sky to protect us. Do you think it's a coincidence that there's a storm tonight? It's not."

As if on cue, lightning sent multicolored light slashing through the rose window above them, and thunder grumbled. Liana laughed. "Look at yourself, Varina," she said. "You nearly jumped out of your skin just now. You *want* to believe; you just won't let yourself. Can't you feel your husband's soul calling to you from the afterlife?"

"No," Varina told the young woman. "You believe in a

chimera. You say 'I don't understand this' and you make up a myth to explain it. We Numetodo look for explanations—we don't need to call on Cénzi to create magic; we call on logic and reason."

Nico was frowning now. "You slap the face of Cénzi with your heresy," he snapped. "You have no idea how powerful Cénzi has made me."

"You would have been this powerful regardless," Varina told him. "The power is within *you*, Nico. It has nothing to do with Cénzi. It's *your* power. You've always had it, and I've always known it."

Nico drew himself up, releasing Liana. In the dimness of the temple, he seemed larger, and his voice—Varina realized—crackled with the power of the Scáth Cumhacht. She wondered whether he even realized what he was doing: without a spell, without calling on Cénzi at all. She was amazed: this was nothing she could do herself, nothing any Numetodo could do. He was tapping the Second World instinctively and naturally, as if he were a part of it. She wondered, knowing this, what else he was capable of doing. *Karl, I could use you now. Together, perhaps we could understand this* . . . "Is this what you've come to do, Varina?" Nico continued. "To insult me here in the very house of Cénzi? If so, you're wasting your breath and we are done talking."

Varina started to respond angrily, then stopped herself. She took a long, slow breath. "Look at me, Nico," she said. "I'm an old woman. I don't want this. I'm here because I cared about you when you were a child, and I still care about you. I don't want you to be hurt. I don't want the death and destruction that will come if the Kraljica hauls you and your people out of here by force. And she *will* do that, Nico. She's determined that she *must* do this, and unless you surrender yourself, that's what will happen. Is that what you want? Do you want your followers here to die?"

Nico laughed again, hearty and rich, so loud that the others in the main portion of the temple glanced their way. Liana smiled with him. "That's all you have, Varina?—to appeal to fear, to play on my sympathy? Do you think me that naive? I have been charged by Cénzi to do this—perhaps you can't understand what that means, but because of that charge, I have no choice. No choice at all. I do

His bidding; I am His vehicle. This is not *my* action nor my battle. If the Kraljica and the Archigos wish to defy Cénzi, then it will be their own souls and everlasting salvation that they risk, and the same for those who support them. Each of you out there is *damned,* Varina. Damned. You want me to surrender? That won't happen. Rather, let me give you this task: go to your Kraljica, who coddles you and your heresy. Tell her that, instead, I demand *her* surrender. Tell her that otherwise she risks the destruction of everything she has built. Tell her that she will find that Cénzi will send fire and flame to assault her, that those she commands will tremble and quake with fear, that they will run in terror from what awaits them. Tell her *that.*"

As he spoke, Nico's voice also rose in power and volume. Varina had to force herself not to step back from him, as if his very words might catch fire and ignite her. She could not deny the power he had; she could feel the cold rage of the Scáth Cumhacht surrounding her—what he would call the Ilmodo—and she realized that she had lost here, that he was beyond any poor capability she had to convince him. The sparkwheel sagged heavily on the belt under her cloak, and she realized that she had no choice. No choice. Her own life didn't matter. But Nico was the heart and the will of the Morelli sect, and if he were gone, the body would collapse.

She took out the sparkwheel. She pointed it at his chest, her hand trembling. He glanced at it, contemptuously. "What is this?" he asked. "Some foolish Numetodo thing?"

She could not hesitate—if she did, he would call up a spell and the moment would be over. Sobbing at what she was doing, weeping because she was about to kill someone both she and Karl had loved, she pressed the trigger. The wheel spun, sparks flared.

But there was only a hiss and sputter from the black sand in the pan, and she saw with despair the dampness beaded on the metal. She dropped the sparkwheel; it clattered on the marble tiles of the floor.

Liana laughed, but Varina could feel Nico studying her face. "I'm sorry," he said to her. "It should never have come to this between us. I'm sorry," he repeated, and it was the voice of the boy she remembered. Nico turned; he unbarred the door and opened it: outside, the wind threw rain across the plaza and black clouds rolled overhead. "Go, Varina," he said. "Go for the sake of our old friendship. Go and tell the Kraljica that if she wants battle, she shall have it—and the blame will be on her head."

Varina was staring at her hand, at the sparkwheel on the floor. Stiffly, she bent down and picked it up again, placing it back on her belt. She took a step toward Nico, and she hugged him. "At least let Liana come with me, for the sake of the child she carries. I'll keep her safe."

"No." The answer came from Liana. "I stay here, with Nico."

Nico smiled at her and his arm went around her again. "I'm sorry, Varina. You have your answer."

"I'm sorry, too," Varina told him, told both of them.

She nodded once to Liana, and went out into the storm, drawing her hood over her face.

~

Jan ca'Ostheim

THE STORM SHOOK THE TENTS like a dog worrying at a stubborn bone. Canvas boomed and rattled above Jan so fiercely that everyone glanced up. "Don't worry," he told Brie. "I've been out in worse."

"I know it's silly, but I worry that this storm's an omen," Brie answered, and Jan laughed, drawing her close and embracing her.

"The weather is just the weather," he told her. "It means that crops will grow and the rivers will run fast and clean. It means that the men will grumble and curse and the roads will be a muddy ruin. But that's all. I promise." He kissed her forehead. "Paulus and the staff will escort you back to Stag Fall," he told her.

"I'm not going to Stag Fall and Brezno. I'm going with you."

He was already shaking his head before she had finished. "No. We have no idea how serious a threat we're facing at Nessantico. I won't have our children orphaned. You're staying with them."

"They're my children as well," Brie persisted. "And I will have to answer to them when they're older. If you *were* to die, they'd want to know why I was so cowardly as to stay behind."

"You didn't go with me when we put down the rebellion in West Magyaria," he countered, though he knew immediately the answer to that. It came as swiftly as he expected.

"I had just given birth to Eria then. Or I would have. Besides, Jan, you need me to be between you and your matarh. The two of you . . ." She shook her head. "It won't be a pretty sight, and you're going to need a mediator."

"I can handle my matarh." He grasped her shoulders, holding her gaze. "Brie, I love you. That's why I can't have you there. If you're there, I'll be too worried about you."

He saw her soften at that, though she was still shaking her head. She wanted to believe him. And it *was* true, at least part of it. He did love her: a quiet love, not the burning intensity he'd once felt for Elissa, not even the lust that arose with the lovers he'd taken. He hurried into the opening. "Give Elissa, Kriege, Caelor, and little Eria kisses for me, and tell them that their vatarh will be back soon, and not to worry."

"Kriege will want to come after you," Brie told him, "and so will Elissa."

He knew then that he'd won the argument. He laughed, pulling her close. "There's time enough for that," he said, "and given the way of things, there will probably be ample opportunity as well. Tell them to be patient, and to study hard with the arms master."

"I'll do that, and I'll be waiting for you as well," she answered.

She rose on her toes and kissed him suddenly. Since Rhianna's sudden departure, since it had become obvious that it was unlikely that the young woman would be found, Brie had been far more affectionate toward him. He'd said nothing to her about what the girl had stolen—though he suspected that Brie knew. He had especially not told Brie about Rhianna's shocking, unbelievable last words. He was still reeling from them, though he'd made every effort to pretend otherwise. *"I'm your daughter. Elissa's daughter. The White Stone's daughter."*

He wanted to shout his denial of that to the world, yet he found that the words stuck in his throat like a burr on the hem of his bashta. *You found Rhianna attractive because she reminded you of Elissa—the Elissa you remembered...* Was it possible? Could she be his daughter? Could she, or could Elissa, have been responsible for Rance's death?

Yes... The word kept surfacing in his mind.

When this war was over, he told himself, he would find her again. He would put a thousand men on her trail, he would track her down, he would have them bring her to him, and he would discover the truth.

And if she is *your and Elissa's daughter?* There was no answer to that question.

So Jan smiled at Brie and pretended that there was nothing between them, as Brie pretended the same, as he knew she'd pretended before with the other mistresses he'd taken. They kissed each other again, and Brie tucked his rain cloak around him as she might have for one of the children. "You must be careful," she told him. "Come back to me a victor."

"I will," he told her. "Firenzcia always does."

He embraced her again for a moment, inhaling the scent of her hair and remembering, instead, the smell of Elissa. Then he released her, and Paulus lifted back the painted flap of the tent, and he went out into the rain, pulling his hood over his head.

Starkkapitän ca'Damont and the a'offiziers stiffened to attention and saluted as he emerged, and he saluted them in return. Sergei ca'Rudka was there as well, dry in a carriage. "It's time," Jan said simply, and ca'Damont and the offiziers saluted again, and ca'Damont barked orders at them as they scattered off to ready their divisions. Jan strode through the muck to Sergei's carriage. In the shadows of the vehicle, Jan could see the gleam of Sergei's nose. "Ambassador?" Jan said. "You have what you need?"

In the dimness, Sergei's hand touched his diplomatic pouch. "I do, Hïrzg. Your matarh will be pleased to see this."

"I suspect she'll be more pleased to see the army of Firenzcia," Jan said. "You're certain you don't want to travel with the army?"

Sergei shook his head. "I need to return to Nessantico as

soon as I can," he said, "if only to let her know that help is coming. I can travel much faster this way. I'll see you there."

Jan nodded, and gestured to the driver. "May Cénzi speed your path," he said. "And may this rain stop before the rivers rise."

Sergei was about to respond, but they heard a voice hailing the Hïrzg. Jan turned—Archigos Karrol's carriage had arrived. The Archigos was helped down by his téni attendants, holding a large umbrella over him. Despite that, Jan could see the gold-threaded hem of the Archigos' robe was spattered with mud, and the man seemed out of breath. "My Hïrzg," the Archigos called out, waving toward Jan.

"The Archigos seems upset," Sergei said. He'd poked his head out from the carriage window. Rain plastered the few strands of his gray hair to his skull and bounced from his nose. "I wonder . . ."

"You wonder what?" Jan asked, but the the Archigos reached them before Sergei answered.

"My Hïrzg," Archigos Karrol said again, giving the sign of Cénzi. "I'm glad that I found you. I . . ." He stopped, glancing at the carriage and seeing Sergei. He scowled.

"Go on, Archigos," Jan told him. "If you've something to say, I'm certain the Ambassador should hear it as well."

"Hïrzg . . . I . . ." The man paused as if to catch his breath. His eternally bowed head strained to look Jan in the eyes. "I had ordered the war-téni to meet with me this morning, to give them a final blessing and my orders, but . . ." He stopped, let his head drop again. The rain beat a quick rhythm on the umbrella above him.

"But . . ." Jan prompted, but he already knew. He glanced at Sergei, who had withdrawn back into the shelter of the carriage.

"Most of them . . . They're gone, my Hïrzg. The ones who stayed told me that a message came during the night, that most of them left the camp afterward. The note . . ."

"Was from Nico Morel," Jan finished for him. He spat. "Cénzi's balls."

The profanity brought Karrol's head up again. Rheumy eyes looked at Jan reproachfully. "Yes, my Hïrzg," Karrol said. "The note was from Morel. The man had the audacity to *order* the war-téni to stand down, as if *he* were the Archigos. I tell you, Hïrzg, once we find these traitors, I will punish them to limits of the Divolonté. They will never again listen to a heretic."

"And in the meantime?" Jan asked him. "What is my army to do for war-téni?"

"There are still two hands of them, Hïrzg."

"Two hands of ten. How impressive. Two hands obey you, and eight hands obey Morel. Perhaps Morel *should* be the Archigos. He seems to have more influence than you."

Archigos Karrol blinked. "I'm confident that the others will soon see the error of their ways. Cénzi will punish them, will make them unable to perform their spells, will haunt their dreams. They will come back, repentant. I'm confident of that."

"I'm so pleased to hear of your confidence," Jan replied flatly. He heard Sergei chuckle softly in his carriage.

"What will bring them back is Nico Morel's death," Sergei commented. "If we kill Morel, we end whatever authority he has."

"Or we make him a martyr," Archigos Karrol retorted, but Sergei answered quickly.

"No. Nico Morel says that Cénzi is leading him, that Cénzi protects him, that he is the voice of Cénzi. If Cénzi allows him to die, then that gives the lie to everything that Morel claims to be. The Morellis will vanish like a spring snowstorm."

"It seems, Ambassador, that you and the Kraljica have but one answer for any problem that faces Nessantico," Karrol muttered.

"And it seems, Archigos," Sergei retorted, "that you have none."

"Enough!" Jan snarled. He waved his hand through the rain. A lightning stroke sliced down nearby, and he waited until the thunder passed. "I expect that you, Archigos, are willing to accompany me—so that I don't lose more war-téni than I already have." The sour look on Karrol's face was enough to tell Jan what the Archigos thought of the idea, but the man managed to lift his hands into the sign of Cénzi, and said nothing. His attendants all glanced at each other. "Ambassador, we're delaying your departure. Tell my matarh to send either Commandant ca'Talin or one of his a'offiziers riding toward us as soon as possible, so we can coordinate with the Holdings' Garde Civile."

"Certainly, Hïrzg," Sergei said. "And I give you my own thanks—you'll be a fine Kraljiki." With that, Sergei tapped on the roof of the carriage with his cane. "Driver!" he called out. The driver slapped the reins and the carriage lurched forward, its wheels digging long and deep furrows in the mud. Jan turned back to the Archigos, still dry under his umbrella while the cold rain dripped from the oiled fabric of Jan's hood.

"We're leaving before Second Call, Archigos," he said. "I would suggest you make yourself ready."

"Hïrzg Jan, I'd ask you to reconsider. I'm an old man, and I have duties to attend to in Brezno. Perhaps if my staff remains with you . . ." The umbrella shook as his attendants' eyes widened.

"I appreciate your frailty, Archigos," Jan told him, "but perhaps it's time you go examine your temples in Nessantico, since you need to replace A'Téni ca'Paim, and since once I'm Kraljiki, the seat of the Faith will be returning there." Archigos Karrol didn't reply, his eternally-bowed back making it appear that he was examining the muddy hem of his robes of office. "You're wasting time, Archigos," Jan told him. "I'll expect to see your carriage join the train of the army in a half-turn of the glass, without any more complaints or suggestions."

With that, Jan spun on his heel. He called out for his horse and weapons, and made his way to where Starkkapitän ca'Damont waited for him.

~

Allesandra ca'Vörl

ALLESANDRA HAD COMMANDEERED a balcony that overlooked the plaza. The Old Temple loomed across the way, though it was difficult to see much in the driving rain and the gloom of the storm. Erik stood behind her and at her shoulder, and his solicitude nagged at her.

"Really, Allesandra, you should move back from the window. Those are war-téni inside the Old Temple, and you've no idea what they can do, especially if they notice that the Kraljica is watching."

"I know *exactly* what war-téni are capable of," she told him tartly. "Probably better than you, Erik. And I don't appreciate you talking to me as if I were a child."

"I'm sorry," he said, but there seemed to be no apology in his voice at all. "I'm just concerned for your safety, my love."

"And I'm concerned for the safety of my people," she answered. "The Garde Kralji isn't the Garde Civile. Their job is to police Nessantico—they've never faced war-téni before, they haven't faced an armed insurrection in a century and a half, and their Commandant is a prisoner in the place they're about to assault."

"That's why I suggested that you place me in charge of them," Erik said. "They need a strong hand guiding them."

So I'm not *a strong hand, in your estimation?* "You've never commanded an organized force either," she reminded him. Truly, the man was becoming tiresome. She was beginning to wonder what she'd seen in him. "I'm the symbol of Nessantico. I rule the Holdings. They deserve to see that I am here, with them. I'd appreciate it if—" She stopped, peering into the rain. "Ah, Varina's returning . . . And there's the signal from A'Offizier ci'Santiago—Morel has refused to negotiate." Allesandra sighed. She'd hoped it wouldn't come to this, that somehow Varina would be able to negotiate the removal of the Morellis from the temple—she couldn't see this ending well, no matter how it was resolved. Yet she had no choice. She especially had no choice if Jan were bringing the Firenzcian army here—she had to end this now or she would appear to be extraordinarily weak.

Talbot had placed two flags on the balcony on which she stood: one a deep blood-red, the other a pale green. Both dripped rain from sodden folds. Allesandra plucked the green flag from its holder and let it fall on the stones of balcony. As if in response, a red star rose from below, arcing high above the plaza. It lingered there for a moment, lending a bloody hue to the gloomy afternoon and hissing audibly in the rain.

A breath later, triple arcs of flame shot out from nearly directly below the balcony—from the Numetodo. The flames guttered and spat, trailing a noxious smoke, and arrowed away to slam into the front portico of the Old Temple. There were terrible explosions as they hit their target, flashes of white that shook the entire plaza. Allesandra could feel the balcony shudder under her feet. A moment later, a wave of heated air rushed past Allesandra, lifting her hair. Through the rain and the smoke, it was difficult to tell what had happened, but now the gardai of the Garde Kralji were rushing toward the Old Temple from all around the plaza, shouting as they ran. She could see ci'Santiago leading them—whatever she might think of the man's competence, he was at least brave.

The gardai were only a quarter of the way across the plaza when the response came from the Old Temple. A dozen fireballs shot from the smoke surrounding the main entrance and from the windows of the buildings attached to the temple. Allesandra heard the Numetodo call out their release words, and all but two of the fireballs from the war-téni sputtered and failed. But those two careened down into the mass of onrushing gardai. Shrill screams rent the storm as they exploded. For a moment, there was chaos in the plaza, the gardai pausing. She could hear ci'Santiago shouting orders as the Numetodo sent their own spells shooting forward toward the Old Temple. The gardai surged forward once more, but choking, acrid smoke was now obscuring the temple plaza, making it difficult to see. Allesandra leaned forward, her hands grasping the rails.

Almost too late, she saw a globe of fire rushing out of the smoke toward her. She recoiled, throwing herself backward into the room. The fireball crashed against the side of the building, billowing out in a great gout of flame a little below and to the right of the balcony where she'd been standing. The building shook, knocking Erik from his feet. The chandelier in the room swayed madly, the cut-glass ornaments clashing and falling. Chunks of plaster and lathework cascaded down from the ceiling, and two long, gaping cracks snaked from floor to ceiling of the outside wall. Part of the balcony on which she'd been standing fell away.

She could smell sulfur, and smoke was billowing up from outside. "Allesandra!" Erik was shouting, pulling her to her feet as she coughed in the fetid, choking air, and the gardai who had been in the corridor outside came rushing in, surrounding her with drawn swords. "We have to leave!"

"Wait!" She staggered to the opening of the balcony, looking out through the shattered doors. The plaza was all a confusion; she could see nothing, though there were flames and explosions around the Old Temple. On the floor below, flames were crawling up the outside of their building.

"Filthy bastardos!" Erik was shouting gesturing toward the Old Temple. "Kill them! Kill them all!"

She stared at him. He grimaced and subsided. "All right," she told Erik and the gardai. "I've done all I can here. Let's go."

~

Sergei ca'Rudka

THE RAIN HAMMERED THE ROOF of the carriage and dripped through every conceivable crevice in the carriage's roof and sides. Sergei could not imagine how miserable the poor driver must be, huddled on his seat as they made their way ahead of the army on the road.

Sergei took a half-turn to eat a quick midday meal at one of the inns in Ville Colhelm, just across the border of the Holdings, and to let the current driver attempt to get the worst of the dampness out of his sodden clothing by sitting in front of the tavern's roaring fire. The new driver he hired didn't seem particularly thrilled at the idea of long turns of the glass out in the weather.

Sergei didn't tarry long. He ate quickly and was back in the carriage with its new driver, jouncing and squelching along the roads made nearly impassable by the horrid weather. By afternoon, the rain had subsided into a persistent, sullen drizzle, the lightning and heaviest rain careening off east and north.

Sergei tried to sleep in the rocking, lurching coach, and failed. The roof was leaking in the corner where he tried to huddle, and the ruts on the road didn't seem to match the carriage wheels, so that every time they dropped into them, the carriage springs threatened to throw him off his seat. He wondered whether the driver did that deliberately to make him as miserable as the driver himself undoubtedly was.

They encountered few people on the road, mostly farmers either sitting on their own heavy and slow plow horses, or with the animal in the traces of an equally heavy and slow wagon laden with goods destined for the markets of the nearest town. Sergei closed his eyes. He yearned to be back in Nessantico, back in his own lush apartments there. Why, he might even visit the Bastida again—surely by this time, Allesandra would have a brace of Morellis ensconced there in the darkness, and he could indulge in the delicious pain . . .

"Out of the road, girl!" he heard the driver call. "Are you blind and deaf?"

Sergei slid aside the curtains of the door in time to see the carriage passing a young woman walking the road. She was drenched, with only a small parcel in her hand and mud up to her knees with stray spatters over her tashta from the carriage wheels. He saw her give the driver's back an obscene gesture.

Her face seemed oddly familiar. He'd let the curtain drop and the carriage lurch ahead for a few breaths before it came to him. "Driver!" he called, using the end of his cane to lift the window between them. "Stop a moment."

"Vajiki?"

"That girl. Stop."

Sergei thought he heard a sigh from the driver. "She hardly seems comely enough to bother about, Vajiki, and she's drenched besides. But as you wish . . ."

The driver pulled on the reins. Sergei opened the curtains again and put his hand out in the rain, gesturing to the girl. "Come on," he told her. "Get out of the weather."

She hesitated, then walked slowly to the carriage. She stood at the door, looking up at him. "Begging your pardon, Vajiki, but how do I know I can trust you?" she said. If she was taken aback by his false nose, she didn't seem to react. And that face . . . *The hair is different. Lighter and shorter—and clumsily cut. But those eyes, and that presence . . .*

"You don't," Sergei told her. "I could give you my word, but what would that mean? If I'm someone who meant you harm, I'd just lie about that, too. It's your choice, lass; you can come in and ride a ways with me, or you can stay out there. If it's the latter, at least you can't get any wetter than you already are."

She laughed. "Aye to that," she said. "Ah, well . . ." She reached up and opened the door of the carriage, stepping onto the footrest there as the carriage sagged under her weight. She dropped into the narrow seat across from him. Water dripped from her hair and the sodden clothes.

She stared at him as Sergei pulled the door closed and rapped on the roof of the carriage with the knob of his cane. "Let's go, driver."

The driver flicked the reins and called to the horse, and the carriage lurched forward again. The young woman continued to stare. In the dimness of the carriage and with his old eyes, it was difficult to see her features that well, but he knew she could see the silver nose glued to his wrinkled visage. If she *was* who he thought she was, she said nothing, didn't acknowledge his name. "Do you make a habit of giving rides to unranked peasants, Vajiki?" she asked.

"No," Sergei answered. "Only to those who seem interesting." She didn't react to that except to brush rain-plastered hair from her forehead. "If we're going to share this uncomfortable coach, we might as well introduce ourselves," he said finally. "You are . . . ?"

"Remy," she said. "Remy Bantara." There was the slightest hesitation as she spoke the last name. *She's lying . . .* Sergei suppressed a twitch of satisfaction. She was a better liar than most, extremely skilled at it, which told him that she was also used to doing so. The hesitation was hardly noticeable, but he'd heard too many lies and evasions in his life. She also kept her right hand under the folds of her overcloak, near the top of her boot. He suspected that she had a weapon there—a knife, most likely. That made him wonder—what else might she be hiding? "And you're Ambassador Sergei ca'Rudka. The Silvernose," she added.

"Ah, we've met before?"

She shook her head, spraying droplets of water from the spikes of hair. "No. But I've heard of you. Everyone has."

And everyone who sees me for the first time does nothing but stare at my nose. Yet you don't . . . Sergei smiled at her. "Where are you going, Vajica Bantara?"

"Nessantico," she told him. "And you may call me Remy, if you prefer."

"That's a long walk, Remy."

"I'm not required to keep a schedule. I will get there when I get there, Ambassador."

"You may call me Sergei, if you like. Nessantico, eh? I'm on my way there as well," he told her. He was certain now. The timbre of her voice, the way she stared intently when she thought she wasn't being observed, the lack of true subservience in her tone. She'd dyed her hair lighter, and probably cut it herself. This was Rhianna—the girl who Paulus had said that the Hïrzg's people were searching for. Knowing Jan as he did, and hearing the interplay between the Hïrzg and Brie, he suspected he knew why. "I'll be stopping at Passe a'Fiume tonight to sleep and change driver and horse, then on to Nessantico in the morning." He hesitated. "You're welcome to accompany me. It's a far shorter ride than a walk."

"And what payment would you be expecting, Amba . . . Sergei?"

"Just the pleasure of conversation," he told her. "As you said, it's a long way to Nessantico, and lonely."

"As I said a moment ago, I've heard of you. And some of those tales . . ." She let her statement trail off into silence. She continued to stare at him.

"I'm not one to believe tales and gossip, myself," Sergei told her. "I prefer to discover the truth on my own. Someone who's strong enough to walk to Nessantico is certainly strong enough to fend off an old man who can barely walk, should he go beyond the bounds of politeness. At the very least, you can certainly outrun me."

She laughed again, a genuine, throaty amusement that made him smile in return. Her hand came out from under her tashta: again, a practiced, effortless movement, not that of a frightened young girl in an uncertain situation, but that of someone who was used to such conditions. He began to wonder if there were more to the story of Jan and Rhianna than he thought.

You could make her talk. You could make her tell you everything.

The thought was sweet and tempting, but he thrust it away. Instead, he continued to smile. "I can arrange a room for you at the Kraljica's apartments in Passe a'Fiume," he said. "I can also assure you that the locks work perfectly well. In exchange, you can tell me your story. Are we agreed?"

"Only if you tell me yours as well," she answered. "Yours would be far more interesting, I assure you."

"The other person's tale is always more interesting," he said. "Frankly, my tale is rather boring. But—we have an agreement, then. So—let's start. Tell me, why is a young woman walking to Nessantico in the rain?"

She looked away then. He could almost hear her thinking. He wondered what she would say, but he was certain that whatever it was would not be the truth.

"It's because of my great-vatarh," she said. "We lived not far outside Ville Colhelm, and he had decided that I had to marry this boy from the farm next to ours—"

"That's a lie," Sergei interrupted. He kept his voice calm. Unperturbed. "I'm sure you'd make it a very entertaining and convincing lie, but it's a lie nonetheless."

Her hand drifted back under her tashta—smoothly, a movement that would have gone unnoticed by most eyes, since at the same time she shifted her position on the seat, placing both legs down as if she were readying herself to move. "I'm sorry," she said. "You're right. I'm not from Ville Colhelm, not from the Holdings at all. I'm from Sesemora, from a town on the Lungosei, but my family is largely from Il Trebbio, and so they were under constant suspicion. The Pjathi's soldiers came one day, and—"

Sergei was already shaking his head and she stopped. "Why don't you tell me your real name," he asked. "Rhianna, perhaps? Or is that one also a lie?" He saw her gaze dart to the door of the carriage. "Don't," he told her. "There's no need for you to be alarmed. As you said, you know me. I have done terrible things in my lifetime, and there's nothing you can tell me, I suspect, that will shock me. Whatever you've done, whatever's happened to you, I've no intention of holding you. Especially since you have your hand on a knife at the moment, and my only weapon is this cane." He lifted it, moving deliberately slowly and grimacing as if it pained him to lift his shoulder—he also neglected to mention the blade he could draw from the sheath of the cane at need, or the fact that Varina had enchanted the cane for him: with the release word she had taught him—she claimed—he could kill an attacker instantly. He had never used the release word, since Varina had said that the spell was incredibly costly and she could not (or would not) do it again. *"Use it only in dire need,"* she had told him. *"Only when there is no other option open for you . . ."*

"The door is unlocked, and I will sit over here away from it," he told the young woman. Grunting, he slid on the seat to the side opposite the door. "You can reach it long before I could stop you. There—now you can escape into this horrible weather whenever you like. But if you're staying, I would like to hear your story. The true one."

She stared at him, and he held her gaze placidly. He saw her relax slowly, though the hand never left her hidden weapon. "I could kill you, Sergei," she told him. "Easily."

"I've no doubt of that. And if it happens, well, I've lived a long life and I'll trust you are skilled enough to make my end fast and easy."

"I'm not joking."

"Neither am I," he answered. "So, is your name even Rhianna?"

The silence stretched long enough that he thought she wasn't going to answer. There was only the creaking of the carriage and the rocking motion of the ruts of the Avi. She slid closer to the door, and he thought she would bolt out into the rain again to be gone forever. Then she let all the air out of her body in one great sigh. She looked away from him, lifting the flap of the door to stare at the rain.

"Rochelle is what my matarh named me," she said.

Nico Morel

FIRE SLITHERED UP THE WALLS, licking at the faces of painted Moitidi and long-dead Archigi. Smoke hid the summit of the dome from view, coiling toward the openings of the great lantern at its very top. The chanting of the war-téni and the shrieking of their spells was a backdrop to the screaming of the injured and the calls of the

Morellis as Nico half-ran, half-stumbled toward the main
gates with Liana struggling behind him. "Absolute!" Ancel
shouted, and he saw the man's gaunt figure through the
haze. "The gardai are charging toward the temple!"

"Tell the war-téni to respond," Nico called. "They'll
break. They'll run." He said it with a confidence that he no
longer felt, and he apologized to Cénzi for his doubt. *I'm
sorry, Cénzi. I believe. I do . . .*

The ferocity of the initial attack had surprised him.
Nothing he'd seen in the dreams that Cénzi had given him
had prepared him for the reality of this battle. The war-téni
had been unable to turn that initial attack—it had happened too quickly, and they had mistakenly thought that
the fireballs were created from the Ilmodo when they were
purely physical: black sand projectiles that exploded on
contact. The blasts tore open the doors they'd so carefully
barricaded: broken timbers and stone shot backward like
terrible missiles into the main temple, hurling pews and
raining dust and debris. At least two hands of his people
had died in that first, horrible moment, and many more had
been injured. The screams of the wounded still echoed in
his head. He'd gone to them, comforting them as best he
could, praying to Cénzi that He move through Nico's hands
and heal them—and for some, He had responded, though it
left Nico as tired as if he'd used the Ilmodo himself against
the tenets of the Divolonté, which forbade the use of Cénzi's Gift for healing.

It had been Ancel who had taken command of the defense of the Old Temple as Nico and Liana tended to the
wounded and prayed for the dead. The war-téni who had
responded to Nico's call now retaliated, sending out their
war-spells toward the onrushing gardai. Their low chants
filled the nave, and they gestured angrily as they sent volley
after volley out into the storm. Nico could hear the screams
and cries of the heretics outside; he could see the fires beginning to consume the buildings around the plaza.

The destruction was terrible to see. It made Nico want to
weep. "This is what You wanted of me, Cénzi," he prayed.
"Let me continue to do Your will . . ." He hugged Liana. "I
have to go," he told her. "I have to help. Take care of those
who are hurt. And be careful."

"Nico . . ." He could see the fear in her soot-streaked

face, and he embraced her quickly, kissing her. She clung to him and he let himself sink into her for just that moment, trying to sear it into his mind and keep it forever. He wondered at the impulse. Then he pushed away and kissed her again. "Be safe in Cénzi's love, and mine," he told her.

"I love you, Nico," she answered. "Be careful."

He smiled. "I have Cénzi's protection," he told her. "They can't harm me.."

And with that, he left her.

He pushed his way through the wreckage, toward where Ancel was standing. He peered out from the ruins of the main doors toward the plaza. "Where are they?" he asked, but then he saw them. A line of gardai rushed out of the pelting rain, with swords raised, their mouths open as they shouted, all jumbled together so he couldn't hear what they said, if there were words at all. Nico raised his own arms as the chanting of the war-téni intensified. He felt the coldness of the Ilmodo envelop him, wrapping all about him, and he gathered that power with the language of Cenzi and his gestures, and he threw it away from him. He didn't know the spell he created; it came to him unbidden and complete—a gift as natural as breathing.

A wave pulsed outward from him, visible in the broken doors and pillars of the temple it sent flying outward, as it threw the rain backward as if storm-wind were blowing it, as it slammed hard into the gardai and sent them tumbling and crashing backward, the power ripping and tearing at them. When it passed, they were gone, the plaza before the doors was swept clean as the rain returned. "Absolute . . ." Ancel breathed. "I have never seen the like . . ." The war-téni had stopped their chanting as well, staring at him with awe on their faces.

But there were sounds of battle now behind him, in the temple itself; Ancel and Nico turned as one to see gardai pouring in from the aisles of the side-chapels as well as from behind the quire. There was hand-to-hand fighting among the pews, with scattered spells being cast by the Morellis who were also téni. Nico could feel other spells being cast, far too quickly to be done by téni—so the Numetodo were here as well. However, the war-téni's spells—meant for mass destruction in open battle—were useless here in a confined space; they would kill Morellis as well as gardai and Numetodo. The war-téni, trained also as swordsmen, drew their weapons instead.

The battle was raging all around, and under the great dome itself, Nico could see Liana, her face pale, chanting and gesturing as she readied a spell. Varina was there also, entering into the temple from the same door she'd left not long before, and she, too, was casting spells.

Cénzi, I need You now. Please help me . . . The prayer rose up in Nico, and he felt the coldness rise again around him. He started to gather it, but one of the Numetodo— was that Talbot, the Kraljica's aide?—had seen him, and with a gesture and a word, the man sent fire hurtling toward Nico. Nico had to use the Ilmodo to cast the spell aside. "There's Morel!" he heard Talbot cry as he pointed toward Nico, and he could feel the Ilmodo being twisted and warped all about him as the Numetodo turned their attention to him. They gave him no respite. As fast as he gathered the Ilmodo, he had to use it to fend off their attacks, and now he was tiring, the exhaustion of using the Ilmodo so strongly and often making his mind and limbs heavy. Once, there was a moment, and he sent Varina, Talbot, and another of the heretics hurtling backward into the walls of the Old Temple, but there were so many of them, and the gardai were closing in around them also . . .

Cénzi, I need You . . .

He ignored his weariness. He closed his eyes, pulling in the power and encasing himself in it so that their spells reflected from him like the sun from a mirror. He could barely see the temple through the swirling haze around him. *I will take them all, Cénzi. I will destroy them as You want me to . . .*

The war-téni were quickly preparing smaller spells. He could see them readying to cast them at the Numetodo and gardai spilling into the Old Temple. The Numetodo were wielding devices like those Varina had carried, and they pointed them at the war-téni. There were loud reports, and puffs of smoke, and the war-téni cried out in the middle of their chants and collapsed to the ground. There was blood soaking their green robes. This was a magic he'd never seen before, a terrible magic.

Cénzi, please . . .

He saw Liana readying her own spell, saw Talbot staggering up with his head bloodied. The man pulled out a strange mechanism much like the one Varina had, and—still on his knees—pointed it toward Liana. Sparks glittered, and there was a loud bang, and smoke curled from the long end of it.

And Liana . . . Liana staggered backward, clutching at herself, and there was a growing dark stain on her tashta between her breasts.

"No!" Nico roared, but his voice was lost in the chaos swirling around him. "No!" He released the Ilmodo wildly, the energy spilling outward without control, sending gardai and Morellis and Numetodo alike tumbling. A wind rushed through the Old Temple, extinguishing the guttering fires and bringing down more of the walls. There were screams and wails, but none were as loud as that which issued from his own throat. "No!"

He was running toward Liana, who had crumpled to the ground, but there were gardai everywhere and hands clutching at him, and they were bearing him down, taking him to the ground even as he fought and kicked and scratched at them. Something hard collided with his head, and the room spun once wildly around him and he could no longer see Liana and the world descended into darkness . . .

~

Brie ca'Ostheim

THE CARRIAGE LURCHED AND JOUNCED and shivered. The ride from Stag Fall to Brezno Palais was nearly as uncomfortable a ride as any Brie had experienced, and the rain and two unhappy children made it no better. Elissa and Kriège were with her; Caelor and Eria were in the following carriage with the nursemaids. A carriage before them carried Paulus and her *domestiques de chambre;* those following held the rest of the staff. Gardai from the Garde Brezno rode on the horses flanking the train, miserable in the weather.

"Matarh, are we there yet?" Elissa grumbled. She stuck

her head out from the nearest window but pulled it back
in quickly, water beading her hair and face. Thunder grumbled at the intrusion. "I want to be there."

"So do I, dear one," Brie told her wearily. "Why don't
you rest, if you can? Look, your brother's asleep. See if you
can sleep like him; that's what a good soldier does—you
sleep whenever there's a chance, because you never know
how long you'll need to stay awake."

Elissa glanced over at the sleeping Kriege, and Brie
knew she was tempted—as Elissa always was when she
thought she was in competition with her brother. But she
scowled. "I'm not sleepy. I just want to be *home*. When
is Vatarh coming back? Why can't I go with him the way
Great-Matarh Allesandra went with Great-Great-Vatarh
Jan?"

"Because your vatarh would send you back, and I was
here to make certain you didn't hide in the supply train like
your great-matarh did, that's why. Here, I brought a deck of
cards; we can play Landsknecht; I'll be dealer, and we can
play for pins . . ."

They played for a time, and despite the lurching of the
carriage, Brie saw Elissa's eyelids growing heavier, until finally her cards dropped from her fingers and spilled over
her lap. Brie picked them up and stored the deck in its box,
setting it under the seat. She leaned her own head back
against the cushions and closed her eyes.

She fell asleep faster than she thought possible, but it
was a sleep haunted by dreams.

*Jan stood in moonlight, arms crossed over his chest. He
was in Nessantico, or at least she believed with dream-cer-
tainty that the city with its strange architecture was Nessantico. Behind Jan was the facade of a huge palais, stained glass
windows cracked and broken, its walls blackened by smoke.
The dream shifted, and Brie realized that there was a woman
with Jan. For a moment she thought it must be Allesandra,
but the hair was dark and when the figure turned slightly she
saw Rhianna's face. The two were close, yet not touching,
but Brie still felt a hot surge of jealousy. Both of them stared
at the palais. There was a blade in Rhianna's hand, and she
drew it back as if to strike . . .*

*. . . But the dream shifted again and she saw her own chil-
dren, but there was another one with them. Strangely, Brie felt*

that all the children were siblings. The new one was a young woman perhaps four or five years older than Elissa, yet Brie couldn't see her face at all no matter how she looked. Jan came into the room, and he went to her and embraced her, kissing first her, then Elissa. "Vatarh!" the woman said . . .

. . . and Brie was holding a baby, looking down into the face of an infant. "Dear little girl," she whispered. "You poor thing . . ." The baby curled its tiny fingers around one of Brie's own and she smiled, but there were shadows in the room, and black smoke and fire, and she clutched the baby to her, trying to run. She thought she could see Jan, and she started toward him, but the fire enveloped him and she heard him scream . . .

"Matarh?"

Brie woke up and realized where she was, the carriage jerking and bouncing over the road. She rubbed at her eyes, dispelling the panic of the nightmare. She realized her heart was racing; she could hear the blood pounding in her temples. Elissa was looking at her; Kriege was still sleeping. "What is it, Elissa?" Brie asked her daughter.

"Why didn't you go with Vatarh?" the girl said.

"Because he asked me to take care of you and your brothers and sister."

Elissa frowned. "I would have gone with him," she said. "I would have helped protect him. I wouldn't have cared what he said."

"Having you there, dear, would only have made your vatarh worry more."

"Did you want to go with him?"

She remembered the argument they'd had. The echo of the nightmare haunted her. "I did," she answered truthfully. "At least part of me still wishes I had, yes."

"Then why didn't you?"

"I would have gone with him . . . I wouldn't have cared what he said . . ." Brie had the nagging sense that Elissa was right. She had made a terrible mistake; she should have insisted. He would need her with Allesandra, if nothing else—the two of them were too much alike, and Brie could nearly see how they would spark against each other. She should be there.

It might be essential that she was there. The premonition seared her, as strongly as if she held her hand in a fire.

Elissa was staring at her.

"Driver, stop!" Brie pounded on the roof of the carriage, waking Kriege, who looked around groggily. The driver pulled up the reins; Brie heard quizzical, worried calls outside, and Paulus came running to the carriage. "Hïrzgin, is there a problem?"

"No, and yes," Brie told him. "I need to have Elissa and Kriege put in one of the other carriages. Take their trunks with them; leave mine on this carriage. I'll be rejoining the Hïrzg and the army. The children and the rest of the staff are to go on to Brezno."

Paulus was shaking his head by the time she was halfway through, and the children were protesting. "Enough!" Brie said to all of them. She gave Elissa and Krieg hugs and a kiss, and pushed them in the direction of Paulus. "Go now!" she told them. "I'll come back when I can. But go now!"

Elissa was smiling.

"Hïrzgin, are you certain . . . ?" Paulus began, but Brie gave him no chance to voice his protest.

"I've already given you my orders," she told him. "Now, take my children and go, or I'll appoint a new aide here and now."

Paulus gulped and bowed his head. "Yes, Hïrzgin," he said. He took Elissa and Kriege's hands, and began shouting orders. Brie laid her head back on her seat and thought of what she would say to Jan when she arrived.

~

Varina ca'Pallo

SHE STARED AT HIM and there were no words she could summon up.

"I'm so sorry, Nico," she said. "So sorry . . ."

He only stared back at her. His hands were bound in chains, his head encased in the metal cage of a silencer. His hair was caked with blood, his face and arms a patchwork of cuts and scratches. In the chill of the cell of the Bastida, he curled against the wall like a broken doll.

I warned you, Nico. I tried to tell you it would end this way . . . She wanted to say the words, but she couldn't. They would only have been further wounds to this already terribly injured man. She sank down to her knees in front of him, on the wet, dirty straw of the Bastida, not caring that she soiled her tashta or that her joints ached with the effort. She reached out to touch his face, as she'd done years ago when he'd been just a child. He turned his head and closed his eyes, and she stopped the gesture just short of him.

"I have nothing to say that can comfort you," she said. "I don't believe in your afterlife or the mercy of your Cénzi, but I've lost people I've loved myself. I've lost Karl, and so I can at least understand a portion of the pain you're feeling." His eyes opened again, though he wasn't looking at her but at the filthy floor of his cell. The place reeked of ancient urine and feces, the foulness contained in the very stones of the cell. She spoke to break the horrible silence as much as anything, because if she didn't speak, she didn't think she could bear to be here. Her breath was a white cloud before her in the dungeon's chill.

"The baby . . ." Liana gasped the words as she died in Varina's arms, as the blood poured from the terrible wound in her chest. *"Take the baby, now. She should be named . . ."* Liana paused, her eyes closing, and Varina thought she was gone, but she took another gurgling breath and opened her eyes again. *". . . Serafina."* Liana's bloody hands clutched at Varina's sleeves. *"Take her. You must . . ."*

And she did. It was the most horrific thing she'd ever done in her life, carving open the woman even as she died, but from the body she lifted a child who squalled and squirmed with life.

"You have a daughter, Nico. Liana . . . There was nothing we could do for her, but we took the child from her as she died. Your child, Nico. Liana told me that she wanted her to be called Serafina. I have her in my house, and she's safe and healthy and beautiful."

Tears were running down Nico's cheeks, leaving clear trails on his filthy skin, and he made a terrible strangled sound as he sobbed.

"I have lost a lover, but that was a long time coming and I had the memory of a long time with Karl. I had time to prepare, to expect the end," she told him. "Still, I really can't imagine what you must be feeling."

He stared at her, choking off the tears and sorrow, his eyes hardening. "And children ... I've never had one, though I sometimes thought of you as my child. I would have taken you as my own, Nico, after those awful days when the Tehuantin came and killed your matarh, but you'd vanished, and when I finally heard your name again, you were already a grown man. I don't know what you went through or what you endured ... I can only imagine what happened to you to turn you into what you've become."

He tried to speak, but all the words were distorted and unintelligible around the silencer. The sound tore at her.

"I made certain that Liana's body was taken care of with respect. The Kraljica ..." Varina paused. Her legs ached and she stood again, afraid that if she didn't she might have to call the garda to help her up. "The Kraljica was having many of the bodies gibbeted and displayed." She saw him recoil visibly at that. "I know, but it's what is always done and I can't entirely blame her; the public anger against the Morellis is strong. But I want you to know that I didn't let that happen to Liana. I had her cleaned and dressed, and paid for the o'téni at the Archigos' Temple to give her the proper service, though they didn't want to do it. I was there when they cremated her in the Ilmodo-fire. I might not believe, but I know it's what she would have wanted. I will do the same for you when the time comes, if I can. But I don't know ..."

She stopped again. She could hear the garda outside the cell door: the creak of his leather armor, the jingle of the keys at his belt, the sound of his breathing. She knew he was listening, and she wondered whether he was amused by her sympathy for Nico. "As for you ... I don't know that I'll be allowed to have your body. You're too famous, Nico. They need to make an example of you, so someone else doesn't do what you did. But if there's anything I can do, I will do it. I tell you this, Nico: I'll make certain that Serafina is safe, too. As long as I'm alive, she will have a home, and I'll make provisions for her on my death. I promise you that much. She'll be safe, and she'll be loved."

She stared down at him, huddled at her feet, his head still averted.

"I hate what you've preached and what you've done in the name of your beliefs," she told him. "I hate the death and injury that have been suffered in your name. I despise what you stand for. But I don't hate *you,* Nico. I will never hate you. I can't. I wanted you to understand that, to know that before … before …"

She stopped. His head had turned, and he looked her once in the eyes before his gaze slid away again. She wasn't certain what she saw there, his expression too distorted by the silencer around his head and the dimness of the cell. This wasn't the Nico she'd met before, not the self-assured Absolute confident in the favor of his god. No, this was a shattered soul, wounded inside as well as outside.

She wondered whether that internal wound might not be as mortal as the one that would eventually kill him. There would be no trial for Nico—he was already judged and condemned. The Faith would insist on having his tongue and hands first, to pay for his disobedience of the Archigos; the state would demand the end of what was left for the death and destruction he'd caused. It would almost certainly all be done publicly, so the citizens could watch and cheer his torment and death. His body would swing in a cage from the Pontica Kralji until there was nothing left but his disconnected bones.

Nico was already dead, even though there was still misery he must endure.

She was crying. The sob pulsed once in her throat, a sound that the stone walls of the Bastida seemed to absorb greedily, as if it were the prison's cold nourishment. She wiped at her face almost angrily. "I wanted to tell you about Liana and Serafina," she said to him. "I hoped it would give you at least some small peace." She wanted him to lift his head again, to look at her and perhaps nod, to give her at least that tiny recognition that he heard her and that he understood.

He did not. The iron chains around his hands rattled dully as he clutched them to his chest.

She called out through the tiny, barred window of the cell door to the garda. "Get me out of here," she said.

~

Niente

THE FLAP OF NIENTE'S TENT WAS THRUST back, and Atl came stalking through. He was holding a brass scrying bowl—a new one, the metal still bright—and it dripped water onto the trampled grass at his feet.

"You lied, Taat," he said. There was as much dismay in his voice as anger. "Axat has let me look at the path you've set us on. I looked at it again and again, and there is no victory for us down that road. None."

"Then you've seen wrongly," Niente told him, even though fear shivered through him. "That is not what Axat has shown me."

"Then take out your bowl now," Atl insisted. "Take it out and let us look together. Prove to me that you're leading the Tecuhtli to where he wishes to go. Prove it, and I'll be silent." Niente could hear desperation in his son's voice, and he rose from the blankets, using his spell-staff to steady him. He went to Atl, who was standing at the tent's entrance like a bronzed statue. Outside, he could hear the army stirring in the early morning, striking the tents to prepare for the day's march. The rain from the day before had ended; the air smelled fresh and clean.

Atl stared down at Niente as he approached. He clasped his son's arm with his free hand, bringing him close. He could feel the young man resisting, then yielding to the embrace. "Atl," he said quietly, finally releasing him and taking a step back. "I ask you to trust me: as your Taat, as your Nahual. Trust that I would not lead the Tehuantin to death. Trust that I want what you want: I want our people to prosper and to be safe. I love you; I love your brothers and sister, your mother. I love Tlaxcala and the lands of our home. I would not see those I love hurt or the land I know so well destroyed. Why would I want that? Why would I do that to you and to the Tehuantin?"

Atl was shaking his head. "I don't know, Taat. It makes

no sense to me either." He lifted the bowl in his hand, and his voice was full of anguish and confusion. "But I know what I've seen. It was as clear as if I saw it happening before me. I had to tell the Tecuhtli what I saw. I had to, because you wouldn't listen to me, and Axat was showing me what you insisted wasn't true."

"I know," Niente told him, nodding. "You only did as I would have done in your place. I'm not angry with you."

"I don't *care* if you're angry or not, Taat. You keep telling me that I'm not seeing correctly, but I know I have the far-sight. I know it."

"You do," Niente told him. "Though that makes me more sad than pleased. It's a terrible gift to have, Atl. You don't believe that now, but in time you will."

"Yes, yes," Atl waved the bowl between them. " 'Look at what it did to me,' You keep saying that, but you had years before it disfigured you so badly. I remember, Taat. I remember what you looked like when I was young. I know the pain of it; I've already felt it, and I can bear it. If you're going to insist that I'm not seeing correctly, then *show me!*" The final words were nearly a shout through clenched teeth. He closed his eyes, opened them, and his voice was a soft plea. "Damn it, Taat, show me. Please . . ."

He had seen this moment in the scrying bowl. He had seen his son's fury, his disbelief. He had heard the accusations flung at him, had seen Atl rushing to Tecuhtli Citlali and telling him all—and he had seen where that path led. Yet the other path, the other choice he could make here, was far less clear, clouded with blood and the haze on the long sight, and he could only hope that somewhere in the mist was the Long Path he wanted.

There is no certainty to the future. There is only Possibility. It was what old Mahri had told Niente when he'd first begun to use Axat's gift, before Tecuhtli Necalli had sent Mahri to Nessantico. Then, Niente had been much like Atl, scoffing at Mahri's warnings, not quite believing the older man. He was young, he was invincible, he knew better than those who had come before him, who were timid and frail.

After all, Tecuhtli Necalli had raised Niente to the title of Nahual after he'd sent Mahri away—but only after forcing him to confront the nahualli who currently held that title: Ohtli, whom Niente had killed.

Tecuhtli Citlali, who had in turn killed Tecuhtli Zolin in challenge, would likely do the same with the next Nahual: force challenge on Niente. He had seen that in visions, also, and he was afraid that he knew the mist-clothed person who stood over his broken body. He was terrified to see that face, and he would turn his eyes from the scrying bowl before the mists cleared.

"Get your bowl, Taat," Atl said again, "or use mine, but let's do this together. Show me what you say I fail to see. Prove it to me."

"No," Niente said. It was the only answer he could give.

"No? By the seven mountains, Taat, is that the only answer you can give me? 'No'—just that single word?"

"I've given you my answer. Be content with it." He turned and started to pack his things for the day's march.

"Is that my Taat's answer, or is that the Nahual's answer?" Atl looked deliberately at the golden band on Niente's forearm.

"It is both."

"It's not sufficient. I'm sorry, Taat. It's not. Don't do this. I beg you."

"It's time for us to break camp," Niente answered, not looking at him. He couldn't—if he did, he'd be lost. "Go, and prepare yourself."

"Taat—"

Niente was holding his own scrying bowl. His hands were trembling around the incised rim, the animals carved there seeming to move of their own accord. He thrust the bowl into his bag. "Go," he repeated.

He could feel Atl staring at him, could feel the anger rising in him. "Why are you forcing this on me?"

"I'm not forcing anything on you, Atl." He turned, finally. He wanted to weep at the look on his son's face. "You must make your own choices. All I'm asking is that you believe in me as you once did."

"I want to do that, Taat. I want that more than anything. And all I'm asking is that you show me that I should. I want to learn from you. I want that more than anything. Teach me."

"I have," Niente told him. "And if I've taught you well, then you know to obey me."

Atl's face changed then. It went stern and closed, as if

Niente were staring at a stranger. "There are other authorities I have to obey, Taat," he said. "I'll ask only once more. Take out your bowl. Show me."

Niente only shook his head. Atl's face went to stone. His hands tightened around his own bowl. "Then you leave me no choice, Taat. I'm sorry, but I can't let you take us down to defeat. I can't let the deaths of thousands of good warriors be on your head, and on mine because of my silence. I can't . . ."

With that, Atl turned. "Atl, wait!" Niente called after him, but he was already through the flap of the tent and gone. "Atl . . ."

Niente sagged to the ground. He prayed to Axat to take him now, to end his stay here and carry him up to the star-heavens. But that was nothing he had ever seen in the bowl, and Axat remained silent.

PRETENSIONS

Rochelle Botelli
Niente
Varina ca'Pallo
Sergei ca'Rudka
Nico Morel
Jan ca'Ostheim
Allesandra ca'Vörl
Brie ca'Ostheim
Niente

Rochelle Botelli

SHE STARTED AT THE BEGINNING. "Rochelle is what my matarh called me. Rochelle was also the name of the first woman my matarh ever killed. I didn't realize that for a long time, didn't realize I'd been named after the first female voice to ever haunt her."

The tale had come far easier than she'd thought it would. Perhaps it was because Sergei listened so well and intently, leaning forward eagerly to hear her words; perhaps it was because she found that it was something she'd wanted to share with someone, all unknowingly, for a long time. Whichever it was, the long story came tumbling out, with Sergei prodding her occasionally with questions: "Your matarh was the White Stone? The same?" or "Nico Morel? You say the boy was your *brother*?" or "You're Jan's daughter . . . ?"

The first half of the tale took the rest of the day, as she told him about her apprenticeship with her matarh, about the White Stone's madness and eventual death in raving insanity, and how she herself had taken up of the mantle of the White Stone—though given Sergei's position, she didn't mention the promise that Matarh had extracted from her on her deathbed.

Once the carriage had stopped at Passe a'Fiume, Sergei hadn't pressed her for more. He told the staff at the Kraljica's apartments to prepare a meal for two and a separate room for her, and had sent the servants out for a new tashta, cosmetics, and some jewelry for her, saying that they'd lost her luggage during the storm. She stared

at herself in the mirror afterward, nearly not recognizing
herself. She wondered what payment Sergei might demand,
and made certain that her vatarh's dagger was accessible
under the tashta.

The town's Comté joined them for dinner; Sergei intro-
duced Rochelle as "Remy, my great-niece from Graubundi,"
traveling with him to Nessantico; she felt him watching her
as she followed his lead, making up tales of their relatives.
He seemed mostly amused by her efforts and the polite
responses by the Comté and his family. The talk around the
table was mostly of old politics and the coming passage of
Jan's army through the town, as the servants served them
dinner in the dining room and various personages of dis-
tinction paraded through to give their greetings. After the
Comté and the last of the dignitaries of the city had left,
Sergei had pleaded exhaustion and a desire to retire for
the evening.

That, she discovered, was a lie. Rochelle heard the
door of his room open not long after; she'd slid Jan's dagger from its scabbard then, ready to defend herself if he
came into her room, but she heard his cane and footsteps
recede down the hall; not long after, she heard the groan of
the main doors on the floor below. From her window, she
watched him go out along the dark streets of the town.

She locked the door to her room anyway.

She didn't know when he returned. She woke in the
morning to the horns of First Call and the knock of one
of the servants. She dressed, and found Sergei already at
breakfast. A half-turn of the glass later, they were back in
the privacy of the carriage, and he asked her to resume her
tale. She did, beginnings with her wanderings from the site
of her matarh's grave, her first tentative contracts as the
new White Stone, and how she felt when she heard the tales
of the White Stone beginning to arise again, and her wanderings through the Coalition.

There were details she still kept to herself, certainly.
Yet . . . This was catharsis, releasing the story. Once she
started, she didn't think she could have stopped. She hadn't
realized the strain of holding it all in. She'd thought that
perhaps one day she might have been able to tell a trusted
lover, but with Sergei . . . He was a stranger, and yet she
could tell him.

She wondered if that was because—if she decided it would be necessary—she could keep it all *still* a secret, wrapped in the silence of a dead man. She kept her hand close to the hilt of Jan's dagger, and she watched the Silvernose's face carefully.

By the time they were approaching Nessantico's walls, she was telling him of the final confrontation with Jan, though she left unsaid the details of how physical it had become. He seemed to understand, his face sympathetic and almost sad as he listened.

"Poor Jan . . ." he'd said, and his empathy for her vatarh irritated Rochelle. "I came to Firenzcia not long after Fynn's assassination, and there were already whispers about this Elissa whom the new Hïrzg had loved, and who had vanished. I don't think he's ever entirely stopped loving her—or at least loving the person he thought she was. I heard the gossip that perhaps she was the White Stone, then when Jan saw her again in Nessantico, that became certain." He stopped, clamping his mouth shut as if to hold back more that he might have said, the folds under his chin waggling with the movement. She wondered whether what he had decided not to tell her was how Kraljica Allesandra, Rochelle's great-matarh, had been the one who had hired Matarh to kill Fynn. She wondered whether he realized that she must know that as well.

If so, neither of them mentioned it.

"So now *you've* come to Nessantico," Sergei said. His rheum-filled eyes held her own, close enough that she could see her warped reflection crawl over his nostrils. "The White Stone's daughter. Jan's daughter, and the great-daughter of the Kraljica, too. Nico Morel's sister. I have to ask *why* you've come."

"Everyone comes to Nessantico eventually."

He seemed to chuckle inwardly. "Once, you might have been able to get away with that answer, Rochelle. Not now. Not with the Coalition as her great rival. Not with the Tehuantin pressing on her borders once again. Not with your brother's people making their violent presence known here. You're being disingenuous, Rochelle, and it doesn't become you." He stared; Rochelle's fingertips brushed the smooth, worn hilt of Jan's dagger. *Will you have to kill him now? Can you let him walk away knowing what he knows?*

"I don't know why I've come," she answered, "and that's only the truth, Sergei. I couldn't stay where I was and I didn't know where else to go, and I just started walking. Nessantico seemed to be calling to me."

"Calling for *what*," he persisted. "Revenge? A reunion?"

"Neither," she said. *Yes, revenge* . . . She could almost hear her matarh's voice whispering that inside. "I didn't know for certain that Nico was here. I swear that by Cénzi."

"Ah, a murderer swearing by Cénzi. How ironic. Your brother might appreciate that. If he's still alive."

That sentence sent a winter breeze swirling down her back, causing the newly-chopped hairs at the back of her neck to rise. "What?"

She couldn't tell if he shrugged or only adjusted himself on the bench seat of the carriage. "You left the encampment before the news came," Sergei said. "Your brother and his followers assaulted the Old Temple in Nessantico. They took it over and barricaded themselves inside. By now, Kraljica Allesandra will have ordered the attack on them; they wouldn't have been able to hold out there. I would suspect that Nico Morel is either dead or in the Bastida by now. I'm sorry; I see that worries you, but I'm sorry—I've no sympathy for him, I'm afraid."

She *was* stunned. She sat back in her seat across from him. Nico dead? No, she hadn't seen him or talked to him for years, but she could still see him as a young man, just leaving to become an acolyte in the Faith, Matarh clinging to him as he lifted a bag in his hand with the few possessions he had, the carriage driver calling out impatiently. She'd glimpsed him once or twice since then; Matarh had taken her to see his induction as téni, but then he'd been sent to Brezno, and the visits stopped. They'd heard the tales of his rise and sudden fall within the ranks of téni; when Matarh had died, he hadn't come, even though Rochelle had expected him. She wondered if he would even recognize her. She wondered if he would care; she wondered if he would condemn her for what she'd done and what she'd become.

"I wasn't here for him," she said. "I didn't know . . ."

"Then why *are* you here? You still haven't answered me."

Outside, she saw houses and other carriages on the road with them, as well as people on horses or walking toward or from the city—leaning out, she could see the gates of the city just ahead. "Stop the carriage," she said. "I'd like to get out here."

Sergei stared for another moment, then he tapped on the roof of the carriage twice; the driver pulled on the reins, calling to the horses and moving them to the side of the road. "Do you kill me now?" Sergei asked. "You're thinking that you could probably get away with it—easy enough to get lost in the crowds here before the driver raised the alarm."

He knows what you're thinking . . . And that, Rochelle realized, meant that he probably had anticipated the act and had a plan to counter it. His hand was on the knob of his cane. Still, he was too old and slow to stop her. "Don't," Sergei told her. His voice almost sounded amused. "I'm not a threat to you, Rochelle. Not at this moment, anyway—though if you become a threat to Nessantico, then we'll be meeting again. We're very much alike, you and I—did you know that? I know you, better than you would believe. The difference is that you're still young. You have a chance to escape becoming me, or becoming like your matarh: a madwoman haunted by the deaths she's caused and too enamored of death to give it up. You just have to stop. Stop being the White Stone—because if you don't, soon you won't *want* to stop. You won't be *able* to stop. Listen to me—I know what I'm speaking of. You don't want that, Rochelle. You truly don't."

He was still holding the cane, still watching her. She saw his gaze fasten on her right hand under her tashta, on the hidden knife.

A quick upward slash. It would come before he could even move, and the blood would be spilling from him even as I leap from the carriage. He'd be dead by my first step . . .

She was breathing hard. *But there'd be no time to use the stone.* The voice might have been her matarh. *You'll be in his eyes, caught there forever at the moment of his death. His eyes will betray you* . . .

The noise of the city was loud in the carriage. "Ambassador?" the driver called down through the closed curtain.

Stop being the White Stone . . .

"Well, Rochelle?" Sergei asked her. "What is it to be?"

A few breaths later, she descended from the carriage. She

looked up at the driver. "The Ambassador says to go on," she told him. He slapped the reins, and the carriage started forward again, slipping into the stream of traffic heading toward the gate. She watched it until it had passed the half-tumbled stone arches, then she slipped into the crowds herself.

~

Niente

THE TECUHTLI CALLED A HALT TO THE march at midday; almost immediately afterward, one of the warriors came panting up to Niente, telling him that Citlali required his presence. His stomach churning with unease, Niente followed the man to where most of the High Warriors were gathered in a wide circle. They parted to let him pass through; in the center, Tecuhtli Citlali was seated, with the High Warrior Tototl, as usual, at his right side. Atl was standing at his left hand, stern and unsmiling as Niente entered the open space.

The burning in Niente's stomach increased.

"Your son tells me disturbing things, Nahual Niente," Citlali said without preamble. "He says that your path leads to defeat, not victory. He says that he sees another way, and he tells me that we must take it now before it is too late."

Split the army in three arms, one of which must go back toward Villembouchure and cross the river. Come to the city from west, north, and south, and come at a fast march, so that you reach the city before the other army can reach it . . . He had seen that vision himself. He'd seen the warriors push howling into the streets, the city's defenses too stretched to offer resistance. The city would fall, in a single, bloody day.

"My son is wrong," Niente said. He could not look at Atl's face. "I've already told the Tecuhtli this."

"You have," Citlali answered. "And I've listened to you, and to Atl. I find it rather compelling that a son who has always loved, respected, and obeyed his Taat feels so strongly that he would go against him: not only as a Taat, but as Nahual."

"Atl believes what he has seen in the bowl, and he does have Axat's gift," Niente answered. "But he doesn't yet have the skill to interpret what he sees in the mists, nor to see far enough through them. What he doesn't realize is that one day's victory may lead to the next day's defeat."

"Hmm . . ." Citlali's fingers stroked his chin as if he were petting a cat. "Or an old man could be so weakened by years of using his gift that he's no longer strong enough to see well, and instead sees only what he wants to see."

"Don't mistake physical weakness for something else, Tecuhtli," Niente said. "I am still stronger in the ways of the X'in Ka than any of the other nahualli." Now he did look at Atl, almost in apology. "And that includes my own son."

In his visions, Axat had granted him only momentary glimpses of this moment—or perhaps that had been his own fears influencing the direction of his far-sight. Whichever, Axat had never let him see it fully. In the original vision he'd had, back in Tlaxcala, this moment had not been on the paths of the future at all. Yet the twisted snarl of possibilities had led him here, despite his attempts to evade it. It was yet another reminder that the future was malleable and changeable, and that there were other influences than Axat's at work.

Mahri and Talis had learned that, to their doom. Perhaps it was now Niente's own turn to be given the lesson.

Citlali was smiling, an expression that Niente had never liked in the man's face, since what amused the Tecuhtli was often unpleasant for others. Tototl was watching also, though the High Warrior's face was stoic—whatever he was thinking, it was hidden from Niente. "Perhaps we should let Axat decide, then," the Tecuhtli said. "You should demonstrate your strength for me, if you're to remain Nahual. And if not . . ." Citlali shrugged then, broadly, the tattoos on his body moving like painted shadows. ". . . then perhaps Atl will be the Nahual."

Niente saw his son's eyes widen as he realized the implication of what Citlali had just said. "Tecuhtli, this is not why I came to you." He glanced toward Niente, shaking his head.

"Perhaps, but it's what I'm asking of you. You've your spell-staff, and Niente has his. Let us see who is stronger. Let us see who Axat wishes to be Nahual—now, while there's still time."

Atl looked over at Niente desperately again. "I can't. Taat, this isn't—"

"You've no choice now," Citlali answered, and his voice was firm but not unkind. "That's the way of things: the weak fall to the stronger, as Necalli fell to Zolin, and when Zolin fell, the red eagle came to me." He touched his skull, where the blood-hued bird was inked. Tototl glanced at it as well. "As one day, I will fall. Or are you telling me that Nahual Niente is correct, and that you've not seen correctly?"

Atl was shaking his head, and Niente saw him caught, snared like a rabbit between truth and his love for Niente. "Taat," he said, "I ask you, for our love, for the good of all the warriors here, to give up the golden band and your bowl."

Niente could feel himself standing at a crossroads. Even without the scrying bowl, the air around him seemed to be filled with the emerald mist of Axat, waiting for him to choose. There: he could lay down the bowl, take off the armband, and simply become Niente who had once been a nahualli, letting Atl come into his legacy. Or he could refuse . . . And down that road there was only mist and confusion and uncertainty. He wasn't certain he had either the strength or the will to defeat Atl, not when it would almost certainly mean the death of one or the other of them.

Yet it had come to this. There were no other paths open. *Axat, why have you given me this burden? Xaria, could you ever forgive me for this, for killing our son?*

"Niente?" Citlali said. "Atl awaits your answer, as do I." *In the mists, his son standing in his way, barring the entrance to the path . . .*

Strangely, there were no tears, even though the sorrow seemed to press on his shoulders as if he bore the Teocalli Axat itself there. His spine bowed under the weight. He could barely lift his head, and his voice was as faint as the voice of the stars.

There is no certainty that you can succeed now, even if you sacrifice Atl. The path has grown faint and difficult to find. It could all be wasted . . .

"I am Nahual," Niente said. "I see the way." He looked at his son, wondering if Atl could see the bleak despair in his face. "I'm sorry, Atl."

Atl looked away, as if there might be an answer written in the clouds above them.

"Then tonight, under Axat's gaze, the two of you will settle this, so that I can make my decision as Tecuhtli," Citlali declared. He rose from his nest of cushions. Tototl and the other High Warriors snapped to attention. "Go, and prepare yourselves," Citlali told them.

"Taat, I don't want this."

"Then you should have considered what going to Tecuhtli Citlali a second time would mean," Niente told Atl. "Didn't you see *that* in the scrying bowl?" It was difficult to keep the concern and irritation from his voice.

The sun was setting in the west behind the army, sending golden shafts of light down on the encampment. The warmth was a mockery. Niente sat cross-legged in front of his tent, his spell-staff laid across his lap. The warriors pretended to ignore the two; the other nahualli had vanished; he'd seen none of them since the sun had started to fall. They would be waiting to see how this ended, and where it might leave them.

The moon would rise soon. Axat's Eye.

"I'm not mistaken about what I saw, Taat," Atl insisted. "The signs and portents were terrible for the path you've set us on. I saw the banner of the red eagle trampled on the ground. I saw hundreds of dead warriors. I saw you, Taat; I saw you dead as well." He was shaking his head, his nostrils flaring with emotion. "I *saw* it. There was no mistake. What Axat showed me couldn't have been victory."

"And down *your* path?" Niente asked.

"That way has become clouded," he admitted, "and it has become more uncertain each day we move forward. But the first time, I saw it clearly: with the army split, with speed, we reached the great city before an army coming from the east could help them. I saw our banners above their towers."

Niente nodded. *Yes, he does see true* . . . "And afterward," he asked his son. "What did you see beyond that? What did you see when that eastern army came to Nessantico?"

Atl shook his head. "The mists were confusing there. I saw many possibilities, and many shadows. But I'm certain at least some of them would lead to victory as well."

They do, some of them, though nearly all are still grim and deadly for us. Yet the path I saw . . . Niente sighed. "Atl, my son, my beloved . . ." He took a long breath. "You have seen truly."

Atl took a step back, his hand slicing air. "You admit that? Then you'll give up the band of the Nahual and the bowl? We can go to Tecuhtli Citlali and tell him that we've reached agreement?"

"No," Niente answered. "Not yet, anyway. You see correctly but you don't see far enough. No, listen to me and be silent—this is something I will say only to you and I'll deny having said it if you repeat it. You're right, Atl. The path I've put us on will probably not lead to victory in Nessantico."

Atl blinked, stunned. His mouth hung open like a fish gasping for air. "I . . . I don't understand. How . . . If that's true, why . . . why would you give theTecuhtli this advice?"

"Because Axat has let me see further. Atl, if we *were* to take Nessantico, then the full fury of the Easterners will fall on us. It won't be enough for them to crush us here— they will pursue us back to our homes in the west, and they won't rest until Tlaxcala lies as tumbled stones in Lake Ixtapatl, a mirror of Nessantico. There is no peace in that future, there is only death and more death, ruin and more ruin. A temporary victory is no victory at all, Atl."

"So you would have us defeated—because in the mists you believe you see more war?" Atl scowled. "That makes no sense. I *know* Axat's visions, Taat, and I know that the further you go from now, the more paths there are and it becomes less clear where they lead. How do you know that *you* have seen correctly? There *must* be other ways. This dire future of yours can't be the only outcome."

"No. There are worse . . . And there may be better, yes, but the way to them is dark to me. What I have seen is the most likely outcome."

"So you say. I say it's your own despair that is coloring the visions. You've told me yourself, Taat—you've said that the far-seer's mood can shape Axat's vision. This is what's happened to you."

"I've seen what happens if we *fall* here, Atl. If we fall, then I've seen West and East eventually reconcile. I've seen ships going back and forth between our lands with goods. I've seen a generation of peace."

"Peace forever?" Atl scoffed. "There's no such thing, Taat. Never has been, never will. How do you know that this lovely future of yours doesn't just lead to an even greater war and even more death for the Tehuantin? You don't—I see it in your face. You could be sacrificing all our warriors and nahualli here for nothing. Don't you see that?"

Niente wanted to shake his head. He wanted to rage and deny what Atl had said. Back in Tlaxcala the vision had been so clear, so certain, so definite. But now . . . He hadn't seen it so clearly since they'd left their own land, and what he saw now was wrapped in doubt and uncertainty, with only tantalizing, mocking glimpses of the future he'd seen. Now, he found he wasn't so certain.

Can you do this? Are you willing to kill Atl for a possibility?

Only the tip of the sun was visible over the trees on the horizon. The sky in the east was already purple, with the evening star that was the gate to the afterlife already visible. The eye of Axat would be peering over the rim of the world soon.

"Go, and prepare yourself," he told Atl. "There isn't much time."

All the hope in Atl's face collapsed. He clamped his lips together and nodded, then turned on the balls of his toes and strode away. Niente watched him go. When he could no longer see Atl, he reached into his pouch and pulled out his scrying bowl.

He knew that the lesser nahualli would be watching. "Bring me clean water," he called out loudly into the evening. "Quickly!"

~

Varina ca'Pallo

SHE WASN'T CERTAIN WHY SHE DID THIS. She only knew that she couldn't live with herself if she didn't. "I know Nico deserves death for what he's done," she told Allesandra. She glanced quickly at Erik ca'Vikej, seated in a chair just behind the Kraljica; she didn't like the man's presence, but Allesandra had made no move to ask him to leave. Varina was seated herself, with an untouched

plate of pastries and a steaming cup on the table next to
her. "But I'm asking that you spare him. I ask it for our
friendship, Allesandra."

Allesandra was pacing, not looking at Varina. She
passed in front of the fireplace, glancing up at the portrait
of Kraljica Marguerite that was placed there, then going to
the balcony. Varina could see the vista outside. The dome
of the Old Temple rose above the intervening buildings on
the Isle a'Kralji, and she could see the streaks of soot from
the fires still marring the gilded curves. It would be months,
perhaps a year or more, before the Old Temple could be restored and the damage to it repaired. But the memories . . .
Those could never be erased.

"I don't understand," Allesandra said. "Morel has condemned himself. He knew the consequences of his actions
and he went ahead with them. There were hands upon
hands of people killed, Varina. We lost A'Téni ca'Paim, and
Commandant cu'Ingres has been gravely injured. You were
nearly killed yourself."

"And so were the Kraljica and I," ca'Vikej interjected.
When Allesandra turned—with what Varina thought was
an odd glare—he shrugged. "It's only the truth," he said.

"In any case, there's not only my judgment involved, but
that of the Faith," Allesandra continued. Her gaze stayed
on ca'Vikej for several moment before returning to her
contemplation of the scene outside the balcony. "They will
insist on his hands and tongue for using the Ilmodo, and his
life for A'Téni ca'Paim. The citizens of Nessantico will also
insist on his life for the lives of our own that he's killed."

"Many of those same citizens supported him when he
talked about the Faith, when he said that the Faith should
be less about accumulating wealth to itself and more about
helping its people, when he said that the téni should pay
more attention to the Toustour and less to their purses."

Allesandra's lips twisted in a wry smile. "And those same
citizens also cheered when he talked about how the Faith
shouldn't tolerate heretics, or are you forgetting that?"

Varina shook her head. "No, I'm not. It's just . . . I don't
want to give up on Nico. He's been gifted with a great
power, and I hate to see that wasted."

"He's not the sweet child you remember, Varina. He's
using that great power against you. And me."

"I know that. But I also want to believe that he's not the person he should have become. Given the right—or wrong—circumstances, any of us could end up the way he has. And his abilities . . ." Varina shook her head slowly. "I've never, *never*, seen someone do what he's doing. It's as if he just reaches into the Second World with his mind and pulls out the power, without any spell at all. If nothing else, that's worthy of study." Varina lifted the cup of tea at her side from the saucer, then set it down again without taking a sip. The sound of porcelain on porcelain was loud in the room. "I'm not asking you to release him. He deserves punishment. I'm asking that you don't kill him."

Ca'Vikej snorted. "The bastardo might prefer a quick death to a life in the Bastida. Cénzi knows I would."

"Erik, please!" Allesandra snapped, and ca'Vikej's eyes narrowed, his mouth closing. He pushed himself up from the chair and gave Allesandra a mockingly low bow, as if he were a petitioner before her.

"I should go," he said. "I have a meeting with the Ambassador from Namarro in a turn." As he passed Varina, he leaned down and whispered: "If you want, I can make certain he dies quickly. Believe me, that would be a blessing." He smiled at Varina and patted her shoulder as if she were an old friend as he left.

"Sometimes, I'm not sure what it was that I saw in him," Allesandra said after he left. "Was it ever that way with you and Karl?"

"With Karl, the problem was getting him to see me in the first place," Varina told her. "But no, I never had second thoughts about him. I knew he was the one."

"I envy you that, then. I've never had that luxury. Well, only once, when I was very young . . ." She seemed to drift off into reverie for a moment, then Varina saw her shiver as if a cold breeze had touched her. "I'm told by the gardai that the Numetodo were critical to the success of the assault. I'm also told by Talbot that you used some . . . interesting devices—weapons that used black sand and yet could be carried in one's hand. They were very effective against the war-téni, he said. You called them 'sparkwheels,' I believe he said."

That brought back the memory of Liana: of the young woman falling backward after Talbot shot her with his

sparkwheel, of the terrible hole gouged in her chest and
the gurgling rattle of her last breaths, of Nico's scream at
seeing her fall and the madness and inconsolable grief that
took him then, of the young woman dying in Varina's arms
as Varina and a healer cut her child from her womb. They
were images that Varina desperately wanted to wipe from
her memory, like chalk from a board. But they could not
be erased, would not be erased. She was afraid they would
haunt her for the rest of her life.

She would also remember pulling the trigger of her own
sparkwheel with Nico's body right there in front of her,
and the misfire of the weapon. *You were willing to kill him
yourself...*

"Talbot tells me that you developed the weapon,"
Allesandra was saying. "Is this what you've been hiding
yourself away working on since Karl passed?"

Varina nodded; it was all she could muster.

"I have a proposal for you," Allesandra said. She was
looking out toward the Old Temple again. "You want Nico
left alive. I think that's foolish, but I'm willing to grant you
that wish—at least temporarily—if you'll give the Holdings
the secret of this sparkwheel."

She was looking directly at Varina now, with the question written on her face. Varina couldn't hold her gaze for
long; she looked away, toward the painting of Marguerite.
"Allesandra . . ." She began, but couldn't continue. How
could she tell her how frightened and guilt-ridden that
made her feel, how the future she imagined—a world
where the formula for black sand was common knowledge,
where anyone could construct a sparkwheel—would be
like. She had no illusions that someone wouldn't improve
upon the black sand formula: make it more powerful, more
deadly. She had no doubt that some skilled artisan would
be able—like Pierre Gabrelli—to take her design and perfect it; make a better and more effective weapon.

She could imagine that world. She wasn't certain she
wanted to live in it.

*You won't. How much longer will you live, even if you
survive the coming siege by the Tehuantin? Five years? Ten?
You won't see the world you create.*

But it would be hers, nonetheless. Her name, and the
name of the Numetodo would be attached to it.

"I know what you're thinking," Allesandra said. "What would Karl have told you, Varina?"

"You can't stop knowledge: it wants to be born, and it will force its way into the world no matter what you do." She heard his voice in her ear, as clearly as if he were standing alongside her. She gasped, an intake of breath that was almost a sob. "I'm afraid of what we would be unleashing, Allesandra. You're a believer in Cénzi, but this . . . This would shake the foundations of the Faith. This would say to the world that magic is less important and less effective than simple knowledge. We Numetodo already defy the Faith—we refute the idea that magic must be confined only to the Faithful, that it comes from Cénzi. This would go further, Allesandra. I'm afraid . . ." She shook her head. "But Karl would say that once the duck is cooked it can't ever be uncooked, so you might as well eat it."

"Then tell us how to make your sparkwheels, and I'll set the smithies and artisans of the city to work. It may be our only hope."

She was still shaking her head, still haunted by the vision of the world she might be creating. They both heard Talbot's knock on the door of the chamber, and the aide opened the door. He inclined his head to Varina before addressing Allesandra. "Kraljica, Ambassador Sergei is in the palais; he's just come from Firenzcia."

"Send him up," Allesandra told him, and Talbot bowed and shut the door again. Varina started to rise, and Allesandra gestured to her to stay. "No," she said. "We both have things to tell him."

There was a new knock on the door, and Talbot announced Sergei, who hobbled into the room with his cane. He looked more tired than Varina remembered, as if he hadn't slept well.

"Sergei," Allesandra said. "You're back quickly. Did you have a good trip?" Allesandra's voice had a strange tremor to it that jerked Varina's head around.

"I had an *interesting* trip, in many ways," he answered, but under the metal nose, he was smiling as he lifted a scroll from his diplomatic pouch and handed it to Allesandra. "Your treaty, Kraljica," he said. "Signed. Hïrzg Jan is on his way with the Firenzcian army."

Varina saw mingled relief and concern war in Allesan-

dra's face, as if the news simultaneously cheered and sad-
dened her. She wondered at that. "Excellent," Allesandra
said, but the enthusiasm for the word was missing from her
voice.

"I saw Vajiki ca'Vikej in the hall as I was coming up, and
he asked about it," Sergei said, almost too offhandedly. "I
told him that I didn't report to him, but to you. He didn't
look happy at the answer." Then he glanced at Varina. "Varina, I understand that the Numetodo were instrumental in
removing Nico Morel and his people from the Old Temple.
I'm glad to see that you're unhurt. Is it true that you have
Nico's child?"

Varina nodded. *Holding her . . . Looking into her innocent, trusting face and seeing Nico's face there as well . . .
Watching the wet nurse she'd employed feeding her . . .* "A
daughter," she said. "Her name is Serafina."

Sergei nodded, staring at her strangely. "Good. I'm glad
she's in your hands. And I'm sorry, also—I know how this
must make you feel. I promise you that I'll talk to Capitaine ce'Denis and make certain that when the time comes,
Nico's death is quick. If the Faith wants his hands and
tongue, they can take them afterward."

Varina shuddered at the image, though there was nothing but empathy in Sergei's eyes. "There may not *be* a
death," Allesandra said before Varina could compose an
answer. "If the Numetodo cooperate."

"Ah?" The white wings of Sergei's eyebrows lifted. He
glanced again at Varina. "Cooperate how?"

"Varina's developed a black sand device, a mechanism—
something anyone can operate with no magic required, and
yet it's devastating. Several of the Morellis and war-téni
were killed with them during the assault. I believe it could
literally change the way of warfare."

So she understands that as well as do I . . . Varina shifted
uncomfortably in her chair. If Allesandra glimpsed the
same future that Varina saw, then it didn't seem to trouble
her. "I haven't yet agreed," she reminded Allesandra. "I
have to think about this."

Allesandra left the balcony window to crouch down in
front of Varina, almost like a supplicant. She took Varina's
hands in her own. "Varina," she said, her eyes not allowing Varina to look away, "there isn't *time* to think. There

isn't time to hesitate at all. The Westlanders will be here in a few days. It's good that Jan is bringing his army, but that still might not be enough—not given what the Tehuantin did at Karnmor and at Villembouchure. Commandant ca'Talin says there are four or five times the numbers who came here last time. The longer we wait, the fewer of your sparkwheels we can make and the less time we have to train people to use them. You *can't* think on this. You need to give me an answer—because it's not just Nico's life that is at stake here, but that of everyone in this city, yourself included."

"I don't care about my life," Varina answered. "Not anymore. Not since Karl died."

"Don't say that," Allesandra answered, squeezing her hands. "I won't listen to talk like that. And you don't mean it either. You have the child to think about now."

Varina tried to smile back at Allesandra. She felt exhausted, and sore from the exertions of the assault. Sergei knelt down alongside Allesandra, groaning with the effort. "Listen to the Kraljica," he said to her. "She's saying what we both feel—and Talbot and the rest of the Numetodo as well."

Varina sighed. She closed her eyes. Outside, she could hear birds twittering in the garden of the palais and the faint clamor of people out on the Avi. Quiet sounds. The sounds of peace. Allesandra's hands were warm on hers, which felt like cold stone on her lap.

Dead things. Broken things.

"All right," she told them. "Tell Talbot to come to my laboratory this evening. I'll give him the plans and formulae."

Sergei ca'Rudka

CAPITAINE ARI CE'DENIS LOOKED WEARY, as if he hadn't slept well for a few days. That was probably true, since the Bastida's cells were stuffed as they had rarely been: with the rebellious war-téni, with the Morellis

who had survived the assault on the Old Temple. And there
was their prized prisoner: Nico Morel.

"I've good news for you, Ari. I'm told that those war-
téni who ask forgiveness and recant all Morelli views will
be released," Sergei told ce'Denis. The Capitaine did not
look at the roll of stained leather that Sergei had set down
alongside the chair in which he sat. He didn't look at Sergei
at all; it seemed that the papers on his desk were far more
interesting. He picked them up, shuffled them, and set them
down again as he listened to Sergei. "Archigos Karrol has
already sent a message to that effect, and the Archigos
himself should be here in a few days. If the war-téni agree
to fight with the army, he'll send them to the front line and
let Cénzi decide whether to allow them to live or not."

Ce'Denis nodded. "And the Morellis? What of their
disposition?"

"Those who were téni but not war-téni will be judged
individually by a Concord of Peers, which Archigos Karrol
intends to convene on arrival. Those who were not téni will
go through the usual judicial procedures and be brought
before the Council of Ca' for their judgment."

"And Nico Morel?"

Sergei smiled. "He is a special case, and he will be han-
dled as such. The Kraljica has placed him entirely under my
jurisdiction."

The Capitaine did glance at the leather roll then, a look
that seemed equal parts disgust and fascination. "I take it
that you're here to *talk* with the prisoner." There was just
the slightest hesitation and stress to the word "talk," as if
another term had first intruded into ce'Denis' mind.

"I am," Sergei told him. "The Kraljica has determined
that there will be no execution of Morel, and she will be
refusing to hand him over to the Concénzia Faith. He is . . ."
A smile. "Mine."

The Capitaine's eyebrows lifted at that, but he said
nothing: a good soldier. "Morel is in the Kralji's Cell of the
main tower," he told Sergei. "You know the way."

Sergei smiled again. "I do, indeed. And I'll leave you
to your duties, Ari. We should have lunch together one of
these days—after the current crisis has passed, perhaps."

Ce'Denis nodded; neither of them took the suggestion
for anything more than politeness. Sergei stood, pushing

himelf up with the knob of his cane and tucking the leather roll under his free arm. He inclined his head to ce'Denis— he'd risen at the same time, and now saluted Sergei. He left the man's office, walking across the courtyard and glancing up at the skull of the dragon mounted on the wall above.

The gardai at the door of the main tower saluted him as he approached. As they opened the massive steel-clad door, a wave of cold air scented with human waste and despair washed over him. Sergei took a deep breath—the familiar smell made him feel momentarily young. Even his own brief interment here had not changed that response.

He slowly made his way up the winding staircase, peering occasionally into the cells that opened on either side, resting on each landing to recover his breath. Once, he could have leaped these stairs two at a time, from bottom to top. Now, each step was a separate mountain that must be surmounted. He was panting heavily despite the frequent stops when he reached the top level.

The garda stationed there saluted Sergei, stiffening to attention. "Open the door, and then go get yourself some refreshment," Sergei told him. "I'll take responsibility for the prisoner."

"Ambassador?" The garda's forehead creased with puzzlement. "You shouldn't be alone with the prisoner. It's not safe for you."

"I'll be fine," Sergei told him.

"At least let me chain him to the wall first."

"I'll be fine," Sergei repeated, more firmly this time. "Go on."

The garda frowned and almost audibly sighed—perhaps with disappointment at missing Sergei's "interview" with the prisoner—and finally saluted again. His keys rattled and hinges groaned as he opened the cell door. Sergei waited until he heard the man's bootsteps fade down the stairs. Then he peered into the cell itself.

This was the cell for the most important prisoners. It had held pretenders to the Sun Throne, it had even held a few who beforehand had given themselves the title of Kraljiki or Kraljica. Karl had once been imprisoned here, and Sergei himself—they had both managed to escape: Karl through Mahri's magic, and Sergei with Karl and Varina's help. Sergei remembered the cell all too well: a frigid stone floor covered with filthy straw, a single bed with a thin blanket, a small wooden table for meals, an opening in the outer wall leading to a narrow balcony from where the prisoner could look out over the city (and from which more than one prisoner had decided to end his incarceration by falling into the courtyard far below.)

Nico was standing on that balcony now, staring outward. Sergei didn't know if the young man hadn't heard him enter, or if he didn't care. His hair was mussed and greasy, standing up erratically between the straps of the silencer laced around his head. His hands and feet were bound with iron chains and manacles so he could only manage a rattling shuffle.

Sergei stepped inside the cell. Leaning on his cane, he spoke loudly, as if declaiming from a stage.

> "A single dew drop
> lingers on black iron, reflecting a free sky,
> waiting to be breathed up by the fierce sun
> and fall yet again, exhaled by cloud.
> So a soul, eternal,
> will also never vanish
> but only cloak itself anew and return."

Nico had turned at Sergei's recitation. He stared at Sergei now, with those eyes that were still compelling and powerful. "The poem 'Rebirth' by Levo ca'Niomi," he said to Nico. "You've heard of him, yes? I think I have that one right—I once spent far too many turns of the glass memorizing his poetry while sitting in the Capitaine's office here. We have the original manuscripts of ca'Niomi's poetry here, did you know that? He had a very nice hand, rather ornate. He spent decades here after his thankfully short reign as Kraljiki; this very cell is where he composed all the verses for which he's so famous. So you see, a life spent imprisoned need not be an entirely wasted one."

Nico stared through the straps of the silencer. Saliva dripped from the leather-wrapped piece protruding into his mouth, shining among the strands of his beard and darkening the front of his plain tunic. Sergei could hear his breath rattling around the device.

"If you promise me that you'll not use the Ilmodo—not

that I think you can with your hands bound that way—and if you promise to make no attempt to escape, I will remove the silencer. I will expect you to swear to Cénzi that you'll do neither. Nod your head if you agree."

Nico nodded, slowly, and Sergei set down the leather roll on the bed, then came over to the young man. "Turn around," he said, "and crouch down a little so I can get to the buckles . . ." Carefully, he unbuckled the straps and lifted the device from Nico's head, the man gagging as the metal piece was removed from his mouth. Sergei stepped back, the silencer dangling from his hand, the buckles jingling.

"Stay where you are," he told Nico. He walked slowly outside the open cell door and, groaning, bent over to pick up the garda's water flask. He brought it inside, handing it to Nico. "Go on . . ."

He watched the young man drink, gulping down the water. Nico handed the flask back to Sergei, who set it on the table. "Are you going to torture me now?" Nico asked. His beautiful voice was harshened and torn by having worn the silencer for so long. He cleared his throat, and Sergei heard the breath rattling in his lungs—prisoners often became sick here, and many died from the wet lung disease. He wondered if Nico would be one.

"Is that what you think I am, your torturer?" he asked Nico. "Does the thought frighten you? Do you wonder what it will feel like, whether you'll be able to stand the pain, whether you'll scream and scream until your throat is raw, when you hear your bones snap, when you see the blood flowing, when you're forced to watch parts of your body flayed and torn and crushed? Do you wonder if you'll beg for it to end, that you'll promise me anything if I would just stop?" He could not entirely keep the eagerness from his voice; he knew Nico heard it.

Nico gulped audibly, his throat moving under the thin scraggly beard. Sergei saw his eyes glance over to the leather roll on his bed. "I know about you, Silvernose," Nico said. "Everyone does."

"Do they? What is it they say, I wonder? No, don't answer. I've a question for you instead—how does it feel to know that you're going to be remembered as someone even more reviled than me? How does it feel to know that, because of your pride and arrogance and misplaced faith, the woman who was carrying your child is dead?"

Sergei saw tears form in Nico's eyes, saw them grow and fall down his cheeks untouched. "You can't hurt me more than that," Nico said, his voice breaking with emotion. "You can't cause me more pain than I've already caused myself."

"Brave words," Sergei answered, "even if they're not true."

Deliberately, he went over to the roll of leather, leaning his cane against the bed. He bent down as if he were about to open the ties that held it closed, then straightened again. "I met an interesting young woman on the way back to Nessantico," he said.

Nico scowled. "I'm not interested in your filthy debauchery, ca'Rudka."

Sergei almost laughed. "There was no 'debauchery,' I'm afraid. Not that I wouldn't have been interested, mind you, especially since I wonder if she might not have shared my, umm, *preferences*. But there was conversation. Strangely, I saw a mirror of myself in her, and it wasn't a pretty sight. Even worse than the genuine one." He touched his nose for emphasis. "But I wondered . . . Can she change herself? Can she avoid becoming what I've become, or is that a hopeless task? Are we what Cénzi makes us, or can we change what we're given? It's an interesting question, isn't it?"

He bent down again to the leather roll. He pulled on the ties, unknotting them. He paused, fingertips on the old, soft leather, looking back over his shoulder at Nico, who was staring in dread fascination: as they all did, all of them whom he was about to torture.

They all looked. They could not fail to look.

"It's a question we might discuss, you and I," Sergei said. "I'd be curious to hear your thoughts on the matter."

With that, he flicked open the leather roll. Inside, cushioned, was a loaf of bread, a wedge of cheese, and a bottle of wine. He heard Nico's gasp of relief and disbelief. "Varina ca'Pallo sent these," Sergei told him. "You have her to thank for your life."

"My life?" Sergei heard the breath of hope in his voice, and he nodded.

"She pleaded for you with the Kraljica. As you might have expected, you were to be given first to the Archigos so he could take your hands and your tongue, and then tortured and executed by the Garde Kralji—all in public so the citizens could hear your screams and see the blood. But your life has been spared—by a Numetodo. By a woman you profess to hate. Isn't that interesting?"

"Why?" he asked. "I don't understand."

"Neither do I," Sergei answered. "Had it been my choice, you would already be dead and your body, hands, and tongue would be hanging from the Pontica a'Kralji as a lesson to others. But Varina . . ." He shrugged. "She loved you, Nico. Both she and Karl would have taken you for their own son, if they'd had the chance. In another life, you might have been Numetodo yourself."

Nico shook his head in denial, but the movement of his head was slow and faint.

~

Nico Morel

"IN ANOTHER LIFE, YOU MIGHT HAVE BEEN Numetodo yourself."

No. That would never have been. Cénzi wouldn't have allowed it. He wanted to rage and deny the accusation, but he couldn't. He couldn't feel Cénzi at all; he hadn't felt Him since he'd watched Liana fall. Cénzi had forsaken him. Nico had spent his time praying as best he could in the midst of his black despair. *Save me if that is Your Will. I am in Your Hands. Save me if there is still more that I need to do for You here, or take me to Your Bosom. I am Your servant, I am Your Hand and Your Voice. I am nothing without You . . .* He had once felt so full of Cénzi that it seemed impossible not to be one with Him. Now, he was empty and alone.

Instead, it was Varina who offered to save him, not Cénzi.

He stared at the food and wine atop the leather, which he had been certain contained the instruments of torture that ca'Rudka was rumored to carry with him whenever he visited the Bastida. Sergei was already breaking off a piece of the bread. He handed it to Nico, and his stomach growled loudly in response. The first taste was stunning; the bread might have come from the Second World itself. He had to force himself not to cram all of it into his mouth.

He could feel Sergei watching him as he ate. He saw ca'Rudka pulling the cork on the wine, taking a long swig himself, then handing the bottle to Nico. He swallowed— like the bread, the wine tasted like nectar in his dry, abused mouth.

Reluctantly, he handed the bottle back to Sergei and accepted some of the cheese and another piece of bread.

"Slowly," Sergei told him. "You'll be sick if you eat too much and too quickly."

Nico took a small bite of the cheese. "I could never have been Numetodo," he told Sergei.

Sergei chuckled dryly, shaking his white-haired, balding head. The silver nose sent light motes scattering around the walls. "You answer too quickly and easily," he said. "It tells me that either you're giving no thought to what you're saying, or that you've no idea how much a person's early life can influence them."

"I could never not believe in Cénzi," Nico told him stubbornly. "My faith is too strong. I am too close to Him."

"Yes, I notice how well He protected you and yours in the Old Temple."

"Blasphemy," Nico hissed reflexively.

"I would be careful with insults, were I you," Sergei said. The man's voice held a dangerous calmness, and the smile was sharp enough to cut skin. "The Kraljica has given you into my care. I will honor Varina's desire to keep you alive because she's my friend, but that leaves open so many possibilities."

Nico could feel the darkness within the man, like an approaching storm striding forward with legs of lightning and grumbling with thunder. He shuddered at the vision. *Cénzi, are You with me again?* No, he couldn't feel the Divine's presence. He was alone. Abandoned.

"You see," Sergei was saying, "that's your problem, Nico. You think everything is preordained. You think that Cénzi always meant for you to be what you are, that He's *still* directing your life. You think you would have ended up in the same place no matter what. But I don't think that's so. I think no one's future is preordained at all. I think you could have *easily* been a Numetodo. In fact, I would wager that by now you'd be the A'Morce of the Numetodo the same way you became Absolute of the Morellis. You *do* have a gift, Nico."

"*Cénzi's* Gift," Nico answered.

"Perhaps," Sergei said. He took another swig of wine and handed the bottle to Nico, whose throat was ravaged and as dry as the Daritria desert; he took it again gratefully. "I believe in Cénzi, so, yes, I would say the gift came to you from him, but Varina certainly doesn't, nor did Karl, and they were both nearly as gifted as you. So maybe we're both wrong. Maybe Cénzi simply doesn't interfere quite so directly in people's lives."

"If you believe that, then you deny one of the tenets of the Toustour."

"Or perhaps I don't believe that Cénzi is cruel enough to have wanted Liana to die and for you never to see your daughter."

Nico started to answer. The Nico who had been Cénzi's Voice would have had no trouble. He would have opened his mouth, and Cénzi would have filled him with the answer. His words would have burned and throbbed, and ca'Rudka would have trembled under their power. Now, he only gaped, and no words came. *When I saw her fall, my faith fell with her . . .*

"I told you about the young woman I met on the way here—I told her that she still had time to change, to find a path that wouldn't end where I am," Sergei said. "I think that's what Varina believes of you, Nico. She believes in you, in your gift, and she believes you can do better with it than you've done."

"I do what Cénzi demands I do," Nico answered. "That's all."

"I watched a Kraljiki descend into madness, listening to voices he thought he heard," Sergei answered.

"I'm not mad."

"Audric didn't think he was mad either."

"You can't compare my relationship to Cénzi with someone who believed a painting was talking to him."

"I can't? At least you can see and touch a painting. You can be certain that it's actually there. You can't do that with

Cénzi." Sergei picked up the bread, twisted off a piece and placed it in his mouth. "What I see here," he said, chewing and swallowing, "is that Cénzi has brought you here, but it's *Varina* who has spared your child, your life, your hands, and your tongue, and thus your gift: a person who doesn't believe in Cénzi, but who believes in *you*."

Cénzi works through her, he wanted to say, but the words wouldn't come. Sergei, groaning, had sat on the bed next to the roll of leather. Nico could see loops and pockets on the inside, all of them empty, though the leather had been imprinted with the shapes of the devices that normally resided there. Ominous dark stains dappled the interior. "Finish what you want of the food and wine, but quickly," Sergei said. "I have other appointments today, and I'm afraid I have to put this back on." He lifted the silencer, dangling by a strap from his finger. Nico's mouth suddenly filled with the memory of the ancient, soiled leather and he nearly vomited. "You should think about this, Nico," the man continued. "You've nothing else to do, after all."

"You act like you have something to offer me."

"I do," Sergei answered easily. "Your life, and whatever comfort you have with it."

"In exchange for what?"

Sergei groaned again as he rose. "We can start with a declaration from you to the war-téni, telling them that they should return to their duties and give themselves to the authority of the Faith once more."

"Cénzi told me that they should not fight," Nico persisted. "He said that the Tehuantin are a punishment for the failure of the Faith, the failure of the Archigos and the a'Téni. How can I deny Cénzi's very words to me, Ambassador?"

"There are two ways," Sergei answered. "You can do so of your own will, or I can return here tomorrow with a different gift for you." Sergei glanced back at the bed, where the empty roll lay. "Either way, you *will* make that statement. I promise you that. It's for you to decide how. Either way, I'll get something I want." He smiled at Nico. "You see, it's too late for *me* to change."

Sergei lifted the silencer; the buckles on the straps jingled. "I really must go now," he said, "but I'll return. Tomorrow. And you can tell me what you've decided."

~

Jan ca'Ostheim

THE VANGUARD OF THE ARMY was still a day or
more away under the direction of the a'offiziers, but
Jan rode ahead of the troops with Archigos Karrol and
Starkkapitän ca'Damont, as well as several of the Firenzcian chevarittai.

He'd not been in Nessantico in fifteen years, not since
Firenzcia had last come to the Holdings' aid against the
Tehuantin. He'd forgotten how magnificent the city looked.
They'd halted on the crest of the last hill along the Avi
a'Firenzcia, where they could see Nessantico laid out before them on either side of the glittering expanse of the
A'Sele. When he'd last glimpsed Nessantico, it had been
cloaked in fire and ruin, nearly destroyed. The city had rebuilt itself anew. The domes of the temples were golden,
the white spires of the Kraljica's Palais seemed to nearly
prick the clouds from the Isle a'Kralji, and the city utterly
filled the flat hollow that held it. Even tarnished and threatened, the city was magnificent.

"It *is* a stunning sight, isn't it, my Hïrzg?" Archigos Karrol said. The Archigos, with his bent spine, couldn't ride a
horse, but he'd descended from his carriage to take in the
scene, standing on the road next to Jan's stallion. "But I still
prefer Brezno and our terraces."

Jan wasn't certain that he entirely agreed. Yes, Brezno
had its beauties as a city, and there were vistas on approach
that made a traveler stop and gaze, but this . . . There was a
power here, somehow. Maybe it came from the multitudes
of people here, thousands more than Brezno held. Maybe
it was a product of the long history of the city, which had
seen empires rise and fall, which had become the seat of
the greatest empire ever seen, at least on this side of the
Strettosei. Even Jan felt the tug of it. *This will be yours
soon enough. All of it . . . If you can save it now.*

"Look," Starkkapitän ca'Damont said, pointing. "The

Avi's crowded with people at the Eastern Gate. The evacuation's already begun. The Tehuantin must be close." He leaned forward on the saddle of his horse, peering down at the vista in front of them. "I wonder if they're coming from the North Bank, the South, or both. If we can engage them before they reach the city itself, we should. Without the war-téni, especially, we need to keep them from the city." Ca'Damont cast a venomous glance at Archigos Karrol, but the man seemed to be staring down at the road.

"There will be war-téni from the temples here," Archigos Karrol said. "You will have the war-téni you need."

"Let's hope so," ca'Damont answered curtly. "But it seems they'd rather follow Morel than you."

"We'll find out what the situation is soon enough," Jan said quickly, interrupting the response that Archigos Karrol started to make. "Archigos, if you'll return to your carriage, we'll ride on. If we make good time, we could be within the walls by Third Call."

As Archigos Karrol, helped by the quartet of his aide ténis, climbed slowly back to his carriage seat, Jan stared westward toward the city, and especially to the Isle a'Kralji and the palais. He wondered if his matarh was there, and how she felt about his impending arrival. He wondered if she both dreaded and looked forward to it all at once, contradictorily.

As he did.

"Let's go," he said to the others, waving his hand. "The city awaits us."

They entered along the Avi a'Firenzcia, proceeding slowly toward the Eastern Gate of the city. The city *was* beginning to evacuate, the road clogged with people and carts, most of them moving away from Nessantico. The people were largely women with children, along with some elderly men—conspicuously absent were able-bodied men; Jan assumed that the Garde Kralji and Garde Civile were pressing them into service of the defense of the city. The houses and buildings along the Avi became more numerous and set closer to the main road as they approached, until they were moving between tightly-packed houses even though they were still outside the city walls proper. Someone had alerted the authorities; as they moved on, suddenly the citizenry was pausing to stop and cheer, and people were peering at them from windows and balconies, waving their hands and producing battered and ancient banners in the Firenzcian colors of black and silver—banners that had evidently been moldering in chests for years. Jan could see many of them looking eastward along the Avi as if expecting to see the army immediately following them, then looking back to them in puzzlement.

He heard his name being called out, greeting him as if he had already liberated the city. "Hïrzg Jan! Hïrzg Jan!" The chevarittai with him smiled, but they also closed ranks around him protectively, and they watched the houses and the growing crowds carefully for any signs of trouble.

Too many of them had fought against Holdings troops. Too many of them had felt the enmity of the Holdings to the Coalition. Like Jan, they wondered what the real thoughts were behind the cheers.

By the time they could see the the ancient gates looming ahead of them, the crowds had grown even larger, filling either side of the street. There were people waving from atop the remnants of the old city walls, and every window and balcony was filled. Starkkapitän ca' Damont leaned over toward Jan. "You'd think the Tehuantin were already running back across the sea."

Jan shrugged. "I think they're remembering that when I last brought the army here, we came after the Tehuantin had already taken the city. They're hoping that this means they're saved. Though judging by the faces ahead of us, some people are less convinced of that."

He nodded toward where the blue-and-gold banner of the Holdings waved in the middle of the Avi just under the ramparts of the city gate. One of the group there wore the livery of the Kraljica's staff; the rest seemed to be a contingent of chevarittai and—judging by the fancy bashtas of two or three—members of the Council of Ca'.

If the citizens were smiling, they were not. They were entirely grim-faced and solemn. Jan found himself somehow disappointed that Allesandra herself wasn't there, though he knew that—had the Kraljica deigned to visit Brezno—he would have done the same, would have let her come to him.

Jan felt keenly now the loss of his aide Rance, who

would have been riding alongside him and who would have been able to identify many of the people waiting for them. "Do you know them?" Jan asked ca'Damont, leaning toward the Starkkapitän. "Is that Matarh's aide? What's his name? Talbot ci'Noel or something like that . . ."

"Talbot ci'Noel it is, I believe," ca'Damont answered. "And that's probably him. The other ones . . ." He shook his head. "I'm afraid I don't know any of the councillors other than Vajica ca'Pallo, and she's not present. I'm sorry, Hïrzg." Jan saw his eyes narrow then. "That man behind ci'Noel, dressed Magyarian style. I would swear that's Erik ca'Vikej, that traitor Stor's son. Look at that smirk on his face—this could be a trap, Hïrzg."

Ca'Damont's hand had gone to his sword hilt, and Jan touched his arm. "Not now," he told the Starkkapitän. "Matarh wouldn't be that obvious. Let's get the lay of the land first."

The aide ci'Noel stepped forward with the councillors as Jan reached them, his chevarittai moving aside to let Jan be the first to enter the city. The aide bowed low; the councillors less so. "Hïrzg Jan," he said. "I welcome you again to Nessantico after far too long an absence. Kraljica Allesandra sends her greetings and her gratitude, and she awaits you at the palais. If you will permit us to escort you to her . . ."

"Thank you, Vajiki ci'Noel," Jan answered, pleased when the man nodded in acknowledgment—the name was either right or close enough. "And Councillors and Chevarittai," he said to the others. He ignored ca'Vikej. It would have been better to have called a few of the councillors and chevarittai out by name, but instead he simply inclined his head to them. "This is Starkkapitän ca'Damont of the Garde Civile, and—" He had heard the carriage door open, and glanced back to see the Archigos being helped down. "Archigos Karrol," he finished.

Ci'Noel inclined his head to ca'Damont, but significantly did not give Archigos Karrol the sign of Cénzi. Instead, he bowed to him as he might to anyone. Jan remembered then that his matarh's aide was one of the Numetodo. Archigos Karrol was frowning, his hands halfway up to his bowed forehead to return the the expected sign. The councillors and chevarittai, however, did clasp their hands to forehead, and the Archigos returned their gesture perfunctorily, with a visible scowl. "Welcome, Starkkapitän," ci'Noel said. "I'm certain that Commandant ca'Talin will welcome your arrival and your advice; he will be waiting at the palais also. Archigos, you're welcome as well, especially since A'Téni ca'Paim's death has left the Faithful here bereft of leadership. I know Commandant ca'Talin is desperate for the help of your war-téni."

Ci'Noel said that last with a trace of a smile, and Jan realized that he probably suspected how few war-téni had followed the Archigos. The Archigos sniffed audibly. "I will be going to the Archigos' Temple immediately to take up residence there and see what needs to be done," he said to the aide. "I assume someone will guide us to the easiest way there."

"Certainly, Archigos," ci'Noel answered, "as soon as you've seen the Kraljica. She has asked that you be present at the meeting also."

"It's been a long ride," the Archigos answered, "and as you can see, I'm not as young as others here . . ."

"The Kraljica expects your presence *first,*" ci'Noel interrupted, and that brought up the Archigos' head to glare at the man. "I'm certain the Hïrzg understands the importance of state precedents, and has explained them to you."

He's taken lessons from Matarh . . . Jan almost smiled at the clever impertinence of the man. "The Archigos will undoubtedly want to hear the latest regarding Nico Morel," Jan agreed, and Karrol's glare now turned to him. "So he can make the best decision regarding Morel's fate and that of his followers."

"Indeed," ci'Noel said, nodding vigorously before the Archigos could object. "There is news there that I'm sure she's waiting to tell you." He bowed again. "If you'll follow me, Hïrzg Jan. The citizenry, as you can see, are waiting to give you their own welcome."

With that, one of the chevarittai led a horse forward and ci'Noel pulled himself onto the saddle. He nodded his head to Jan and tugged at the reins, turning his horse to continue westward.

The populace cheered as they proceeded under the arch of the gate and into Nessantico.

~

Allesandra ca'Vörl

SHE WAS MORE NERVOUS than she'd imagined she would be. The hall of the Sun Throne had been set for the reception, and as she waited in the small room behind the throne's dais with three palais e-téni and two of the hall servants, she could hear the servants bustling about making certain that everything was set. She'd been told that Hïrzg Jan and the others were on the palais grounds, that Talbot and the Council of Ca' were escorting them to the hall, and she went to the nearly transparent scrim to peer into the hall. There was a loud knock on the far door, and the palais door wards hurried to open it. Talbot entered, bowing and indicating that the Hïrzg should enter.

For the first time in fifteen years, she saw her son.

He'd changed; he hadn't changed. She certainly knew him immediately. The image of him as a young man burned in her mind was still there in this adult in the prime of his life. His hair had darkened and receded a bit, and there was a trace of gray at his temples that surprised her. She touched her own hair, knowing that the white was rapidly overpowering the color in her long, bound tresses. But his features: those were the eyes she remembered, with a hawk's gaze that could send an arrow flying unerringly to the heart of a stag. The set of his mouth, the strong line of his jaw, his confident stride; they were still as she remembered.

She wanted to part the curtain and run to him, yet she could not. This was to be a dance as intricate and tightly choreographed as any ce'Miella minuet. This was not the time for emotions to rule, but for diplomacy. Even with the challenge of the Tehuantin pressing against their doorstep, the niceties of society and position must be followed. So Allesandra waited as Jan and the Firenzcian contingent were escorted up to the open space before the throne's dais, until the servants had hurried forward with trays of refreshments. Her councillors (with Varina joining them and holding Nico's daughter) were standing in their own huddle; the Firenzcian chevarittai, like most warriors fresh from a long march, took the offered food and drink eagerly, Starkkapitän ca'Damont with them. Archigos Karrol stood in front of the steps of the dais and waved away the servants (to the evident consternation of the téni clustered around him); he seemed to be contemplating whether his position as Archigos would permit him to ascend the steps up to the dais, his face—when he lifted it from staring at the floor—was a mask of irritation. Jan took water but waved away the food, standing and speaking softly to Talbot in front of ci'Recroix's massive painting of a peasant family. Jan was staring over Talbot's shoulder at the stunningly lifelike figures on the canvas.

Erik was standing alone. Isolated. Ignored by both Firenzcians and Nessanticans. Somehow, Allesandra found that fitting.

Talbot glanced over toward the screen and nodded. He bowed briefly to Jan, then brushed past Archigos Karrol to ascend the dais and stand to one side of the Sun Throne. Conversation in the room failed as everyone looked at him. Faintly, Allesandra heard one of the e-téni with her start to chant and gesture. "Kraljica Allesandra ca'Vörl of the Holdings," Talbot intoned, and the e-téni's spell made his words boom and thunder in the hall, as if a Moitidi had spoken them. The other two e-téni were chanting now, and as the hall servants parted the curtain, they cast their own spells, surrounding Allesandra in a bath of faint golden light as she stepped out, as if she'd been caught in a moving shaft of noon sunlight. Those in the room bowed to her as one, the Archigos and téni instead favoring her with the sign of Cénzi. Talbot took to one knee as she approached.

Her heart was beating hard, her breath was too fast. Jan alone had not bowed his head. Instead, he stared at her, as she did toward him. Their gazes locked, and she hoped that he saw the affection there.

She took three steps forward, until she stood alongside the Sun Throne, but she didn't sit, as she would have for a normal reception. Instead, she paused there, and she extended her hands toward Jan. "Hïrzg," she said. "Jan . . . Please . . ."

At the invitation, he bounded up the steps of the dais—

more like a young man than a ruler, more like the child she remembered. He took her proffered hands. "Matarh," he said. "It's good to see you."

She'd played out this moment a hundred times in her mind, anticipating a thousand different reactions. She'd imagined him angry or sullen or terribly proper and aloof. She'd even dared to imagine a tearful reunion. This . . . This tugged her lips into a wide, helpless smile, and she pressed her fingers against his.

"It's good to see you, Jan," she said, softly enough that only he could hear her. "I mean that, my son. I should never have waited this long, and you have my sincere apology for that."

He smiled, but there was a caution there, and a wariness in his eyes. She saw him glance at the Sun Throne. "Would it light up if I sat there?" he asked her.

"It will," she answered. "Soon enough." *And if you have the light-téni prepare beforehand.* He would learn that soon enough, too; though the Sun Throne still shone when the Kraljica or Kraljiki sat on it, that light had been but a dim spark since Kraljica Marguerite's time, visible only in twilight darkness. It now required the aid of light-téni to be noticeable in the day. She'd also learned that the trigger for the light wasn't herself, but the signet ring of the Kralji— the light that the famous Archigos Siwel ca'Elad had enchanted within the crystalline depths would arise whenever *anyone* wearing the ring sat on the throne.

He had dropped her hands, though he was still smiling—as were all of those watching the historic encounter. He was too like her; he knew the importance of this moment, knew that it would set the tone for the future. "Matarh," he said, loudly enough that all could hear him, "the army of Firenzcia has come again to help the Holdings and the Sun Throne."

Applause and cheers broke at that statement, the sound washing over them as they stood on the dais. They both turned as they accepted the ovation. Allesandra felt a lightness she had not felt in a long time. She saw Erik among the audience, still isolated, near the Holdings councillors and chevarittai but not with them, and well away from the Firenzcians. He applauded as loudly as the others, but his grin was smug and self-satisfied. She hated it.

She took Jan's hand in hers, lifting them both in the air. "To a new union," she said loudly. "Of family, and of countries."

The applause and cheers redoubled. The light and glow in the room brightened around both of them, and if Allesandra knew that it was only an effect of the light-téni huddled in the room behind the dais, it still seemed fitting and right.

That evening, after the reception and a brief Third Call blessing by Archigos Karrol, Talbot escorted them to the private dining room within her apartments in the palais. Allesandra walked with her arm linked in Jan's; Archigos Karrol stumped along behind with a cane and a single téni attendant and Starkkapitän ca'Damont, while Erik trailed the company by a pace.

Waiting for them in the room were Sergei and Varina. Varina was empty-armed now, having given Nico's daughter to the care of servants for the duration.

"Kraljica! Hïrzg Jan!" Sergei's voice boomed as Talbot opened the door and stepped aside. "You don't know how delighted I am to see the two of you together! Matarh and son, as it should be. Hïrzg Jan, you certainly remember Varina ca'Pallo, A'Morce of the Numetodo . . ."

Varina bowed to Jan, who returned the bow, but Allesandra heard a distinct hiss of distaste from Archigos Karrol. The man muttered something Allesandra couldn't hear to his attendant.

"Please, sit," Allesandra told them, gesturing to the round table Talbot had set up in the room, laden with decanters and covered plates. "There are refreshments, and we'll have dinner brought in later. Jan, if you would sit next to me . . ." She watched the others settle around the table: Sergei to her left hand with Varina next to him; Archigos Karrol to Jan's right, then Starkkapitan ca'Damont. Erik sat between the Firenzcians and the Nessanticans, with Varina and ca'Damont on either side of him; she saw him glance uncomfortably at ca'Damont, who had defeated his vatarh. The Archigos' téni attendant and Talbot took a small table to one side of the room, near the servants' door. Allesandra waited until they'd all settled and Talbot had gestured to the wait staff to pour wine.

"This is a momentous occasion," she said finally, lifting her glass. "I would propose a toast to the renewed Holdings, and to my son, Hïrzg of Firenzcia and now A'Kralj of the Holdings."

"And to victory over the Tehuantin," Sergei added.

Allesandra nodded. "To the Holdings, and to victory." The phrase was echoed around the table, though Jan only lifted his glass with a smile, without saying anything.

"Kraljica, I appreciate the hospitality you've shown us," Archigos Karrol said, though the expression on his face belied the words. "But the work of the Faith awaits me. I should go to the Old Temple and see what the vile Morellis have done. And I would like Nico Morel given over to me tonight, so that I may immediately place the judgment of the Faith on him."

"So you may take his hands and tongue, you mean?" Allesandra asked the man, and Varina gasped. She stared at Allesandra, as if afraid that Allesandra would hand Nico over despite her promise. "So you may then execute him?"

The Archigos sniffed. "Indeed. Morel has placed this fate on himself, Kraljica. It's not my doing. I will, of course, take hands and tongue publicly, in the Temple Square, so that everyone may see what happens to heretics who defy the Faith." He glanced at Varina as he said the last.

"I'm afraid, Archigos, that I have changed Nico Morel's fate, at the A'Morce Numetodo's request," Allesandra answered. "Nico Morel currently resides in the Bastida, and he will remain there at my pleasure."

Karrol's head turned toward Allesandra, like a turtle looking sideways. Both his hands were on the table, as if he were trying to decide whether to stand. Across the room, she saw his attendant start to rise; Talbot placed his hand on the young man's arm, shaking his head. "How strange that a Numetodo unbeliever would be concerned with Morel's life, since if Morel had his way, she would be in the Bastida or worse herself. But in any case, Nico Morel is the Faith's business, not the crown's or the Numetodo's," Karrol declared. "This is a matter of religion, not of state."

"Ah." Allesandra placed steepled hands under her chin. "Though war *is* a matter of state, Archigos. Tell me, how many war-téni did you bring with you?"

The Archigos hissed like a turtle, too, Allesandra decided. "I hear that it was less than two hands," Allesandra continued. "So few . . . However, Sergei has promised me that Nico Morel will give us the war-téni of Nesssantico, and that he will also send word to those who refused to follow you, and that they will come at his call." She saw Sergei nod at that, as Varina glanced at the silver-nosed man strangely. "It seems, Archigos, that Nico Morel is able to provide the state far more war-téni than *you* can. So I don't think your business at the Old Temple is quite so pressing. I've already pardoned the téni and war-téni who followed Morel, provided they go to the front. Those few who still refused . . ." She lifted an uncaring shoulder. "Well, I will permit you to do with them as you will."

Archigos Karrol's face had gone white, as if he were choking. "You will *permit* . . . You have no authority to do that, Kraljica. None at all. I am Archigos, and I—"

"And you, Archigos Karrol, don't seem to realize just how fragile and precarious your position is. The majority of your téni followed Nico Morel rather than the unfortunate A'Téni ca'Paim, and your own war-téni did the same. Where is this power you seem to think you possess, Archigos? You couldn't defeat Nico Morel, but *I* did—with the great help, I would remind you, of the Numetodo. It would seem that the Faith is no longer the only ally to which a Kralji can turn in time of need, nor the strongest. I suggest that if you wish to demonstrate how the Faith can help, you do so, Archigos. My faith in Cénzi is as strong as ever, but frankly I don't think the defense of Nessantico would be any less strong if you shared the same cell as Morel."

Karrol slammed his hands on the table, causing glasses to ring and china to clatter. "My Hïrzg, will you let this . . . this . . . *heretic* speak to me this way?"

Allesandra saw Jan shrug from the side of her vision. "If the Kraljica can actually produce the war-téni for my army, Archigos, perhaps she has a point." He turned to her. "Matarh, you haven't changed a whit. You still somehow manage to have things your way."

"I won't stay here," Archigos Karrol spat. "I don't need to listen to this apostasy."

"Then I will permit you to leave," Allesandra told him. "But be cautious with what you say and what you do, Archigos. You *will* consult either my son or me before you take any significant action—either that, or you'll find that you'll be replaced by one of the a'téni who *does* realize that the Faith is the servant of the state rather than the reverse."

"You have *no* authority to replace me," the Archigos blustered. "The Concord A'Téni won't stand for it. The need of the Faith supersedes that of any state."

"If you would like to test that theory, Archigos, I invite you to try. Talbot, would you have the palais gardai escort Archigos Karrol to the Old Temple, so he may survey the damage there? Perhaps he'd like to supervise the work crews, since he can't give us the war-téni we require."

Karrol's assistant came forward with his cane as the Archigos stood. He glared at Allesandra, who calmly gave him the sign of Cénzi in return. Karrol stalked from the room with what little dignity remained to him. Jan applauded ironically as the doors closed behind the man.

"Huzzah, Matarh," he said. "That was well-played. I've been trying to find an excuse to get rid of that ineffective old *bastardo* for a year or more now, and here you've done it for me."

"You can thank Sergei," she told him. "He's the one who will convince Nico Morel to cooperate." She saw Varina glare at Sergei with that—as if she realized the meaning underneath the words. "And now—to our own business. Have you spoken with the nations of the Coalition? Are they all in accord?"

"I've not spoken to them all, though I've sent messages to them," Jan told her. "Sesemora is the strongest of them outside Firenzcia, and therefore the most dangerous, but Brie is the first cousin of Pjathi ca'Brinka and the family connections will prevail. Miscoli will fall in with Sesemora. East Magyaria knows that Tennshah's troops would be swarming over its borders without Firenzcia's protection. West Magyaria . . ." Here he stopped and glanced—once—in Erik's direction. "The Gyula is our man."

Allesandra saw Erik grimace, then slip a smile like a mask back over his face. "Perhaps the fate of West Magyaria isn't quite as settled as you believe, Hïrzg Jan," Erik said. "Perhaps the Kraljica has other plans."

"Oh?" Jan asked. "Is this true, Matarh? Do rebels, traitors, and incompetents give commands in the Holdings? Are you planning to make the Hïrzg of Firenzcia as irrelevant as you did the Archigos? That won't work, I'm afraid—I hold the high cards in this game, unless you want Nessantico overrun by the Westlanders." There was genuine anger in his voice now. She glanced at Erik once more. He nodded to her and smiled. She looked away.

"Even with Firenzcia, I'm afraid there's still no guarantee that the Tehuantin won't prevail," she told Jan. "Their army is far larger than the one they brought before, Commandant ca'Talin has been unable to slow their advance, and what they did at Karnmor . . ." She shivered, involuntarily. "But in answer to your question, no" she said, more firmly. "I make my own decisions as to what is best for Nessantico—as you will, too, Jan. As we will together."

She paused. *You're still certain you want to do this?* Erik was grinning, confident, and the presumption there irked her. She already knew the answer—because she knew that, inevitably, with Erik and Jan it would come down to choosing between the two of them. She raised her glass to Jan. "If the current Gyula is satisfactory to you," she told him, "then he will remain Gyula."

"What!" Erik gave a shout of outrage, rising to his feet. Talbot rose at the same time, and the gardai at the door stiffened. "You *promised* me," he shouted at Allesandra, his face gone red. His finger stabbed air. "I trusted you. You and I have shared your—"

"*Silence!*" Allesandra thundered in return. "If you say a word more, Vajiki, you'll find yourself in the Bastida. *That* is my promise. You're no longer welcome in my presence. You have this night to leave Nessantico. Go where you will, but if you're here at First Call tomorrow, you will be declared a traitor to the Sun Throne and hunted down accordingly. If you're caught, you'll be sent to West Magyaria for trial by the Gyula's court."

"You can't mean this."

"Oh, but I do," Allesandra told him.

"I meant nothing to you, then? The time we spent together—"

"—is done with," she finished for him. "It's one thing

for a Kralji to make a mistake, Erik. It's entirely another to continue to make it. Did you think I would exchange the good of the Holdings for simple affection? If you did, you never knew me at all."

"I know you now," Erik spat. "You're a cold, cold bitch."

It should have stung. It didn't. She felt nothing at all. "Erik, you are wasting what little time you have."

Erik glared. He fumed. But he clamped his mouth shut and stalked away from the table. The gardai opened the door for him. His bootsteps faded away down the long hall as the doors closed again.

"Matarh, you *do* amaze me," Jan said. He looked around the table at Starkkapitän ca'Damont, at Sergei and Varina. "Which one of us leaves next?"

She ignored the sarcasm. "The Archigos needed to re-alize his place," Allesandra told him. "We don't need the distraction of having to placate the Concénzia Faith in this crisis. And as for Erik . . ." She shrugged. "I'm afraid I made a poor decision, and it was time to rectify it."

"Actually, if you don't mind the correction, you made two poor decisions—you also backed his vatarh."

She started to argue. *No, let him have that much of a victory here. He's uncertain and worried.* "I'll accept that." She nod-ded to Sergei, Varina, and ca'Damont, who sat silent through the exchange. "I'm sorry all of you had to witness that. I hope you know how much I value your advice and your counsel, Sergei, Varina. Both of you are vital to the Holdings, especially now. And Starkkapitän ca'Damont, your expertise will be es-sential in the coming days. Now . . . Let us talk of what faces Nessantico, and how we might prevail . . ."

~

Brie ca'Ostheim

IT TOOK TWO DAYS TO CATCH UP with the supply train of the army, and another half-day to move through seemingly endless triple lines of infantry toward the com-mand battalion. The soldiers cheered as her carriage approached with the insignia of the Hïrzg on its side. They moved off the road to allow the carriage to pass, and she waved to them. She also saw riders being sent ahead of her farther up the line, galloping through the fields and meadows alongside the road, and she knew that word of her arrival would be going to the offiziers, and from them to Jan. Brie expected Jan to be among those to greet her when she finally came within sight of the banner of the Hïrzg and the starkkapitän, but it was instead Armond cu'Weller, a chevaritt and a'offizier, who strode up to the carriage as the driver pulled the reins. Brie pushed open the door of the carriage and descended the steps before either the Garde Brezno riders with her or cu'Weller could move to help her.

"Hïrzgin," he said, saluting her. His face was worried and anxious, and he glanced from her to the trio of mounted Garde Brezno gardai with her. Around them, the army had come to a sluggish halt. "Is there a problem? Was your train attacked? The children . . . ?"

"The children are fine, and should be in Brezno by now," she answered. "I returned to be with my husband, that's all, and to stand with him when he meets the Kraljica. If you would tell him that I've come, I'd appreciate it. I thought he'd be here . . ."

Cu'Weller looked away a moment, his lips pressing together. "I regret, Hïrzgin, to have to tell you that the Hïrzg, Starkkapitän ca'Damont, and several of the chevarittai had ridden ahead of the army. They are likely in Nessantico already."

"Oh." The vision of Jan standing in flame came back to her, and the mysterious woman with him . . . She bit at her lower lip, and that gave cu'Weller the chance to hurry in. He opened the door of the carriage for her, as if expecting her to immediately return inside.

"I'm sorry, Hïrzgin." He glanced again at the mounted gardai with him. "I'll assign a squad of additional troops to accompany you back to Stag Fall, and give you new horses and driver. The cook can put together provisions for the road . . ."

"I won't be leaving," she told him, and surprise lifted his eyebrows.

"Hïrzgin, this isn't a place for you. An army on the march . . ."

"My husband isn't here. That means that I am the authority of the throne of Firenzcia, does it not, A'Offizier?"

Cu'Keller looked as if he wanted to protest, but shook his head slightly. "Yes, Hïrzgin, I suppose so but . . ."

"Then my commands supersede yours, and I will continue on with you to Nessantico," she told him, "until such a time as the Starkkapitän and my husband return. Do you have an issue with that, A'Offizier?"

"No, Hïrzgin. No issue." The words were an acceptance, but the look on his face belied them.

She didn't care. Something told her that she needed to be with Jan, and she would. "Good," she told him. She opened the door of the carriage, one foot on the step. "Then let us not keep the army waiting," she told him. "We've a long march ahead."

~

Niente

*T*HE WATERS OF AXAT BETRAYED HIM. *He could see little of the Long Path in the mist. Even the events just before them were clouded. There were too many conflicting signs, too many possibilities, too many powers in opposition. Everything was in flux, everyone was in movement. He could no longer see his Long Path at all. It was gone, as if Axat had withdrawn Her favor from him, as if She were angry with him for his failures.*

He saw only one thing. He saw himself and Atl, facing each other, and lightning flashed between them, and through the mist, he saw Atl fall . . .

With an angry shout and a sweep of his arm, Niente sent the scrying bowl flying. The trio of nahualli who had brought him the bowl and the water and were in attendance on him, scrambled to their feet in surprise. "Nahual?"

"Leave me!" he told them. "Go on! Get out!"

They scattered, leaving him alone in the tent.

It's gone. The future you sought to have has been taken

from you. Can you find it again? Is there still time, or has the possibility passed entirely now?

He didn't know. The uncertainty was a fire in his stomach, a hammer pounding on his skull.

He collapsed to the ground, burying his head in his hands. The bowl sat accusingly upside down on the grass before him, orange-tinted water dewing the green blades. *The foreign grass, the foreign soil ...*

He didn't know how long he sat there when he saw a wavering shadow against the fabric, cast from the great fire in the center of their encampment. "Nahual?" a tentative voice called. "It's time. The Eye of Axat has risen. Nahual?"

"I'm coming," he called out. "Be patient."

The shadow receded. Niente pulled himself up. His spell-staff was still on the table. He took it in his hand, feeling the tingling of the spells caught within the whorled grain. *Can you do this? Will you do this?*

He went to the flap of the tent, pushed it aside. He stepped out.

The army had encamped along the main road where it descended a long hill. The tents of the Nahual and the Tecuhtli had been placed on the crown of the hill, surrounded by the tents of the High Warriors and nahualli. Below, Niente could see the glimmering of hundreds of campfires; above, the ribbon of the Star River cleaved the sky, dimmed by the brilliance of Axat's Eye, staring down at them. The High Warriors and the nahualli stood in a ring around the trampled grasses of the meadow. Near the campfire, blazing in the open space between the Nahual's tent and that of the Tecuhtli, stood Tecuhtli Citlali, Tototl, and Atl. His son was bare to the waist, his skin glistening. He held his spell-staff in one hand, the end tapping nervously on the ground.

"You still want this, Atl?" Niente asked him. "You are so certain of your path?"

Atl shook his head. "Do I *want* it, Taat? No. I don't. But I am certain of the path Axat has shown, and I'm confident that the path you want us to take leads to defeat, despite what you believe. You were the one who taught me that even when someone in authority tells you that they're right, they might still be wrong—and that in order

to serve them, you have to persist. You said that was the
Nahual's role to the Tecuhtli, and that of the nahualli to
the Nahual." He took a long, slow breath, tapping his
spell-staff on the ground again. "No, I don't want this. I
don't want to fight you. I hate this. But I don't see that I
have a choice."

Citlali stepped forward between the two. "Enough talk,"
he said. "We've wasted enough time on this already—and
the city waits for us. Do what you must, so I know who
my Nahual is, so I know which of you is seeing the paths
correctly." He looked from Niente to Atl. "Do it," he said.
"Now!"

He stepped back, gesturing to Niente and Atl. Niente
knew that Citlali wanted them to raise their spell-staffs,
wanted the night to blaze suddenly with lightnings and
fire, to see one of the two of them crumple to the ground
broken, burned, and dead. He could see it in the eagerness of the man's face, the ways the red eagle's wings
moved on the sides of his shaved skull. The nahualli, the
High Warriors, they all shared that same hunger—they
stared and leaned forward, their mouths half-open in
anticipation.

No one had seen a Nahual battle a challenger in a generation. They looked forward to the historic scene. Neither
Atl nor Niente had moved, though. Niente saw the muscles
bunch in his son's arm, and he knew that Atl *would* do this.
He knew that the vision in the bowl would be kept. At the
first lifting of his staff, it would begin—and Atl would die.

"No!" Niente shouted, and he cast his spell-staff to the
ground. "I won't."

"If you are my Nahual, you will," Citlali roared, as if
disappointed.

"Then I am not the Nahual," Niente said. "Not any longer. Atl is right. Axat has clouded my vision of the Path. I'm
no longer in her favor, and I no longer See true."

He bowed to his son, as a nahualli to the Nahual. He
stripped the golden bracelet from his forearm. His skin felt
cold and naked without it. "I yield," he said. He knelt, and
he proffered the bracelet to Atl. "You are the Techutli's
Nahual now," he told him. "I am simply a nahualli. Your
servant."

He could feel the Long Path fading in his mind. *You took*

it from me, Axat. This is Your fault. If he could no longer see, then he would trade his vision for Atl's. If there was no Long Path, then he would take victory for the Tehuantin.

He would be satisfied. He wouldn't live to see the consequences.

FAILINGS

Nico Morel
Sergei ca'Rudka
Jan ca'Ostheim
Niente
Varina ca'Pallo
Rochelle Botelli
Varina ca'Pallo
Brie ca'Ostheim
Niente

Nico Morel

CÉNZI . . .

Cénzi had abandoned him, and he could only wonder what he'd done wrong, how he could have misinter-
preted things so badly that Cénzi would have allowed this
to happen. Nico had spent the time since Sergei had left
him on his knees, refusing all food and water. He used the
chains binding his hands and legs as flails, to break open
again the scabs of the wounds he'd sustained in the battle
for the Old Temple, letting the hot blood and the pain take
away all thought of the outside world. He accepted the
pain; he bathed in it; he gave it up to Cénzi as an offering in
hopes that He might speak again to him.

*You've taken my lover and stolen my child. You've al-
lowed the people who followed me to die horribly. You've
taken my freedom. How did I offend You? What did I fail
to see or do for You? How have I misheard Your message?
Tell me. If you wish to punish me, then I give myself to You
freely, but tell me why I must be punished. Please help me to
understand . . .*

That was his prayer. That is what he repeated, over and
over: as the wind-horns spoke Third Call over the city, as
night came, as the stars wheeled past and the moon rose.
He prayed, on his knees, lost inside himself and trying
again to find the voice of Cénzi somewhere in his despair.

He couldn't keep the other thoughts from intruding. His
mind drifted, unfocused. He could hear Sergei's voice, telling him over and over, "It's Varina who has spared your
life, your hands, and your tongue, and thus your gift: a

person who doesn't believe in Cénzi, but who believes in you . . . It's Varina who saved your child . . ." Muffled by the silencer, Nico shouted against that terrible voice, screwing his eyes shut as if he could deny the memory entrance to his mind if he denied himself sight. "I told you about the young woman—I told her that she still had time to change, to find a path that wouldn't end where I am," Sergei persisted. "I think that's what Varina believes of you, Nico. She believes in you, in your gift, and she believes you can do better with it than you've done."

No! If Varina saved me, it was because she was unwittingly being twisted to Your will. It must be. Tell me that it's so! Give me Your sign . . .

But what surfaced in his mind was instead the image of Liana's broken and torn body, of the way her eyes stared blindly toward the dome of the Old Temple, and the way her hands clutched her stomach as if trying to cradle the unborn child inside her. He called upon Cénzi to change this horrible act, to return her to life, to take his own life in her place, but she only stared and her chest did not move and the blood thickened and stopped around her as he tried to rouse her, as he held her, as the gardai tore him away as he screamed . . .

Cénzi, I know Your gift was given to me—why did You give it to me if not to serve You? What do You ask of me? I will do it. I thought I had done it, but if that's not true, then show me. Just take this torment from me. Make me understand . . .

He thought he felt a hand on his shoulder and he turned, but there was no one there. It must have been the dead turns of the night, when even the great city was at its most quiet. He must have been kneeling there for turns, with his legs gone dead under him. The still, foul air of the cell shivered and he heard Varina's voice. "I hate what you've preached and what you've done in the name of your beliefs. But I don't hate *you*, Nico. I will never hate you."

"Why not?" he tried to say but his tongue was pressed down by the silencer, and he could only make strangled, unintelligible noises. "Why don't you hate me? How can you not?"

The air shivered and he thought he heard a laugh.

Cénzi? Varina?

Again, he tried to return to his prayer but his mind wouldn't allow it. His head was full of voices, but not the one he so desired to hear. He fell backward into memory, lurched forward again into the squalid, filthy present, then fell back again.

He was eleven, in the house where they lived after Elle took him away from Nessantico, where she stayed when her belly was at its fullest with the child inside, the one she said would be his brother or sister. He could hear Elle groaning and crying in the next room, and he huddled in the common room, scared and frightened by the obvious pain in her voice and praying to Cénzi that she'd be all right. He'd heard many times about women dying in childbirth, and he didn't know what would happen to him if Elle died—not with his own matarh and vatarh dead, not with Varina and Karl probably dead also for all he knew. Elle was all he had in the world, and so he prayed as hard as he could that she would live. He promised Cénzi that he would devote his life to Him if he would keep Elle alive.

Elle moaned again, and this time gave a long, shrill scream that was quickly muffled, as if someone had placed a hand or a pillow over Elle's mouth, and he heard the oste-femme in attendance give a call to her assistants. Nico uncurled himself from the corner and went to the closed door, opening it carefully. He could see Elle propped up in a seated position on the bed, two of the attendants holding her. "Where's my baby?" she was saying, weeping. "Where ... No, be quiet, be quiet! I can't hear! Where is it?" Nico knew she was talking not only to those in the room, but to the voices in her head.

There was a lot of blood on the sheets. He tried not to look at it.

A wet nurse sat on chair nearby, but the laces of her tashta were still tied and her face was drawn. The oste-femme was crouched over a bundle at the foot of the bed. She was shaking her head. "I'm sorry, Vajica," she said to Elle. "The cord was—what is that *boy* doing here?"

Nico realized the oste-femme was staring at him in the doorway. "I can help," he said.

"Out!" the oste-femme shouted, pointing at the door. She gestured to one of the attendants. "Get him out!" she ordered, and turned back to the bundle. Nico ran into the room. He could feel the cold of power around him. He had felt it since he'd begun praying, growing more frigid and more powerful with each breath he took. Now it seared his lungs and his throat, and he couldn't hold it back. He pushed forward even as the attendant grabbed at him, as Elle shouted either at him or the voices in her head or the oste-femme. Between the arms of the oste-femme he could see a baby, though her skin was a strange blue-white color and there was a flesh-colored rope around her neck. He reached toward her . . . And when he touched her, he felt the cold energy surge out of him as he spoke words he didn't know at all and his hands moved in an odd pattern. His fingers touched her leg, and he gasped as the power ran out of him, leaving him as exhausted as if he'd been running all day. The baby's leg jerked, and then the body convulsed and the rope dissolved: the child's mouth opened and there was a wail and cry. The oste-femme had taken a step back as Nico had pushed past her; now she gasped. "The child," she said. "She was dead . . ."

The baby was crying now, and the wet nurse came forward, untying the blouse of her tashta and taking the baby in her arms. "What is going on?" Elle was saying, but then . . .

. . . then the memory shifted. It no longer possessed the soft haze of recollection. Everything was sharp-edged and too brightly colored, the way it was when Cénzi gave him a vision. It was no longer Elle on the childbirth bed but Varina, and she opened her arms. Nico cuddled himself happily in her arms. She stroked his hair. "You saved her life," Varina said. "It was you."

"I prayed to Cénzi," he told her. "It was Him."

"No," Varina/Elle answered softly, her hands stroking his back. "It was *you*, Nico. You alone. You reached into the Second World and took its power, which doesn't come from Cénzi or any other god but just *is*. You are able to tap that. Rochelle owes you her life. She will always owe you that."

"Rochelle? Is that going to be her name?"

"Yes. It was my own matarh's name," Varina/Elle said, "and I will teach her all I know, and one day she might give you back what you gave her."

The woman who was both Elle and not-Elle hugged him

hard, and Nico hugged her back, but now there was only empty air there. He opened his eyes.

The sun had risen, and now he heard the wind-horns sounding First Call, as sunlight crawled reluctantly down the black tower of the Bastida a'Drago toward the opening of his cell. He wanted, suddenly, to look outside, to see the rising light. He tried to get to his feet, but they were as stiff and unyielding as stone, and when he tried to move them, the pain made him scream behind the gag of the silencer. He couldn't stand. Instead, he dragged himself forward on his chained hands, crawling to the opening that led to the small open ledge in the tower. He pulled himself up on the railing there, moaning with the sharp prickling in his legs as life returned to them. He stared out at the morning. A mist had risen from the A'Sele, and the Avi a'Parete outside the gates of the Bastida was beginning to fill with people walking to temple or to early morning errands.

One figure snared his gaze . . . A woman was standing near the Bastida gates, underneath the leering grin of the dragon's head. She wasn't moving, but staring at the Bastida, and at the tower in which he was held. Even at the distance, there was something about her, something familiar. "Rochelle . . . ?" he breathed. He didn't know if he was dreaming, or if it was even possible; he'd not seen her in years. But those features . . .

He tried to pull himself upright on the ledge, but his hand slipped on the rail, his legs couldn't hold him, and he fell. He pulled himself up again, hating that he couldn't shout her name. But he could wave, he could make her see him . . .

She wasn't there. She'd vanished. He scanned the Avi for some sign of her—there, could that be her, hurrying away north over the Pontica?—but he couldn't be certain and he couldn't shout after her. The figure vanished into the crowds and distance.

He let himself fall again on the ledge.

Was it her, Cénzi? Did you send her to me?

It wasn't Cénzi who answered. Instead, he thought he heard the soft laughter of Varina.

~

Sergei ca'Rudka

"HOW LONG HAS HE been this way?"

The garda at Nico's cell shrugged at Sergei's question. His gaze kept dropping to the roll of leather under Sergei's arm. "All night," he said. "He started praying when you left; he won't drink, won't eat. Just prays."

"Open the door," Sergei told the man, "and come inside with me. I may need your help."

The garda nodded. There might have been the flicker of a smile on his lips as he took the ring of keys from his belt and unlocked the cell, pushing the door open. He stepped inside and gestured toward Nico. "You want me to drag him back inside?"

Sergei shook his head as he stepped into the cell, sliding past the garda. "Nico?" he called.

Nico didn't respond.

He was kneeling on the ledge of the tower, the sun throwing a long shadow from his huddled form across the cell. Sergei could see that he'd soiled his bashta sometime in the night. "Nico?" he called again, and again there was no response. Moving carefully over the filthy straw on the stone floor, placing the roll of leather on his bed, Sergei stepped around Nico's body until he could see his face. His eyes were closed, but his chest heaved with his breaths. His hands were clasped together, and his mouth was moving around the silencer as if he were praying. "Nico!" he said, more loudly this time, stepping into the sunlight so that his shadow covered Nico.

The eyes opened sluggishly, and Nico squinted up at Sergei through slitted, pouched eyes. "You look terrible," Sergei told him.

Nico gave a strangled laugh around the gag.

"Let me take the silencer off. You'll promise not to try to use the Ilmodo?"

Nico gave a slow nod, and Sergei unbuckled the straps of

the device and lifted it from Nico's head. Nico coughed and swallowed hard, wiping awkwardly at his face with chained hands and the sleeve of his bashta. "Thank you," he said. His gaze fixed on the leather roll, on the garda standing silently near the door with an eager grin on his face. "Why is it that I think there's no food this time? Do you want to hear me scream? Is that it?"

"It doesn't have to be that way," Sergei told him. "It's not . . . not what I want. Not from you. But we need the war-téni and they listen to you."

"And you think that you can torture me into cooperation." Slowly, he stood, rubbing at his legs and grimacing.

Sergei shrugged. "I don't think it. I know it. I've done it many times."

"Ah, dear Silvernose. You enjoy that, don't you, forcing someone to do what they don't want to do?" Strangely, he was still smiling. "You enjoy their pain."

Sergei didn't answer. He went to the bed, untied the strings. He pushed at the end of the roll, letting it open. The garda chuckled as he did so. His instruments were all there, the ones he'd collected and cared for over the long years, the ones he'd used so many times, with so many prisoners. He knew Nico was looking at them also; he knew the thrill of fear that would be surging through Nico's body as he imagined those devices twisting and tearing and gouging his flesh. Nico would already be feeling the pain, before Sergei even plucked the first tool from its loop.

Can this be the time that it changes?

But it couldn't be, not if he wanted to save Nessantico. Not this time.

But Nico wasn't staring at the array of instruments with fear just as the myriad others had. He regarded them with a steady gaze, and only then looked slowly back to Sergei. His cracked and battered lips still twitched with a smile, and through the purpling bruises on his face, his eyes were unafraid. *Has the boy gone mad entirely?* "Which first?" Nico asked him. "That one?" He pointed to a clawed pincer. "Or that one?" His finger moved, to the brass hammer. "You like that one especially, don't you?"

"Will you sign the document?" Sergei asked. "Will you stand before the Old Temple and recant? Will you tell the war-téni that they must serve?"

"Cénzi gave me a vision tonight," Nico said conversationally, making Sergei's eyes narrow at the evasion. "I prayed for turn after turn, and He wouldn't answer me. When He finally did, it was strange, and I'm still not sure that I understood. Varina was there. And my sister."

"Nico," Sergei said softly, gently, as if speaking to a child. "Listen to me. There's no other way for you. I must have your recantation. I must have it for Nessantico. I must have it to save lives and for the good of all here. Tell me that you'll recant and none of this has to happen. Tell me."

"Varina told me that I still had the Gift, that it hadn't been taken from me."

"Nico . . ."

He raised his manacled hands. "You said Varina saved my life."

"She did."

"Tell me, my friend Silvernose, do you think she saved me for this?" He gestured at the bed and the instruments there. The chains clinked dully with the motion.

"It's for Varina's sake that I haven't already forced you," Sergei told him. "It's for her that I still won't—as long as you swear to me and Cénzi that you'll recant. But you make one mistake, Nico—it's not Varina who has spared your life, but the Kraljica at Varina's request. The Kraljica will let you live if you confess your mistake; she has given me the charge to force that from you if you refuse, and if you *still* will not . . ." Sergei lifted his hands. He plucked the brass hammer from its loop and fitted the handle to it. "If you will not—then after I am finished with you, you'll be handed over to the Archigos. I guarantee you that you'll find no compassion there."

"You and I both believe in Cénzi, Ambassador. We both believe that His will should be followed."

"I don't believe Cénzi talks to me," Sergei answered. He tapped the battered end of the brass hammer in one palm. "I do the best I can, but I'm only a weak human being. I do what I think is best for Cénzi, but most especially what I think is best for Nessantico."

Nico nodded. He turned his back to Sergei and shuffled gingerly to the ledge of the cell. He stood there looking out. "I could let myself fall," he said to the air. "It would all be over in a few breaths."

"Others have done that," Sergei said. "If you do, I'll produce a signed confession from you and have it read aloud in the plaza. It won't be as effective, but it might suffice."

Nico smiled over his shoulder. Sergei thought then that he would do it. There was nothing he could do to stop Nico; by the time he reached the young man, his body would already be broken on the stones of the courtyard below; even if he did, Sergei no longer had the strength to hold him back—they might both end up falling.

But Nico didn't fall. He took a long breath, looking out over the city. "I thought I saw my sister out there," he told Sergei. "Varina and my sister, and poor dead Liana, whose only sin was that she loved me and followed me—that's what Cénzi gives me when I pray to Him."

He looked back at Sergei, and his face was bleak. "All I wanted—all I *ever* wanted—was to serve Him, in gratitude for the Gift He has given me."

"Then serve Him, and admit that you were wrong."

"How do you do that?" Nico asked. "How do you suddenly change what you've done for years? How?"

Sergei came forward to stand next to him. He remembered this ledge; all the stones he'd come to know so well in the time he'd been held here himself. Nico was crying, twin tears leaving a clean path on his grimy cheeks. "I don't know how," he told Nico. "I only know that you have to start with one step."

He was still holding the brass hammer. He lifted it, showing it to Nico. "Put your hands on the railing there," he told Nico sternly. "Do it!" The garda started forward to force Nico's cooperation, but Sergei gestured to him to stay back.

Nico, his hands trembling in their chains, placed them flat on the weathered, chipped stone, his fingers splayed out. Sergei lifted the hammer. He could imagine the brass head coming down, crushing flesh and bone, and the sweet, sweet cry of agony that Nico would make and the pleasure that would surge through him with it.

. . . and he let the hammer fall from his hands, tumbling over the edge of the balcony to clatter loudly on the flagstones below. Chips of stone flew, the wooden handle splintered into two pieces; the hammer leaving a deep gouge in the stone The gardai stationed at the gates jumped, startled, looking back at the courtyard.

"Come with me," Sergei told Nico. "We're going to the Old Temple. I think you have something to say."

Nico lifted his hands. He stared at them wonderingly and clenched them into fists.

He nodded.

～

Jan ca'Ostheim

JAN VIEWED THE LANDSCAPE FROM THE TOP of the hill along the Avi a'Sele, some fifteen miles out of Nessantico, and his mind reeled. "Cénzi's balls . . ." Starkkapitän ca'Damont breathed alongside him, and Commandant Eleric ca'Talin gave a sympathetic laugh at the curse.

"It's rather impressive, isn't it?" the Commandant said. "They're swarming along the road and a good mile or two on either side. I have reports that companies of their warriors crossed the A'Sele and are now on the south side as well. We haven't been able to do more than annoy them, much less stop them."

Jan had seen armies on the march before, but rarely so large a force. The Westlanders spread out before them, dark specks crawling like ants along the road and through the tilled fields to either side, the scales sewn onto their bamboo-and-leather armor glistening in sunlight. They made the army at Commandant ca'Talin's back look like but a single squad. The Firenzcian force that would be arriving was little more than half the size of the Tehuantins. "I feel better now that we have at least a few hands of warténi with us," ca'Talin continued, "and we have adequate supplies of black sand, but these Westerner sorcerers are terribly strong, and we already know what their own black sand weapons can do against city walls. They cut through Villembouchure's defense like rats through soft cheese; it was all I could do to hold the town for a single day and make it as costly for them as I could. Still, they forced me to retreat just to preserve the troops I had so I could continue to harry them on the way here." The Commandant shook his head. "If I thought we had any realistic chance of cutting them down significantly, I would say we should bring your troops here and engage the Tehuantin here and now, before they reach Nessantico. We have the advantage of height, and beyond these last hills the land flattens in front of Nessantico, and we'll have less room to maneuver. But if we do that and fail, then we've abandoned the city's defenses to those who manage to live and retreat, and to the Garde Kralji. If you have some better strategy, Hïrzg, Starkkapitän, I'd be happy to hear it."

Ca'Damont only shook his gray head. Jan stared downward. "Watch," ca'Talin said. "I've sent out a group of chevarittai to attack their left flank there, by the river where the Westerners are exposed. The chevarittai are in that copse of trees..."

Before the Commandant had finished speaking, a group of two hands of mailed riders rushed outward from the cover of the trees, hurtling toward a group of Tehuantin warriors who had become slightly separated from the main group. They saw the Westlander warriors bring down their pikes, grounding them against the charge. But the lead chevaritt hurled something that glistened in the sun toward their front ranks. It exploded, shattering as it reached them. They saw the brilliance of the explosion and the smoke rising from the Tehuantin ranks before the sound of the explosion came, a thunder that rolled from the hillside. There was a hole in the pike line, with several of the Westlanders on the ground. The chevarittai slammed into that hole, swords and spears slashing, but now they could see other warriors hurrying toward the gap, and plume-helmeted sorcerers raising their spell-staffs. Lightnings flashed, and—with the shrill call of a cornet—the chevarittai were retreating back through the hole they'd torn in the line. There were only six of them now, with two riderless horses accompanying them, and two more horses down. They hurried back into the cover of the trees as arrows plummeted down around them— Jan saw another rider fall under the assault just before they reached the tree line.

Then it was over.

"Five dead," ca'Damont said. "But I count at least twice that number of the Westlanders down. Still..." He licked at his lips. "That's not a margin of loss we can sustain. There's bravery—and our chevarittai have that in abundance—and there's stupidity. We can pick off the Tehuantin a hand at a time, but even if we do, they'll be at the gates of Nessantico in five days at their current pace. With the black sand they have, we won't be able to keep them out—and if they can do at Nessantico something like they did at Karnmor . . ." Ca'Damont shuddered. "I thank Cénzi for your reconciliation with the Kraljica, Hïrzg Jan. Without Firenzcia, we would be doomed. Even with your support, nothing is certain. I cede control of the Garde Civile to you, and I'll cooperate with you and the Starkkapitän in any way I can."

"Thank you, Commandant," Jan told him. "My matarh chose well when she named you Commandant, and she's fortunate to have someone of your skill at her side. You've done as well as could be expected. No one could have done better." Starkkapitän ca'Damont nodded at that appraisal.

He looked again at the deadly array before them, then over his shoulder at the land behind: the Avi a'Sele winding through woods until it vanished. He could, faintly, see the roofs of Pre a'Fleuve above the distant treetops. Only a few miles beyond that lay Nessantico. And somewhere just to the west of Nessantico, his own army should be nearly within sight of the city, weary from a long, fast march from Firenzcia.

To the immediate south, the great ribbon of the River A'Sele curled through the rolling landscape, oblivious to the drama that was unfolding so near to it. Whether the Holdings prevailed or the Tehuantin, it would continue to flow to the sea, unperturbed and uncaring.

"I agree with your assessment, Commandant," he said. "We can't stand here, not with the troops we have, though it's a shame since we have the high ground. Still, I think we might yet slow them down. We need more time to prepare, for my own troops to arrive and rest, and for Sergei to get more of the war-téni here also. We'll meet their main force outside Nessantico because it's our only choice, but I think we'll also give them a taste of what they're up against—if only so we can see how they'll react. Starkkapitän, Commandant, let's retire to the tents and make our plans . . ."

Niente

FOR THE LAST FEW DAYS, the Easterners had harassed their forces, nipping at the outlying flanks like angry dogs, then pulling back without ever fully engaging. Niente wondered at the tactics—the Easterners still held the high ground while most of their own warriors were concentrated along the road and the fields alongside it, in the valleys of this land. Niente knew that if Citlali had been the Easterner general, he would have rained down storms of arrows on them, would have hurled spells from the heavens toward them, would have sent wave upon wave of soldiers down from the hills. He would have forced decisive battle on them while he held the advantage of the land.

But the Easterners would only sometimes use their archers as the warriors moved through the passes. They sent out only small groups of riders who would try to pick off squads who had strayed from the main body of the army. They only rarely used their spellcasters.

Perhaps Atl had been right. Perhaps the best path was that leading to a victory here. Perhaps they could achieve such a devastating blow to their empire that they could never force the horrible retaliation that Niente had glimpsed in the scrying bowl.

Perhaps.

Niente trudged with the rest of the nahualli in the train of Nahual Atl. His feet ached, his legs trembled with exhaustion whenever they stopped, and he wondered if he could keep up even this slow pace until they reached the city. As Nahual, he had ridden and rarely walked, but now . . . The other nahualli mostly ignored him, as if he were invisible. When he'd been Nahual, they'd been eager to seek him out, to ask his advice, to listen to what he had to say. No longer. Now he watched them fawn over his son as they once had him. He watched Atl bask in their adoration. He saw the jealousy in their hearts, and the appraisal in their eyes as they searched him for any weakness that they might exploit.

They measured themselves against Atl as they had once done against Niente, to see if they might become Nahual themselves.

"Taat!" He heard Atl call him, and he quickened his pace as they walked, moving through the nahualli to where his son rode—on the horse Niente had once ridden himself—a careful six paces behind Tecuhtli Citlali in the middle of the train.

"Nahual," Niente said, and found that he found himself secretly pleased to see the pain in his son's eyes at the use of the title. "What is it you need?"

"Did you use the scrying bowl last night?"

Niente shook his head. He'd not used the bowl since he'd abdicated his title. He could still feel its weight in the leather bag sung over his shoulder. Atl's lips pursed at the answer. Niente thought that Atl already looked visibly older than before they'd left their own country: the cost of using the far-sight. In time—too little time—he would look as haggard and ancient and scarred as Niente did now. His face would be a horror, a constant reminder of the power of Axat's grip. One day he would realize that all Niente's warnings had been true.

Niente hoped that he wasn't alive to see that day.

"I can see little in my own bowl," Atl said, his voice a whisper that only the two of them could hear. "Everything is confused. There are so many images, so many contradictions. And Tecuhtli Citlali keeps asking what I think of his strategies."

Again, Niente felt a guilty stab of satisfaction. "Do you still see victory for us?"

A nod. "I do. Yet . . ."

"Yet?"

An uncomfortable shrug. He looked forward, not at Niente. "I was so sure, Taat. Right after Karnmor, I could nearly *touch* it, everything was so clear. Yet since then, a mist has begun to overlay everything, there are shadows moving in the future and forces I can't quite see. It's become worse since, well, since you stepped down."

"I know," Niente told him. "I felt the forces and the changes, too."

Atl looked back at Niente, and lifted his right arm

slightly, so that the golden bracelet of the Nahual shone briefly. "This isn't what I wanted, Taat. I would rather you were still wearing this, and that is the truth. It was only . . . I know what I had seen in the bowl, and it wasn't what you said was there."

"I know that also."

"Could you have killed me, had we fought as the Tecuhtli wanted?"

Niente nodded. "Yes." His answer was certain and quick. Yes, he was still stronger than his son with the X'in Ka. Even now. He was sure of that. "But . . . I wouldn't. I wouldn't kill my own son so I could continue to call myself Nahual. I couldn't."

Atl didn't answer, seeming to ponder that. "I need your help, Taat. You were Nahual for so long. I need your advice, your counsel, your skill."

"You have it," he told Atl, and for the first time in days, he smiled. Slowly, Atl returned the gesture.

"Good," Atl said. "Then tonight when we stop, we will both use our scrying bowls, and we will talk with each other about what we see, and that way I will give Tecuhtli Citlali the best advice I can. Will you do that with me, Taat?"

Niente patted his son's leg. "I will."

"Good. Then it's settled. You!" Atl called out to one of the nahualli. "Go and find a horse for the Uchben Nahual. I need to speak to him and borrow from his wisdom, and he should not be walking. Hurry!" *Uchben Nahual*—the Old Nahual.

He could be that. He could serve that way.

If that was the role Axat had given him, he would perform it.

~

Varina ca'Pallo

SHE MIGHT HAVE UNDERSTOOD instinctively if she had borne children of her own with Karl, but that had never happened. But Karl had his children, back in Paeti.

"It's different with your own children," Karl had told her once. *"It doesn't matter what they do—there's very little they could do, even some horrible things, that would change the way you feel about them. You might hate their actions, but you can never hate them."*

She thought she might realize that, finally.

She'd accosted Sergei after the meeting with Hïrzg Jan, pulling at the old Silvernose's bashta as they left the palais. "If you hurt him, Sergei, I will never forgive you," she said. "Never. I don't care how long we've been friends. If you torture him, I will never call you friend again."

His face was pained, the wrinkles deep around his false nose and eyes. "Varina, the war-téni—"

"I don't care," she told him. "Remember that Karl and I risked our lives to save you from the same fate. Pay us back now."

Sergei had only shaken his head. *"I can promise nothing,"* he'd answered. *"I'm sorry, Varina. Nessantico needs the war-téni."*

Strange how Nico had become the son she'd never had. The son she'd lost for years after the first invasion of Nessantico. The son who hated everything she and Karl believed and for which they'd struggled over the decades. The son who seemed perfectly comfortable with the thought of killing her for his own beliefs.

You might hate their actions, but you can never hate them.

She could not hate him. It made no sense, but the feelings were there.

The page had come to her at the Numetodo House from the palais, bearing a letter from the Kraljica. "The Kraljica requires your presence at the Old Temple in a turn of the glass," he said, bowing to her. And he'd left. The letter had said little more, only that Allesandra herself would be there, and that she requested her presence both as a friend and as a member of the Council of Ca', and that the Archigos would also be present. She knew that it must be something to do with Nico. The thought terrified her.

She wasn't certain what she'd do if he'd been abused, how she might react. She didn't know what she *could* do, since Talbot had already started manufacturing the sparkwheels for the Garde Kralji and Garde Civile. Her single bargaining chip was gone.

So she watched the carriage with the Garde Kralji's insignia on it as it clattered into the open space of the plaza. A dais had been erected near the blackened, shattered front facade of the Old Temple, with a viewing stand no more than five strides from it. The dais was only large enough for a few people to stand on; in the center was a wooden pillar with chains attached. Allesandra was already seated on the viewing stand with a cadre of Garde Kralji gardai around her; there was a sea of téni also present, though if Archigos Karrol was indeed watching, he did so from somewhere else—Varina wondered if Allesandra had insisted on that. Behind the téni there was a dense crowd of onlookers, as if this were a holiday and they were there for the celebration. They were strangely silent, the citizens of Nessantico; Varina had no sense of what they were thinking or where their sympathies might lie.

Varina wanted to go toward the carriage, knowing that Nico would be inside, but Allesandra gestured to her from the stand and Talbot had already come up to her. "Follow me, A'Morce," he said. Varina looked back at the carriage, then followed Talbot to the stand, the gardai sliding aside as they climbed the short set of stairs. Varina curtsied to Allesandra, then to the other members of the Council of Ca', who were seated immediately behind the Kraljica.

"Sit here, my dear," Allesandra told her, gesturing to a seat at her right side. The seat to the left was vacant; Varina wondered if Archigos Karrol was supposed to be sitting there—which also made her wonder at the significance of placing the Archigos to the left, lower position, but then Talbot seated himself there.

The carriage—its windows shuttered so that no one could see inside, and pulled by a single black horse—had come alongside the smaller dais. Gardai hurried forward, surrounding it as two of them opened the doors. From the side facing the Kraljica, Sergei was helped down. Leaning on his cane, he bowed to the stand with its dignitaries, then went around to the far side of the carriage. Varina glimpsed Nico's head over the top of the carriage, then more of him as he ascended the stairs alongside Sergei. Was he limping, or was that only due to the chains that bound his ankles and hands? There were bruises on his face, but they seemed old, not fresh, and there were no ob-

vious disfigurements. His head was free of the terrible cage
of the silencer. He seemed to incline himself toward Sergei
as they reached the top of the dais, saying something to the
man. He appeared to nearly smile as he looked out at the
crowd—would that be the reaction of a man who'd been
tortured?

Now Nico, too, faced the Kraljica, and he bent low at the
waist toward her, giving her the sign of Cénzi as best he could
with manacled hands. "Kraljica," he said. "Councillors." He
seemed to be scanning the crowd. Varina wondered if he were
looking for the Archigos. "And especially, téni. I've come to
plead for your forgiveness, and your understanding."

His voice was a husk, containing but a memory of the
power Varina remembered. He sounded weak and exhausted. But he lifted his head, and he looked out at each
of them, his eyes finding all of them in turn. Varina felt the
shock of connection when his gaze came to her. He smiled
again then, nodding ever so slightly to her, and she could
not stop herself from giving him a smile in return. Then
his gaze drifted on, and Varina thought that he stared for
a long time past the téni into the citizenry, and she half-
turned to see who had caught his eye. But he finally cleared
his throat and began to speak again.

"I acted in the belief that I was doing what Cénzi required of me," he said, more loudly. "Nothing more. I say
that not to excuse my actions, but so you understand that
there was no malice in them, only faith. A terribly mistaken
faith." His voice ignited with the last few words. They shivered, they pulsed, they rang from the ramparts of the buildings around the plaza with impossible clarity. Varina found
herself looking around to see if some téni were chanting,
adding the power of the Ilmodo to his words, but she could
see no movement among the green-robed ranks, and she
realized that it must be from Nico himself. She wondered if
Sergei realized that Nico was able to use the Ilmodo even
with his hands chained, as no téni should be able to do.
Even Allesandra's head moved back as if trying to escape
the sound, and now Sergei glanced over at Nico, his head
cocked as if he were puzzled.

"I thought I was Cénzi's Voice," Nico continued. "I
thought I was the Absolute. But I was not. It was actually
my own voice I heard, my own hatred and prejudices. I

apologize to all of those who listened to me then, and I tell you this: I was, all unwittingly, a false prophet and you would have been better not to have listened to me. I might still have the love of the most important person in my life had I not been so foolish." Varina heard his voice choke at that, and she thought of Serafina—she'd left the baby asleep at the Numetodo House, with the wet nurse Belle watching over her.

"I apologize to you," Nico continued, "and I am profoundly sorry for what I've done. Your sins are on my head, and when Cénzi calls me I will need to answer for them. I release you. I tell you now: follow your Archigos. Follow your Kraljica and your Hïrzg."

"There," Allesandra whispered to Varina. "That is what we've come for. We have you to thank for this, Varina . . ." She seemed almost ready to rise and respond, but Nico had taken a breath, and now his voice was ice and fire at once.

"I believed," Nico said. "I still believe. I have prayed now for days for His direction. What I've come to realize is that the gift Cénzi has given me is not constrained by laws and restrictions that the Faith placed on me. Cénzi's revelation to me in the wake of my folly was both enlightening and freeing." He raised his bound hands as if offering them to the sky. "I had allowed the Archigos and those within the Faith to chain and bind my gift in their human fetters, when, in fact, Cénzi places no such limitation on them. That's what the Numetodo have known all along, to their credit—" and there Nico's gaze found Varina again, and he smiled broadly toward her. "That's what I finally realized myself, and what I demonstrate to you now."

Varina stood. "Nico, no . . ." she began, her voice a pale shadow of his own, but it was already too late.

Nico's hands were still raised, and now he gestured once with both of them together, and he shouted a single word—a word in the language of the Ilmodo, of the Scáth Cumhacht, of the X'in Ka. A darkness, a fragment of a starless and moonless night, seemed to wrap around him, hiding him. Sergei gave a shout and reached toward Nico, only to draw his hand back with a cry when he touched the darkness. The gardai did the same, but when they reached the darkness, the false night in which Nico had wrapped himself suddenly vanished.

And where Nico had been, they found only the chains in which he'd been fettered, lying on the wooden planks of the dais. Nico himself had vanished.

Varina blinked. "Well," she said, "it seems he listened to me more than I thought."

~

Rochelle Botelli

ROCHELLE WATCHED NICO, weighed down in chains as he was helped up to the dais, with Old Silvernose standing right alongside him. She felt helpless, the emotion even more acute now than when she'd glimpsed him in the tower of the Bastida from the Avi a'Parete. Then, she'd had no hope that she could help him. Now, he was so close: without the horrid black stones of the Bastida holding him; without the unknown corridors between them; with only the téni and some gardai separating them.

Yet she still couldn't help him. They would catch her and drag her down before she reached him even though several of them would be dead as a result. But she would fail. Must fail. That was another thing Matarh had taught her, even in her madness. *"Make certain the odds are well in your favor before you move. Sometimes, you must just accept that you can't win and not even try."*

To be so achingly close to him, to see her brother again and not be able to help him . . .

It hurt. It wounded her as surely as a sword's edge. Yet there was something she might accomplish today, if she had the chance. The Kraljica was here, her great-matarh, and though Allesandra was as well guarded as her brother, perhaps there might be a moment, a chance. Rochelle's hand went to the dagger under her clothing, the dagger she'd stolen from her vatarh. The vow she'd made to her matarh burned in her mind.

If she couldn't save a life, perhaps she could take one just as important.

On the dais, Nico bowed to the ca'-and-cu' on their own

raised platform. "Kraljica, Councillors. And especially, téni. I've come to plead for your forgiveness, and your understanding." His voice sounded tired, and he was looking around. His gaze flitted over each of them, and Rochelle stood on her toes, trying to see better over the people around her. Then it happened. Nico's eyes found hers. She could *feel* the connection and acknowledgment. Nico was staring right at her, and his lips curled in the faintest of smiles, as if he *knew* her. He nodded toward her, as if telling her that he knew why she was there and to be patient. She wanted to wave toward him, to shout out his name, but then his gaze moved back to the dignitaries on their stand, and his voice had gained volume and power. She half-listened to him as she tried to push through the crowd closer to the stand. Nico's voice continued to swell and pulse; it was like the beating of summer sunlight on her. She caught words here and there:

"I thought I was Cénzi's Voice . . . I am profoundly sorry for what I've done . . . I believed. I still believe . . ." Above the crowd, she saw Nico lifting his hands and the gesture caught her. She stopped, wondering.

"I had allowed the Archigos and those within the Faith to chain and bind my gift in their human fetters, when, in fact, Cénzi places no such limitation on them. That's what the Numetodo have known all along, to their credit. That's what I finally realized myself, and what I demonstrate to you now."

Nico?

She never saw clearly what happened next. It was as if Nico had wrapped himself completely in a black cloak. She heard people shouting and gesturing, saw Old Silvernose withdraw his hand from the darkness with a curse, then . . .

Nico was gone, and people all around the plaza were shouting wordlessly. The gardai were buzzing like a hive of bees whose nest had just been struck. Rochelle had moved to the rear edge of the Kraljica's dais, just behind the ring of gardai. They jumped up onto the stage now, closing around the Kraljica with their swords drawn, and Rochelle drew back. There was no hope of getting to Allesandra now. None. Again, this was one of the times when she must allow herself to fail.

She drifted back in the crowd, away from the suspicious eyes of the gardai, away from the green-robed téni who seemed just as upset and on edge.

A hand touched her shoulder from behind and she

whirled, the dagger already drawn. She could kill someone in this crowd easily enough and still escape in the confusion . . .

But her hand stopped in mid-thrust. "Nico—"

"Hush!" he said. He'd drawn a hood over his head; his face was visible only to those who looked directly at him. But even half-hidden as he was, he looked incredibly exhausted and drawn. His hand on her shoulder trembled, and she felt him sag, as if he was barely able to stand. In the shadow of the hood, there were darker circles under his eyes. "Cénzi told me you were here. He showed you to me. Come on!" She looked back at the dais and he shook his head. "No. Not now, Rochelle. Come! I need your help."

He put his arm around her. Leaning heavily on her, he guided her away, through the thinning edge of the crowd and away from the growing uproar and the plaza itself, until they were walking down a street adorned with shop signs and busy with hustling people, though few of them seemed to be interested in the wares displayed in the open windows or in the sidewalk cabinets. Their faces were grim and harried, and Rochelle remembered the same looks on the faces of those fleeing the city when she'd arrived.

Nico finally stopped near a café. "You have money?" he asked her, and she nodded. "Good. I need to sit and to eat—they will hardly look for me here."

They took a table against the wall of the cafe and ordered wine, cheese, bread, and some meats. The waiter seemed genuinely pleased to have a patron; no doubt those had been far more sparse than usual in the past few weeks.

She watched Nico as he ate. He had changed a great deal from the boy she remembered. The Nico of her memory had been eager and apprehensive all at the same time as he prepared to go to Brezno Temple as an acolyte. She'd been with him again, when he'd taken the green robe of the téni and made his pledge to Cénzi in that same temple, and he'd seemed so sure of himself then..

The Nico who stood before her now was thinner, his cheeks drawn in. The lines of his face were harsher and more deeply drawn, and she could see the pain of his life written there. There had always been an intensity to him, one that she remembered from her earliest memory of him, but was changed now. It had turned into something harder, deeper inside himself, and more dangerous.

She knew she had changed as well. Perhaps more than Nico had. Neither of them were the person they'd been back then. Brother and sister they might be, but time had pulled them apart and she didn't know if they could ever fit together again.

"You're staring." Nico set down the cup and poured himself more wine from the flagon.

"I haven't seen you in years, Nico."

He smiled. "You've grown into an attractive young woman." Then the smile faded. "You've also taken on Matarh's legacy. I've heard the gossip that the White Stone still walks. That's you?"

She nodded.

"Do you hear their voices, too?"

"No. I'm not mad, Nico."

"Not yet," he answered. "But you can't do what you do and stay sane. You can't do what you do and expect anything but the soul shredders after your death. Cénzi will find you wanting, my sister."

It was so similar to what Sergei had told her that she wanted to laugh. "You're going to lecture *me*?" Rochelle sniffed in derision. "They had you in chains, Nico. How many died when you and your people took the Old Temple?" She saw him flush with that accusation, and she remembered. "I'm sorry, Nico," she said, putting her hand on his. "I forgot. I wish I could have met Liana."

He nodded, and she saw his eyes swim in sudden moisture. He wiped at them, almost angrily. "I wish that, too. You see, that was *my* punishment. My madness. Cénzi always gives us warnings, one way or another. It's just that we sometimes don't pay attention to them or even see them for what they are."

"You still believe, after all this?" she asked him. "You still think your destiny is within the Faith?"

"Yes." He said it firmly, without hesitation, the strength returning to his voice. "And what about your own faith, Rochelle? Do you still believe?"

"I don't know," she answered. "I think so, but . . ." A shoulder rose under her tashta. "I don't know," she repeated. "But you do?"

"I do," he said. "Still. Cénzi contains everything, Rochelle. He contains all that is good, and He contains all that is evil as well. That is why the Moitidi fought each other and Him; because they were His children and thus contained within themselves were all possibilities. And He brought you here, now, for a reason."

Rochelle laughed bitterly. "You have no idea why I'm here."

"Don't I?" Nico reached across the table and plucked up a baguette. He broke off a piece of the bread and pushed it into his mouth with a forefinger. He chewed contentedly for a moment, then took a sip of the wine. Then he leaned forward toward her conspiratorially. "You're here to kill the Kraljica," he whispered, and leaned back again.

Rochelle felt her face flush, and he laughed. "Oh, it's not such a revelation," he told her. "Matarh asked the same of me, when I became a téni. 'You'll be close to her one day,' she told me. 'When you're an a'téni or maybe even the Archigos. You'll be close to her, and I want you to kill her for me, because of what she did to ruin my life.' Isn't that what she told you as well?"

"It was similar," Rochelle admitted.

"I thought so. But that's not why you're here, Rochelle. You're here because Cénzi wanted you to see me. He wanted to reunite us."

She felt a chill touch her spine at that, as if a winter breeze had somehow lingered behind to caress her at that moment, and she wondered where that feeling came from as she shivered and hugged herself. *He had been there, then he had wrapped himself in darkness and gone somewhere else. If I could do that, why, the White Stone could go anywhere. The White Stone could easily kill the Kraljica . . .* "What you did out there—can you do that again? Could you teach me how to do it?" she asked Nico.

"A month ago I would have said no," he told her. "I would have told you that only the pure of faith can or should use the Ilmodo. But now . . ." He drained the wine in front of him. "I don't know. Perhaps anything is possible."

"And why do you think that Cénzi wanted us together?"

"I really don't know yet," he answered, "but perhaps we'll find out."

~

Varina ca'Pallo

VARINA MADE RUSHED APOLOGIES to Kraljica
Allesandra and hurried away from the Old Temple
with a quartet of gardai assigned to her. Allesandra, the
councillors, Sergei—they were all surrounded by gardai, and everyone seemed panicked. Varina, though, was
gripped by a terrifying certainty. She made her way quickly
to the Numetodo House with her stomach burning and
worry furrowing her forehead.

The chains lying empty on the dais and Nico gone . . .

She was afraid that she knew where he'd gone.

Even before the carriage had stopped she was half-run-
ning toward the door, something she hadn't done in years.
"A'Morce," Johannes said as she pushed into the house,
looking surprised at Varina's appearance and her lack of
breath, "we didn't expect you back . . ."

"Where is she?" Varina said, interrupting him. "Serafina—
where is she?" Her voice was shrill but she didn't care.

"Why, she's upstairs with Belle, of course. I think that—"

She pushed past him, pounding up the stairs with her
heart racing. She tore open the door. Belle, a young recruit
of the Numetodo, and also a wet nurse with a new child of
her own, was sitting in a chair at the window of Varina's
office there. Startled, Belle covered herself; Varina realized
she'd been nursing the baby. "A'Morce? Is everything all
right?"

Her heart, which seemed to have been trying to force its
way from her throat, settled back into her chest. The terrible scenes she'd imagined all the way here faded slowly
in her mind: Belle lying still on the carpeted floor, the Numetodo House afire or wrecked, her other friends dead or
wounded, and Nico's child gone.

Vanished like Nico himself.

She closed her eyes for a moment, her hand to her
mouth. "I thought . . ." she began, then shut off the thought

with a shake of her head. Her heart was starting to slow, her breath to return, and now she was beginning to feel foolish at her panic. "Never mind, Belle. I don't know what I was thinking. How's Sera?"

Belle smiled. She lifted the cloth over her shoulder, showing Varina the baby suckling at her breast, the little mouth working hard even though her eyes were closed. "Hungry as a wolf cub," Belle answered. "I'm wondering if there's going to be anything left for my own little one." She laughed, stroking Sera's head, with its crown of fine golden hair. "I've found another wet nurse for her, also; my cousin Michelle lost her own baby at birth, and said she'd be willing to come to your house mornings. Between the two of us, we'll keep the little dear well fed. Now that the Firenzcians are coming, we should be safe enough."

I wish I was as certain . . . Varina forced a smile to her face. "Thank you," Varina told her. "Tell her I'll pay her double the usual rate for her trouble."

"You're very generous, A'Morce." Sera lost the nipple for a moment and started to cry with tears sparkling in her blue eyes, and Belle lifted her breast to Sera's mouth. The infant settled again. "How was the . . . ?" She stopped, uncertain of the word. "Apology?" she finished.

"Unsatisfying, I'm afraid," Varina told her. "Nico showed again why he was Absolute of the Morellis. He's escaped. Disappeared."

Varina saw Belle's arms tighten protectively around Sera—Varina could see the suspicions running through the young woman's head. "A'Morce? Perhaps you should stay here at the Numetodo House tonight where you have protection. We could make up a place for the baby . . ."

"I can deal with Nico myself if I need to," she told Belle, hoping that her voice sounded more confident than she felt. Now that she had calmed somewhat, now that she knew Serafina was safe, she was less concerned. Surely Nico would be hiding somewhere; he might have even left the city. She went to the drawer of her desk and took out the spark-wheel there. She checked that the pan was filled with black sand and that a bullet pack was in the barrel. She thrust the weapon into the sash of her tashta under her cloak. "Finish up, and I'll take her," Varina said.

Belle nodded. "I have to get back to my sister's, anyway. By now my own little one's waking up from her nap and she'll be crying for attention. This one's almost done, I think." Belle sat back; Sera let the nipple slide from her mouth, opening her eyes for a breath, then settling back. Her breathing was slow and quiet. "There, you see? Already asleep, the greedy little thing. I've a cup on your desk with more milk if you need it. I'll send Michelle over tomorrow before First Call. Here you are, A'Morce . . ."

Rising, she handed Sera to Varina, then covered herself again, tying the shoulder sash of her tashta. As Belle bustled about the room gathering her things, Varina stared down at the sleeping face: the pudgy, reddened cheeks; the contented, trusting ease with which she slept; the tiny fingers, one curled into a fist, the other clutching at the blanket in which she was wrapped. Varina felt a surge of . . . she wasn't sure what the emotion was, but inside her there was a fierce need to protect this child, as she had once felt the same urge toward Nico.

And you failed back then. You let him escape you, and that madwoman ended up taking him.

Varina leaned down and kissed Sera's forehead. Belle smiled at her. "I'll see you tomorrow, A'Morce."

"Thank you, Belle."

"It's my pleasure to help, A'Morce. The poor thing didn't deserve to lose her matarh and vatarh this way."

"No," Varina agreed. "She didn't."

Belle leaned down and kissed Sera, then bowed her head to Varina. "I'll see you in the morning with my cousin."

After Belle left, Varina sat in the chair near the window for a time, rocking back and forth and watching Sera sleep while she listened to people passing in the corridor outside or walking in the garden below her window. She thought briefly of putting Sera down and letting her sleep while she worked for a bit, then thought better of it. She wrapped Sera more tightly, then picked up her own cloak and left the office. Coming down the stairs, she passed Johannes. "I'm sorry for my abruptness earlier," she told him. "I was worried."

He nodded. "I've heard since about what happened at the Old Temple. I can understand, A'Morce. You're heading home? Why don't you let me or someone accompany you?"

"I'll be fine," she told him. "It's still early enough, and

there are plenty of people about. I'll see you tomorrow morning. There's to be a meeting with Allesandra on our progress with sparkwheels."

He bowed to her and she left the house, walking quickly across the front courtyard and out the gates, turning left on the Avi a'Parete toward their house a few blocks away. That's how she still thought of it: *their* house, as if Karl were still alive, as if she might open the door of his library there and find him sitting at the desk poring over some old tome. She still sometimes heard a noise and would turn, expecting to see him standing there, but he never was.

She hugged Sera tighter as she walked. The faces she passed would sometimes nod to her, but most of them were strained and serious: people hurrying to their own tasks and worrying about the city and what might happen. The sparseness of traffic made it look as if it were far later than it actually was; usually the Avi was at its most crowded and noisy between Second and Third Call, but not today.

Varina turned the corner onto her own street, then down the curving lane in the direction of the A'Sele. She reached the gate to their manor and unlocked it, not bothering to ring for one of the house servants. She closed the gate behind her.

"Varina." The voice to her left made her jump and clutch Sera so tightly that the baby cried in her sleep. She turned slowly, seeing two figures in the vine-wrapped shadows of the gate's stone pillar.

"Nico," she said. "You shouldn't be here." Behind Nico, a young woman stared at her intently.

Nico smiled. "Probably," he agreed. "But you have something I needed to see."

Varina took a step back. She could feel the weight of the sparkwheel under her cloak; she could feel the energy of the spells in her mind waiting to be released. Sera fussed in her arms, awake now. "Nico, I'm warning you. I'm not giving her to you. If you try to take her, I will fight you to protect her."

"I don't want to take her from you," he answered. "I'm glad they gave her to you for the time being, since I know you'll do exactly what you just said you'd do. I just want to see her—to see my daughter. Please, Varina?"

"I won't let you hold her."

"That's fair enough."

"And tell that woman to stand well back."

Nico nodded to his companion, who slid back a few steps. Varina tucked the cloth back from Sera's face as Nico came up to her. She watched his face as he stared down at the baby, watched as his face softened, as his lips curved upward in a smile, as he half-laughed at the sight of her. "The shape of her eyes—I can see Liana," he said huskily.

He reached out toward her, and Varina clutched tighter at her. She felt the spell energy boiling in her head. But he only stroked her cheek with a finger, then laughed again when Sera reached up with her hand, fisting her fingers around his. "Strong, too," he said. "That's good. Hey, Serafina. I'm your vatarh . . ." He glanced at Varina. "That's a good name. Serafina."

"Nico, if they catch you again, they won't be so kind this time."

"Then I'll need to be careful, won't I?" he said. "Are you leaving Nessantico?"

Varina shook her head. "No?" Nico said. He sounded disappointed, or perhaps concerned "Even with the baby?"

"If it comes to that, I'll send Sera away with someone I can trust." She paused. "That won't be you, Nico. I'm sorry."

He inclined his head. A sadness deepened the lines around his eyes. "I understand. But . . . At your age, Varina, we have to be realistic. And it's not just age—look at you: your study of magic has taken its own toll. The baby needs a matarh who's younger."

Varina thought he glanced sidewise toward the woman with him. Varina looked at her also. She didn't recognize the face, but there was something about her, something vaguely familiar . . . She shook her head.

"I'm aware that I'm her great-matarh's age," she told them, "and I know what my studies have done as well. I've seen the face in the mirror. I've already made inquiries. But for now, Sera's in my charge, and I will protect her. I'm serious, Nico."

"And that's understood," he told her. "I've already told you that I'm glad they gave her to you. You were always kind to me back then. Sometimes I wished . . ." He glanced again at the woman with him, then took a long breath. "Keep her safe," he said. "Maybe sometime I can actually be her vatarh."

"You *are* her vatarh," Varina told him. "And I'll tell her about you. She'll know you. I promise you that much."

Another nod. He pulled his finger away from her hand and she fussed. He stroked her cheek again. "It's time to go," he said. "Good-bye, little Serafina." He leaned down and kissed her, then straightened. The woman with him had moved to the gate.

"Let me unlock it again for you," Varina said, but the young woman only gave her a look of disdain. She plucked two thin pieces of steel from somewhere in her cloak, leaned down, and a moment later pushed the gate open. She grinned back at Varina. Nico bowed, almost as if he were leaving her house after a visit.

A moment later, he and his companion were gone. Varina pulled the gate shut again, listening to the lock click into place. Sera was whimpering.

She hugged the baby, rocking her in her arms until she settled again.

~

Brie ca'Ostheim

THE DRUMS BEAT CADENCE as the army approached the city. The a'offiziers, following orders relayed from Stakkapitän ca'Damont, steered the army toward the fields north of the Avi a'Firenzcia and didn't enter the city itself. The citizenry of the villages just outside the gates cheered the advancing battalions and the silver-and-black banners that waved above them. And they especially cheered the Hïrzgin who accompanied them.

Brie waved back to them, smiling the smile she'd perfected over the years for state affairs, a mask behind which she could hide her own uncertainty and fears, a cheerful gesture to the crowds detached from any true awareness. On the nearest of the fields where the army was to encamp, a tent had been erected, flying both the banners of Nessantico and Firenzcia, blue and gold mingling with black and silver. As Brie's carriage approached, the flaps of the tent opened and a crowned figure appeared flanked by Garde Brezno in the uniform of the Holdings, and Brie saw Sergei ca'Rudka standing just behind the crowned figure. Brie recognized the woman immediately from the paintings she'd seen of her: Allesandra. The Kraljica strode forward with her arms wide, her own smile nearly as wide. Sergei limped after her. "Where is my marriage-daughter?" Allesandra said as she approached Brie's carriage. "Where is the Hïrzgin?"

Soldiers hurried forward to open the doors of her carriage and place a step below for her. Brie took the offered hand and stepped out into the sun, blinking and keeping her own smile fastened to her face. She allowed Allesandra to fold her in her embrace, kissing her on one cheek, then the other. Allesandra smelled of rose and pomegranate; her grip was surprisingly strong and surprisingly genuine. "This moment should have come years ago," she whispered in Brie's ear. "I apologize for that; it was my fault. I have wanted to know you and your children for so long . . ."

Her voice trailed off. Brie held Allesandra's hands. She gazed at the older woman's eyes, at the folds that cushioned them, at the powder dusting the skin and the blue shadows under her painted and plucked brows. She could see Jan in the shape of those eyes and in the lines of her face; she could see a reflection of Elissa, Kriege, Caelor, and Eria as well. Even that voice, taken down in pitch . . .

"I've wanted this moment myself," Brie told her. "For longer than you might imagine, Kraljica. We have so much to talk about." She knew that Jan would scold her for saying what she said next, but she didn't care. She had looked into Allesandra's face and she had seen no monster there. 'I want my children to know their great-matarh—as she is, not as Jan has portrayed her."

Brie saw pain pass over Allesandra's face at that. "I believe it's Venerable Carin in the Toustour who advises us that the distress of truth is always preferable to the balm of lies," Allesandra answered. "Still, there are times when I think we all prefer the lies. I'm certain that Jan, in his mind, spoke what he believed to be the truth about me. I'm afraid I've not always been a good matarh to him, and I have done things—"

Brie hurried to cut off whatever admission Allesandra

intended to make, squeezing Allesandra's hands. "You have done, I'm sure, what was necessary for you to do as Kraljica. I believe that Venerable Carin is also the one who admonishes us that the past can't be changed, only the present. Let's grasp this moment, Kraljica, you and I, and make the present good."

Allesandra smiled again. "I hope my son appreciates the wife and counselor he has in you," she said.

Brie only returned the smile, perfect and practiced. "He appreciates me as much as he is able," she answered, "and as little as he can get away with."

Allesandra laughed. "Isn't that the way of things?" she exclaimed. She hugged Brie again, then took her hand. She raised it in the air, turning to the soldiers and chevarittai around them. "This is Hïrzgin Brie," she proclaimed, "and I welcome her to Nessantico as my marriage-daughter, and as the wife of the next Kraljiki and the matarh to his heirs."

Cheers erupted from the ranks around them, and Brie bowed and waved to the assembly. She wondered if they would still be cheering in a few days. "Are you hungry?" Allesandra asked. "I have dinner waiting for us in the tent . . ."

Brie let Allesandra escort her to the tent. As she passed Sergei, she stopped and gave the man the sign of Cénzi. "Hïrzgin," the Silvernose said. "It's good to see you again." He leaned closer to her then, his voice a harsh, bare whisper. "And I have things to tell you as well."

With that, he leaned away again, smiling at her, and waving her into the tent in Allesandra's wake.

"You're certain the girl was Rhianna?"

"Rochelle is her real name; at least that's what she claims. But yes, it was the same young woman. I'm certain of it."

"And she also claims to be the daughter of the White Stone and Jan?"

Sergei nodded silently. Brie sat back in her chair, shaking her head but not knowing how to respond. She wanted to protest, wanted to cry, wanted to scream in rage.

This explains so much. He's still in love with her, after all these years.

Allesandra had returned to the city; Sergei remained

behind after their dinner, telling Allesandra that he would escort Brie to the palais himself as soon as she was ready. The table that had held the dinner still lay between them, though the servants had cleared it of everything but a flagon of wine and some bread and cheese. Brie leaned forward and tipped the flagon into her goblet, watching the wine splash into the bottom. She leaned back again and sipped.

"I think it's quite possible she's telling the truth," Sergei continued. "I'm fairly certain of it, in fact. I know that's not what you wish to hear, Hïrzgin, but we have to acknowledge that—given the history we both know—it's plausible."

"But not certain."

He smiled under the silver nose. "No, not certain. I have people out making inquiries and checking some of the references she gave to me, but it will be a long time before I hear from them given the current situation, and who knows if they will ever uncover enough to prove things one way or the other." He shrugged. "Regardless, that *is* what Rochelle believes, true or not."

"And she's *here*."

"She is."

Brie pondered that. *Did she and Jan plan this? Or is it just coincidence?* "Does Jan know? Does Allesandra?"

Sergei shook his head. "Allesandra definitely doesn't, nor have I spoken to Jan. I wanted to tell you first. But they also need to be told." Sergei took in a long breath through his metal nose; the sound whistled slightly. "The girl is dangerous, Hïrzgin. She has taken the mantle of the White Stone to herself. She says that it was she who killed Rance—hired by a man whose daughter you'd sent away for some reason."

"Oh." The statement was like a blow to the stomach. Brie set down the wine. Her hand went to her throat. "By Cénzi, no ... Mavel cu'Kella—she was with child. Jan's child. I had to remove her from the court and send her away. It must have been her vatarh. He had been petitioning to be a chevaritt, but after that ..." She looked at Sergei, distraught. "*I* caused Rance's death," she said. "It was because of me."

"It was because of the girl's vatarh," Sergei answered. "Not you. You're not responsible for his actions."

"And Rhianna, or Rochelle ... She was in the palais all

that time, taking care of me and my children, and Jan . . ." She went silent. Sergei said nothing. She could feel him watching her. *The woman in my nightmare. Could that have been Rochelle?* "I feel sick," she told Sergei. "That girl, Jan's *daughter,* half sister to my own children . . ."

"She's a *bastarda.* She has no real claim to the throne."

"I know. There have been enough of those," she answered with a wry, self-deprecating twist of her lips. "Still, she was the first, and Jan . . ." She stopped, looked at Sergei. "I'm told you once met the woman who was the White Stone."

"No," Sergei answered. "I didn't. But I came to Brezno not long after she, well, after she assassinated Hïrzg Fynn. From what I remember, Rochelle must look much as her matarh did at the time."

Brie felt her heart pounding hard in her chest. She felt the wine and her dinner churning in her stomach. Again, the realization rose up inside her: *Jan still loves this Elissa, has never stopped loving her.* "Elissa," Brie said. "That's what the White Stone called herself then. I didn't know the history when Jan wanted to name our daughter. I just thought it was a name he liked . . ." She gave a bitter laugh. "I didn't find out for another year or more, when it was too late to change. I've never quite forgiven him for that."

"Do you want me to tell Allesandra and Jan about Rochelle?"

Brie shivered with a sudden chill. "You may inform Allesandra. But I'd like to be the one to tell Jan. I'd like to see his face when he learns."

Sergei inclined his head. He rose from his chair. "Then I'll leave the Hïrzg to you," he said. "I'll get our carriage ready, Hïrzgin. The Kraljica will be wondering what happened to us."

"Yes," Brie said. "Do that. I'll be along in a moment."

Sergei bowed and left the room. Brie poured herself another goblet of wine. She sat there for several breaths, just staring at the red liquid shimmering against the golden surface. *I want to see his face . . .*

She wondered how she could tell him.

Niente

NIENTE HAD BEGUN TO BELIEVE that they might come within sight of the great city's walls uncontested.

The Tehuantin army was descending from the hills into a lush valley, green and fragrant with the strange trees of the region, dotted with pockets of farmland and vineyards carved from the forest. It was land that Niente remembered, land that Niente had often recalled in his dreams. The army had split into three arms, as Atl had seen in the bowl—the southern arm crossing the river, a northern arm moving north to the higher road, and the main bulk continuing to follow the road that paralleled the river.

That's where Tecuhtli Citlali was ensconced; that's where Atl, as Nahual, and Niente followed.

They knew that the Easterners were pacing them. There had been the occasional strange and brief skirmishes with their horsed warriors, who would come shouting challenge and then plunge madly into their ranks—even the High Warriors were talking about the undoubted bravery of the Easterners, while at the same time shaking their heads at the foolhardy and useless tactics. There were occasional flurries of arrows from the heights as they passed through the winding valleys, but the shields of the warriors took most of them, and the nahualli used their spell-staffs to great effect. Of the Easterner spellcasters, their war-téni, there was no sign at all.

All of the Easterner attempts to impede their progress were little more than the buzzing of flies to the army.

They followed the curve of the river, with the spires of a village just visible over the tops of the trees. They rode through a pastoral landscape, though the ordered fields had been emptied of crops and livestock. That was undoubtedly so that the Tehuantin army would have to forage farther afield to provision themselves, which they did—raiding parties were sent out wide from the arms,

taking cattle and other livestock and stripping the fields
as bare as if locusts had descended on them, all the food
sent back to feed the demanding stomachs of the warriors. The occasional farmhouse or mansion they encountered was abandoned and silent. The sounds of the army
drowned out the sounds that Niente imagined they might
have heard had they been riding unaccompanied along the
road: the calls of the Easterner birds, the wind rustling the
leaves, the lowing of cattle.

But even so, this land felt *too* quiet. Niente began to
peer around, uneasy; he noticed Citlali and the High Warriors around him doing the same, and he realized that the
vanguard riders, who should have reported back some time
ago, were still absent.

There was movement on the low ridges around them:
in the afternoon sun, bright stalks of men rose from the
ground. "Atl!" he said warningly, grasping for his spell-staff,
but the warning was already late.

Fireballs arced in the sky toward them, fuming black
smoke trailing behind, and the air was feathered with the
shafts of arrows. They fell, hissing, and warriors snapped
up shields against them; still, Niente saw several warriors
fall even as he sent counter-spells toward the fireballs.
The nearest exploded far above them, with a *boom* that
made him want to clap his hands over his ears. Atl was
also chanting release words, and another of the fireballs
careened wildly to one side, plowing into the meadow and
spewing mud and grass and liquid fire where it landed. But
another was streaking too fast toward the banners of the
Tecuhtli; Niente slammed a counter-spell against it, but it
was already too close. He could feel the heat as the war-
spell erupted into sticky gouts of flame, and the concussion
washed over them. Niente was thrown from his horse as
screams came from the closest warriors. For a moment,
Niente was pinned under his horse as the beast tried to
scramble up again. The grass was afire on either side of the
dirt road. Easterner trumpets shrilled a rising sequence of
notes, followed by the roar of their soldiers charging and
the shouts of the High Warriors as they tried to restore
order to the the startled and shattered ranks.

Metal clanged against metal as Niente struggled to rise,

using his spell-staff as a cane. A hand took his arm and pulled: Atl, his face sooty and stained.

All around him was chaos. There were scores of dead warriors near the road, where the fireball had struck, but Tecuhtli Citlali and High Warrior Tototl were yet alive, shouting and gesturing to the left, where a full-scale battle was underway between the Easterners and the Tehuantin forces. *I have never seen this attack,* Niente realized. *This is new* ... Bellowing, his spear out, Citlali was seating himself again on his horse, held by two warriors. "Nahual Atl!" Niente heard Citlali shout. "To me! To me!"

Atl's hand left Niente's arm. He leaped astride his own mount. "Nahualli!" Atl called, "to the Tecuhtli!" Citlali and Tototl already galloping toward the front line of the fray, and now Atl yanked at the reins of his horse in pursuit. Niente looked for his own horse, saw the animal standing with head down a few paces away. He went to the creature—limping, feeling muscles pulling angrily all along his side. The horse shied away as he approached, and he saw that its right foreleg was broken; it could put no weight on it. Niente cursed. He began a shuffling run, joining the rush of warriors toward the battle line halfway across the meadow. Ahead, he could see the nahualli casting their own war-spells toward the enemy ranks, and he lifted his own spell-staff to join the barrage even as he ran, shouting the release words.

Fire and lightnings flickered down from sudden, low clouds. They slammed to the ground well up the ridge and in the midst of the charging Easterners. The warriors roared—a war cry to Sakal, calling down the wrath of the sun-god—and surged forward. Niente could see the banners of Citlali flying up the rise with the Easterners already fleeing before him, their front lines broken, their wounded being dragged ignominiously away. The retreat was humiliating and complete. Citlali called a halt to the counterattack as the Easterners melted away into the forest and the strips of wooded area between the fields. Easterner trumpets shrilled a falling sequence. The banner of the Tecuhtli fluttered briefly at the top of the rise— Niente could see Atl alongside him—then Citlali began to canter down the hill toward the road again, Tototl following behind him. Niente couldn't see his face past the red eagle tattooed on his face and the blood spattered over it. Niente pushed forward through the milling warriors to where Citlali was dismounting. The Tecuhtli's sword blade was covered in gore.

Now he could see the expression on Citlali's face: he was furious as he gazed at the dead and injured warriors, as healers scurried forward to care for the living and the priests to give rites to the dead. Citlali bent down to several of them, touching faces that he and Niente had known for years. The smell of burnt flesh was strong, and the grass of the meadow was still afire around some of them.

Atl was standing not far from Citlali and Tototl. His spell-staff hung from his hand as if it were exhausted. His head was shaking, as if in denial. "I didn't see this, Taat," he said to Niente as he approached. "I looked, but this was hidden. Why didn't I see it?"

"Why, indeed?" Another voice intruded before Niente could answer. Citlali had turned to the two of them. "I have two nahualli who are reputed to be the strongest since Mahri at far-sight, yet neither of you gave me any hint of this. I don't grieve for the loss—our warriors died the good death, in battle, as they should. But you, Atl, told me that the Easterners wouldn't engage us fully again until we reached the great city." His red-eyed gaze turned to Niente. "And you said you could see very little at all. Why? Has Axat abandoned us?"

Both Niente and Atl shook their heads simultaneously. "Something has changed," Niente said. "I've told you many times before, Tecuhtli, that Axat shows what *can* be, not what *will* be. Something has changed with the Easterners."

Citlali sniffed derisively. "That's clear enough," he said, waving his hand at the smoke and bodies around them. "Find out what, and what it means to us. Find out now."

The sun was a golden bowl dying in the west, and the mist of the future rose green around their faces. The nahualli watched them, silent; Tecuhtli Citlali watched as well, with the High Warriors grouped around him.

In the scrying bowl, the present split and tore, and the shreds of the future twisted and curled away. Niente chased after them with his mind; alongside him, Atl was doing the same. The chase was as exhausting as any physical one.

So close to the moment, the threads of possibilities were snarled and interwoven. Images kept rising from the mist and it was difficult to see them long enough to understand their meanings.

There: the face of a king, or so Niente assumed it was from the golden band around his head, waved a sword with a host behind him dressed in black and silver, rather than the blue-and-gold livery of the army of the great city. Niente remembered those colors—the colors of the army that had come to the succor of the city after Tecuhtli Zolin had taken it. Niente trembled, seeing that . . .

But the mist rolled over the king, and he saw a queen sitting on a glowing throne with red fire all around her. A young woman lifted a knife that glittered in the fire's glow, and a man stood near the throne as well, and the furious blaze within the room seemed to issue from his uplifted hands . . .

Cold mist extinguished the fire and bore it away. Now Niente stared down at ranks of people, but these were not soldiers in glittering armor, but plain-clothed folks, and they pointed odd devices toward Niente, not unlike the eagle claws that the nahualli used for sacrifice. The devices spat smoke and fire, and black bumblebees came spitting from them, rushing toward Niente . . .

But the mist took them, too.

A wind blew through the mist, and there before him, for an enticing moment, he glimpsed again the Long Path. It had changed since the last time Niente had seen it. This future was still strewn with the fallen banners of the Tehuantin. Far down the path, he saw the banners of the Tehuantin flying alongside the blue-and-gold banners of the Easterners, and two men underneath, one with the red eagle tattoo of the Tecuhtli and a woman wearing the clothing of the Easterners with a golden scepter in her hand. The two stood together, and they smiled at each other, and there was no animosity between them at all. They stood on a hill, and to one side were the odd, domed buildings of the Easterner and to the other stepped pyramids like those of Tlaxcala, and people were passing back and forth between them.

The mist hid the middle ground of the Long Path, but close to Niente, the mists now rolled away, and he saw Citlali there, dead, and a nahualli alongside him. Niente bent closer to the bowl. On the nahualli's youthful, muscular arm, gold sparkled: the band of the Nahual. Standing over them, as if responsible for their deaths, he glimpsed the back of another nahualli: an old man's bald skull, a wisp of hair, and—as the nahualli turned—a crumpled and scarred visage with a blind left eye.

Niente recoiled with a gasp . . .

"No . . ." Niente whispered, and the breath of his denial shifted the mists so that the Long Path vanished, only to reveal yet another Long Path. At the end of this one, he could see Tlaxcala, but the floating city burned in the center of the lake and the great pyramids were broken and tumbled. As with the previous vision of the Long Path, the middle ground again was obscured, but images flickered closer to him. There, Tecuhtli Citlali sat on a glowing throne under a domed roof, with the blue-and-gold banner on the tiled floor before him, and several Easterners prostrate before him as if ready to be sacrificed to Axat and Sakal so that the rest of their people might live.

Niente breathed again, and the cold green vapors wrapped around his face. He felt his face suddenly wet, and he realized that he had touched the water of the scrying bowl. With the touch, the visions dissolved and he was staring only at a bowl.

He came back to reality slowly, gasping for breath as if from a long run. Tecuhtli Citlali was staring at him grimly, and at his left, Atl had already lifted his head from his own bowl. Several of the lesser nahualli came forward quickly and took away the bowls and tables. "Well?" Citlali said. "What did Axat show you?"

Niente said nothing; from the side of his vision, he saw Atl glance briefly at him. "The vision I saw still shows our victory, Tecuhtli," he said. "I saw you on the Easterner's throne."

Citlali's gaze had remained on Niente. "And you, Uchben Nahual? Is that what you saw also?"

Niente lifted his head. He could feel his hands shaking, and one of the lesser nahualli came rushing forward to hand him his spell-staff. He took it gratefully, leaning heavily on it. He blinked, trying to clear his head of the visions.

The Long Path . . . Axat has gifted you with two choices . . .
"I saw the same, Tecuhtli," he said truthfully.

"Hah!" Tecuhtli Citlali rose to his feet, stamping once on the ground as Tototl and the other High Warriors roared their approval. "Then we go forward, and we will take their great city, and we will make widows of their wives and orphans of their children if they resist us."

RESURRECTIONS

The Gathering Storm
The Storm's Fury
The Storm's Passing
The Dawn

The Gathering Storm

JAN SMELLED OF HORSE, sweat, smoke, and blood. But then, so did Starkkapitän ca'Damont and Commandant ca'Talin. There'd been no time for them to bathe or change clothes. They'd stripped themselves of their sweaty and battered armor after the engagement with the Westlanders and ridden hard back to Nessantico, leaving the grudging retreat of the Garde Civile to the a'offiziers. Their boots clattered—grimy, mud-splattered, and out of place—on the polished tiles of the Kraljica's Palais on the Isle; the hall gardai, the servants, and the courtiers milling in the corridors stared at the trio apprehensively, as if trying to gauge from their faces and demeanor the severity of the threat to the city.

If they could read those expressions correctly, they would be frightened.

Allesandra's aide Talbot met Jan as they passed the outer reception chambers, and escorted them through the private servants' corridor to the Council of Ca's chambers. He gestured to the hall gardai to open the doors as they approached. The murmur of conversation within stopped. Allesandra was waiting for them there, with Sergei ca'Rudka and the councillors; a map of the surrounding area already open on the table.

They all looked at Jan expectantly.

"If you're looking for good news," he told them without preamble, "I have none." He stopped. A woman standing alongside Allesandra turned from perusing the map to face him. "Brie? I thought—"

Brie went to him, embracing him as openly as if he wore finery for a ball. He tried to step back, knowing how he looked, but if she felt any revulsion at his smell or appearance, she showed none of it. She kissed his stubbled cheek, then his mouth; it took a moment, but he returned the kiss. "I came with our army, my dear," she said. "The children are in Brezno, but I felt my place was here, with my husband in the city he will rule one day."

"You shouldn't have come, Brie."

"*Why* should I not have?" she asked, her head cocked. The tone of her voice was strange—almost coy and too light. He could sense another question underneath, one she wasn't asking.

"That's not obvious?" he answered. "It's dangerous for you to be here."

"I thought it might be more dangerous for me to *not* be here," she responded. He could hear a subtext in her words, but the meaning eluded him. She smiled at him: again with the same strangeness. "I'm here, my husband, and I have brought your army with me. Why, you should be pleased."

Jan nodded—yes, there was more going on here with Brie than what she was saying on the surface, but there was no time for him to puzzle it out now, and to try to do so would only make him angry with her. He kissed her again, perfunctorily, then looked around at the others in the room. *Focus . . .*

"Kraljica, Ambassador, Councillors—the Westlanders have a force significantly larger than ours, even with the Firenzcian addition," he told them. He went to the map, sweeping a hand across the inked features. "They are advancing along a front that would have them entering Nessantico all along the western edge on the north side of the A'Sele, from the banks of the A'Sele to above the Avi a'Nostrosei or even to the Avi a'Nortegate. That's bad enough, but our scouts tell us that they've sent another force across the river to attack the city from the south. At the moment, we have no more than twenty war-téni, all from Nessantico; we'll need at least a few hundred to even try to match the Westlanders in that respect. And judging from what they did at Villembouchure, they also have adequate supplies of black sand, which means that none of the buildings here are safe if they come close. As for what they did at Karnmor, well, we can only hope that they have no way to repeat that horror. If they can, then there's no hope at all."

"You make it sound as if we have already lost and should be emptying the city," his matarh said, and Jan shook his head.

"No, Matarh," he said. "That's not what I'm saying. Nessantico isn't lost, but it *is* in grave and immediate danger and we can't underestimate that. I've seen the Westlanders, and we've engaged with them to test them. That's told us that we'll need all the forces we can muster: all the war-téni, every able-bodied citizen, every possible resource. Even with all that, we'll also need the grace of Cénzi, or we'll once again see Nessantico burning."

The silence after he spoke stretched long. "That's not what any of us want. Here's what the Starkkapitän, Commandant, and I propose," he said finally, pointing to the map. "The A'Sele curves north just after Pré a'Fleuve; that will necessarily compress their forces. I intend to station our troops just beyond the River Infante from the village of Certendi and south. We'll hold there as long as we can, then destroy the bridges if we need to retreat to the other side. I want earthworks to be built from the Avi a'Certendi to the A'Sele along the eastern side of the Infante. Commandant ca'Tali, Starkkapitän ca'Damont, and I will make the Westlanders fight for every stride of land between the Infante and Nessantico, and hopefully keep them from the city entirely on the North Bank. As for the South ..."

He looked at Allesandra and Sergei. "I will leave that in your hands."

". . . there's a Long Path, Atl. A way that leads to a better place for us even though it won't seem so at first, and Citlali would never believe me. But *you* must believe me. Victory here isn't victory; it will mean eventual defeat for us. Tlaxcala itself might fall."

Atl was shaking his head all through Niente's explanation. "I know you keep saying that, Taat, but that's not what I see. Even if I wanted to believe you ..." He waved a hand in exasperation, accompanied by a sigh. "I see nothing of this Long Path at all."

"You're not looking far enough ahead. It's not something you're capable of yet."

That was a mistake. He could see it in the way the firelight in the tent found the hard lines of Atl's face. "I *can* see Axat's paths, Taat. I think I may see them better than you do. You just don't want to admit that. I'm going to my own tent. Fill your spell-staff, then get some sleep, Taat. I'm going to do the same."

He nodded to Niente and started to leave, but Niente clutched at his son, his fingers around the gold band of the Nahual that had once been around his own forearm. "Atl, this is terribly important. I *saw t*he Long Path; I saw it ever so clearly back in Tlaxcala and even here for a time. I haven't glimpsed it since—there are so many elements fouling the mists, as you know yourself. But it's there—it must be. Between the two of us, we may be able to find it again. If we glimpse it just once more, if we can see how we must respond . . ."

Niente rummaged in his pack. He pulled out two small wooden birds, crudely carved and painted a bright red, the lines of their bodies rough and simple. He handed one to Atl. "I made these earlier this evening. I've put a spell inside them, so that if we're separated in the battle, we can still give each other a message. If one of us sees the way, then we can tell the other that the Long Path is open."

Atl looked at the bird. He started to hand it back. "I don't need—"

Niente closed his son's fingers around the sculpture. "Please," he said to Atl. "Please take it."

Atl sighed: as he had sighed as a child when his parents had insisted that he do something he didn't want to do. "Fine," he said. "I'll keep it. But, Taat, there's no Long Path. I don't know where this war will lead us—none of us can know that—but I *do* know that we can have victory here. I've seen it, and I intend to lead Tecuhtli Citlali to that point." He looked down at Niente, the firelight reflecting in his dark eyes. "Fill your spell-staff," he told him, as if addressing one of the lesser nahualli. "You'll need it soon. I need to use the scrying bowl myself tonight." He went to the tent flap and opened it. Outside, the moon shone over his shoulder. "There won't be a Long Path there, Taat.

I know this," he said. "You're seeing what you want to see, not what Axat is willing to give us."

He let the tent flap fall behind him as he left.

"You will cross the river this morning with Tototl and join the southern force with two hands of nahualli under you."

That was the order Niente received from Tecuhtli Citlali. Atl and Tototl stood at the warrior's side as he delivered it. His son's face was unreadable and troubled, and Niente wondered—after the previous night's conversation—whether the order had come from Citlali or Atl. He had to admit the sense of it—to have the former Nahual with the Tecuhtli to second-guess the new Nahual could lead to hesitation and contradictions. In the south, Niente would have no rival ... and neither would Atl with the main force. In the south, Niente would be a potent resource for the nahualli, and a tested leader. If Niente had still been Nahual, had he been looking for an overwhelming victory here instead of the chimera of his Long Path, he might have suggested something similar, sending Atl with the southern arm.

Citlali gave him no chance to argue. "Uchben Nahual, the boat with the other nahualli is waiting for you on the bank," he told Niente. "You will leave as soon as you gather your things. Nahual Atl, I wish to discuss our strategy with you ..." With that dismissal, Tecuhtli Citlali turned from Niente, gesturing to Atl to follow him. Atl glanced once at Niente.

"Taat," he said, "I will see you again in the great city. Keep yourself safe." He nodded, then followed Citlali.

Not long after, Niente found himself in a boat with three others alongside crossing the A'Sele, the brown water churned to momentary white by oars pulled by young warriors. The scent of fresh water touched his nose, though the trees on the far bank were clouded by haze in the poor vision of his one good eye. He could feel the stares of the other nahualli with him, feel their appraisal as he crouched in the stern of the small craft.

Niente looked westward down the river—they had received a message from the captain of their fleet that the river had been cleared and they were bringing the warships upriver to meet them. Niente saw no sails yet, but the river curved away in the near distance, and the fleet might have been only around the bend. The High Warrior Tototl, in one of the other boats, stared only straight ahead to the other shore.

What do I do now? This strategy was not in any of the paths I glimpsed. He wondered if Atl had seen this, and knew where the path led. He felt lost and adrift in the currents of the present. *Can I find the Long Path in this, and if I do, dare I take it?* He'd already given up the Long Path once because of the implied cost. That vision had been clear, as if Axat had wanted him to know. Citlali's death mattered little to Niente; a warrior expected and even welcomed death in battle. But Niente had been dead as well in that glimpse; could he truly *do* that, if that was what Axat demanded as payment? And if Axat demanded Atl's life as well as Axat had once hinted . . .

His hands were shaking, and not from the damp morning chill.

Did Atl see this? Is that why you were sent away?

He wanted desperately to talk to Atl, but that was no longer possible. He felt in his pouch for the carved bird. The touch of it gave him no comfort.

The shore was growing closer; he could nearly make out the individual trees rather than just a green mass, and he glimpsed a half-dozen warriors gathered under the verdant canopy ready to escort them to the road. The prow of the boat squelched into mud on the reed-masked bank, jolting him. The warriors waiting for them hurried down the bank to help them out. He heard Tototl shouting orders. Niente allowed the warriors to pull him up onto dry land. At the top of the bank, he looked across the river once more. Through the cataract-haze, he thought he could see figures moving.

He wondered if one of them was Atl.

"By Cénzi, it's true, then . . ." Jan's hand prowled his beard. His eyes widened, and Brie could swear there was genuine shock in them. Not just feigned surprise. Perhaps she'd guessed wrongly and Jan had actually not sent the girl ahead of them to meet her in the city. "I promise you, Brie, I didn't know she was here. That's Cénzi's own truth. I swear it. I know you must have been thinking that I sent Rhianna here—or Rochelle or whatever her true name is—but I never thought . . ."

"No, you didn't," Brie chided him. She continued to watch his face. The shock on his face had seemed genuine enough when she'd told him Sergei's news. "She claims she's your *daughter,* Jan."

"She told me that also."

"She told *you*? When?"

"When she took Matarh's knife from me. It was her parting volley as she fled." He ran his fingers through hair newly dampened by a quick bath. "She killed Rance. I *knew* it, even then. She looks so much like El—" He stopped and glanced at Brie. "Her matarh," he finished.

"So is it possible she's telling the truth, that she's your daughter?"

Jan's shoulders slumped. Now his hands were plowing nervously through his hair. "I suppose so. She's about the right age."

"Did you ever . . . With Rhi . . . Rochelle?"

He shook his head angrily, his hand making a sweeping denial that swept air across her cheek. "No! I swear it, Brie. She never allowed me to—" He exhaled loudly. "For good reason, evidently." He paced the dressing room in the apartments that Allesandra had given them in the palais, snatching up the padded undertunic of his Garde Civile uniform. "Brie, I'm sorry, but I can't worry about this. Not now. I don't know why Sergei didn't clap her in the Bastida when he had the chance."

She went to him, pushing his hands aside as he fumbled at the ties of the undertunic. "Here, let me do that. Is that what you want for her?" Brie asked. "The Bastida? Judgment for the deaths she's caused?"

She felt his chest heave under her hands. "Yes. And no. I don't know what I want, Brie. If she's my daughter, by the White Stone . . ."

"Not your daughter. Just a *bastarda* you fathered." She'd finished tying the laces and stepped away.

"Back then, I would have married Elissa." This time he said the name without hesitation, and Brie found that it hurt to hear it, to hear her own daughter's name attached to that woman. Jan's word stung her. "I would have married her without hesitation and without my parents' permission if they wouldn't give it," he continued. "The girl wouldn't have been a *bastarda*. I'd already asked Matarh to open negotiations with Elissa's family—or at least the family she claimed to be part of. Oh, I'll bet Matarh is finding this a most wonderful jest."

She was certain that Jan had intended the words to hurt; she forced herself to show nothing of it. "Your matarh was doing what she thought she needed to do to protect her family. As I do also, when I must."

"Yes, that's undoubtedly why Matarh hired the White Stone to kill Fynn; to protect her family." He finished putting on the rest of his uniform, sitting on one of the chairs to pull on his boots. "Brie, I need to meet with ca'Damont and ca'Talin within a mark of the glass. You need to be careful—I don't know what this Rhianna or Rochelle might be after. Cénzi alone knows who the White Stone might go after next. I'd be far more comfortable if you were out of the city entirely."

Where you'd be free to do whatever you want. Brie would have been more pleased if she felt that his concern was genuine and not just self-serving. *Like his matarh—his needs always come first.* "I'm staying, my husband," Brie told him firmly. "You have your duty; I have mine. Allesandra will be directing the southern defense; I'll help her."

"Brie . . ." He stood up, buckling on his sword belt and adjusting it.

"No, I mean it, Jan. I've trained with my brothers and can hold my own with them with a sword. You know that. My vatarh's schooled me on military strategy and has even consulted with me many times in the past, when raiders came over the border from Shenkurska. Allesandra has directed armies herself—I've heard you screaming in frustration about some of the tactics and strategies she's used over the last several years. I'm no less safe here in Nessantico than I would be traveling on the roads, even with an escort."

He was shaking his head. "I know that face you're wearing now. There's no use talking to you."

"Then why are you still arguing?" she asked him. She wasn't certain whether he was irritated or whether it was simply the stress. "I don't *want* to argue with you, my love. We need each other, and I only want you to be as safe as you can be. You've a destiny, Jan—to be the next Kraljiki. I want to see that happen; I intend to sit next to you on the Sun Throne." She brushed imaginary lint from his shoulders and smiled up at him: the practiced smile, the required smile. "Now . . . Go on—meet with the Starkkapitän and the Commandant. You and I will worry about Rochelle later, when the Tehuantin are no longer a threat."

"And you?"

"I have my own meeting with Allesandra."

"Not with Sergei, too?"

She shrugged. "He said he had other business this evening." She stood on her toes and kissed his cheek. "Go," she told him.

"You can't wear the green robes," Rochelle told Nico, and he favored her with an indulgent smile that touched his lips and vanished a breath later. It seemed his lips no longer remembered how to truly smile. Joy had vanished from life, when before it had filled him.

"There's a large difference between 'not permitted to' and 'can't,'" he answered. "I'm a téni, and it's my right to wear the robes. *More* than a right; it's my obligation. I follow Cénzi, not that half-dead fool who calls himself the Archigos. It's time for me to make that statement fully and to stop hiding like a criminal."

"You *are* a criminal in the eyes of the Holdings and the Faith. They'll kill you if they can."

"They can try." He tried to smile at her again, but it collapsed. "And there's a large difference between 'try' and 'will,' too. You needn't look so worried, little sister."

She shrugged. They were on the second floor of one of the Morelli safe houses in Oldtown; the owner—a draper—had been visibly distressed to see Nico there, but had dismissed his apprentices for the rest of the day, sent his family to visit cousins two streets over, and had agreed to send out the word to the remaining Morelli sect that the Absolute desired to meet with them.

Nico had also learned that Ancel had been among those captured and executed after the storming of the Old Temple—another soul laid at his feet, another death for which he must atone. There were so many, and they weighed so heavily on his shoulders that he wanted to fall to his knees under them.

Liana, Ancel, I promise you—I will find peace for you . . .

He could still see the face of his and Liana's daughter snuggled in Varina's arms. He could feel Sera's fingers wrapped around his, clutching him as if she knew she belonged to him. That memory, and the memory of Liana and Ancel and all of those who had died for him caused tears to gather in his eyes again, and he wiped them away.

Downstairs, among the draperies hung on wires waiting to be arranged into folds, Nico could hear the buzz and rumble of conversation through the floorboards: several of the war-téni had slipped away from the temple to come here; there were also, he was told, many of Brezno's war-téni present as well, who had entered the city over the last few days following after the train of the Firenzcian army. He'd already talked to some of them—Archigos Karrol had declared that all war-téni would be sent to the battle-field with Hïrzg Jan tomorrow.

"We won't go, if that's what you tell us, Absolute." They'd all told him that. They'd all sworn that they would follow him rather than the Archigos, if he asked them. Their loyalty gratified him at the same time that it added to the guilt he bore.

How can you follow me after what I've done, after my failures? How can you still have faith when I struggle with it?

Nico still wasn't sure what he intended to tell them. He would leave that to Cénzi. But he suspected he already knew. The choices had narrowed with the arrival of the Westlanders, and he had spent the night before praying to Cénzi for guidance while Rochelle watched him, her face more curious than devout. She reminded him of Elle, her matarh and Nico's adopted-matarh. *What did you do to her, Elle? Did you twist her beyond saving?*

But he couldn't worry about Rochelle now. Not yet. His followers, those who were left, waited for him, and the words of Cénzi burned inside him. "Let's go," he told Rochelle, holding out his hand to her. "It's time."

He let her descend first, then followed her down the stairs. The astringent smell of dyes and the stiffeners for the fabric was strong in the single large room below, a room that also functioned as a store and showroom for the draper.

There were at least five double hands of people crowded into the space, packed so tightly that the air was heated with their presence. No greetings split that atmosphere as he appeared; everyone seemed as somber as Nico felt himself. He gave them the sign of Cénzi, and bowed to them meekly as they returned the gesture. A few lamps set on the draper's walls provided the only light, but he could see many green robes like the one he wore, even though their faces were largely unfamiliar. He could feel their stares on his bruised and battered face, on the purple blotches that covered his forearms, at the way he limped as he descended the stairs. He saw them gazing curiously at Rochelle.

"May Cénzi bless you all," he told them, spreading his hands wide. He could feel their affection for him, and he returned it; the room was filled with a pale glow that emanated from nowhere and everywhere. "I'm humbled that you would come, and even more humbled that you would still listen to what I have to say."

"You're still Cénzi's Voice, Absolute," someone called out from their midst. "We follow you. We saw Cénzi perform the miracle in the square. We saw you vanish without casting a spell; we saw the empty chains." The others murmured their agreement, and the sound made Nico want to embrace them all, to try to burn away the grief and loss in the heat of their approval and support.

He clasped his hands together in front of him as if in prayer. "Yes," he told them. "Cénzi came to me as I stood before the Kraljica, and He released me from the poor shackles this life placed on me. But . . ." He stopped, shaking his head. "Cénzi has also shown me that I've let my own pride lead me away from His path, and He has punished me for that. He's taken into Himself too many of those whom I loved, He has sent others into pain and misery, and He has filled me with grief and sorrow. Their pain came because they followed me. I realize now that I must become entirely Cénzi's vessel, that I must give myself over completely to Him and must accept whatever He gives me to bear. I realize that I am nothing."

He brought his head up and lowered his hands, his gaze sweeping over them, making eye contact with each of them in the room. "You must also understand that," he told them. "This is your task as well, as it has always been for the téni—to perform the will of Cénzi and nothing more."

"What is it that Cénzi wants us to do?" someone asked. "Tell us, Absolute."

Nico hesitated even though he felt the words filling him. *Am I right this time, Cénzi? Am I hearing You and not myself? Is this truly what You want me to tell them?* The words remained in his mind, and he could rid himself of them only by speaking them.

"Our Faith is being directly threatened," he said. "We have the Westlanders ready to overwhelm Nessantico and the Holdings, and if that happens, then the Faithful will suffer greatly. I have prayed, and I have opened myself to Cénzi and listened to Him, and this is what He tells me." He paused and took several breaths, looking at each of them. "Now is the time to set aside our struggles with the false leaders of the Faith—not forever, but for a short time. We must first beat back the heathens and heretics who threaten us before we can look to the heresy within the Holdings and the Coalition."

He paused, nodding to them. "I said this the other day on the plaza, and I tell you again here: for now, you should obey the Archigos. War-téni, go to war. Téni, perform whatever duty is given you. For the rest of you, do what you must. Obey the authorities that are over you. For now."

He waited. The glow in the room increased. "Do this for the moment," he told them. "And afterward . . . Afterward, we will again look inward. Afterward, we will turn our attention to reforming the Concénzia Faith. We will take the glory we have earned, and we will shape the Faith as Cénzi intended it to be, as the Toustour and the Divolonté demand, and we will listen to the commands of no one, *no one,* who is not with us. That is all I have to say tonight."

The glow in the room faded, and the lamplight seemed dull in comparison. They shuffled, they hesitated, they stared. Then someone opened the door; one by one, they gave him the sign of Cénzi and shuffled from the room. Nico returned the sign to each of them, murmuring a blessing to each. When they had all gone, he felt Rochelle's hand on his shoulder.

"They weren't happy," she said. "You didn't give them what they came to hear. They were disappointed."

"I know," he told her. "But it's all I had."

Rochelle nodded. "You're tired."

"Exhausted," he admitted. He looked at the stairs leading to the second floor. "But there's still one more meeting before I can sleep."

"What do you mean?" she asked. He said nothing, only gestured for her to follow him. He trudged up the stairs, his feet heavy on the treads. There was lamplight coming from the rear bedroom, where there had been no light before. He heard Rochelle's knife blade slide from its sheath, and he shook his head at her.

"You won't need that. Not yet."

He walked easily down the corridor to the room and pushed the door open. "Did you hear what you wanted to hear?" he asked the person in the room.

"Did you hear what you wanted to hear?" Nico said, and Sergei shrugged.

"Overall, yes," he answered. "You just saved yourself, and saved the war-téni along with you."

"My safety isn't in your hands, Silvernose," Nico said, but the bravado in his voice was tired and unheated.

"Ah, but actually it is," Sergei answered. He glimpsed movement behind Nico and saw a face. "Rochelle. Please, why don't the two of you come in and sit down? There's no reason we can't have a civil conversation, just the three of us."

Nico entered with a shrug and sat on the edge of the bed in the room. Sergei saw him glance at the far door on the rear of the house. Sergei had left it open, displaying the stairway leading down to an alley behind the draper's. Rochelle entered and immediately put her spine to the wall to one side of the corridor doorway, remaining standing. She stared at Sergei, her eyes intent and dangerous. Sergei lifted his own hands from the arms of his chair, his right holding his cane. He imagined he could feel Varina's spell hidden within the wood. "There, you see. I'm no threat to either of you at the moment."

Nico's mouth twitched with the ghost of amusement. "And neither of us believe that."

"I didn't expect you to," Sergei told him. In his mind, he repeated the release word for the spell Varina had placed

on his cane so it would be clear if he needed to use it. He
wondered how effective it might be against Nico—not as
much as he might hope, he suspected.

"You have a better information network than I thought,
Sergei."

"I was lucky. A few of your Morelli téni had guilty con-
sciences. After the debacle in the Old Temple, they're not
all quite so trusting of you anymore, Nico. They came and
told me where you'd be."

"I can't say I blame them." Nico leaned back on the bed.
"I don't trust myself either. What would you have done had
I not told the war-téni to obey the Archigos?"

"There were enough gardai, loyal téni, and Numetodo
spellcasters in the streets outside to have arrested twice the
rabble you managed to cobble together tonight, even with
the war-téni." Sergei closed his eyes, imagining the scene.
"Let me tell you what would have happened. They were
waiting for my signal. I would have all of you taken immediately to the courtyard outside the Kraljica's Palais,
driving the pack of you down the A'Parete like a herd of
pigs being taken to slaughter, so that everyone could see
you. By the time we reached the palais, there would be a
huge crowd of citizens there to watch the spectacle, and I
would set you and your people at the front. I would drag
you forward, Nico, with tourniquets tied hard around your
forearms. I would tell the citizens that you and the war-téni
who follow you would rather see Nessantico burned to the
ground and all of them dead rather than fulfill their oath
to Cénzi, the Faith, and the people. I would have handed
a volunteer from the citizenry an executioner's ax—and
I would have many volunteers, Nico. I'd have that person
strike your hands from your arms. Your screams would re-
bound from the walls of the palais, so loud that you'd think
that all of Nessantico could hear them. Then I'd have another citizen pull your tongue from your mouth and slice
it off with red-hot scissors, so that the wound would be immediately cauterized. I wouldn't want you to die. Not yet. I
would tell them all—the citizenry, the war-téni watching—
that this was the Faith's punishment, and that now I would
show them the punishment of the Sun Throne. I would bind
you to a post, and have one of the Bastida garda open your
stomach and pull out a loop of your intestines. I'd tie that to

a windlass, and have the garda slowly extract your guts, the windlass creaking as it turned. If you were still alive, afterward, then I'd have you flayed, the skin stripped from your living body. When you finally died, in misery and torment, your body would be put into a gibbet and displayed, with your hands and tongue nailed to your skull."

Neither had spoken during his long tale. Sergei opened his eyes. Nico still watched him from the bed, but his face was an inscrutable mask. Rochelle appeared horrified. Her mouth hung slightly open, and she would not look directly at him. "You enjoy that fantasy," she said angrily.

"I do, indeed," Sergei admitted, glancing at her before returning his attention to Nico. "Then, when it was all over," Sergei continued, scratching at the base of his metal nose with a forefinger, "I would tell the war-téni that they have two choices set before them. One is to renounce you, obey the Archigos, and serve Nessantico, and they might live. The other is to immediately suffer your fate. I would give each of them the choice. How many do you think would have followed you into martyrdom, Nico?"

"I don't know," Nico answered. "Nor do I think it does much good to speculate about any of this, since it didn't happen. I told them to obey the Archigos, and you've let them go. What matters is what happens now." He shifted position, sitting upright at the bed's edge. "So what *does* happen now, Sergei? Do you try to arrest me again?"

"I could try," Sergei answered, then lifted his hand as Nico started to protest. "Despite my fantasy—" there he stopped and smiled at Rochelle, "—after your performance in the plaza, I do have doubts as to my ability to manage that."

"I have no idea how that happened," Nico said. "That was Cénzi, not me."

"Then maybe Cénzi—if it's truly Him—would make arresting you both difficult and costly, and it's entirely possible I might not survive the attempt. But there are enough gardai and utilinos waiting for my command that I'm fairly sure we'd eventually succeed, Cénzi aside."

"That's blasphemy," Nico snapped.

"It might be if I actually thought Cénzi were responsible. Still . . ."

"Why are you here then, if not to arrest me?"

"I'm here because Varina is my friend, and she asked me to do this. Personally, I think that she's too forgiving of you, but she seems to think that you're worth saving, that you *are* in fact savable, and that we also need you. I'm not so certain, myself." Sergei tapped his cane on the rug underneath his chair. "What is it that *you* want, Nico?"

"That's easy," the young man answered. "I want to continue to serve Cénzi."

"And for right now, what is it Cénzi demands you do, in your mind? Could it be to help defend Nessantico, as you've told the war-téni?"

Nico understood; Sergei could see it. "If it were, if I happened to believe that, what might be gained by it?"

"There's still much you need to answer for, Nico," Sergei told him. "A'Téni ca'Paim's death, the death of all the others who tried to defend the Old Temple, the destruction, the injuries. Varina might be willing to see past all that, but not the Kraljica. Not entirely. Still—perhaps the argument could be made that the death of ca'Paim was accidental and unintended, that the gardai who died did so fulfilling their duty, and that if the Morellis and their Absolute have served the Holdings well and pledged to work with the Holdings in the future, then perhaps much of what has happened might be forgiven. Not forgotten, never forgotten, of course, but it would be understood how *unfortunate* it all was."

"You make a promise you have no authority to keep, Sergei, nor does Varina."

"I have authority to offer it from someone who does," Sergei told him. "It's your choice as to whether or not to consider it."

Nico *hmmed* low in his throat. "The Archigos is in agreement as well?"

"The Archigos has nothing to do with any of this. It's a purely secular matter. You and the Concénzia Faith will have to come to your own separate understanding, but if you serve the state, the state will see that the Faith does nothing that would, well, compromise your abilities." He tapped the cane again, harder this time. "Nessantico needs your help, Nico. I've seen what you can do. You would be the most formidable war-téni we have." Sergei rubbed his nose again. "If that's what Cénzi wills."

"Don't make this a joke, Sergei."

"I assure you that I'm entirely serious."

"I need to pray first. I can't give you an answer now."

Sergei sighed. "And I can't wait, Nico. I'm sorry." Sergei groaned to his feet, moving to the rear door. He raised his cane; out in the alleyway, forms moved, and he heard running footsteps downstairs, moving through the house. He turned back to the room. "I'm really am sor—" he began, but the cold of the Ilmodo hit him then, and he saw the darkness in the midst of the room, and when it dissipated a breath later, neither Nico nor Rochelle were there. A garda thrust his face into the room. "Ambassador?"

"It appears the Absolute lied to me," he said to the man.

Varina held Sera in her arms, rocking slowly back and forth as she stood at the window. Outside, in the street beyond the front courtyard of her house, a seemingly endless line of troops in black-and-silver uniforms were marching westward. Their boots beat a solemn funereal cadence on the Avi a'Parete, as if the city itself were a drum. They'd been marching past for a turn of the glass already, since just after First Call, the noise of the cornets that had heralded their arrival waking Serafina from her sleep. Varina had taken up the child, cuddling her and soothing her fussing. She kissed the infant's brow, feeling the downy softness of Sera's hair on her lips.

"Don't be frightened, Sera," she whispered against the low thunder of boots on cobblestones. "They're here to protect us, dear one. They're here to keep you safe."

There was a soft knock at the door to the bedroom, followed by the the creak of hinges. "A'Morce, I'm sorry I'm late. The streets are a mess, as you can imagine. I had to come in the back way ..." The wet nurse Michelle entered the bedroom, already striding forward and unlacing her blouse. "The poor little one must be starving. Here, let me take her for a bit ..."

Varina handed Sera to Michelle, watching as the infant fussed for a moment before her searching mouth found the nipple and began to suck. "Yes, famished, aren't we?" Michelle said, smiling at Sera before looking to Varina. "It feels so ..." She stopped, and Varina saw moisture gathering in Michelle's eyes. "I'm sorry," the young woman said.

"Sometimes when I hold her, I think of my own . . ." She stopped again, swallowing hard.

"I can't imagine the pain you've felt, losing your own baby," Varina told her. "I'm so sorry, Michelle."

Michelle nodded. "The whole city seems to be in an uproar," she said. The change of subject was abrupt and, Varina was certain, entirely deliberate. Michelle lifted her shoulder and leaned her head down to blot away tears. Sera stirred and settled again in her arms. "They say that you can see the Westlanders already from the top of the Bastida's tower. Don't know that it's true, but . . ." Michelle shivered, and Sera stopped sucking for a moment, her large blue eyes opening, then closing again as she returned to the breast. "A'Morce, my husband wants me to go to my brother's home in Ile Verte. I thought, well, I thought, if you wanted . . . I could . . ."

Varina sighed. She stroked Sera's head. The child's eyes opened again, finding Varina's gaze. Sera smiled for a moment around the nipple, a white bubble escaping her lips before she returned to feeding. "I think that would be an excellent idea, Michelle. If you don't mind."

"Not at all," Michelle answered. "It would be my pleasure to take care of her. A'Morce, you should come as well. My brother has a large home there, and I'm sure . . ."

Varina shook her head. She glanced again at the army marching past: it was the rear supply train now—wagons and horses. "My place is here," she told Michelle. "When are you leaving?"

"This evening, after Third Call."

"Then why don't you come and get Sera at Second Call? I'll have her things ready for you then."

Michelle nodded. "She's a beauty," she said. "It a shame about her vatarh, and her poor matarh. She's lucky to have you, A'Morce."

Varina attempted a smile and found that she couldn't. She stroked Sera's head again. "Michelle, if something should happen to me—"

"Nothing will happen," Michelle said quickly, not letting her finish. Varina shook her head.

"We don't know that," Varina said. "If something should happen, something that would mean that I can't care for

Sera, would you take her? Belle speaks so highly of you, and perhaps it might ease your own loss, if only a little."

Michelle *was* crying now, her head down as she watched Serafina at her breast. "A'Morce . . ."

"Just say yes," she said. She stroked Sera's head. "That's all."

Michelle nodded, and Varina folded both of them softly into her arms. "Good," Varina said. "That will ease my mind."

Jan watched the offiziers directing the troops into position. He, Starkkapitän ca'Damont, and Commandant ca'Talin had taken a position on the second-floor balcony of a farmhouse, situated on a small rise a few hundred strides from the River Infante. On the roof of the farmhouse, Jan had placed pages with message banners as well as the signal-callers with their cornets and zinkes. A hole had been torn into the ceiling of the room behind them, with a ladder extending up to the roof so that pages could move from the command post to the roof and orders could be called up. From their vantage point, they could see the companies being placed on this side of the river, as well as the sappers who were placing obstacles along the riverbank against the Westlanders' crossing.

On the far side of the river, closer to Nessantico, workers were digging a double line of earthwork ramparts, where the army—should it need to retreat—could fall back and hold at need.

Jan hoped that those wouldn't be used, but he suspected they would be.

The Westlander troops were discernible in the verzehen—a lensed tube, designed by the Numetodo, that allowed one to see at a great distance. Through the warped and somewhat blurred, circular vision granted by the verzehen, Jan watched the offiziers of the Tehuantin, their High Warriors, giving their own orders. He saw the banner of a snake on an emerald field. Their troops marched through fields that had been farmland and through the groves. The very trees of the woods that bordered the fields seemed to sway under their numbers. They were already approaching the village of Certendi.

There were too many. Too many. Like the swarming scarlet ants of Daritria, it appeared that they could simply cross the Infante on the bodies of their own dead. Jan handed the verzehen to ca'Talin. "They're here," he said. "They'll be within arrow shot of our lines by evening. If I were their general, I'd stop there to mass the troops and attack in the new light, but . . ." He shrugged. "They've done the opposite before. We may be fighting in darkness. Are the war-téni here?"

"They came in last night, most of them, Hïrzg," ca'Damont told him. "Nearly all of the Holdings' group, and most of ours. They said that Nico Morel told them to come."

"Then Sergei was good to his word," Jan answered. "Excellent. Cénzi knows we'll need them all." He gestured to one of the pages; the boy came hurrying over. "Have the horns call back the a'offiziers." The page saluted and scooted up the ladder; a few breaths later, they heard the clear, shrill call of the cornets.

"We're set, then," Jan said. "We'll talk to the offiziers, then it's time to go to your commands and get yourselves ready. We'll see if we have the pieces placed where they need to be. Let's pray to Cénzi that that's the case."

He looked through the verzehen once more, watching the blurred forms of the warriors approaching. He doubted that the person commanding them felt the same burning doubt that he felt. "We'll hold them here," he told the others, "because we must."

The great ring boulevard of the Avi a'Parete had once defined the limits of the city of Nessantico, with a fortified wall running its entire length except for the Isle a'Kralji, which was adequately protected by the waters of the A'Sele. All of Nessantico had fit inside the wall—and that wall had been necessary in those times of endless war between the fiefdoms of Nessantico and those of her neighbors.

Now, most of that ancient city wall was gone, its great stones buried or reused in the city's buildings, with only a few small sections of the edifice still remaining. Nessantico had spilled well outside the confines of the Avi a'Parete, though less so in the south than other directions. Not far outside the remnants of the old Sutegate of the city, there were still open fields and farmland, and it was there that Allesandra watched the new sparkwheeler corps practice. They were dressed in normal clothing, most of them looking as if they'd just been plucked off the streets of Oldtown—which was actually the case. Talbot walked away from the group as Allesandra approached. He helped Allesandra down from her carriage; he was still dressed in his palais staff uniform. Allesandra peered across the field toward the men. "Forgive their appearance, Kraljica," Talbot said, as if realizing how they looked. "I've only had two days to work with them."

"Where's Varina? I thought these devices were her idea," Allesandra asked.

"She's settling things with the child. Then she's going to the northern front with the Hïrzg, along with most of the Numetodo. I thought you knew. The Hïrzg asked for as many spellcasters as were available."

Allesandra nodded—had Varina told her that, or had she forgotten? Someone in the group of sparkwheelers shouted the order to "fire!" The reports of the sparkwheels barked, and white smoke bloomed at the end of metal tubes. Across the field, paper targets set on straw bales fluttered as lead pellets peppered them.

The horses jumped in the carriage's traces, their eyes white and wide. The driver yanked back on the reins, calling to them.

Allesandra found that she'd taken an involuntary step backward herself at the violence of the sound, nearly falling back into the carriage. "You might stuff some paper in your ears, Kraljica," Talbot said. "These devices do make an infernal racket."

"Unless the enemy is stationary, it would seem that one shot is all that your new corps are going to have before the warriors are on them," Allesandra observed—the sparkwheelers were all reloading their weapons, and that process seemed to take an inordinate amount of time. "The Tehuantin are used to the noise of black sand; they're not going to be frightened away by it."

Talbot smiled. "That was my concern also, Kraljica. We've made a few small modifications to Varina's original design. The black sand and pellet packets are all pre-made, so no measurements need be made in the field. We also thought by extending the barrel somewhat, we could increase the distance and accuracy of the shot. That seems to be the case, though it's made the weapon heavier and bulkier." Out in the field, men were replacing the targets with fresh ones. The sparkwheelers were still reloading.

"Accurate or not, it's still one shot. If all I were given was one strike with my sword while the enemy was allowed to hit me freely as often as he wished, then the battle would be over quickly. It wouldn't matter if I had the sharper weapon."

"Indeed," Talbot said. "Which is why we've given some thought to tactics. Let me demonstrate . . . Cartier—form a squadron into lines of four," he called out. One of the men bowed slightly toward them and shouted more orders. A dozen men formed three wide-spaced lines of four as Cartier arranged them. Talbot stepped forward toward them.

"First line, kneel!' he shouted. "First line, fire!" Four sparkwheels spun and ignited, the echo of the reports rolling across the field. The men from the first line stood, each took a step to the left, and stepped backward to the rear. They began to reload their weapons. "Second line, kneel," Talbot shouted. "Second line, fire!" Again, reports sounded and white smoke drifted away. The men stood and fell back behind the first line. "Third line, kneel! Third line, fire!" Another roll of thunder, and the third line fell back. The first line had finished reloading by this time. "First line, kneel! First line, fire!"

Another volley, and Talbot grinned at Allesandra. "Stand down!" he called to the sparkwheelers, then walked back to Allesandra. "Kraljica?"

The flanks of the horses were trembling as they pulled anxiously at their bits, the driver working hard to stop them from bolting. Allesandra's ears rang with the noise of the weapons. "That was impressive, Talbot," Allesandra told him, and Talbot's grin widened.

"A three-line squadron can fire three volleys in nine breaths, and continue to do so until they're out of black sand packets, though after several shots, the sparkwheels become too hot to safely fire."

"But it's one thing to stand here with nothing but straw bales to face, and another when it's a charging enemy who intends to kill you," Allesandra continued. "These aren't soldiers, Talbot. They're not chevarittai. They're not even Numetodo. They look like they're just bakers and grocers, butchers and apothecaries."

"That's true of most of them," Talbot admitted. "I *don't* know how they're going to react when it comes time. But the effectiveness . . . The black sand weapons we've used before required large quantities of the material, and they're indiscriminate—the explosion might kill no one at all or several people, or might kill your own people if you're not careful. Spells are costly in time and exhaustion and they require years of training before most people can use them well. To use a sword or pike effectively requires weeks or months of training, too. These . . ." He gestured toward the field. "Varina's sparkwheels use very little black sand, they're as precise as a spell, and they require only a turn or two of training to use. They change the entire equation."

"That's what I'm afraid of," Allesandra interjected. "The power you've given the untrained rabble . . ."

"I'm afraid that the rabble is nearly all we have between us and the Tehuantin at the moment, Kraljica, unless you think that the Garde Brezno can do the impossible."

She frowned. "I know," Allesandra answered. "Still, something about this . . ." She clapped Talbot on the shoulder. "I'm sorry, Talbot. I worry what this means for the future: for the Holdings, for the Faith, for our society." She pressed her lips together, cutting off the rest of her thought. "You've done a fine job," she told Talbot. "Everything we've asked for and more. I just hope it all works when the time comes—because it will have to."

She drew herself up, mounting onto the step of her carriage. "Continue your work. In the meantime, I need to check with Sergei and the Garde Brezno."

Talbot bowed to her; she stepped fully into the carriage, gesturing to the driver. He slapped the reins on the back of the horses, and with a grumbling of wheels, the carriage lurched forward.

His feet ached, his back throbbed with every step. They had passed three villages so far in the day's march, all of them deserted—Tototl had allowed the warriors to scavenge for food and supplies, then ordered the houses burned. The smoke was still smeared across the sky behind them.

Niente wanted to do little more than lie down and let the warriors and nahualli leave him in the dirt. He was grateful when Tototl called a halt to the quick march. He sank down in the grass alongside the road and accepted the bread, cheese, and water that one of the nahualli handed him, gulping down the sweet coolness. He saw a shadow looming near him, and sat up. Tototl was watching him.

"I will get you a horse, Uchben Nahual."

"I'll be fine in a few moments, High Warrior."

"I will get you a horse," Tototl answered. "I need the Uchben Nahual to be ready when we begin the attack tonight."

Niente had rarely talked to Tototl, since the High Warriors, with the exception of the Tecuhtli with the Nahual, rarely had interaction with the nahualli. He found himself looking at the man's painted face and wondering what he might actually be thinking. "We're that close, then?"

"We'll see the tops of the houses when we cross the next rise. The scouts have told me that there are troops readying to meet us. The battle will begin very soon now." For a few breaths, Tototl was silent, and Niente was content to sit on the grassy bank of the road. The breeze was fragrant with the scent of this land. Then Tototl stirred. "What did you see when you looked in the scrying bowl, Uchben Nahual? I watched you, watched your face, and I don't believe that you told Tecuhtli Citlali everything."

"I told him the truth," Niente insisted. "Nahual Atl saw the same."

Tototl's mouth twisted under the paint and ink that adorned his face. "Your son is not you, Uchben Nahual. He may be one day, but not yet. You were holding back something you saw, something that frightened you. I saw it in your face, Niente. I want to know—did you see us defeated?"

Niente shook his head. *I saw our victory here, and its terrible cost. I saw that it might be averted, and I saw that there the future was too confused and tangled to predict.* "No," he said.

"I'm not afraid of dying," Tototl said. He was staring northward along the road, as if he could already see the city. "Dying well in battle is the end that every High Warrior looks for. It's not a fear of dying; I'm afraid of the cost of this to the Tehuantin." Tototl looked down again at Niente, and hope sprang up in him, a hope that the warrior might understand what Citlali could not. "Is that what you're afraid of also, Uchben Nahual?" Tototl asked

Niente's throat seemed to close under Tototl's steady, unblinking regard. He nodded silently.

"So you've seen something." This time Tototl said it with certainty. Niente shook his head.

"I don't know," he answered. "I've seen too many paths, High Warrior. Too many, and all of them uncertain. But . . ." He inhaled, long and slow. *Can you trust this man? Could this be a trap he's set for you, maybe even one that Citlali and Atl have set?* "Let me ask you this: if you killed a warrior in challenge, you would claim that you have won a victory. But what if in killing that warrior, you have in turn so inflamed his son that when *he* becomes a warrior, he brings an army and destroys everything that you've built, destroys everything you cherish so completely that it cannot be recovered? Was your initial victory worth winning, then?"

"That would depend," Tototl said, "on whether you could tell me—without doubt—that the son would do all this."

Niente was shaking his head. "The future is never entirely certain," he told the warrior. "Even what happens in the next moment might change, if Axat wills it. But what if I could tell you that this was the likely outcome? Would you hold your sword stroke, then?"

"It would depend on whether holding my sword stroke cost me my own life," Tototl said. "No warrior wants to give the enemy their life freely. I would think the same would be true of a nahualli."

"That's what I might say in your place," Niente said.

Tototl's head cocked slightly to one side. He grunted something that might have been assent. "Since you say the future is always uncertain, would *you* give your full support to a High Warrior, Uchben Nauhual, even if you thought it might be the wrong path?"

"That's a nahualli's duty," Niente answered. A quick amusement crossed Tototl's face, and he knew the warrior understood that he hadn't fully answered the question.

"I will get you a horse, Uchben Nahual," Tototl said to Niente.

*   *   *

"She was with him? You're *certain* it was her?"

Sergei nodded. "It was Rochelle, Hïrzgin. So at least
that much of what she told me would seem to be the truth.
Rochelle was raised as Nico's sister by the White Stone.
Whether she knows that he's not really her brother . . . ?"
Sergei raised a tired shoulder. "I'm not sure she under-
stands that."

Sergei and Brie were sitting astride their horses, overlooking the fields around the Avi a'Sutegate where the
Garde Kralji was encamped. There were too few of them,
Sergei knew—given the report the scouts had brought
back of the size of the Westlander forces advancing toward
them. Though the offiziers were running the gardai through
maneuvers, the troops looked sluggish and lost. They were
not trained for this: open, full-scale combat against another
organized and trained force. That much had been shown
in the debacle of the Old Temple, when even the equally
untrained Morellis had been able to hold them at bay for
too long. The Garde Kralji was a glorified personal guard
and policing unit, not an army battalion.

The battle won't be won here, Sergei reminded himself.
*It will be won across the River A'Sele, with the Hïrzg and
the Garde Civile. We just have to hold our own here, hold
them back long enough that the Garde Civile can return and
rescue us.*

He was fairly certain they would need that rescue, and
he wasn't particularly hopeful that it would be coming.

"They look terribly clumsy and slow, and I'm not at
all impressed with their offiziers," Brie said next to him,
as if she had overheard his thoughts. She was dressed
in full armor over a quilted tashta and wore a sword at
her side, though her helm was still lashed to the pommel of her saddle, her brown hair braided and hanging
low down her back. She looked entirely comfortable in
the martial outfit—much, he thought, as Allesandra did
when she commanded the field troops. It was a shame,
he thought, that the two of them had been so long sundered. Allesandra's son had married someone much like
his matarh, either unwittingly or consciously. "I wish I
had brought the Garde Brezno as well. These Garde

Kralji are going to need strong leadership on the field, or they'll break the first time the fighting gets difficult."

"Indeed," Sergei answered. "The Kraljica and the Hïrzgin must be the ones to give them that. Commandant cu'Ingres, I'm afraid, is still troubled by his injuries, and A'Offizier ci'Santiago is, well, let's just call him inexperienced."

"Where *is* the Kraljica?"

"On her way, I expect. We should see her any time now."

Brie made a noise of assent. He saw her lean forward in her saddle, leather creaking. She was peering toward the south. "Is that another of our scouts? He's riding fast . . ." She pointed, and Sergei saw a cloud of dust far away along the avi. His own vision was poor, and he couldn't quite make out the rider or the colors.

"It may be," he said. "Whoever it is, they're coming fast. There must be news."

The two of them flicked the reins of their horses, cantering down to the road to meet the rider. They were joined by A'Offizier ci'Santiago as the rider came galloping up, his mount lathered with effort. The rider saluted them.

"The Westlanders," he said, panting. "Not far down the road . . . A thousand or more . . . All along the road." He stopped, catching his breath. "A few turns of the glass and they'll be here," he said. "They're coming at a fast march, and they have several of their spellcasters with them, and the makings of siege machines with them as well. We need to be ready."

Ci'Santiago nodded, but he did nothing. Sergei sighed. "We'll need to send for Talbot and the sparkwheelers— A'Offizier, perhaps you can give this man a fresh horse and have him bear the message. Hïrzgin . . ."

"I'll take the field command of the troops until the Kraljica arrives," she told Sergei. "Ambassador, you and Commandant cu'Ingres can see to the main strategy here in the command tents." Sergei could see her already looking at the landscape and deciding where to place the troops for best advantage. "I'll need signalers, cornets, and runners, and I'll want to talk to the offiziers. A'Offizier ci'Santiago, I need you to arrange that immediately. What are you waiting here for? There's no time, man. Go!"

Ci'Santiago was gaping at her, but he shut his mouth

and saluted as Sergei stifled a laugh. The man turned his horse and galloped away; the scout following him. Brie was staring south, her mouth set. Sergei thought he could see smoke rising from the horizon.

"I do believe you frightened the poor man," Sergei told her, and she sniffed through her nose. "He's probably already complaining about the demon woman from Firenzcia."

"I'm happy to be the demon woman if it means we survive this," she told him. "Do you think we can, Ambassador?"

"Would I be here if I didn't?" he answered, and hoped she couldn't hear the lie.

Nico heard the lock to the house gates snick open under Rochelle's ministrations; she grinned toward Nico as she slipped the thin pieces of metal back into their packet. "Easy," she said, pushing the gates open; Nico slid inside ahead of her, but he felt her put a hand on his shoulder almost immediately. He glanced back at her from under the hood that masked his head, the cloak that disguised his green robes heavy around him.

"Something's wrong here," Rochelle said.

"What do you mean?"

"Listen," she answered.

The street outside the gates was crowded with people leaving the city. They could hear their voices: the calls, the arguments, the cries of children too young to understand the panic of their parents and relatives. There were the creak and groans of the carts, the shuffling of feet on the pavement, the whistles of utilinos vainly trying to direct traffic and quell the inevitable confrontations. "There's all this noise out there," she told him. "But inside here—the staff should be scurrying around, getting things ready for whatever, but there's *nothing*. The shutters to the windows are all closed and probably locked, and I don't hear anything at all. It's too quiet here."

"What are you telling me?" His voice was a husk. He already knew the answer, could feel it in a despair that settled low in his stomach.

"I don't think she's there, Nico. I think she's gone already. I'm sorry."

Nico pushed past Rochelle, striding angrily toward the

front doors of Varina's house. It was locked, but rather than wait for Rochelle, he kicked hard at it and the wood around the lock cracked. He kicked again, and the door opened.

"Subtle," Rochelle said behind him.

He ignored her, stepping into the marbled entranceway. He was certain now that Rochelle was right; the servants should have come running, perhaps ready to defend the house, but there was no one in sight. "Varina?" he called. He thought he saw a cat dart across the hallway ahead of him. Otherwise, there was no response. He heard Rochelle enter the house behind him; glancing over his shoulder, he saw that she was holding her knife, the blade naked in her hand. "We won't need that," he said.

"Probably not. But it makes me feel better."

He shrugged. He walked slowly down the hallway, glancing into the reception rooms to either side. The furniture there was covered with sheets; the cat glared at him from atop a blanketed couch, then went back to licking its front paws. He continued to move through the house: the sunroom, a library, the kitchens—they were all the same, empty, with every indication that Varina didn't expect to return here soon. He heard Rochelle calling him from upstairs, and he followed the sound of her voice. She'd put the knife in its sheath, and was standing at the door to what had to be a nursery. The furniture here, too, was covered. She opened the drawers of a dresser along one wall. "Empty," she told him. "I told you—Serafina's not here, Nico. The Numetodo's taken her elsewhere."

Nico was shaking his head. "Varina's still here in the city. I can *feel* it."

One eyebrow rose on Rochelle's face. "Well, if she is, she's not staying here, and the baby's not here either."

"She's sent Sera away," Nico said.

"I gathered that. So can Cénzi tell you where?"

He scowled at her, a warning about blasphemy on his lips, but he held it back. She seemed to realize it as well, holding up a hand. "All right, so you don't know. What do we do now?" Rochelle asked, but Nico could only shake his head.

"I don't know," he told her. After his confrontation with Sergei, he'd hoped to take Sera, to leave the city with his daughter and his sister, and find a place to think and pray: to know what Cénzi wanted of him, to know how to assuage the guilt and pain he bore . . . He'd hoped—he'd prayed—that Cénzi would give him his daughter, but it seemed that Cénzi still had other plans for him. He looked upward. "Cénzi, what are You trying to tell me?"

He listened to the whispers in his head and in his heart, and his face grew grim. "I think it's time for us to part for a while," he told Rochelle.

~

The Storm's Fury

IN THE LATE AFTERNOON, the sun hung low in the west, but where there had been clear sky before, a storm had birthed itself across the River Infante. Thunderheads rose high in the sky, though these were clouds that lurked impossibly close to the ground. Underneath them, the army of the Tehuantin was cloaked in shadow, and the storm walked itself forward on jagged legs of flickering lightning. The black, roiling clouds stretched off southward along the front the Tehuantin had established. Jan's horse shifted uneasily under him, nostrils flaring as low thunder growled like some great beast. There was a sharp odor in the air that wrinkled Jan's nostrils.

"War-storm," one of the chevarittai near Jan muttered. "The cowards—they won't even give us a chance for honorable single combat first." Jan nodded—he'd heard of the Tehuantin war-storms, called up by their spellcasters: a co-operative spell. The Westlanders had used them to great effectiveness when they'd last been here, as well as during their battles with the Holdings in the Hellins, but Jan had never seen one himself. He doubted he was going to enjoy the firsthand experience.

"Alert the war-téni," he said, patting his horse's neck to calm it. "We're going to need them. The attack's starting."

Jan, with several companies of Firenzcian troops and chevarittai, was on the western side of the River Infante just below the village of Certendi. The bridge over the river was at their backs. On the eastern side of the river, he could see the earthen ramparts they'd built; he had little hope that they would be able to keep the western bank for long. Starkkapitän ca'Damont was farther downriver, with the remainder of the Firenzcian army; Commandant ca'Talin, with the Holdings' Garde Civile, at the southern end of their line, near where the Infante joined with the A'Sele.

"Tell your men they must hold," Jan told the chevarittai. He yanked on his horse's reins, riding up and down just between the lines of infantry and archers. "Hold!" he told them all. "We need to hold here." As the war-storm stalked forward, the rumbling of the great cloud growing louder and more ominous, the war-téni came up to the front. He gestured to the green robes. "Here's where you begin to earn your forgiveness," he told them. "There—that storm must come down."

The storm lurched nearer with every breath. The air smelled of the lightning strikes but not of rain. Ahead of the troops, in what had formerly been a field planted with wheat and grain, Jan had placed entrapments for the Tehuantin warriors: sharpened iron spikes set in the ground, covered pits whose bottoms were festooned with wooden stakes, packets of black sand that Varina and her Numetodo had enchanted so that they would explode when someone stepped near them. But the storm was marching across the field, not yet the Westlander warriors. The lightning strikes tore at the ground, uprooting the stakes and exposing the pits, tossing earth everywhere and causing the black sand packets to explode harmlessly.

Jan cursed at the war-téni. "Now!" he shouted at them. "Now!"

The war-téni began their chants, sending the energy of the Ilmodo surging outward toward the false storm. With each spell that was released, the storm began to fall apart, and underneath, they could see the Tehuantin warriors hidden below, marching steadily toward them. "Archers!" Jan shouted, and behind him, bows creaked under tension, then a thin flurry of arrows arched upward, curving back down to rain upon the Westlanders. They snapped up shields. Jan saw several of the warriors fall despite the protection, though wherever one fell, another took up his place. To the south, the war-storm loomed over the ranks of the Holdings, and Jan heard cries of pain and alarm as the lightning tore at the soldiers there. But the storm was already falling apart—the power behind it released. Now, he heard the guttural shouts of the Westlander spellcasters; fireballs shrieked like angry Moitidi in their direction. The war-téni chanted their counter-spells; Jan saw several of the fireballs explode harmlessly above, but others came through, slamming into the ranks and spewing their fiery, terrible destruction and gouging holes in the lines. His horse reared in terror. "Move the lines forward! Fill the gaps!" Jan shouted as he tried to calm his mount. The offiziers shouted directions; signal flags waved.

Then, with a great shout, the warriors charged, and there was little time for thought at all. Jan unsheathed his sword and kicked his horse forward. The chevarittai gave a cry of fury and followed him, the gardai infantry rising in a black-and-silver wave to meet the Westlanders.

They crashed together in a flurry of swords, spears, and pikes.

Jan had fought the legions of Tennshah. These Westlanders were equally ferocious as fighters, but they were also far more disciplined. He could hear their own offiziers calling out crisp orders in their language, and their spellcasters were embedded in their midst, wielding staffs that crackled and flared with spells. He remembered that much from the last time. Jan hacked with his sword at a sea of brown faces painted in red and black, and wherever one fell to him, another sprang up to take his place. They were being pushed slowly back, and still the Westlanders kept coming. Jan realized that they couldn't hold here on this side of the river—if they were pushed much closer to the river, there could be no orderly retreat; they'd be slaughtered.

"Back!" he shouted. "To the bridge! To the bridge!"

The offiziers took up the cry; the flag-bearers waved their signal flags, the cornets shrilled their call. The Firenzcian troops, disciplined and precise as always, gave ground grudgingly and as they had been trained to do, allowing the archers and war-téni to cover their retreat and carrying away their wounded wherever possible.

The dead they left.

Here, there were two bridges crossing the Infante, a half-mile apart. The northern bridge, along the Avi a'Nostrosei, had already been destroyed. The one over the Avi a'Certendi still remained. The Infante could be forded but not easily, since its current was swift and there were deep pools that only the locals knew. The archers and war-téni were first over the bridge as the foot troops and cheva-rittai held back the Westlanders, the offiziers hurrying them across toward ramparts that had been erected on the far side. Jan stayed with his men, his armor blood-splattered and dented, the gray Firenzcian steel of his sword stained with gore, until the bridge was cleared and the archers had re-formed on the far side.

"Break away!" he called finally when he heard the horns from the far side of the Infante, and they rushed toward the bridge. Jan turned again there, keeping back the war-riors who pursued them, howling. The ground was thick with bodies around him and the chevarittai. A spellcaster gestured with his stick, and the chevaritt alongside Jan went down with a scream and the smell of brimstone, but the spellcaster was cut down himself in the next moment. Most of the infantry was across. "Across!" Jan shouted. "Chevarittai, across!" They turned their horses; they fled. The hooves of the war-steeds pounded on the planks of the bridge, and Jan gestured to the war-téni who were waiting on the far side. The Tehuantin pursued, too closely. Already, the warriors were on the western end of the bridge.

"Now!" Jan cried as he reached ground on the far side. "Take it down!"

"Hïrzg, not before we're behind the ramparts," someone said, and Jan stood up in his stirrups, furious, and roared.

"Take it down *now*!"

The war-téni chanted; fire began to crawl the wooden support beams. The flames licked at the paper that wrapped the black sand lashed there.

The explosions flung pieces of the bridge high in the air, huge, rough-cut beams tumbling end over end, the bricks and stones of the pilings slicing through the air. Warriors and gardai alike were struck. One of the bricks slammed into Jan, the impact unhorsing him. He heard his horse scream as well, an awful sound. As he fell, he saw the center of the bridge collapse, falling into the Infante with a huge splash, taking a mass of Westlander warriors with it.

Then he hit the ground. For a moment, everything went

black around him. When he came back to consciousness,
he saw faces above him and hands. "Hïrzg, are you hurt?"

Jan let them pull him to his feet. His chest ached as if
his horse had fallen on him, and the armor was heavily in-
dented where the brick had struck him. His chest burned
with every inhale; he had to sip the air as he shook off the
hands. His horse was thrashing on the ground, a plank embedded in the creature's side.

The bridge was down. The sun was already sinking to
the level of the trees, throwing long shadows over the battlefield. The Westlanders had retreated back from the water's edge to be out of arrow range. Jan limped to his horse.
One of the stallion's front legs was broken, and blood
gushed from the long wound along its flank. "My sword?"
he asked, and someone handed it to him. Kneeling down
alongside the horse, he patted its neck. "Rest," he said.
"You've served well." Grunting with pain, he raised the
sword high and brought it down hard, slicing deep into the
neck. The horse tried to stand one last time, then went still.
The world seemed to dance around Jan, the edges of his
vision darkening again. He forced himself to stand, leaning
on the sword.

"Get the lines formed behind the ramparts," he said
to those around him. "Tend to the wounded and set the
watches. Send the a'offiziers to me, and get word to the
Starkkapitän and the Commandant of what's . . .." *Happened here* . . . The words were in his mind, but they didn't
seem to come out. The darkness was moving too fast even
though the sun was still visible in the sky.

He felt himself falling.

There weren't enough nahualli with Niente to create a war-
storm. Ahead of them, in the golden light of late afternoon,
they could see the Easterner troops arrayed on the hillsides
on either side of the road. Their own numbers appeared to
be significantly greater than that of the Easterners unless
they had troops hidden in reserve on the far slope.

Tototl sniffed in disdain.

"This is all they bring against us?" he said, and the warriors closest to them chuckled. "Uchben Nahual, it's time to
do as we've discussed."

Niente inclined his head to Tototl and turned his horse,

riding back to where the other nahualli were sheltered in the midst of the warriors. He'd had them fill their spell-staffs the night before as usual, so that they could perform this spell at need and still be rested for the battle. They could not create the war-storm, but they *could* create cloud enough to mask them. That was what they did now, their mass chant pulling power from the X'in Ka, the energy rising into the air and becoming visible. Wisps of cloud began to sway in front of the warriors, from the road to nearly the banks of the river, a fog that thickened and became dense, a wall shaped by the nahualli so that the Easterners could no longer see them. This wall would not need to move with the troops, nor would it need to generate the lightnings of the war-storm. Niente gestured when he could no longer see the Easterner troops ahead of them nor the hills on which they stood, and the nahualli stopped their chant.

Niente swayed on his feet, as if he'd run from here to the river and back: the payment for the chant and his channeling of the energy, but he forced himself to stay upright, even though a few of the younger nahualli collapsed, panting. Using the X'in Ka this way—creating the spell without giving yourself time to recover from the effort—was costly; Niente didn't understand why the Easterner spellcasters usually performed their magic this way, rather than storing the spells to be released later. "Get up," he told them. "Take up your spell-staffs. There's still a battle to be fought."

With the fog-wall shutting off sight of the Easterner troops, Tototl shouted his orders, gesturing to the lesser warriors and the High Warriors in charge of them. Two companies slid away to the left, toward the river—they would outflank the Easterners and come upon them from the side and rear. Tototl waited as the flanking arm moved away and Niente rode back to him. "If this is all that is between us and the city, we'll be there by evening, Uchben Nahual," Tototl said. "It would seem that your son has seen well—sending us across the river was the path to victory. They weren't prepared for this. We will push through their city and come upon the rest of their army from the rear as Citlali and Nahual Atl attack them from the front. We will crush them between us like a shelled nut between stones."

The comment only made Niente scowl. He'd tried to use the scrying bowl the night before: everything was confus-

ing, and powers moved on the side of the Easterners that
he could not clearly see while the Long Path eluded him
entirely. Tototl seemed to find Niente's irritation amusing—he laughed. "Don't worry, Uchben Nahual," he said.
"I still have faith in you. Is your spell-staff full?"

Niente lifted the staff, the ebony hardwood he'd carved
so carefully decades ago with the symbols of power. His
hands over the long years had polished the knobbed end
and the middle of the staff to a gleaming satiny finish. The
staff felt like part of him; he could feel the energy within,
waiting for the release words to burst forth in fury and
death. Yet even as he displayed the staff to Tototl and the
warriors and nahualli around him gave a shout of affirmation, Niente felt little but despair.

There was no life in this victory, if victory it was to be. No
joy. Not if it were to lead to the place he'd once glimpsed.

Tototl unsheathed his sword. He lifted it with Niente's
staff as the shouts redoubled. "It is time for blood!" Tototl
declared. "It is time for death or glory!" He pointed the
sword toward the cloudbank. "For Sakal!" he roared, and
they shouted with him as they charged forward. Niente was
carried along with the flood, but he was silent.

They entered the cold, gray blankness of the cloud, and
emerged into sun and heat and battle.

Brie had positioned the troops on the two hillsides that
flanked the road, with only a single company on the road
itself, and the archers in position on either side—they
would at least have the high ground to begin this battle.
The Westlanders would have to charge uphill if they wished
to engage them.

If they had chevarittai, they could have come charging
down at terrible speed, like a gigantic spear thrusting into
the Westlanders' midst. But they had no chevarittai and too
few archers, only three of the Numetodo—of whom Brie
was rather suspicious, there being no Numetodo in Firenzcia at all; at least none who openly showed themselves—
and no war-téni at all.

Allesandra had arrived a turn earlier, dressed in her own
armor, and Brie had ceded field command to her, as was
proper given that the Garde Kralji was hers. The Kraljica

had given her approval of Brie's placement of the gardai. "I see you've been taught well," she said. "I expected no less." Brie and the Kraljica, along with Sergei and Commandant cu'Ingres, watched the approach of the Westlander troops, under the banner of a winged snake. Brie was sobered by the frightening size of their force; she was even more concerned as they watched their spellcasters—safely out of the range of the archers they had—place a fog-wall between them to mask their formation.

Brie had not been able to conceal a shudder at the sight. "Kraljica, Ambassador, is there some better and more defensible ground between here and Sutegate? Perhaps we should try to harry them rather than stop them? We could send smaller groups against their flanks, create a defensive wall at the city . . ."

Allesandra had glanced at Sergei and cu'Ingres, neither of whom spoke. "It's too late for that, Hïrzgin," Allesandra said. "We must stand here, we must hold them as long as we can, and we must make them pay for every stride of ground they take."

Brie clenched her hands around the reins of her warhorse. "Then I'll stand with you, Kraljica, at the front."

"No." Allesandra shook her head. "That's my place and responsibility," she said, "and Jan would never forgive me if you were hurt here. I want you to take the river flank with Talbot's sparkwheelers," she said. "They'll need a steady heart and commander to guide them. Talbot can stay with you, but I need the other Numetodo here—we have too few of them, since most went with Commandant ca'Talin."

Brie had wanted to argue—to her mind, the Garde Kralji would also need strong leadership or they would break, but she grudgingly inclined her head. "As you say, Kraljica . . ."

Reluctantly, she rode to the western side of the road and up the hill through the Garde Kralji—staring at her worriedly—to the rear flank where the sparkwheelers had been placed. She shook her head at the sight of them: clothed in whatever they already had on their backs. They had no armor at all, except for the few who wore scraps of rusted metal curaisses or ripped and ill-fitting chainmail. Except for the strange-looking devices each of them carried, they were armed only with ancient swords, farm implements,

and cudgels. They looked more like a mob than a fighting
force—a mob that a bare squadron of Garde Brezno would
have been able to rout and send screaming into the streets.

Brie informed Talbot of the Kraljica's orders; he seemed
as distressed by them as she was, but Talbot had hurriedly
sent his fellow Numetodo down to where the Kraljica's
banner flew on the eastern side of the road.

"I'm her aide," he said as he watched the Numetodo
moving toward the Kraljica's banner. "I should be with her.
This is madness."

"Which is why," Brie said, "she has kept us both back.
She knows the odds. Do these sparkwheelers actually have
a purpose?"

In answer, Talbot ran them through their drills, forming the sparkwheelers into lines and moving them back
in sequence. Brie tried to imagine the the sparkwheels firing, tried to imagine the corps not breaking and fleeing
in terror at the sight of the enemy. As Talbot shouted his
orders, she also watched the impossible bank of fog that
blanketed the road below, sliding off past the side of the
hill on which she stood.

The gray wall was silent.

"What happens when they 'fire'?" she asked.

"The sparkwheels discharge. They're actually quite effective. Varina invented them." He cocked his head slightly
at Brie. "There's no magic involved at all, Hïrzgin, if that's
your worry. No flaunting of 'Cénzi's Gift,' as you of the
Faith might term it."

She started to retort, then . . .

"Talbot . . ." She pointed down the hill.

It began with a muffled roar from behind the cloud: the
sound of clashing armor and shouting warriors. From out
of the fog, the Tehuantin came rushing toward them, wave
upon wave of them, filling the road as well as the fields to
either side. Brie, from her vantage point, heard Allesandra
call for the archers to fire, and the Numetodo sent fireballs
and lightnings crackling toward them. The spells and the
arrows cut brief holes in the line that were immediately
filled, and now the Westlander spellcasters raised their
spell-staffs and sent their own lightnings hurtling toward
Allesandra and the troops. There were explosions along
both hills, and screams.

The clamor grew louder; the lines came close . . .

. . . and collided with a clash of metal. From the heights where the sparkwheelers were set, Brie could see the battle laid out before her, the two armies swarming like a plague of insects over the landscape. Some of the sparkwheelers were visibly frightened by what they saw and some of them stepped backward up the hill—northward, toward the city. Talbot and Brie both shouted at them to hold, and Brie turned her horse to cut them off, like a sheepdog with its herd. "Retreat, and I will cut you down," Brie shouted at them, her sword held high, her warhorse stamping its feet in response to her agitation.

"Talbot, let's move them down so we can . . ." she began, but suddenly clamped her mouth shut.

The battle was already failing below—she could see it. The front line of the Garde Kralji had already buckled, and Allesandra's banner was moving north along the road, giving ground. The Westlanders were no longer issuing from the fog-wall, and despite their numbers, there seemed to be fewer of them than Brie remembered. Brie looked to Talbot, worried and suddenly suspicious.

"Stay here," she said. She urged her horse up the slope of the hill toward the ridge, staying in the cover of the trees. When she reached the summit, she peered down. She could see the gray fog-wall arrowing off toward the ribbon of the river. And out in front of it . . .

"Oh, no . . ." She breathed a curse.

Below her, already ascending the slope below, was the remainder of the Westlander army.

The war-storm was both terrifying and deadly, but it was only a chimera: a ghost from the Second World. Even as Varina tore at it with the Scáth Cumhacht, she still had to admire its power, its precision, and its making. She could feel the many individual threads of the storm, how it was woven from the spells of many spellcasters and formed by a single one of them: a particularly strong presence, and one who was close to her.

This was nothing that the téni of the Faith could do, nor the Numetodo—another skill that those of the Eastern world didn't have. Even as she shredded the clouds and dissipated the spell-threads that held it together, Varina found herself thinking of how she would put together a spell like this herself.

If you live, this is something you should work on, so the Numetodo learn to do it as well.

If you live . . .

That, she was afraid, was no certainty.

She was with Commandant ca'Talin's Garde Civile at the southern terminus of the front, in the narrowing triangle between the River Infante and the River A'Sele. Here, the Infante broke into two arms as it joined the A'Sele, and the Avi a'Sele arched over it with two bridges. As with Starkkapitän ca'Damont's command just to the north, and with Hïrzg Jan's command at the northern end of the front, they had placed themselves on the western side of the Infante. The Tehuantin were set in a long, curving front that stretched from the Avi a'Sele to the Avi a'Nostrosei, somewhat over two miles long.

The war-storm, from what she could see, may have covered their entire length.

The other Numetodo were also ripping into the war-storm with her. The lightning was fading, the black cloud rent and shredded. They could see men moving behind it, charging forward. "Back, back!" Commandant ca'Talin was shouting at her and the others. "Stay behind the line. Archers, fire!" Flags waved; cornets blasted the air, and all along the line flights of arrows rose to meet the war-storm. Varina could see the shields of the warriors flick up, saw the arrows fall mostly to embed themselves in the shields. Swords hacked at the arrows stuck on the shields, shearing them off, and an answering hail of arrows came from the Tehuantin. Varina heard Mason cry out near her and go down, an arrow fletched with gray feathers in his chest. Another arrow thudded into the ground at her feet. "Back!" ca'Talin shouted again, and this time they obeyed, Johannes and Niels dragging Mason with them.

Varina could see little of the battle other than the bodies jostling around her, but she could hear it: the clash of steel against steel, the cries from the soldiers on both sides, the shrill calls of the horns. She could smell it as well: the smoke from the spell-fires, the scent of blood, the nose-wrinkling stench of brimstone. But ahead of her there was only a writhing mass of soldiers. Ca'Talin, on his horse, surrounded by chevarittai, went hurtling into that chaos, and for a moment Varina and the others were alone. They sent fire-spells arcing over their gardai into the Tehuantin lines beyond; they used counter-spells to blast away the fire hurled at them by the Westlander spellcasters. Black sand exploded to Varina's right, sending dirt and body parts hurtling through the air and half-deafening her.

Varina could feel the terrible exhaustion of using the Scáth Cumhacht this way. All the spells she'd stored the night before were gone, and her mind was too tired and confused to create new spells easily. She was done; she was empty.

If you live . . .

She was less certain of that now than ever.

The cornets had altered their call. Varina saw the Commandant and chevarittai emerge from the smoke and confusion of the battle. Behind them, gardai were turning and fleeing eastward. "To the bridges!" ca'Talin shouted as he passed them. "To the bridges!"

Varina was swept up with them, helpless. The retreat was a rout, a confusion. She found herself pushed, stumbling and nearly falling. All around her, people were shoving and she couldn't stand. It would be easy, she thought, to just lay down here, to let it end. She felt herself starting to fall once again.

A hand went around her waist. "Here, pull yourself up." Ca'Talin had returned, and he pulled her up onto his warhorse, her arms and shoulders aching. She could see the bridges ahead, clotted with gardai fleeing toward the earthern ramparts on the far side.

"We've lost here," ca'Talin half-shouted to her as they plunged into the press of men. "The Westlanders have this side of the river, all the way north. May Cénzi preserve us for tomorrow."

Seeing the Tehuantin advancing up the far side of the hill toward them, Brie turned her steed and rode hard down to the sparkwheelers, the horse sending rocks and pebbles cascading down ahead of them.

"Talbot! This way," she cried. "Bring your people and follow me!" Once she saw Talbot's acknowledgment, saw him begin to shout orders and shove at the sparkwheelers nearest him, she headed up the slope again until she was on the ridge. The Tehuantin were still ascending the hill, with the obvious intention of flanking the main battle and coming on the Garde Kralji from the side and rear while they were intent on the main assault from along the road. The hill's summit was flat and mostly treeless; the Westlanders were advancing through a meadow. She'd been seen by them, also; she heard an arrow hiss past her head, and she moved downslope slightly.

Talbot and the sparkwheelers were nearly to the top; she quickly told Talbot what she'd seen. They arranged the lines just below the summit, the sparkwheelers checking their weapons again to make certain they were loaded, and opening the leather pouches they wore that held, Brie had been told, the tiny packets of black sand to reload the weapons. She'd seen the packets; they were hardly impressive—they'd only added to her doubts as to the efficiency of the spark-wheel as a weapon.

But she had no other choice. She had to hope that what Talbot had told her wasn't an elaborate lie. "All right," she said. "On my command, we'll move up to the ridge. Talbot, be ready to fire as soon as you're there—they have archers, so you're going to be under attack yourselves." She saw some of the men blanch at that. "You have the high ground and the advantage. Hit them hard, and the archers will be useless," she told them, though she didn't believe that at all. She thought their archers would make a wall of bodies on the summit from the sparkwheelers. "Now—forward!"

Almost grudgingly, the men trudged up to the ridgeline, Brie and Talbot alongside them. She heard the calls in the strange Westlander tongue as they appeared, but Talbot was already shouting out the cadence before the first arrows came. "First line, kneel! First line, fire!"

The racket that ensured made Brie's horse rear up in terror. White, acrid smoke bloomed along the line, and down the hill . . . Brie could scarcely believe what she saw: Westlanders went down as if a divine blade had scythed through their ranks. She gave a cry of surprise, almost a laugh. "Second line kneel! Second line, fire!"

Again, the reports from the sparkwheels echoed; again, more Westlanders fell, their bodies tumbling back down the hill or crumpling where they stood. A few arrows were

slicing into the sparkwheelers now as well, and she saw
three or four of the men go down. "Damn it, stand, you bastardos!" Talbot shouted as the lines wavered and started to
dissolve. Brie rode behind them as the line in the rear fal-
tered and tried to break rather than reload their weapons.

"No!" she told them. "Stay and fight, or you'll face my
blade! Stay!"

"Third line, kneel. Third line, fire!" Talbot cried, and this
time the volley was a stutter rather than a concerted explosion, but still more Tehuantin were falling. Brie could
see the enemy wavering. "Again!" she shouted to Talbot.
"Hurry!"

"First line, kneel! First line, fire!" Another stuttering,
and some of the men could not fire at all, still clumsily
trying to load their pieces with trembling hands. But yet
more of the Tehuantin were down and the arrow fire had
stopped entirely. Down the hill, injured and dying warriors
were screaming in their language, and other painted warriors were shouting in return. "Second line, kneel. Second
line, fire!"

Again the sparkwheels gave their roar, and as more warriors fell, the Tehuantin finally broke. The warriors turned
and began running back down the hill despite the efforts of
their offiziers to hold them, and it was suddenly a panicked
retreat. The sparkwheeler corps gave a shout of triumph,
and a few, without orders from Talbot, fired their sparkwheels at the retreating backs. At the top of the hill, fists
punched the air in triumph.

Brie shouted a huzzah with them, but then she looked
behind and the joy died in her throat. Well below, on the
road, the Garde Kralji was in full flight. She could see
Allesandra's banner waving and hear the cornets calling
retreat. Behind them, the Tehuantin warriors were pursuing: a black wave of them that overspread the road along
both hills, a wave that would overwhelm their cadre of
sparkwheelers if they stayed. "Talbot!" Brie shouted. "To
the Kraljica! We can't stay here."

They may have won a small victory in their skirmish,
but there would be no greater victory here. She led Talbot
and the sparkwheelers down the hill to join the Kraljica in
her flight.

*   *   *

Niente had thought that Tototl would chase the Easterners straight back into their city, or even overrun their retreat and slay them here. He might have done exactly that,
except one of the High Warriors came gasping back to
them raving of a massacre: the group that had been sent
to the western flank had been nearly destroyed. Tototl
called a halt to the advance, sending only a few squadrons to to pursue the fleeing Easterners. Tototl and Niente
had followed the High Warrior around to the far side of
the hill. Now Niente was looking up on a terrible carnage
on the hillside before him—though he'd seen worse in
his long deades of warfare, certainly. He'd witnessed men
hacked to pieces, had viewed corpses piled on corpses.
But this: there was an eerie quiet here, and the bodies
were strangely whole. There was too little blood.

Tototl had leaped down from his horse, going from body
to body strewn over the grassy slope. "What magic did
this?" he demanded of Niente.

Niente shook his head. "A magic I haven't seen before,"
he said to Tototl.

"Why didn't you *see* this?" Tototl raged, and Niente
could only continue to shake his head. His hands were
trembling. He could smell black sand in the air.

Black sand.

This was no magic . . . The thought kept coming back to
him with the scent. The fact that black sand was not created
from the X'in Ka was something Niente had kept from the
Tecuhtli and the warriors. He wanted the warriors to believe that black sand was something magical. He hadn't
wanted them to know that *anyone* could make it if they
knew the ingredients, the measures of the formula, and the
method of preparation. He and the few nahualli he'd en-
trusted with the secret kept it so—they all suspected that if
the warriors could make black sand themselves, they might
decide they had no need of nahualli at all.

This was no magic . . .

He knew this, but he could not admit it to Tototl.

If Atl is facing this also . . . Fear ran cold through him,
and he nearly reached for the carved bird, nearly spoke the
word that would allow him to communicate with his son
and warn him. But he would be too late: that battle was
undoubtedly also underway. Too late. And while the East-

erners had this deadly skill, it still hadn't made a difference in this battle. They had taken out the flanking troops, but they'd still be routed.

But Tototl was right in one respect: he had not seen this. *What would the scrying bowl say now?*

"The Easterners have learned a spell they've never shown us before," he told Tototl. The wounded bled from deep, jagged, but nearly circular holes. The dead were the worst—it looked as if they been struck by invisible arrows that had—impossibly—torn through metal-and-bamboo armor to plunge deep into the bodies, sometimes lancing entirely through them. And on the top of the hill, where the surviving warriors had said that the terrible barrage had come from, there were no bodies at all, very few signs of blood, though there were a few Tehuantin arrows on the ground. But the ground wasn't disturbed as it would have been had they needed to drag away bodies. The Easterners had been able to inflict this damage on them without significant loss of their own.

Could they have done this with the main troops? Are they holding this back, waiting for a better place to use this power?

It may not have been magic, but something both awful and unbelievable had happened here. They had used black sand in some way that Niente could not comprehend. "I need to use the scrying bowl again," he said to Tototl. "Something has changed, something Axat didn't show me before. This is important. I worry about the Tecuhtli." *The Long Path: could it still be there? Could it have changed, too? Or has everything changed? Has Atl seen this?* He had to know. He had to find out. He was missing something that was critical to understanding their situation—he could feel it in the roiling in his gut, a burning. He felt old, used up, useless.

"There isn't time," Tototl answered. "The Tecuhtli will take care of himself, and he has the Nahual with him. The city is open to us. All we need to do is chase them. They're running; I can't give them time to regroup."

"Then as soon as we can after we reach the city," Niente told him. "Look at this! Do you want this to happen to us or to Citlali?"

Tototl scowled. "Pour oil on the bodies and burn them,"

he ordered the warriors. "Then rejoin us. Niente, come with me—the city awaits us."

He spat on the ground. Then, with a final scowl, he remounted. Niente was still staring, still trying to make some sense of this. "Come, Uchben Nahual," Tototl told him. "The answers you want are running from us as we stand here."

In that, the warrior was right. Niente sighed, then went to his own horse and—with the help of one of the warriors— pulled himself back into the saddle.

They rode away, Tototl already calling out to resume their advance.

If the day had been terrible, the night was hideous. Varina was huddled with the Garde Civile, pressed between the two earthen ramparts that had been built over the previous few days, and the night rained spark and fire, as if hands were plucking the very stars from the heavens and hurling them to earth. Both sides now used catapults to throw black sand fire into each other's ranks. The explosions thundered every few breaths: sometimes distant, sometimes distressingly close.

There was no rest this night and no sleep. She watched the fireballs arc overhead to fall westward, and cowered as the return barrage hammered at their ramparts. She tried to blot out the sounds of screams and wails whenever one of the Tehuantin missiles struck.

This was worse than open combat. At least there she had a semblance of control. There was no control in this: her life, and the lives of all of those around her were up to the whims of fate and accident. The next fireball could fall on her and it would be over, or it would miss and take someone else's life. Varina felt helpless and powerless, cowering with her back against cold dirt and trying to recover as much of her strength as she could so that she could replenish her spells for the attack that would come in the morning.

It would come. They all knew it.

The news from the north had been disheartening. Neither Starkkapitän ca'Damont nor Hïrzg Jan, with the Firenzcian troops, had been able to hold the west bank of the Infante. Both had been forced to retreat across the river.

Worse, the word had come that Hïrzg Jan had been injured during the retreat, as the a'Certendi bridge was destroyed. The rumors were wild and varied: Varina heard that Jan was dying; she heard that he had been carried back to the city to the healers; she heard that he was directing the defense from his tent-bed; she heard that he'd had himself lashed to his horse so that he would appear unhurt to his men as he rode about encouraging them; she'd heard that his injuries were minor and he was fine.

She had no idea which rumors were false and which true. What was apparent was that the battle of the day before had been only a prelude. The Infante would be forded; they all knew that. The Tehuantin would find the shallow places and they would cross as soon as it was light.

She trembled, closing her eyes as another fireball shrieked overhead and exploded well to her left. Had she believed in Cénzi, she would have prayed—there were certainly prayers being mumbled all around her. She almost envied the comfort the soldiers might find in them.

"Varina?" Commandant ca'Damont crouched next to her. In the noise, she hadn't heard his approach. She started to stand, but he shook his head and motioned to her to stay down.

"I'm sorry," she said. "I was trying to rest."

He smiled wanly. "There's not much rest around here. I wanted to tell you—Mason, your Vajiki ce'Fieur: the healers say he'll recover. They're going to evacuate him back to the city."

"Good. Thank you. I appreciate your telling me that."

"I want you to go with him," ca'Damont continued. "This is no place for you."

An old, frail woman . . . She could nearly hear the unsaid comment. "No," she told him. "You need me here. I'm A'Morce Numetodo; this is where I belong."

"More war-téni have arrived," he said. "A full double hand. And I have the other Numetodo you brought with you. You proved yourself earlier, Varina. No one could ask more of you. And you have a child to think of."

She wanted to agree. She wanted to take his offer and go running back to the city—but even there she wouldn't be safe. She could flee as far as she wanted, she could take Serafina and go east or north, but if they lost here—and she could see no way that they could win—she would always wonder whether she should have stayed, whether her presence might have made a difference.

Karl would not have fled. He would have stayed, even if he thought that the battle was lost. She knew that for a certainty. "Most of the gardai here have children to think of," she told him firmly. "That's *why* they're here."

"Still . . ."

"I'm not leaving," she told him.

The Commandant nodded. He stood and saluted her. "You're certain?"

She gave a shuddering laugh as another fireball howled past. Firelight bloomed and shadows moved as it exploded. "No," she answered. "But I'm staying, and you're interrupting my rest."

They heard the low rumble of another explosion somewhere beyond the rampart. "Rest?" the Commandant said. "I doubt any of us will be getting that tonight. But all right. Stay if you want. Cénzi knows that we need all the help we can get." He seemed to realize what he'd said, giving a wry half-smile. "Forgive me, A'Morce."

"Don't apologize," she told him. "If your Cénzi exists, I hope He's listening to you."

It wasn't supposed to have been this way. Sergei had prayed to Cénzi, but Cénzi hadn't answered—not that he expected any help from that quarter. The Tehuantin pursued Kraljica Allesandra and the Garde Kralji all the way back into the city. The Kraljica had tried to re-form and stand at Sutegate, but the Tehuantin were moving across too wide a swath now, pouring into the city's streets from everywhere along the southern reaches. Allesandra didn't have troops enough to cover the city's entire southern border. It had become quickly obvious that they couldn't hold the South Bank: not with the Garde Kralji, not even with the sparkwheelers, who had proved oddly effective during the retreat. They'd pulled back even farther, abandoning the entire South Bank for the Isle A'Kralji.

They *could* keep the Tehuantin from pouring through the bottlenecks that were the two bridges.

Sergei had urged Allesandra to destroy the Pontica a'Brezi Veste and Pontica a'Brezi Nippoli entirely, to take down the spans so that the Tehuantin couldn't cross the southern fork of the A'Sele without ships. She refused. "The ponticas stay up," she said. "I will not just give up half the city. The bridges stay up, we defend them tonight, and tomorrow we'll go back across them to take back our streets."

Sergei had argued vehemently with her, and Commandant cu'Ingres had agreed with Sergei; neither of their arguments convinced her to change her mind.

And it was on the Pontica a'Brezi Veste and the Pontica a'Brezi Nippoli that the sparkwheelers truly excelled. With Brie and Talbot's guidance, the corps had controlled the small spaces. Though the Westlanders had thrown wave after wave at them through the late afternoon and into the dusk, they'd left both bridges full of corpses. After several vain attempts and with the sunlight dying, the Westlanders had finally pulled back.

From the roof of the Kraljica's Palais, Sergei could see fires burning in the South Bank where once the téni had lit the lanterns along the Avi a'Parete. The yellow flames were a mockery. To the west and north, across the A'Sele but still outside the city, there were constant rumbles and the flashes of explosions, as if a rainless, cloudless thunderstorm had taken up residence there. Below, beyond the outer walls of the courtyards and entrance to the palais, in the Avi, Brie was still awake, on foot now. Sergei could hear her voice in the stunned silence of the palais: setting the watches on the bridge and exhorting the sparkwheelers to see to their weapons, get what rest they could, but be ready to respond at need.

Hïrzgin Brie had proved to be as valuable as her husband in this fight. Perhaps more so.

Sergei felt Allesandra come alongside him. She was still dressed in her armor, though it was no longer gleaming and polished: in the moonlight, he could see the scratches and scorch marks of the battle. Her graying hair was matted to her head. A sextet of Garde Kralji were with her, as well as the few remaining members of the Council of Ca' who had not fled the city. "Tomorrow," she told Sergei, told the councillors, "we will take back the South Bank."

"We will try as best we can," Sergei said. His tone betrayed his feeling as to the success they would find.

"We *will*," Allesandra answered sternly. The councillors looked frightened, and Sergei knew that they all believed that as unlikely as he did. A flash, and—belatedly—another rumble came from the west. He could feel the building trembling under his feet with the sound. The councillors looked around as if searching for shelter; the gardai shuffled nervously, clenching their pikes. "A runner's come from the North Bank," Allesandra said. "The Tehuantin have the west side of the Infante, and the Garde Civile has pulled back to the earthworks. They're safe for now. They'll try to ford the river tomorrow and we will push them back. Let the Infante and then the A'Sele take their bodies back to the sea."

"We will try, I'm sure," Sergei answered again. "Have you heard further news of the Hïrzg?"

Her face tightened. "I'm told that Hïrzg Jan has refused to return to the city. How badly he's been injured . . ." She shrugged. "No one is saying. He's my son, and he's a soldier. He will continue to fight as long as he can."

Sergei glanced down again to where Brie was patrolling. "Does *she* know?"

"I told Brie myself. I offered to let her go to him while she can. She said her place was here for now, and that Cénzi could keep Jan safe better than she could." Allesandra almost smiled. "I think she's learned to have a fondness for these sparkwheelers."

Sergei grunted. "I hope she's right," he said. "We can't hold back the Tehuantin, Kraljica. Soon, they're going to start bombarding us with black sand until we can't station the sparkwheelers at the bridgeheads any longer, and once the sparkwheelers have pulled back they'll come across. We need to take down the ponticas to the South Bank and cut them off. Let them throw what they want at us, but they won't be able to cross—not until they build boats."

Alesandra drew back. Her eyes narrowed, her lips pursed. "You've said all this too many times already, Sergei. I won't give up the South Bank. I *will not* abandon my city. Not while I can draw breath. No." She took in a breath through her nose, loud in the night. "I've asked Commandant ca'Talin or Starkkapitän ca'Damont to send us a company or two of gardai to help."

"Kraljica, they can't spare them. Not with the Tehuantin force they're facing. You can't ask that of them."

"The message has already been sent," she told him. "I said that they needed to make their best judgment as to whether they could spare the troops or not. They'll send them," she said firmly.

It was obvious that he wasn't going to change her mind. He was also certain that whether they had an additional company of gardai or not, the Garde Kralji weren't going to be sufficient to take back the South Bank. If the bridges continued to stand, they would not even be sufficient to hold the Isle, even with the help of the sparkwheelers. He tapped the tip of his cane on the roof tiles uneasily. In the west, there were more flashes. "If you'll excuse me, Kraljica, I need to find Talbot . . ."

He left Allesandra still on the roof with the gardai and the councillors. He found Talbot on the ground floor of the palais, looking frazzled and angry as he snapped orders to a quartet of the palais staff. They scurried off as Sergei approached. "I don't have enough staff here," Talbot said. "Thee quarters of them evidently fled the city as soon we left here yesterday."

"You can't blame them, my friend. Anyone with more sense than loyalty would leave."

"I know, but how am I supposed to run the palais without people?" He ran his fingers through his hair. "Listen to me. I've just been chased halfway across Nessantico by the Tehuantin; I've managed to survive spells and arrows and swords, and I'm worrying about whether the beds are made and meals are served."

"It's your job."

"It doesn't feel important, given the circumstances. By Cénzi, I'm exhausted."

"You can sleep later. We can both sleep later. Come with me."

"Where?"

Sergei rubbed at his nose. "You know where the black sand for the Garde Kralji is kept? You have the keys to that storeroom?"

"Yes, but . . ."

"Then come along."

A turn of the glass later, he and Talbot approached the Pontica a'Brezi Veste with several bundles of black sand carried by gardai. Brie greeted them; she glanced at their burdens, and she cocked her head. "I thought that the Kraljica said that the ponticas were to be left intact," she said.

Sergei glanced up at the roof of the palais, at the balconies studding the southern wall. No one was there. "I've managed to convince the Kraljica that we may need to take the bridges down if our attack tomorrow doesn't go well. We're to set the black sand on the supports around this side, so that we can set them off at need. That's all."

Brie nodded. "Sounds like a good plan to me. I'll get the sparkwheelers to help," she said.

Another turn of the glass, and Sergei and Talbot, with the rest of the black sand, came to the Pontica a'Brezi Nippoli. Sergei gave the offizier in charge of the Garde Kralji there the same tale that he'd given Brie. As he'd done at the previous bridge, he supervised the placement of the black sand packets, making certain that they were linked together with black sand-infused oiled cotton ropes so that touching off the length of fuse would cause all the packets to explode at once.

Sergei held the fuse, hefting it in his hand; a lantern burned at his feet in the grass of the riverbank. "We're done here," he told Talbot. "Now—go tell everyone to stand back."

Sergei could not see Talbot's face as he stood farther up the embankment, the moon almost directly behind him. "Stand back? Sergei, have you gone insane? The Kraljica gave specific orders—"

Sergei leaned down. He tucked his cane under his arm, picked up the lantern and opened the glass front, holding the fuse cord in his other hand. "When a tooth goes bad, you don't have a choice but to pluck it out," he said to Talbot. "If you leave it in, it just causes you more pain and misery, and eventually rots all the rest."

"You can't do this," Talbot protested. "The Kraljica said—"

"The Kraljica and I disagree. Be honest, Talbot: do you think we can take back the South Bank from the Westlanders tomorrow? The best defense for the Isle and the entire city is to take down the ponticas and leave the Westlanders stranded."

"That's not your decision to make," Talbot told him.

Sergei grinned up at him, lifting the lantern. "At the moment, it appears that it is," he answered. He touched the end of the fuse cord to the flame. It hissed and sparked, and fire began to crawl along its length. Sergei dropped the fuse and began to hurry up the riverbank as fast as he could, using his cane for leverage.

"Cénzi's balls," Talbot cursed; he stared for a breath as if considering hurrying down the bank after the fuse, then waved to the gardai at the bridge's abutments. "Back!" he shouted to them. "Get away from the bridge! Take cover!" He half-slid down the embankment and grabbed Sergei's arm, hauling him up. Together, they fled as the fuse cord hissed and sputtered and the blue glow of its fire slid toward the bridge.

The blast nearly lifted Sergei off his feet. The concussion slammed into him like a falling wall; he could feel the heat scorching his back, and the sound . . . He could hear timbers snapping as rocks and planking slammed into the ground around them, falling like a hard, dangerous rain. Sergei and Talbot cowered, covering their heads. When it had ended, his ears still ringing, Sergei turned. The bridge had collapsed, the span sloping into the waters of the A'Sele midway across. The stubs of piling and pillars rose from the water like broken teeth.

Sergei grinned. "They won't be coming across there soon," he said. "All these men stationed here can get some rest. Now, let's finish the job . . ."

Talbot was shaking his head. "Sorry, Sergei, I can't let you. You lied to me. You disobeyed the Kraljica's direct orders."

"I'm trying to save the damned city," Sergei retorted.

"It's not *your* damned city."

Ah, but it is . . . He knew Talbot realized the worth of what he'd done. He knew Talbot actually agreed with him. "Talbot, you know I'm right."

"What I know doesn't matter," Talbot told him. "I'm the Kraljica's aide, not the Kraljiki. Damn you to the soul shredders, Sergei . . ." He shook his head, glaring at the ruins of the bridge. The Garde Brezno were sidling closer to the edge, staring at the wreckage. Shouts and lanterns were hurrying toward them. "Allesandra's going to be furious."

"She'll be more furious when we take down the other

pontica," Sergei answered, "but she also won't be able to undo that." But Talbot wasn't going to admit that Sergei was right. He knew it before Talbot responded, knew it from the way the aide's thin face closed up.

"That's not going to happen," Talbot said. He looked at the people running toward them. "Sergei, you can still survive this: admit that you disobeyed her and set the black sand packets, but that you were doing it in case we had to retreat tomorrow and there was no other way to stop the Tehuantin from crossing over to the Isle and onto the North Bank. You can tell her that this was an accident; your lamp set off the fuse. She won't believe you; she'll be terribly angry at what you've done, but she won't be able to prove anything. I'll back you that far, Sergei. But no further. The other bridge stays up."

"Talbot . . ."

"No," Talbot said firmly, interrupting Sergei. "It's either that, or I tell her exactly what happened here and that you intended this all along. She'll have you executed as a traitor then, Sergei, and I wouldn't blame her. Which is it to be? You decide."

Talbot was right. Sergei knew that, knew Allesandra well enough to realize that even if she understood his reasoning, he'd gone beyond the bounds of what she could forgive if she knew the whole truth. Dead, he could do nothing for the city. Dead, he could do nothing more to atone for all he'd done over his life. Dead, he couldn't take down the other bridge.

"All right," he told Talbot. "I'll take your offer."

She'd followed Nico back into the maze of Oldtown, to another nondescript house in another nondescript narrow lane. There was nobody there, nobody came to Nico's knock. The door had been locked, but that was no issue—not to Rochelle. She'd picked the lock and they'd gone in. Nico had nearly immediately told her that he needed to pray. She told him that both of them needed to eat—but there had been nothing in the house. She'd gone foraging, finding stale bread in an abandoned bakery, and moldy cheese elsewhere. She'd taken water from the nearest well. When she returned to the house, Nico was in the front room on his knees. He'd paid no attention when she tried to get him to eat, when she tried to force some water between his cracked and bruised lips, when she'd jostled and yelled at him to try to get his attention.

Her brother was lost, mumbling half-intelligible prayers to Cénzi and unresponsive. He ignored her, as if he no longer cared or even knew that she was there. She could get no reaction from him at all. He seemed to be in a trance.

Fine. She was used to madness. She'd dealt with it long enough with their matarh.

She slept a little on the floor next to him, but couldn't sleep long. She found herself awake in the dark with Nico still praying next to her. By now, she thought, it must be only a few turns before close to First Call. "Nico? Nico— talk to me."

There was no answer. He was in the same position he'd been in for turn upon turn. So, Nico had abandoned her, too—well, she was used to being alone, to making her own decisions. She couldn't help Nico, couldn't go wherever it was he was, but there were still things she could do, that she was supposed to do. She touched the hilt of the knife she'd stolen from her vatarh, stroking the bejeweled hilt.

Promise me you will do what I couldn't do. Promise me ...

"I will," she told her matarh's ghost. "I will."

She went back to Nico, kneeling on the bare wooden floor. His legs must have long ago lost any feeling. His hands were clasped in the sign of Cénzi, his head bowed down toward them, his eyes closed. She could hear him mumbling. "Nico?" she said, touching his shoulder. "Nico, I need you to answer me."

He did not. The mumbling continued, unabated. She hugged him once. "Then pray for me," she told him. "Pray for both of us."

There was no sign he'd heard. She stood, watching him, then finally left the room. She closed the door behind her, and went out into the streets of Oldtown. In the early morning, the streets were dark and deserted. Most of the inhabitants, those who could, had fled eastward out of the city. There were strange flashes in the sky to the west, accompanied by distant thunder, and southward, clouds of smoke were touched underneath with the glow of fires.

South. Rochelle went that way, sliding easily through the shadows cast by the moon.

She had no idea how long it was before she came to the Pontica Kralji, linking the North Bank to the Isle. There were no gardai on the bridge, no traffic at all. The moon was setting and the sky was beginning to lighten in the east, extinguishing the stars at the zenith. The waters of the A'Sele roiled around the pilings, dark and mysterious. The smell of burning wood mingled with the scent of mud and river water.

Something bright flared in the sky ahead of her, trailing sparks and painting the currents of the A'Sele with its bright reflections. The apparition brightened and swelled, descending rapidly. She saw it fall, felt the impact through the soles of her boots, saw the fire of the explosion. Someone shrieked distantly in pain and alarm and the smell of burning grew stronger, overlaid now with a sulfurous stench. Another fireball shrieked into the southern sky; this one exploded high above the Isle, sending black shadows racing.

A rider appeared from the Isle a'Kralji end of the pontica, galloping over the bridge toward her, his cloak billowing behind. Rochelle shrank back against the bridge supports; the rider hurtled past her without a glance, turning sharply left toward the River Market. She could see the leather pouch around his body: a fast-rider carrying a message.

That meant that the Kraljica was most likely on the Isle. Allesandra. Her great-matarh. Her matarh's voice seemed to whisper in her ears: *"Promise me . . ."*

Another fireball played false sun, this one also slamming to earth somewhere on the Isle. She could hear the wind-horns of the Old Temple growling a low alarm.

Rochelle ran across the pontica, half-expecting someone to shout after her, or perhaps for an arrow to find her. Nothing happened. She was on the Avi a'Parete on the Isle. All about her were the Isle's grand buildings, dominated here by the Kraljica's Palais, directly ahead on the left. She slid to her left, following a street dominated by government buildings. Farther south, she could hear activity: horns calling, people shouting, She turned the corner, moving southward again; ahead, she could see people far down the street. She hurried to the wall surrounding the palais. A servants' door was set there to one side. She knocked on it, waited, knocked again. No one answered. She crouched down and took out her lockpick kit. A few breaths later, she pushed the door open and slipped inside the grounds.

She found herself standing in the gardens of the palais. The scent of flowers was strong, and she could hear a fountain trickling water nearby. There was no one in the gardens at all, and few of the palais windows were lit.

Another fireball lifted its bright head over the far wall of the palais grounds. It seemed to be heading directly toward her and the palais, but at the last moment when it seemed to be about to strike the palais itself, it shattered into a thousand fragments, each hissing and glowing as they fell—a counterspell must have found it. She wondered how many fires the sparks would set, and whether the fire-téni would come to put them out.

Rochelle ran to the nearest palais door. Locked: again, she took out the picks, manipulating them until she heard the *snick* of the mechanism opening. She opened the door just enough to slide inside.

She found herself in what must have been the servants' corridor: a plain narrow hallway with cross-corridors opening off to either side and a large door at the end. If this was like Brezno Palais, as she expected it would be, then most of these doors would be unlocked. The servants needed to have access to all parts of the palais to serve their masters and mistresses, and to do so in the most unobtrusive manner possible. Doubtless, the palais was honeycombed with such passages.

But the back corridors of Brezno Palais had also been a bustle of activity. This one was silent, and Rochelle found that strange. She moved quickly to the main door, easing the door open a crack. She glimpsed one of the main public hallways of the palais; she could also hear voices. There were several people walking hurriedly away from another room just farther down. One of the men she recognized immediately: Sergei ca'Rudka, the silver nose gleaming on his wrinkled, pasty face, his cane tapping an erratic rhythm on the tiles. The woman alongside him was talking, in a hurried and angry voice. "... don't care what you were thinking or what your reasons were. I'm *furious* with you, Sergei. Absolutely furious. And Talbot; why in Cénzi's name didn't you check with me? You knew I'd ordered the ponticas to stay up."

"I must apologize profusely, Kraljica," Sergei said, though Rochelle thought he sounded more pleased than apologetic. So that *was* the Kraljica. *Great-matarh, I'm here for you . . .* But not now. Not yet. There were too many people around her: Sergei, the one called Talbot, as well as a quartet of gardai.

"Your 'accident'—if that's what it really was—may have jeopardized our chance to assault the Tehuantin on the South Bank. Now there's only one route over, so . . ."

Their voices drifted into unintelligibility as they walked down the corridor. Rochelle risked opening the door wider. There were two gardai stationed at the door from where the group had come. Rochelle ducked back into the servants' corridor. She took the corridor that led off in the direction of the room with the gardai, counting her steps to judge when she'd walked the distance. There was another door a few strides farther down the corridor. She opened that door.

She found herself in the Hall of the Sun Throne. The crystalline mass of the Sun Throne itself dominated the hall on its dais. Fine. This would do: the Kraljica must come back here in time, and Rochelle could fulfill her promise.

She saw a flash of light through the high windows of the hall, and the palais itself shook as thunder grumbled. She could smell woodsmoke and the windows of the palais were alight with a dawn of flame.

Rochelle settled herself in to wait.

Niente dusted the water in the scrying bowl with the orange powder and chanted the spell to open his mind to Axat. The green mist began to rise, and he bent his head over the bowl.

They were encamped in the city itself, with warriors securing the streets and plundering the houses and buildings there—for food and supplies, had been Tototl's orders, but Niente was certain that many of the warriors were also taking whatever treasures they could carry. Others had been set to building a catapult, and Niente had tasked the nahualli with enchanting the bags of black sand that the catapult would hurl onto the island so that they would explode upon impact. The chanting of the nahualli and the hammering of the warrior engineers filled the wide boulevard outside the fortress prison at the river's edge. From the gates of the edifice, the skull of a horrible, many-toothed creature leered down at Niente—almost as if it could be the head of the winged serpent that flew on the Tecuhtli's banner. That, Niente thought, was nearly an irony. Axat's Eye had risen, and it seemed to watch Niente as he performed the ritual, watched him as intently as did Tototl.

The visions came quickly, rushing toward him almost too fast for him to see, the paths of the future twisting and intertwining. Niente could still see victory along the clearest, closest path, but now it was a victory won at terrible cost. There were changes wrought on the landscape, powers rising that hadn't been glimpsed before, or that had been hinted at only in wisps of possibilities: the king of black-and-silver; the old woman who smelled of black sand; the young man with the wild, strange power. That last one . . . He was the most difficult of all for Niente to see, wrapped in mist and mystery. Around him, all the possible paths of the future seemed to be coiled. Niente wanted to stay with this one, but the mists kept pushing him away no matter how hard he tried.

In the mist, Niente could also feel Atl, so close that he almost thought that his son was standing beside him, peering into his bowl at the same time. *Here.* He tried to cast his thoughts toward Atl. *See what I see. Let me find the Long Path, and hope you see it also . . .*

But there was no response. He couldn't show Atl what he had seen, nor could he see what Atl saw. In the mist, they stayed separate.

"Will they take down the other bridge?" Tototl asked. "If they do that . . ."

"If they do that, then we can't get across to help Tecuhtli Citlali. I know. Now let me look . . ."

He'd already seen that: in the primary path, the Easterners inexplicably never destroyed either bridge. He didn't understand that. With the bridges up, Tototl would win through to the Isle, though at terrible cost. The strange black sand weapons that the Easterners wielded would take down far too many warriors before they could, inevitably, overwhelm them. They would reach Citlali and still

crush the Easterners between them, but this was no longer
the overwhelming victory that Niente had seen in Tlaxcala.
Everything had changed.

Which meant the Long Path had changed as well. If the
Long Path were still there at all.

Niente bent his head into the mist again, searching.
Please, Axat. Show me . . .

And She did.

~

The Storm's Passing

"WELL?" TOTOTL ASKED NIENTE as he poured
the water from the scrying bowl onto the cobbles
of the boulevard. Niente cleaned the bowl with the sleeve
of his shirt and looked solemnly at the High Warrior.

"Do you remember, Tototl, that we talked about how
something that appeared to be a victory might not be so?"

Tototl's painted visage remained impassive. "I remember you saying that," he said. "And I remember that I told
you that I believed you saw more in the bowl than you
were telling Tecuhtli Citlali. So tell me now, Uchben Nahual, what did you see? Tell me the truth."

Niente placed the scrying bowl back in its pouch, feeling
the texture of the incised patterns along its rims. He took up
his spell-staff; he could feel the energy of the X'in Ka throbbing within the wood, captured and ready to be loosed. The
smells filled his nostrils: burning wood, the scent of water,
the odor of clothing worn too long. He swallowed, and he
tasted the lingering tang of the green mist he had inhaled.
His senses seemed too full and too sharp. He glanced up at
the leering skull on the wall above him, and he could imagine the thing alive once more—teeth like ivory knives slicing
open a victim caught in its powerful jaws.

"Listen to me, Tototl," he said. "I said nothing to Tecuhtli
Citlali because he couldn't see beyond now and beyond his
own ambitions. You have the imagination to do that. You

could become a great Tecuhtli. One whose name would ring for generations."

Tototl couldn't entirely conceal the eagerness those words brought to him: Niente saw it in the the faint movement of the warrior's mouth, in the slight widening of his eyes in their pools of red paint. There was ambition in the warrior. "You saw that?" he asked.

A nod. "It's one of the futures. A possibility." Niente paused. He looked at the catapult, nearly finished now. He looked at the bridge arching near them at the end of the boulevard, at the great building that loomed just beyond it, at the golden dome rising above the other rooftops in the middle of the island. "Tototl, victory right now hinges on a thread. You are that thread, Tototl. Without you, there is no victory at all. I've seen that."

"What must I do?"

"You must win through to the island and to the other side, as you said earlier. You must bring your warriors to attack the Easterners from their rear. If you want victory, that's what you have to accomplish."

"Why would I not? That's why we came here: to take the city, to avenge our loss with Tecuhtli Zolin, to rule this land."

Niente wondered if he should tell him. Certainly Citlali would have heard none of it; he would have stopped Niente already, and Niente—he had to admit—would have bowed to the Tecuhtli. *I will have victory here . . .* That was all Citlali wanted to hear. He would scoff at the Long Path; he wouldn't care what happened years afterward. But then, Tototl might feel the same. Niente took a breath. He watched the nahualli place the first of the black sand charges in the carrier of the catapult as the warriors winched down the arm.

"Citlali's victory here will be too costly for us in the end," Niente said. "He might yet take the city, but he won't be able to hold it for long. Other Easterner armies will come from the far corners of their empire. This land is huge, and we have too few warriors here and not enough time to send for more from across the sea. And when the Easterners have killed all of us who are left, they will look toward our homeland and they will return there with an even greater army than the one they brought before. They will hunt us down until they're certain we can never trouble them again."

"You *know* this?"

Niente shook his head. "No," he admitted. "But it's a future I see; the likely one."

"Has the new Nahual seen this also?"

Niente shook his head. "No. But Atl's still learning. He sees only the near future, not the Long Path."

"Before, *you* saw an easy victory. You said that before we ever left our own land."

"I did," Niente admitted. "At the time, that was the truth. But that has changed. There are forces here that were hidden from me, situations that have changed from what they were when I first consulted Axat. Nothing in the future is ever solid and fixed."

"Then this future you see might also change. *Will* also change."

"It might. Still . . . Tototl, I would tell you to take the warriors here and leave. Find our ships—by now, they should be nearly to the city. Take them and return home. I would tell you to become the Tecuhtli so that when the Easterners come back to our land—and they *will* come back—we will still be strong enough to resist them. They'll understand that as we couldn't conquer them, also they can't conquer us, and our empires will have to deal with each other as equals."

Tototl was already shaking his head. "I won't run," he said. "I won't abandon Citlali. Not without knowing that I have no other choice."

"Then here are the signs, Tototl. When the magic is snatched away from all the nahualli, when you see me fall to a weapon that shouldn't kill—those are the signs that what I tell you is true. Will you retreat then, Tototl? Will you listen to my advice, as Tecuhtli Citlali would not."

Tototl seemed to laugh. "You're like a length of smoked beef, Uchben Nahual," he said, "too old and tough to die. And who could snatch away the power of the nahualli?"

"If it happens," Niente pleaded, "if you see those signs, will you go?"

"If it happens," Tototl told him, "I will remember what you said, and I'll do what I think I must."

As he said the words, the catapult sang its deadly song,

and a fireball went hissing across the river toward the island. They both watched it fall and explode in a roar of orange flame.

Jan wondered if this would be his final day.

Smoke smudged the southeastern sky from fires burning unchecked on the South Bank of the city. Runners had come from his matarh during the night with a message—the Tehuantin were on the South Bank; they would try to push them back in the morning; send a company of your gardai if you can spare them.

But he couldn't spare them. They were already too few for the task before them. The night before had been hideous, with the ground shaking as both sides pounded at each other with black sand. Now the eastern sky was pink and orange, and the Tehuantin would be renewing the ground attack. He was certain of that; it was what he would have done himself.

One of the pages was assisting him with his armor, and Jan winced as the boy tightened the lacings of his cuirass—an armorer having pounded out the indentation from the brick the night before. "Go on," he told the page. "Make them tight. Can't have it falling off in the middle of battle."

Any movement hurt. It hurt to breathe. He'd coughed up blood last night after he'd recovered consciousness, though that, thankfully, had stopped. Binding his chest in the armor actually felt good, but he wondered if he could take a sword blow to the ribs without collapsing. He wondered if he could lead his men the way a Hïrzg should: at the head of the charge into the enemy. "Bring my horse to me," Jan said, and the page saluted and scurried away.

He had spent the night in a tent beyond the second wall of earthworks. Most of the black sand had fallen well short of that encampment, but there were still craters of dark earth here and there, and smoke from grass fires that had to be extinguished. The offiziers had reported the losses to him a half-turn earlier after calling the rolls. Jan had been appalled. He had brought over 4,000 gardai and some 300 chevarittai to Nessantico. He and Starkkapitän ca'Damont had split them nearly equally. Jan now had less than 1,000

gardai and five double hands of chevarittai; ca'Damont had
less.

No, he could not send a company to the Kraljica. He
would be lucky to return to Nessantico with a full company
himself. He'd read the message from ca'Talin: *Outlook
grim. Recommend holding as long as possible, then falling
back to the city itself.* Under it, in his spidery handwriting,
ca'Damont had added a brief *I concur.* Jan had sent his own
message in return to the two:

*Agreed. Make them pay for crossing the river, then fall
back to the River Market. We'll regroup there and consult
with the Kraljica.*

The page came back leading a warhorse that had once
borne one of the dead chevarittai. The boy placed a step
next to the horse, then helped hoist Jan into the saddle.
He managed to get himself seated without groaning aloud.
"Thank you," he told the boy, saluting. He cantered away,
wincing as every step jarred his body. He rode up the short
slope to the top of the second embankment. He waited
there for several breaths, looking out over the landscape.

Most of his troops were gathered below, in the wide
trough between the earthworks, snaking away far to the
south and the Starkkapitän ca'Damont's command, and
past there to Commandant ca'Talin, and extending north
for a half-mile or so to the Avi a' Nostrosei. Beyond the
slope of the first embankment across from Jan, there was a
quarter mile or less of flat ground between the earthworks
and the River Infante—the field was torn by horses and the
boots of the soldiers, and pockmarked with craters from
the black sand bombardment. On the other side of the Infante, Jan could see the army of the Tehuantin. Their offiziers were already setting the formations, and Jan could
see small flags planted here and there along the far riverbank—he assumed their scouts had marked the shallows
where the river could be forded.

There were far too many flags. The Infante was neither
deep nor wide like the A'Sele; there were too many places
where the Tehuantin could cross. Last night, Jan had asked
one of the local gardai to map the spots where footmen
could wade across; he had archers placed across from the
potential fords.

Make them pay for crossing the river . . . He might not
be able to stop them, but he could charge them a steep toll.

A few Westlander archers sent futile arrows in his direction; they fell short, and Jan gestured obscenely at
them. "Come on!" he shouted at them, his chest burning
with the effort. "Come on; we're waiting for you, bastardos! We ready to make your wives widows and your children orphans!" He said it for the benefit of the gardai in
the trench between the embankments, who looked up at
him and cheered; he doubted that any of the Westlanders
understood his words at all, even if they understood the
tone. He wanted to double over from the stabbing pain in
his chest as he roared his defiance, but instead he smiled
and gestured again at the Tehuantin. A few hundred strides
away, he saw his banners, and he saluted the men and went
to where his offiziers had gathered.

"Another sunrise," he told them. "That's always a good
sight. The sun is at our backs and in their eyes. Let's make
this day the last they see."

Allesandra paraded on her warhorse before those gathered
in the courtyard of the palais. In the false dawn, her armor
gleamed, yesterday's gore scrubbed and polished away.
Brie, Talbot, and that damned fool Sergei were behind her
on their own horses, watching as she stalked the line. She
let her anger and frustration ride freely in her words.

"We have no choice," she told them. "It is my duty—it
is *our* duty—to protect this city, and I will not let us betray that trust. Right now, the Westlanders hold the South
Bank. They walk streets that should be safe for our citizens,
plundering our houses and our temples, killing and raping
those who have remained behind. The Hïrzg's forces and
our own Garde Civile are facing their main army on the
North Bank; they have tasked us with protecting their rear
flank, and with keeping the city a safe place for their return.
We must hold the South Bank. I *will* hold the South Bank."

She paused as another fireball screamed through the
brightening sky—they all watched it. Her horse trembled
underneath her, and she patted its muscular neck, calming
it as the fireball fell to earth behind them across the Avi.
"You see?" she said. "The Tehuantin mean nothing less

than the destruction of the Holdings and Nessantico. Stay here, and all of you will die anyway. If I'm to die, I would rather die with my sword in my hand and my enemy bleeding at my feet."

The cheer that came from them was loud but ragged. Even some of those shouting looked unsure. The spark-wheelers, to one side, shuffled uneasily; she noticed Brie glaring at them. "We march today to glory," she told them, pulling her sword from its sheath and holding it aloft. "We march for the Holdings. We march for Nessantico. And I will march with you, at your head."

An open-top, téni-driven carriage rattled down the streets through the smoke, moving slowly around the rubble in the street; Allesandra could see the symbol of Cénzi's cracked globe on the doors of the vehicle. "Today, the Archigos himself will march with us," she added. "Make yourselves ready. We will begin the attack in two marks of the glass, and we'll show these Westlanders how the Holdings responds to those who threaten it."

They cheered again, because—Allesandra knew—it was expected of them, because they wanted to believe her even as fear made their bowels want to turn to water. She rode toward the Archigos' carriage with Brie, Talbot, and Sergei trailing her. Archigos Karrol's balding head peered over the side of the carriage; he did not look pleased to be here. Two pale, younger faces were visible behind him. "Archigos, I'm glad to see you," Allesandra said. "However belatedly."

"Let's not pretend that you or the Hïrzg left me any choice, Kraljica," he answered. "But I'm here."

"And the war-téni?"

"There are four more who have arrived from the east today. I sent two to the Hïrzg; the other two are with me. They understand the consequences if they fail to serve." He gestured to the other two téni in the carriage.

"Good," she told him. "I hope they're well-rested. We need them now. Talbot, if you'd take charge of the war-téni and the archers. Brie, you have the sparkwheelers." She scowled at Sergei, still feeling anger at the man's insolence in disregarding her orders. "Sergei, you'll be with me and the Archigos."

They assembled quickly. While Allesandra remained furious with Sergei for having destroyed the eastern bridge, she had to admit that a two-pronged attack across both bridges would have divided and thinned their forces too much. Still, the difficulty was that they would all need to cross the Pontica a'Brezi Veste. The fact that the Tehuantin had left the bridge standing and not destroyed it from their end told Allesandra that they wanted the bridge intact as much as she did—so they could meet up with their army on the North Bank. Sergei's urging to retreat to the Isle and the North Bank, destroying all the southern bridges across the A'Sele to isolate this arm of the Tehuantin, made tactical sense.

Allesandra knew that intellectually, yet emotionally . . .

This was her city, the seat of the Holdings. She would *not* allow it to be taken from her. She'd already had to rebuild this city once; she didn't want to do that yet again. She would rather fall here and leave it to her successor—whomever that might be—to do that.

Their attack began with a barrage of spells from Talbot and the few Numetodo, as well as the new war-téni and the Archigos. Nearly all the spells were neutralized or deflected by the Tehuantin spellcasters, but those that went through sent the Tehuantin scrambling back from the Bastida and the area immediately around the South Bank end of the bridge. "Now!" Allesandra shouted, and she led the Garde Kralji in a charge across the bridge while Talbot directed their archers to provide a cover of arrows ahead of them. Sergei was behind her, and the Archigos' carriage, rattling over the timbers. The Tehuantin sent their own shower of arrows toward them as they started across, but the Archigos chanted and gestured from his carriage seat; the arrows were swept wide with a spell-wind to fall harmlessly in the A'Sele.

In a few breaths, they were across. The warriors came shrieking and shouting toward them. "To the Bastida!" she shouted to the gardai; they pushed forward, riding and shoving through the open gates of the prison, not caring that they were leaving the Avi full of Tehuantin behind them, that they were surrounded.

Behind the Garde Kralji, Brie led the sparkwheelers across the pontica. At the foot of the bridge, they formed their lines and their weapons bellowed a rhythmic call of death. The warriors in the Avi began to fall, and none of them could reach the sparkwheelers to stop them. From the gates of the Bastida, Allesandra could see Brie, dismounted, prowling behind the sparkwheelers, her voice exhorting them to stay, to keep the lines moving, to move faster. Her strong voice called out the commands; the stuttered roar of the sparkwheels echoing around the Avi. The Tehuantin fell back. Allesandra and the gardai were no longer pressed on all sides.

"Follow me!" Allesandra shouted, and led the Garde Kralji in a furious charge from the Bastida gates.

The night had been horrible; the dawn was simply brutal. As the sun hauled itself over the trees and the roofs of Nessantico, the Westlanders came: with a roar and a shout, with their swords and spears waving, with volleys of black sand and shrieking, violent spells. They plunged into the waters of the Infante. Water splashed high and white around them while arrows from the Garde Civile rained down on them. At first, it was slaughter and the gardai shouted in exultation and relief, but there were more and more of them, and they just kept coming, and now their nahualli were casting enchantments that sent the arrows to ash in the air.

They were across, more warriors coming with every passing breath. The war-téni and the Numetodo poured fire on them; it did not stop the advance. The Tehuantin left hands upon hands of warriors dead on the ground, but they still came, relentless.

"Pull back!" the offiziers and the cornets called, and the Garde Civile scrambled out from between the double wall of embankments, retreating to the higher crest of the second wall. As they retreated, they tipped over barrels of oil that had been brought up from the city, soaking the ground with it and leaving black pools behind. As the Tehuantin crested the first wall, they were again greeted by arrow fire. Bodies tumbled into the slick trench before them, but now their companions, unhurt, were with them.

The prepared spells pounded in Varina's head, in the minds of all the Numetodo along the earthworks. "Wait!" Varina heard ca'Damont order the war-téni and Numetodo. "Not yet! Wait!"

The Tehuantin warriors had reached the trench and

were beginning to ascend the second embankment, where the Garde Civil troops waited. "Now!" ca'Damont shouted; Varina gestured and spoke the release word, as did the two Numetodo alongside her, Leovic and Niels, as did the war-teni farther up the line. Fire arced out from between their hands. The oil-soaked ground between the earthworks erupted into a pit of hissing, smoky flame. Those caught in the inferno screamed—Varina saw them writhing among the flames. The heat beat on her skin as the horrible stench of blistered flesh wafted over them. Just below her, a warrior staggered out of the flames, his body horribly charred, flames still licking about his armor and clothing. She saw his face, terribly young, the mouth open as he screamed in his own language. Varina didn't know if he called for help or for his god or simply from the pain. She could imagine him at home, embracing his wife or holding his children, laughing at something one of them might have said. She hardly noticed the sword he held, or the fact that he raised it above her.

Arrows sprouted along the man's front, and he collapsed, forever silent. Varina gagged and vomited on the ground, falling to her knees next to the dead warrior. As she spat out the bile, she wondered: *so strange; I've seen hundred of people die in the last few days, and this one face has affected me the most . . .*

"You must come with us, A'Morce!" Leovic and Niels closed around her, pulling her up and half-dragging her down the far side of the slope. The Tehuantin had momentarily pulled back as the fires roared in the trench, but the flames were dying quickly as the oil was consumed. The Tehuantin pushed forward again, spilling over the earthwork and up the other side. The waiting Garde Civile drew their swords, and Varina, along with the other Numetodo and war-téni, retreated as hand-to-hand combat flared all along the ridge. She could hear the cornets blaring and see the flags waving, but they meant little to her now as Leovic and Niels continued to help her retreat, one on each arm. She simply moved with the flow of people in blue-and-gold uniforms: back toward the city, always back. The retreat was slow at first, but gained momentum, and suddenly they were not walking but running, giving their spines to the Tehuantin as they fled. She could hear the pounding of

the hooves of warriors' horses, saw people fall around her,
struck by arrows or felled by spells.

Leovic and Niels were half-carrying her as they ran. She
didn't dare stop to look back. She didn't want to.

"Move, move, move!" Brie screamed at the sparkwheelers
as she saw the Kraljica, with Sergei on their horses, the Archigos in his carriage, and the Garde Kralji, pour out from
the brief shelter of the Bastida. "Let's go! Keep up!"

They had made an abattoir of the Avi at the bridge-
head. The sparkwheelers ran over cobbles slick with blood,
around bodies that still moaned and writhed. The faces of
the sparkwheelers looked alternately horrified and pleased
with the carnage they'd caused, but Brie gave them no time
to ponder or exult. She pushed them forward toward the
Bastida's gates.

In the open, the sparkwheelers were most vulnerable;
they were best at defending a confined space. And if their
lines were broken, they would be overwhelmed quickly.
She shepherded them, not letting them separate, screaming
at them.

Allesandra's people charged into a clot of warriors at
the end of the Bastida walls. More of the Westlanders hurried from the side streets, led by a mounted warrior whose
face was painted red and his skull shaved clean. Brie could
see a spellcaster with him: an old man whose face was ravaged as if by some disease, his left eye white and blind. As
Brie lined up the sparkwheelers near the Bastida gate to
deal with the renewed assault, she saw the Archigos chanting and moving his withered hands in a new spell with his
green-and-gold robes swaying. The Westlander spellcaster
raised a wooden staff, shouting a single word in his strange
tongue.

His spell came immediately.

The Archigos and his carriage were enveloped in flame.
The téni-driver fell from his seat, shrieking and flailing at
his burning robes with his hands. She heard the old man
shrilling in surprise and agony. He pushed open the door
and fell from the carriage to the street, his robes seeming
to drip liquid flame. He rolled on the pavement, a long, thin
wail coming from him that ended suddenly, but Brie could
no longer see the Archigos, not in the swirl of the battle.

As she shouted at the sparkwheelers, trying to get them into their proper lines, she glimpsed the red-skulled warrior with a spear in his hand urging his horse into a gallop toward Allesandra. The Kraljica brought up her sword, but the red-painted warrior's spear thrust was quicker; with horror, Brie saw the tip of his spear drive hard into and through the Kraljica's armor. The warrior leaped from his horse, still holding the spear that impaled Allesandra, dragging her down. Brie, shouting at the sparkwheelers desperately, saw Sergei jump from his horse as if he were a young man.

They, too, vanished in the melee.

The spellcasters on both sides were hurling spells, and yet more warriors were arriving, filling the streets. She could feel the chill of the Ilmodo all around them. "Fire!" she screamed at the sparkwheelers, who were staring in confusion. "Fire!"

But then it all changed.

Nico was abandoned. Bereft. Even Rochelle had left him sometime during the night. He had felt her departure, even if he hadn't responded to her.

He had been praying for over a full day now without eating, drinking, or sleeping, and Cénzi remained silent. Or perhaps He was saying too much. Nico was afflicted by visions, but he couldn't tell whether they emanated from Cénzi or from the sounds he was hearing outside or from his own fevered imagination. He was cold and shivering, as if wrapped in an impossible winter as cold as the Ilmodo itself. Behind his closed eyes, he felt that he watched the battle to the west as the sun touched him through the window of the hovel in Oldtown. He could see the troops running from the Westlanders, could see the mounted chevarittai vainly trying to protect the rear of the retreating men from the mounted High Warriors with their painted faces and strange armor. Those in black and silver, those in blue and gold were failing; too many of them taken by arrows or by the warrior riders.

Nico witnessed it as if he drifted above the battlefield in the cold arms of his prayers, staring down at the scene. He was a bird, a falcon, drifting on the cold wind. He could see the banner of Commandant ca'Talin, and farther north,

those of the Starkkapitän and the Hïrzg. They were all flying back toward the city, the foremost of them already in
the streets near the Avi a'Certendi, the westernmost limb
of the sprawling city.

He drifted above it all, watching . . .

. . .and he saw her: Varina. She was exhausted, being
pulled along by two other Numetodo heretics; the three
of them dangerously separated from the main mass of the
Garde Civile. The mounted warriors were close by, only a
few strides away and the grim foot-soldiers of the Tehuantin weren't far behind them. They were going to be overrun
and killed. All too soon.

*Why do you show me this, Cénzi? Why do you show me
the heretic so clearly?*

As he watched Varina, he felt the cold wrap its arms
even tighter around him. He was falling, tumbling down toward Varina as he saw the warriors on the warhorses rushing at her, as her companions turned to hurl futile spells
toward the attackers, as they surrounded her.

Then he was *there,* on the ground and standing not far from
Varina. He heard her gasp and call his name—"Nico?"—but
there was so much energy here that he could barely hear for
the buzzing of it. The Second World seemed to gape open in
the sky above him, a cold fire, the frigid power of the Ilmodo
pouring down. He could feel them all pulling at the energy
above him: the war-téni, the heretics, the spellcasters of the
Tehuantin, even those across the A'Sele in the city. He could
feel the power stored in the spell-sticks of the Tehuantin, in
the minds of the Numetodo.

All of them channeled the Ilmodo from the Second
World where Cénzi still lived.

Nico felt vast. He could stretch out his fingers and touch
the threads of all of their connections to the Ilmodo; he
could pull on them, take them for himself . . .

So he did.

It wasn't a conscious movement. He acted as if someone else had control of his body, without volition. He heard
himself saying words he couldn't comprehend, felt his
hands moving in patterns he had never used before. *Cénzi?*
But if it was Cénzi, there was no answer.

He shouted the final words, made the final gesture. He
snatched the cords of power that tied the Westlanders to

the Second World, but he left that of the téni and even the Numetodo alone. He stood on the battlefield with his arms wide, and the Second World took him as it never had before.

He had never felt so full of the power of the Ilmodo. It filled him, burning and too dangerous to handle for more than a breath. He took it all in, breathed in the gift of Cénzi, and exhaled it again, shouting.

What do I do with this? he asked Cénzi, and he heard the answer:

Do what you should do . . .

The wave of energy pulsed out from him, radiating westward and north along the line of battle. Where it touched, the Tehuantin were thrown back, flung wildly backward into their own ranks. They toppled like game pieces swept aside by an angry hand.

The warrior riders about to slay Varina and her companions were taken in the storm, both steeds and riders hurled away. "Go!" Nico told them. "This is Cénzi's Gift!" His voice was that of Cénzi; it roared, a thunder that could be heard all along the lines. "Go!"

And it was over. The threads of power snapped; the Second World shut with a deep thunder. A terrible exhaustion filled him, so overpowering that he couldn't stand. His legs gave way, and he collapsed into cold darkness.

"Let them come across," Tototl said. "Once they're in the boulevard, they'll be easy targets and we'll hit them from all sides at once."

The tactic had worked initially. The Easterners used their spells as the sun rose; Niente told the nahualli to let them waste their energy even though they could have easily countered them all with the spells in their spell-staffs. The warriors drew back, abandoning the catapult. Niente waited on his horse next to Tototl, just down the first major cross street of the great boulevard. Their archers sent volleys into the sky; an ancient nahualli Easterner riding in a carriage showed his strength and sent the arrows flying harmlessly away. The Tecuhtli of the Easterners—the woman clad in steel—escorted her warriors across.

They heard the rush of warriors who were hidden near the river and in the courtyard of where the monster's skull was set, but Tototl raised his hand as the warriors behind them pressed forward, eager to join the battle. "Wait," he said. "Not yet."

Through the gaps between the buildings, Niente glimpsed the Easterners pressing farther up the street, the woman, strangely, leading them into the courtyard from which the warriors had come. He wondered at that for a moment, then the answer came: the terrible shrill chatter of the black sand weapons, sounding eerily like the eagle claws used in the sacrifice of captives. They heard the screams that followed, and saw the warriors falling like maize being harvested. The warriors grumbled now behind Tototl, wanting revenge for the fallen, and still he held them back. The Easterner Tecuhtli called out, and their warriors poured back into the boulevard, pushing back the remnants of the warriors in the boulevard.

"Now!" Tototl cried, and they surged out into the fray. Tototl charged directly toward the woman, snatching the riding spear from its holder on his saddle, his sword still sheathed. Niente tried to follow him. The Easterner spell-caster in the carriage, clad in green and gold and older than Niente, was chanting, his hands moving in familiar patterns. Niente could feel the power gathering around him, and so Niente raised his spell-staff, shouting a release word. The X'in Ka shot from the staff, a sun-blast that enveloped the spellcaster in blue flame. The man screamed, the blast covering carriage and rider.

So slow. The Easterner way of magic was so slow.

Niente saw Tototl's spear skewer the Easterner Tecuhtli like a haunch of meat. The High Warrior leaped down from his horse with the spear still grasped in his hands, wrenching the helpless woman down from her horse to the cobblestones. Tototl shouted in triumph. Niente heard the impact as the woman's body hit the ground.

He could feel their spellcasters readying spells, could hear the woman commanding the terrible eagle claws shouting orders to her people, a long brown braid swaying from underneath her helm. Niente raised his spell-staff ready to take down the braided woman—to his mind, she was the most dangerous of their enemies.

He shouted the release word, but in that same moment, a terrible force pulled at him, at all the nahualli. The frigid air of the X'in Ka swirled over them, above them, and it swept away his spell—and he knew: he had seen this, though he had not believed it possible.

The misted man, the hidden one—he had made his decision. He had acted.

The Long Path was open.

Niente gasped. This was a raw force he had never felt before.

An invisible vortex sat over them, like the hungry mouth of a fierce tornado, and it sucked at the energy locked in Niente's staff, in *all* of their spell-staffs, ripping away the power stored there and leaving their staffs as empty as if they'd cast all the spells they'd so laboriously placed within them the previous night. It was not only the nahualli that felt it: he could see everyone pause and look about, glancing upward, searching for something they could not see. Tototl had ripped the spear from the body of the Tecuhtli; he stood over her, the spear poised to strike again, and he, too, hesitated.

Then the vortex was gone, vanished, and Niente was holding only an empty length of wood. He could see the other nahualli staring or dropping their staffs in alarm. "Niente!" Tototl shouted from the cobble, his spear still raised. Niente showed him his staff.

"I have nothing," he said in amazement. "The magic has been taken from all the nahualli. Tototl, I saw this . . . I told you . . ."

"You're still alive," Tototl grunted. "We stay. We fight!"

He lifted the spear again. Niente saw the strangest sight then: an old man with a silver nose, rushing toward Tototl. He brandished not a sword but a cane as he shouted at the High Warior, and yet . . .

Niente felt the threat of that stick. Tototl saw the man also, but he did nothing, only smiled. Niente shouted as the man thrust the tip of his cane toward Tototl, and he leaped between them, trying to knock away the cane with his staff, but he wasn't strong enough. The cane touched Niente's own body.

The impact was like the fist of Axat. He thought he saw Her face above him, nodding as he fell. Niente saw a carved bird flying away in front of Her.

A last gift . . .

*   *   *

Sergei saw the warrior's vicious spear thrust pierce Allesandra's armor. He saw her mouth open in silent surprise and shock, saw the warrior use the spear's shaft to pull Allesandra down from her horse. He stood over her, yanking the spear from the Kraljica's body with blood spattering as he prepared to thrust down again at her prone figure. He shouted something toward an ancient Westlander spellcaster standing near him.

Sergei had stopped himself. Something felt strange: a furious cold wind swirled in the Avi, and the fury of the spells all around seemed to have stopped.

Sergei shook himself. He limped toward Allesandra, cane in one hand, his rapier in the other. Another Westlander sprang from his left side, and he thrust underneath the man's cut, the thin blade of the rapier finding a gap between the bamboo slats of his armor and sliding into his abdomen. The Westlander doubled over, falling, the motion taking the sword from Sergei's grasp. He left it there; he had no strength to hold it. "No!" he shouted at the warrior standing over Allesandra. He brandished his cane at the man, who looked at him and seemed to nearly laugh.

Sergei prayed that he remembered the word that Varina had taught him, that he would pronounce it correctly, that the spell she said she'd placed within the cane would actually work. "Scaoil!" he cried, and he plunged the brass ferrule of his cane toward the warrior.

But as he did so, the ancient spellcaster moved with surprising speed for his evident age, interposing himself between Sergei and the warrior, waving his spell-staff. The cane struck the spellcaster instead. In the instant the cane touched him, the ferrule seemed to explode. A loud, percussive sound nearly deafened Sergei. The blast sent splinters of his cane flying, it sent the old spellcaster flying backward in a spray of blood and gore, dying if not already dead. A red carved bird flew up from the spellcaster's ripped pouch and landed again on the old man's chest. He grasped the bird, seemed to whisper to it, then his head fell to one side.

The red-painted warrior dropped his spear from his hand as he stared at the body of the spellcaster, lying in the Avi near the wounded Allesandra.

Time stopped then for Sergei. The warrior stood, the cool rictus of battle fury still on his face. Sergei thought that the man would reach to his side and draw his sword, that he would cut Sergei down in the next instant. There were no gardai who would save him, no sparkwheelers close enough.

He wondered what death would feel like.

But the warrior stared at the spellcaster's body and he shook his head. He shouted something that Sergei did not understand: a prayer, a curse, a query. He stepped back and away from Sergei: one step, another, then another. Then he turned completely, and he roared a command that echoed in the street. The warriors in the Avi began to give ground, slowly at first, then more quickly. Sergei saw Brie and Talbot pursuing them with the sparkwheelers, but he called to them. "Wait! The Kraljica . . ."

He bent down to her. "Sergei," she said. "It hurts . . ."

"I know," he told her. A few gardai had gathered around—bloody and battered and appearing dazed. They stared at the Kraljica, at the shattered body of the spellcaster.

"Help me," Sergei told them. "Help me get her back to the palais . . ."

Jan, with the chevarittai and a few of the war-téni, fought a rear action to protect their retreat, engaging the mounted warriors and keeping the Westlander foot troops away from the the stragglers. In his role in command of the Firenzcian army, Jan had rarely needed to coordinate a full-scale retreat, but he'd been on the other side of one many times, and he knew a retreat was often the most dangerous time for the troops as the advancing force could pick off the stragglers, sending arrows and spells to decimate and even obliterate the rearmost companies. Too often, the advancing army could often overtake their demoralized and exhausted foe and inflict terrible casualties.

Retreat might allow the commander to fight another day, but it also might lead to a total and ignominious defeat. They were not even falling back to fortifications, but to an open and unprotected city.

The Westlander spellcasters hurled spells at them that their war-téni had little time and little energy to deflect. Their archers barbed the very sky with arrows. Their mounted troops—thankfully few—dashed toward the back of the running gardai, picking them off. The front ranks of their army pushed forward at a full charge. Jan could glimpse, through the smoke and confusion of the battle-field, the banners of the Tehuantin commander: a winged serpent flying on rippling, bright green cloth. Most of the spells seemed to come from the group around that banner.

Jan was exhausted and in terrible pain. His fingers longed to release the weight of heavy Firenzcian steel, the hilt of his sword already slippery with blood. He swayed in his saddle, nearly falling from the horse as spell-lightning hissed and boomed directly in front of him, causing his war-horse to rear. He settled the animal.

"Hïrzg!" he heard someone call, and a chevaritt to his right pointed to a quartet of mounted warriors about to run down a group of gardai.

Jan sighed. He forced his fingerss to tighten on his sword. He ignored the pain searing his chest. He kicked his horse into a gallop toward the warriors.

You aren't going to survive this. This is going to be your last battle.

The thought came to him as a certainty. A prophecy. He shivered even as he shouted encouragement to the cheva-rittai, even as they pounded toward the warriors.

Then . . .

A wave of intense cold washed over him, as if winter had come early; as it passed, even with the fury of their charge, he realized that the constant rain of spells from the Tehu-antin forces had stopped. The warriors ahead of them had realized it as well. They'd pulled up their horses, looking back toward their own lines. Jan worried that the spellcast-ers were preparing another mass spell like the war-storm. But instead, a visible wave rushed across the land from east to west, one that caused Jan to pull back on the reins in amazement. They could all see it: in the shimmering air, in the dust it raised from the ground as it moved. Where the pulse touched the advancing front line of the Westlanders, the warriors were tossed and thrown back even though it left their own people untouched. Jan heard screams and wails, then a greater single voice.

"Go! This is Cénzi's Gift. Go!"

The shout seemed to come from everywhere and nowhere.

Jan felt a sudden faint hope. A war-téni's fireball went

screaming overhead toward the Tehuantin. There was no response to the spell: no deflection, no impotent explosion far above. The fireball shrieked death and plowed into the Westlanders ranks, exploding untouched. Another followed, and another—all of them went through. The hope within him surged, and his injuries no longer mattered. "Turn!" he shouted to the troops, to the offiziers. "Turn! Follow me!"

He raised his sword as the chevarittai took up his shout. He heard it echoing faintly down the the lines, and the retreat halted, then slowly turned. Jan was already riding hard toward the Tehuantin. All along the battlefield, as far to the south as Jan could see, the retreat was turning. Black and silver began to flow westward.

With the chevarittai around him, Jan plowed into the stunned line of the Westlanders, driving toward the banner of the winged snake. The first warriors he passed were strewn on the ground; whether dead or rendered unconscious by the massive unknown spell, he didn't know. Then he hit resistance, and he pushed through a sea of flashing blades, his pains forgotten in the fury of battle. The chevarittai shouted as they hewed through the Westlanders toward their commander, all of them pushing forward. They could hear the roar of the onrushing gardai behind them.

There was no answer from the Tehuantin spellcasters. Whatever had happened had stolen their magic. But the Tehuantin warriors—at least those away from the initial pulse, were unaffected. They fought as fiercely as ever, and now that the initial euphoria had passed, the exhaustion and the pain were making themselves felt again. The assault slowed, though now the banners of the winged snake were agonizingly close. Every strike of his sword into the press of warriors sent a shock streaking up Jan's sword arm. His legs ached, and he could barely hold his seat on the warhorse. His ribs stabbed him with ivory knives at every breath.

He wondered where Brie was. He wondered who would tell his children, and what they would say.

You must at least make the story worth the telling.

Groaning, he brought his sword up to protect his side against a sword thrust, his blade cleaving down past the attack into the warrior's neck. He saw the man's mouth open,

his eyes go wide. Something stabbed hard at his thigh on
the left, and he swung around to face the warrior with a
spear, the point embedded in his leg just above the cuisse. Jan yanked the reins hard to the left and the warhorse
lifted its hooves, striking the attacker and trampling him
as the spear's tip was torn from Jan's thigh. He could feel
blood soaking the padding under the cuisse.

He was closer. He could hear the snake banner flapping. "To me!" he called the chevarittai, but he heard
no reply. He didn't know where they were, had no time
to search for them. Scowling, he plunged forward, letting
the horse run over the warriors between. He broke into
a small opening:, he could see the Tehuantin leader, his
shaved skull adorned with a red eagle that spread its wings
over his cheeks. The man was older than Jan, bulky in the
Westlander armor and astride his own horse, a magnificent piebald. Next to him was one of the Westlander spellcasters, a young one, with his spell-staff in his hand and a
golden band on his arm.

Jan gathered what strength he still had. He raised his
sword and shouted challenge. He kicked the warhorse
forward.

From her hiding place behind the tapestries along the rear
wall, Rochelle watched them carry the Kraljica into the hall.
Allesandra's armor was spattered with red, and there was
a hole punched through the chest plate from which blood
still flowed. Her face was pale and drawn, her graying hair
disheveled and as stiff as straw around her face. "Put me on
the throne," she heard Allesandra husk. The woman's voice
was an exhausted, skeletal croak. The gardai bearing her
obeyed, placing the woman on the Sun Throne. Rochelle
expected the throne to blaze into light as the Kraljica sat in
its crystalline embrace, as all the tales said, but the throne
responded with only the palest of glows, barely visible in
the sunlight.

She wondered if that was because the Kraljica was close
to death.

"Someone find the Kraljica's healers," she heard Sergei
say. "The rest of you, go to the Hïrzgin for orders; she is in
command. Go!"

They scattered. Rochelle watched as Sergei crouched

beside the throne. "What can I do for you, Kraljica?" he said.

"Water, Sergei," she whispered. "I'm so thirsty."

He limped toward a stand near the servants' door; he was missing his cane and moved slowly. Rochelle slipped out from behind the tapestry. With a few bounding steps, she was on the dais, the knife in her hand. Sergei heard her, and he cried out her name—"Rochelle!"—but he was too far away and too slow to stop her. The pale stone—laced in its pouch around Rochelle's neck—seemed to pulse white-hot against her skin.

"You will kill her, and as she dies, you will tell her why so she goes to Cénzi knowing it . . ."

Allesandra looked at Rochelle with confusion in her pained eyes. "Hello, Great-Matarh," Rochelle said. "I'm Rochelle."

"Rochelle? Great-Matarh?" The confusion deepened on the woman's face. She glanced at the knife and her eyes narrowed. "I know that weapon," she said, licking her dry lips. She coughed, and bubbles of red froth flecked the corners of her mouth. "I killed Mahri with that. Where did you . . . ?"

"From your son," Rochelle said. "From my vatarh."

Her eyes widened again. "Your vatarh? Jan?"

"Rochelle, don't do this." That was Sergei. He took a few faltering steps toward the dais, his hand stretching out toward her. She ignored him. A swipe of the blade, and she could be through any of the doors and away before he could do anything to stop her.

"Yes, Jan is my vatarh," Rochelle told Allesandra. Her free hand clutched at the tiny leather bag that held the flat, nearly white pebble that contained her matarh and all their victims. "And my matarh . . . She was the White Stone. Elissa, you called her at the time, though that wasn't her real name."

"Elissa . . ." Allesandra's eyes closed for a moment. Her breath rattled; the eyes opened again. "Jan . . ."

"She loved him," Rochelle told Allesandra, leaning close to her. She placed the blade against her great-matarh's neck. Allesandra put her hand over Rochelle's, but there was no power in her grasp. Her skin felt like wrinkled parchment.

"Rochelle, the woman's dead already," Sergei said. "You don't need to do this. The White Stone's dead. Leave her that way."

Rochelle glanced at him. "Why do you care, Ambassador? Your hands are far bloodier than mine."

"I said it to you in the carriage: it's not too late for you, Rochelle. You're not your matarh. You don't have to become what she became."

The knife trembed in her hand. *"Promise me . . ."*

"Do this," Sergei said, "and you are forever the White Stone, the hated assassin who murdered the Kraljica. You'll be hunted for the rest of your short and miserable life. You'll never feel safe, never feel comfortable. Eventually you'll make a mistake and be caught, and you'll be dragged back here in chains and executed. That's your fate, Rochelle, the only fate you have if you do this."

"And if I don't? Aren't I still the White Stone, who killed Rance and others?"

Sergei shrugged. "I don't know," he said. "Your life will be your book to write. If the White Stone vanishes, there's no one to chase."

Rochelle's mind was in torment. The blade pressed into Allesandra's skin, the keen edge drawing blood. All she had to do was press a little harder. Just lean into the woman slightly; the knife would do the rest. Allesandra's fingers pressed against her own, almost as if the woman were willing her to do this. "My matarh loved Jan," Rochelle said to her. Her voice trembled more than her hands.

"I know," Allesandra said. Her lips were slick with blood, and a long thick line drooled down one side of her mouth. "And Jan loved her. I know that too." Her breath gurgled, and the smell of it was vile. "I'm sorry."

"Sorry?" Rochelle nearly shouted the word. She almost plunged the knife into her neck with the violence of the word. "You should have said that to *her.*"

Allesandra gave no answer. Her breathing had gone thin and slow, and her body jerked once spasmodically. She stared at Rochelle, blinking heavily.

"Rochelle . . ."

Rochelle lifted the knife away from Allesandra's neck and sheathed it. *Kill her . . .* She heard her matarh's voice whisper, but the sound was faint, and Rochelle found that she had no will to do it. Not anymore. All the rage had left her, all the certainty.

She didn't have to do this. She didn't have to be the White Stone. Matarh had been insane; that didn't have to be her fate as well.

"I want to watch you die," she told the Kraljica. She glanced at Sergei. "I need to see it."

"All right," Sergei told her. He came ponderously up the steps of the dais to stand next to her. "We'll watch together."

Allesandra's mouth opened, as if she were about to protest, but she said nothing. They heard her breath go out. The Kraljica was looking at Sergei. "Nessantico . . ." Her voice was hardly more than a zephyr. He eyes were fixed somewhere between the two of them, staring blindly. "Sergei, is she safe?"

"Yes," Sergei told her. "She's safe."

There was no reaction from Allesandra. After a time, they realized that she had not taken in another breath. Her eyes were still open. Rochelle took the white stone from the pouch. She placed it over Allesandra's right eye. "There, Matarh," she said. "She's yours . . ."

She started down the dais. "Wait," Sergei called after her. "The stone . . ."

"Leave it there," Rochelle told him. "Take it for a memento. Throw it away. I don't care. I don't need it."

She left the hall as the healers—too late—came in.

The wave of cold, then the surge that passed over them harmlessly but slammed into the Westlanders . . .

Nico's presence and his voice, impossibly loud . . .

The silence that seemed to last several breaths, as they realized that none of the Westlanders were casting spells toward them . . .

What had happened?

Varina could still feel the Scáth Cumhacht within herself. She had felt something—someone?—tug at the spells she had stored in her mind as if it wanted to steal them, but the presence had passed by her untouched. Well to the north, she saw a war-téni's fireball sizzling across the horizon, streaking toward the enemy, then another and yet another, this one from a téni near her. None of them were touched.

She could hear the offiziers shouting, turning the gardai, facing them westward once more. The tide which had pulled them along slowed, stopped, then began to flow the other way. They stood motionless against the current. Leovic and Niels were still holding her arms, but she could see them watching. "Go," she told them. "They need you. I'll follow as best I can."

"A'Morce," Niels protested.

"Go," she repeated.

They left her, running toward one of the chevarittai offiziers. She watched them be gathered up in the rush. Then, far more slowly, limping, she followed. Gardai swarmed past her, shouting. She heard the din of the battle renewed ahead of her, but all the spells seemed to be coming from the Faith's war-téni and the Numetodo, not from the Westlanders.

She was standing among the bodies of those who had fallen in the retreat, most in blue and gold. It was difficult to ignore them. The worst were the ones who were not dead but too wounded to walk, who reached out toward her for succor as she passed or were still crawling toward the city. To them, she could only say that help would be coming soon to rescue them—and hope that she was telling them the truth.

But she was looking for one person in particular.

She saw a body off to her left and ahead of her—dressed in a green téni's robes. She thought it might be one of the war-téni, then she saw the face.

Nico's face.

Ignoring her aching legs, she ran to him, sinking down to her knees alongside him. He seemed unharmed: no blood on his robes, his face dirty and dark with old bruises and cuts, but he looked otherwise untouched. "Nico?" she said, rolling him on his back, looking desperately at the robes for a sign of what had hurt him.

He opened his eyes. He smiled. "Hi, Varina. I guess I was sleeping. Have you seen my matarh?" It was a boy's voice. A child's voice. He sat up and glanced around, his eyes widening as he took in the gardai running past shouting and waving their swords; the bodies lying nearby; the fumes and smoke of the battlefield; the trampled earth that had once been a farmer's field. He pushed himself to a sitting position. "Varina," he said, his voice trembling with obvious fear. He clutched at her arms. "I'm scared, Varina. Take me home. Please. I don't want to be here."

"Nico, what did you do?"

He looked frightened at the question, shrinking away from her. "I didn't do nothing, honest. I just want to go home. I want to see Matarh. I want to see Talis."

Varina hugged him. "Nico, Talis and Serafina are . . . gone."

"Where did they go?" he asked. In his eyes there was no mockery, only the innocent question.

"Nico . . ." She couldn't answer him. Varina hugged him again. Whatever Nico had done, however he'd done it, the effort had obviously taken his mind with it. This was no longer the Absolute of the Morellis. This was no longer Nico the great téni. He clung to her like a child to his matarh, and she could feel him shivering with panic and dismay.

Gardai were still flowing past them; the din of battle and the thundering of war-téni spells was deafening. "Nico, come on," she said. "Let's get you out of here. It's not safe. You can come to my house. Would you like that?"

He nodded urgently, clinging to her. She pulled him to his feet.

Together, they stumbled eastward toward the city.

Atl felt naked and unprotected, his spell-staff impossibly emptied in a few breaths by that terrible spell from the east, and now the battle was suddenly renewed when it was supposed to have ended.

In victory. In the victory he'd seen. In the victory he'd told the Tecuhtli would be his. He remembered his taat's vision, the one Niente claimed to have glimpsed, the path that Atl had been unable to see, the one he'd believed to be his taat's lie. This was not possible.

Citlali raged at him as fireballs from the Easterner nahualli fell near them. "Stop them!" the Tecuhtli shouted. "Damn you, Nahual! Stop them!"

But all Atl could do was shake his head. "I have no power, Tecuhtli. None of the nahualli have. It's been taken from us." The spells were gone, and there was no time now to craft new ones to place in the spell-sticks.

"You promised me victory, Nahual! You promised me

the city!" Citlali wailed like a child deprived of his favorite
toy, but there was no answer at all to that. His face was so
flushed with his anger that the red eagle seemed to blend
into his flesh.

There will be no victory, Atl wanted to tell him. *Or if
there is to be one, it's not one that I've glimpsed in the bowl.
The paths in the scrying bowl had been wiped away. Everything had changed. I have never seen this path at all. I don't
know where it leads.*

As his taat had warned. His hand felt for his pouch,
where the carved bird his taat had given him was nestled.
*If one of us sees the way, then we can tell the other that the
Long Path is open....* Could Niente have been right: could
this Long Path exist, the one Atl could never see?

He wished Niente were here.

Citlali was still raving, but Atl's attention was on the
carved bird in his pouch. It seemed to rustle, as if it were
alive and flapping its wings in panic. He opened the leather
flap, reached in. Yes, the thing was moving. It went still in
his hand as he took it out, and as he did, he heard, unmis-
takably, Niente's voice.

*"Tototl is returning to the ships. You must go too! The
Long Path is here."*

"Taat?"

There was no answer. Atl dropped the bird from fingers
that had lost their strength. He watched it tumble to the
ground, to be lost among the stalks of grain that the armies
had crushed into the dirt. His taat's voice had sounded so
weak, so lost, and there came to him a certainty that he
would never hear it again.

"Tecuhtli," Atl called. "We must retreat and find the
ships. We have no magic. We'll have none until we can rest
again."

"No!" Citlali spat. "I will have the city today."

"It's not possible now," Atl said.

"How would you know?" Citlali scoffed. "Nothing you
have told me has been true. You are no longer Nahual. I'll
find another. I'll make Niente Nahual again."

Citlali raised his sword against Atl as if he were about to
strike, and Atl lifted his spell-stick uselessly.

Someone called toward them in the tongue of the Easterners, and a warhorse broke through the ring about Citlali

and Atl, bearing a warrior covered in blood and dirt, his helm lost, a notched sword clutched in his hand. He bore down directly toward Citlali, and the Tecuhtli turned from Atl to parry the the man's stroke. Steel rang against steel, and Atl saw a shard of Citlali's blade fly away, spinning. As their warhorses came close, Citlali pushed hard at the Easterner, and the man fell from his saddle. Citlali laughed. "You see?" he said. "You see how easily they fall? And you tell me to *retreat*?"

The Easterner was struggling groggily to his feet, favoring one leg. He seemed barely able to lift his weapon. All around them, Atl could see the black-and-silver and blue-and-gold uniforms of the Easterners, though the three of them stood alone in a quiet nexus of the chaos. Warriors were falling under the press, and their spellcasters hurled their magic with the nahualli unable to respond. Citlali jumped from his horse; Atl saw his boot crush the carved red bird into the muddy, torn ground. The Tecuhtli lifted his sword again. The strike, Atl saw, would take the Easterner's head.

Atl lifted back his empty spell stick. He brought it down hard on Citlali's skull. The sound was strangely quiet, like a stick thumping a ripe melon, but Citlali fell senseless at the Easterner's stunned feet. The Easterner looked at Atl, who stared back. For a breath, neither of them moved, then—as Atl watched from his horse, the Easterner lifted his sword. He brought it down through Citlali's neck. "The Tecuhtli is lost!" Atl called out loudly so that the warriors nearest him could hear. "The Tecuhtli is lost. Retreat! Back to the ships!"

As the warriors began to respond, as they began to disengage and fall back, as the Easterners shouted in triumph, Atl stared down at the Easterner. The man leaned on his sword, still buried in Citlali's neck. Atl nodded to him.

Then he jerked the reins of his horse and began the long flight westward.

The Dawn

THEY WERE PURSUED BY THE ARMY of blue and gold and the army of black and silver, hounding them as they retreated toward the river and the waiting ships, but not hotly. The stragglers had been picked off, but the main armies had never reengaged. It was apparent that the Easterners were content to chase them from their land, but they would not demand their extermination if the Tehuantin were willing to leave.

The army had seen the masts of their fleet the second day, ten miles upriver from Nessantico, and they'd boarded as quickly as they could. Tototl, now calling himself Tecuhtli, had boarded the *Yaoyotl,* and he had turned the fleet westward as soon as the surviving warriors and nahualli were aboard. The empty boats—far too many of them—he'd scuttled in the middle of the river to discourage any of the Holdings' navy from pursuing them.

They sailed down the A'Sele, moving quickly with its current toward the sea.

Toward home.

Atl, aboard the *Yaoyotl,* stared into the green mist of his scrying bowl. Tototl watched him carefully, the warrior's skull painted now with the red eagle pattern that would soon be tattooed permanently on his flesh.

The myriad futures spread out before Atl, no longer blanketed and dim as they once had been. It was as if Axat had lifted a veil from before his face. He could see far more clearly than he'd ever seen before, all the uncertainties that had shrouded things for so long blown away like passing storm clouds. The futures were open before him, all the possibilities.

What he saw made him gasp. *The Long Path . . . This was the future that Taat saw, that he always said was there.* He realized then that Niente had known what that Long Path would cost: that to achieve it he must die; that Tecuhtli

Citalali would be killed as well if this future was ever to rise; that a multitude of warriors would die as well. *How long did you keep this secret, Taat? Did you know before we even left?*

Atl suspected that he had. It explained so much. It explained why Niente had never wanted him to use the scrying bowl himself. That had been the act of a protective father, not that of a jealous Nahual. The realization made Atl regret the harsh words they'd exchanged.

"Will I return here?" Tototl asked Atl harshly, interrupting his thoughts and making the green mist waver as he exhaled so that he almost lost the vision. "Will I avenge our defeat?"

Atl could see that future as well: their ships loaded again with an army, one yet larger than Citlali's, returning a third time to those shores. Only this time, the armies of the Holdings were one, and they descended upon them furiously and early, the bulk of them armed with terrible weapons like the ones that Tototl and Niente had witnessed during their battles. The warriors of the Tehuantin were cut down like wheat with a scythe and the earth drank their blood.

It was a terrible future, but it was one that could easily come to pass.

But the other . . . the one stretching out until the mists swallowed it. *That* one was also possible if Atl could direct Tototl that way. It would take skill, and it would demand sacrifice, but it was there and he could see Niente's hand upon it.

"You will do better than that, Tecuhtli," Atl told him. "You will one day bring us to peace with the Easterners. Your name will be honored everywhere in our land. All the Tecuhtli who come after will compare themselves to you. You will be forever the Great Tecuhtli."

The mists were failing now, and Atl took the bowl and threw the water within it over the side of the ship. He handed the bowl to one of the lesser nahualli. "Clean this," he told the man, "and put it back in my cabin." He could feel the weariness of the X'in Ka hammering at him, and his left eye twitched uncomfortably. Atl squeezed his eyes shut and opened them again. Tototl was watching him.

"Peace?" he said. "How does a warrior find honor

in peace? How does one become great without war and victory?"

Atl took a long breath. He looked westward, toward the smoke and fumes of Nessantico, toward the place where Niente's body would forever lie. "I will show you," he told Tototl. "Together, we will keep to that path."

"Watch me," she told Nico. "Then I want you to try it yourself. Are you watching? See, you loop one string like this, then take the other and go around the bottom of the loop once, and . . ."

There was a knock on Varina's bedroom door as she was tying the laces of Nico's boots. "A'Morce?"

"Come in," Varina said, and Michelle entered, carrying Serafina in her arms. The baby was bundled in lace, and Michelle held the child protectively as she glanced warily at Nico, who sat on the bed. His guileless face turned to look at Michelle.

"Is that Serafina?" he asked Varina, his voice eager.

"Yes," she told him.

He looked down, almost shyly. "May I . . . May I hold her?"

Michelle was shaking her head slightly, but Varina smiled at him. "Just for the tiniest bit," she told him. "And you must be very careful with her." Varina nodded to Michelle; still frowning, the wet nurse came forward and placed the baby in Nico's outstretched hands. "Make sure you hold her head," Varina told him. "Yes, like that. That's good . . ."

Nico grinned, cradling Serafina in his arms. The baby fussed for a moment, then quieted as Nico rocked her unconsciously, staring down into the baby's face. "Her eyes are so big," he said wonderingly. "And her hands are awful small. She's really my daughter?"

"Yes. Yours and Liana's." Varina reached down and stroked Sera's head. Her hair was fine as down, the skin smooth and warm. Her tiny hand waved, finding Varina's finger and clutching it. She laughed.

Nico shook his head. He was watching the interplay. "I don't remember Liana," he said. "I don't know how . . ."

"I'll tell you one day," Varina told him. "Right now, we still have to get ready to go to the Kraljica's funeral.

Here ..." She held out her hands, and Nico carefully placed Sera there. Varina heard Michelle's audible sigh of relief. Varina kissed Sera's forehead, hugging her for a few breaths before handing her back to Michelle. "She's fed?"

"Fed and dressed and ready to go," Michelle answered. "I have a change of clothes and diapers. I came up to tell you that the carriage is here from the palais."

"Good," Varina told her. "Go ahead and get her in and settled. Nico and I will be down in a few moments. I just have to finish his boots."

Michelle glanced at Nico again. "A'Morce, the young man's dangerous. What he did ..."

"What he did with the Tehuantin saved us," Varina answered. "And cost him far more than most would have been willing to give."

"He could be faking his condition, or he could recover his wits. What then?"

Nico said nothing as they discussed him. He only looked from one woman to the other as they spoke.

"Then," Varina answered, "we will deal with that when it happens." It was the same question she'd heard already a dozen times or more. There were those on the Council and among the ca'-and-cu' of the city and the téni of the Faith who wanted Nico tried and executed for the deaths he'd caused and the damage to the Old Temple during the Morelli takeover. For that matter, there was a part of Varina's own heart that was still angry with him for the destruction and deaths he'd caused, unapologetically, to her own friends during Karl's funeral.

Nico, truly, had much to answer for, yet he had nearly single-handedly saved the city when it was about to fall. There was also no denial of that—or of the fact that his efforts had cost him greatly, and perhaps, perhaps that had been punishment enough. The Nico in front of her seemed to remember nothing of that day or much of his previous life at all. The Nico before her was an innocent—he might inhabit the same body, but he was not the Nico who had claimed to be the Absolute. Perhaps the Kraljiki would demand punishment for the past, but Varina would fight that, with all the efforts she could muster. "For now, he's a child, and he needs to be treated as such."

"As you say, A'Morce," Michelle answered. Serafina

cried, and Michelle rocked her gently. "I'll get her quieted
down again, and we'll see you in the carriage."

As Michelle left the room, Varina bent down again to
the laces of Nico's boots. He was watching her, frowning.
"It's all right, Nico," she said. "Michelle's not angry with
you. She's just concerned about you, as I am. Now, watch
me and let's see if you can tie the other one. Loop the lace
like this, then pass the other end around it . . ."

The téni were already in attendance at the Archigos' Temple. A'Téni Valerie ca'Beranger of Prajnoli would conduct
the service—the rumors were that she would most likely be
elected Archigos when the Concord A'Téni convened in a
few days. Brie escorted the children up an aisle lined with e-
téni in white robes—the color of death—trimmed in green.
The téni watched, silent: like lines of white bone arrowing
toward the Stone of Cénzi as Brie and the children ascended
the dais and approached the altar, the great Stone of Cénzi,
draped in a brilliant azure cloth.

"There," Brie whispered to Elissa, Kriege, Caelor, and
Eria. Her voice sounded loud under the dome and she
glanced up once at the frescoes of Cénzi and the Moitidi
far above them. "This is your great-matarh Allesandra.
She was a great woman, and she told me that she wanted
so much to get to know all of you. I wish you could have
known her when she was alive."

This was not how she'd intended for the children to
meet their great-matarh. She'd hoped to introduce them
to the woman, not the dead container that had once held
her. She wondered whether it might not have been better
to let the children remain in Brezno for the funeral, but for
the fact that they would then have missed their vatarh's
coronation.

"It's ugly here," Elissa had proclaimed on disembark-
ing from the carriage at the palais. She looked around at the
buildings, broken and scarred by fire and war. "It smells horrible, too. Brezno is much prettier, Matarh. Why can't we just
stay there?"

"Nessantico is our new home now," she'd told them. "And
we'll make it prettier and more impressive than Brezno—as
it was once before. We'll help your vatarh make it that way,
all of us."

She hoped that had not been a lie.

Now, in the Archigos' Temple, they stared at yet another broken ruin, that of the Kraljica.

The toddler Eria hung back, a thumb firmly planted in her mouth. She refused to approach the bier at all, content to look at the body while hanging onto Brie's tashta. Caelor approached only hesitantly, and then moved quickly away close to Brie. Kriege stalked forward with a firm grimace on his face, stared down at the white-painted face there, then took a step back, sniffing as if he could smell the corruption through the scent-shield that the téni had placed around the body. Elissa, who had walked forward with Kriege, remained there, staring down at the body as if she were trying to memorize every detail: the lines of her great-matarh's face; the golden funeral mask that the téni would place on her face in just a turn of the glass, when the doors of the Archigos' Temple were opened so that the funeral could begin; the iron rod of Kraljiki Henri VI cradled in her left hand; the signet ring of the Kralji displayed on her upturned right palm, which Jan would take when the funeral rite was finished. The blue cloth over the altar was covered in wreaths of yellow trumpet-flowers. Seven candelabra were set around the stone; they were alight not with flame but with brilliant téni-light, bathing the body in a yellow-white light so intense it seemed that the dome of the temple had been lifted so the sun could shine down on the Kraljica.

Elissa touched Allesandra's arm with a tentative finger, then looked at the fingertip as if it were a foreign object. "She's cold," Elissa reported. "And kind of hard."

"That's what happens when you die."

"Oh." Elissa seemed to consider that. "Her face looks pretty, though."

Brie could hear Jan's voice, talking with Sergei ca'Rudka, Starkkapitän ca'Damont, and Commandant ca'Talin to one side of the quire. Talbot, Allesandra's aide who had agreed to stay on as Jan's aide, cleared his throat near the pews. "Hïrzgin, they're ready to let the ca'-and-cu' enter the temple. I'm going to go get the Hïrzg and the others— you have a bit yet, but . . ."

She nodded to him, and he stepped away. "Don't touch that," she told Elissa, who was reaching out with a tentative hand toward the ring. Elissa snatched back her hand as if she'd burned it.

"I wasn't going to touch it," she told Brie. "Is that going to be Vatarh's ring?"

"Yes, very soon," Brie told her.

"And will it be mine one day?"

Kriege glared at Elissa. "That's not *fair,* Matarh," he howled, his voice shrill under the dome. Brie saw the white lines of the téni ripple and someone laughed, a quick sound that was choked off. "She gets *everything.*"

She could hear Talbot chuckling as he strode across the nave toward Jan. She laughed, too. "No one's going to get the ring—at least not for a long, long time, when you're all grown up. We'll see then. It may be that neither of you will want it."

"Then I'll take it," Caelor interjected. "It's a pretty ring."

Brie laughed. "Come on," she told her children. "We need to take our seats ..."

The wind-horns called mournfully, their low wail sending the pigeons erupting from the ground on the plaza outside. Inside, Rochelle could feel the temple wall throbbing against her back. She'd slipped into the temple via a back door much earlier, picking the lock well before dawn, sliding up to the choir loft and along the side to a shadowed corner behind the arch of one of the buttresses, where she could look down at the quire, the bier and the closest pews.

She thought she could smell smoke here: not just the spiced aroma from the censers on the altar, but a fume that was a remnant of the black sand bombardment of the Tehuantin, lingering here below the painted arches of the dome. She had sat there hidden for several turns, waiting. She'd watched the white-robed téni file in; the choir settling into their seats not far from her.

She'd seen her vatarh and his family enter to view the body midmorning, had watched Brie escort the children forward after she and Jan had paid their own respects.

The children ... The thought came to her that this could have been her matarh and her, if only things had been different, but then she shook her head. *No,* she told herself firmly. *Their relationship could never have survived the falsehoods and Matarh's madness. It would never have been.*

This was never meant for you. Don't lie to yourself. You can only be his bastarda, *never his true daughter.*

She wondered what her future held, and she had no answer for that. Her hand went to the jeweled hilt of the knife she'd taken from her vatarh, the knife with which she'd hoped to kill the Kraljica. The smooth wood of the pommel seemed to throb against her fingers.

The family stepped back from the bier. She saw them settle into their pews, heard the doors open as the windhorns began their throbbing, mournful call once again, and the ca'-and-cu' entered the temple. The choir, startling her, began to sing one of Darkmavis' ethereal, mournful pieces. The rising tones and the close harmonies echoed, loud and insistent, near here to the dome of the temple that they enveloped her like a cloak.

It seemed to take forever for the mourners to enter between the lines of white-robed téni and settle in their pews. From her hiding place, Rochelle watched the front pews, gazing at her vatarh and her half siblings, as well as the woman who had taken her own matarh's place: Brie, whom they were calling the Victor of the South Bank and who the crowds cheered as loudly as they did Jan. She could see Sergei in the row behind them, sitting next to the Numetodo woman, who had a child in her arms.

And beside her was Nico, fidgeting like a bored child. The A'Morce kept turning to him and speaking softly to him, and Rochelle noticed that Sergei was watching the young man closely. Nico—she wondered if it was true, what they said of him, that his wits were gone and that he was no more than a child. Seeing him this way hurt most of all, she thought.

A'Téni ca'Beranger finally emerged from behind the quire and began the service, attended by a covey of high-ranking téni who fluttered around her with censers and goblets, with the staff of the broken globe, with the scrolls of the Toustour and Divolonté. Rochelle half-dozed through most of it, stirring only when Jan arose to give the Admonition. She watched him move to the High Lectern— walking like an old man, leaning on a cane with one arm clutched tight to his body. Talbot moved to assist him, and she saw Jan shake his head at the man. Slowly, he ascended the steps of the High Lectern, refusing to allow his injuries to stop him. She saw him gaze out over the crowd, then stare at the body of his matarh for several breaths before speaking.

"It's customary to say how kind and wonderful one's matarh was in life," he said finally, his baritone voice swelling with the fine acoustics of the temple. "I won't tell you that lie. She was not, perhaps, the best matarh I could have had. I was her only child, but I was still not the child she cared most about.

"That child, her only true child, was Nessantico. The Holdings. To Nessantico, she was an excellent matarh: a strong and forceful one, who accomplished what few others could have. She restored Nessantico when the city was in ruins. She kept the Holdings from falling apart when in lesser hands it would have crumbled and dissolved. She protected Nessantico when, for the second time, it came under the attack of foreign invaders. She gave all her love and all her energy and all her attention to this city and this empire, and when the sacrifice was demanded, she was willing to give Nessantico her life as a final payment."

He paused, taking several breaths as if speaking had exhausted him. Rochelle leaned forward. *I was willing to take her life. I would have, Matarh, but I was too late.* Her hand was still on the knife hilt. Her vatarh glanced upward, as if he'd glimpsed her movement or could somehow feel the pull of the knife she'd stolen from him. She slid back into shadow. His eyes, far below, seemed to hold her despite the great distance.

"Celebrate Allesandra ca'Vörl," Jan continued, his gaze returning to the audience. "Celebrate her stewardship of the Holdings, because in a time when the Holdings teetered on the brink, she kept the empire from the edge. That was masterful. That was genius. That was passion. *Those* were the qualities that Matarh possessed in abundance. They were exactly the qualities that Nessantico needed, and she arrived at exactly the time Nessantico required her presence. Nessantico was fortunate to have her—with her abilities and in this moment. Even if I didn't exactly appreciate that most of the time."

A faint chuckle ran through the crowd at that comment, sounding out of place in the temple. "We have emerged victorious from a terrible war," Jan said, "in no small part because of Kraljica Allesandra's actions. I can only hope, in going forward, that I am able to emulate her, that I *can* be her son and build upon her legacy. The Holdings are one again, the Faith is one again, but there are challenges ahead that will test us—all of us. I know that she will be watching from the arms of Cénzi. I hope that we can make her proud of what we accomplish."

Jan bowed his head. Rochelle thought that he might say more, but he gave the sign of Cénzi to the crowd and left the High Lectern—slowly, again, the sound of his cane loud in the silence. He returned to his seat as the A'Téni and her attendants moved back to the altar. As they began to circle the bier, chanting and waving censers, Rochelle sank back into her niche, putting her spine to the cold stone.

What do I do, Vatarh? What do I do to make you proud of me?

She could feel the hilt of the knife pressing into her side as she crouched against the temple's buttress. If Nessantico was to be her vatarh's passion, as it had been Allesandra's, if—as he had said was true of Allesandra—the Holdings were to be his one true child, then she would share that passion with him. Rochelle's matarh had given her a singular skill; she would use it, then.

I won't be the White Stone, no, but I can become the Blade of Nessantico.

She nodded. She would stay in the shadows. She would truly be Jan's daughter. She would serve the Holdings in her own way.

Yes.

The choir began to sing once more, and she closed her eyes, letting herself sink into the ethereal sound, as insubstantial and mysterious as she would be.

The procession around the ring boulevard of the Avi a'Parete was long and slow and—Jan could see by the throngs that lined the Avi waiting for the Kraljica to pass by—necessary. The populace stood several hands deep on both sides of the Avi for the entire length of the boulevard, as far he could see. Their faces were solemn; many were weeping openly. Jan realized then that as Allesandra had loved the city, it had come to love and appreciate her in return.

He could only hope they would do the same for him in
the coming years.

He grimaced as the carriage in which he rode found
a jagged hole in the pavement, the impact pushing his
cracked ribs together, the pain radiating all the way to his
shoulders. The cuts the healers had sewn closed days ago
pulled as he tried to make himself comfortable in the seat.
He struggled to show as little of his discomfort as possible
to the crowds. He smiled; he waved. And on his hand, the
signet ring of the Kralji glistened.

The funeral procession for Allesandra echoed that for
the great and beloved Kraljica Marguerite. None of the
Kralji between Marguerite and Allesandra had been given
such a formal display. Kraljiki Justi, Marguerite's son, had
been mocked and loathed; the people of the city had actually *rejoiced* at his death, and his bier had gone directly from
the Archigos' Temple to the palais. His son Audric's reign
had been worse, though Sergei's short regency had kept
the city stable. But once the regency ended prematurely,
Audric's madness and erratic behavior had damaged the
Holdings even further, and his assassination had—many
thought—been a blessing. Kraljica Sigourney, Audric's successor, had committed suicide as the Tehuantin sacked and
burned the city, and her body had been desecrated by the
Westlanders: Jan remembered that all too vividly.

With Sigourney's death, with the city a smoking ruin
around him, Jan could have taken the title of Kraljiki himself; he'd chosen to give Nessantico and the Holdings to his
matarh instead: a gesture of mockery.

She had turned his mockery into a true gift, he had to
admit. That was evident now.

Jan's carriage, drawn by three white horses in a four-
horse harness, followed immediately behind the bier. He
could hear the chanting of the téni who walked alongside
the bier, which appeared to float in a white cloud. Above
the body, huge images of the Kraljica appeared and vanished again: there she was as she appeared in her official
portrait; there she dedicated the rebuilt dome of the Old
Temple, there she smiled as she descended from the balcony during the Gschnas.

The smell of trumpet-flowers accompanied her, and the
sound of the musicians in the open carriage ahead of the

bier, playing Darkmavis and ce'Miella: a fusing of ancient and modern.

The old giving way to the new. Jan found it compelling.

"Look—they're cheering for you, Vatarh," Elissa said happily, pointing and waving herself. And it was true, as the bier passed, as their open carriage followed, the mourning morphed into applause and smiles. "They like you."

"They're cheering because they don't have a choice," Jan told her, and Brie frowned.

"Jan . . ."

"It's true, and the children should understand that," he answered her. He leaned forward across to where the children were sitting, ignoring the pull of the stitches and the twinge in his chest. "The people will applaud you as long as they think you're going to keep food in their bellies and a roof over their heads. They'll applaud you when they fear you, too, because they're afraid that if they don't, they'll be punished. Don't mistake their smiles and applause for anything more than a facade."

He felt Brie's hand on his arm. "Darling, please. They don't understand what you're saying, and you're just scaring them. And you shouldn't be so cynical. Not today of all days."

She was right, and he knew it. He glimpsed the ornate handle of the sparkwheel fitted to an embossed leather holder on her belt: the gorgeous sparkwheel Varina and the Numetodo had presented to her after the battle. The citizens of Nessantico *were* cheering Brie, he knew: the success of the sparkwheeler corps in the battle was already a legend in the city, and it appeared that the A'Hïrzg in Brie had become the favorite of the city. "I'm sorry," he told her, told the children. "You're right . . ."

They continued around the ring boulevard, and he continued to smile and wave. Because it was expected. Because it was his duty. They clattered over the Pontica A'Kralji, where, in iron gibbets, the skeletal body of the Westlander war-téni Sergei had killed and the Westlander Tehuantin were displayed in gory triumph. Jan barely glanced at their bodies.

The procession ended at the courtyard of the Kraljica's Palais at dusk. The bier floated on its mage-cloud to the summit of the pile of oil-soaked timbers set well away from the wings of the palais: the pyre that would send Allesandra's soul into the arms of Cénzi, placed in the center of the Kraljica's gardens. The ca'-and-cu' of the city and of the Holdings and Coalition both, the chevarittai in their dress uniforms of blue and gold or black and silver, Sergei ca'Rudka, Starkkapitän ca'Damont, Commandant ca'Talin of the Garde Civile: they were all here, watching as Jan and his family descended from their carriage.

Jan looked a last time at his matarh's body. He nodded to Talbot, who gestured to the fire-téni arrayed around the pyre. Their hands danced an intricate ballet together; their voices mingled in a slow chant. Fire bloomed orange-red between their hands as they gestured, as if tossing petals toward the pyre. Flames crackled and hissed in fury, licking at the oil and climbing rapidly. The mage-cloud vanished under a pall of writhing white that rose to the height of the palais roof before the wind smeared it across the sky. The flames touched the bier itself; Jan could see trumpet-flowers withering and curling under as Allesandra's body became lost in the heat waver and smoke. The furious crackling and popping of the fire echoed from the walls of the palais and the insistent heat drove everyone a few steps back from the pyre.

A log collapsed in the pyre, sending sparks coiling wildly upward. Jan realized that he'd been watching the fire burn for far longer than he'd thought, that the sky was growing dark.

"We can go now, Kraljiki," Talbot said. The title sounded strange to Jan. "They're ready in the hall . . ."

The Hall of the Sun Throne was packed. The windows in the long room flickered red with the flames of the pyre, while the great window behind the throne showed the dusk sky, already a deep violet with the first stars beginning to glisten above. The Council of Ca' was seated before the throne, with the other dignitaries. A'Téni ca'Beranger waited with Talbot alongside the Sun Throne. Brie gave the children to the nursemaids and approached the dais of the throne alongside Jan.

The Sun Throne. The massive chair sculpted from a single massive crystal towered more than two men high, a mottled, semitransparent white. It loomed over Jan and Brie. As he stared at the throne, he twisted the signet ring on his hand, the gold and silver of the ring cold and smooth on his flesh. "This is what you were meant for, my husband," Brie whispered to him. He glanced over to her, saw that she was looking at his hands. "You know that," she said. "Your matarh did, too."

"She had a strange way of showing it."

"She was meant for it also. That was the problem." She gestured toward the throne. "There it is," she said. "It's yours, my love."

Jan glanced toward Talbot. He nodded. Behind a door at the far rear of the hall, just behind the throne, two light-téni were chanting. Talbot had told him how in the last century, the Sun Throne barely reacted to the signet ring, that it was instead the work of especially trusted and skilled light-téni who ensured that the proper response came when a Kralji sat on the crystal.

Jan had laughed at that revelation—another sham, another show.

Jan ascended the dais, A'Téni ca'Beranger giving him the sign of Cenzi as he passed. On reaching the throne, he turned to face the crowd. They were watching him, all of them.

He sat. The crystal around him erupted with brilliant yellow light, seeming to emerge from the hidden depths of the throne. Kraljiki Jan sat, bathed in that light, as the audience rose in thunderous applause.

"I'll always wonder what the Holdings might have been had you lived," Sergei said to the portrait of Kraljica Marguerite. "I'd love to know what you think of things now."

The wine he'd had was making his head spin a bit. Downstairs, in the palais, the celebration for the new Kraljiki was still going on while, outside, the embers of Allesandra's pyre glowed red in the night. Sergei had slipped away from the festivities via the servants' corridors to come up here—to the chambers that had been Allesandra's and which were now Jan's. A goblet of wine still in his hand, he raised it to Marguerite's portrait as he lounged in a chair. A small fire—set to take away the evening chill—crackled in the hearth below the portrait, the fire and the candles lit to either side giving a wavering illumination that lent animation to Marguerite's painted, stern face. He could imagine her stirring, opening her mouth to talk to him . . .

It was an unnerving sensation, bringing back memories of Audric and his madness.

Sergei took a long sip of the wine and, with his free hand, reached into a pocket of his bashta. He retrieved a smooth, pale pebble. He rubbed its polished surface between his fingers. Wine sloshed over the rim of his glass with the motion and threw bloody droplets on his bashta. He didn't care.

"Marguerite, we both loved this city and this empire so much that we were willing to do anything for her. Anything at all. I wonder . . . Did she love us back for our passion and our faith? Did you care? Did you sometimes regret your life the way I do? Hmm . . . Somehow, knowing you, I doubt it. You were always so sure of yourself." He lifted the goblet to her in salute, then brought it to his mouth and tilted it, draining the wine in a long gulp. He set the goblet down on the table next to him and reached for his new cane, lifting himself from the chair with a grunt and a moan. "You'll have a new relative to stare at tonight," he told Marguerite. "Let's hope he's a good one, as strong as you were."

He realized he was still holding the stone. He held it up to his ear. "I don't hear anyone," he said. He tapped the stone on his nose, listening to the ring of stone on metal. He laughed, weaving slightly as he stood there, and placed the stone back in his pocket. "What becomes of us when we're gone?" he asked the painting. "Does Cénzi really wait there to judge us? I'd appreciate a sign, Marguerite. I really would."

The painting stared at him in the firelight. Marguerite's painted gaze refused to let him go. Finally, Sergei rubbed at his nose and sniffed. "No answer, eh?" he said. "You always did keep your secrets. Well, I suppose I'll find out soon enough."

He bowed to the painting, nearly falling as he did so. He patted the stone in his pocket. He left the room, leaving the goblet on the table, and, stumbling, made his way down the back stairs again. As he reached the servants' corridor nearest the Hall of the Sun Throne, he could hear the noise of the revelers, still chattering. He went in the other direction, making his way out into the garden. The cool night air seemed to clear his mind. He could smell the odor of ash and woodfire—far out in the gardens, servants were raking and spreading the coals of the pyre. He shook his head, rubbed at his stubbled cheeks. He walked around the side of the palais toward the Avi a'Parete, still crowded with pedestrians and carriages even this late. Across the Pontica a'Brezi Veste, he could see the tower and walls of the Bastida.

He took a long breath. The tower was dark against the moonlit clouds, and a small light glistened in one of the upper windows, seeming to beckon to him. Sergei's hand, in the pocket of his bashta, touched again the pebble of the White Stone.

He sighed, and he began walking the other way.

Epilogue: Nessantico

ANOTHER KRALJIKI SAT on the Sun Throne, bathed in its golden light—yet another relative of the great Kraljica Marguerite. The Holdings were unified once again, with the new Kraljiki also holding the title of Hïrzg of Firenzcia. A new Archigos sat on the throne in the Archigos' Temple, where Archigi had sat for centuries, but this was an altered Faith and a weakened Faith, and many who walked Nessantico's streets were no longer believers.

In the far west, across the Strettosei, there was a new Tecuhtli, with a young Nahual beside him.

A child who had become a powerful young man had become little more than a child again. And the White Stone had vanished once more, perhaps to return or perhaps gone to oblivion entirely.

Nessantico—the city, the woman—didn't care. Such movements didn't trouble her. The story was not done. There would be more strife, more conflicts. Thrones would pass. Victory and defeat, the rival twins of war, would contend against each other with new players.

She didn't care. The story was not done because the story never ends. It could not.

The people moving in her streets had been born and would die to be replaced by others. The Sun Throne would feel the weight of dozens of future Kralji yet unborn, and they would be good leaders or bad, but in time they would all—no matter how good, no matter how bad—eventually pass from the long, endless tale.

But *she* never would. She had been in the tale from the

beginning. The tale was hers, and it would not end until she ended, and she . . .

She was deathless.

Her fortunes had risen again. From a shattered kingdom, a new and stronger one would arise. The face that the A'Sele reflected back to her would change. Perhaps even one day the line of the Kralji itself would vanish. Perhaps.

But not her. Never her.

She would continue. Nessantico would stride into that long future: living, breathing, eternal, the central character of the land's story. Her face would be rewritten, her old lines stripped away to be replaced by new ones. She would age; she would be renewed, again and again.

The tale would not end.

That tale could not end until she herself was gone.

And that, she told herself, could never happen.

APPENDICES

PRIMARY VIEWPOINT CHARACTERS
(alphabetical order by rank, then family name):

Varina ca'Pallo [*Vah-REE-nah Kah-PAHL-low*]
A'Morce (Head) of the Numetodo, and member of the Council of Ca'. Wife of Karl ca'Pallo.

Sergei ca'Rudka [*SARE-zhay Kah-ROOD-kah*]
Advisor to Allesandra and Ambassador to Frirenzcia.

Allesandra ca'Vörl [*Ahl-ah-SAHN-drah Kah-VOORL*]
Kraljica of Nessantico; Jan ca'Ostheim's matarh.

Brie ca'Ostheim [*Bree Kah-OHST-hime*]
Jan's wife and Hïrzgin of Firenzcia

Jan ca'Ostheim [*Yahn Kah-OHST-hime*] (née ca'Vörl)
Hïrzg of Firenzcia, son of Allesandra.

Nico Morel [*NEE-koh Mohr-ELL*]
A former téni, now defrocked and the charismatic leader of a fundamentalist movement.

Rochelle Botelli [*Row-SHELL Bott-TAHL-lee*]
The half-sister of Nico Morel, operating as the "White Stone," an assassin-for-hire.

Niente [*Nee-EHN-tay*]
The Nahual (chief spellcaster) of the Westlanders.

SUPPORTING CAST
(alphabetical order by rank, then family name):

The Ca':

Karrol ca'Asano [*CARE-ohl Kah-ahh-SAH-noh*]
The Archigos in Brezno.

Valerie ca'Beranger [*VALL-err-ee Kah-BEHR-enn-jer*]
The A'Téni of Prajnoli.

Audric ca'Dakwi [*AHD-ric Kah-DAWK-whee*]
Kraljiki from 544-548.

Simon ca'Dakwi [*See-MOHN Kah-DAWK-whee*]
member of the Council of Ca'.

Armen ca'Damont [*AHR-mehn Kah-DAH-mon*]
Starkkapitän of the Firenzcian Garde Civile.

Anaïs ca'Gerodi [*Ahn-ahh-EES Kah-ger-OH-dee*]
Member of the Council of Ca'.

Edouard ca'Matin [*EDD-ooh-ard Kah-Mah-TEEN*]
Member of the Council of Ca'

Karl ca'Pallo [*Karhl K- PAHL-low*] (nee ca'Vliomani)
A'morce, head of the Numetodo in Nessantico; husband of Varina.

Caelor ca'Ostheim [*KAY-lohr Kah-OHST-hime*]
Third child (son) of Jan and Brie, age 8.

Elissa ca'Ostheim [*Eh-LISS-ah Kah-OHST-hime*]
Jan and Brie's firstborn, a daughter, now 11.

Eria ca'Ostheim [*EHR-ree-ah Kah-OHST-hime*]
Youngest child and daughter of Jan and Brie, age 3.

Jan ca'Ostheim [*Yahn Kah-OHST-hime*]
Second child (son) of Jan and Brie, age 9. He is usually
referred to as "Kriege" rather than Jan.

Soleil ca'Paim [*Soh-LAY Kah-PAYM*]
A'Téni of Nessantico.

Jager ca'Schisler [*YAY-ger Kah-SIS-lehr*]
Ambassador of the Coalition to the Holdings in
Nessantico.

Ana ca'Seranta [*AHN-ah Kah-sir-AHN-tah*]
Former Archigos of Nessantico

Henri ca'Sibelli [*AHN-ree Kah-Sah-BEHL-lee*]
Member of the Council of Ca'.

Eleric ca'Talin [*EHL-eh-ric Kah-TAHL-inn*]
Commandant of the Garde Civile in Nessantico.

Erik ca'Vikej [*AIR-ick Kah-VEE-kahg*]
Claimant to the throne of West Magyaria, and suitor to
Allesandra.

Stor ca'Vikej [*STOHR Kah-VEE-kahg*]
Vatarh of Erik and self-proclaimed Gyula of West
Magyaria, killed in the War of Union (561-562).

The Cu':

Eris cu'Bloch [*AIR-ess Koo-BLOCK*]
Commandant of the Garde Brezno.

Cu'Brunelli [*Koo-Broon-ELL-ee*]
A famous architect in the Holdings, responsible for the
design of the great dome of the Old Temple.

Talo cu'Ingres [*TAH-low Koo-AHNG*]
Commandant of the Garde Kralji in Nessantico.

Josef cu'Kella [*YOH-seff Koo-KEHL-lah*]
An ambitious businessman in Brezno who hires the
White Stone.

Mavel cu'Kella [*Mah-vehl-ah Koo-KEHL-lah*]
Daughter of Josef cu'Kella, mistress of Hïrzg Jan.

Colin cu'Mullin [*KOHL-inn Koo-MUHL-linn*]
Son of Karl ca'Pallo (nee ca'Vliomani), living on the
Isle of Paeti.

Armond cu'Weller [*ARRH-mohnd Koo-WEHL-lerr*]
A chevaritt and a'offizier in the Firenzcian Garde
Civile.

The Ci':

Aaros ci'Bella [*AHR-roos Kee-BEHL-lah*]
A suspected spy held in the Bastida.

Sinclair ci'Braun [*Sin-CLAHR Kee-BRAWN*]
A goltschlager (maker of gold foil) in Brezno.

Rance ci'Lawli [*Rahns Kee-LAWH-lee*]
Chief secretary and aide for Hïrzg Jan in Brezno.

Talbot ci'Noel [*TAHL-bott Kee-no-ELL*]
Allesandra's chief aide.

Edouard ci'Recroix [*EDD-ward Kee-reh-KROI*]
A famous artist.

Pierre ci'Santiago [*Pee-AIR Kee-Sahn-tee-AHH-goh*]
An a'offizier in the Garde Kralji.

Paulus ci'Simone [*PAHL-us Kee-See-MOHN*]
Rance ci'Lawli's assistant.

Timos ci'Stani [*TEE-mohs Kee-STAH-nee*]
A war-teni and Morelli sympathizer.

The Ce':

Johannes ce'Agrippa [*Yoh-HAHN-ess Keh-Ahh-GREEP-ahh*]
A Numetodo magician.

Ancel ce'Breton [*ANN-cehl Keh-Breh-TAHN*]
A follower of Nico Morel.

Leovic ce'Darci [*LEE-oh-vik Keh-DARR-cee*]
A Numetodo architect and engineer.

Ari ce'Denis [*AIR-ee Keh-DEHN-nees*]
Capitaine of the Bastida a'Drago in Nessantico.

Mason ce'Fieur [*MAY-sohn Keh-FEARH*]
A Numetodo.

Belle ce'Josse [*Bel Keh-JOSS-eh*]
A young Numetodo.

Liana ce'Kein [*Lee-AHN-ah Keh-KINE*]
A follower of Nico Morel, and his lover.

Ari ce'Miella [*AHH-ree Keh-Me-ELL-ahh*]
A famous composer of the time.

Henri ce'Mott [*AHN-ree Keh-MOHT*]
A gilder in Brezno.

Martin ce'Mollis [*MAHR-tinn Keh-MOHL-liss*]
A fisherman from Karnmor.

Niels ce'Sedgwick [*NEELS Keh-SEDGH-wick*]
A Numetodo geologist.

Emerin ce'Stego [*EMM-air-inn Keh-STEH-goh*]
A member of the Garde Brezno, stationed in Brezno
Palais. Also the lover of Rochelle Botelli.

The Unranked:

Elle Botelli [*ELL-ahh Boe-TELL-ee*]
The original White Stone, the matarh of Rochelle
Botelli and the "stepmatarh" of Nico Morel. Also used
the name Elissa ca'Karina, and "Elle Botelli" may or
may not be her real name.

Pierre Gabrelli [*Pee-AIR Gah-BRELL-ee*]
An artisan and craftsman with the Numetodo.

Serafina Morel [*Sair-ah-FEEN-ah more-ELL*]
Matarh of Nico Morel.

Serafina Morel [*Sair-ah-FEEN-ah more-ELL*]
Daughter of Nico Morel and Liana ce'Kein.

Albertus Paracel [*Al-BERT-us PAIR-ah-sell*]
A Numetodo scribe and librarian.

Nicolau Petros [*NEE-koh-low PET-rohs*]
A Numetodo astronomer.

Talis Posti [*TAWL-iss POHS-tee*]
Vatarh of Nico Morel, a Tehuantin.

Atl [*AH-tull*]
   Son of Niente and Xaria.

Citlali [*See-TAHL-lee*]
   The Tecuhtli (warrior-king) of the Tehuantin.

Darkmavis [*Dark-MAY-viss*]
   A well-known composer.

Tototl [*Toe-TOE-tull*]
   High Warrior of the Tehuantin, second to Tecuhtli
   Citlali.

Xaria [*SAHR-ee-ahh*]
   Wife of Niente.

DICTIONARY:

A'Morce [*Ah-MORS*]
   A generic title meaning "head" or "leader." See also
   "Téte."

A'Sele [*Ah-SEEL*]
   The river that divides the city of Nessantico.

Acal
   A small Tehuantin watercraft like a canoe.

Archigos [*ARR-chee-ghos*]
   The leader of the Concénzia Faith. The plural is
   "Archigi."

Avi a'Parete [*Ahh-VEE Ah-pah-REET*]
   The wide boulevard that forms a circle within the
   city of Nessantico, and also serves as a focus for city
   events.

Axat [*Ahh-SKIAT*]
   The moon-god of the Tehuantin people.

Bashta [*BAASH-tah*]
   A one-piece blouse and pants, usually tied with a wide
   belt around the waist, and generally loose and flowing
   elsewhere. Bashtas are generally worn by males, though
   there are female versions, and can be either plain or

extravagantly ornate, depending on the person's status and the situation.

Bastida a'Drago [*Bahs-TEE-dah Ah-DRAH-goh*]
The "Fortress of the Dragon," an ancient tower that now serves as a state prison for Nessantico. Originally built by Kraljiki Selida II.

Besteigung [*BEHZ-tee-gung*]
"Ascension" The ceremony where a new Hïrzg or Hïrzgin of Firenzcia is officially recognized after the prescribed mourning period for the previous ruler.

"Ca'-and-cu'" [*Kaw-and-Koo*]
The term for the high status families in the Holdings. The rich. See: Family Names.

Cabasab [*KAW-bah-sahn*]
The title of the ruler of Daritria.

Calli
The Tehuantin term for "house."

The "Calls"
In the Concénzia Faith, there are Three Calls during the day for prayer. First Call is in the morning, when the sun has risen above the horizon the distance of a fist held at arm's length. Second Call is when the sun is at zenith. Third Call is when the sun is a fist's length above the horizon at sunset.

Calpulli
Tehuantin word for "neighborhood," the subdivisions of their cities.

Cénzi [*SHEN-zee*]
Main god of the Nessantico pantheon, and the patron of the Concénzia Faith.

Chevaritt [*Sheh-vah-REE*], *Chevarittai* [*Sheh-vah-REE-tie*]
The "knights" of Nessantico—men of the ca'-and-cu' families. The title of "chevaritt" is bestowed by the Kraljiki or Kraljica, or by the appointed ruler of the various countries within the Holding; in times of genuine war, the chevarittai (the plural form of the word) are called upon to prove their loyalty and courage.

The chevarittai will follow (usually) the orders of the
Commandant of the Garde Civile, but not particularly
those of the common offiziers of the Garde Civile.
Their internal status is largely based on familial rank.
In the past, occasional conflicts have been decided by
honorable battle between chevarittai while the armies
watched.

Coinage

There are three primary coinages in use in Nessantico:
the bronze "folia" in tenth (d'folia), half (se'folia),
and full (folia) denominations; the silver "siqil" in half
(se'siqil) and full denominations; the gold "sola" in half
(se'sola) and full denominations. Twenty folias equal
a se'siqil; fifty siqils (or two thousand folias) equal a
se'sola. The daily wage for a simple laborer is generally
around a folia; a competent craftsperson might command four or five folias a day or a se'siqil a week. The
price (and size) of a loaf of common brown bread in
Nessantico is fixed at a d'folia.

Colors

Each of the various countries within the Holdings
retained their colors and flags. Here are the basic banner structures: East Magyaria: horizontal stripes of red,
green, and orange; Firenzcia: alternating vertical stripes
of black and silver; Graubundi: a field of yellow with
black stars; Hellin: red and black fields divided diagonally; Il Trebbio: a yellow sun on a blue field; Namarro:
a red crescent moon on a field of yellow; Nessantico:
blue and gold fields divided diagonally. Used by both
North and South Nessantico. Miscoli: a single white
star on a field of midnight blue; Paeti: vertical stripes
of green, white, and orange; Sesemora: a field of silver
with a mailed fist in the center; Sforzia: a field of white
with a diagonal blue bar; West Magyaria: horizontal
stripes of orange, red, and blue

Comté [KOM-tay]

The head of a town or city, usually a ca' and a chevaritt

Concénzia [*Kon-SEHN-zee-ah*]

The primary theology within Nessantico, whose primary deity is Cénzi, though Cénzi is simply the chief god of a pantheon.

Concord A'Téni

The gathering of all a'Téni within Concénzia—a Concord A'Téni is called to elect a new Archigos or to make changes to the Divolonté.

Cornett

A straight wind instrument made of wood or brass, and played like a trumpet.

Council of Ca'

The advisory council for the Kralji of the Holdings. Usually consists of five members. The Council of Ca' will sometimes serve as the quasi-official governing body of the Holdings if the current Kraljica or Kraljiki is underage, incapacitated, or absent.

Days of the Week

The six days of the week in Nessantico are named after major deities in the Toustour. The week begins with Cénzidi (Cénzi's Day), and follows with Vuctadi, Mizzkdi, Gostidi, Draiordi, and Parladi

Divolonté [*Dee-voh-LOHN-tay*]

"God's Will"—the rules and regulations that make up the tenets followed by those of the Concénzia Faith.

Domestiques de chambre

"Chamber servants," the servants whose task it is to attend to the Kraljiki or Kraljica in their bedchamber. Only highly trusted servants are given this assignment.

Family Names

Within Nessantico and most of the Holdings, the family names follow the female line. A man will (except in rare cases) upon marriage take his wife's family name, and all children (without exception) take the family name of the matarh. In the event of the death of a wife, the widower will usually retain his wife's family name until remarried. Status within society is determined by a prefix to the family name. In rising order, they are:

none, ce'(pronounced Keh), ci' (Kee), cu' (Koo), ca'
(Kah).

Firenzcian Coalition
The loose alliance between Firenzcia and states that
have seceded from the Holdings: Firenzcia, Sesemora,
Miscoli, East and West Magyaria.

Fjath [*Phiy-AHTH*]
The title for the ruler of Sforzia.

Garda
"Guard" or "soldier" (used interchangeably). The
plural is Gardai.

Gardai's Disease
A euphemism for homosexuality.

Garde Brezno [*GAR-duh BREHZ-noh*]
The city guard of Brezno in Firenzcia.

Garde Civile [*GAR-duh Sih-VEEL*]
The army of the country of Nessantico. Not the largest
force (that's the army of Firenzcia), but the Garde
Civile directs all the armies of the Holdings in war
situations.

Garde Kralji [*GAR-duh KRAHL-jee*]
The city guard of Nessantico. Based in the Bastida, their
insignia is a bronze dragon's skull. The common ranks
are "gardai" (ranging from a prefix of e' to a'), the officers are "offizier" (also ranging from a prefix of e' to a').
The highest rank in the Garde Kralji is Commandant.

Gardes a'Liste [*GAR-dess Ah-LEEST*]
The bureaucratic organization responsible for maintaining the rolls of family names, and for assigning the
official prefixes of rank to them.

Généra a'Pace [*Jhen-AH-rah Ah-pah-SAY*]
"Creator of Peace"—the popular title for the late
Kraljica Marguerite I. For three decades under her
rule, there were no major wars within the Holdings.

Grandes horizontales [*GRAHN-days Hor-eh-ZHON-tah-leh*]
The term for the high-class courtesans with ca'-and-cu'
patrons.

Greaves
Leg armor.

Gschnas [*Guh-SHWAZ*]
The "False World" Ball—takes place every year in
Nessantico.

Gyula [*G-YUH-lah*]
Ruler of West Magyaria. East Magyaria also uses the
same title.

Hauberk
A short chain mail coat.

Hïrzg [HAIRZG (almost two syllables)]
The title for the ruler of Firenzcia. "Hïrzgin" is the
feminine form, and "A'Hïrzg" is the term for either the
female or male heir.

Ilmodo [*Eel-MOH-doh*]
"The Way." The Ilmodo is a pervasive energy that
can be shaped through the use of ritualized chants,
perfected and codified by the Concénzia Faith. The
Numetodo call the Ilmodo "Scáth Cumhacht." Other
cultures that are aware of it will have their own name.
Niente's people call it "X'in Ka."

Instruttorei [*Inn-struh-TORR-ay*]
Instructor

Kraljica [*Krahl-JEE-kah*]
Title most similar to "Empress." The masculine form
is "Kraljiki" (Krahl-jee-kee). To refer to a ruler non-
gender-specifically, "Kralji" is generally used, which is
also the plural.

Kusah [*KOO-sah*]
The title for the ruler of Namarro

Lake Ixtapatl [*Ish-tah-PAH-ull*]
The large, brackish lake in which the island city of
Tlaxcala rests.

Marque
The document given to an acolyte who is to be taken
into the Order of Téni and placed in the service of the
Concénzia Faith.

Matarh [*MAH-tarr*]
"Mother".

Moitidi [*Moy-TEE-dee*]
The "half-gods"—the demigods created by Cénzi, who in turn created all living things.

Montbataille [*Mont-bah-TEEL*]
A city set on the long slopes of a mountain in the east of North Nessantico; also the site of a famous battle between Nessantico and the province of Firenzcia, and the only good pass through the mountains between the Rivers Clario and Loi.

Morellis
The disciples and followers of the self-proclaimed prophet Nico Morel.

Na' [*NAHH*]
"Mother" in the Tehuantin language.

Nahual [*NAH-hu-all*]
The proper title for the chief spellcaster of the Westlanders. The spellcasters are called "nahualli"—which is both singular and plural.

Namarro [*Nah-MARR-oh*]
The southernmost province of the Holdings of Nessantico.

Nessantico [*Ness-ANN-tee-ko*]
The capital city of the Holdings, ruled by the Kraljica.

Note of Severance
A document that releases an acolyte from his or her instruction toward being in the Order of Téni. Typically, 5% or less of acolytes complete their training and are accepted into the Order. The vast majority will receive a note.

Onczio [*AHNK-zhee-oh*]
"Uncle."

Offizier [*OFF-ih-zeer*]
"Officer" the various ranks of offizier follow the ranks of téni. In ascending order: e'offizier, o'offizier,

u'offizier, a'offizier. Often, an offizier in one of the armies also is a Chevaritt.

Oste-femme [*OHS-tah-femm*]
Midwife.

Passe a'Fiume [*PASS-eh ah-fee-UHM*]
The city that sits on the main river crossing of the Clario in eastern Nessantico.

Pjathi [*Peh-HAH-thee*]
Title for the ruler of Sesemora.

Pontica a'Brezi Nippoli [*Phon-TEE-kah Ah-BREHZ-ee Nee-POHL-ee*]
One of the Four Bridges of Nessantico.

Pontica a'Brezi Veste [*Phon-TEE-kah Ah-BREHZ-ee VESS-tee*]
One of the Four Bridges of Nessantico.

Pontica Kralji [*Phon-TEE-kah KRAWL-jee*]
One of the Four Bridges of Nessantico.

Pontica Mordei [*Phon-TEE-kah MHOR-dee*]
One of the Four Bridges of Nessantico.

Quibela [*Qwee-BELL-ah*]
A city in the province of Namarro.

Sakal [*Sah-KHAL*] The sun-god of the Tehuantin people.

Sapnut
The fruit of the sapnut tree, from which a rich yellow dye is made.

Scarlet Pox
A childhood illness, often deadly.

Scáth Cumhacht [*Skawth Koo-MOCKED*]
The Numetodo term for the Ilmodo.

Sesemora [*Say-seh-MOHR-ah*]
A province in the northeast of the Holdings of Nessantico.

Southern Fever
An affliction that kills a high percentage of those affected—the fever causes the brain to swell, bring-

ing on dementia and/or coma, while the lungs fill with
liquid from the infection, causing pneumonia-like
symptoms. Often, even if the victim recovers from the
coughing, they are left brain-damaged.

Starkkapitän [*Starkh-KAHP-ee-tahn*]
"High Captain"—the title for the commander of Firenzcian troops.

Stone
A measure of weight for dry goods. Merchants are
required to have a set of weights, certified by the local
board. A stone is approximately a pound and a half in
our measures.

Strettosei [*STRETT-oh-see*]
The ocean to the west of Nessantico.

T'Sha [*Ti-SHAH*]
The ruler of Tennshah.

Taat [*Taaht*]
"Father" in the Tehuantin tongue.

Ta'Mila [*Tah-MEE-ah*]
The ruler of Il Trebbio.

Tantzia
"Aunt."

Tashta [*TAWSH-tah*]
A robe-like garment in fashion in Nessantico.

Tecuhtli [*Teh-KOO-uhl-ee*]
The title for "Lord" or "War-King" in the Tehuantins'
language.

Tehuantin [*Teh-WHO-ahn-teen*]
"The People"—the name the Westlanders call
themselves.

Téni [*TEHN-ee*]
"Priest." Those of the Concénzia who have been tested
for their mastery of the Ilmodo, have taken their vows,
and are in the service of the church. The téni priest-
hood also uses a ranking similar to the Families of

Nessantico. In ascending order, the ranks are e'Téni,
o'Téni, u'Téni, and a'Téni.

Teocalli [*Teh-o-CAHL-ee*]
The Tehuantin term for "temple." The plural form is
teocaltin.

Téte [*teh-TAY*]
"Head"— title for the leaders of an organization, such
as the Guardians of the Faith or the Council of Ca'.
Another title for an organizational leader is "A'Morce"
(used by the Numetodo, among others . . .).

Tlaxcala [*Tlash-TAH-lah*]
The capital city of the Tehuantin nations.

Toustour [*TOOS-toor*]
The "All-Tale"—the bible for the Concénzia Faith.

Turn of the glass
An hour. The glass referred to is an hourglass, the sides
of which are typically incised with lines marking the
quarter-hours. Thus, a "mark of the glass" is roughly
fifteen minutes.

Utilino [*Oo-teh-LEE-noh*]
A combination concierge and watchman who patrols a
small area (no more than a block each) of the city. The
utilino—who is also a téni of the Concénzia faith—is
there to run errands (for a fee) as well as to keep order,
and is considered to be part of the Garde Kralji.

Vajica [*Vah-JEE-kah*]
Title most similar to "Madam," used in polite address
with adults who have no other title, or where the title is
unknown. The masculine form is "Vajiki." The plurals
are "Vajicai" and "Vajik."

Vambrace
Armor protecting the lower arm.

Vatarh [*VAH-ter*]
"Taat."

Venerable Carin
One of the books contained in the Toustour.

Verzehen [*Ver-ZAY-hehn*]
Foreign term for a telescope.

Ville Colhelm [*VEE-ah KOHL-helm*]
A town on the border of Nessantico and Firenzcia, at
the River Clario.

War-téni
Téni whose skills in Ilmodo have been honed for
warfare

White-Peak Wall
Tehuantin name for the mountain range between the
Tehuantin empire and the Helllins.

Zink
A wind instrument similar to a cornett but curved
rather than straight.

THE RECENT LINE OF THE KRALJI:

471–521: **Marguerite ca'Ludovici** [*Marhg-u-REET Kah-
loo-doh-VEE-kee*]—also known as the "Généra a'Pace"

521–544: **Justi ca'Dakwi** [*JUSS-tee Kah-DAWK-whee*]
(née ca'Ludovici, nee ca'Mazzak)—also known as the
"One-Legged." Son of Marguerite.

544–548: The Regency of Sergei ca'Rudka: for **Kraljica
Audric ca'Dakwi** [*AHD-ric- Kah-DAWK-whee*], son of
Justi, who is still in his minority.

548–548: **Audric ca'Dakwi** [*AHD-ric Kah-DAWK-
whee*]—for the last few months of Audric's reign before
his assassination, Regent ca'Rudka is dismissed and Audric (later known as "The Mad") holds the Sun Throne.

548–548: **Sigourney ca'Ludovici** [*Si-GOHR-nee Kah-
loo-doh-VEE-kee*]—great grand-niece of Marguerite.

548–present: **Allesandra ca'Vörl** [*Ahl-ah-SAHN-drah
Kah-VOORL*]—great grand-niece of Marguerite

THE RECENT LINE OF THE HÏRZGIN:

493–516: **Karin ca'Belgradin** [*KAH-reen
Kah-bell-GRAH-deen*]

516–548: **Jan ca'Vörl** [*Yahn Kah-VOORL*]—Son of
Karin. Seceded from the Holdings in 522 to form the
Coalition of Firenzcia.

548–548: **Fynn ca'Vörl** [*Finn Kah-VOORL*]—Son of
Jan. Assassinated by the White Stone.

548–present: **Jan (II) ca'Vörl** [*Yahn Kah-VOORL*]—
Grandson of Jan (via Allesandra).

THE RECENT LINE OF THE ARCHIGI:

503–521: **Dhosti ca'Millac** [*DOST-ee Kah-MEE-lok*]—
"the Dwarf." Committed suicide (though some still whisper that it was murder).

521–521: **Orlandi ca'Cellibrecca** [*Orh-LAHN-dee Kah-
sell-eh-BREK-ah*]—Left the throne to join with Firenzcia
during the War of Secession. This began the Division of
the Faith (521–548).

The Line in Nessantico:

521–548: **Ana ca'Seranta** [*AHN-ah Kah-sir-AHN-
tah*]—Assassinated by Tehuantin sorcerer under orders
from Archigos Semini.

548–548: **Kenne ca'Fionta** [*KENN-ah Kah-fee-ON-
tah*]—Tortured to death by Kraljica Sigourney.

The Line in Brezno:

521–525: **Orlandi ca'Cellibrecca** [*Orh-LAHN-dee Kah-
sell-eh-BREK-ah*]—Died of natural causes.

525–548: **Semini ca'Cellibrecca** [*SEH-meen-eh Kah-
sell-ee-BREK-ah*]—marriage-son of Orlandi.

The Line of the Reunited Faith:

549–present: **Karrol ca'Asano** [*CARE-ohl Kah-ahh-
SAH-noh*]—Named Archigos after the deposing of Semini
ca'Cellibrecca. The line is now seated at Brezno rather
than in Nessantico.

HISTORICAL PERSONAGES:

Falwin I [*FAHL-win*]—Hïrzg Falwin of Firenzcia led a brief, unsuccessful revolt against Kraljiki Henri VI, which was quickly and brutally put down.

Henri VI [*OHN-ree*]—First Kralji of the ca'Ludovici line (413–435), from whom Marguerite I was descended.

Kalima III [*Kah-LEE-mah*]—Archigos from 215–243.

Kelwin [*KEHL-win*]—First Hïrzg of Firenzcia

Levo ca'Niomi [*LEHV-oh Kah-nee-OH-mee*]—Led a coup in 383 and was Kraljiki for three days. Forcibly removed, he would be imprisoned for almost two decades in the Bastida, and there would write poetry that would long survive his death.

Maria III—Kraljica of Nessantico from 219–237

Misco [*MEEZ-koh*]—The legendary "founder of Brezno."

Pellin I [*PEH-Lihn*]—Archigos of the Faith from 114–122.

Selida II [*Seh-LEE-dah*]—Kraljiki of Nessantico. Finished building the city walls and the Bastida d'Drago.

Sveria I [*seh-VERH-ee-ah*]—Kraljiki of Nessantico 179-211. The Secession War occupied nearly all his reign. He finally brought Firenzcia fully into the Holdings.

SNIPPETS FROM THE "NESSANTICO CONCORDIA"
(4th Edition, Year 642)

Family Names in the Holdings:
Within Nessantico, lineage follows the matrilineal line. A husband might, in rare cases, retain his own family name (especially if it were considered higher in status than his wife's), but the wife can never take his name. In the vast majority of cases, however, the husband will legally take on his wife's family name, thus becoming a member of that family in the eyes of Nessantico law—the husband will continue to bear that name and be considered to be part of that family even upon the death of his spouse, unless and until he remarries and thus acquires his new wife's name. (Divorces and annulments are rare in Nessantico, requiring the signature of the Archigos,

and each divorce is a special situation where the rules are sometimes fluid.) Children are, without exception, given the mother's family name: "One always is certain of the mother," as the saying goes in Nessantico.

The prefix to a family name can change, depending on the relative status of the immediate family within Nessantico society. The prefixes, in order of rising status, are:

- none
- ce' (keh)
- ci' (kee)
- cu' (koo)
- ca' (kah).

One of the functionary roles of the Kralji was to sign the official family rolls every three years wherein the prefixes are recorded, though the Kraljiki or Kraljica rarely determined any changes personally; that was the role of the bureaucracy within Nessantico known as the Gardes a'Liste.

Thus, it is possible that the husband or wife of the ci'Smith family might gain status in some manner and be awarded a new prefix by the Gardes a'Liste. Husband, wife, their children and any surviving maternal parents thus become cu'Smith, but brothers, sisters, and any cousins would remain ci'Smith.

Royalty Succession Within The Holdings:

Various countries within the Holdings, not surprisingly given the variance of customs, have various rules of succession within their societies. This is especially true when those countries are independently ruled. For instance, in East Magyaria, the closest male relative of the previous ruler who is also *not* a direct child of that ruler is named as the successor. However, with the ascension of Nessantico and the Holdings, those countries within Nessantico's influence tend to follow the lead of the Kralji.

For the royal families of Nessantico, title succession is normally to the Kralji's children by birth order regardless of gender. However, it is possible for the Kralji to legally designate a favorite child as the heir and bypass earlier-born children, if the Kralji deems them unfit to rule or if for some reason they fall out of favor. This is an uncommon occurrence, though hardly rare throughout history. For the Kralji, it means that his or her children will tend to curry favor so as to remain in good graces or perhaps to unseat one of their brothers or sisters from being named the a'Kralj.

The Ilmodo and Spellcasting:

Some people have the ability to sense the power that exists all around us: the invisible potent energy of the Second World that surrounds us. In the Nessantico-controlled regions of the world, usage of magic has always been linked to religious faith, all the way back into prehistory. The myth of Cénzi extends deep into the historical mist, and it is the followers of Cenzi who have always possessed the power to manipulate the Ilmodo through chants and hand-motions.

The chanting that binds the power of the Ilmodo is the "Ilmodo language" that all acolyte téni are taught. The Ilmodo language actually has its linguistic roots in the speech of the Westlands, though neither those of the Concénzia Faith nor the Numetodo realized that for centuries. Those of the Westlands also take power from the Second World via the instrument of religion, though through a different god and mythology, and they have their own name for the Ilmodo: X'in Ka

The Numetodo have taken the most recent path to this power: not through faith at all, but essentially by making a "science" of magic. The cult of the Numetodo first arose in the late 400s, originally from the Isle of Paeti, and spread mostly west and south from there, sometimes reacting violently with the culture of Nessantico and the Concénzia Faith.

However the power is gained, there is a necessary "payment" for spell use: using spells costs the wielder physically; the greater the effect, the higher the cost in exhaustion and weariness for the caster.

Different paths have resulted in different abilities— for Concénzian téni, there is no "storage" of spells—their spells take time to cast and once prepared, they must be cast or they are lost. However, the téni of the Faith have the advantage of being able to cast spells that linger for

some time after the casting (see "The Lights of Nessantico" or "The Sun Throne of the Kralji"). Téni who cast
spells quickly and effectively are unusual, and have in
historical times been suspected of heresy.

The Numetodo, in contrast, have found a way to cast
their spells several turns of the glass earlier (though such
spells can't be stored indefinitely). Like all users of this
power, they "pay" for it with exhaustion but hold the
power with their minds to be released with a single gesture and word. Their spells are generally longer and more
arduous to create (even more so than that of the téni), but
do not require "faith"—as is required by both the path of
Concénzia and the Westlanders. All they require is that
the spellcaster follows a "formula." However, any variation from the formula, even small, will generally ruin the
spell.

The Westlanders, following what they call X'in Ka,
must perform the chants and hand gestures much like the
téni, but they can also "enchant" an object with a spell
(something neither téni nor Numetodo can do), so that
the object (e.g.: a walking stick) manipulated in a particular way (e.g. striking someone) can release a spell (e.g. a
shocking jolt that renders the struck person unconscious).

In all cases and whatever the path of the spellcaster,
the spells of the Second World tend to be linked to
elementals in our world: fire, earth, air, and water. Most
spellcasters have an ability sharply stronger in one element and much weaker in the others. Rarely does a spellcaster have the ability to handle two or more elements
with any skill; even more rare are those who can move
easily between any of the elements.

The Ranks of Téni in the Concénzia Faith:

The téni are ranked in the following order, from lowest
to highest:

Acolyte—those who are receiving instruction to become one of the téni—generally, the instructions requires
tuition be paid to Concénzia by the students' families. The
Concénzia Faith brings in both male and female students
to become téni, though realistically the classes tend to
be largely male, and there are fewer women than men
represented in the higher ranks of the téni. (There have

been only six female Archigi in the long history of the Faith.) During the acolyte period (typically three years), the students serve within the Faith, doing menial tasks for the téni, and also begin to learn the chants and mental discipline necessary for Ilmodo, the manipulation of the universe-energy. Typically, only about 10% of the acolytes receive the Marque of the Téni. There are schools for acolytes in all the major cities of Nessantico, each presided over by the a'Téni of the region.

E'Téni—the lowest téni rank for those brought into the service of the Faith. The acolytes who receive their Marque are, with exceedingly few exceptions, awarded this rank, which denotes that they have some small skill with Ilmodo. At this point, they are generally tasked with menial labor that requires the magic of Cénzi, such as lighting the city lamps, and are expected to increase their skill and demonstrate their continuing mastery of the Ilmodo.

O'Téni—an e'téni will be awarded this rank, generally after one to five years of service, at which point they are either put in service of one of the temples, administering to the needs of the community, or they are placed in charge of one of the téni-powered industries within the city. This is where most téni will end their careers. Only a select few will pass this rank to become u'téni.

U'Téni—u'teni serve directly under the a'teni of the region. An u'téni is generally responsible for maintaining one of the temples of the city, and overseeing the activities of the o'téni attached to that temple.

A'Téni—the highest rank within the Faith with the exception of that of Archigos. The a'téni each are in charge of a region centered around one of the large cities of the Holdings. There, they generally wield enormous power and influence with the political leaders and over the citizenry. At times, this can be a contentious relationship; most often, however, it is neutral or mutually beneficial. In the year of Kraljica Marguerite's Jubilee, there were twenty-three a'téni in the Faith, an increase of three from the time she ascended the throne. Generally, the larger and more influential the city where they are based, the more influence the a'téni has within the Faith.

Archigos—the head of the Faith. This is not necessarily an elective office. Often, the Archigos designates his or her own successor from among the a'téni or even potentially a favorite u'téni. However, in practice, there have been "coups" within Concénzia where either the Archigos died before naming a successor, or where the right of the successor to ascend to the position has been disputed, sometimes violently. When that happens, those a'téni who aspire to the seat of the Archigos are locked in a special room within the Archigos's Temple for the Concord A'Téni. What happens there is a matter of great speculation and debate. One will, however, emerge as Archigos.

The Creation of Cénzi:

At the start of all things, there was only Vucta, the Great Night, the eyeless female essence who had always existed, wandering alone through the nothingness of the universe. Though Vucta could not see the stars, she could feel their heat, and when she was cold she would come to them and stay for a time. It was near one star that she found something she had never experienced before: a world—a place of rocks and water, and she stayed there for a time, wondering and dreaming as she walked in this strange place, touching everything to feel its shape and listening to the wind and the surf, feeling the rain and the snow and the touch of the clouds. She hoped that here, in this strange place near the star, there might be another like her, but there were no animals here yet, nor trees, nor anything living.

As Vucta walked the world, wisps of her dream-thoughts gathered around her like a mist, coalescing and hardening and finally growing heavy from their sheer volume. The dream-thoughts began to shape themselves, a white shroud around Vucta that grew longer and more substantial as she walked, heavier and heavier with each step until the weightiest part of it drooped to the ground and snagged on a rock. Eyeless, Vucta could not see that. She continued her walking and her thinking, and her dream-thoughts poured from her, but now they lay solid where they had fallen, stretching and thinning as she strode away from where they were caught. Vucta, in truth was already growing tired of this place and her search, and she desired the heat of another sun, so she leaped away from the world and the shroud of her dream-thoughts snapped as she flew.

*Vucta's dream-thoughts lay there, all of them co-
alescing, and when the sun shone on the first day after
Vucta's departure, there was a form like hers curled on
the ground. On the second day, the sun's light made the
dream-thoughts stir, and the form moved arms and legs,
though it did not know itself. The dream-thoughts that
were the yearning of Vucta gathered in its head, and from
Vucta's desire to know the place where she walked, they
made eyes in the face.*

*On the third day, when the sun touched it once more, it
opened those eyes and it saw the world. "I am Cénzi," the
creature said, "and this place is mine." And he rose then
and began to walk about . . .*

That is the opening of the Toustour, the All-Tale. In
time, as the creation tale continues, Cénzi would become
lonely and he would create companions—the Moitidi—
fashioning them from the breath of his body, which still
contained Vucta's strong power. Those companions, in
turn, would imitate their creator and fashion all the living
creatures of the earth: plant and animal, including the
humans. The Moitidi's own breaths were weak, and thus
those they created were correspondingly more flawed.
But it was Cénzi's breath and the weaker breaths of the
Moitidi that permeated the atmosphere of the world and
would become the Ilmodo, which humans through prayer,
devotion to Cénzi, and intense study could learn to shape.

But the relationship between Cénzi and his offspring
would always be contentious, marred by strife and jealousy. Cénzi had given his creations laws that they were
to follow, but in time, they began to change and ignore
those laws, flaunting themselves over Cénzi. Cénzi would
become angry with his creations for their attitudes, but
they were unrepentant, and so they began to war openly
against Cénzi. It was a long and brutal conflict, and few
of the living creatures would survive it, for in that past
there had been many types of creatures who could speak
and think. Cénzi's throwing down of the Moitidi as they
wrestled and fought would cause mountains to rise up and
valleys to form, shaping the world which had until then
been flat, with but one great ocean. The final blow that destroyed most of the Moitidi would fracture the very earth,

tear apart the land and create the deep rift into which the Strettosei would flow.

After that immense blow that shook the entire world, those few Moitidi who remained fled and hid and cowered. Cénzi, though, was haunted by what had happened, and he wished to find Vucta and speak with her, whose dream-thoughts had made him. Only a single speaking and thinking species were left of all of Cénzi's grandchildren, and he made this promise to them, our own ancestors: that if they remained faithful to him, he would always listen to them and send his power back to them, and that one day, he would return here and be with them forever.

With that promise, he left the world to wander the night between the stars.

In the view of the Concénzia Faith, Cénzi is the only god worthy of worship (Vucta being considered by the Concénzian scholars to be more an all-pervading spirit rather than an entity), and it is His laws, given to the Moitidi, that the Faith has codified and now follows. The gods worshipped by other religions within and without the Holdings are those cowardly Moitidi who came out of hiding when Cénzi left and have deceived their followers into thinking they are true gods. The surviving Moitidi remain in mortal fear of Cénzi's return and flee whenever Cénzi's thoughts turn back to this world, as they do, reputedly, when the faithful pray strongly enough.

The truth of this is shown in that the laws of humankind, wherever they may live and whomever they may claim to worship, have a similarity at the core—because they all derive from the original tenets of Cénzi.

The Divolonté:

The Divolonté is a loose collection of rules and regulations by which the Concénzia Faith is governed, the majority of which derive from the Toustour. However, the Divolonté is secular in origin, created and added to by the various Archigi and a'téni through the centuries, while the Toustour is considered to be derived from Cénzi's own words. The Divolonté is also a dynamic document, undergoing slow, continual evolution through the auspices of the Archigos and the a'téni. Many of its precepts and commands are somewhat archaic, and are ignored or even flaunted by the current Faith. It is, however, the Divolonté that the conservative element within the Faith quotes when they look at the threat of other faiths and belief systems, such as that of the Numetodo.

A RECENT HISTORY OF NESSANTICO:

YEAR 521 (the events of A *Magic of Twilight*): This is Kraljica Marguerite's Jubilee Year—under her half a century of rule, Nessantico has flourished. However, in the spring, Kraljica Marguerite is assassinated. Kraljiki Justi (her son) takes the Sun Throne. Archigos Dhosti dies; Archigos Orlandi becomes head of the Concénzia Faith. Hïrzg Jan leads the army of Firenzcia into the Holdings, intending to take Nessantico. Archigos Ana becomes head of the Concénzia Faith after Archigos Orlandi defects to Hïrzg Jan at Passe a'Fiume. Nessantico is attacked by Firenzcian forces. Allesandra, daughter of Hïrzg Jan of Firenzcia, is taken as hostage by Archigos Ana and Kraljiki Justi. Firenzcian forces retreat.

522: Orlandi formally declares himself Archigos in Brezno—the Concénzia Faith is sundered. A son, Fynn, is born to Hïrzg Jan and Greta ca'Vörl. Hïrzg Jan refuses to pay ransom for Allesandra, and declares Firenzcia independent of the Holdings. Semini cu'Kohnle marries Francesca ca'Cellibrecca, daughter of Orlandi.

523: Envoy Karl ci'Vliomani of the Isle of Paeti is elevated to Ambassador and given the rank of cu'. The Numetodo influence begins to grow within the Holdings. Sesemora secedes from the Holdings and allies with Firenzcia—the first country within what will be known as the Coalition of Firenzcia. Hïrzgin Greta ca'Vörl dies under "suspicious" circumstances; the Numetodo sect is blamed.

524: Miscoli and East Magyaria join Sesemora in seceding and joining the Coalition of Firenzcia. War is declared between the two rival Holdings. It will drag on for years without a decisive victory by either side. The Eastern and Western branches of the Concénzia Faith declare each other heretical and invalid.

525: Kraljiki Justi marries Marie ca'Dakwi of Il Trebbio,

daughter of the current Ta'Mila (local ruler) of Il Trebbio.
Justi takes the ca'Dakwi name (as is proper and expected
in their society). Archigos Orlandi of Brezno dies of natural
causes. A'Téni Semini ca'Cellibrecca becomes Archigos
there.

526: A first child is born to Justi and Marie, a son. He
will die within three months. Hïrzg Jan formally declares
his son Fynn to be the A'Hïrzg—the heir to his throne.
This leaves Allesandra in limbo, no longer the official heir
to her vatarh's throne.

527: A second child is born to Justi and Marie, a daughter. Like her sibling, she will die within three months

529: A third child is born to Justi and Marie, another
daughter who is named Marguerite. She is stronger than
her siblings and lives. She becomes the A'Kralj (heir).

531: The Treaty of Passe a'Fiume is signed, ending open
hostilities between Nessantico and Firenzcia. As part of
the negotiations, Allesandra (now 21 years old and having
lived nearly as long in Nessantico as in Firenzcia) is finally
ransomed and returns to Firenzcia.

532: Allesandra marries Pauli ca'Xielt of West Mag-
yaria, son of the Gyula (local ruler) of West Magyaria.
West Magyaria secedes from the Holdings and joins the
Firenzcian Coalition.

533: A male child is born to Allesandra and Pauli: Jan.
This will be their only child. Their marriage is rumored
to be "troubled." In Nessantico, Marie dies bearing the
fourth child of Justi, another son. Though sickly, Audric
will survive.

535: Nessantican forces push farther westward in the
Hellins (and also on the Isle of Paeti, which they will come
to control).

537: Southern Fever rises again in the cities. Marguerite
ca'Dakwi, vacationing in Namarro, is infected and dies.
Audric becomes the a'Kralj in her place.

540: The Commandant of the Holdings forces in the
Hellins, Petrus ca'Helfier, is killed by a Westlander after
ca'Helfier either "rapes" a Westlander's daughter or
the two of them fall in love (the truth here will probably never be known). The new Commandant, Donatien
ca'Sibelli, takes the murderer forcibly and executes
him without trial; the Westlanders protest. Retaliations

escalate, and there is suddenly open war—and Commandant ca'Sibelli finds that there are new forces with the
Westlanders: soldiers with faces marked by tattoos and
spellcasters with skills that match those of the téni. In
the Coalition, A'Hïrzg Fynn, now 18, leads the Firenzcian
army successfully against Tennshah, taking land in the east
for the Holdings of Firenzcia.

542: There are attacks by Westlanders inside the
Hellins frontier—the magic used by the Westlanders
proves formidable. Westlanders win a large-scale battle
with Holdings forces in the Hellins. The towns around
Lake Malik and Lake Udar are lost, as is control of the
western frontier. The Hellins Holdings are reduced to thin
strips of land around the cities of Tobarro and Munereo.

543: Hïrzg Jan suffers a heart attack. His health begins
a slow, steady decline.

544: Justi, realizing he is dying, names Sergei ca'Rudka
as his choice for Regent until Audric reaches his majority
at 16. Kraljiki Justi dies, and Audric becomes Kraljiki at
age 11.

YEAR 548: (the events of *A Magic of Nightfall*):
Hïrzg Jan of the Coalition dies; Hïrzg Fynn crowned.
Archigos Ana of Nessantico assassinated, Archigos Kenne
crowned. Assassination attempt on Hïrzg Fynn fails. Ser-
gei ca'Rudka deposed as Regent by Kraljiki Audric and
imprisoned. The White Stone assassinates Hïrzg Fynn;
Fynn's nephew Jan (son of Allesandra) becomes Hirzg
Jan II. Sergei ca'Rudka escapes from the Bastida aided
by Numetodo and flees to the Coalition. In the Hellins,
the capital of Munereo falls to the Tehuantin Westland-
ers. The Tehuantin send an invasion force to the Holdings;
Karnor razed. Kraljiki Audric assassinated by ensorceled
offizier; Kraljica Sigourney crowned. Coalition troops
march into the Holdings from the East. City of Nessan-
tico taken by Tehuantin, burned and plundered; Kraljica
Sigourney commits suicide. Coalition forces sweep away
the Tehuantin army. The White Stone kills a Tehuantin
spellcaster, saving Hïrzg Jan's life. Allesandra is named
Kraljica.

YEAR 549: Rochelle, daughter of the White Stone and
Hïrzg Jan II of the Coalition, is born. Archigos Semini is

stripped of his title upon Hïrzg Jan's return to Brezno, though he accepts the lesser position of A'Téni of Nessantico. A'Téni Karrol ca'Asano of Malacki is elevated to Archigos, and the Concénzia Faith is reunited, though the new seat of the Archigos is in Brezno, not Nessantico. Karl ca'Vliomani marries Varina (becoming Karl ca'Pallo). Sergei ca'Rudka is named Special Ambassador to Firenzcia for the Holdings.

YEAR 550: The Numetodo become an official political entity within the Holdings. Varina is named as their head (A'Morce), and becomes a member of Council of Ca'.

YEAR 551: Jan ca'Vörl marries Brie ca'Ostheim of Sesemora—as is customary in this society, he takes her name and becomes Jan ca'Ostheim.

YEAR 552: Kraljica Allesandra, despite the protests of the Faith and A'Téni Semini, declares that the Numeteodo may not be prosecuted or harmed for their beliefs within the Holdings. Semini commits suicide in protest. Soleil ca'Paim is named the new A'Téni for Nessantico. Jan and Brie's first child is born, a girl named Elissa.

YEAR 553: Pauli ca'Vörl, Allesandra's estranged husband (and Hïrzg Jan's vatarh), becomes Gyula of West Magyaria when his vatarh dies.

YEAR 554: Due to diplomatic efforts by Kraljica Allesandra and Ambassador Karl ca'Pallo, the Isle of Paeti rejoins the Holdings. A son Jan (nicknamed "Kriege") is born to Hïrzg Jan and Brie.

YEAR 556: West Magyaria secedes from the Coalition (but does not rejoin the Holdings). Caelor (son) born to Jan and Brie.

YEAR 557: The army of Firenzcia invades West Magyaria. It quickly becomes obvious that the army of West Magyaria is no match for the Firenzcians. Gyula Pauli is assassinated by his own Council of Ca' when he refuses the terms of surrender. West Magyaria returns to control by the Coalition.

YEAR 558: Nico ce'Morel, an extremely charismatic e'téni with radically conservative views, begins to gain a following in the Holdings and the Coalition.

YEAR 560: Eria (daughter) born to Jan and Brie.

YEAR 560: Nico Morel defrocked by the Concénzia

Faith. However, his popularity continues to grow. He espouses a fundamentalist, harsh reshaping of the Faith.

YEAR 561: Nico Morel comes to Nessantico. War again breaks out in West Magyaria, as a pretender to the Gyula's throne, Stor ca'Vikej, supported by the Holdings and Nessantico, attempts a coup. Firenzcian troops are quickly involved. The Holdings forces, undermanned, are forced to retreat. Stor ca'Vikej is killed.

YEAR 562: Nico's popularity is growing, which doesn't sit well with Kraljica Allesandra and her rather secular government. There are violent conflicts between the followers of Nico (called "Morelli") and the Garde Kralji.

YEAR 563: A *Magic of Dawn* **begins . . .**

S.L. Farrell

The Nessantico Cycle

"[Farrell's] best yet, a delicious melange of politics, war, sorcery, and religion in a richly imagined world."
—George R. R. Martin,
New York Times bestselling author

"Readers who appreciate intricate world building, intrigue and action will immerse themselves effortlessly in this rich and complex story."
—*Publishers Weekly*

A MAGIC OF TWILIGHT
978-0-7564-0536-6

A MAGIC OF NIGHTFALL
978-0-7564-0599-1

A MAGIC OF DAWN
978-0-7564-0646-2

To Order Call: 1-800-788-6262
www.dawboks.com

DAW 120

Sherwood Smith

Inda

"A powerful beginning to a very promising series by a writer who is making her bid to be a major fantasist. By the time I finished, I was so captured by this book that it lingered for days afterward. I had lived inside these characters, inside this world, and I was unwilling to let go of it. That, I think, is the mark of a major work of fiction…you owe it to yourself to read *Inda*." —Orson Scott Card

INDA
978-0-7564-0422-2

THE FOX
978-0-7564-0483-3

KING'S SHIELD
978-0-7564-0500-7

TREASON'S SHORE
978-0-7564-0573-1 (hardcover)
978-0-7564-0634-9
(paperback)

To Order Call: 1-800-788-6262
www.dawbooks.com

Violette Malan

Kristen Britain

The GREEN RIDER series

"Wonderfully captivating...a truly enjoyable read."
—Terry Goodkind

"A fresh, well-organized fantasy debut, with a
spirited heroine and a reliable supporting cast."
—*Kirkus*

"The author's skill at world building and her feel for
dramatic storytelling make this first-rate fantasy
a good choice." —*Library Journal*

"Britain keeps the excitement high from beginning
to end." —*Publishers Weekly*

GREEN RIDER
0-88677-858-1 (mass)   978-0-7564-0548-9 (trade)

FIRST RIDER'S CALL
0-7564-0209-3 (mass)   978-0-7564-0572-4 (trade)

THE HIGH KING'S TOMB
978-0-7564-0588-5 (mass)   978-0-7564-0489-5 (trade)

BLACKVEIL
(Available February 2011)
978-0-7564-0660-8 (hardcover)

To Order Call: 1-800-788-6262
www.dawbooks.com

DAW 7

Patrick Rothfuss

THE NAME OF THE WIND
The Kingkiller Chronicle: Day One

"It is a rare and great pleasure to come on somebody writing not only with the kind of accuracy of language that seems to me absolutely essential to fantasy-making, but with real music in the words as well.... Oh, joy!"　　　—Ursula K. Le Guin

"Amazon.com's Best of the Year...So Far Pick for 2007: Full of music, magic, love, and loss, Patrick Rothfuss's vivid and engaging debut fantasy knocked our socks off."　　　—Amazon.com

"One of the best stories told in any medium in a decade. Shelve it beside *The Lord of the Rings* ...and look forward to the day when it's mentioned in the same breath, perhaps as first among equals."
　　　—*The Onion*

"[Rothfuss is] the great new fantasy writer we've been waiting for, and this is an astonishing book."
　　　—Orson Scott Card

ISBN: 978-0-7564-0474-1

To Order Call: 1-800-788-6262
www.dawbooks.com